# HERCULE POIROT'S CASEBOOK

# HERCULE POIROT'S CASEBOOK

Agatha Christie

DODD, MEAD & COMPANY
*New York*

No part of this book may be reproduced in any form
without permission in writing from the publisher.
Published by Dodd, Mead & Company, Inc.
79 Madison Avenue, New York, N.Y. 10016
Distributed in Canada by
McClelland and Stewart Limited, Toronto
Manufactured in the United States of America
First Edition

*Library of Congress Cataloging in Publication Data*

Christie, Agatha, 1890–1976.
  Hercule Poirot's casebook.

  1. Detective and mystery stories, English.   I. Title.
PR6005.H66H4   1984      823'.912      84–13488
ISBN 0–396–08417–6

# CONTENTS

## FROM THE REGATTA MYSTERY

## FROM THE LABORS OF HERCULES

## FROM THREE BLIND MICE

# FROM THE UNDER DOG

# FROM DOUBLE SIN

# HERCULE
# POIROT'S
# CASEBOOK

# POIROT
# INVESTIGATES

# The Adventure of "The Western Star"

I WAS standing at the window of Poirot's rooms looking out idly on the street below.

"That's queer," I ejaculated suddenly beneath my breath.

"What is, *mon ami?*" asked Poirot placidly, from the depths of his comfortable chair.

"Deduce, Poirot, from the following facts! Here is a young lady, richly dressed—fashionable hat, magnificent furs. She is coming along slowly, looking up at the houses as she goes. Unknown to her, she is being shadowed by three men and a middle-aged woman. They have just been joined by an errand boy who points after the girl, gesticulating as he does so. What drama is this being played? Is the girl a crook, and are the shadowers detectives preparing to arrest her? Or are *they* the scoundrels, and are they plotting to attack an innocent victim? What does the great detective say?"

"The great detective, *mon ami*, chooses, as ever, the simplest course. He rises to see for himself." And my friend joined me at the window.

In a minute he gave vent to an amused chuckle.

"As usual, your facts are tinged with your incurable romanticism. That is Miss Mary Marvell, the film star. She is being followed by a bevy of admirers who have recognized her. And, *en passant*, my dear Hastings, she is quite aware of the fact!"

I laughed.

"So all is explained! But you get no marks for that, Poirot. It was a mere matter of recognition."

"*En vérité!* And how many times have you seen Mary Marvell on the screen, *mon cher?*"

I thought.

"About a dozen times perhaps."

"And I—once! Yet *I* recognize her, and *you* do not."

"She looks so different," I replied rather feebly.

"Ah! *Sacré!*" cried Poirot. "Is it that you expect her to promenade herself in the streets of London in a cowboy hat, or with bare feet and a bunch of curls, as an Irish colleen? Always with you it is the non-essentials! Remember the case of the dancer, Valerie Saintclair."

I shrugged my shoulders, slightly annoyed.

"But console yourself, *mon ami,*" said Poirot, calming down. "All cannot be as Hercule Poirot! I know it well."

"You really have the best opinion of yourself of anyone I ever knew!" I cried, divided between amusement and annoyance.

"What will you? When one is unique, one knows it! And others share that opinion—even, if I mistake not, Miss Mary Marvell."

"What?"

"Without doubt. She is coming here."

"How do you make that out?"

"Very simply. This street, it is not aristocratic, *mon ami!* In it there is no fashionable doctor, no fashionable dentist—still less is there a fashionable milliner! But there *is* a fashionable detective. *Oui,* my friend, it is true—I am become the mode, the *dernier cri!* One says to another, *'Comment?* You have lost your gold pencil case? You must go to the little Belgian. He is too marvellous! Everyone goes! *Courez!'* And they arrive! In flocks, *mon ami!* With problems of the most foolish!" A bell rang below. "What did I tell you? That is Miss Marvell."

As usual, Poirot was right. After a short interval, the American film star was ushered in, and we rose to our feet.

Mary Marvell was undoubtedly one of the most popular actresses on the screen. She had only lately arrived in England in company with her husband, Gregory B. Rolf, also a film actor. Their marriage had taken place about a year ago in the States and this was their first visit to England. They had been given a great reception. Everyone was prepared to go mad over Mary Marvell, her wonderful clothes, her furs, her jewels, above all one jewel, the great diamond which had been nicknamed, to match its owner, "the Western Star." Much, true and untrue, had been written about this famous stone which was reported to be insured for the enormous sum of fifty thousand pounds.

All these details passed rapidly through my mind as I joined with Poirot in greeting our fair client.

Miss Marvell was small and slender, very fair and girlish-looking, with the wide innocent blue eyes of a child.

Poirot drew forward a chair for her, and she commenced talking at once.

"You will probably think me very foolish, Monsieur Poirot, but Lord Cronshaw was telling me last night how wonderfully you cleared up the mystery of his nephew's death, and I felt that I just must have your advice. I dare say it's only a silly hoax—Gregory says so—but it's just worrying me to death."

She paused for breath. Poirot beamed encouragement.

"Proceed, madame. You comprehend, I am still in the dark."

"It's these letters." Miss Marvell unclasped her handbag, and drew out three envelopes which she handed to Poirot.

The latter scrutinized them closely.

"Cheap paper—the name and address carefully printed. Let us see the inside." He drew out the enclosure.

I had joined him, and was leaning over his shoulder. The writing consisted of a single sentence, carefully printed like the envelope. It ran as follows:

"The great diamond which is the left eye of the god must return whence it came."

The second letter was couched in precisely the same terms, but the third was more explicit:

"You have been warned. You have not obeyed. Now the diamond will be taken from you. At the full of the moon, the two diamonds which are the left and right eye of the god shall return. So it is written."

"The first letter I treated as a joke," explained Miss Marvell. "When I got the second, I began to wonder. The third one came yesterday, and it seemed to me that, after all, the matter might be more serious than I had imagined."

"I see they did not come by post, these letters."

"No; they were left by hand—by a *Chinaman.* That is what frightens me."

"Why?"

"Because it was from a Chinaman in San Francisco that Gregory bought the stone three years ago."

"I see, madame, that you believe the diamond referred to to be—"

" 'The Western Star,' " finished Miss Marvell. "That's so. At the same time, Gregory remembers that there was some story attached to the stone, but the Chinaman wasn't handing out any information. Gregory says he seemed just scared to death, and in a mortal hurry to get rid of the thing. He only asked about a tenth of its value. It was Greg's wedding present to me."

Poirot nodded thoughtfully.

"The story seems of an almost unbelievable romanticism. And yet— who knows? I pray of you, Hastings, hand me my little almanac."

I complied.

"*Voyons!*" said Poirot, turning the leaves. "When is the date of the full moon? Ah, Friday next. That is in three days' time. *Eh bien,* madame, you seek my advice—I give it to you. This *belle histoire* may be a hoax—but it may not! Therefore I counsel you to place the diamond in my keeping until after Friday next. Then we can take what steps we please."

A slight cloud passed over the actress's face, and she replied constrainedly:

"I'm afraid that's impossible."

"You have it with you—*hein?*" Poirot was watching her narrowly.

The girl hesitated a moment, then slipped her hand into the bosom of her gown, drawing out a long thin chain. She leaned forward, unclosing her hand. In the palm, a stone of fire, exquisitely set in platinum, lay and winked at us solemnly.

Poirot drew in his breath with a long hiss.

"*Épatant!*" he murmured. "You permit, madame?" He took the jewel in his own hand and scrutinized it keenly, then restored it to her with a little bow. "A magnificent stone—without a flaw. Ah, *cent tonnerres!* and you carry it about with you, *comme ça!*"

"No, no, I'm very careful really, Monsieur Poirot. As a rule it's locked up in my jewel case, and left in the hotel safe deposit. We're staying at the *Magnificent*, you know. I just brought it along today for you to see."

"And you will leave it with me, *n'est-ce pas?* You will be advised by Papa Poirot?"

"Well, you see, it's this way, Monsieur Poirot. On Friday we're going down to Yardly Chase to spend a few days with Lord and Lady Yardly."

Her words awoke a vague echo of remembrance in my mind. Some gossip—what was it now? A few years ago Lord and Lady Yardly had paid a visit to the States, rumor had it that his lordship had rather gone the pace out there with the assistance of some lady friends—but surely there was something more, some gossip which coupled Lady Yardly's name with that of a "movie" star in California—why! it came to me in a flash! of course it was none other than Gregory B. Rolf.

"I'll let you into a little secret, Monsieur Poirot," Miss Marvell was continuing. "We've got a deal on with Lord Yardly. There's some chance of our arranging to film a play down there in his ancestral pile."

"At Yardly Chase?" I cried, interested. "Why, it's one of the showplaces of England."

Miss Marvell nodded.

"I guess it's the real old feudal stuff all right. But he wants a pretty stiff price, and of course I don't know yet whether the deal will go through, but Greg and I always like to combine business with pleasure."

"But—I demand pardon if I am dense, madame—surely it is possible to visit Yardly Chase without taking the diamond with you?"

A shrewd, hard look came into Miss Marvell's eyes which belied their childlike appearance. She looked suddenly a good deal older.

"I want to wear it down there."

"Surely," I said suddenly, "there are some very famous jewels in the Yardly collection, a large diamond amongst them?"

"That's so," said Miss Marvell briefly.

I heard Poirot murmur beneath his breath, "Ah, *c'est comme ça!*" Then he said aloud, with his usual uncanny luck in hitting the bull's-eye (he dignifies it by the name of psychology): "Then you are without doubt already acquainted with Lady Yardly, or perhaps your husband is?"

"Gregory knew her when she was out West three years ago," said Miss Marvell. She hesitated a moment, and then added abruptly: "Do either of you ever see *Society Gossip?*"

We both pleaded guilty rather shamefacedly.

"I asked because in this week's number there is an article on famous jewels, and it's really very curious—" She broke off.

I rose, went to the table at the other side of the room and returned with the paper in question in my hand. She took it from me, found the article, and began to read aloud:

". . . Among other famous stones may be included the Star of the East, a diamond in the possession of the Yardly family. An ancestor of the present Lord Yardly brought it back with him from China, and a romantic story is said to attach to it. According to this, the stone was once the right eye of a temple god. Another diamond, exactly similar in form and size, formed the left eye, and the story goes that this jewel, too, would in course of time be stolen. 'One eye shall go West, the other East, till they shall meet once more. Then, in triumph shall they return to the god.' It is a curious coincidence that there is at the present time a stone corresponding closely in description with this one, and known as 'the Star of the West,' or 'the Western Star.' It is the property of the celebrated film actress, Miss Mary Marvell. A comparison of the two stones would be interesting."

I stopped.

"*Épatant!*" murmured Poirot. "Without doubt a romance of the first water." He turned to Mary Marvell. "And you are not afraid, madame? You have no superstitious terrors? You do not fear to introduce these two Siamese twins to each other lest a Chinaman should appear and, hey presto! whisk them both back to China?"

His tone was mocking, but I fancied that an undercurrent of seriousness lay beneath it.

"I don't believe that Lady Yardly's diamond is anything like as good a stone as mine," said Miss Marvell. "Anyway, I'm going to see."

What more Poirot would have said I do not know, for at that moment the door flew open, and a splendid-looking man strode into the room.

From his crisply curling black head, to the tips of his patent-leather boots, he was a hero fit for romance.

"I said I'd call round for you, Mary," said Gregory Rolf, "and here I am. Well, what does Monsieur Poirot say to our little problem? Just one big hoax, same as I do?"

Poirot smiled up at the big actor. They made a ridiculous contrast.

"Hoax or no hoax, Mr. Rolf," he said dryly, "I have advised madame your wife not to take the jewel with her to Yardly Chase on Friday."

"I'm with you there, sir. I've already said so to Mary. But there! She's a woman through and through, and I guess she can't bear to think of another woman outshining her in the jewel line."

"What nonsense, Gregory!" said Mary Marvell sharply. But she flushed angrily.

Poirot shrugged his shoulders.

"Madame, I have advised. I can do no more. *C'est fini.*"

He bowed them both to the door.

"Ah! *la la*," he observed, returning. "*Histoire des femmes!* The good husband, he hit the nail on the head—*tout de même*, he was not tactful! Assuredly not."

I imparted to him my vague remembrances, and he nodded vigorously.

"So I thought. All the same, there is something curious underneath all this. With your permission, *mon ami*, I will take the air. Await my return, I beg of you. I shall not be long."

I was half asleep in my chair when the landlady tapped on the door, and put her head in.

"It's another lady to see Mr. Poirot, sir. I've told her he was out, but she says as how she'll wait, seeing as she's come up from the country."

"Oh, show her in here, Mrs. Murchison. Perhaps I can do something for her."

In another moment the lady had been ushered in. My heart gave a leap as I recognized her. Lady Yardly's portrait had figured too often in the Society papers to allow her to remain unknown.

"Do sit down, Lady Yardly," I said, drawing forward a chair. "My friend Poirot is out, but I know for a fact that he'll be back very shortly."

She thanked me and sat down. A very different type, this, from Miss Mary Marvell. Tall, dark, with flashing eyes, and a pale proud face—yet something wistful in the curves of the mouth.

I felt a desire to rise to the occasion. Why not? In Poirot's presence I have frequently felt a difficulty—I do not appear at my best. And yet there is no doubt that I, too, possess the deductive sense in a marked degree. I leant forward on a sudden impulse.

"Lady Yardly," I said, "I know why you have come here. You have received blackmailing letters about the diamond."

There was no doubt as to my bolt having shot home. She stared at me open-mouthed, all color banished from her cheeks.

"You know?" she gasped. "How?"

I smiled.

"By a perfectly logical process. If Miss Marvell has had warning letters—"

"Miss Marvell? She has been here?"

"She has just left. As I was saying, if she, as the holder of one of the twin diamonds, has received a mysterious series of warnings, you, as the holder of the other stone, must necessarily have done the same. You see how simple it is? I am right, then, you have received these strange communications also?"

For a moment she hesitated, as though in doubt whether to trust me or not, then she bowed her head in assent with a little smile.

"That is so," she acknowledged.

"Were yours, too, left by hand—by a Chinaman?"

"No, they came by post; but, tell me, has Miss Marvell undergone the same experience, then?"

I recounted to her the events of the morning. She listened attentively.

"It all fits in. My letters are the duplicates of hers. It is true that they came by post, but there is a curious perfume impregnating them— something in the nature of joss-stick—that at once suggested the East to me. What does it all mean?"

I shook my head.

"That is what we must find out. You have the letters with you? We might learn something from the postmarks."

"Unfortunately I destroyed them. You understand, at the time I regarded it as some foolish joke. Can it be true that some Chinese gang are really trying to recover the diamonds? It seems too incredible."

We went over the facts again and again, but could get no further towards the elucidation of the mystery. At last Lady Yardly rose.

"I really don't think I need wait for Monsieur Poirot. You can tell him all this, can't you? Thank you so much, Mr.—"

She hesitated, her hand outstretched.

"Captain Hastings."

"Of course! How stupid of me. You're a friend of the Cavendishes, aren't you? It was Mary Cavendish who sent me to Monsieur Poirot."

When my friend returned, I enjoyed telling him the tale of what had occurred during his absence. He cross-questioned me rather sharply over the details of our conversation and I could read between the lines that he was not best pleased to have been absent. I also fancied that the dear old fellow was just the least inclined to be jealous. It had become rather a pose with him to consistently belittle my abilities, and I think he was chagrined at finding no loophole for criticism. I was secretly rather pleased with myself, though I tried to conceal the fact for fear of irritating him. In spite of his idiosyncrasies, I was deeply attached to my quaint little friend.

"*Bien!*" he said at length, with a curious look on his face. "The plot develops. Pass me, I pray you, that *Peerage* on the top shelf there." He turned the leaves. "Ah, here we are! 'Yardly . . . 10th viscount, served South African War' . . . *tout ça n'a pas d'importance* . . . 'mar. 1907 Hon. Maude Stopperton, fourth daughter of 3rd Baron Cotteril' . . . um, um, um, . . . 'has iss. two daughters, born 1908, 1910. . . . Clubs . . . residences.' . . . *Voilà,* that does not tell us much. But tomorrow morning we see this milord!"

"What?"

"Yes. I telegraphed him."

"I thought you had washed your hands of the case?"

"I am not acting for Miss Marvell since she refuses to be guided by my advice. What I do now is for my own satisfaction—the satisfaction of Hercule Poirot! Decidedly, I must have a finger in this pie."

"And you calmly wire Lord Yardly to dash up to town just to suit your convenience. He won't be pleased."

"*Au contraire,* if I preserve for him his family diamond, he ought to be very grateful."

"Then you really think there is a chance of its being stolen?" I asked eagerly.

"Almost a certainty," replied Poirot placidly. "Everything points that way."

"But how—"

Poirot stopped my eager questions with an airy gesture of the hand. "Not now, I pray you. Let us not confuse the mind. And observe that *Peerage*—how you have replaced him! See you not that the tallest books go in the top shelf, the next tallest in the row beneath, and so on. Thus we have order, *method,* which, as I have often told you, Hastings—"

"Exactly," I said hastily, and put the offending volume in its proper place.

Lord Yardly turned out to be a cheery, loudvoiced sportsman with a rather red face, but with a good-humored bonhomie about him that was distinctly attractive and made up for any lack of mentality.

"Extraordinary business this, Monsieur Poirot. Can't make head or tail of it. Seems my wife's been getting odd kinds of letters, and that this Miss Marvell's had 'em too. What does it all mean?"

Poirot handed him the copy of the *Society Gossip*.

"First, milord, I would ask if these facts are substantially correct?"

The peer took it. His face darkened with anger as he read.

"Damned nonsense!" he spluttered. "There's never been any romantic story attaching to the diamond. It came from India originally, I believe. I never heard of all this Chinese god stuff."

"Still, the stone *is* known as 'The Star of the East.' "

"Well, what if it is?" he demanded wrathfully.

Poirot smiled a little, but made no direct reply.

"What I would ask you to do, milord, is to place yourself in my hands. If you do so unreservedly, I have great hopes of averting the catastrophe."

"Then you think there's actually something in these wildcat tales?"

"Will you do as I ask you?"

"Of course I will, but—"

"*Bien!* Then permit that I ask you a few questions. This affair of Yardly Chase, is it, as you say, all fixed up between you and Mr. Rolf?"

"Oh, he told you about it, did he? No, there's nothing settled." He hesitated, the brick-red color of his face deepening. "Might as well get the thing straight. I've made rather an ass of myself in many ways, Monsieur Poirot—and I'm head over ears in debt—but I want to pull up. I'm fond of the kids, and I want to straighten things up, and be able to live on at the old place. Gregory Rolf is offering me big money— enough to set me on my feet again. I don't want to do it—I hate the thought of all that crowd playacting round the Chase—but I may have to, unless—" He broke off.

Poirot eyed him keenly. "You have, then, another string to your bow? Permit that I make a guess? It is to sell the Star of the East?"

Lord Yardly nodded. "That's it. It's been in the family for some generations, but it's not entailed. Still, it's not the easiest thing in the world to find a purchaser. Hoffberg, the Hatton Garden man, is on the lookout for a likely customer, but he'll have to find one soon, or it's a washout."

"One more question, *permettez*—Lady Yardly, which plan does she approve?"

"Oh, she's bitterly opposed to my selling the jewel. You know what women are. She's all for this film stunt."

"I comprehend," said Poirot. He remained a moment or so in thought, then rose briskly to his feet. "You return to Yardly Chase at once? *Bien!* Say no word to anyone—to *anyone*, mind—but expect us there this evening. We will arrive shortly after five."

"All right, but I don't see—"

"*Ça n'a pas d'importance,*" said Poirot kindly. "You will that I preserve for you your diamond, *n'est-ce pas?*"

"Yes, but—"

"Then do as I say."

A sadly bewildered nobleman left the room.

It was half-past five when we arrived at Yardly Chase, and followed the dignified butler to the old paneled hall with its fire of blazing logs. A pretty picture met our eyes: Lady Yardly and her two children, the mother's proud dark head bent down over the two fair ones. Lord Yardly stood near, smiling down on them.

"Monsieur Poirot and Captain Hastings," announced the butler.

Lady Yardly looked up with a start, her husband came forward uncertainly, his eyes seeking instruction from Poirot. The little man was equal to the occasion.

"All my excuses! It is that I investigate still this affair of Miss Marvell's. She comes to you on Friday, does she not? I make a little tour first to make sure that all is secure. Also I wanted to ask of Lady Yardly if she recollected at all the postmarks on the letters she received?"

Lady Yardly shook her head regretfully. "I'm afraid I don't. It is stupid of me. But, you see, I never dreamt of taking them seriously."

"You'll stay the night?" said Lord Yardly.

"Oh, milord, I fear to incommode you. We have left our bags at the inn."

"That's all right." Lord Yardly had his cue. "We'll send down for them. No, no—no trouble, I assure you."

Poirot permitted himself to be persuaded, and sitting down by Lady Yardly, began to make friends with the children. In a short time they were all romping together, and had dragged me into the game.

"*Vous êtes bonne mère,*" said Poirot, with a gallant little bow, as the children were removed reluctantly by a stern nurse.

Lady Yardly smoothed her ruffled hair.

"I adore them," she said with a little catch in her voice.

"And they you—with reason!" Poirot bowed again.

A dressing gong sounded, and we rose to go up to our rooms. At that moment the butler entered with a telegram on a salver which he handed to Lord Yardly. The latter tore it open with a brief word of apology. As he read it he stiffened visibly.

With an ejaculation, he handed it to his wife. Then he glanced at my friend.

"Just a minute, Monsieur Poirot. I feel you ought to know about this. It's from Hoffberg. He thinks he's found a customer for the diamond—an American, sailing for the States tomorrow. They're sending down a chap to night to vet the stone. By Jove, though, if this goes through—" Words failed him.

Lady Yardly had turned away. She still held the telegram in her hand.

"I wish you wouldn't sell it, George," she said, in a low voice. "It's been in the family so long." She waited, as though for a reply, but when none came her face hardened. She shrugged her shoulders. "I must go and dress. I suppose I had better display 'the goods.'" She turned to Poirot with a slight grimace.

"It's one of the most hideous necklaces that was ever designed! George has always promised to have the stones reset for me, but it's never been done." She left the room.

Half an hour later, we three were assembled in the great drawing room awaiting the lady. It was already a few minutes past the dinner hour.

Suddenly there was a low rustle, and Lady Yardly appeared framed in the doorway, a radiant figure in a long white shimmering dress. Round the column of her neck was a rivulet of fire. She stood there with one hand just touching the necklace.

"Behold the sacrifice," she said gaily. Her ill humor seemed to have vanished. "Wait while I turn the big light on and you shall feast your eyes on the ugliest necklace in England."

The switches were just outside the door. As she stretched out her hand to them, the incredible thing happened. Suddenly without any warning, every light was extinguished, the door banged, and from the other side of it came a long-drawn piercing woman's scream.

"My God!" cried Lord Yardly. "That was Maude's voice! What has happened?"

We rushed blindly for the door, cannoning into each other in the darkness. It was some minutes before we could find it. What a sight met our eyes! Lady Yardly lay senseless on the marble floor, a crimson mark on her white throat where the necklace had been wrenched from her neck.

As we bent over her, uncertain for the moment whether she were dead or alive, her eyelids opened.

"The Chinaman," she whispered painfully. "The Chinaman—the side door."

Lord Yardly sprang up with an oath. I accompanied him, my heart beating wildly. The Chinaman again! The side door in question was a small one in the angle of the wall, not more than a dozen yards from the scene of the tragedy. As we reached it, I gave a cry. There, just short of the threshold, lay the glittering necklace, evidently dropped by the thief in the panic of his flight. I swooped joyously down on it. Then I uttered another cry which Lord Yardly echoed. For in the middle of the necklace was a great gap. The Star of the East was missing!

"That settles it," I breathed. "These were no ordinary thieves. This one stone was all they wanted."

"But how did the fellow get in?"

"Through this door."

"But it's always locked."

I shook my head. "It's not locked now. See." I pulled it open as I spoke.

As I did so something fluttered to the ground. I picked it up. It was a piece of silk, and the embroidery was unmistakable. It had been torn from a Chinaman's robe.

"In his haste it caught in the door," I explained. "Come, hurry. He cannot have gone far as yet."

But in vain we hunted and searched. In the pitch darkness of the night, the thief had found it easy to make his getaway. We returned reluctantly, and Lord Yardly sent off one of the footmen post haste to fetch the police.

Lady Yardly, aptly ministered to by Poirot, who is as good as a woman in these matters, was sufficiently recovered to be able to tell her story.

"I was just going to turn on the other light," she said, "when a man sprang on me from behind. He tore my necklace from my neck with such force that I fell headlong to the floor. As I fell I saw him disappearing through the side door. Then I realized by the pigtail and the embroidered robe that he was a Chinaman." She stopped with a shudder.

The butler reappeared. He spoke in a low voice to Lord Yardly.

"A gentleman from Mr. Hoffberg's, m'lord. He says you expect him."

"Good heavens!" cried the distracted nobleman. "I must see him, I suppose. No, not here, Mullings, in the library."

I drew Poirot aside.

"Look here, my dear fellow, hadn't we better get back to London?"

"You think so, Hastings? Why?"

"Well"—I coughed delicately—"things haven't gone very well, have they? I mean, you tell Lord Yardly to place himself in your hands and all will be well—and then the diamond vanishes from under your very nose!"

"True," said Poirot, rather crestfallen. "It was not one of my most striking triumphs."

This way of describing events almost caused me to smile, but I stuck to my guns.

"So, having—pardon the expression—rather made a mess of things, don't you think it would be more graceful to leave immediately?"

"And the dinner, the without doubt excellent dinner, that the *chef* of Lord Yardly has prepared?"

"Oh, what's dinner!" I said impatiently.

Poirot held up his hands in horror.

*"Mon Dieu!* It is that in this country you treat the affairs gastronomic with a criminal indifference."

"There's another reason why we should get back to London as soon as possible," I continued.

"What is that, my friend?"

"The other diamond," I said, lowering my voice. "Miss Marvell's."

*"Eh bien,* what of it?"

"Don't you see?" His unusual obtuseness annoyed me. What had happened to his usually keen wits? "They've got one, now they'll go for the other."

*"Tiens!"* cried Poirot, stepping back a pace and regarding me with admiration. "But your brain marches to a marvel, my friend! Figure to yourself that for the moment I had not thought of that! But there is plenty of time. The full of the moon, it is not until Friday."

I shook my head dubiously. The full-of-the-moon theory left me entirely cold. I had my way with Poirot, however, and we departed immediately, leaving behind us a note of explanation and apology for Lord Yardly.

My idea was to go at once to the *Magnificent,* and relate to Miss Marvell what had occurred, but Poirot vetoed the plan, and insisted that the morning would be time enough. I gave in rather grudgingly.

In the morning Poirot seemed strangely disinclined to stir out. I began to suspect that, having made a mistake to start with, he was singularly loath to proceed with the case. In answer to my persuasions, he pointed out, with admirable common sense, that as the details of the affair at Yardly Chase were already in the morning papers the Rolfs would know quite as much as we could tell them. I gave way unwillingly.

Events proved my forebodings to be justified. About two o'clock, the telephone rang. Poirot answered it. He listened for some moments, then with a brief *"Bien, j'y serai"* he rang off, and turned to me.

"What do you think, *mon ami?"* He looked half ashamed, half excited. "The diamond of Miss Marvell, it has been stolen."

"What?" I cried, springing up. "And what about the 'full of the moon' now?" Poirot hung his head. "When did this happen?"

"This morning, I understand."

I shook my head sadly. "If only you had listened to me. You see I was right."

"It appears so, *mon ami*," said Poirot cautiously. "Appearances are deceptive, they say, but it certainly appears so."

As we hurried in a taxi to the *Magnificent*, I puzzled out the true inwardness of the scheme.

"That 'full of the moon' idea was clever. The whole point of it was to get us to concentrate on the Friday, and so be off our guard beforehand. It is a pity you did not realize that."

*"Ma foi!"* said Poirot airily, his nonchalance quite restored after its brief eclipse. "One cannot think of everything!"

I felt sorry for him. He did so hate failure of any kind.

"Cheer up," I said consolingly. "Better luck next time."

At the *Magnificent*, we were ushered at once into the manager's office. Gregory Rolf was there with two men from Scotland Yard. A pale-faced clerk sat opposite them.

Rolf nodded as we entered.

"We're getting to the bottom of it," he said. "But it's almost unbelievable. How the guy had the nerve I can't think."

A very few minutes sufficed to give us the facts. Mr. Rolf had gone out of the hotel at 11:15. At 11:30, a gentleman, so like him in appearance as to pass muster, entered the hotel and demanded the jewel case from the safe deposit. He duly signed the receipt, remarking carelessly as he did so, "Looks a bit different from my ordinary one, but I hurt my hand getting out of the taxi." The clerk merely smiled and remarked that he saw very little difference. Rolf laughed and said, "Well, don't run me in as a crook this time, anyway. I've been getting threatening letters from a Chinaman, and the worst of it is I look rather like one myself—it's something about the eyes."

"I looked at him," said the clerk who was telling us this, "and I saw at once what he meant. The eyes slanted up at the corners like an Oriental's. I'd never noticed it before."

"Darn it all, man," roared Gregory Rolf, leaning forward, "Do you notice it now?"

The man looked up at him and started.

"No, sir," he said. "I can't say that I do." And indeed there was nothing even remotely Oriental about the frank brown eyes that looked into ours.

The Scotland Yard man grunted. "Bold customer. Thought the eyes might be noticed, and took the bull by the horns to disarm suspicion. He must have watched you out of the hotel, sir, and nipped in as soon as you were well away."

"What about the jewel case?" I asked.

"It was found in a corridor of the hotel. Only one thing had been taken—'the Western Star.'"

We stared at each other—the whole thing was so bizarre, so unreal.

Poirot hopped briskly to his feet. "I have not been of much use, I fear," he said regretfully. "Is it permitted to see Madame?"

"I guess she's prostrated with the shock," explained Rolf.

"Then perhaps I might have a few words alone with you, monsieur?"

"Certainly."

In about five minutes Poirot reappeared.

"Now, my friend," he said gaily. "To a post office. I have to send a telegram."

"Who to?"

"Lord Yardly." He discounted further inquiries by slipping his arm through mine. "Come, come, *mon ami*, I know all that you feel about this miserable business. I have not distinguished myself! You, in my place, might have distinguished yourself! *Bien!* All is admitted. Let us forget it and have lunch."

It was about four o'clock when we entered Poirot's rooms. A figure rose from a chair by the window. It was Lord Yardly. He looked haggard and distraught.

"I got your wire and came up at once. Look here, I've been round to Hoffberg, and they know nothing about that man of theirs last night, or the wire either. Do you think that—"

Poirot held up his hand.

"My excuses! I sent that wire, and hired the gentleman in question."

"*You*—but why? What?" The nobleman spluttered impotently.

"My little idea was to bring things to a head," explained Poirot placidly.

"Bring things to a head! Oh, my God!" cried Lord Yardly.

"And the ruse succeeded," said Poirot cheerfully. "Therefore, milord, I have much pleasure in returning you—this!" With a dramatic gesture he produced a glittering object. It was a great diamond.

"The Star of the East," gasped Lord Yardly. "But I don't understand—"

"No?" said Poirot. "It makes no matter. Believe me, it was necessary for the diamond to be stolen. I promised you that it should be preserved to you, and I have kept my word. You must permit me to keep my little secret. Convey, I beg of you, the assurances of my deepest respect to Lady Yardly, and tell her how pleased I am to be able to restore her jewel to her. What *beau temps*, is it not? Good day, milord."

And smiling and talking, the amazing little man conducted the bewildered nobleman to the door. He returned gently rubbing his hands.

"Poirot," I said. "Am I quite demented?"

"No, *mon ami*, but you are, as always, in a mental fog."

"How did you get the diamond?"

"From Mr. Rolf."

"Rolf?"

"*Mais oui!* The warning letters, the Chinaman, the article in *Society Gossip,* all sprang from the ingenious brain of Mr. Rolf! The two diamonds, supposed to be so miraculously alike—bah! they did not exist. There was only *one* diamond, my friend! Originally in the Yardly collection, for three years it has been in the possession of Mr. Rolf. He stole it this morning with the assistance of a touch of greasepaint at the corner of each eye! Ah, I must see him on the film, he is indeed an artist, *celui-là!*"

"But why did he steal his own diamond?" I asked, puzzled.

"For many reasons. To begin with, Lady Yardly was getting restive."

"Lady Yardly?"

"You comprehend she was left much alone in California. Her husband was amusing himself elsewhere. Mr. Rolf was handsome, he had an air about him of romance. But *au fond,* he is very businesslike, *ce monseiur!* He made love to Lady Yardly, and then he blackmailed her. I taxed the lady with the truth the other night, and she admitted it. She swore that she had only been indiscreet, and I believe her. But, undoubtedly, Rolf had letters of hers that could be twisted to bear a different interpretation. Terrified by the threat of a divorce, and the prospect of being separated from her children, she agreed to all he wished. She had no money of her own, and she was forced to permit him to substitute a paste replica for the real stone. The coincidence of the date of the appearance of the Western Star struck me at once. All goes well. Lord Yardly prepares to *range* himself—to settle down. And then comes the menace of the possible sale of the diamond. The substitution will be discovered. Without doubt she writes off frantically to Gregory Rolf who has just arrived in England. He soothes her by promising to arrange all—and prepares for a double robbery. In this way he will quiet the lady, who might conceivably tell all to her husband, an affair which would not suit our blackmailer at all, he will have £50,000 insurance money (aha, you had forgotten that!), and he will still have the diamond! At this point I put my finger in the pie. The arrival of a diamond expert is announced. Lady Yardly, as I felt sure she would, immediately arranges a robbery—and does it very well too! But Hercule Poirot, he sees nothing but facts. What happens in actuality? The lady switches off the light, bangs the door, throws the necklace down the passage, and screams. She has already wrenched out the diamond with pliers upstairs—"

"But we saw the necklace round her neck!" I objected.

"I demand pardon, my friend. Her hand concealed the part of it where the gap would have shown. To place a piece of silk in the door beforehand is child's play! Of course, as soon as Rolf read of the robbery, he arranged his own little comedy. And very well he played it!"

"What did you say to him?" I asked with lively curiosity.

"I said to him that Lady Yardly had told her husband all, that I was empowered to recover the jewel, and that if it were not immediately handed over proceedings would be taken. Also a few more little lies which occurred to me. He was as wax in my hands!"

I pondered the matter.

"It seems a little unfair on Mary Marvell. She has lost her diamond through no fault of her own."

"Bah!" said Poirot brutally. "She has a magnificent advertisement. That is all she cares for, that one! Now the other, she is different. *Bonne mère, très femme!*"

"Yes," I said doubtfully, hardly sharing Poirot's views on femininity. "I suppose it was Rolf who sent her the duplicate letters."

*"Pas du tout,"* said Poirot briskly. "She came by the advice of Mary Cavendish to seek my aid in her dilemma. Then she heard that Mary Marvell, whom she knew to be her enemy, had been here, and she changed her mind, jumping at a pretext that *you,* my friend, offered her A very few questions sufficed to show me that *you* told her of the letters, not she you! She jumped at the chance your words offered."

"I don't believe it," I cried, stung.

*"Si, si, mon ami,* it is a pity that you study not the psychology. She told you that the letters were destroyed? Oh, la la, *never* does a woman destroy a letter if she can avoid it! Not even if it would be more prudent to do so!"

"It's all very well," I said, my anger rising, "but you've made a perfect fool of me! From beginning to end! No, it's all very well to try to explain it away afterwards. There really is a limit!"

"But you were so enjoying yourself, my friend. I had not the heart to shatter your illusions."

"It's no good. You've gone a bit too far this time."

*"Mon Dieu!* but how you enrage yourself for nothing, *mon ami!"*

"I'm fed up!" I went out, banging the door. Poirot had made an absolute laughing stock of me. I decided he needed a sharp lesson. I would let some time elapse before I forgave him. He had encouraged me to make a perfect fool of myself!

# The Tragedy at
# Marsdon Manor

I HAD been called away from town for a few days, and on my return found Poirot in the act of strapping up his small valise.

"*A la bonne heure*, Hastings. I feared you would not have returned in time to accompany me."

"You are called away on a case, then?"

"Yes, though I am bound to admit that, on the face of it, the affair does not seem promising. The Northern Union Insurance Company have asked me to investigate the death of a Mr. Maltravers who a few weeks ago insured his life with them for the large sum of fifty thousand pounds."

"Yes?" I said, much interested.

"There was, of course, the usual suicide clause in the policy. In the event of his committing suicide within a year the premiums would be forfeited. Mr. Maltravers was duly examined by the Company's own doctor, and although he was a man slightly past the prime of life was passed as being in quite sound health. However, on Wednesday last—the day before yesterday—the body of Mr. Maltravers was found in the grounds of his house in Essex, Marsdon Manor, and the cause of his death is described as some kind of internal hemorrhage. That in itself would be nothing remarkable, but sinister rumors as to Mr. Maltravers' financial position have been in the air of late, and the Northern Union have ascertained beyond any possible doubt that the deceased gentleman stood upon the verge of bankruptcy. Now that alters matters considerably. Maltravers had a beautiful young wife, and it is suggested that he got together all the ready money he could for the purpose of paying the premiums on a life insurance for his wife's benefit, and then committed suicide. Such a thing is not uncommon. In any case, my friend Alfred Wright, who is a director of the Northern Union, has asked me to investigate the facts of the case, but, as I told him, I am not very hopeful of success. If the cause of the death had been heart failure, I should have been more sanguine. Heart failure may always be translated as the inability of the local

G. P. to discover what his patient really did die of, but a hemorrhage seems fairly definite. Still, we can but make some necessary inquiries. Five minutes to pack your bag, Hastings, and we will take a taxi to Liverpool Street."

About an hour later, we alighted from a Great Eastern train at the little station of Marsdon Leigh. Inquiries at the station yielded the information that Marsdon Manor was about a mile distant. Poirot decided to walk, and we betook ourselves along the main street.

"What is our plan of campaign?" I asked.

"First I will call upon the doctor. I have ascertained that there is only one doctor in Marsdon Leigh, Dr. Ralph Bernard. Ah, here we are at his house."

The house in question was a kind of superior cottage, standing back a little from the road. A brass plate on the gate bore the doctor's name. We passed up the path and rang the bell.

We proved to be fortunate in our call. It was the doctor's consulting hour, and for the moment there were no patients waiting for him. Dr. Bernard was an elderly man, high-shouldered and stooping, with a pleasant vagueness of manner.

Poirot introduced himself and explained the purpose of our visit, adding that insurance companies were bound to investigate fully in a case of this kind.

"Of course, of course," said Dr. Bernard vaguely. "I suppose, as he was such a rich man, his life was insured for a big sum?"

"You consider him a rich man, doctor?"

The doctor looked rather surprised.

"Was he not? He kept two cars, you know, and Marsdon Manor is a pretty big place to keep up, although I believe he bought it very cheap."

"I understand that he had had considerable losses of late," said Poirot, watching the doctor narrowly.

The latter, however, merely shook his head sadly.

"Is that so? Indeed. It is fortunate for his wife, then, that there is this life insurance. A very beautiful and charming young creature, but terribly unstrung by this sad catastrophe. A mass of nerves, poor thing. I have tried to spare her all I can, but of course the shock was bound to be considerable."

"You have been attending Mr. Maltravers recently?"

"My dear sir, I never attended him."

"What?"

"I understand Mr. Maltravers was a Christian Scientist—or something of that kind."

"But you examined the body?"

"Certainly. I was fetched by one of the under-gardeners."

"And the cause of death was clear?"

"Absolutely. There was blood on the lips, but most of the bleeding must have been internal."

"Was he still lying where he had been found?"

"Yes, the body had not been touched. He was lying on the edge of a small plantation. He had evidently been out shooting rooks, a small rook rifle lay beside him. The hemorrhage must have occurred quite suddenly. Gastric ulcer, without a doubt."

"No question of his having been shot, eh?"

"My dear sir!"

"I demand pardon," said Poirot humbly. "But, if my memory is not at fault, in the case of a recent murder, the doctor first gave a verdict of heart failure—altering it when the local constable pointed out that there was a bullet wound through the head!"

"You will not find any bullet wounds on the body of Mr. Maltravers," said Dr. Bernard dryly. "Now, gentlemen, if there is nothing further—"

We took the hint.

"Good morning, and many thanks to you, doctor, for so kindly answering our questions. By the way, you saw no need for an autopsy?"

"Certainly not." The doctor became quite apoplectic. "The cause of death was clear, and in my profession we see no need to distress unduly the relatives of a dead patient."

And, turning, the doctor slammed the door sharply in our faces.

"And what do you think of Dr. Bernard, Hastings?" inquired Poirot, as we proceeded on our way to the Manor.

"Rather an old ass."

"Exactly. Your judgments of character are always profound, my friend."

I glanced at him uneasily, but he seemed perfectly serious. A twinkle, however, came into his eye, and he added slyly:

"That is to say, when there is no question of a beautiful woman!"

I looked at him coldly.

On our arrival at the manor house, the door was opened to us by a middle-aged parlormaid. Poirot handed her his card, and a letter from the insurance company for Mrs. Maltravers. She showed us into a small morning room, and retired to tell her mistress. About ten minutes elapsed, and then the door opened, and a slender figure in widow's weeds stood upon the threshold.

"Monsieur Poirot?" she faltered.

"Madame!" Poirot sprang gallantly to his feet and hastened towards her. "I cannot tell you how I regret to derange you in this way. But what will you? *Les affaires*—they know no mercy."

Mrs. Maltravers permitted him to lead her to a chair. Her eyes were red with weeping, but the temporary disfigurement could not conceal her extraordinary beauty. She was about twenty-seven or eight, and very fair, with large blue eyes and a pretty pouting mouth.

"It is something about my husband's insurance, is it? But must I be bothered *now*—so soon?"

"Courage, my dear madame. Courage! You see, your late husband insured his life for rather a large sum, and in such a case the company always has to satisfy itself as to a few details. They have empowered me to act for them. You can rest assured that I will do all in my power to render the matter not too unpleasant for you. Will you recount to me briefly the sad events of Wednesday?"

"I was changing for tea when my maid came up—one of the gardeners had just run to the house. He had found—"

Her voice trailed away. Poirot pressed her hand sympathetically.

"I comprehend. Enough! You had seen your husband earlier in the afternoon?"

"Not since lunch. I had walked down to the village for some stamps, and I believe he was out pottering round the grounds."

"Shooting rooks, eh?"

"Yes, he usually took his little rook rifle with him, and I heard one or two shots in the distance."

"Where is this little rook rifle now?"

"In the hall, I think."

She led the way out of the room and found and handed the little weapon to Poirot, who examined it cursorily.

"Two shots fired, I see," he observed, as he handed it back. "And now, madame, if I might see—"

He paused delicately.

"The servant shall take you," she murmured, averting her head.

The parlormaid, summoned, led Poirot upstairs. I remained with the lovely and unfortunate woman. It was hard to know whether to speak or remain silent. I essayed one or two general reflections to which she responded absently, and in a very few minutes Poirot rejoined us.

"I thank you for all your courtesy, madame. I do not think you need be troubled any further with this matter. By the way, do you know anything of your husband's financial position?"

She shook her head.

"Nothing whatever. I am very stupid over business things."

"I see. Then you can give us no clue as to why he suddenly decided to insure his life? He had not done so previously, I understand."

"Well, we had only been married a little over a year. But, as to why he insured his life, it was because he had absolutely made up his mind that he would not live long. He had a strong premonition of his own death. I gather that he had had one hemorrhage already, and that he knew that another one would prove fatal. I tried to dispel these gloomy fears of his, but without avail. Alas, he was only too right!"

Tears in her eyes, she bade us a dignified farewell. Poirot made a characteristic gesture as we walked down the drive together.

"*Eh bien,* that is that! Back to London, my friend, there appears to be no mouse in this mousehole. And yet—"

"Yet what?"

"A slight discrepancy, that is all! You noticed it? You did not? Still, life is full of discrepancies, and assuredly the man cannot have taken his own life—there is no poison that would fill his mouth with blood. No, no, I must resign myself to the fact that all here is clear and above board—but who is this?"

A tall young man was striding up the drive towards us. He passed us without making any sign, but I noted that he was not ill-looking, with a lean, deeply bronzed face that spoke of life in a tropic clime. A gardener who was sweeping up leaves had paused for a minute in his task, and Poirot ran quickly up to him.

"Tell me, I pray you, who is that gentleman? Do you know him?"

"I don't remember his name, sir, though I did hear it. He was staying down here last week for a night. Tuesday, it was."

"Quick, *mon ami,* let us follow him."

We hastened up the drive after the retreating figure. A glimpse of a black-robed figure on the terrace at the side of the house, and our quarry swerved and we after him, so that we were witnesses of the meeting.

Mrs. Maltravers almost staggered where she stood, and her face blanched noticeably.

"You," she gasped. "I thought you were on the sea—on your way to East Africa?"

"I got some news from my lawyers that detained me," explained the young man. "My old uncle in Scotland died unexpectedly and left me some money. Under the circumstances I thought it better to cancel my passage. Then I saw this bad news in the paper and I came down to see if there was anything I could do. You'll want someone to look after things for you a bit perhaps."

At that moment they became aware of our presence. Poirot stepped forward, and with many apologies explained that he had left his stick in the hall. Rather reluctantly, it seemed to me, Mrs. Maltravers made the necessary introduction.

"Monsieur Poirot, Captain Black."

A few minutes' chat ensued, in the course of which Poirot elicited the fact that Captain Black was putting up at the Anchor Inn. The missing stick not having been discovered (which was not surprising), Poirot uttered more apologies and we withdrew.

We returned to the village at a great pace, and Poirot made a beeline for the Anchor Inn.

"Here we establish ourselves until our friend the Captain returns," he explained. "You notice that I emphasized the point that we were returning to London by the first train? Possibly you thought I meant it. But no—you observed Mrs. Maltravers' face when she caught sight of this young Black? She was clearly taken aback, and he—*eh bien*, he was very devoted, did you not think so? And he was here on Tuesday night—the day before Mr. Maltravers died. We must investigate the doings of Captain Black, Hastings."

In about half an hour we espied our quarry approaching the inn. Poirot went out and accosted him and presently brought him up to the room we had engaged.

"I have been telling Captain Black of the mission which brings us here," he explained. "You can understand, *monseiur le capitaine*, that I am anxious to arrive at Mr. Maltravers' state of mind immediately before his death, and that at the same time I do not wish to distress Mrs. Maltravers unduly by asking her painful questions. Now, you were here just before the occurrence, and can give us equally valuable information."

"I'll do anything I can to help you, I'm sure," replied the young soldier, "but I'm afraid I didn't notice anything out of the ordinary. You see, although Maltravers was an old friend of my people's, I didn't know him very well myself."

"You came down—when?"

"Tuesday afternoon. I went up to town early Wednesday morning, as my boat sailed from Tilbury about twelve o'clock. But some news I got made me alter my plans, as I dare say you heard me explain to Mrs. Maltravers."

"You were returning to East Africa, I understand?"

"Yes. I've been out there ever since the War—a great country."

"Exactly. Now what was the talk about at dinner on Tuesday night?"

"Oh, I don't know. The usual odd topics. Maltravers asked after my people, and then we discussed the question of German reparations, and then Mrs. Maltravers asked a lot of questions about East Africa, and I told them one or two yarns, that's about all, I think."

"Thank you."

Poirot was silent for a moment, then he said gently: "With your permission, I should like to try a little experiment. You have told us all that your conscious self knows, I want now to question your subconscious self."

"Psychoanalysis, what?" said Black, with visible alarm.

"Oh, no," said Poirot reassuringly. "You see, it is like this, I give you a word, you answer with another, and so on. Any word, the first one you think of. Shall we begin?"

"All right," said Black slowly, but he looked uneasy.

"Note down the words, please, Hastings," said Poirot. Then he took from his pocket his big turnip-faced watch and laid it on the table beside him. "We will commence. Day."

There was a moment's pause, and then Black replied:

"*Night.*"

As Poirot proceeded, his answers came quicker.

"Name," said Poirot.

"*Place.*"

"Bernard."

"*Shaw.*"

"Tuesday."

"*Dinner.*"

"Journey."

"*Ship.*"

"Country."

"*Uganda.*"

"Story."

"*Lions.*"

"Rook Rifle."

"*Farm.*"

"Shot."

"*Suicide.*"

"Elephant."

"*Tusks.*"

"Money."

"*Lawyers.*"

"Thank you, Captain Black. Perhaps you could spare me a few minutes in about half an hour's time?"

"Certainly." The young soldier looked at him curiously and wiped his brow as he got up.

"And now, Hastings," said Poirot, smiling at me as the door closed behind him. "You see it all, do you not?"

"I don't know what you mean."

"Does that list of words tell you nothing?"

I scrutinized it, but was forced to shake my head.

"I will assist you. To begin with, Black answered well within the normal time limit, with no pauses, so we can take it that he himself has no guilty knowledge to conceal. 'Day' to 'Night' and 'Place' to 'Name' are normal associations. I began work with 'Bernard' which might have suggested the local doctor had he come across him at all. Evidently he had not. After our recent conversation, he gave 'Dinner' to my 'Tuesday,' but 'Journey' and 'Country' were answered by 'Ship' and 'Uganda,' showing clearly that it was his journey abroad that was important to him and not the one which brought him down here. 'Story' recalls to him one of the 'Lion' stories he told at dinner. I proceed to 'Rook Rifle' and he answered with the totally unexpected word 'Farm.' When I say 'Shot,' he answers at once 'Suicide.' The association seems clear. A man he knows committed suicide with a rook rifle on a farm somewhere. Remember, too, that his mind is still on the stories he told at dinner, and I think you will agree that I shall not be far from the truth if I recall Captain Black and ask him to repeat the particular suicide story which he told at the dinner table on Tuesday evening."

Black was straightforward enough over the matter.

"Yes, I did tell them that story now that I come to think of it. Chap shot himself on a farm out there. Did it with a rook rifle through the roof of the mouth, bullet lodged in the brain. Doctors were no end puzzled over it—there was nothing to show except a little blood on the lips. But what—"

"What has it got to do with Mr. Maltravers? You did not know, I see, that he was found with a rook rifle by his side."

"You mean my story suggested to him—oh, but that is awful!"

"Do not distress yourself—it would have been one way or another. Well, I must get on the telephone to London."

Poirot had a lengthy conversation over the wire, and came back thoughtful. He went off by himself in the afternoon, and it was not till seven o'clock that he announced that he could put it off no longer, but must break the news to the young widow. My sympathy had already gone out to her unreservedly. To be left penniless, and with the knowledge that her husband had killed himself to assure her future was a hard burden for any woman to bear. I cherished a secret hope, however, that young Black might prove capable of consoling her after her first grief had passed. He evidently admired her enormously.

Our interview with the lady was painful. She refused vehemently to believe the facts that Poirot advanced, and when she was at last convinced broke down into bitter weeping. An examination of the body turned our suspicions into certainty. Poirot was very sorry for the poor lady, but, after all, he was employed by the insurance company, and what could he do? As he was preparing to leave he said gently to Mrs. Maltravers:

"Madame, you of all people should know that there are no dead!"

"What do you mean?" she faltered, her eyes growing wide.

"Have you never taken part in any spiritualistic séances? You are mediumistic, you know."

"I have been told so. But you do not believe in spiritualism, surely?"

"Madame, I have seen some strange things. You know that they say in the village that this house is haunted?"

She nodded, and at that moment the parlormaid announced that dinner was ready.

"Won't you just stay and have something to eat?"

We accepted gratefully, and I felt that our presence could not but help distract her a little from her own griefs.

We had just finished our soup, when there was a scream outside the door, and the sound of breaking crockery. We jumped up. The parlormaid appeared, her hand to her heart.

"It was a man—standing in the passage."

Poirot rushed out, returning quickly.

"There is no one there."

"Isn't there, sir?" said the parlormaid weakly. "Oh, it did give me a start!"

"But why?"

She dropped her voice to a whisper.

"I thought—I thought it was the master—it looked like 'im."

I saw Mrs. Maltravers give a terrified start, and my mind flew to the old superstition that a suicide cannot rest. She thought of it too, I am sure, for a minute later, she caught Poirot's arm with a scream.

"Didn't you hear that? Those three taps on the window? That's how *he* always used to tap when he passed round the house."

"The ivy," I cried. "It was the ivy against the pane."

But a sort of terror was gaining on us all. The parlormaid was obviously unstrung, and when the meal was over Mrs. Maltravers besought Poirot not to go at once. She was clearly terrified to be left alone. We sat in the little morning room. The wind was getting up, and moaning round the house in an eerie fashion. Twice the door of the room came unlatched and the door slowly opened, and each time she clung to me with a terrified gasp.

"Ah, but this door, it is bewitched!" cried Poirot angrily at last. He got up and shut it once more, then turned the key in the lock. "I shall lock it, so!"

"Don't do that," she gasped, "if it should come open now—"

And even as she spoke the impossible happened. The locked door slowly swung open. I could not see into the passage from where I sat, but she and Poirot were facing it. She gave one long shriek as she turned to him.

"You saw him—there in the passage?" she cried.

He was staring down at her with a puzzled face, then shook his head.

"I saw him—my husband—you must have seen him too?"

"Madame, I saw nothing. You are not well—unstrung—"

"I am perfectly well, I—Oh, God!"

Suddenly, without any warning, the lights quivered and went out. Out of the darkness came three loud raps. I could hear Mrs. Maltravers moaning.

And then—I saw!

The man I had seen on the bed upstairs stood there facing us, gleaming with a faint ghostly light. There was blood on his lips, and he held his right hand out, pointing. Suddenly a brilliant light seemed to proceed from it. It passed over Poirot and me, and fell on Mrs. Maltravers. I saw her white terrified face, and something else!

"My God, Poirot!" I cried. "Look at her hand, her right hand. It's all red!"

Her own eyes fell on it, and she collapsed in a heap on the floor.

"Blood," she cried hysterically. "Yes, it's blood. I killed him. I did it. He was showing me, and then I put my hand on the trigger and pressed. Save me from him—save me! He's come back!"

Her voice died away in a gurgle.

"Lights," said Poirot briskly.

The lights went on as if by magic.

"That's it," he continued. "You heard, Hastings? And you, Everett? Oh, by the way, this is Mr. Everett, rather a fine member of the theatrical profession. I 'phoned to him this afternoon. His make-up is good, isn't it? Quite like the dead man, and with a pocket torch and the necessary phosphorescence he made the proper impression. I shouldn't touch her right hand if I were you, Hastings. Red paint marks so. When the lights went out I clasped her hand, you see. By the way, we mustn't miss our train. Inspector Japp is outside the window. A bad night—but he has been able to while away the time by tapping on the window every now and then.

"You see," continued Poirot, as we walked briskly through the wind and rain, "there was a little discrepancy. The doctor seemed to think the deceased was a Christian Scientist, and who could have given him that impression but Mrs. Maltravers? But to us she represented him as being in a grave state of apprehension about his own health. Again, why was she so taken aback by the reappearance of young Black? And lastly, although I know that convention decrees that a woman must make a decent pretense of mourning for her husband, I do not care for such heavily rouged eyelids! You did not observe them, Hastings? No? As I always tell you, you see nothing!

"Well, there it was. There were the two possibilities. Did Black's story suggest an ingenious method of committing suicide to Mr. Maltravers, or did his other listener, the wife, see an equally ingenious method of committing murder? I inclined to the latter view. To shoot himself in the way indicated, he would probably have had to pull the trigger with his toe—or at least so I imagine. Now if Maltravers had been found with one boot off, we should almost certainly have heard of it from someone. An odd detail like that would have been remembered.

"No, as I say, I inclined to the view that it was a case of murder, not suicide, but I realized that I had not a shadow of proof in support of my theory. Hence the elaborate little comedy you saw played to-night."

"Even now I don't quite see all the details of the crime," I said.

"Let us start from the beginning. Here is a shrewd and scheming woman who, knowing of her husband's financial debacle and tired of the elderly mate she has only married for his money, induces him to insure his life for a large sum, and then seeks for the means to accomplish her purpose. An accident gives her that—the young soldier's strange story. The next afternoon when *monsieur le capitaine,* as she thinks, is on the high seas, she and her husband are strolling round the grounds. 'What a curious story that was last night!' she observes. 'Could a man shoot himself in such a way? Do show me if it is possible!' The poor fool—he shows her. He places the end of the rifle in his mouth. She stoops down, and puts her finger on the trigger, laughing up at him. 'And now, sir,' she says saucily, 'supposing I pull the trigger?'

"And then—and then, Hastings—she pulls it!"

# The Adventure
# of the Cheap Flat

SO far, in the cases which I have recorded, Poirot's investigations have started from the central fact, whether murder or robbery, and have proceeded from thence by a process of logical deduction to the final triumphant unravelling. In the events I am now about to chronicle, a remarkable chain of circumstances led from the apparently trivial incidents which first attracted Poirot's attention to the sinister happenings which completed a most unusual case.

I had been spending the evening with an old friend of mine, Gerald Parker. There had been, perhaps, about half a dozen people there beside my host and myself, and the talk fell, as it was bound to do sooner or later wherever Parker found himself, on the subject of house hunting in London. Houses and flats were Parker's special hobby. Since the end of the War, he had occupied at least half a dozen different flats and maisonnettes. No sooner was he settled anywhere than he would light unexpectedly upon a new find, and would forthwith depart bag and baggage. His moves were nearly always accomplished at a slight pecuniary gain, for he had a shrewd business head, but it was sheer love of the sport that actuated him, and not a desire to make money at it. We listened to Parker for some time with the respect of the novice for the expert. Then it was our turn, and a perfect Babel of tongues was let loose. Finally the floor was left to Mrs. Robinson, a charming little bride who was there with her husband. I had never met them before, as Robinson was only a recent acquaintance of Parker's.

"Talking of flats," she said, "have you heard of our piece of luck, Mr. Parker? We've got a flat—at last! In Montagu Mansions."

"Well," said Parker, "I've always said there are plenty of flats—at a price!"

"Yes, but this isn't at a price. It's dirt cheap. Eighty pounds a year!"

"But—but Montagu Mansions is just off Knightsbridge, isn't it? Big handsome building. Or are you talking of a poor relation of the same name stuck in the slums somewhere?"

"No, it's the Knightsbridge one. That's what makes it so wonderful."

"Wonderful is the word! It's a blinking miracle. But there must be a catch somewhere. Big premium, I suppose?"

"No premium!"

"No prem—oh, hold my head, somebody!" groaned Parker.

"But we've got to buy the furniture," continued Mrs. Robinson.

"Ah!" Parker brisked up. "I knew there was a catch!"

"For fifty pounds. And it's beautifully furnished!"

"I give it up," said Parker. "The present occupants must be lunatics with a taste for philanthropy."

Mrs. Robinson was looking a little troubled. A little pucker appeared between her dainty brows.

"It *is* queer, isn't it? You don't think that—that—the place is *haunted?*"

"Never heard of a haunted flat," declared Parker decisively.

"N-o." Mrs. Robinson appeared far from convinced. "But there were several things about it all that struck me as—well, queer."

"For instance—" I suggested.

"Ah," said Parker, "our criminal expert's attention is aroused! Unburden yourself to him, Mrs. Robinson. Hastings is a great unraveler of mysteries."

I laughed, embarrassed but not wholly displeased with the role thrust upon me.

"Oh, not really queer, Captain Hastings, but when we went to the agents, Stosser and Paul—we hadn't tried them before because they only have the expensive Mayfair flats, but we thought at any rate it would do no harm—everything they offered us was four and five hundred a year, or else huge premiums, and then, just as we were going, they mentioned that they had a flat at eighty, but that they doubted if it would be any good our going there, because it had been on their books some time and they had sent so many people to see it that it was almost sure to be taken—'snapped up' as the clerk put it—only people were so tiresome in not letting them know, and then they went on sending, and people get annoyed at being sent to a place that had, perhaps, been let some time."

Mrs. Robinson paused for some much needed breath, and then continued:

"We thanked him, and said that we quite understood it would probably be no good, but that we should like an order all the same—just in case. And we went there straightaway in a taxi, for, after all, you never know. No. 4 was on the second floor, and just as we were waiting for the lift, Elsie Ferguson—she's a friend of mine, Captain Hastings, and they are looking for a flat too—came hurrying down the stairs. 'Ahead of you for once, my dear,' she said. 'But it's no good. It's already let.' That seemed to finish it, but—well, as John said, the place was very cheap, we could afford to give more, and perhaps if we offered a premium—. A horrid thing to do, of course, and I feel quite ashamed of telling you, but you know what flat-hunting is."

I assured her that I was well aware that in the struggle for houseroom the baser side of human nature frequently triumphed over the higher, and that the well known rule of dog eat dog always applied.

"So we went up and, would you believe it, the flat wasn't let at all. We were shown over it by the maid, and then we saw the mistress, and the thing was settled then and there. Immediate possession and fifty pounds for the furniture. We signed the agreement next day, and we are to move in tomorrow!" Mrs. Robinson paused triumphantly.

"And what about Mrs. Ferguson?" asked Parker. "Let's have your deductions, Hastings."

" 'Obvious, my dear Watson,' " I quoted lightly. "She went to the wrong flat."

"Oh, Captain Hastings, how clever of you!" cried Mrs. Robinson admiringly.

I rather wished Poirot had been there. Sometimes I have the feeling that he rather underestimates my capabilities.

The whole thing was rather amusing, and I propounded the thing as a mock problem to Poirot on the following morning. He seemed interested, and questioned me rather narrowly as to the rents of flats in various localities.

"A curious story," he said thoughtfully. "Excuse me, Hastings, I must take a short stroll."

When he returned, about an hour later, his eyes were gleaming with a peculiar excitement. He laid his stick on the table, and brushed the nap of his hat with his usual tender care before he spoke.

"It is as well, *mon ami,* that we have no affairs of moment on hand. We can devote ourselves wholly to the present investigation."

"What investigation are you talking about?"

"The remarkable cheapness of your friend's, Mrs. Robinson's, new flat."

"Poirot, you are not serious!"

"I am most serious. Figure to yourself, my friend, that the real rent of those flats is £350. I have just ascertained that from the landlord's agents. And yet this particular flat is being sublet at eighty pounds! Why?"

"There must be something wrong with it. Perhaps it is haunted, as Mrs. Robinson suggested."

Poirot shook his head in a dissatisfied manner.

"Then again how curious it is that her friend tells her the flat is let, and, when she goes up, behold, it is not so at all!"

"But surely you agree with me that the other woman must have gone to the wrong flat. That is the only possible solution."

"You may or may not be right on that point, Hastings. The fact still remains that numerous other applicants were sent to see it, and yet, in spite of its remarkable cheapness, it was still in the market when Mrs. Robinson arrived."

"That shows that there *must* be something wrong about it."

"Mrs. Robinson did not seem to notice anything amiss. Very curious, is it not? Did she impress you as being a truthful woman, Hastings?"

"She was a delightful creature!"

"*Évidemment!* Since she renders you incapable of replying to my question. Describe her to me, then."

"Well, she's tall and fair; her hair's really a beautiful shade of auburn—"

"Always you have had a penchant for auburn hair!" murmured Poirot. "But continue."

"Blue eyes and a very nice complexion and—well, that's all, I think," I concluded lamely.

"And her husband?"

"Oh, he's quite a nice fellow—nothing startling."

"Dark or fair?"

"I don't know—betwixt and between, and just an ordinary sort of face."

Poirot nodded.

"Yes, there are hundreds of these average men—and, anyway, you bring more sympathy and appreciation to your description of women. Do you know anything about these people? Does Parker know them well?"

"They are just recent acquaintances, I believe. But surely, Poirot, you don't think for an instant—"

Poirot raised his hand.

"*Tout doucement, mon ami.* Have I said that I think anything? All I say is—it is a curious story. And there is nothing to throw light upon it; except perhaps the lady's name, eh, Hastings?"

"Her name is Stella," I said stiffly, "but I don't see—"

Poirot interrupted me with a tremendous chuckle. Something seemed to be amusing him vastly.

"And Stella means a star, does it not? Famous!"

"What on earth—"

"And stars give light! *Voilà!* Calm yourself, Hastings. Do not put on that air of injured dignity. Come, we will go to Montagu Mansions and make a few inquiries."

I accompanied him, nothing loath. The Mansions were a handsome block of buildings in excellent repair. A uniformed porter was sunning himself on the threshold, and it was to him that Poirot addressed himself:

"Pardon, but could you tell me if a Mr. and Mrs. Robinson reside here?"

The porter was a man of few words and apparently of a sour or suspicious disposition. He hardly looked at us and grunted out:

"No. 4. Second floor."

"I thank you. Can you tell me how long they have been here?"

"Six months."

I started forward in amazement, conscious as I did so of Poirot's malicious grin.

"Impossible," I cried. "You must be making a mistake."

"Six months."

"Are you sure? The lady I mean is tall and fair with reddish gold hair and—"

"That's 'er," said the porter. "Come in the Michaelmas quarter, they did. Just six months ago."

He appeared to lose interest in us and retreated slowly up the hall. I followed Poirot outside.

"*Eh bien,* Hastings?" my friend demanded slyly.

"Are you so sure now that delightful women always speak the truth?" I did not reply.

Poirot had steered his way into Brompton Road before I asked him what he was going to do and where we were going.

"To the house agents, Hastings. I have a great desire to have a flat in Montagu Mansions. If I am not mistaken, several interesting things will take place there before long."

We were fortunate in our quest. No. 8, on the fourth floor, was to be let furnished at ten guineas a week. Poirot promptly took it for a month. Outside in the street again, he silenced my protests:

"But I make money nowadays! Why should I not indulge a whim? By the way, Hastings, have you a revolver?"

"Yes—somewhere," I answered, slightly thrilled. "Do you think—"

"That you will need it? It is quite possible. The idea pleases you, I see. Always the spectacular and romantic appeal to you."

The following day saw us installed in our temporary home. The flat was pleasantly furnished. It occupied the same position in the building as that of the Robinsons, but was two floors higher.

The day after our installation was a Sunday. In the afternoon, Poirot left the front door ajar, and summoned me hastily as a bang reverberated from somewhere below.

"Look over the banisters. Are those your friends? Do not let them see you."

I craned my neck over the staircase.

"That's them," I declared in an ungrammatical whisper.

"Good. Wait awhile."

About half an hour later, a young woman emerged in brilliant and varied clothing. With a sigh of satisfaction, Poirot tiptoed back into the flat.

"*C'est ça.* After the master and mistress, the maid. The flat should now be empty."

"What are we going to do?" I asked uneasily.

Poirot had trotted briskly into the scullery and was hauling at the rope of the coal-lift.

"We are about to descend after the method of the dustbins," he explained cheerfully. "No one will observe us. The Sunday concert, the Sunday 'afternoon out,' and finally the Sunday nap after the Sunday dinner of England—*le rosbif*—all these will distract attention from the doings of Hercule Poirot. Come, my friend."

He stepped into the rough wooden contrivance and I followed him gingerly.

"Are we going to break into the flat?" I asked dubiously.

Poirot's answer was not too reassuring:

"Not precisely today," he replied.

Pulling on the rope, we descended slowly till we reached the second floor. Poirot uttered an exclamation of satisfaction as he perceived that the wooden door into the scullery was open.

"You observe? Never do they bolt these doors in the daytime. And yet anyone could mount or descend as we have done. At night yes—though not always then—and it is against that that we are going to make provision."

He had drawn some tools from his pocket as he spoke, and at once set deftly to work, his object being to arrange the bolt so that it could be pulled back from the lift. The operation only occupied about three minutes. Then Poirot returned the tools to his pocket, and we reascended once more to our own domain.

On Monday Poirot was out all day, but when he returned in the evening he flung himself into his chair with a sigh of satisfaction.

"Hastings, shall I recount to you a little history? A story after your own heart and which will remind you of your favorite cinema?"

"Go ahead," I laughed. "I presume that it is a true story, not one of your efforts of fancy."

"It is true enough. Inspector Japp of Scotland Yard will vouch for its accuracy, since it was through his kind offices that it came to my ears. Listen, Hastings. A little over six months ago some important naval plans were stolen from an American Government department.

They showed the position of some of the most important harbor defenses, and would be worth a considerable sum to any foreign government—that of Japan, for example. Suspicion fell upon a young man
named Luigi Valdarno, an Italian by birth, who was employed in a
minor capacity in the department and who was missing at the same
time as the papers. Whether Luigi Valdarno was the thief or not, he
was found two days later on the East Side in New York, shot dead.
The papers were not on him. Now for some time past Luigi Valdarno
had been going about with a Miss Elsa Hardt, a young concert singer
who had recently appeared and who lived with a brother in an apartment in Washington. Nothing was known of the antecedents of Miss
Elsa Hardt, and she disappeared suddenly about the time of Valdarno's
death. There are reasons for believing that she was in reality an accomplished international spy who has done much nefarious work under
various aliases. The American Secret Service, while doing their best
to trace her, also kept an eye upon certain insignificant Japanese gentlemen living in Washington. They felt pretty certain that, when Elsa
Hardt had covered her tracks sufficiently, she would approach the
gentlemen in question. One of them left suddenly for England a fortnight ago. On the face of it, therefore, it would seem that Elsa Hardt
is in England." Poirot paused, and then added softly: "The official description of Elsa Hardt is: Height 5 ft. 7, eyes blue, hair auburn, fair
complexion, nose straight, no special distinguishing marks."

"Mrs. Robinson!" I gasped.

"Well, there is a chance of it, anyhow," amended Poirot. "Also, I
learn that a swarthy man, a foreigner of some kind, was inquiring
about the occupants of No. 4 only this morning. Therefore, *mon ami*,
I fear that you must forswear your beauty sleep tonight, and join me
in my all-night vigil in the flat below—armed with that excellent revolver of yours, *bien entendu!*"

"Rather," I cried with enthusiasm. "When shall we start?"

"The hour of midnight is both solemn and suitable, I fancy. Nothing
is likely to occur before then."

At twelve o'clock precisely, we crept cautiously into the coal-lift
and lowered ourselves to the second floor. Under Poirot's manipulation,
the wooden door quickly swung inwards, and we climbed into the
flat. From the scullery we passed into the kitchen where we established
ourselves comfortably in two chairs with the door into the hall ajar.

"Now we have but to wait," said Poirot contentedly, closing his
eyes.

To me, the waiting appeared endless. I was terrified of going to
sleep. Just when it seemed to me that I had been there about eight
hours—and had, as I found out afterwards, in reality been exactly one
hour and twenty minutes—a faint scratching sound came to my ears.

Poirot's hand touched mine. I rose, and together we moved carefully in the direction of the hall. The noise came from there. Poirot placed his lips to my ear.

"Outside the front door. They are cutting out the lock. When I give the word, not before, fall upon him from behind and hold him fast. Be careful, he will have a knife."

Presently there was a rending sound, and a little circle of light appeared through the door. It was extinguished immediately and then the door was slowly opened. Poirot and I flattened ourselves against the wall. I heard a man's breathing as he passed us. Then he flashed on his torch, and as he did so, Poirot hissed in my ear:

"*Allez.*"

We sprang together, Poirot with a quick movement enveloped the intruder's head with a light woolen scarf while I pinioned his arms. The whole affair was quick and noiseless. I twisted a dagger from his hand, and as Poirot brought down the scarf from his eyes, whilst keeping it wound tightly round his mouth, I jerked up my revolver where he could see it and understand that resistance was useless. As he ceased to struggle Poirot put his mouth close to his ear and began to whisper rapidly. After a minute the man nodded. Then enjoining silence with a movement of the hand, Poirot led the way out of the flat and down the stairs. Our captive followed, and I brought up the rear with the revolver. When we were out in the street, Poirot turned to me.

"There is a taxi waiting just round the corner. Give me the revolver. We shall not need it now."

"But if this fellow tries to escape?"

Poirot smiled.

"He will not."

I returned in a minute with the waiting taxi. The scarf had been unwound from the stranger's face, and I gave a start of surprise.

"He's not a Jap," I ejaculated in a whisper to Poirot.

"Observation was always your strong point, Hastings! Nothing escapes you. No, the man is not a Jap. He is an Italian."

We got into the taxi, and Poirot gave the driver an address in St. John's Wood. I was by now completely fogged. I did not like to ask Poirot where we were going in front of our captive, and strove in vain to obtain some light upon the proceedings.

We alighted at the door of a small house standing back from the road. A returning wayfarer, slightly drunk, was lurching along the pavement and almost collided with Poirot, who said something sharply to him which I did not catch. All three of us went up the steps of the house. Poirot rang the bell and motioned us to stand a little aside. There was no answer and he rang again and then seized the knocker which he plied for some minutes vigorously.

A light appeared suddenly above the fanlight, and the door was opened cautiously a little way.

"What the devil do you want?" a man's voice demanded harshly.

"I want the doctor. My wife is taken ill."

"There's no doctor here."

The man prepared to shut the door, but Poirot thrust his foot in adroitly. He became suddenly a perfect caricature of an infuriated Frenchman.

"What you say, there is no doctor? I will have the law of you. You must come! I will stay here and ring and knock all night."

"My dear sir—" The door was opened again, the man, clad in a dressing gown and slippers, stepped forward to pacify Poirot with an uneasy glance round.

"I will call the police."

Poirot prepared to descend the steps.

"No, don't do that, for Heaven's sake!" The man dashed after him.

With a neat push Poirot sent him staggering down the steps. In another minute all three of us were inside the door and it was pushed to and bolted.

"Quick—in here." Poirot led the way into the nearest room switching on the light as he did so. "And you—behind the curtain."

"Si, signor," said the Italian and slid rapidly behind the full folds of rose-colored velvet which draped the embrasure of the window.

Not a minute too soon. Just as he disappeared from view a woman rushed into the room. She was tall with reddish hair and held a scarlet kimono round her slender form.

"Where is my husband?" she cried, with a quick frightened glance. "Who are you?"

Poirot stepped forward with a bow.

"It is to be hoped your husband will not suffer from a chill. I observed that he had slippers on his feet, and that his dressing gown was a warm one."

"Who are you? What are you doing in my house?"

"It is true that none of us have the pleasure of your acquaintance, madame. It is especially to be regretted as one of our number has come specially from New York in order to meet you."

The curtains parted and the Italian stepped out. To my horror I observed that he was brandishing my revolver, which Poirot must doubtless have put down through inadvertence in the cab.

The woman gave a piercing scream and turned to fly, but Poirot was standing in front of the closed door.

"Let me by," she shrieked. "He will murder me."

"Who was it dat croaked Luigi Valdarno?" asked the Italian hoarsely, brandishing the weapon, and sweeping each one of us with it. We dared not move.

"My God, Poirot, this is awful. What shall we do?" I cried.

"You will oblige me by refraining from talking so much, Hastings. I can assure you that our friend will not shoot until I give the word."

"Youse sure o' dat, eh?" said the Italian leering unpleasantly.

It was more than I was, but the woman turned to Poirot like a flash.

"What is it you want?"

Poirot bowed.

"I do not think it is necessary to insult Miss Elsa Hardt's intelligence by telling her."

With a swift movement, the woman snatched up a big black velvet cat which served as a cover for the telephone.

"They are stitched in the lining of that."

"Clever," murmured Poirot appreciatively. He stood aside from the door. "Good evening, madame. I will detain your friend from New York while you make your getaway."

"Whatta fool!" roared the big Italian, and raising the revolver he fired point-blank at the woman's retreating figure just as I flung myself upon him.

But the weapon merely clicked harmlessly and Poirot's voice rose in mild reproof.

"Never will you trust your old friend, Hastings. I do not care for my friends to carry loaded pistols about with them and never would I permit a mere acquaintance to do so. No, no, *mon ami.*" This to the Italian who was swearing hoarsely. Poirot continued to address him in a tone of mild reproof, "See now, what I have done for you. I have saved you from being hanged. And do not think that our beautiful lady will escape. No, no, the house is watched, back and front. Straight into the arms of the police they will go. Is not that a beautiful and consoling thought? Yes, you may leave the room now. But be careful—be very careful. I— Ah, he is gone! And my friend Hastings looks at me with eyes of reproach. But it was all so simple! It was clear, from the first, that out of several hundred, probably, applicants for No. 4, Montagu Mansions only the Robinsons were considered suitable. Why? What was there that singled them out from the rest—at practically a glance? Their appearance? Possibly, but it was not so unusual. Their name, then!"

"But there's nothing unusual about the name of Robinson," I cried. "It's quite a common name."

"Ah! *Sapristi,* but exactly! That was the point. Elsa Hardt and her husband, or brother or whatever he really is, come from New York, and take a flat in the name of Mr. and Mrs. Robinson. Suddenly they learn that one of these secret societies, the Mafia, or the Camorra, to which doubtless Luigi Valdarno belonged, is on their track. What do they do? They hit on a scheme of transparent simplicity. Evidently they knew that their pursuers were not personally acquainted with either of them. What then can be simpler? They offer the flat at an absurdly low rental. Of the thousands of young couples in London looking for flats, there cannot fail to be several Robinsons. It is only a matter of waiting. If you will look at the name of Robinson in the telephone directory, you will realize that a fair-haired Mrs. Robinson was pretty sure to come along sooner or later. Then what will happen? The avenger arrives. He knows the name, he knows the address. He strikes! All is over, vengeance is satisfied, and Miss Elsa Hardt has escaped by the skin of her teeth once more. By the way, Hastings, you must present me to the real Mrs. Robinson—that delightful and truthful creature! What will they think when they find their flat has been broken into! We must hurry back. Ah, that sounds like Japp and his friends arriving."

A mighty tattoo sounded on the knocker.

"How did you know this address?" I asked as I followed Poirot out into the hall. "Oh, of course, you had the first Mrs. Robinson followed when she left the other flat."

"*A la bonne heure,* Hastings. You use your gray cells at last. Now for a little surprise for Japp."

Softly unbolting the door, he stuck the cat's head round the edge and ejaculated a piercing "Miaow."

The Scotland Yard inspector, who was standing outside with another man, jumped in spite of himself.

"Oh, it's only Monsieur Poirot at one of his little jokes!" he exclaimed, as Poirot's head followed that of the cat. "Let us in, moosior."

"You have our friends safe and sound?"

"Yes, we've got the birds all right. But they hadn't got the goods with them."

"I see. So you come to search. Well, I am about to depart with Hastings, but I should like to give you a little lecture upon the history and habits of the domestic cat."

"For the Lord's sake, have you gone completely balmy?"

"The cat," declaimed Poirot, "was worshiped by the ancient Egyptians. It is still regarded as a symbol of good luck if a black cat crosses your path. This cat crossed your path tonight, Japp. To speak of the interior of any animal or any person is not, I know, considered polite in England. But the interior of this cat is perfectly delicate. I refer to the lining."

With a sudden grunt, the second man seized the cat from Poirot's hand.

"Oh, I forgot to introduce you," said Japp. "Mr. Poirot, this is Mr. Burt of the United States Secret Service."

The American's trained fingers had felt what he was looking for. He held out his hand, and for a moment speech failed him. Then he rose to the occasion.

"Pleased to meet you," said Mr. Burt.

# The Mystery of Hunter's Lodge

"AFTER all," murmured Poirot, "it is possible that I shall not die this time."

Coming from a convalescent influenza patient, I hailed the remark as showing a beneficial optimism. I myself had been the first sufferer from the disease. Poirot in his turn had gone down. He was now sitting up in bed, propped up with pillows, his head muffled in a woolen shawl, and was slowly sipping a particularly noxious *tisane* which I had prepared according to his directions. His eye rested with pleasure upon a neatly graduated row of medicine bottles which adorned the mantelpiece.

"Yes, yes," my little friend continued. "Once more shall I be myself again, the great Hercule Poirot, the terror of evildoers! Figure to yourself, *mon ami,* that I have a little paragraph to myself in *Society Gossip.* But yes! Here it is! 'Go it—criminals—all out! Hercule Poirot—and believe me, girls, he's some Hercules!—our own pet society detective can't get a grip on you. 'Cause why? 'Cause he's got *la grippe* himself'!"

I laughed.

"Good for you, Poirot. You are becoming quite a public character. And fortunately you haven't missed anything of particular interest during this time."

"That is true. The few cases I have had to decline did not fill me with any regret."

Our landlady stuck her head in at the door.

"There's a gentleman downstairs. Says he must see Monsieur Poirot or you, Captain. Seeing as he was in a great to-do—and with all that quite the gentleman—I brought up 'is card."

She handed me the bit of pasteboard. "Mr. Roger Havering," I read.

Poirot motioned with his head towards the bookcase, and I obediently pulled forth *Who's Who.* Poirot took it from me and scanned the pages rapidly.

"Second son of fifth Baron Windsor. Married 1913 Zoe, fourth daughter of William Crabb."

"Hm!" I said. "I rather fancy that's the girl who used to act at the Frivolity—only she called herself Zoe Carrisbrook. I remember she married some young man about town just before the War."

"Would it interest you, Hastings, to go down and hear what our visitor's particular little trouble is? Make him all my excuses."

Roger Havering was a man of about forty, well set up and of smart appearance. His face, however, was haggard, and he was evidently laboring under great agitation.

"Captain Hastings? You are Monsieur Poirot's partner, I understand. It is imperative that he should come with me to Derbyshire today."

"I'm afraid that's impossible," I responded. "Poirot is ill in bed— influenza."

His face fell.

"Dear me, that is a great blow to me."

"The matter on which you want to consult him is serious?"

"My God, yes! My uncle, the best friend I have in the world, was foully murdered last night."

"Here in London?"

"No, in Derbyshire. I was in town and received a telegram from my wife this morning. Immediately upon its receipt I determined to come round and beg Monsieur Poirot to undertake the case."

"If you will excuse me a minute," I said, struck by a sudden idea.

I rushed upstairs, and in a few brief words acquainted Poirot with the situation. He took any further words out of my mouth.

"I see. I see. You want to go yourself, is it not so? Well, why not? You should know my methods by now. All I ask is that you should report to me fully every day, and follow implicitly any instructions I may wire you."

To this I willingly agreed.

An hour later I was sitting opposite Mr. Havering in a first-class carriage on the Midland Railway, speeding rapidly away from London.

"To begin with, Captain Hastings, you must understand that Hunter's Lodge, where we are going, and where the tragedy took place, is only a small shooting box in the heart of the Derbyshire moors. Our real home is near Newmarket, and we usually rent a flat in town for the season. Hunter's Lodge is looked after by a housekeeper who is quite capable of doing all we need when we run down for an occasional weekend. Of course, during the shooting season, we take down some of our own servants from Newmarket. My uncle, Mr. Harrington Pace (as you may know, my mother was a Miss Pace of New York), has, for the last three years, made his home with us. He never got on well with my father, or my elder brother, and I suspect that my being somewhat of a prodigal son myself rather increased than diminished his affection towards me. Of course I am a poor man, and my uncle was a rich one—in other words, he paid the piper! But, though exacting in many ways, he was not really hard to get on with, and we all three lived very harmoniously together. Two days ago my uncle, rather wearied with some recent gayeties of ours in town, suggested that we should run down to Derbyshire for a day or two. My wife telegraphed to Mrs. Middleton, the housekeeper, and we went down that same afternoon. Yesterday evening I was forced to return to town, but my wife and my uncle remained on. This morning I received this telegram." He handed it over to me:

Come at once uncle Harrington murdered last night bring good detective if you can but do come—Zoe.

"Then, as yet you know no details?"

"No, I suppose it will be in the evening papers. Without doubt the police are in charge."

It was about three o'clock when we arrived at the little station of Elmer's Dale. From there a five-mile drive brought us to a small gray stone building in the midst of the rugged moors.

"A lonely place," I observed with a shiver.

Havering nodded.

"I shall try and get rid of it. I could never live here again."

We unlatched the gate and were walking up the narrow path to the oak door when a familiar figure emerged and came to meet us.

"Japp!" I ejaculated.

The Scotland Yard inspector grinned at me in a friendly fashion before addressing my companion.

"Mr. Havering, I think? I've been sent down from London to take charge of this case, and I'd like a word with you, if I may, sir."

"My wife—"

"I've seen your good lady, sir—and the housekeeper. I won't keep you a moment, but I'm anxious to get back to the village now that I've seen all there is to see here."

"I know nothing as yet as to what—"

"Exactly," said Japp soothingly. "But there are just one or two little points I'd like your opinion about all the same. Captain Hastings here, he knows me, and he'll go on up to the house and tell them you're coming. What have you done with the little man, by the way, Captain Hastings?"

"He's ill in bed with influenza."

"Is he now? I'm sorry to hear that. Rather the case of the cart without the horse, your being here without him, isn't it?"

And on his rather ill-timed jest I went on to the house. I rang the bell, as Japp had closed the door behind him. After some moments it was opened to me by a middle-aged woman in black.

"Mr. Havering will be here in a moment," I explained. "He has been detained by the inspector. I have come down with him from London to look into the case. Perhaps you can tell me briefly what occurred last night."

"Come inside, sir." She closed the door behind me, and we stood in the dimly lighted hall. "It was after dinner last night, sir, that the man came. He asked to see Mr. Pace, sir, and, seeing that he spoke the same way, I thought it was an American gentleman friend of Mr. Pace's and I showed him into the gun room, and then went to tell Mr. Pace. He wouldn't give any name, which, of course, was a bit odd, now I come to think of it. I told Mr. Pace, and he seemed puzzled like, but he said to the mistress, 'Excuse me, Zoe, while I just see what this fellow wants.' He went off to the gun room, and I went back to the kitchen, but after a while I heard loud voices, as if they were quarreling, and I came out into the hall. At the same time, the mistress she comes out too, and just then there was a shot and then a dreadful silence. We both ran to the gun room door, but it was locked and we had to go round to the window. It was open, and there inside was Mr. Pace, all shot and bleeding."

"What became of the man?"

"He must have got away through the window, sir, before we got to it."

"And then?"

"Mrs. Havering sent me to fetch the police. Five miles to walk it was. They came back with me, and the constable he stayed all night, and this morning the police gentleman from London arrived."

"What was this man like who called to see Mr. Pace?"

The housekeeper reflected.

"He had a black beard, sir, and was about middle-aged, and had on a light overcoat. Beyond the fact that he spoke like an American I didn't notice much about him."

"I see. Now I wonder if I can see Mrs. Havering?"

"She's upstairs, sir. Shall I tell her?"

"If you please. Tell her that Mr. Havering is outside with Inspector Japp, and that the gentleman he has brought back with him from London is anxious to speak to her as soon as possible."

"Very good, sir."

I was in a fever of impatience to get at all the facts. Japp had two or three hours' start on me, and his anxiety to be gone made me keen to be close at his heels.

Mrs. Havering did not keep me waiting long. In a few minutes I heard a light step descending the stairs, and looked up to see a very handsome young woman coming towards me. She wore a flame-colored jumper, that set off the slender boyishness of her figure. On her dark head was a little hat of flame-colored leather. Even the present tragedy could not dim the vitality of her personality.

I introduced myself, and she nodded in quick comprehension.

"Of course I have often heard of you and your colleague, Monsieur Poirot. You have done some wonderful things together, haven't you? It was very clever of my husband to get you so promptly. Now will you ask me questions? That is the easiest way, isn't it, of getting to know all you want to about this dreadful affair?"

"Thank you, Mrs. Havering. Now what time was it that this man arrived?"

"It must have been just before nine o'clock. We had finished dinner, and were sitting over our coffee and cigarettes."

"Your husband had already left for London?"

"Yes, he went up by the 6:15."

"Did he go by car to the station, or did he walk?"

"Our own car isn't down here. One came out from the garage in Elmer's Dale to fetch him in time for the train."

"Was Mr. Pace quite his usual self?"

"Absolutely. Most normal in every way."

"Now, can you describe this visitor at all?"

"I'm afraid not. I didn't see him. Mrs. Middleton showed him straight into the gun room and then came to tell my uncle."

"What did your uncle say?"

"He seemed rather annoyed, but went off at once. It was about five minutes later that I heard the sound of raised voices. I ran out into the hall and almost collided with Mrs. Middleton. Then we heard the shot. The gun room door was locked on the inside, and we had to go right round the house to the window. Of course that took some time, and the murderer had been able to get well away. My poor uncle"—her voice faltered—"had been shot through the head. I saw at once that he was dead. I sent Mrs. Middleton for the police. I was careful to touch nothing in the room but to leave it exactly as I found it."

I nodded approval.

"Now, as to the weapon?"

"Well, I can make a guess at it, Captain Hastings. A pair of revolvers of my husband's were mounted upon the wall. One of them is missing. I pointed this out to the police, and they took the other one away with them. When they have extracted the bullet, I suppose they will know for certain."

"May I go to the gun room?"

"Certainly. The police have finished with it. But the body has been removed."

She accompanied me to the scene of the crime. At that moment Havering entered the hall, and with a quick apology his wife ran to him. I was left to undertake my investigations alone.

I may as well confess at once that they were rather disappointing. In detective novels clues abound, but here I could find nothing that struck me as out of the ordinary except a large bloodstain on the carpet where I judged the dead man had fallen. I examined everything with painstaking care and took a couple of pictures of the room with my little camera which I had brought with me. I also examined the ground outside the window, but it appeared to have been so heavily trampled underfoot that I judged it was useless to waste time over it. No, I had seen all that Hunter's Lodge had to show me. I must go back to Elmer's Dale and get into touch with Japp. Accordingly I took leave of the Haverings, and was driven off in the car that had brought us up from the station.

I found Japp at the Matlock Arms and he took me forthwith to see the body. Harrington Pace was a small, spare, clean-shaven man, typically American in appearance. He had been shot through the back of the head, and the revolver had been discharged at close quarters.

"Turned away for a moment," remarked Japp, "and the other fellow snatched up a revolver and shot him. The one Mrs. Havering handed over to us was fully loaded and I suppose the other one was also. Curious what darn fool things people do. Fancy keeping two loaded revolvers hanging up on your wall."

"What do you think of the case?" I asked, as we left the gruesome chamber behind us.

"Well, I'd got my eye on Havering to begin with. Oh, yes!" noting my exclamation of astonishment. "Havering has one or two shady incidents in his past. When he was a boy at Oxford there was some funny business about the signature on one of his father's checks. All hushed up, of course. Then, he's pretty heavily in debt now, and they're the kind of debts he wouldn't like to go to his uncle about, whereas you may be sure the uncle's will would be in his favor. Yes, I'd got my eye on him, and that's why I wanted to speak to him before he saw his wife, but their statements dovetail all right, and I've been to the station and there's no doubt whatever that he left by the 6:15. That gets up to London about 10:30. He went straight to his club, he says, and if that's confirmed all right—why, he couldn't have been shooting his uncle here at nine o'clock in a black beard!"

"Ah, yes, I was going to ask you what you thought about that beard?"

Japp winked.

"I think it grew pretty fast—grew in the five miles from Elmer's Dale to Hunter's Lodge. Americans that I've met are mostly clean-shaven. Yes, it's among Mr. Pace's American associates that we'll have to look for the murderer. I questioned the housekeeper first, and then her mistress, and their stories agree all right, but I'm sorry Mrs. Havering didn't get a look at the fellow. She's a smart woman, and she might have noticed something that would set us on the track."

I sat down and wrote a minute and lengthy account to Poirot. I was able to add various further items of information before I posted the letter.

The bullet had been extracted and was proved to have been fired from a revolver identical with the one held by the police. Furthermore, Mr. Havering's movements on the night in question had been checked and verified, and it was proved beyond doubt that he had actually arrived in London by the train in question. And, thirdly, a sensational development had occurred. A city gentleman, living at Ealing, on crossing Haven Green to get to the District Railway Station that morning, had observed a brown-paper parcel stuck between the railings. Opening it, he found that it contained a revolver. He handed the parcel over to the local police station, and before night it was proved to be the one we were in search of, the fellow to that given us by Mrs. Havering. One bullet had been fired from it.

All this I added to my report. A wire from Poirot arrived while I was at breakfast the following morning:

> Of course black-bearded man was not Havering only
> you or Japp would have such an idea wire me
> description of housekeeper and what clothes she wore
> this morning same of Mrs. Havering do not waste time
> taking photographs of interiors they are
> underexposed and not in the least artistic.

It seemed to me that Poirot's style was unnecessarily facetious. I also fancied he was a shade jealous of my position on the spot with full facilities for handling the case. His request for a description of the clothes worn by the two women appeared to me to be simply ridiculous, but I complied as well as I, a mere man, was able to.

At eleven a reply wire came from Poirot:

> Advise Japp arrest housekeeper before it is too
> late.

Dumbfounded, I took the wire to Japp. He swore softly under his breath.

"He's the goods, Monsieur Poirot! If he says so, there's something in it. And I hardly noticed the woman. I don't know that I can go so far as arresting her, but I'll have her watched. We'll go up right away, and take another look at her."

But it was too late. Mrs. Middleton, that quiet middle-aged woman, who had appeared so normal and respectable, had vanished into thin air. Her box had been left behind. It contained only ordinary wearing apparel. There was no clue in it to her identity or as to her whereabouts.

From Mrs. Havering we elicited all the facts we could:

"I engaged her about three weeks ago when Mrs. Emery, our former housekeeper, left. She came to me from Mrs. Selbourne's Agency in Mount Street—a very well-known place. I get all my servants from there. They sent several women to see me, but this Mrs. Middleton seemed much the nicest, and had splendid references. I engaged her on the spot, and notified the agency of the fact. I can't believe that there was anything wrong with her. She was such a nice quiet woman."

The thing was certainly a mystery. While it was clear that the woman herself could not have committed the crime, since at the moment the shot was fired Mrs. Havering was with her in the hall, nevertheless she must have some connection with the murder, or why should she suddenly take to her heels and bolt?

I wired the latest development to Poirot and suggested returning to London and making inquiries at Selbourne's Agency.

Poirot's reply was prompt:

```
   Useless to inquire at agency they will never have
heard of her find out what vehicle took her up to
Hunter's Lodge when she first arrived there.
```

Though mystified, I was obedient. The means of transport in Elmer's Dale were limited. The local garage had two battered Ford cars, and there were two station flies. None of these had been requisitioned on the date in question. Questioned, Mrs. Havering explained that she had given the woman the money for her fare down to Derbyshire and sufficient to hire a car or carriage to take her up to Hunter's Lodge. There was usually one of the Fords at the station on the chance of its being required. Taking into consideration the further fact that nobody at the station had noticed the arrival of a stranger, black-bearded or otherwise, on the fatal evening, everything seemed to point to the conclusion that the murderer had come to the spot in a car, which had been waiting near at hand to aid his escape, and that the same car had brought the mysterious housekeeper to her new post. I may mention that inquiries at the agency in London bore out Poirot's prognostication. No such woman as "Mrs. Middleton" had ever been on their books. They had received the Hon. Mrs. Havering's application for a housekeeper, and had sent her various applicants for the post. When she sent them the engagement fee, she omitted to mention which woman she had selected.

Somewhat crestfallen, I returned to London. I found Poirot established in an armchair by the fire in a garish silk dressing gown. He greeted me with much affection.

"*Mon ami* Hastings! But how glad I am to see you. Veritably I have for you a great affection! And you have enjoyed yourself? You have run to and fro with the good Japp? You have interrogated and investigated to your heart's content?"

"Poirot," I cried, "the thing's a dark mystery! It will never be solved."

"It is true that we are not likely to cover ourselves with glory over it."

"No, indeed. It's a hard nut to crack."

"Oh, as far as that goes, I am very good at cracking the nuts! A veritable squirrel! It is not that which embarrasses me. I know well enough who killed Mr. Harrington Pace."

"You know? How did you find out?"

"Your illuminating answers to my wires supplied me with the truth. See here, Hastings, let us examine the facts methodically and in order. Mr. Harrington Pace is a man with a considerable fortune which at his death will doubtless pass to his nephew. Point No. 1. His nephew is known to be desperately hard up. Point No. 2. His nephew is also known to be—shall we say a man of rather loose moral fiber? Point No. 3."

"But Roger Havering is proved to have journeyed straight up to London."

"*Précisément*—and therefore, as Mr. Havering left Elmer's Dale at 6:15, and since Mr. Pace cannot have been killed before he left, or the doctor would have spotted the time of the crime as being given wrongly when he examined the body, we conclude quite rightly, that Mr. Havering did *not* shoot his uncle. But there is a Mrs. Havering, Hastings."

"Impossible! The housekeeper was with her when the shot was fired."

"Ah, yes, the housekeeper. But she has disappeared."

"She will be found."

"I think not. There is something peculiarly elusive about that housekeeper, don't you think so, Hastings? It struck me at once."

"She played her part, I suppose, and then got out in the nick of time."

"And what was her part?"

"Well, presumably to admit her confederate, the black-bearded man."

"Oh, no, that was not her part! Her part was what you have just mentioned, to provide an alibi for Mrs. Havering at the moment the shot was fired. And no one will ever find her, *mon ami*, because she does not exist! 'There's no such person,' as your so great Shakespeare says."

"It was Dickens," I murmured, unable to suppress a smile. "But what do you mean, Poirot?"

"I mean that Zoe Havering was an actress before her marriage, that you and Japp only saw the housekeeper in a dark hall, a dim middle-aged figure in black with a faint subdued voice, and finally that neither you nor Japp, nor the local police whom the housekeeper fetched, ever saw Mrs. Middleton and her mistress at one and the same time. It was child's play for that clever and daring woman. On the pretext of summoning her mistress, she runs upstairs, slips on a bright jumper and a hat with black curls attached which she jams down over the gray transformation. A few deft touches and the makeup is removed, a slight dusting of rouge, and the brilliant Zoe Havering comes down with her clear ringing voice. Nobody looks particularly at the housekeeper. Why should they? There is nothing to connect her with the crime. She, too, has an alibi."

"But the revolver that was found at Ealing? Mrs. Havering could not have placed it there?"

"No, that was Roger Havering's job—but it was a mistake on their part. It put me on the right track. A man who has committed a murder with a revolver which he found on the spot would fling it away at once, he would not carry it up to London with him. No, the motive was clear, the criminals wished to focus the interest of the police on a spot far removed from Derbyshire; they were anxious to get the police away as soon as possible from the vicinity of Hunter's Lodge. Of course the revolver found at Ealing was not the one with which Mr. Pace was shot. Roger Havering discharged one shot from it, brought it up to London, went straight to his club to establish his alibi, then went quickly out to Ealing by the district, a matter of about twenty minutes only, placed the parcel where it was found and so back to town. That charming creature, his wife, quietly shoots Mr. Pace after dinner—you remember he was shot from behind? Another significant point, that!—reloads the revolver and puts it back in its place, and then starts off with her desperate little comedy."

"It's incredible," I murmured, fascinated, "and yet—"

"And yet it is true. *Bien sur*, my friend, it is true. But to bring that precious pair to justice, that is another matter. Well, Japp must do what he can—I have written him fully—but I very much fear, Hastings, that we shall be obliged to leave them to Fate, or *le bon Dieu,* whichever you prefer."

"The wicked flourish like a green bay tree," I reminded him.

"But at a price, Hastings, always at a price, *croyez-moi!*"

Poirot's forebodings were confirmed. Japp, though convinced of the truth of his theory, was unable to get together the necessary evidence to ensure a conviction.

Mr. Pace's huge fortune passed into the hands of his murderers. Nevertheless, Nemesis did overtake them, and when I read in the paper that the Hon. Roger and Mrs. Havering were among those killed in the crashing of the Air Mail to Paris I knew that justice was satisfied.

# The Million Dollar Bond Robbery

"WHAT a number of bond robberies there have been lately!" I observed one morning, laying aside the newspaper. "Poirot, let us forsake the science of detection, and take to crime instead!"

"You are on the—how do you say it?—get-rich-quick tack, eh, *mon ami?*"

"Well, look at this last *coup,* the million dollars' worth of Liberty Bonds which the London and Scottish Bank were sending to New York, and which disappeared in such a remarkable manner on board the *Olympia.*"

"If it were not for the *mal de mer,* and the difficulty of practicing the so excellent method of Laverguier for a longer time than the few hours of crossing the channel, I should delight to voyage myself on one of these big liners," murmured Poirot dreamily.

"Yes, indeed," I said enthusiastically. "Some of them must be perfect palaces; the swimming-baths, the lounges, the restaurant, the palm courts—really, it must be hard to believe that one is on the sea."

"Me, I always know when I am on the sea," said Poirot sadly. "And all those bagatelles that you enumerate, they say nothing to me; but, my friend, consider for a moment the geniuses that travel as it were incognito! On board these floating palaces, as you so justly call them, one would meet the elite, the *haute noblesse* of the criminal world!"

I laughed.

"So that's the way your enthusiasm runs! You would have liked to cross swords with the man who sneaked the Liberty Bonds?"

The landlady interrupted us.

"A young lady as wants to see you, Mr. Poirot. Here's her card."

The card bore the inscription: Miss Esmée Farquhar, and Poirot, after diving under the table to retrieve a stray crumb, and putting it carefully in the wastepaper basket, nodded to the landlady to admit her.

In another minute one of the most charming girls I have ever seen was ushered into the room. She was perhaps about twenty-five, with big brown eyes and a perfect figure. She was well-dressed and perfectly composed in manner.

"Sit down, I beg of you, mademoiselle. This is my friend, Captain Hastings, who aids me in my little problems."

"I am afraid it is a big problem I have brought you today, Monsieur Poirot," said the girl, giving me a pleasant bow as she seated herself. "I dare say you have read about it in the papers. I am referring to the theft of Liberty Bonds on the *Olympia*." Some astonishment must have shown itself in Poirot's face, for she continued quickly: "You are doubtless asking yourself what I have to do with a grave institution like the London and Scottish Bank. In one sense nothing, in another sense everything. You see, Monsieur Poirot, I am engaged to Mr. Philip Ridgeway."

"Aha! and Mr. Philip Ridgeway—"

"Was in charge of the bonds when they were stolen. Of course no actual blame can attach to him, it was not his fault in any way. Nevertheless, he is half-distraught over the matter, and his uncle, I know, insists that he must carelessly have mentioned having them in his possession. It is a terrible setback in his career."

"Who is his uncle?"

"Mr. Vavasour, joint general manager of the London and Scottish Bank."

"Suppose, Miss Farquhar, that you recount to me the whole story?"

"Very well. As you know, the bank wished to extend their credits in America, and for this purpose decided to send over a million dollars in Liberty Bonds. Mr. Vavasour selected his nephew, who had occupied a position of trust in the bank for many years and who was conversant with all the details of the bank's dealings in New York, to make the trip. The *Olympia* sailed from Liverpool on the 23rd, and the bonds were handed over to Philip on the morning of that day by Mr. Vavasour and Mr. Shaw, the two joint general managers of the London and Scottish Bank. They were counted, enclosed in a package, and sealed in his presence, and he then locked the package at once in his portmanteau."

"A portmanteau with an ordinary lock?"

"No, Mr. Shaw insisted on a special lock being fitted to it by Hubbs's. Philip, as I say, placed the package at the bottom of the trunk. It was stolen just a few hours before reaching New York. A rigorous search of the whole ship was made, but without result. The bonds seemed literally to have vanished into thin air."

Poirot made a grimace.

"But they did not vanish absolutely, since I gather that they were sold in small parcels within half an hour of the docking of the *Olympia!*

Well, undoubtedly the next thing is for me to see Mr. Ridgeway."

"I was about to suggest that you should lunch with me at the Cheshire Cheese. Philip will be there. He is meeting me, but does not yet know that I have been consulting you on his behalf."

We agreed to this suggestion readily enough, and drove there in a taxi.

Mr. Philip Ridgeway was there before us, and looked somewhat surprised to see his fiancée arriving with two complete strangers. He was a nice-looking young fellow, tall and spruce, with a touch of graying hair at the temples, though he could not have been much over thirty.

Miss Farquhar went up to him and laid her hand on his arm.

"You must forgive my acting without consulting you, Philip," she said. "Let me introduce you to Monsieur Hercule Poirot, of whom you must often have heard, and his friend, Captain Hastings."

Ridgeway looked very astonished.

"Of course I have heard of you, Monsieur Poirot," he said, as he shook hands. "But I had no idea that Esmée was thinking of consulting you about my—our trouble."

"I was afraid you would not let me do it, Philip," said Miss Farquhar meekly.

"So you took care to be on the safe side," he observed, with a smile. "I hope Monsieur Poirot will be able to throw some light on this extraordinary puzzle, for I confess frankly that I am nearly out of my mind with worry and anxiety about it."

Indeed, his face looked drawn and haggard and showed only too clearly the strain under which he was laboring.

"Well, well," said Poirot. "Let us lunch, and over lunch we will put our heads together and see what can be done. I want to hear Mr. Ridgeway's story from his own lips."

While we discussed the excellent steak and kidney pudding of the establishment, Philip Ridgeway narrated the circumstances leading to the disappearance of the bonds. His story agreed with that of Miss Farquhar in every particular. When he had finished, Poirot took up the thread with a question.

"What exactly led you to discover that the bonds had been stolen, Mr. Ridgeway?"

He laughed rather bitterly.

"The thing stared me in the face, Monsieur Poirot. I couldn't have missed it. My cabin trunk was half out from under the bunk and all scratched and cut about where they'd tried to force the lock."

"But I understood that it had been opened with a key?"

"That's so. They tried to force it, but couldn't. And, in the end, they must have got it unlocked somehow or other."

"Curious," said Poirot, his eyes beginning to flicker with the green light I knew so well. "Very curious! They waste much, much time trying to prise it open, and then—*sapristi!* they find that they have the key all the time—for each of Hubbs's locks are unique."

"That's just why they couldn't have had the key. It never left me day or night."

"You are sure of that?"

"I can swear to it, and besides, if they had had the key or a duplicate, why should they waste time trying to force an obviously unforcible lock?"

"Ah! there is exactly the question we are asking ourselves! I venture to prophesy that the solution, if we ever find it, will hinge on that curious fact. I beg of you not to assault me if I ask you one more question: Are you perfectly certain you did not leave the trunk unlocked?"

Philip Ridgeway merely looked at him, and Poirot gesticulated apologetically.

"Ah, but these things can happen, I assure you! Very well, the bonds were stolen from the trunk. What did the thief do with them? How did he manage to get ashore with them?"

"Ah!" cried Ridgeway. "That's just it. How? Word was passed to the Customs authorities, and every soul that left the ship was gone over with a toothcomb!"

"And the bonds, I gather, made a bulky package?"

"Certainly they did. They could hardly have been hidden on board— and anyway we know they weren't because they were offered for sale within half an hour of the *Olympia's* arrival, long before I got the cables going and the numbers sent out. One broker swears he bought some of them even before the *Olympia* got in. But you can't send bonds by wireless."

"Not by wireless, but did any tug come alongside?"

"Only the official ones, and that was after the alarm was given when everyone was on the lookout. I was watching out myself for their being passed over to someone that way. My God, Monsieur Poirot, this thing will drive me mad! People are beginning to say I stole them myself."

"But you also were searched on landing, weren't you?" asked Poirot gently.

"Yes."

The young man stared at him in a puzzled manner.

"You do not catch my meaning, I see," said Poirot, smiling enigmatically. "Now I should like to make a few inquiries at the bank."

Ridgeway produced a card and scribbled a few words on it.

"Send this in and my uncle will see you at once."

Poirot thanked him, bade farewell to Miss Farquhar, and together we started out for Threadneedle Street and the head office of the

London and Scottish Bank. On production of Ridgeway's card, we were led through the labyrinth of counters and desks, skirting paying-in clerks and paying-out clerks and up to a small office on the first floor where the joint general managers received us. They were two grave gentlemen, who had grown gray in the service of the bank. Mr. Vavasour had a short white beard, Mr. Shaw was cleanshaven.

"I understand you are strictly a private inquiry agent?" said Mr. Vavasour. "Quite so, quite so. We have, of course, placed ourselves in the hands of Scotland Yard. Inspector McNeil has charge of the case. A very able officer, I believe."

"I am sure of it," said Poirot politely. "You will permit a few questions, on your nephew's behalf? About this lock, who ordered it from Hubbs's?"

"I ordered it myself," said Mr. Shaw. "I would not trust to any clerk in the matter. As to the keys, Mr. Ridgeway had one, and the other two are held by my colleague and myself."

"And no clerk has had access to them?"

Mr. Shaw turned inquiringly to Mr. Vavasour.

"I think I am correct in saying that they have remained in the safe where we placed them on the 23rd," said Mr. Vavasour. "My colleague was unfortunately taken ill a fortnight ago—in fact on the very day that Philip left us. He has only just recovered."

"Severe bronchitis is no joke to a man of my age," said Mr. Shaw ruefully. "But I am afraid Mr. Vavasour has suffered from the hard work entailed by my absence, especially with this unexpected worry coming on top of everything."

Poirot asked a few more questions. I judged that he was endeavoring to gauge the exact amount of intimacy between uncle and nephew. Mr. Vavasour's answers were brief and punctilious. His nephew was a trusted official of the bank, and had no debts or money difficulties that he knew of. He had been entrusted with similar missions in the past. Finally we were politely bowed out.

"I am disappointed," said Poirot, as we emerged into the street.

"You hoped to discover more? They are such stodgy old men."

"It is not their stodginess which disappoints me, *mon ami*. I do not expect to find in a bank manager a 'keen financier with an eagle glance' as your favorite works of fiction put it. No, I am disappointed in the case—it is too easy!"

"*Easy?*"

"Yes, do you not find it almost childishly simple?"

"You know who stole the bonds?"

"I do."

"But then—we must—why—"

"Do not confuse and fluster yourself, Hastings. We are not going to do anything at present."

"But why? What are you waiting for?"

"For the *Olympia*. She is due on her return trip from New York on Tuesday."

"But if you know who stole the bonds, why wait? He may escape."

"To a South Sea island where there is no extradition? No, *mon ami*, he would find life very uncongenial there. As to why I wait—*eh bien*, to the intelligence of Hercule Poirot the case is perfectly clear, but for the benefit of others, not so greatly gifted by the good God—the Inspector McNeil, for instance—it would be as well to make a few inquiries to establish the facts. One must have consideration for those less gifted than oneself."

"Good Lord, Poirot! Do you know, I'd give a considerable sum of money to see you make a thorough ass of yourself—just for once. You're so confoundedly conceited!"

"Do not enrage yourself, Hastings. In verity, I observe that there are times when you almost detest me! Alas, I suffer the penalties of greatness!"

The little man puffed out his chest, and sighed so comically that I was forced to laugh.

Tuesday saw us speeding to Liverpool in a first-class carriage of the L. & N. W. R. Poirot had obstinately refused to enlighten me as to his suspicions—or certainties. He contented himself with expressing surprise that I, too, was not equally *au fait* with the situation. I disdained to argue, and intrenched my curiosity behind a rampart of pretended indifference.

Once arrived at the quay alongside which lay the big transatlantic liner, Poirot became brisk and alert. Our proceedings consisted in interviewing four successive stewards and inquiring after a friend of Poirot's who had crossed to New York on the 23rd.

"An elderly gentleman, wearing glasses. A great invalid, hardly moved out of his cabin."

The description appeared to tally with one Mr. Ventnor who had occupied the cabin C 24 which was next to that of Philip Ridgeway. Although unable to see how Poirot had deduced Mr. Ventnor's existence and personal appearance, I was keenly excited.

"Tell me," I cried, "was this gentleman one of the first to land when you got to New York?"

The steward shook his head.

"No, indeed, sir, he was one of the last off the boat."

I retired crestfallen, and observed Poirot grinning at me. He thanked the steward, a note changed hands, and we took our departure.

"It's all very well," I remarked heatedly, "but that last answer must have damped your precious theory, grin as you please!"

"As usual, you see nothing, Hastings. That last answer is, on the contrary, the coping stone of my theory."

I flung up my hands in despair.

"I give it up."

When we were in the train, speeding towards London, Poirot wrote busily for a few minutes, sealing up the result in an envelope.

"This is for the good Inspector McNeil. We will leave it at Scotland Yard in passing, and then to the Rendezvous Restaurant, where I have asked Miss Esmée Farquhar to do us the honor of dining with us."

"What about Ridgeway?"

"What about him?" asked Poirot with a twinkle.

"Why, you surely don't think—you can't—"

"The habit of incoherence is growing upon you, Hastings. As a matter of fact I *did* think. If Ridgeway had been the thief—which was perfectly possible—the case would have been charming; a piece of neat methodical work."

"But not so charming for Miss Farquhar."

"Possibly you are right. Therefore all is for the best. Now, Hastings, let us review the case. I can see that you are dying to do so. The sealed package is removed from the trunk and vanishes, as Miss Farquhar puts it, into thin air. We will dismiss the thin-air theory, which is not practicable at the present stage of science, and consider what is likely to have become of it. Everyone asserts the incredibility of its being smuggled ashore—"

"Yes, but we know—"

"*You* may know, Hastings. I do not. I take the view that, since it seemed incredible, it *was* incredible. Two possibilities remain: it was hidden on board—also rather difficult—or it was thrown overboard."

"With a cork on it, do you mean?"

"Without a cork."

I stared.

"But if the bonds were thrown overboard, they couldn't have been sold in New York."

"I admire your logical mind, Hastings. The bonds were sold in New York, therefore they were not thrown overboard. You see where that leads us?"

"Where we were when we started."

"*Jamais de la vie!* If the package was thrown overboard, and the bonds were sold in New York, the package could not have contained the bonds. Is there any evidence that the package *did* contain the bonds? Remember, Mr. Ridgeway never opened it from the time it was placed in his hands in London."

"Yes, but then—"

Poirot waved an impatient hand.

"Permit me to continue. The last moment that the bonds are seen as bonds is in the office of the London and Scottish Bank on the morning of the 23rd. They reappear in New York half an hour after the *Olympia* gets in, and according to one man, whom nobody listens to, actually *before* she gets in. Supposing then, that they have never been on the *Olympia* at all? Is there any other way they could get to New York? Yes. The *Gigantic* leaves Southampton on the same day as the *Olympia,* and she holds the record for the Atlantic. Mailed by the *Gigantic,* the bonds would be in New York the day before the *Olympia* arrived. All is clear, the case begins to explain itself. The sealed packet is only a dummy, and the moment of its substitution must be in the office in the bank. It would be an easy matter for any of the three men present to have prepared a duplicate package which could be substituted for the genuine one. *Très bien,* the bonds are mailed to a confederate in New York, with instructions to sell as soon as the *Olympia* is in, but someone must travel on the *Olympia* to engineer the supposed moment of the robbery."

"But why?"

"Because if Ridgeway merely opens the packet and finds it a dummy, suspicion flies at once to London. No, the man on board in the cabin next door does his work, pretends to force the lock in an obvious manner so as to draw immediate attention to the theft, really unlocks the trunk with a duplicate key, throws the package overboard and waits until the last to leave the boat. Naturally he wears glasses to conceal his eyes, and is an invalid since he does not want to run the risk of meeting Ridgeway. He steps ashore in New York and returns by the first boat available."

"But who—which was he?"

"The man who had a duplicate key, the man who ordered the lock, the man who has *not* been severely ill with bronchitis at his home in the country—*enfin,* that 'stodgy' old man, Mr. Shaw! There are criminals in high places sometimes, my friend. Ah, here we are. Mademoiselle, I have succeeded! You permit?"

And, beaming, Poirot kissed the astonished girl lightly on either cheek!

# The Adventure of
# the Egyptian Tomb

I have always considered that one of the most thrilling and dramatic of the many adventures I have shared with Poirot was that of our investigation into the strange series of deaths which followed upon the discovery and opening of the Tomb of King Men-her-Ra.

Hard upon the discovery of the Tomb of Tutankh-Amen by Lord Carnarvon, Sir John Willard and Mr. Bleibner of New York, pursuing their excavations not far from Cairo, in the vicinity of the Pyramids of Gizeh, came unexpectedly on a series of funeral chambers. The greatest interest was aroused by their discovery. The tomb appeared to be that of King Men-her-Ra, one of those shadowy kings of the Eighth Dynasty, when the Old Kingdom was falling to decay. Little was known about this period, and the discoveries were fully reported in the newspapers.

An event soon occurred which took a profound hold on the public mind. Sir John Willard died quite suddenly of heart failure.

The more sensational newspapers immediately took the opportunity of reviving all the old superstitious stories connected with the ill luck of certain Egyptian treasures. The unlucky mummy at the British Museum, that hoary old chestnut, was dragged out with fresh zest, was quietly denied by the museum, but nevertheless enjoyed all its usual vogue.

A fortnight later Mr. Bleibner died of acute blood poisoning, and a few days afterwards a nephew of his shot himself in New York. The Curse of Men-her-Ra was the talk of the day, and the magic power of dead-and-gone Egypt was exalted to a fetish point.

It was then that Poirot received a brief note from Lady Willard, widow of the dead archaeologist, asking him to go and see her at her house in Kensington Square. I accompanied him.

Lady Willard was a tall, thin woman, dressed in deep mourning. Her haggard face bore eloquent testimony to her recent grief.

"It is kind of you to have come so promptly, Monsieur Poirot."

"I am at your service, Lady Willard. You wished to consult me?"

"You are, I am aware, a detective, but it is not only as a detective that I wish to consult you. You are a man of original views, I know, you have imagination, experience of the world—tell me, Monsieur Poirot, what are your views on the supernatural?"

Poirot hesitated for a moment before he replied. He seemed to be considering. Finally he said:

"Let us not misunderstand each other, Lady Willard. It is not a general question that you are asking me there. It has a personal application, has it not? You are referring obliquely to the death of your late husband?"

"That is so," she admitted.

"You want me to investigate the circumstances of his death?"

"I want you to ascertain for me exactly how much is newspaper chatter, and how much may be said to be founded on fact. Three deaths, Monsieur Poirot—each one explicable taken by itself, but taken together surely an almost unbelievable coincidence, and all within a month of the opening of the tomb! It may be mere superstition, it may be some potent curse from the past that operates in ways undreamed of by modern science. The fact remains—three deaths! And I am afraid, Monsieur Poirot, horribly afraid. It may not yet be the end."

"For whom do you fear?"

"For my son. When the news of my husband's death came I was ill. My son, who has just come down from Oxford, went out there. He brought the—the body home, but now he has gone out again, in spite of my prayers and entreaties. He is so fascinated by the work that he intends to take his father's place and carry on the system of excavations. You may think me a foolish, credulous woman, but, Monsieur Poirot, I am afraid. Supposing that the spirit of the dead king is not yet appeased? Perhaps to you I seem to be talking nonsense—"

"No, indeed, Lady Willard," said Poirot quickly. "I, too, believe in the force of superstition, one of the greatest forces the world has ever known."

I looked at him in surprise. I should never have credited Poirot with being superstitious. But the little man was obviously in earnest.

"What you really demand is that I shall protect your son. I will do my utmost to keep him from harm."

"Yes, in the ordinary way, but against an occult influence?"

"In volumes of the Middle Ages, Lady Willard, you will find many ways of counteracting black magic. Perhaps they knew more than we moderns with all our boasted science. Now let us come to facts, that I may have guidance. Your husband had always been a devoted Egyptologist, hadn't he?"

"Yes, from his youth upwards. He was one of the greatest living authorities upon the subject."

"But Mr. Bleibner, I understand, was more or less of an amateur?"

"Oh, quite. He was a very wealthy man who dabbled freely in any subject that happened to take his fancy. My husband managed to interest him in Egyptology, and it was his money that was so useful in financing the expedition."

"And the nephew? What do you know of his tastes? Was he with the party at all?"

"I do not think so. In fact I never knew of his existence till I read of his death in the paper. I do not think he and Mr. Bleibner can have been at all intimate. He never spoke of having any relations."

"Who are the other members of the party?"

"Well, there is Dr. Tosswill, minor official connected with the British Museum; Mr. Schneider of the Metropolitan Museum in New York; a young American secretary; Dr. Ames, who accompanies the expedition in his professional capacity; and Hassan, my husband's devoted native servant."

"Do you remember the name of the American secretary?"

"Harper, I think, but I cannot be sure. He had not been with Mr. Bleibner very long, I know. He was a very pleasant young fellow."

"Thank you, Lady Willard."

"If there is anything else—?"

"For the moment, nothing. Leave it now in my hands, and be assured that I will do all that is humanly possible to protect your son."

They were not exactly reassuring words, and I observed Lady Willard wince as he uttered them. Yet, at the same time, the fact that he had not pooh-poohed her fears seemed in itself to be a relief to her.

For my part I had never before suspected that Poirot had so deep a vein of superstition in his nature. I tackled him on the subject as we went homewards. His manner was grave and earnest.

"But yes, Hastings. I believe in these things. You must not underrate the force of superstition."

"What are we going to do about it?"

"*Toujours pratique*, the good Hastings! *Eh bien*, to begin with we are going to cable to New York for fuller details of young Mr. Bleibner's death."

He duly sent off his cable. The reply was full and precise. Young Rupert Bleibner had been in low water for several years. He had been a beachcomber and a remittance man in several South Sea islands, but had returned to New York two years ago, where he had rapidly sunk lower and lower. The most significant thing, to my mind, was that he had recently managed to borrow enough money to take him to Egypt. "I've a good friend there I can borrow from," he had declared. Here, however, his plans had gone awry. He had returned to New York cursing his skinflint of an uncle who cared more for the bones of dead and gone kings than his own flesh and blood. It was during his sojourn in Egypt that the death of Sir John Willard occurred. Rupert had plunged once more into his life of dissipation in New York, and then, without warning, he had committed suicide, leaving behind him a letter which contained some curious phrases. It seemed written in a sudden fit of remorse. He referred to himself as a leper and an outcast, and the letter ended by declaring that such as he were better dead.

A shadowy theory leapt into my brain. I had never really believed in the vengeance of a long-dead Egyptian king. I saw here a more modern crime. Supposing this young man had decided to do away with his uncle—preferably by poison. By mistake, Sir John Willard receives the fatal dose. The young man returns to New York, haunted by his crime. The news of his uncle's death reaches him. He realizes how unnecessary his crime has been, and stricken with remorse takes his own life.

I outlined my solutions to Poirot. He was interested.

"It is ingenious what you have thought of there—decidedly it is ingenious. It may even be true. But you leave out of count the fatal influence of the tomb."

I shrugged my shoulders.

"You still think that has something to do with it?"

"So much so, *mon ami,* that we start for Egypt tomorrow."

"What?" I cried, astonished.

"I have said it." An expression of conscious heroism spread over Poirot's face. Then he groaned. "But, oh," he lamented, "the sea! The hateful sea!"

It was a week later. Beneath our feet was the golden sand of the desert. The hot sun poured down overhead. Poirot, the picture of misery, wilted by my side. The little man was not a good traveler. Our four days' voyage from Marseilles had been one long agony to him. He had landed at Alexandria the wraith of his former self, even his usual neatness had deserted him. We had arrived in Cairo and had driven out at once to the Mena House Hotel, right in the shadow of the Pyramids.

The charm of Egypt had laid hold of me. Not so Poirot. Dressed precisely the same as in London, he carried a small clothesbrush in his pocket and waged an unceasing war on the dust which accumulated on his dark apparel.

"And my boots," he wailed. "Regard them, Hastings. My boots, of the neat patent leather, usually so smart and shining. See, the sand is inside them, which is painful, and outside them, which outrages the eyesight. Also the heat, it causes my mustaches to become limp— but limp!"

"Look at the Sphinx," I urged. "Even I can feel the mystery and the charm it exhales."

Poirot looked at it discontentedly.

"It has not the air happy," he declared. "How could it, half-buried in sand in that untidy fashion. Ah, this cursed sand!"

"Come, now, there's a lot of sand in Belgium," I reminded him, mindful of a holiday spent at Knocke-sur-mer in the midst of *"les dunes impeccables"* as the guidebook had phrased it.

"Not in Brussels," declared Poirot. He gazed at the Pyramids thoughtfully. "It is true that they, at least, are of a shape solid and geometrical, but their surface is of an unevenness most unpleasing. And the palm trees I like them not. Not even do they plant them in rows!"

I cut short his lamentations, by suggesting that we should start for the camp. We were to ride there on camels, and the beasts were patiently kneeling, waiting for us to mount, in charge of several picturesque boys headed by a voluble dragoman.

I pass over the spectacle of Poirot on a camel. He started by groans and lamentations and ended by shrieks, gesticulations and invocations to the Virgin Mary and every saint in the calendar. In the end, he descended ignominiously and finished the journey on a diminutive donkey. I must admit that a trotting camel is no joke for the amateur. I was stiff for several days.

At last we neared the scene of the excavations. A sunburnt man with a gray beard, in white clothes and wearing a helmet, came to meet us.

"Monsieur Poirot and Captain Hastings? We received your cable. I'm sorry that there was no one to meet you in Cairo. An unforeseen event occurred which completely disorganized our plans."

Poirot paled. His hand, which had stolen to his clothesbrush, stayed its course.

"Not another death?" he breathed.

"Yes."

"Sir Guy Willard?" I cried.

"No, Captain Hastings. My American colleague, Mr. Schneider."

"And the cause?" demanded Poirot.

"Tetanus."

I blanched. All around me I seemed to feel an atmosphere of evil, subtle and menacing. A horrible thought flashed across me. Supposing I were the next?

"*Mon Dieu,*" said Poirot, in a very low voice, "I do not understand this. It is horrible. Tell me, monsieur, there is no doubt that it was tetanus?"

"I believe not. But Dr. Ames will tell you more than I can do."

"Ah, of course, you are not the doctor."

"My name is Tosswill."

This, then, was the British expert described by Lady Willard as being a minor official at the British Museum. There was something at once grave and steadfast about him that took my fancy.

"If you will come with me," continued Dr. Tosswill, "I will take you to Sir Guy Willard. He was most anxious to be informed as soon as you should arrive."

We were taken across the camp to a large tent. Dr. Tosswill lifted up the flap and we entered. Three men were sitting inside.

"Monsieur Poirot and Captain Hastings have arrived, Sir Guy," said Tosswill.

The youngest of the three men jumped up and came forward to greet us. There was a certain impulsiveness in his manner which reminded me of his mother. He was not nearly so sunburnt as the others, and that fact, coupled with a certain haggardness round the eyes, made him look older than his twenty-two years. He was clearly endeavoring to bear up under a severe mental strain.

He introduced his two companions, Dr. Ames, a capable-looking man of thirty-odd, with a touch of graying hair at the temples, and Mr. Harper, the secretary, a pleasant, lean young man wearing the national insignia of horn-rimmed spectacles.

After a few minutes' desultory conversation the latter went out, and Dr. Tosswill followed him. We were left alone with Sir Guy and Dr. Ames.

"Please ask any questions you want to ask, Monsieur Poirot," said Willard. "We are utterly dumfounded at this strange series of disasters, but it isn't—it can't be, anything but coincidence."

There was a nervousness about his manner which rather belied the words. I saw that Poirot was studying him keenly.

"Your heart is really in this work, Sir Guy?"

"Rather. No matter what happens, or what comes of it, the work is going on. Make up your mind to that."

Poirot wheeled round on the other.

"What have you to say to that, *monsieur le docteur?*"

"Well," drawled the doctor, "I'm not for quitting myself."

Poirot made one of those expressive grimaces of his.

"Then, *évidemment,* we must find out just how we stand. When did Mr. Schneider's death take place?"

"Three days ago."

"You are sure it was tetanus?"

"Dead sure."

"It couldn't have been a case of strychnine poisoning, for instance?"

"No, Monsieur Poirot. I see what you're getting at. But it was a clear case of tetanus."

"Did you not inject antiserum?"

"Certainly we did," said the doctor dryly. "Every conceivable thing that could be done was tried."

"Had you the antiserum with you?"

"No. We procured it from Cairo."

"Have there been any other cases of tetanus in the camp?"

"No, not one."

"Are you certain that the death of Mr. Bleibner was not due to tetanus?"

"Absolutely plumb certain. He had a scratch upon his thumb which became poisoned, and septicemia set in. It sounds pretty much the same to a layman, I dare say, but the two things are entirely different."

"Then we have four deaths—all totally dissimilar, one heart failure, one blood poisoning, one suicide, and one tetanus."

"Exactly, Monsieur Poirot."

"Are you certain that there is nothing which might link the four together?"

"I don't quite understand you?"

"I will put it plainly. Was any act committed by those four men which might seem to denote disrespect to the spirit of Men-her-Ra?"

The doctor gazed at Poirot in astonishment.

"You're talking through your hat, Monsieur Poirot. Surely you've not been guyed into believing all that fool talk?"

"Absolute nonsense," muttered Willard angrily.

Poirot remained placidly immovable, blinking a little out of his green cat's eyes.

"So you do not believe it, *monsieur le docteur?*"

"No, sir, I do not," declared the doctor emphatically. "I am a scientific man, and I believe only what science teaches."

"Was there no science then in Ancient Egypt?" asked Poirot softly. He did not wait for a reply, and indeed Dr. Ames seemed rather at a loss for the moment. "No, no, do not answer me, but tell me this. What do the native workmen think?"

"I guess," said Dr. Ames, "that, where white folk lose their heads, natives aren't going to be far behind. I'll admit that they're getting what you might call scared—but they've no cause to be."

"I wonder," said Poirot noncommittally.

Sir Guy leant forward.

"Surely," he cried incredulously, "you cannot believe in—oh, but the thing's absurd! You can know nothing of Ancient Egypt if you think that."

For answer Poirot produced a little book from his pocket—an ancient tattered volume. As he held it out I saw its title, *The Magic of the Egyptians and Chaldeans.* Then, wheeling round, he strode out of the tent. The doctor stared at me.

"What is his little idea?"

The phrase, so familiar on Poirot's lips, made me smile as it came from another.

"I don't know exactly," I confessed. "He's got some plan of exorcising the evil spirits, I believe."

I went in search of Poirot, and found him talking to the lean-faced young man who had been the late Mr. Bleibner's secretary.

"No," Mr. Harper was saying, "I've only been six months with the expedition. Yes, I knew Mr. Bleibner's affairs pretty well."

"Can you recount to me anything concerning his nephew?"

"He turned up here one day, not a bad-looking fellow. I'd never met him before, but some of the others had—Ames, I think, and Schneider. The old man wasn't at all pleased to see him. They were at it in no time, hammer and tongs. 'Not a cent,' the old man shouted. 'Not one cent now or when I'm dead. I intend to leave my money to the furtherance of my life's work. I've been talking it over with Mr. Schneider today.' And a bit more of the same. Young Bleibner lit out for Cairo right away."

"Was he in perfectly good health at the time?"

"The old man?"

"No, the young one."

"I believe he did mention there was something wrong with him. But it couldn't have been anything serious, or I should have remembered."

"One thing more, has Mr. Bleibner left a will?"

"So far as we know, he has not."

"Are you remaining with the expedition, Mr. Harper?"

"No, sir, I am not. I'm for New York as soon as I can square up things here. You may laugh if you like, but I'm not going to be this blasted old Men-her-Ra's next victim. He'll get me if I stop here."

The young man wiped the perspiration from his brow.

Poirot turned away. Over his shoulder he said with a peculiar smile: "Remember, he got one of his victims in New York."

"Oh, hell!" said Mr. Harper forcibly.

"That young man is nervous," said Poirot thoughtfully. "He is on the edge, but absolutely on the edge."

I glanced at Poirot curiously, but his enigmatical smile told me nothing. In company with Sir Guy Willard and Dr. Tosswill we were taken round the excavations. The principal finds had been removed to Cairo, but some of the tomb furniture was extremely interesting. The enthusiasm of the young baronet was obvious, but I fancied that I detected a shade of nervousness in his manner as though he could not quite escape from the feeling of menace in the air. As we entered the tent which had been assigned to us, for a wash before joining the evening meal, a tall dark figure in white robes stood aside to let us pass with a graceful gesture and a murmured greeting in Arabic. Poirot stopped.

"You are Hassan, the late Sir John Willard's servant?"

"I served my Lord Sir John, now I serve his son." He took a step nearer to us and lowered his voice. "You are a wise one, they say, learned in dealing with evil spirits. Let the young master depart from here. There is evil in the air around us."

And with an abrupt gesture, not waiting for a reply, he strode away.

"Evil in the air," muttered Poirot. "Yes, I feel it."

Our meal was hardly a cheerful one. The floor was left to Dr. Tosswill, who discoursed at length upon Egyptian antiquities. Just as we were preparing to retire to rest, Sir Guy caught Poirot by the arm and pointed. A shadowy figure was moving amidst the tents. It was no human one: I recognized distinctly the dog-headed figure I had seen carved on the walls of the tomb.

My blood literally froze at the sight.

"*Mon Dieu!*" murmured Poirot, crossing himself vigorously. "Anubis, the jackal-headed, the god of departing souls."

"Someone is hoaxing us," cried Dr. Tosswill, rising indignantly to his feet.

"It went into your tent, Harper," muttered Sir Guy, his face dreadfully pale.

"No," said Poirot, shaking his head, "into that of the Dr. Ames."

The doctor stared at him incredulously; then, repeating Dr. Tosswill's words, he cried:

"Someone is hoaxing us. Come, we'll soon catch the fellow."

He dashed energetically in pursuit of the shadowy apparition. I followed him, but, search as we would, we could find no trace of any living thing having passed that way. We returned, somewhat disturbed in mind, to find Poirot taking energetic measures, in his own way, to ensure his personal safety. He was busily surrounding our tent with various diagrams and inscriptions which he was drawing in the sand. I recognized the five-pointed star, or pentacle, many times repeated. As was his wont, Poirot was at the same time delivering an impromptu lecture on witchcraft and magic in general, white magic as opposed to black, with various references to the Ka and the Book of the Dead thrown in.

It appeared to excite the liveliest contempt in Dr. Tosswill, who drew me aside, literally snorting with rage.

"Balderdash, sir," he exclaimed angrily. "Pure balderdash. The man's an impostor. He doesn't know the difference between the superstitions of the Middle Ages and the beliefs of Ancient Egypt. Never have I heard such a hodgepodge of ignorance and credulity."

I calmed the excited expert, and joined Poirot in the tent. My little friend was beaming cheerfully.

"We can now sleep in peace," he declared happily. "And I can do with some sleep. My head, it aches abominably. Ah, for a good *tisane!*"

As though in answer to prayer, the flap of the tent was lifted and Hassan appeared, bearing a steaming cup which he offered to Poirot. It proved to be camomile tea, a beverage of which he is inordinately fond. Having thanked Hassan and refused his offer of another cup for myself, we were left alone once more. I stood at the door of the tent some time after undressing, looking out over the desert.

"A wonderful place," I said aloud, "and a wonderful work. I can feel the fascination. This desert life, this probing into the heart of a vanished civilization. Surely, Poirot, you, too, must feel the charm?"

I got no answer, and I turned, a little annoyed. My annoyance was quickly changed to concern. Poirot was lying back across the rude couch, his face horribly convulsed. Beside him was the empty cup. I rushed to his side, then dashed out and across the camp to Dr. Ames's tent.

"Dr. Ames!" I cried. "Come at once."

"What's the matter?" said the doctor, appearing in pajamas.

"My friend. He's ill. Dying. The camomile tea. Don't let Hassan leave the camp."

Like a flash the doctor ran to our tent. Poirot was lying as I left him.

"Extraordinary," cried Ames. "Looks like a seizure—or—what did you say about something he drank?" He picked up the empty cup.

"Only I did not drink it!" said a placid voice.

We turned in amazement. Poirot was sitting up on the bed. He was smiling.

"No," he said gently. "I did not drink it. While my good friend Hastings was apostrophizing the night, I took the opportunity of pouring it, not down my throat, but into a little bottle. That little bottle will go the analytical chemist. No"—as the doctor made a sudden movement—"as a sensible man, you will understand that violence will be of no avail. During Hastings' brief absence to fetch you, I have had time to put the bottle in safe keeping. Ah, quick, Hastings, hold him!"

I misunderstood Poirot's anxiety. Eager to save my friend, I flung myself in front of him. But the doctor's swift movement had another meaning. His hand went to his mouth, a smell of bitter almonds filled the air, and he swayed forward and fell.

"Another victim," said Poirot gravely, "but the last. Perhaps it is the best way. He has three deaths on his head."

"Dr. Ames?" I cried, stupefied. "But I thought you believed in some occult influence?"

"You misunderstood me, Hastings. What I meant was that I believe in the terrific force of superstition. Once get it firmly established that a series of deaths are supernatural, and you might almost stab a man in broad daylight, and it would still be put down to the curse, so strongly is the instinct of the supernatural implanted in the human race. I suspected from the first that a man was taking advantage of that instinct. The idea came to him, I imagine, with the death of Sir John Willard. A fury of superstition arose at once. As far as I could see, nobody could derive any particular profit from Sir John's death. Mr. Bleibner was a different case. He was a man of great wealth. The information I received from New York contained several suggestive points. To begin with, young Bleibner was reported to have said he had a good friend in Egypt from whom he could borrow. It was tacitly understood that he meant his uncle, but it seemed to me that in that case he would have said so outright. The words suggest some boon companion of his own. Another thing, he scraped up enough money to take him to Egypt, his uncle refused outright to advance him a penny, yet he was able to pay the return passage to New York. Some one must have lent him the money."

"All that was very thin," I objected.

"But there was more. Hastings, there occur often enough words spoken metaphorically which are taken literally. The opposite can happen too. In this case, words which were meant literally were taken metaphorically. Young Bleibner wrote plainly enough: 'I am a leper,' but nobody realized that he shot himself because he believed that he had contracted the dread disease of leprosy."

"What?" I ejaculated.

"It was the clever invention of a diabolical mind. Young Bleibner was suffering from some minor skin trouble. He had lived in the South Sea Islands, where the disease is common enough. Ames was a former friend of his, and a well-known medical man, he would never have dreamed of doubting his word. When I arrived here, my suspicions were divided between Harper and Dr. Ames, but I soon realized that only the doctor could have perpetrated and concealed the crimes, and I learnt from Harper that he was previously acquainted with young Bleibner. Doubtless the latter at some time or another had made a will or had insured his life in favor of the doctor. The latter saw his chance of acquiring wealth. It was easy for him to inoculate Mr. Bleibner with the deadly germs. Then the nephew, overcome with despair at the dread news his friend had conveyed to him, shot himself. Mr. Bleibner, whatever his intentions, had made no will. His fortune would pass to his nephew and from him to the doctor."

"And Mr. Schneider?"

"We cannot be sure. He knew young Bleibner too, remember, and may have suspected something, or, again, the doctor may have thought that a further death motiveless and purposeless would strengthen the coils of superstition. Furthermore, I will tell you an interesting psychological fact, Hastings. A murderer has always a strong desire to repeat his successful crime, the performance of it grows upon him. Hence my fears for young Willard. The figure of Anubis you saw tonight was Hassan, dressed up by my orders. I wanted to see if I could frighten the doctor. But it would take more than the supernatural to frighten him. I could see that he was not entirely taken in by my pretenses of belief in the occult. The little comedy I played for him did not deceive him. I suspected that he would endeavor to make me the next victim. Ah, but in spite of *la mer maudite*, the heat abominable, and the annoyances of the sand, the little gray cells still functioned!"

Poirot proved to be perfectly right in his premises. Young Bleibner, some years ago, in a fit of drunken merriment, had made a jocular will, leaving "my cigarette case you admire so much and everything else of which I die possessed which will be principally debts to my good friend Robert Ames who once saved my life from drowning."

The case was hushed up as far as possible, and, to this day, people talk of the remarkable series of deaths in connection with the Tomb of Men-her-Ra as a triumphal proof of the vengeance of a bygone king upon the desecrators of his tomb—a belief which, as Poirot pointed out to me, is contrary to all Egyptian belief and thought.

# The Jewel Robbery at
# the Grand Metropolitan

"POIROT," I said, "a change of air would do you good."

"You think so, *mon ami?*"

"*I am sure of it.*"

"Eh—eh?" said my friend, smiling. "It is all arranged, then?"

"You will come?"

"Where do you propose to take me?"

"Brighton. As a matter of fact, a friend of mine in the City put me on to a very good thing, and—well, I have money to burn, as the saying goes. I think a weekend at the Grand Metropolitan would do us all the good in the world."

"Thank you, I accept most gratefully. You have the good heart to think of an old man. And the good heart, it is in the end worth all the little gray cells. Yes, yes, I who speak to you am in danger of forgetting that sometimes."

I did not quite relish the implication. I fancy that Poirot is sometimes a little inclined to underestimate my mental capacities. But his pleasure was so evident that I put my slight annoyance aside.

"Then, that's all right," I said hastily.

Saturday evening saw us dining at the Grand Metropolitan in the midst of a merry throng. All the world and his wife seemed to be at Brighton. The dresses were marvellous, and the jewels—worn sometimes with more love of display than good taste—were something magnificent.

"*Hein,* it is a sight this!" murmured Poirot. "This is the home of the profiteer, is it not so, Hastings?"

"Supposed to be," I replied. "But we'll hope they aren't all tarred with the profiteering brush."

Poirot gazed round him placidly.

"The sight of so many jewels makes me wish I had turned my brains to crime, instead of to its detection. What a magnificent opportunity for some thief of distinction! Regard, Hastings, that stout woman by the pillar. She is, as you would say, plastered with gems."

I followed his eyes.

"Why," I exclaimed, "it's Mrs. Opalsen."

"You know her?"

"Slightly. Her husband is a rich stockbroker who made a fortune in the recent oil boom."

After dinner we ran across the Opalsens in the lounge, and I introduced Poirot to them. We chatted for a few minutes, and ended by having our coffee together.

Poirot said a few words in praise of some of the costlier gems displayed on the lady's ample bosom, and she brightened up at once.

"It's a perfect hobby of mine, Mr. Poirot. I just *love* jewelry. Ed knows my weakness, and every time things go well he brings me something new. You are interested in precious stones?"

"I have had a good deal to do with them one time and another, madame. My profession has brought me into contact with some of the most famous jewels in the world."

He went on to narrate, with discreet pseudonyms, the story of the historic jewels of a reigning house, and Mrs. Opalsen listened with bated breath.

"There now!" she exclaimed, as he ended. "If it isn't just like a play! You know, I've got some pearls of my own that have a history attached to them. I believe it's supposed to be one of the finest necklaces in the world—pearls so beautifully matched and so perfect in color. I declare I really must run up and get it!"

"Oh, madame," protested Poirot, "you are too amiable. Pray do not derange yourself!"

"Oh, but I'd like to show it to you."

The buxom dame waddled across to the lift briskly enough. Her husband, who had been talking to me, looked at Poirot inquiringly.

"Madame, your wife is so amiable as to insist on showing me her pearl necklace," explained the latter.

"Oh, the pearls!" Opalsen smiled in a satisfied fashion. "Well, they *are* worth seeing. Cost a pretty penny too! Still, the money's there all right; I could get what I paid for them any day—perhaps more. May have to, too, if things go on as they are now. Money's confoundedly tight in the City. All this infernal E.P.D." He rambled on, launching into technicalities where I could not follow him.

He was interrupted by a small pageboy who approached and murmured something in his ear.

"Eh—what? I'll come at once. Not taken ill, is she? Excuse me, gentlemen."

He left us abruptly. Poirot leaned back and lit one of his tiny Russian cigarettes. Then, carefully and meticulously, he arranged the empty coffee cups in a neat row, and beamed happily on the result.

The minutes passed. The Opalsens did not return.

"Curious," I remarked, at length. "I wonder when they will come back."

Poirot watched the ascending spirals of smoke, and then said thoughtfully:

"They will not come back."

"Why?"

"Because, my friend, something has happened."

"What sort of thing? How do you know?" I asked curiously.

Poirot smiled.

"A few moments ago the manager came hurriedly out of his office and ran upstairs. He was much agitated. The liftboy is deep in talk with one of the pages. The liftbell has rung three times, but he heeds it not. Thirdly, even the waiters are distrait; and to make a waiter distrait—" Poirot shook his head with an air of finality. "The affair must indeed be of the first magnitude. Ah, it is as I thought! Here come the police."

Two men had just entered the hotel—one in uniform, the other in plain clothes. They spoke to a page, and were immediately ushered upstairs. A few minutes later, the same boy descended and came up to where we were sitting.

"Mr. Opalsen's compliments, and would you step upstairs."

Poirot sprang nimbly to his feet. One would have said that he awaited the summons. I followed with no less alacrity.

The Opalsens' apartments were situated on the first floor. After knocking on the door, the pageboy retired, and we answered the summons, "Come in!" A strange scene met our eyes. The room was Mrs. Opalsen's bedroom, and in the center of it, lying back in an armchair, was the lady herself, weeping violently. She presented an extraordinary spectacle, with tears making great furrows in the powder with which her complexion was liberally coated. Mr. Opalsen was striding up and down angrily. The two police officials stood in the middle of the room, one with a notebook in hand. A hotel chambermaid, looking frightened to death, stood by the fireplace; and on the other side of the room a Frenchwoman, obviously Mrs. Opalsen's maid, was weeping and wringing her hands, with an intensity of grief that rivaled that of her mistress.

Into this pandemonium stepped Poirot, neat and smiling. Immediately, with an energy surprising in one of her bulk, Mrs. Opalsen sprang from her chair towards him.

"There now; Ed may say what he likes, but I believe in luck, I do. It was fated I should meet you the way I did this evening, and I've a feeling that if you can't get my pearls back for me nobody can."

"Calm yourself, I pray of you, madame." Poirot patted her hand soothingly. "Reassure yourself. All will be well. Hercule Poirot will aid you!"

Mr. Opalsen turned to the police inspector.

"There will be no objection to my—er—calling in this gentleman, I suppose?"

"None at all, sir," replied the man civilly, but with complete indifference. "Perhaps now your lady's feeling better she'll just let us have the facts?"

Mrs. Opalsen looked helplessly at Poirot. He led her back to her chair.

"Seat yourself, madame, and recount to us the whole history without agitating yourself."

Thus abjured, Mrs. Opalsen dried her eyes gingerly, and began.

"I came upstairs after dinner to fetch my pearls for Mr. Poirot here to see. The chambermaid and Célestine were both in the room as usual—"

"Excuse me, madame, but what do you mean by 'as usual'?"

Mr. Opalsen explained.

"I make it a rule that no one is to come into this room unless Célestine, the maid, is there also. The chambermaid does the room in the morning while Célestine is present, and comes in after dinner to turn down the beds under the same conditions; otherwise she never enters the room."

"Well, as I was saying," continued Mrs. Opalsen, "I came up. I went to the drawer here,"—she indicated the bottom right-hand drawer of the kneehole dressing table—"took out my jewel case and unlocked it. It seemed quite as usual—but the pearls were not there!"

The inspector had been busy with his notebook. "When had you last seen them?" he asked.

"They were there when I went down to dinner."

"You are sure?"

"Quite sure. I was uncertain whether to wear them or not, but in the end I decided on the emeralds, and put them back in the jewel case."

"Who locked up the jewel case?"

"I did. I wear the key on a chain round my neck." She held it up as she spoke.

The inspector examined it, and shrugged his shoulders.

"The thief must have had a duplicate key. No difficult matter. The lock is quite a simple one. What did you do after you'd locked the jewel case?"

"I put it back in the bottom drawer where I always keep it."

"You didn't lock the drawer?"

"No, I never do. My maid remains in the room till I come up, so there's no need."

The inspector's face grew graver.

"Am I to understand that the jewels were there when you went down to dinner, and that since then *the maid has not left the room?*"

Suddenly, as though the horror of her own situation for the first time burst upon her, Célestine uttered a piercing shriek, and, flinging herself upon Poirot, poured out a torrent of incoherent French.

The suggestion was infamous! That she should be suspected of robbing madame! The police were well known to be of a stupidity incredible! But monsieur, who was a Frenchman—

"A Belgian," interjected Poirot, but Célestine paid no attention to the correction.

Monsieur would not stand by and see her falsely accused, while that infamous chambermaid was allowed to go scot-free. She had never liked her—a bold, red-faced thing—a born thief. She had said from the first that she was not honest. And had kept a sharp watch over her too, when she was doing madame's room! Let those idiots of policemen search her, and if they did not find madame's pearls on her it would be very surprising!

Although this harangue was uttered in rapid and virulent French, Célestine had interlarded it with a wealth of gesture, and the chambermaid realized at least a part of her meaning. She reddened angrily.

"If that foreign woman's saying I took the pearls, it's a lie!" she declared heatedly. "I never so much as saw them."

"Search her!" screamed the other. "You will find it as I say."

"You're a liar—do you hear?" said the chambermaid, advancing upon her. "Stole 'em yourself, and want to put it on me. Why, I was only in the room about three minutes before the lady come up, and then you were sitting here the whole time, as you always do, like a cat watching a mouse."

The inspector looked across inquiringly at Célestine. "Is that true? Didn't you leave the room at all?"

"I did not actually leave her alone," admitted Célestine reluctantly, "but I went into my own room through the door here twice—once to fetch a reel of cotton, and once for my scissors. She must have done it then."

"You wasn't gone a minute," retorted the chambermaid angrily. "Just popped out and in again. I'd be glad if the police *would* search me. *I've* nothing to be afraid of."

At this moment there was a tap at the door. The inspector went to it. His face brightened when he saw who it was.

"Ah!" he said. "That's rather fortunate. I sent for one of our female searchers, and she's just arrived. Perhaps if you wouldn't mind going into the room next door."

He looked at the chambermaid, who stepped across the threshold with a toss of her head, the searcher following her closely.

The French girl had sunk sobbing into a chair. Poirot was looking round the room, the main features of which I have made clear by a sketch.

"Where does that door lead?" he inquired, nodding his head towards the one by the window.

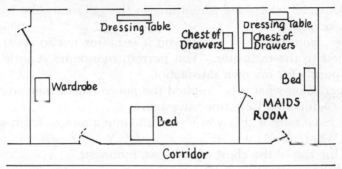

"Into the next apartment, I believe," said the inspector. "It's bolted, anyway, on this side."

Poirot walked across to it, tried it, then drew back the bolt and tried it again.

"And on the other side as well," he remarked. "Well, that seems to rule out that."

He walked over to the windows, examining each of them in turn.

"And again—nothing. Not even a balcony outside."

"Even if there were," said the inspector impatiently, "I don't see how that would help us, if the maid never left the room."

"*Évidemment,*" said Poirot, not disconcerted. "As mademoiselle is positive she did not leave the room—"

He was interrupted by the reappearance of the chambermaid and the police searcher.

"Nothing," said the latter laconically.

"I should hope not, indeed," said the chambermaid virtuously. "And that French hussy ought to be ashamed of herself taking away an honest girl's character!"

"There, there, my girl; that's all right," said the inspector, opening the door. "Nobody suspects you. You go along and get on with your work."

The chambermaid went unwillingly.

"Going to search *her?*" she demanded, pointing at Célestine.

"Yes, yes!" He shut the door on her and turned the key.

Célestine accompanied the searcher into the small room in her turn. A few minutes later she also returned. Nothing had been found on her.

The inspector's face grew graver.

"I'm afraid I'll have to ask you to come along with me all the same, miss." He turned to Mrs. Opalsen. "I'm sorry, madame, but all the evidence points that way. If she's not got them on her, they're hidden somewhere about the room."

Célestine uttered a piercing shriek, and clung to Poirot's arm. The latter bent and whispered something in the girl's ear. She looked up at him doubtfully.

"*Si, si, mon enfant*—I assure you it is better not to resist." Then he turned to the inspector. "You permit, monsieur? A little experiment—purely for my own satisfaction."

"Depends on what it is," replied the police officer noncommittally.

Poirot addressed Célestine once more.

"You have told us that you went into your room to fetch a reel of cotton. Whereabouts was it?"

"On the top of the chest of drawers, monsieur."

"And the scissors?"

"They also."

"Would it be troubling you too much, mademoiselle, to ask you to repeat those two actions? You were sitting here with your work, you say?"

Célestine sat down, and then, at a sign from Poirot, rose, passing into the adjoining room, took up an object from the chest of drawers, and returned.

Poirot divided his attention between her movements and a large turnip of a watch which he held in the palm of his hand.

"Again, if you please, mademoiselle."

At the conclusion of the second performance, he made a note in his pocket book, and returned the watch to his pocket.

"Thank you, mademoiselle. And you, monsieur,"—he bowed to the inspector—"for your courtesy."

The inspector seemed somewhat entertained by this excessive politeness. Célestine departed in a flood of tears, accompanied by the woman and the plainclothes official.

Then, with a brief apology to Mrs. Opalsen, the inspector set to work to ransack the room. He pulled out drawers, opened cupboards, completely unmade the bed, and tapped the floor. Mr. Opalsen looked on skeptically.

"You really think you will find them?"

"Yes, sir. It stands to reason. She hadn't time to take them out of the room. The lady's discovering the robbery so soon upset her plans.

No, they're here right enough. One of the two must have hidden them—and it's very unlikely for the chambermaid to have done so."

"More than unlikely—impossible!" said Poirot quietly.

"Eh?" The inspector stared.

Poirot smiled modestly.

"I will demonstrate. Hastings, my good friend, take my watch in your hand—with care. It is a family heirloom! Just now I timed mademoiselle's movements—her first absence from the room was of twelve seconds, her second of fifteen. Now observe my actions. Madame will have the kindness to give me the key of the jewel case. I thank you. My friend Hastings will have the kindness to say 'Go!'"

"Go!" I said.

With almost incredible swiftness, Poirot wrenched open the drawer of the dressing table, extracted the jewel-case, fitted the key in the lock, opened the case, selected a piece of jewelry, shut and locked the case, and returned it to the drawer, which he pushed to again. His movements were like lightning.

"Well, *mon ami?*" he demanded of me breathlessly.

"Forty-six seconds," I replied.

"You see?" He looked round. "There would not have been time for the chambermaid even to take the necklace out, far less hide it."

"Then that settles it on the maid," said the inspector with satisfaction, and returned to his search. He passed into the maid's bedroom next door.

Poirot was frowning thoughtfully. Suddenly he shot a question at Mr. Opalsen.

"This necklace—it was, without doubt, insured?"

Mr. Opalsen looked a trifle surprised at the question.

"Yes," he said hesitatingly, "that is so."

"But what does that matter?" broke in Mrs. Opalsen tearfully. "It's my necklace I want. It was unique. No money could be the same."

"I comprehend, madame," said Poirot soothingly. "I comprehend perfectly. To *la femme* sentiment is everything—is it not so? But monsieur, who has not the so fine susceptibility, will doubtless find some slight consolation in the fact."

"Of course, of course," said Mr. Opalsen rather uncertainly. "Still—"

He was interrupted by a shout of triumph from the inspector. He came in dangling something from his fingers.

With a cry, Mrs. Opalsen heaved herself up from her chair. She was a changed woman.

"Oh, oh, my necklace!"

She clasped it to her breast with both hands. We crowded around.

"Where was it?" demanded Opalsen.

"Maid's bed. In among the springs of the wire mattress. She must have stolen it and hidden it there before the chambermaid arrived on the scene."

"You permit, madame?" said Poirot gently. He took the necklace from her and examined it closely; then handed it back with a bow.

"I'm afraid, madame, you'll have to hand it over to us for the time being," said the inspector. "We shall want it for the charge. But it shall be returned to you as soon as possible."

Mr. Opalsen frowned.

"Is that necessary?"

"I'm afraid so, sir. Just a formality."

"Oh, let him take it, Ed!" cried his wife. "I'd feel safer if he did. I shouldn't sleep a wink thinking someone else might try and get hold of it. That wretched girl! And I would never have believed it of her."

"There, there, my dear, don't take on so." I felt a gentle pressure on my arm. It was Poirot.

"Shall we slip away, my friend? I think our services are no longer needed."

Once outside, however, he hesitated, and then, much to my surprise, he remarked:

"I should rather like to see the room next door."

The door was not locked, and we entered. The room, which was a large double one, was unoccupied. Dust lay about rather noticeably, and my sensitive friend gave a characteristic grimace as he ran his finger round a rectangular mark on a table near the window.

"The *service* leaves to be desired," he observed dryly.

He was staring thoughtfully out of the window, and seemed to have fallen into a brown study.

"Well?" I demanded impatiently. "What did we come in here for?"

He stared.

"*Je vous demande pardon, mon ami.* I wished to see if the door was really bolted on this side also."

"Well," I said, glancing at the door which communicated with the room we had just left, "it *is* bolted."

Poirot nodded. He still seemed to be thinking.

"And, anyway," I continued, "what does it matter? The case is over. I wish you'd had more chance of distinguishing yourself. But it was the kind of case that even a stiff-backed idiot like that inspector couldn't go wrong over."

Poirot shook his head.

"The case is not over, my friend. It will not be over until we find out who stole the pearls."

"But the maid did!"

"Why do you say that?"

"Why," I stammered, "they were found—actually in her mattress."

"Ta, ta, ta!" said Poirot impatiently. "Those were not the pearls."

"What?"

"Imitation, *mon ami*."

The statement took my breath away. Poirot was smiling placidly.

"The good inspector obviously knows nothing of jewels. But presently there will be a fine hullabaloo!"

"Come!" I cried, dragging at his arm.

"Where?"

"We must tell the Opalsens at once."

"I think not."

"But that poor woman—"

"*Eh bien;* that poor woman, as you call her, will have a much better night believing the jewels to be safe."

"But the thief may escape with them!"

"As usual, my friend, you speak without reflection. How do you know that the pearls Mrs. Opalsen locked up so carefully tonight were not the false ones, and that the real robbery did not take place at a much earlier date?"

"Oh!" I said bewildered.

"Exactly," said Poirot, beaming. "We start again."

He led the way out of the room, paused a moment as though considering, and then walked down to the end of the corridor, stopping outside the small den where the chambermaids and valets of the respective floors congregated. Our particular chambermaid appeared to be holding a small court there, and to be retailing her late experiences to an appreciative audience. She stopped in the middle of a sentence. Poirot bowed with his usual politeness.

"Excuse that I derange you, but I shall be obliged if you will unlock for me the door of Mr. Opalsen's room."

The woman rose willingly, and we accompanied her down the passage again. Mr. Opalsen's room was on the other side of the corridor, its door facing that of his wife's room. The chambermaid unlocked it with her passkey, and we entered.

As she was about to depart Poirot detained her.

"One moment; have you ever seen among the effects of Mr. Opalsen a card like this?"

He held out a plain white card, rather highly glazed and uncommon in appearance. The maid took it and scrutinized it carefully.

"No, sir, I can't say I have. But, anyway, the valet has most to do with the gentlemen's rooms."

"I see. Thank you."

Poirot took back the card. The woman departed. Poirot appeared to reflect a little. Then he gave a short, sharp nod of the head.

"Ring the bell, I pray of you, Hastings. Three times, for the valet."

I obeyed, devoured with curiosity. Meanwhile Poirot had emptied the wastepaper basket on the floor, and was swiftly going through its contents.

In a few moments the valet answered the bell. To him Poirot put the same question, and handed him the card to examine. But the response was the same. The valet had never seen a card of that particular quality among Mr. Opalsen's belongings. Poirot thanked him, and he withdrew, somewhat unwillingly, with an inquisitive glance at the overturned wastepaper basket and the litter on the floor. He could hardly have helped overhearing Poirot's thoughtful remark as he bundled the torn papers back again:

"And the necklace was heavily insured. . . ."

"Poirot," I cried, "I see—"

"You see nothing, my friend," he replied quickly, "as usual, nothing at all! It is incredible—but there it is. Let us return to our own apartments."

We did so in silence. Once there, to my intense surprise, Poirot effected a rapid change of clothing.

"I go to London tonight," he explained. "It is imperative."

"What?"

"Absolutely. The real work, that of the brain (ah, those brave little gray cells), it is done. I go to seek the confirmation. I shall find it! Impossible to deceive Hercule Poirot!"

"You'll come a cropper one of these days," I observed, rather disgusted by his vanity.

"Do not be enraged, I beg of you, *mon ami*. I count on you to do me a service—of your friendship."

"Of course," I said eagerly, rather ashamed of my moroseness. "What is it?"

"The sleeve of my coat that I have taken off—will you brush it? See you, a little white powder has clung to it. You without doubt observed me run my finger round the drawer of the dressing table?"

"No, I didn't."

"You should observe my actions, my friend. Thus I obtained the powder on my finger, and, being a little overexcited, I rubbed it on my sleeve; an action without method which I deplore—false to all my principles."

"But what was the powder?" I asked, not particularly interested in Poirot's principles.

"Not the poison of the Borgias," replied Poirot, with a twinkle. "I see your imagination mounting. I should say it was French chalk."

"French chalk?"

"Yes, cabinetmakers use it to make drawers run smoothly."

I laughed.

"You old sinner! I thought you were working up to something exciting."

"Au revoir, my friend. I save myself. I fly!"

The door shut behind him. With a smile, half of derision, half of affection, I picked up the coat, and stretched out my hand for the clothes brush.

The next morning, hearing nothing from Poirot, I went out for a stroll, met some old friends, and lunched with them at their hotel. In the afternoon we went for a spin. A punctured tire delayed us, and it was past eight when I got back to the Grand Metropolitan.

The first sight that met my eyes was Poirot, looking even more diminutive than usual, sandwiched between the Opalsens, beaming in a state of placid satisfaction.

"*Mon ami* Hastings!" he cried, and sprang to meet me. "Embrace me, my friend; all has marched to a marvel!"

Luckily, the embrace was merely figurative—not a thing one is always sure of with Poirot.

"Do you mean—" I began.

"Just wonderful, I call it!" said Mrs. Opalsen, smiling all over her fat face. "Didn't I tell you, Ed, that if he couldn't get back my pearls nobody would?"

"You did, my dear, you did. And you were right."

I looked helplessly at Poirot, and he answered the glance.

"My friend Hastings is, as you say in England, all at the seaside. Seat yourself, and I will recount to you all the affair that has so happily ended."

"Ended?"

"But yes. They are arrested."

"Who are arrested?"

"The chambermaid and the valet, *parbleu!* You did not suspect? Not with my parting hint about the French chalk?"

"You said cabinetmakers used it."

"Certainly they do—to make drawers slide easily. Somebody wanted that drawer to slide in and out without any noise. Who could that be? Obviously, only the chambermaid. The plan was so ingenious that it did not at once leap to the eye—not even to the eye of Hercule Poirot.

"Listen, this was how it was done. The valet was in the empty room next door, waiting. The French maid leaves the room. Quick as a flash the chambermaid whips open the drawer, takes out the jewel case, and, slipping back the bolt, passes it through the door. The valet opens it at his leisure with the duplicate key with which he has provided himself, extracts the necklace, and waits his time. Célestine leaves the room again, and—pst!—in a flash the case is passed back again and replaced in the drawer.

"Madame arrives, the theft is discovered. The chambermaid demands to be searched, with a good deal of righteous indignation, and leaves the room without a stain on her character. The imitation necklace with which they have provided themselves has been concealed in the French girl's bed that morning by the chambermaid—a master stroke, *ca!*"

"But what did you go to London for?"

"You remember the card?"

"Certainly. It puzzled me—and puzzles me still. I thought—"

I hesitated delicately, glancing at Mr. Opalsen.

Poirot laughed heartily.

"*Une blague!* For the benefit of the valet. The card was one with a specially prepared surface—for fingerprints. I went straight to Scotland Yard, asked for our old friend Inspector Japp, and laid the facts before him. As I had suspected, the fingerprints proved to be those of two well-known jewel thieves who have been 'wanted' for some time. Japp came down with me, the thieves were arrested, and the necklace was discovered in the valet's possession. A clever pair, but they failed in method. Have I not told you, Hastings, at least thirty-six times, that without method—"

"At least thirty-six thousand times!" I interrupted. "But where did their method break down?"

"*Mon ami*, it is a good plan to take a place as chambermaid or valet—but you must not shirk your work. They left an empty room undusted; and therefore, when the man put down the jewel case on the little table near the communicating door, it left a square mark—"

"I remember," I cried.

"Before, I was undecided. Then—I *knew!*"

There was a moment's silence.

"And I've got my pearls," said Mrs. Opalsen as a sort of Greek chorus.

"Well," I said, "I'd better have some dinner."

Poirot accompanied me.

"This ought to mean kudos for you," I observed.

"*Pas du tout,*" replied Poirot tranquilly. "Japp and the local inspector will divide the credit between them. But"—he tapped his pocket—"I have a check here, from Mr. Opalsen, and, how say you, my friend? This weekend has not gone according to plan. Shall we return here next weekend—at my expense this time?"

# The Kidnapped
# Prime Minister

NOW that war and the problems of war are things of the past, I think I may safely venture to reveal to the world the part which my friend Poirot played in a moment of national crisis. The secret has been well-guarded. Not a whisper of it reached the press. But, now that the need for secrecy has gone by, I feel it is only just that England should know the debt it owes to my quaint little friend, whose marvelous brain so ably averted a great catastrophe.

One evening after dinner—I will not particularize the date; it suffices to say that it was at the time when "Peace by negotiation" was the parrot cry of England's enemies—my friend and I were sitting in his rooms. After being invalided out of the Army I had been given a recruiting job, and it had become my custom to drop in on Poirot in the evenings after dinner and talk with him of any cases of interest that he might have on hand.

I was attempting to discuss with him the sensational news of that day—no less than an attempted assassination of Mr. David MacAdam, England's Prime Minister. The account in the papers had evidently been carefully censored. No details were given, save that the Prime Minister had had a marvelous escape, the bullet just grazing his cheek.

I considered that our police must have been shamefully careless for such an outrage to be possible. I could well understand that the German agents in England would be willing to risk much for such an achievement. "Fighting Mac," as his own party had nicknamed him, had strenuously and unequivocally combated the pacifist influence which was becoming so prevalent.

He was more than England's Prime Minister—he *was* England; and to have removed him from his sphere of influence would have been a crushing and paralyzing blow to Britain.

Poirot was busy mopping a gray suit with a minute sponge. Never was there a dandy such as Hercule Poirot. Neatness and order were his passion. Now, with the odor of benzine filling the air, he was quite unable to give me his full attention.

"In a little minute I am with you, my friend. I have all but finished. The spot of grease—he is not good—I remove him—so!" He waved his sponge.

I smiled as I lit another cigarette.

"Anything interesting on?" I inquired, after a minute or two.

"I assist a—how do you call it?—'charlady' to find her husband. A difficult affair, needing the tact. For I have a little idea that when he is found he will not be pleased. What would you? For my part, I sympathize with him. He was a man of discrimination to lose himself."

I laughed.

"At last! The spot of grease, he is gone! I am at your disposal."

"I was asking you what you thought of this attempt to assassinate MacAdam?"

"*Enfantillage!*" replied Poirot promptly. "One can hardly take it seriously. To fire with the rifle—never does it succeed. It is a device of the past."

"It was very near succeeding this time," I reminded him.

Poirot shook his head impatiently. He was about to reply when the landlady thrust her head round the door and informed him that there were two gentlemen below who wanted to see him.

"They won't give their names, sir, but they says as it's very important."

"Let them mount," said Poirot, carefully folding his gray trousers.

In a few minutes the two visitors were ushered in, and my heart gave a leap as in the foremost I recognized no less a personage than Lord Estair, leader of the House of Commons; while his companion, Mr. Bernard Dodge, was also a member of the war cabinet, and, as I knew, a close personal friend of the Prime Minister.

"Monsieur Poirot?" said Lord Estair interrogatively. My friend bowed. The great man looked at me and hesitated. "My business is private."

"You may speak freely before Captain Hastings," said my friend, nodding to me to remain. "He has not all the gifts, no! But I answer for his discretion."

Lord Estair still hesitated, but Mr. Dodge broke in abruptly:

"Oh, come on—don't let's beat about the bush! As far as I can see, the whole of England will know the hole we're in soon enough. Time's everything."

"Pray be seated, messieurs," said Poirot politely. "Will you take the big chair, Milord?"

Lord Estair started slightly. "You know me?"

Poirot smiled. "Certainly. I read the little papers with the pictures. How should I not know you?"

"Monsieur Poirot, I have come to consult you upon a matter of the most vital urgency. I must ask for absolute secrecy."

"You have the word of Hercule Poirot—I can say no more!" said my friend grandiloquently.

"It concerns the Prime Minister. We are in grave trouble."

"We're up a tree!" interposed Mr. Dodge.

"The injury is serious, then?" I asked.

"What injury?"

"The bullet wound."

"Oh, that!" cried Mr. Dodge contemptuously. "That's old history."

"As my colleague says," continued Lord Estair, "that affair is over and done with. Luckily, it failed. I wished I could say as much for the second attempt."

"There has been a second attempt, then?"

"Yes, though not of the same nature. Monsieur Poirot, the Prime Minister has disappeared."

"What?"

"He has been kidnapped!"

"Impossible!" I cried, stupefied.

Poirot threw a withering glance at me, which I knew enjoined me to keep my mouth shut.

"Unfortunately, impossible as it seems, it is only too true," continued his lordship.

Poirot looked at Mr. Dodge. "You said just now, monsieur, that time was everything. What did you mean by that?"

The two men exchanged glances, and then Lord Estair said:

"You have heard, Monsieur Poirot, of the approaching Allied Conference?"

My friend nodded.

"For obvious reasons, no details have been given of when and where it is to take place. But, although it has been kept out of the newspapers, the date is, of course, widely known in diplomatic circles. The conference is to be held tomorrow—Thursday—evening at Versailles. Now you perceive the terrible gravity of the situation. I will not conceal from you that the Prime Minister's presence at the conference is a vital necessity. The pacifist propaganda, started and maintained by the German agents in our midst, has been very active. It is the universal opinion that the turning point of the conference will be the strong personality of the Prime Minister. His absence may have the most serious results—possibly a premature and disastrous peace. And we have no one who can be sent in his place. He alone can represent England."

Poirot's face had grown very grave. "Then you regard the kidnapping of the Prime Minister as a direct attempt to prevent his being present at the conference?"

"Most certainly I do. He was actually on his way to France at the time."

"And the conference is to be held?"

"At nine o'clock tomorrow night."

Poirot drew an enormous watch from his pocket.

"It is now a quarter to nine."

"Twenty-four hours," said Mr. Dodge thoughtfully.

"And a quarter," amended Poirot. "Do not forget the quarter, monsieur—it may come in useful. Now for the details—the abduction, did it take place in England or in France?"

"In France. Mr. MacAdam crossed to France this morning. He was to stay tonight as the guest of the commander-in-chief, proceeding tomorrow to Paris. He was conveyed across the Channel by destroyer. At Boulogne he was met by a car from General Headquarters and one of the commander-in-chief's A.D.C.s."

"*Eh bien?*"

"Well, they started from Boulogne—but they never arrived."

"What?"

"Monsieur Poirot, it was a bogus car and a bogus A.D.C. The real car was found in a side road, with the chauffeur and the A.D.C. neatly gagged and bound."

"And the bogus car?"

"Is still at large."

Poirot made a gesture of impatience. "Incredible! Surely it cannot escape attention for long?"

"So we thought. It seemed merely a question of searching thoroughly. That part of France is under military law. We were convinced that the car could not go long unnoticed. The French police and our own Scotland Yard men, and the military are straining every nerve. It is, as you say, incredible—but nothing has been discovered!"

At that moment a tap came at the door, and a young officer entered with a heavily sealed envelope which he handed to Lord Estair.

"Just through from France, sir. I brought it on here, as you directed."

The minister tore it open eagerly, and uttered an exclamation. The officer withdrew.

"Here is news at last! This telegram has just been decoded. They have found the second car, also the secretary, Daniels, chloroformed, gagged, and bound, in an abandoned farm near C—. He remembers nothing, except something being pressed against his mouth and nose from behind, and struggling to free himself. The police are satisfied as to the genuineness of his statement."

"And they have found nothing else?"

"No."

"Not the Prime Minister's dead body? Then, there is hope. But it is strange. Why, after trying to shoot him this morning, are they now taking so much trouble to keep him alive?"

Dodge shook his head. "One thing's quite certain. They're determined at all costs to prevent his attending the conference."

"If it is humanly possible, the Prime Minister shall be there. God grant it is not too late. Now, messieurs, recount to me everything— from the beginning. I must know about this shooting affair as well."

"Last night, the Prime Minister, accompanied by one of his secretaries, Captain Daniels—"

"The same who accompanied him to France?"

"Yes. As I was saying, they, motored down to Windsor, where the Prime Minister was granted an audience. Early this morning, he returned to town, and it was on the way that the attempted assassination took place."

"One moment, if you please. Who is this Captain Daniels? You have his dossier?"

Lord Estair smiled. "I thought you would ask me that. We do not know very much of him. He is of no particular family. He has served in the English Army, and is an extremely able secretary, being an exceptionally fine linguist. I believe he speaks seven languages. It is for that reason that the Prime Minister chose him to accompany him to France."

"Has he any relatives in England?"

"Two aunts A Mrs. Everard, who lives at Hampstead, and a Miss Daniels, who lives near Ascot."

"Ascot? That is near to Windsor, is it not?"

"That point has not been overlooked. But it has led to nothing."

"You regard the Capitaine Daniels, then, as above suspicion?"

A shade of bitterness crept into Lord Estair's voice, as he replied:

"No, Monsieur Poirot. In these days, I should hesitate before I pronounced *anyone* above suspicion."

"*Très bien.* Now I understand, milord, that the Prime Minister would, as a matter of course, be under vigilant police protection, which ought to render any assault upon him an impossibility?"

Lord Estair bowed his head. "That is so. The Prime Minister's car was closely followed by another car containing detectives in plain clothes. Mr. MacAdam knew nothing of these precautions. He is personally a most fearless man, and would be inclined to sweep them away arbitrarily. But, naturally, the police make their own arrangements. In fact, the premier's chauffeur, O'Murphy, is a C.I.D. man."

"O'Murphy? That is a name of Ireland, is it not so?"

"Yes, he is an Irishman."

"From what part of Ireland?"

"County Clare, I believe."

"*Tiens!* But proceed, milord."

"The premier started for London. The car was a closed one. He and Captain Daniels sat inside. The second car followed as usual. But, unluckily, for some unknown reason, the Prime Minister's car deviated from the main road—"

"At a point where the road curves?" interrupted Poirot.

"Yes—but how did you know?"

"Oh, *c'est évident!* Continue!"

"For some unknown reason," continued Lord Estair, "the premier's car left the main road. The police car, unaware of the deviation, continued to keep to the high road. At a short distance down the unfrequented lane, the Prime Minister's car was suddenly held up by a band of masked men. The chauffeur—"

"That brave O'Murphy!" murmured Poirot thoughtfully.

"The chauffeur, momentarily taken aback, jammed on the brakes. The Prime Minister put his head out of the window. Instantly a shot rang out—then another. The first one grazed his cheek, the second, fortunately, went wide. The chauffeur, now realizing the danger, instantly forged straight ahead, scattering the band of men."

"A near escape," I ejaculated, with a shiver.

"Mr. MacAdam refused to make any fuss over the slight wound he had received. He declared it was only a scratch. He stopped at a local cottage hospital, where it was dressed and bound up—he did not, of course, reveal his identity. He then drove, as per schedule, straight to Charing Cross, where a special train for Dover was awaiting him, and, after a brief account of what had happened had been given to the anxious police by Captain Daniels, he duly departed for France. At Dover, he went on board the waiting destroyer. At Boulogne, as you know, the bogus car was waiting for him, carrying the Union Jack, and correct in every detail."

"That is all you have to tell me?"

"Yes."

"There is no other circumstance that you have omitted, milord?"

"Well, there is one rather peculiar thing."

"Yes?"

"The Prime Minister's car did not return home after leaving the Prime Minister at Charing Cross. The police were anxious to interview O'Murphy, so a search was instituted at once. The car was discovered standing outside a certain unsavoury little restaurant in Soho, which is well known as a meeting place of German agents."

"And the chauffeur?"

"The chauffeur was nowhere to be found. He, too, had disappeared."

"So," said Poirot thoughtfully, "there are two disappearances: the Prime Minister in France, and O'Murphy in London."

He looked keenly at Lord Estair, who made a gesture of despair.

"I can only tell you, Monsieur Poirot, that, if anyone had suggested to me yesterday that O'Murphy was a traitor, I should have laughed in his face."

"And today?"

"Today I do not know what to think."

Poirot nodded gravely. He looked at his turnip of a watch again.

"I understand that I have carte blanche, messieurs—in every way, I mean? I must be able to go where I choose, and how I choose."

"Perfectly. There is a special train leaving for Dover in an hour's time, with a further contingent from Scotland Yard. You shall be accompanied by a military officer and a C.I.D. man, who will hold themselves at your disposal in every way. Is that satisfactory?"

"Quite. One more question before you leave, messieurs. What made you come to me? I am unknown, obscure, in this great London of yours."

"We sought you out on the express recommendation and wish of a very great man of your own country."

"*Comment?* My old friend the *Préfet*—?"

Lord Estair shook his head.

"Once higher than the *Préfet*. One whose word was once law in Belgium—and shall be again! That England has sworn!"

Poirot's hand flew swiftly to a dramatic salute. "Amen to that! Ah, but my Master does not forget. . . . Messieurs, I, Hercule Poirot, will serve you faithfully. Heaven only send that it will be in time. But this is dark—dark. . . . I cannot see."

"Well, Poirot," I cried impatiently, as the door closed behind the Ministers, "what do you think?"

My friend was busy packing a minute suitcase, with quick, deft movements. He shook his head thoughtfully.

"I do not know what to think. My brains desert me."

"Why, as you said, kidnap him, when a knock on the head would do as well?" I mused.

"Pardon me, *mon ami,* but I did not quite say that. It is undoubtedly far more their affair to kidnap him."

"But why?"

"Because uncertainty creates panic. That is one reason. Were the Prime Minister dead, it would be a terrible calamity, but the situation would have to be faced. But now you have paralysis. Will the Prime Minister reappear, or will he not? Is he dead or alive? Nobody knows, and until they know nothing definite can be done. And, as I tell you, uncertainty breeds panic, which is what *les Boches* are playing for. Then, again, if the kidnappers are holding him secretly somewhere, they have the advantage of being able to make terms with both sides.

The German Government is not a liberal paymaster, as a rule, but no doubt they can be made to disgorge substantial remittances in such a case as this. Thirdly, they run no risk of the hangman's rope. Oh, decidedly, kidnapping is their affair."

"Then, if that is so, why should they first try to shoot him?"

Poirot made a gesture of anger. "Ah, that is just what I do not understand! It is inexplicable—stupid! They have all their arrangements made (and very good arrangements too!) for the abduction, and yet they imperil the whole affair by a melodramatic attack, worthy of a cinema, and quite as unreal. It is almost impossible to believe in it, with its band of masked men, not twenty miles from London!"

"Perhaps they were two quite separate attempts which happened irrespective of each other," I suggested.

"Ah, no, that would be too much of a coincidence! Then, further— who is the traitor? There must have been a traitor—in the first affair, anyway. But who was it—Daniels or O'Murphy? It must have been one of the two, or why did the car leave the main road? We cannot suppose that the Prime Minister connived at his own assassination! Did O'Murphy take that turning of his own accord, or was it Daniels who told him to do so?"

"Surely it must have been O'Murphy's doing."

"Yes, because if it was Daniels', the Prime Minister would have heard the order, and would have asked the reason. But there are altogether too many 'whys' in this affair, and they contradict each other. If O'Murphy is an honest man, *why* did he leave the main road? But if he was a dishonest man, *why* did he start the car again when only two shots had been fired—thereby, in all probability, saving the Prime Minister's life? And, again, if he was honest, why did he, immediately on leaving Charing Cross, drive to a well-known rendezvous of German spies?"

"It looks bad," I said.

"Let us look at the case with method. What have we for and against these two men? Take O'Murphy first. Against: that his conduct in leaving the main road was suspicious; that he is an Irishman from County Clare; that he has disappeared in a highly suggestive manner. For: that his promptness in restarting the car saved the premier's life; that he is a Scotland Yard man, and, obviously, from the post allotted to him, a trusted detective. Now for Daniels. There is not much against him, except the fact that nothing is known of his antecedents, and that he speaks too many languages for a good Englishman! (Pardon me, *mon ami*, but, as linguists, you are deplorable!) Now *for* him, we have the fact that he was found gagged, bound, and chloroformed— which does not look as though he had anything to do with the matter."

"He might have gagged and bound himself, to divert suspicion."

Poirot shook his head. "The French police would make no mistake of that kind. Besides, once he had attained his object, and the Prime Minister was safely abducted, there would not be much point in his remaining behind. His accomplices *could* have gagged and chloroformed him, of course, but I fail to see what object they hoped to accomplish by it. He can be of little use to them now, for, until the circumstances concerning the Prime Minister have been cleared up, he is bound to be closely watched."

"Perhaps he hoped to start the police on a false scent?"

"Then why did he not do so? He merely says that something was pressed over his nose and mouth, and that he remembers nothing more. There is no false scent there. It sounds remarkably like the truth."

"Well," I said, glancing at the clock, "I suppose we'd better start for the station. You may find more clues in France."

"Possibly, *mon ami*, but I doubt it. It is still incredible to me that the Prime Minister has not been discovered in that limited area, where the difficulty of concealing him must be tremendous. If the military and the police of two countries have not found him, how shall I?"

At Charing Cross we were met by Mr. Dodge.

"This is Detective Barnes, of Scotland Yard, and Major Norman. They will hold themselves entirely at your disposal. Good luck to you. It's a bad business, but I've not given up hope. Must be off now." And the Minister strode rapidly away.

We chatted in a desultory fashion with Major Norman. In the center of the little group of men on the platform I recognized a little ferret-faced fellow talking to a tall, fair man. He was an old acquaintance of Poirot's—Detective-Inspector Japp, supposed to be one of the smartest of Scotland Yard's officers. He came over and greeted my friend cheerfully.

"I heard you were on this job, too. Smart bit of work. So far they've got away with the goods all right. But I can't believe they can keep him hidden long. Our people are going through France with a fine-tooth comb. So are the French. I can't help feeling it's only a matter of hours now."

"That is, if he's still alive," remarked the tall detective gloomily.

Japp's face fell. "Yes. . . . But somehow I've got the feeling he's alive all right."

Poirot nodded. "Yes, yes; he's alive. But can he be found in time? I, like you, did not believe he could be hidden so long."

The whistle blew, and we all trooped up into the Pullman car. Then, with a slow, unwilling jerk, the train drew out of the station.

It was a curious journey. The Scotland Yard men crowded together. Maps of northern France were spread out, and eager forefingers traced the lines of roads and villages. Each man had his own pet theory. Poirot showed none of his usual loquacity, but sat staring in front of him, with an expression on his face that reminded me of a puzzled child. I talked to Norman, whom I found quite an amusing fellow. On arriving at Dover Poirot's behavior moved me to intense amusement. The little man, as he went on board the boat, clutched desperately at my arm. The wind was blowing lustily.

*"Mon Dieu!"* he murmured. "This is terrible!"

"Have courage, Poirot," I cried. "You will succeed. You will find him. I am sure of it."

"Ah, *mon ami,* you mistake my emotion. It is this villainous sea that troubles me! The *mal de mer*—it is horrible suffering!"

"Oh!" I said, rather taken aback.

The first throb of the engines was felt, and Poirot groaned and closed his eyes.

"Major Norman has a map of northern France if you would like to study it?"

Poirot shook his head impatiently.

"But no, but no! Leave me, my friend. See you, to think, the stomach and the brain must be in harmony. Laverguier has a method most excellent for averting the *mal de mer.* You breathe in—and out— slowly, so—turning the head from left to right and counting six between each breath."

I left him to his gymnastic endeavors, and went on deck.

As we came slowly into Boulogne Harbor, Poirot appeared, neat and smiling, and announced to me in a whisper that Laverguier's system had succeeded "to a marvel!"

Japp's forefinger was still tracing imaginary routes on his map. "Nonsense! The car started from Boulogne—here they branched off. Now, my idea is that they transferred the Prime Minister to another car. See?"

"Well," said the tall detective, "I shall make for the seaports. Ten to one, they've smuggled him on board a ship."

Japp shook his head. "Too obvious. The order went out at once to close all the ports."

The day was just breaking as we landed. Major Norman touched Poirot on the arm. "There's a military car here waiting for you, sir."

"Thank you, monsieur. But, for the moment, I do not propose to leave Boulogne."

"What?"

"No, we will enter this hotel here, by the quay."

He suited the action to the word, demanded and was accorded a private room. We three followed him, puzzled and uncomprehending.

He shot a quick glance at us. "It is not so that the good detective should act, eh? I perceived your thought. He must be full of energy. He must rush to and fro. He should prostrate himself on the dusty road and seek the marks of tires through a little glass. He must gather up the cigarette end, the fallen match? That is your idea, is it not?"

His eyes challenged us. "But I—Hercule Poirot—tell you that it is not so! The true clues are within—*here!*" He tapped his forehead. "See you, I need not have left London. It would have been sufficient for me to sit quietly in my rooms there. All that matters is the little gray cells within. Secretly and silently they do their part, until suddenly I call for a map, and I lay my finger on a spot—so—and I say: the Prime Minister is *there!* And it is so! With method and logic one can accomplish anything! This frantic rushing to France was a mistake— it is playing a child's game of hide-and-seek. But now, though it may be too late, I will set to work the right way, from within. Silence, my friends, I beg of you."

And for five long hours the little man sat motionless, blinking his eyelids like a cat, his green eyes flickering and becoming steadily greener and greener. The Scotland Yard man was obviously contemptuous, Major Norman was bored and impatient, and I myself found the time pass with wearisome slowness.

Finally, I got up, and strolled as noiselessly as I could to the window. The matter was becoming a farce. I was secretly concerned for my friend. If he failed, I would have preferred him to fail in a less ridiculous manner. Out of the window I idly watched the daily leave boat, belching forth columns of smoke, as she lay alongside the quay.

Suddenly I was aroused by Poirot's voice close to my elbow.

"*Mes amis,* let us start!"

I turned. An extraordinary transformation had come over my friend. His eyes were flickering with excitement, his chest was swelled to the uttermost.

"I have been an imbecile, my friends! But I see daylight at last."

Major Norman moved hastily to the door. "I'll order the car."

"There is no need. I shall not use it. Thank Heaven the wind has fallen."

"Do you mean you are going to walk, sir?"

"No, my young friend. I am no St. Peter. I prefer to cross the sea by boat."

"To cross the *sea?*"

"Yes. To work with method, one must begin from the beginning. And the beginning of this affair was in England. Therefore, we return to England."

At three o'clock, we stood once more upon Charing Cross platform. To all our expostulations, Poirot turned a deaf ear, and reiterated again and again that to start at the beginning was not a waste of time, but the only way. On the way over, he had conferred with Norman in a low voice, and the latter had dispatched a sheaf of telegrams from Dover.

Owing to the special passes held by Norman, we got through everywhere in record time. In London, a large police car was waiting for us, with some plainclothes men, one of whom handed a typewritten sheet of paper to my friend. He answered my inquiring glance.

"A list of the cottage hospitals within a certain radius west of London. I wired for it from Dover."

We were whirled rapidly through the London streets. We were on the Bath Road. On we went, through Hammersmith, Chiswick and Brentford. I began to see our objective. Through Windsor and on to Ascot. My heart gave a leap. Ascot was where Daniels had an aunt living. We were after *him,* then, not O'Murphy.

We duly stopped at the gate of a trim villa. Poirot jumped out and rang the bell. I saw a perplexed frown dimming the radiance of his face. Plainly, he was not satisfied. The bell was answered. He was ushered inside. In a few moments he reappeared, and climbed into the car with a short, sharp shake of his head. My hopes began to die down. It was past four now. Even if he found certain evidence incriminating Daniels, what would be the good of it, unless he could wring from someone the exact spot in France where they were holding the Prime Minister?

Our return progress towards London was an interrupted one. We deviated from the main road more than once, and occasionally stopped at a small building, which I had no difficulty in recognizing as a cottage hospital. Poirot only spent a few minutes at each, but at every halt his radiant assurance was more and more restored.

He whispered something to Norman, to which the latter replied:

"Yes, if you turn off to the left, you will find them waiting by the bridge."

We turned up a side road, and in the failing light I discerned a second car, waiting by the side of the road. It contained two men in plain clothes. Poirot got down and spoke to them, and then we started off in a northerly direction, the other car following close behind.

We drove for some time, our objective being obviously one of the northern suburbs of London. Finally, we drove up to the front door of a tall house, standing a little back from the road in its own grounds.

Norman and I were left with the car. Poirot and one of the detectives went up to the door and rang. A neat parlormaid opened it. The detective spoke.

"I am a police officer, and I have a warrant to search this house."

The girl gave a little scream, and a tall, handsome woman of middle age appeared behind her in the hall.

"Shut the door, Edith. They are burglars, I expect."

But Poirot swiftly inserted his foot in the door, and at the same moment blew a whistle. Instantly the other detectives ran up, and poured into the house, shutting the door behind them.

Norman and I spent about five minutes cursing our forced inactivity. Finally the door reopened, and the men emerged, escorting three prisoners—a woman and two men. The woman, and one of the men, were taken to the second car. The other man was placed in our car by Poirot himself.

"I must go with the others, my friend. But have great care of this gentleman. You do not know him, no? *Eh bien*, let me present to you, Monsieur O'Murphy!"

O'Murphy! I *gaped* at him open-mouthed as we started again. He was not handcuffed, but I did not fancy he would try to escape. He sat there staring in front of him as though dazed. Anyway, Norman and I would be more than a match for him.

To my surprise, we still kept a northerly route. We were not returning to London, then! I was much puzzled. Suddenly, as the car slowed down, I recognized that we were close to Hendon Aerodrome. Immediately I grasped Poirot's idea. He proposed to reach France by aeroplane.

It was a sporting idea, but, on the face of it, impracticable. A telegram would be far quicker. Time was everything. He must leave the personal glory of rescuing the Prime Minister to others.

As we drew up, Major Norman jumped out, and a plainclothes man took his place. He conferred with Poirot for a few minutes, and then went off briskly.

I, too, jumped out, and caught Poirot by the arm.

"I congratulate you, old fellow! They have told you the hiding place? But, look here, you must wire to France at once. You'll be too late if you go yourself."

Poirot looked at me curiously for a minute or two.

"Unfortunately, my friend, there are some things that cannot be sent by telegram."

At that moment Major Norman returned, accompanied by a young officer in the uniform of the Flying Corps.

"This is Captain Lyall, who will fly you over to France. He can start at once."

"Wrap up warmly, sir," said the young pilot. "I can lend you a coat, if you like."

Poirot was consulting his enormous watch. He murmured to himself: "Yes, there is time—just time." Then he looked up, and bowed politely to the young officer. "I thank you, monsieur. But it is not I who am your passenger. It is this gentleman here."

He moved a little aside as he spoke, and a figure came forward out of the darkness. It was the second male prisoner who had gone in the other car, and as the light fell on his face, I gave a gasp of surprise.

*It was the Prime Minister!*

"For heaven's sake, tell me all about it," I cried impatiently, as Poirot, Norman, and I motored back to London. "How in the world did they manage to smuggle him back to England?"

"There was no need to smuggle him back," replied Poirot dryly. "The Prime Minister has never left England. He was kidnapped on his way from Windsor to London."

"*What?*"

"I will make all clear. The Prime Minister was in his car, his secretary beside him. Suddenly a pad of chloroform is clapped on his face—"

"But by whom?"

"By the clever linguistic Captain Daniels. As soon as the Prime Minister is unconscious, Daniels picks up the speaking tube, and directs O'Murphy to turn to the right, which the chauffeur, quite unsuspicious, does. A few yards down that unfrequented road, a large car is standing, apparently broken down. Its driver signals to O'Murphy to stop. O'Murphy slows up. The stranger approaches. Daniels leans out of the window, and, probably with the aid of an instantaneous anesthetic, such as ethyl chloride, the chloroform trick is repeated. In a few seconds, the two helpless men are dragged out and transferred to the other car, and a pair of substitutes take their places."

"Impossible!"

"*Pas du tout!* Have you not seen music-hall turns imitating celebrities with marvelous accuracy? Nothing is easier than to personate a public character. The Prime Minister of England is far easier to understudy than Mr. John Smith of Clapham, say. As for O'Murphy's 'double,' no one was going to take much notice of him until after the departure of the Prime Minister, and by then he would have made himself scarce. He drives straight from Charing Cross to the meeting place of his friends. He goes in as O'Murphy, he emerges as someone quite different. O'Murphy has disappeared, leaving a conveniently suspicious trail behind him."

"But the man who personated the Prime Minister was seen by everyone!"

"He was not seen by anyone who knew him privately or intimately.

And Daniels shielded him from contact with anyone as much as possible. Moreover, his face was bandaged up, and anything unusual in his manner would be put down to the fact that he was suffering from shock as a result of the attempt upon his life. Mr. MacAdam has a weak throat, and always spares his voice as much as possible before any great speech. The deception was perfectly easy to keep up as far as France. There it would be impracticable and impossible—so the Prime Minister disappears. The police of this country hurry across the Channel, and no one bothers to go into the details of the first attack. To sustain the illusion that the abduction has taken place in France, Daniels is gagged and chloroformed in a convincing manner."

"And the man who has enacted the part of the Prime Minister?"

"Rids himself of his disguise. He and the bogus chauffeur may be arrested as suspicious characters, but no one will dream of suspecting their real part in the drama, and they will eventually be released for lack of evidence."

"And the real Prime Minister?"

"He and O'Murphy were driven straight to the house of 'Mrs. Everard,' at Hampstead, Daniels' so-called aunt. In reality, she is Frau Bertha Ebenthal, and the police have been looking for her for some time. It is a valuable little present that I have made to them—to say nothing of Daniels! Ah, it was a clever plan, but he did not reckon on the cleverness of Hercule Poirot!"

I think my friend might well be excused his moment of vanity.

"When did you first begin to suspect the truth of the matter?"

"When I began to work the right way—from *within!* I could not make that shooting affair fit in—but when I saw that the net result of it was that *the Prime Minister went to France with his face bound up* I began to comprehend! And when I visited all the cottage hospitals between Windsor and London, and found that no one answering to my description had had his face bound up and dressed that morning, I was sure! After that, it was child's play for a mind like mine!"

The following morning, Poirot showed me a telegram he had just received. It had no place of origin, and was unsigned. It ran:

    In time.

Later in the day the evening papers published an account of the Allied Conference. They laid particular stress on the magnificent ovation accorded to Mr. David MacAdam, whose inspiring speech had produced a deep and lasting impression.

# The Disappearance of
# Mr. Davenheim

POIROT and I were expecting our old friend Inspector Japp of
Scotland Yard to tea. We were sitting round the tea table awaiting
his arrival. Poirot had just finished carefully straightening the
cups and saucers which our landlady was in the habit of throwing,
rather than placing, on the table. He had also breathed heavily on
the metal teapot, and polished it with a silk handkerchief. The kettle
was on the boil, and a small enamel saucepan beside it contained some
thick, sweet chocolate which was more to Poirot's palate than what
he described as "your English poison."

A sharp rat-tat sounded below, and a few minutes afterwards Japp
entered briskly.

"Hope I'm not late," he said as he greeted us. "To tell the truth, I
was yarning with Miller, the man who's in charge of the Davenheim
case."

I pricked up my ears. For the last three days the papers had been
full of the strange disappearance of Mr. Davenheim, senior partner
of Davenheim and Salmon, the well-known bankers and financiers.
On Saturday last he had walked out of his house, and had never been
seen since. I looked forward to extracting some interesting details from
Japp.

"I should have thought," I remarked, "that it would be almost impossible for anyone to disappear nowadays."

Poirot moved a plate of bread and butter the eighth of an inch,
and said sharply:

"Be exact, my friend. What do you mean by 'disappear'? To which
class of disappearance are you referring?"

"Are disappearances classified and labeled, then?" I laughed.

Japp smiled also. Poirot frowned at us both.

"But certainly they are! They fall into three categories: First, and
most common, the voluntary disappearance. Second, the much abused
'loss of memory' case—rare, but occasionally genuine. Third, murder,

and a more or less successful disposal of the body. Do you refer to all three as impossible of execution?"

"Very nearly so, I should think. You might lose your own memory, but some one would be sure to recognize you—especially in the case of a well-known man like Davenheim. Then 'bodies' can't be made to vanish into thin air. Sooner or later they turn up, concealed in lonely places, or in trunks. Murder will out. In the same way, the absconding clerk, or the domestic defaulter, is bound to be run down in these days of wireless telegraphy. He can be headed off from foreign countries; ports and railway stations are watched; and, as for conceal- ment in this country, his features and appearance will be known to everyone who reads a daily newspaper. He's up against civilization."

"*Mon ami,*" said Poirot, "you make one error. You do not allow for the fact that a man who had decided to make away with another man—or with himself in a figurative sense—might be that rare ma- chine, a man of method. He might bring intelligence, talent, a careful calculation of detail to the task; and then I do not see why he should not be successful in baffling the police force."

"But not *you*, I suppose?" said Japp good-humoredly, winking at me. "He couldn't baffle *you*, eh, Monsieur Poirot?"

Poirot endeavored, with a marked lack of success, to look modest. "Me, also! Why not? It is true that I approach such problems with an exact science, a mathematical precision, which seems, alas, only too rare in the new generation of detectives!"

Japp grinned more widely.

"I don't know," he said. "Miller, the man who's on this case, is a smart chap. You may be very sure he won't overlook a footprint, or a cigar ash, or a crumb even. He's got eyes that see everything."

"So, *mon ami,*" said Poirot, "has the London sparrow. But all the same, I should not ask the little brown bird to solve the problem of Mr. Davenheim."

"Come now, monsieur, you're not going to run down the value of details as clues?"

"By no means. These things are all good in their way. The danger is they may assume undue importance. Most details are insignificant; one or two are vital. It is the brain, the little gray cells"—he tapped his forehead—"on which one must rely. The senses mislead. One must seek the truth within—not without."

"You don't mean to say, Monsieur Poirot, that you would undertake to solve a case without moving from your chair, do you?"

"That is exactly what I do mean—granted the facts were placed before me. I regard myself as a consulting specialist."

Japp slapped his knee. "Hanged if I don't take you at your word.

Bet you a fiver that you can't lay your hand—or rather tell me where to lay my hand—on Mr. Davenheim, dead or alive, before a week is out."

Poirot considered. *"Eh bien, mon ami,* I accept. *Le sport,* it is the passion of you English. Now—the facts."

"On Saturday last, as is his usual custom, Mr. Davenheim took the 12:40 train from Victoria to Chingside, where his palatial country place, the Cedars, is situated. After lunch, he strolled round the grounds, and gave various directions to the gardeners. Everybody agrees that his manner was absolutely normal and as usual. After tea he put his head into his wife's boudoir, saying that he was going to stroll down to the village and post some letters. He added that he was expecting a Mr. Lowen, on business. If Lowen should come before he himself returned, he was to be shown into the study and asked to wait. Mr. Davenheim then left the house by the front door, passed leisurely down the drive, and out at the gate, and—was never seen again. From that hour, he vanished completely."

"Pretty—very pretty—altogether a charming little problem," murmured Poirot. "Proceed, my good friend."

"About a quarter of an hour later a tall, dark man with a thick black mustache rang the front-door bell, and explained that he had an appointment with Mr. Davenheim. He gave the name of Lowen, and in accordance with the banker's instructions was shown into the study. Nearly an hour passed. Mr. Davenheim did not return. Finally Mr. Lowen rang the bell, and explained that he was unable to wait any longer, as he must catch his train back to town. Mrs. Davenheim apologized for her husband's absence, which seemed unaccountable, as she knew him to have been expecting the visitor. Mr. Lowen reiterated his regrets and took his departure.

"Well, as everyone knows, Mr. Davenheim did *not* return. Early on Sunday morning the police were communicated with, but could make neither head nor tail of the matter. Mr. Davenheim seemed literally to have vanished into thin air. He had not been to the post office; nor had he been seen passing through the village. At the station they were positive he had not departed by any train. His own motor had not left the garage. If he had hired a car to meet him in some lonely spot, it seems almost certain that by this time, in view of the large reward offered for information, the driver of it would have come forward to tell what he knew. True, there was a small race-meeting at Entfield, five miles away, and if he had walked to that station he might have passed unnoticed in the crowd. But since then his photograph and a full description of him have been circulated in every newspaper, and nobody has been able to give any news of him. We have, of course, received many letters from all over England, but each clue, so far, has ended in disappointment.

"On Monday morning a further sensational discovery came to light. Behind a portière in Mr. Davenheim's study stands a safe, and that safe had been broken into and rifled. The windows were fastened securely on the inside, which seems to put an ordinary burglary out of court, unless, of course, an accomplice within the house fastened them again afterwards. On the other hand, Sunday having intervened, and the household being in a state of chaos, it is likely that the burglary was committed on the Saturday, and remained undetected until Monday."

"*Précisément*," said Poirot dryly. "Well, is he arrested, *ce pauvre M. Lowen?*"

Japp grinned. "Not yet. But he's under pretty close supervision."

Poirot nodded. "What was taken from the safe? Have you any idea?"

"We've been going into that with the junior partner of the firm and Mrs. Davenheim. Apparently there was a considerable amount in bearer bonds, and a very large sum in notes, owing to some large transaction having been just carried through. There was also a small fortune in jewelry. All Mrs. Davenheim's jewels were kept in the safe. The purchasing of them had become a passion with her husband of late years, and hardly a month passed that he did not make her a present of some rare and costly gem."

"Altogether a good haul," said Poirot thoughtfully. "Now, what about Lowen? Is it known what his business was with Davenheim that evening?"

"Well, the two men were apparently not on very good terms. Lowen is a speculator in quite a small way. Nevertheless, he has been able once or twice to score a coup off Davenheim in the market, though it seems, they seldom or never actually met. It was a matter concerning some South American shares which led the banker to make his appointment."

"Had Davenheim interests in South America, then?"

"I believe so. Mrs. Davenheim happened to mention that he spent all last autumn in Buenos Aires."

"Any trouble in his home life? Were the husband and wife on good terms?"

"I should say his domestic life was quite peaceful and uneventful. Mrs. Davenheim is a pleasant, rather unintelligent woman. Quite a nonentity, I think."

"Then we must not look for the solution of the mystery there. Had he any enemies?"

"He had plenty of financial rivals, and no doubt there are many people whom he has got the better of who bear him no particular good will. But there was no one likely to make away with him—and, if they had, where is the body?"

"Exactly. As Hastings says, bodies have a habit of coming to light with fatal persistency."

"By the way, one of the gardeners says he saw a figure going round to the side of the house toward the rose garden. The long French window of the study opens on to the rose garden, and Mr. Davenheim frequently entered and left the house that way. But the man was a good way off, at work on some cucumber frames, and cannot even say whether it was the figure of his master or not. Also, he cannot fix the time with any accuracy. It must have been before six, as the gardeners cease work at that time."

"And Mr. Davenheim left the house?"

"About half-past five or thereabouts."

"What lies beyond the rose garden?"

"A lake."

"With a boathouse?"

"Yes, a couple of punts are kept there. I suppose you're thinking of suicide, Monsieur Poirot? Well, I don't mind telling you that Miller's going down tomorrow expressly to see that piece of water dragged. That's the kind of man he is!"

Poirot smiled faintly, and turned to me. "Hastings, I pray you, hand me that copy of the *Daily Megaphone*. If I remember rightly, there is an unusually clear photograph there of the missing man."

I rose, and found the sheet required. Poirot studied the features attentively.

"H'm!" he murmured. "Wears his hair rather long and wavy, full mustache and pointed beard, bushy eyebrows. Eyes dark?"

"Yes."

"Hair and beard turning gray?"

The detective nodded. "Well, Monsieur Poirot, what have you got to say to it all? Clear as daylight, eh?"

"On the contrary, most obscure."

The Scotland Yard man looked pleased.

"Which gives me great hopes of solving it," finished Poirot placidly.

"Eh?"

"I find it a good sign when a case is obscure. If a thing is clear as daylight—*eh bien,* mistrust it! Someone has made it so."

Japp shook his head almost pityingly. "Well, each to their fancy. But it's not a bad thing to see your way clear ahead."

"I do not see," murmured Poirot. "I shut my eyes—and think."

Japp sighed. "Well, you've got a clear week to think in."

"And you will bring me any fresh developments that arise—the result of the labors of the hard-working and lynx-eyed Inspector Miller, for instance?"

"Certainly. That's in the bargain."

"Seems a shame, doesn't it?" said Japp to me as I accompanied him to the door. "Like robbing a child!"

I could not help agreeing with a smile. I was still smiling as I reentered the room.

"*Eh bien!*" said Poirot immediately. "You make fun of Papa Poirot, is it not so?" He shook his finger at me. "You do not trust his gray cells? Ah, do not be confused! Let us discuss this little problem—incomplete as yet, I admit, but already showing one or two points of interest."

"The lake!" I said significantly.

"And even more than the lake, the boathouse!"

I looked sidewise at Poirot. He was smiling in his most inscrutable fashion. I felt that, for the moment, it would be quite useless to question him further.

We heard nothing of Japp until the following evening, when he walked in about nine o'clock. I saw at once by his expression that he was bursting with news of some kind.

"*Eh bien,* my friend," remarked Poirot. "All goes well? But do not tell me that you have discovered the body of Mr. Davenheim in your lake, because I shall not believe you."

"We haven't found the body, but we did find his *clothes*—the identical clothes he was wearing that day. What do you say to that?"

"Any other clothes missing from the house?"

"No, his valet is quite positive on that point. The rest of his wardrobe is intact. There's more. We've arrested Lowen. One of the maids, whose business it is to fasten the bedroom windows, declares that she saw Lowen coming *towards* the study through the rose garden about a quarter past six. That would be about ten minutes before he left the house."

"What does he himself say to that?"

"Denied first of all that he had ever left the study. But the maid was positive, and he pretended afterwards that he had forgotten just stepping out of the window to examine an unusual species of rose. Rather a weak story! And there's fresh evidence against him come to light. Mr. Davenheim always wore a thick gold ring set with a solitaire diamond on the little finger of his right hand. Well, that ring was pawned in London on Saturday night by a man called Billy Kellett! He's already known to the police—did three months last autumn for lifting an old gentleman's watch. It seems he tried to pawn the ring at no less than five different places, succeeded at the last one, got gloriously drunk on the proceeds, assaulted a policeman, and was run in in consequence. I went to Bow Street with Miller and saw him.

He's sober enough now, and I don't mind admitting we pretty well frightened the life out of him, hinting he might be charged with murder. This is his yarn, and a very queer one it is.

"He was at Entfield races on Saturday, though I dare say scarfpins was his line of business, rather than betting. Anyway, he had a bad day, and was down on his luck. He was tramping along the road to Chingside, and sat down in a ditch to rest just before he got into the village. A few minutes later he noticed a man coming along the road to the village, 'dark-complexioned gent, with a big mustache, one of them city toffs,' is his description of the man.

"Kellett was half concealed from the road by a heap of stones. Just before he got abreast of him, the man looked quickly up and down the road, and seeing it apparently deserted he took a small object from his pocket and threw it over the hedge. Then he went on towards the station. Now, the object he had thrown over the hedge had fallen with a slight "chink" which aroused the curiosity of the human derelict in the ditch. He investigated and, after a short search, discovered the ring! That is Kellett's story. It's only fair to say that Lowen denies it utterly, and of course the word of a man like Kellett can't be relied upon in the slightest. It's within the bounds of possibility that he met Davenheim in the lane and robbed and murdered him."

Poirot shook his head.

"Very improbable, *mon ami*. He had no means of disposing of the body. It would have been found by now. Secondly, the open way in which he pawned the ring makes it unlikely that he did murder to get it. Thirdly, your sneak thief is rarely a murderer. Fourthly, as he has been in prison since Saturday, it would be too much of a coincidence that he is able to give so accurate a description of Lowen."

Japp nodded. "I don't say you're not right. But all the same, you won't get a jury to take much note of a jailbird's evidence. What seems odd to me is that Lowen couldn't find a cleverer way of disposing of the ring."

Poirot shrugged his shoulders. "Well, after all, if it were found in the neighborhood, it might be argued that Davenheim himself had dropped it."

"But why remove it from the body at all?" I cried.

"There might be a reason for that," said Japp. "Do you know that just beyond the lake, a little gate leads out on to the hill, and not three minutes' walk brings you to—what do you think?—a *lime kiln.*"

"Good heavens!" I cried. "You mean that the lime which destroyed the body would be powerless to affect the metal of the ring?"

"Exactly."

"It seems to me," I said, "that that explains everything. What a horrible crime!"

By common consent we both turned and looked at Poirot. He seemed lost in reflection, his brow knitted, as though with some supreme mental effort. I felt that at last his keen intellect was asserting itself. What would his first words be? We were not long left in doubt. With a sigh, the tension of his attitude relaxed, and turning to Japp, he asked:

"Have you any idea, my friend, whether Mr. and Mrs. Davenheim occupied the same bedroom?"

The question seemed so ludicrously inappropriate that for a moment we both stared in silence. Then Japp burst into a laugh. "Good Lord, Monsieur Poirot, I thought you were coming out with something startling. As to your question, I'm sure I don't know."

"You could find out?" asked Poirot with curious persistence.

"Oh, certainly—if you *really* want to know."

"*Merci, mon ami.* I should be obliged if you would make a point of it."

Japp stared at him a few minutes longer, but Poirot seemed to have forgotten us both. The detective shook his head sadly at me, and murmuring, "Poor old fellow! War's been too much for him!" gently withdrew from the room.

As Poirot still seemed sunk in a daydream, I took a sheet of paper, and amused myself by scribbling notes upon it. My friend's voice aroused me. He had come out of his reverie, and was looking brisk and alert.

"*Que faites vous là, mon ami?*"

"I was jotting down what occurred to me as the main points of interest in this affair."

"You become methodical—at last!" said Poirot approvingly.

I concealed my pleasure. "Shall I read them to you?"

"By all means."

I cleared my throat.

"'One: All the evidence points to Lowen having been the man who forced the safe.

"'Two: He had a grudge against Davenheim.

"'Three: He lied in his first statement that he had never left the study.

"'Four: If you accept Billy Kellett's story as true, Lowen is unmistakably implicated.'"

I paused. "Well?" I asked, for I felt that I had put my finger on all the vital facts.

Poirot looked at me pityingly, shaking his head very gently. "*Mon pauvre ami!* But it is that you have not the gift! The important detail, you appreciate him never! Also, your reasoning is false."

"How?"

"Let me take your four points.

"One: Mr. Lowen could not possibly know that he would have the chance to open the safe. He came for a business interview. He could not know beforehand that Mr. Davenheim would be absent posting a letter, and that he would consequently be alone in the study!"

"He might have seized his opportunity," I suggested.

"And the tools? City gentlemen do not carry round housebreaker's tools on the off chance! And one could not cut into that safe with a penknife, *bien entendu!*"

"Well, what about Number Two?"

"You say Lowen had a grudge against Mr. Davenheim. What you mean is that he had once or twice got the better of him. And presumably those transactions were entered into with the view of benefiting himself. In any case you do not as a rule bear a grudge against a man you have got the better of—it is more likely to be the other way about. Whatever grudge there might have been would have been on Mr. Davenheim's side.'"

"Well, you can't deny that he lied about never having left the study?"

"No. But he may have been frightened. Remember, the missing man's clothes had just been discovered in the lake. Of course, as usual, he would have done better to speak the truth."

"And the fourth point?"

"I grant you that. If Kellett's story is true, Lowen is undeniably implicated. That is what makes the affair so very interesting."

"Then I did appreciate *one* vital fact?"

"Perhaps—but you have entirely overlooked the two most important points, the ones which undoubtedly hold the clue to the whole matter."

"And pray, what are they?"

"One, the passion which has grown upon Mr. Davenheim in the last few years for buying jewelry. Two, his trip to Buenos Aires last autumn."

"Poirot, you are joking!"

"I am most serious. Ah, sacred thunder, but I hope Japp will not forget my little commission."

But the detective, entering into the spirit of the joke, had remembered it so well that a telegram was handed to Poirot about eleven o'clock the next day. At his request I opened it and read it out:

    Husband and wife have occupied separate rooms
    since last winter.

"Aha!" cried Poirot. "And now we are in mid-June! All is solved!" I stared at him.

"You have no moneys in the bank of Davenheim and Salmon, *mon ami?*"

"No," I said, wondering. "Why?"

"Because I should advise you to withdraw it—before it is too late."

"Why, what do you expect?"

"I expect a big smash in a few days—perhaps sooner. Which reminds me, we will return the compliment of a *dépêche* to Japp. A pencil, I pray you, and a form. *Voilà!* 'Advise you to withdraw any money deposited with firm in question.' That will intrigue him, the good Japp! His eyes will open wide—wide! He will not comprehend in the slightest—until tomorrow, or the next day!"

I remained skeptical, but the morrow forced me to render tribute to my friend's remarkable powers. In every paper was a huge headline telling of the sensational failure of the Davenheim bank. The disappearance of the famous financier took on a totally different aspect in the light of the revelation of the financial affairs of the bank.

Before we were halfway through breakfast, the door flew open and Japp rushed in. In his left hand was a paper; in his right was Poirot's telegram, which he banged down on the table in front of my friend.

"How did you know, Monsieur Poirot? How the blazes could you know?"

Poirot smiled placidly at him. "Ah, *mon ami,* after your wire, it was a certainty! From the commencement, see you, it struck me that the safe burglary was somewhat remarkable. Jewels, ready money, bearer bonds—all so conveniently arranged for—whom? Well, the good Monsieur Davenheim was of those who 'look after Number One' as your saying goes! It seemed almost certain that it was arranged for—himself! Then his passion of late years for buying jewelry! How simple! The funds he embezzled, he converted into jewels, very likely replacing them in turn with paste duplicates, and so he put away in a safe place, under another name, a considerable fortune to be enjoyed all in good time when everyone has been thrown off the track. His arrangements completed, he makes an appointment with Mr. Lowen (who has been imprudent enough in the past to cross the great man once or twice), drills a hole in the safe, leaves orders that the guest is to be shown into the study, and walks out of the house—where?" Poirot stopped, and stretched out his hand for another boiled egg. He frowned. "It is really insupportable," he murmured, "that every hen lays an egg of a different size! What symmetry can there be on the breakfast table? At least they should sort them in dozens at the shop!"

"Never mind the eggs," said Japp impatiently. "Let 'em lay 'em square if they like. Tell us where our customer went to when he left the Cedars—that is, if you know!"

"*Eh bien*, he went to his hiding-place. Ah, this Monsieur Davenheim, there may be some malformation in his gray cells, but they are of the first quality!"

"Do you know where he is hiding?"

"Certainly! It is most ingenious."

"For the Lord's sake, tell us, then!"

Poirot gently collected every fragment of shell from his plate, placed them in the egg cup, and reversed the empty eggshell on top of them. This little operation concluded, he smiled at the neat effect, and then beamed affectionately on us both.

"Come, my friends, you are men of intelligence. Ask yourselves the question which I asked myself. 'If I were this man, where should *I* hide?' Hastings, what do you say?"

"Well," I said, "I'm rather inclined to think I'd not do a bolt at all. I'd stay in London—in the heart of things, travel by tubes and buses; ten to one I'd never be recognized. There's safety in a crowd."

Poirot turned inquiringly to Japp.

"I don't agree. Get clear away at once—that's the only chance. I would have had plenty of time to prepare things beforehand. I'd have a yacht waiting, with steam up, and I'd be off to one of the most out-of-the-way corners of the world before the hue and cry began!"

We both looked at Poirot. "What do *you* say, monsieur?"

For a moment he remained silent. Then a very curious smile flitted across his face.

"My friends, if *I* were hiding from the police, do you know where I should hide? In a prison!"

"What?"

"You are seeking Monsieur Davenheim in order to put him in prison, so you never dream of looking to see if he may not be already there!"

"What do you mean?"

"You tell me Madame Davenheim is not a very intelligent woman. Nevertheless I think that if you took her to Bow Street and confronted her with the man Billy Kellett, she would recognize him! In spite of the fact that he has shaved his beard and mustache and those bushy eyebrows, and has cropped his hair close. A woman nearly always knows her husband, though the rest of the world may be deceived!"

"Billy Kellett? But he's known to the police!"

"Did I not tell you Davenheim was a clever man? He prepared his alibi long beforehand. He was not in Buenos Aires last autumn—he was creating the character of Billy Kellett, 'doing three months,' so that the police should have no suspicions when the time came. He was playing, remember, for a large fortune, as well as liberty. It was worthwhile doing the thing thoroughly. Only—"

"Yes?"

"*Eh bien,* afterwards he had to wear a false beard and wig, had to *make up as himself* again, and to sleep with a false beard is not easy—it invites detection! He cannot risk continuing to share the chamber of madame his wife. You found out for me that for the last six months, or ever since his supposed return from Buenos Aires, he and Mrs. Davenheim occupied separate rooms. Then I was sure! Everything fitted in. The gardener who fancied he saw his master going round to the side of the house was quite right. He went to the boathouse, donned his 'tramp' clothes, which you may be sure had been safely hidden from the eyes of his valet, dropped the others in the lake, and proceeded to carry out his plan by pawning the ring in an obvious manner, and then assaulting a policeman, getting himself safely into the haven of Bow Street, where nobody would ever dream of looking for him!"

"It's impossible," murmured Japp.

"Ask madame," said my friend, smiling.

The next day a registered letter lay beside Poirot's plate. He opened it, and a five-pound note fluttered out. My friend's brow puckered.

"Ah, *sacré!* But what shall I do with it? I have much remorse! *Ce pauvre Japp!* Ah, an idea! We will have a little dinner, we three! That consoles me. It was really too easy. I am ashamed. I, who would not rob a child—*mille tonnerres! Mon ami,* what have you, that you laugh so heartily?"

# The Adventure of
# the Italian Nobleman

POIROT and I had many friends and acquaintances of a rather informal nature. Among these was to be numbered Dr. Hawker, a near neighbor of ours, and a member of the medical profession. It was the genial doctor's habit to drop in sometimes of an evening and have a chat with Poirot, of whose genius he was an ardent admirer. The doctor himself, frank and unsuspicious to the last degree, admired the talents so far removed from his own.

On one particular evening in early June, he arrived about half-past eight and settled down to a comfortable discussion on the cheery topic of the prevalence of arsenical poisoning in crimes. It must have been about a quarter of an hour later when the door of our sitting room flew open, and a distracted female precipitated herself into the room.

"Oh, doctor, you're wanted! Such a terrible voice. It gave me a turn, it did indeed."

I recognized in our new visitor Dr. Hawker's housekeeper, Miss Rider. The doctor was a bachelor, and lived in a gloomy old house a few streets away. The usually placid Miss Rider was now in a state bordering on incoherence.

"What terrible voice? Who is it, and what's the trouble?"

"It was the telephone, doctor. I answered it—and a voice spoke. 'Help,' it said. 'Doctor—help. They've killed me!' Then it sort of trailed away. 'Who's speaking?' I said. 'Who's speaking?' Then I got a reply, just a whisper, it seemed, 'Foscatine'—something like that—'Regent's Court.' "

The doctor uttered an exclamation.

"Count Foscatini. He has a flat in Regent's Court. I must go at once. What can have happened?"

"A patient of yours?" asked Poirot.

"I attended him for some slight ailment a few weeks ago. An Italian, but he speaks English perfectly. Well, I must wish you good night, Monsieur Poirot, unless—" He hesitated.

"I perceive the thought in your mind," said Poirot, smiling. "I shall

114

be delighted to accompany you. Hastings, run down and get hold of a taxi."

Taxis always make themselves sought for when one is particularly pressed for time, but I captured one at last, and we were soon bowling along in the direction of Regent's Park. Regent's Court was a new block of flats, situated just off St. John's Wood Road. They had only recently been built, and contained the latest service devices.

There was no one in the hall. The doctor pressed the lift bell impatiently, and when the lift arrived questioned the uniformed attendant sharply.

"Flat 11. Count Foscatini. There's been an accident there, I understand."

The man stared at him.

"First I've heard of it. Mr. Graves—that's Count Foscatini's man—went out about half an hour ago, and he said nothing."

"Is the count alone in the flat?"

"No, sir, he's got two gentlemen dining with him."

"What are they like?" I asked eagerly.

We were in the lift now, ascending rapidly to the second floor, on which Flat 11 was situated.

"I didn't see them myself, sir, but I understand that they were foreign gentlemen."

He pulled back the iron door, and we stepped out on the landing. No. 11 was opposite to us. The doctor rang the bell. There was no reply, and we could hear no sound from within. The doctor rang again and again; we could hear the bell trilling within, but no sign of life rewarded us.

"This is getting serious," muttered the doctor. He turned to the lift attendant.

"Is there any passkey to this door?"

"There is one in the porter's office downstairs."

"Get it, then, and, look here, I think you'd better send for the police."

Poirot approved with a nod of the head.

The man returned shortly; with him came the manager.

"Will you tell me, gentlemen, what is the meaning of all this?"

"Certainly. I received a telephone message from Count Foscatini stating that he had been attacked and was dying. You can understand that we must lose no time—if we are not already too late."

The manager produced the key without more ado, and we all entered the flat.

We passed first into a small square lounge hall. A door on the right of it was half open. The manager indicated it with a nod.

"The dining room."

Dr. Hawker led the way. We followed close on his heels. As we

entered the room I gave a gasp. The round table in the center bore
the remains of a meal; three chairs were pushed back, as though their
occupants had just risen. In the corner, to the right of the fire-place,
was a big writing table, and sitting at it was a man—or what had
been a man. His right hand still grasped the base of the telephone,
but he had fallen forward, struck down by a terrific blow on the head
from behind. The weapon was not far to seek. A marble statuette
stood where it had been hurriedly put down, the base of it stained
with blood.

The doctor's examination did not take a minute. "Stone dead. Must
have been almost instantaneous. I wonder he even managed to telephone. It will be better not to move him until the police arrive."

On the manager's suggestion we searched the flat, but the result
was a foregone conclusion. It was not likely that the murderers would
be concealed there when all they had to do was to walk out.

We came back to the dining room. Poirot had not accompanied
us in our tour. I found him studying the center table with close attention. I joined him. It was a well-polished round mahogany table. A
bowl of roses decorated the center, and white lace mats reposed on
the gleaming surface. There was a dish of fruit, but the three dessert
plates were untouched. There were three coffee cups with remains
of coffee in them—two black, one with milk. All three men had taken
port, and the decanter, half full, stood before the center plate. One
of the men had smoked a cigar, the other two cigarettes. A tortoise
shell-and-silver box, holding cigars and cigarettes, stood open upon
the table.

I enumerated all these facts to myself, but I was forced to admit
that they did not shed any brilliant light on the situation. I wondered
what Poirot saw in them to make him so intent. I asked him.

"*Mon ami,*" he replied, "you miss the point. I am looking for something that I do *not* see."

"What is that?"

"A mistake—even a little mistake—on the part of the murderer."

He stepped swiftly to the small adjoining kitchen, looked in, and
shook his head.

"Monsieur," he said to the manager, "explain to me, I pray, your
system of serving meals here."

The manager stepped to a small hatch in the wall.

"This is the service lift," he explained. "It runs to the kitchens at
the top of the building. You order through this telephone, and the
dishes are sent down in the lift, one course at a time. The dirty plates
and dishes are sent up in the same manner. No domestic worries,
you understand, and at the same time you avoid the wearying publicity
of always dining in a restaurant."

Poirot nodded.

"Then the plates and dishes that were used tonight are on high in the kitchen. You permit that I mount there?"

"Oh, certainly, if you like! Roberts, the lift man, will take you up and introduce you; but I'm afraid you won't find anything that's of any use. They're handling hundreds of plates and dishes, and they'll be all lumped together."

Poirot remained firm, however, and together we visited the kitchens and questioned the man who had taken the order from Flat 11.

"The order was given from the *à la carte menu*—for three," he explained. "Soup julienne, filet de sole normande, tournedos of beef, and a rice soufflé. What time? Just about eight o'clock, I should say. No, I'm afraid the plates and dishes have been all washed up by now. Unfortunate. You were thinking of fingerprints, I suppose?"

"Not exactly," said Poirot, with an enigmatical smile. "I am more interested in Count Foscatini's appetite. Did he partake of every dish?"

"Yes; but of course I can't say how much of each he ate. The plates were all soiled, and the dishes empty—that is to say, with the exception of the rice soufflé. There was a fair amount of that left."

"Ah!" said Poirot, and seemed satisfied with the fact.

As we descended to the flat again he remarked in a low tone:

"We have decidedly to do with a man of method."

"Do you mean the murderer, or Count Foscatini?"

"The latter was undoubtedly an orderly gentleman. After imploring help and announcing his approaching demise, he carefully hung up the telephone receiver."

I stared at Poirot. His words now and his recent inquiries gave me the glimmering of an idea.

"You suspect poison?" I breathed. "The blow on the head was a blind."

Poirot merely smiled.

We reentered the flat to find the local inspector of police had arrived with two constables. He was inclined to resent our appearance, but Poirot calmed him with the mention of our Scotland Yard friend, Inspector Japp, and we were accorded a grudging permission to remain. It was a lucky thing we were, for we had not been back five minutes before an agitated middle-aged man came rushing into the room with every appearance of grief and agitation.

This was Graves, valet-butler to the late Count Foscatini. The story he had to tell was a sensational one.

On the previous morning, two gentlemen had called to see his master. They were Italians, and the elder of the two, a man of about forty, gave his name as Signor Ascanio. The younger was a well-dressed lad of about twenty-four.

Count Foscatini was evidently prepared for their visit and immediately sent Graves out upon some trivial errand. Here the man paused and hesitated in his story. In the end, however, he admitted that, curious as to the purport of the interview, he had not obeyed immediately, but had lingered about endeavoring to hear something of what was going on.

The conversation was carried on in so low a tone that he was not as successful as he had hoped; but he gathered enough to make it clear that some kind of monetary proposition was being discussed, and that the basis of it was a threat. The discussion was anything but amicable. In the end, Count Foscatini raised his voice slightly, and the listener heard these words clearly:

"I have no time to argue further now, gentlemen. If you will dine with me tomorrow night at eight o'clock, we will resume the discussion."

Afraid of being discovered listening, Graves had then hurried out to do his master's errand. This evening the two men had arrived punctually at eight. During dinner they had talked of indifferent matters— politics, the weather, and the theatrical world. When Graves had placed the port upon the table and brought in the coffee his master told him that he might have the evening off.

"Was that a usual proceeding of his when he had guests?" asked the inspector.

"No, sir, it wasn't. That's what made me think it must be some business of a very unusual kind that he was going to discuss with these gentlemen."

That finished Graves's story. He had gone out about 8:30, and, meeting a friend, had accompanied him to the Metropolitan Music Hall in Edgeware Road.

Nobody had seen the two men leave, but the time of the murder was fixed clearly enough at 8:47. A small clock on the writing table had been swept off by Foscatini's arm, and had stopped at that hour, which agreed with Miss Rider's telephone summons.

The police surgeon had made his examination of the body, and it was now lying on the couch. I saw the face for the first time—the olive complexion, the long nose, the luxuriant black mustache, and the full red lips drawn back from the dazzlingly white teeth. Not altogether a pleasant face.

"Well," said the inspector, refastening his notebook. "The case seems clear enough. The only difficulty will be to lay our hands on this Signor Ascanio. I suppose his address is not in the dead man's pocket book by any chance?"

As Poirot had said, the late Foscatini was an orderly man. Neatly written in small, precise handwriting was the inscription, "Signor Paolo Ascanio, Grosvenor Hotel."

The inspector busied himself with the telephone, then turned to us with a grin.

"Just in time. Our fine gentleman was off to catch the boat train to the Continent. Well, gentlemen, that's about all we can do here. It's a bad business, but straightforward enough. One of these Italian vendetta things, as likely as not."

Thus airily dismissed, we found our way downstairs. Dr. Hawker was full of excitement.

"Like the beginning of a novel, eh? Real exciting stuff. Wouldn't believe it if you read about it."

Poirot did not speak. He was very thoughtful. All the evening he had hardly opened his lips.

"What says the master detective, eh?" asked Hawker, clapping him on the back. "Nothing to work your gray cells over this time."

"You think not?"

"What could there be?"

"Well, for example, there is the window."

"The window? But it was fastened. Nobody could have got out or in that way. I noticed it specially."

"And why were you able to notice it?"

The doctor looked puzzled. Poirot hastened to explain.

"It is to the curtains I refer. They were not drawn. A little odd, that. And then there was the coffee. It was very black coffee."

"Well, what of it?"

"Very black," repeated Poirot. "In conjunction with that let us remember that very little of the rice soufflé was eaten, and we get— what?"

"Moonshine," laughed the doctor. "You're pulling my leg."

"Never do I pull the leg. Hastings here knows that I am perfectly serious."

"I don't know what you are getting at, all the same," I confessed. "You don't suspect the manservant, do you? He might have been in with the gang, and put some dope in the coffee. I suppose they'll test his alibi?"

"Without doubt, my friend; but it is the alibi of Signor Ascanio that interests me."

"You think he has an alibi?"

"That is just what worries me. I have no doubt that we shall soon be enlightened on that point."

The *Daily Newsmonger* enabled us to become conversant with succeeding events.

Signor Ascanio was arrested and charged with the murder of Count Foscatini. When arrested, he denied knowing the count, and declared he had never been near Regent's Court either on the evening of the crime or on the previous morning. The younger man had disappeared entirely. Signor Ascanio had arrived alone at the Grosvenor Hotel from the Continent two days before the murder. All efforts to trace the second man failed.

Ascanio, however, was not sent for trial. No less a personage than the Italian ambassador himself came forward and testified at the police court proceedings that Ascanio had been with him at the embassy from eight till nine that evening. The prisoner was discharged. Naturally, a lot of people thought that the crime was a political one, and was being deliberately hushed up.

Poirot had taken a keen interest in all these points. Nevertheless, I was somewhat surprised when he suddenly informed me one morning that he was expecting a visitor at eleven o'clock, and that that visitor was none other than Ascanio himself.

"He wishes to consult you?"

"*Du tout*, Hastings. I wish to consult him."

"What about?"

"The Regent's Court murder."

"You are going to prove that he did it?"

"A man cannot be tried twice for murder, Hastings. Endeavor to have the common sense. Ah, that is our friend's ring."

A few minutes later Signor Ascanio was ushered in—a small, thin man with a secretive and furtive glance in his eyes. He remained standing, darting suspicious glances from one to the other of us.

"Monsieur Poirot?"

My little friend tapped himself gently on the chest.

"Be seated, signor. You received my note. I am determined to get to the bottom of this mystery. In some small measure you can aid me. Let us commence. You—in company with a friend—visited the late Count Foscatini on the morning of Tuesday the 9th—"

The Italian made an angry gesture.

"I did nothing of the sort. I have sworn in court—"

"*Précisément*—and I have a little idea that you have sworn falsely."

"You threaten me? Bah! I have nothing to fear from you. I have been acquitted."

"Exactly, and as I am not an imbecile, it is not with the gallows I threaten you—but with publicity. Publicity! I see that you do not like the word. I had an idea that you would not. My little ideas, you know, they are very valuable to me. Come, signor, your only chance is to be frank with me. I do not ask to know whose indiscretions brought

you to England. I know this much, you came for the especial purpose
of seeing Count Foscatini."

"He was not a count," growled the Italian.

"I have already noted the fact that his name does not appear in
the *Almanach de Gotha.* Never mind, the title of count is often useful
in the profession of blackmailing."

"I suppose I might as well be frank. You seem to know a good
deal."

"I have employed my gray cells to some advantage. Come, Signor
Ascanio, you visited the dead man on the Tuesday morning—that is
so, is it not?"

"Yes, but I never went there on the following evening. There was
no need. I will tell you all. Certain information concerning a man of
great position in Italy had come into this scoundrel's possession. He
demanded a big sum of money in return for the papers. I came over
to England to arrange the matter. I called upon him by appointment
that morning. One of the young secretaries of the Embassy was with
me. The count was more reasonable than I had hoped, although even
then the sum of money I paid him was a huge one."

"Pardon, how was it paid?"

"In Italian notes of comparatively small denomination. I paid over
the money then and there. He handed me the incriminating papers.
I never saw him again."

"Why did you not say all this when you were arrested?"

"In my delicate position I was forced to deny any association with
the man."

"And how do you account for the events of the evening, then?"

"I can only think that someone must have deliberately impersonated
me. I understand that no money was found in the flat."

Poirot looked at him and shook his head.

"Strange," he murmured. "We all have the little gray cells. And
so few of us know how to use them. Good morning, Signor Ascanio.
I believe your story. It is very much as I had imagined. But I had to
make sure."

After bowing his guest out, Poirot returned to his armchair and
smiled at me.

"Let us hear M. le Capitaine Hastings on the case?"

"Well, I suppose Ascanio is right—somebody impersonated him."

"Never, never will you use the brains the good God has given you.
Recall to yourself some words I uttered after leaving the flat that night.
I referred to the window curtains not being drawn. We are in the
month of June. It is still light at eight o'clock. The light is failing by
half-past. *Ça vous dit quelque chose?* I perceive a struggling impression

that you will arrive some day. Now let us continue. The coffee was, as I said, very black. Count Foscatini's teeth were magnificently white. Coffee stains the teeth. We reason from that that Count Foscatini did not drink any coffee. Yet there was coffee in all three cups. Why should anyone pretend Count Foscatini had drunk coffee when he had not done so?"

I shook my head, utterly bewildered.

"Come, I will help you. What evidence have we that Ascanio and his friend, or two men posing as them, ever came to the flat that night? Nobody saw them go in; nobody saw them go out. We have the evidence of one man and of a host of inanimate objects."

"You mean?"

"I mean knives and forks and plates and empty dishes. Ah, but it was a clever idea! Graves is a thief and a scoundrel, but what a man of method! He overhears a portion of the conversation in the morning, enough to realize that Ascanio will be in an awkward position to defend himself. The following evening, about eight o'clock, he tells his master he is wanted at the telephone. Foscatini sits down, stretches out his hand to the telephone, and from behind Graves strikes him down with the marble figure. Then quickly to the service telephone—dinner for three! It comes, he lays the table, dirties the plates, knives, and forks, etc. But he has to get rid of the food too. Not only is he a man of brain; he has a resolute and capacious stomach! But after eating three tournedos, the rice soufflé is too much for him! He even smokes a cigar and two cigarettes to carry out the illusion. Ah, but it was magnificently thorough! Then, having moved on the hands of the clock to 8:47, he smashes it and stops it. The one thing he does not do is to draw the curtains. But if there had been a real dinner party the curtains would have been drawn as soon as the light began to fail. Then he hurries out, mentioning the guests to the lift man in passing. He hurries to a telephone box, and as near as possible to 8:47 rings up the doctor with his master's dying cry. So successful is his idea that no one ever inquires if a call was put through from Flat 11 at that time."

"Except Hercule Poirot, I suppose?" I said sarcastically.

"Not even Hercule Poirot," said my friend, with a smile. "I am about to inquire now. I had to prove my point to you first. But you will see, I shall be right; and then Japp, to whom I have already given a hint, will be able to arrest the respectable Graves. I wonder how much of the money he has spent."

Poirot *was* right. He always is, confound him!

# The Case of
# the Missing Will

THE problem presented to us by Miss Violet Marsh made rather a pleasant change from our usual routine work. Poirot had received a brisk and businesslike note from the lady asking for an appointment, and he had replied asking her to call upon him at eleven o'clock the following day.

She arrived punctually—a tall, handsome young woman, plainly but neatly dressed, with an assured and businesslike manner. Clearly a young woman who meant to get on in the world. I am not a great admirer of the so-called New Woman myself, and, in spite of her good looks, I was not particularly prepossessed in her favor.

"My business is of a somewhat unusual nature, Monsieur Poirot," she began, after she had accepted a chair. "I had better begin at the beginning and tell you the whole story."

"If you please, mademoiselle."

"I am an orphan. My father was one of two brothers, sons of a small yeoman farmer in Devonshire. The farm was a poor one, and the elder brother, Andrew, emigrated to Australia, where he did very well indeed, and by means of successful speculation in land became a very rich man. The younger brother, Roger (my father), had no leanings towards the agricultural life. He managed to educate himself a little, and obtained a post as a clerk with a small firm. He married slightly above him; my mother was the daughter of a poor artist. My father died when I was six years old. When I was fourteen, my mother followed him to the grave. My only living relation then was my Uncle Andrew, who had recently returned from Australia and bought a small place, Crabtree Manor, in his native county. He was exceedingly kind to his brother's orphan child, took me to live with him, and treated me in every way as though I was his own daughter.

"Crabtree Manor, in spite of its name, is really only an old farmhouse. Farming was in my uncle's blood, and he was intensely interested in various modern farming experiments. Although kindness itself to me, he had certain peculiar and deeply rooted ideas as to the upbringing

of women. Himself a man of little or no education, though possessing
remarkable shrewdness, he placed little value on what he called 'book
knowledge.' He was especially opposed to the education of women.
In his opinion, girls should learn practical housework and dairywork,
be useful about the home, and have as little to do with book learning
as possible. He proposed to bring me up on these lines, to my bitter
disappointment and annoyance. I rebelled frankly. I knew that I possessed a good brain, and had absolutely no talent for domestic duties.
My uncle and I had many bitter arguments on the subject, for, though
much attached to each other, we were both self-willed. I was lucky
enough to win a scholarship, and up to a certain point was successful
in getting my own way. The crisis arose when I resolved to go to
Girton. I had a little money of my own, left me by my mother, and
I was quite determined to make the best use of the gifts God had
given me. I had one long, final argument with my uncle. He put the
facts plainly before me. He had no other relations, and he had intended
me to be his sole heiress. As I have told you, he was a very rich man.
If I persisted in these 'new-fangled notions' of mine, however, I need
look for nothing from him. I remained polite, but firm. I should always
be deeply attached to him, I told him, but I must lead my own life.
We parted on that note. 'You fancy your brain, my girl,' were his
last words. 'I've no book learning, but, for all that, I'll pit mine against
yours any day. We'll see what we shall see.'

"That was nine years ago. I have stayed with him for a weekend
occasionally, and our relations were perfectly amicable, though his
views remained unaltered. He never referred to my having matricu-
lated, nor to my B.Sc. For the last three years his health had been
failing, and a month ago he died.

"I am now coming to the point of my visit. My uncle left a most
extraordinary will. By its terms, Crabtree Manor and its contents are
to be at my disposal for a year from his death—'during which time
my clever niece may prove her wits,' the actual words run. At the
end of that period, 'my wits having proved better than hers,' the house
and all my uncle's large fortune pass to various charitable institutions."

"That is a little hard on you, mademoiselle, seeing that you were
Mr. Marsh's only blood relation."

"I do not look on it in that way. Uncle Andrew warned me fairly,
and I chose my own path. Since I would not fall in with his wishes,
he was at perfect liberty to leave his money to whom he pleased."

"Was the will drawn up by a lawyer?"

"No; it was written on a printed will form and witnessed by the
man and his wife who live in the house and do for my uncle."

"There might be a possibility of upsetting such a will?"

"I would not even attempt to do such a thing."

"You regard it, then, as a sporting challenge on the part of your uncle?"

"That is exactly how I look upon it."

"It bears that interpretation, certainly," said Poirot thoughtfully. "Somewhere in this rambling old manor house your uncle has concealed either a sum of money in notes or possibly a second will, and has given you a year in which to exercise your ingenuity to find it."

"Exactly, Monsieur Poirot; and I am paying you the compliment of assuming that your ingenuity will be greater than mine."

"Eh, eh! but that is very charming of you. My gray cells are at your disposal. You have made no search yourself?"

"Only a cursory one; but I have too much respect for my uncle's undoubted abilities to fancy that the task will be an easy one."

"Have you the will or a copy of it with you?"

Miss Marsh handed a document across the table. Poirot ran through it, nodding to himself.

"Made three years ago. Dated March 25; and the time is given also—11 A.M.—that is very suggestive. It narrows the field of search. Assuredly it is another will we have to seek for. A will made even half an hour later would upset this. *Eh bien,* mademoiselle, it is a problem charming and ingenious that you have presented to me here. I shall have all the pleasure in the world in solving it for you. Granted that your uncle was a man of ability, his gray cells cannot have been of the quality of Hercule Poirot's!"

(Really, Poirot's vanity is blatant!)

"Fortunately, I have nothing of moment on hand at the minute. Hastings and I will go down to Crabtree Manor tonight. The man and wife who attended on your uncle are still there, I presume?"

"Yes, their name is Baker."

The following morning saw us started on the hunt proper. We had arrived late the night before. Mr. and Mrs. Baker, having received a telegram from Miss Marsh, were expecting us. They were a pleasant couple, the man gnarled and pink-cheeked, like a shriveled pippin, and his wife a woman of vast proportions and true Devonshire calm.

Tired with our journey and the eight-mile drive from the station, we had retired at once to bed after a supper of roast chicken, apple pie, and Devonshire cream. We had now disposed of an excellent breakfast, and were sitting in a small paneled room which had been the late Mr. Marsh's study and living room. A roll-top desk stuffed with papers, all neatly docketed, stood against the wall, and a big leather armchair showed plainly that it had been its owner's constant resting place. A big chintz-covered settee ran along the opposite wall, and the deep low window seats were covered with the same faded chintz of an old-fashioned pattern.

"*Eh bien, mon ami,*" said Poirot, lighting one of his tiny cigarettes, "we must map out our plan of campaign. Already I have made a rough survey of the house, but I am of opinion that any clue will be found in this room. We shall have to go through the documents in the desk with meticulous care. Naturally, I do not expect to find the will among them; but it is likely that some apparently innocent paper may conceal the clue to its hiding place. But first we must have a little information. Ring the bell, I pray of you."

I did so. While we were waiting for it to be answered, Poirot walked up and down, looking about him approvingly.

"A man of method, this Mr. Marsh. See how neatly the packets of papers are docketed; then the key to each drawer has its ivory label— so has the key of the china cabinet on the wall; and see with what precision the china within is arranged. It rejoices the heart. Nothing here offends the eye—"

He came to an abrupt pause, as his eye was caught by the key of the desk itself, to which a dirty envelope was affixed. Poirot frowned at it and withdrew it from the lock. On it were scrawled the words: KEY OF ROLL-TOP DESK, in a crabbed handwriting, quite unlike the neat superscriptions on the other keys.

"An alien note," said Poirot, frowning. "I could swear that here we have no longer the personality of Mr. Marsh. But who else has been in the house? Only Miss Marsh, and she, if I mistake not, is also a young lady of method and order."

Baker came in answer to the bell.

"Will you fetch madame your wife, and answer a few questions?"

Baker departed, and in a few moments returned with Mrs. Baker, wiping her hands on her apron and beaming all over her face.

In a few clear words Poirot set forth the object of his mission. The Bakers were immediately sympathetic.

"Us don't want to see Miss Violet done out of what's hers," declared the woman. "Cruel hard 'twould be for hospitals to get it all."

Poirot proceeded with his questions. Yes, Mr. and Mrs. Baker remembered perfectly witnessing the will. Baker had previously been sent in to the neighbouring town to get two printed will forms.

"Two?" said Poirot sharply.

"Yes, sir, for safety like, I suppose, in case he should spoil one— and sure enough, so he did do. Us had signed one—"

"What time of day was that?"

Baker scratched his head, but his wife was quicker.

"Why, to be sure, I'd just put the milk on for the cocoa at eleven.

Don't ee remember? It had all boiled over on the stove when us got back to kitchen."

"And afterwards?"

" 'Twould be about an hour later. Us had to go in again. 'I've made a mistake,' says old master, 'had to tear the whole thing up. I'll trouble you to sign again,' and us did. And afterwards master give us a tidy sum of money each. 'I've left you nothing in my will,' says he, 'but each year I live you'll have this to be a nest egg when I'm gone'; and sure enough, so he did."

Poirot reflected.

"After you had signed the second time, what did Mr. Marsh do? Do you know?"

"Went out to the village to pay tradesmen's books."

That did not seem very promising. Poirot tried another tack. He held out the key of the desk.

"Is that your master's writing?"

I may have imagined it, but I fancied that a moment or two elapsed before Baker replied, "Yes, sir, it is."

"He's lying," I thought. "But why?"

"Has your master let the house?—have there been any strangers in it during the last three years?"

"No, sir."

"No visitors?"

"Only Miss Violet."

"No strangers of any kind been inside this room?"

"No, sir."

"You forget the workmen, Jim," his wife reminded him.

"Workmen?" Poirot wheeled round on her. "What workmen?"

The woman explained that about two years and a half ago workmen had been in the house to do certain repairs. She was quite vague as to what the repairs were. Her view seemed to be that the whole thing was a fad of her master's and quite unnecessary. Part of the time the workmen had been in the study; but what they had done there she could not say, as her master had not let either of them into the room while the work was in progress. Unfortunately, they could not remember the name of the firm employed, beyond the fact that it was a Plymouth one.

"We progress, Hastings," said Poirot, rubbing his hands as the Bakers left the room. "Clearly he made a second will and then had workmen from Plymouth in to make a suitable hiding place. Instead of wasting time taking up the floor and tapping the walls, we will go to Plymouth."

With a little trouble, we were able to get the information we wanted. After one or two essays, we found the firm employed by Mr. Marsh. Their employees had all been with them many years, and it was easy to find the two men who had worked under Mr. Marsh's orders. They remembered the job perfectly. Among various other minor jobs, they had taken up one of the bricks of the old-fashioned fireplace, made a cavity beneath, and so cut the brick that it was impossible to see the join. By pressing on the second brick from the end, the whole thing was raised. It had been quite a complicated piece of work, and the old gentleman had been very fussy about it. Our informant was a man called Coghan, a big, gaunt man with a grizzled mustache. He seemed an intelligent fellow.

We returned to Crabtree Manor in high spirits, and, locking the study door, proceeded to put our newly acquired knowledge into effect. It was impossible to see any sign on the bricks, but when we pressed in the manner indicated, a deep cavity was at once disclosed.

Eagerly Poirot plunged in his hand. Suddenly his face fell from complacent elation to consternation. All he held was a charred fragment of stiff paper. But for it, the cavity was empty.

"*Sacré!*" cried Poirot angrily. "Some one has been before us."

We examined the scrap of paper anxiously. Clearly it was a fragment of what we sought. A portion of Baker's signature remained, but no indication of what the terms of the will had been.

Poirot sat back on his heels. His expression would have been comical if we had not been so overcome.

"I understand it not," he growled. "Who destroyed this? And what was their object?"

"The Bakers?" I suggested.

"*Pourquoi?* Neither will makes any provision for them, and they are more likely to be kept on with Miss Marsh than if the place became the property of a hospital. How could it be to anyone's advantage to destroy the will? The hospitals benefit—yes; but one cannot suspect institutions."

"Perhaps the old man changed his mind and destroyed it himself," I suggested.

Poirot rose to his feet, dusting his knees with his usual care.

"That may be," he admitted. "One of your more sensible observations, Hastings. Well, we can do no more here. We have done all that mortal man can do. We have successfully pitted our wits against the late Andrew Marsh's; but, unfortunately, his niece is no better off for our success."

By driving to the station at once, we were just able to catch a train to London, though not the principal express. Poirot was sad and dissatisfied. For my part, I was tired and dozed in a corner. Suddenly, as we were just moving out of Taunton, Poirot uttered a piercing squeal.

"*Vite*, Hastings! Awake and jump! But jump I say!"

Before I knew where I was we were standing on the platform, bare-headed and minus our valises, while the train disappeared into the night. I was furious. But Poirot paid no attention.

"Imbecile that I have been!" he cried. "Triple imbecile! Not again will I vaunt my little gray cells!"

"That's a good job at any rate," I said grumpily. "But what is this all about?"

As usual, when following out his own ideas, Poirot paid absolutely no attention to me.

"The tradesmen's books—I have left them entirely out of account! Yes, but where? Where? Never mind, I cannot be mistaken. We must return at once."

Easier said than done. We managed to get a slow train to Exeter, and there Poirot hired a car. We arrived back at Crabtree Manor in the small hours of the morning. I pass over the bewilderment of the Bakers when we had at last aroused them. Paying no attention to anybody, Poirot strode at once to the study.

"I have been, not a triple imbecile, but thirty-six times one, my friend," he deigned to remark. "Now, behold!"

Going straight to the desk, he drew out the key, and detached the envelope from it. I stared at him stupidly. How could he possibly hope to find a big will form in that tiny envelope? With great care he cut open the envelope, laying it out flat. Then he lighted the fire and held the plain inside surface of the envelope to the flame. In a few minutes faint characters began to appear.

"Look, *mon ami!*" cried Poirot in triumph.

I looked. There were just a few lines of faint writing stating briefly that he left everything to his niece, Violet Marsh. It was dated March 25, 12:30 P.M., and witnessed by Albert Pike, confectioner, and Jessie Pike, married woman.

"But is it legal?" I gasped.

"As far as I know, there is no law against writing your will in a blend of disappearing and sympathetic ink. The intention of the testator is clear, and the beneficiary is his only living relation. But the cleverness of him! He foresaw every step that a searcher would take—that I, miserable imbecile, took. He gets two will forms, makes the servants sign twice, then sallies out with his will written on the inside of a dirty envelope and a fountain pen containing his little ink mixture. On some excuse he gets the confectioner and his wife to sign their names under his own signature, then he ties it to the key of his desk and chuckles to himself. If his niece sees through his little ruse, she will have justified her choice of life and elaborate education, and be thoroughly welcome to his money."

"She didn't see through it, did she?" I said slowly. "It seems rather unfair. The old man really won."

"But no, Hastings. It is *your* wits that go astray. Miss Marsh proved the astuteness of her wits and the value of the higher education for women by at once putting the matter in *my* hands. Always employ the expert. She has amply proved her right to the money."

I wonder—I very much wonder—what old Andrew Marsh would have thought!

# The Veiled Lady

I HAD noticed that for some time Poirot had been growing increasingly dissatisfied and restless. We had had no interesting cases of late, nothing on which my little friend could exercise his keen wits and remarkable powers of deduction. This morning he flung down the newspaper with an impatient *"Tchah!"*—a favorite exclamation of his which sounded exactly like a cat sneezing.

"They fear me, Hastings; the criminals of your England they fear me! When the cat is there, the little mice, they come no more to the cheese!"

"I don't suppose the greater part of them even know of your existence," I said, laughing.

Poirot looked at me reproachfully. He always imagines that the whole world is thinking and talking of Hercule Poirot. He had certainly made a name for himself in London, but I could hardly believe that his existence struck terror into the criminal world.

"What about that daylight robbery of jewels in Bond Street the other day?" I asked.

"A neat coup," said Poirot approvingly, "though not in my line. *Pas de finesse, seulement de l'audace!* A man with a loaded cane smashes the plate-glass window of a jeweler's shop and grabs a number of precious stones. Worthy citizens immediately seize him; a policeman arrives. He is caught red-handed with the jewels on him. He is marched off to the police station, and then it is discovered that the stones are paste. He has passed the real ones to a confederate—one of the aforementioned worthy citizens. He will go to prison—true; but when he comes out, there will be a nice little fortune awaiting him. Yes, not badly imagined. But I could do better than that. Sometimes, Hastings, I regret that I am of such a moral disposition. To work against the law, it would be pleasing, for a change."

"Cheer up, Poirot; you know you are unique in your own line."

"But what is there on hand in my own line?"

I picked up the paper.

"Here's an Englishman mysteriously done to death in Holland," I said.

"They always say that—and later they find that he ate the tinned fish and that his death is perfectly natural."

"Well, if you're determined to grouse!"

*"Tiens!"* said Poirot, who had strolled across to the window. "Here in the street is what they call in novels a 'heavily veiled lady.' She mounts the steps; she rings the bell—she comes to consult us. Here is a possibility of something interesting. When one is as young and pretty as that one, one does not veil the face except for a big affair."

A minute later our visitor was ushered in. As Poirot had said, she was indeed heavily veiled. It was impossible to distinguish her features until she raised her veil of black Spanish lace. Then I saw that Poirot's intuition had been right; the lady was extremely pretty, with fair hair and large blue eyes. From the costly simplicity of her attire, I deduced at once that she belonged to the upper strata of society.

"Monsieur Poirot," said the lady in a soft, musical voice, "I am in great trouble. I can hardly believe that you can help me, but I have heard such wonderful things of you that I come literally as a last hope to beg you to do the impossible."

"The impossible, it pleases me always," said Poirot. "Continue, I beg of you, mademoiselle."

Our fair guest hesitated.

"But you must be frank," added Poirot. "You must not leave me in the dark on any point."

"I will trust you," said the girl suddenly. "You have heard of Lady Millicent Castle Vaughan?"

I looked up with keen interest. The announcement of Lady Millicent's engagement to the young Duke of Southshire had appeared a few days previously. She was, I knew, the fifth daughter of an impecunious Irish peer, and the Duke of Southshire was one of the best matches in England.

"I am Lady Millicent," continued the girl. "You may have read of my engagement. I should be one of the happiest girls alive; but oh, M. Poirot, I am in terrible trouble! There is a man, a horrible man— his name is Lavington; and he—I hardly know how to tell you. There was a letter I wrote—I was only sixteen at the time; and he—he—"

"A letter that you wrote to this Mr. Lavington?"

"Oh, *no*—not to him! To a young soldier—I was very fond of him— he was killed in the war."

"I understand," said Poirot kindly.

"It was a foolish letter, an indiscreet letter, but indeed, M. Poirot, nothing more. But there are phrases in it which—which might bear a different interpretation."

"I see," said Poirot. "And this letter has come into the possession of Mr. Lavington?"

"Yes, and he threatens, unless I pay him an enormous sum of money, a sum that it is quite impossible for me to raise, to send it to the duke."

"The dirty swine!" I ejaculated. "I beg your pardon, Lady Millicent."

"Would it not be wiser to confess all to your future husband?"

"I dare not, M. Poirot. The duke is a rather peculiar character, jealous and suspicious and prone to believe the worst. I might as well break off my engagement at once."

"Dear, dear," said Poirot with an expressive grimace. "And what do you want me to do, milady?"

"I thought perhaps that I might ask Mr. Lavington to call upon you. I would tell him that you were empowered by me to discuss the matter. Perhaps you could reduce his demands."

"What sum does he mention?"

"Twenty thousand pounds—an impossibility. I doubt if I could raise a thousand, even."

"You might perhaps borrow the money on the prospect of your approaching marriage—but I doubt if you could get hold of half that sum. Besides—*eh bien,* it is repugnant to me that you should pay! No, the ingenuity of Hercule Poirot shall defeat your enemies! Send me this Mr. Lavington. Is he likely to bring the letter with him?"

The girl shook her head.

"I do not think so. He is very cautious."

"I suppose there is no doubt that he really has it?"

"He showed it to me when I went to his house."

"You went to his house? That was very imprudent, milady."

"Was it? I was so desperate. I hoped my entreaties might move him."

"Oh, *là là!* The Lavingtons of this world are not moved by entreaties! He would welcome them as showing how much importance you attached to the document. Where does he live, this fine gentleman?"

"At Buona Vista, Wimbledon. I went there after dark—" Poirot groaned. "I declared that I would inform the police in the end, but he only laughed in a horrid, sneering manner. 'By all means, my dear Lady Millicent, do so if you wish,' he said."

"Yes, it is hardly an affair for the police," murmured Poirot.

" 'But I think you will be wiser than that,' he continued. 'See, here is your letter—in this little Chinese puzzle box!' He held it so that I could see. I tried to snatch at it, but he was too quick for me. With a horrid smile he folded it up and replaced it in the little wooden box. 'It will be quite safe here, I assure you,' he said, 'and the box itself lives in such a clever place that you would never find it.' My eyes turned to the small wall safe, and he shook his head and laughed. 'I have a better safe than that,' he said. Oh, he was odious! M. Poirot, do you think that you can help me?"

"Have faith in Papa Poirot. I will find a way."

These reassurances were all very well, I thought, as Poirot gallantly ushered his fair client down the stairs, but it seemed to me that we had a tough nut to crack. I said as much to Poirot when he returned. He nodded ruefully.

"Yes—the solution does not leap to the eye. He has the whip hand, this M. Lavington. For the moment I do not see how we are to circumvent him."

Mr. Lavington duly called upon us that afternoon. Lady Millicent had spoken truly when she described him as an odious man. I felt a positive tingling in the end of my boot, so keen was I to kick him down the stairs. He was blustering and overbearing in manner, laughed Poirot's gentle suggestions to scorn, and generally showed himself as master of the situation. I could not help feeling that Poirot was hardly appearing at his best. He looked discouraged and crestfallen.

"Well, gentlemen," said Lavington, as he took up his hat, "we don't seem to be getting much farther. The case stands like this: I'll let the Lady Millicent off cheap, as she is such a charming young lady," he leered odiously. "We'll say eighteen thousand. I'm off to Paris today—a little piece of business to attend to over there. I shall be back on Tuesday. Unless the money is paid by Tuesday evening, the letter goes to the duke. Don't tell me Lady Millicent can't raise the money. Some of her gentlemen friends would be only too willing to oblige such a pretty woman with a loan—if she goes the right way about it."

My face flushed, and I took a step forward, but Lavington had wheeled out of the room as he finished his sentence.

"My God!" I cried. "Something has got to be done. You seem to be taking this lying down, Poirot."

"You have an excellent heart, my friend—but your gray cells are in a deplorable condition. I have no wish to impress Mr. Lavington with my capabilities. The more pusillanimous he thinks me, the better."

"Why?"

"It is curious," murmured Poirot reminiscently, "that I should have uttered a wish to work against the law just before Lady Millicent arrived!"

"You are going to burgle his house while he is away?" I gasped.

"Sometimes, Hastings, your mental processes are amazingly quick."

"Suppose he takes the letter with him?"

Poirot shook his head.

"That is very unlikely. He has evidently a hiding place in his house that he fancies to be pretty impregnable."

"When do we—er—do the deed?"

"Tomorrow night. We will start from here about eleven o'clock."

At the time appointed I was ready to set off. I had donned a dark suit, and a soft dark hat. Poirot beamed kindly on me.

"You have dressed the part, I see," he observed. "Come let us take the underground to Wimbledon."

"Aren't we going to take anything with us? Tools to break in with?"

"My dear Hastings, Hercule Poirot does not adopt such crude methods."

I retired, snubbed, but my curiosity was alert.

It was just on midnight that we entered the small suburban garden of Buona Vista. The house was dark and silent. Poirot went straight to a window at the back of the house, raised the sash noiselessly and bade me enter.

"How did you know this window would be open?" I whispered, for really it seemed uncanny.

"Because I sawed through the catch this morning."

"What?"

"But yes, it was the most simple. I called, presented a fictitious card and one of Inspector Japp's official ones. I said I had been sent, recommended by Scotland Yard, to attend to some burglar-proof fastenings that Mr. Lavington wanted fixed while he was away. The housekeeper welcomed me with enthusiasm. It seems they have had two attempted burglaries here lately—evidently our little idea has occurred to other clients of Mr. Lavington's—with nothing of value taken. I examined all the windows, made my little arrangement, forbade the servants to touch the windows until tomorrow, as they were electrically connected up, and withdrew gracefully."

"Really, Poirot, you are wonderful."

"*Mon ami*, it was of the simplest. Now, to work! The servants sleep at the top of the house, so we will run little risk of disturbing them."

"I presume the safe is built into the wall somewhere?"

"Safe? Fiddlesticks! There is no safe. Mr. Lavington is an intelligent man. You will see, he will have devised a hiding place much more intelligent than a safe. A safe is the first thing everyone looks for."

Whereupon we began a systematic search of the entire place. But after several hours' ransacking of the house, our search had been unavailing. I saw symptoms of anger gathering on Poirot's face.

"*Ah, sapristi*, is Hercule Poirot to be beaten? Never! Let us be calm. Let us reflect. Let us reason. Let us—*enfin!*—employ our little gray cells!"

He paused for some moments, bending his brows in concentration; then the green light I knew so well stole into his eyes.

"I have been an imbecile! The kitchen!"

"The kitchen," I cried. "But that's impossible. The servants!"

"Exactly. Just what ninety-nine people out of a hundred would say! And for that very reason the kitchen is the ideal place to choose. It is full of various homely objects. *En avant,* to the kitchen!"

I followed him, completely skeptical, and watched while he dived into breadbins, tapped saucepans, and put his head into the gas oven. In the end, tired of watching him, I strolled back to the study. I was convinced that there, and there only, would we find the *cache.* I made a further minute search, noted that it was now a quarter past four and that therefore it would soon be growing light, and then went back to the kitchen regions.

To my utter amazement, Poirot was now standing right inside the coalbin, to the utter ruin of his neat light suit. He made a grimace.

"But yes, my friend, it is against all my instincts so to ruin my appearance, but what will you?"

"But Lavington can't have buried it under the coal?"

"If you would use your eyes, you would see that it is not the coal that I examine."

I then saw that on a shelf behind the coal bunker some logs of wood were piled. Poirot was dexterously taking them down one by one. Suddenly he uttered a low exclamation.

"Your knife, Hastings!"

I handed it to him. He appeared to insert it in the wood, and suddenly the log split in two. It had been neatly sawn in half and a cavity hollowed out in the center. From this cavity Poirot took a little wooden box of Chinese make.

"Well done!" I cried, carried out of myself.

"Gently, Hastings! Do not raise your voice too much. Come, let us be off, before the daylight is upon us."

Slipping the box into his pocket, he leaped lightly out of the coal bunker, brushed himself down as well as he could, and leaving the house by the same way as we had come, we walked rapidly in the direction of London.

"But what an extraordinary place!" I expostulated. "Anyone might have used the log."

"In July, Hastings? And it was at the bottom of the pile—a very ingenious hiding place. Ah, here is a taxi! Now for home, a wash, and a refreshing sleep."

After the excitement of the night, I slept late. When I finally strolled into our sitting room just before one o'clock, I was surprised to see Poirot, leaning back in an armchair, the Chinese box open beside him, calmly reading the letter he had taken from it.

He smiled at me affectionately, and tapped the sheet he held.

"She was right, the Lady Millicent; never would the Duke have pardoned this letter! It contains some of the most extravagant terms of affection I have ever come across."

"Really, Poirot," I said, rather disgustedly, "I don't think you should have read the letter. That's the sort of thing that isn't done."

"It is done by Hercule Poirot," replied my friend imperturbably.

"And another thing," I said. "I don't think using Japp's official card yesterday was quite playing the game."

"But I was not playing a game, Hastings. I was conducting a case."

I shrugged my shoulders. One can't argue with a point of view.

"A step on the stairs," said Poirot. "That will be Lady Millicent."

Our fair client came in with an anxious expression on her face which changed to one of delight on seeing the letter and box which Poirot held up.

"Oh M. Poirot. How wonderful of you! How did you do it?"

"By rather reprehensible methods, milady. But Mr. Lavington will not prosecute. This is your letter, is it not?"

She glanced through it.

"Yes. Oh, how can I ever thank you! You are a wonderful, wonderful man. Where was it hidden?"

Poirot told her.

"How very clever of you!" She took up the small box from the table. "I shall keep this as a souvenir."

"I had hoped, milady, that you would permit me to keep it—also as a souvenir."

"I hope to send you a better souvenir than that—on my wedding day. You shall not find me ungrateful, M. Poirot."

"The pleasure of doing you a service will be more to me than a check—so you permit that I retain the box."

"Oh, no, M. Poirot, I simply must have that," she cried laughingly.

She stretched out her hand, but Poirot was before her. His hand closed over it.

"I think not." His voice had changed.

"What do you mean?" Her voice seemed to have grown sharper.

"At any rate, permit me to abstract its further contents. You observe that the original cavity has been reduced by half. In the top half, the compromising letter; in the bottom—"

He made a nimble gesture, then held out his hand. On the palm were four large glittering stones, and two big milky white pearls.

"The jewels stolen in Bond Street the other day, I rather fancy," murmured Poirot. "Japp will tell us."

To my utter amazement, Japp himself stepped out from Poirot's bedroom.

"An old friend of yours, I believe," said Poirot politely to Lady Millicent.

"Nabbed, by the Lord!" said Lady Millicent, with a complete change of manner. "You nippy old devil!" She looked at Poirot with almost affectionate awe.

"Well, Gertie, my dear," said Japp, "the game's up this time, I fancy. Fancy seeing you again so soon! We've got your pal, too, the gentleman who called here the other day calling himself Lavington. As for Lavington himself, alias Croker, alias Reed, I wonder which of the gang it was who stuck a knife into him the other day in Holland? Thought he'd got the goods with him, didn't you? And he hadn't. He double-crossed you properly—hid 'em in his own house. You had two fellows looking for them, and then you tackled M. Poirot here, and by a piece of amazing luck he found them."

"You do like talking, don't you?" said the late Lady Millicent. "Easy there, now. I'll go quietly. You can't say that I'm not the perfect lady. *Ta-ta*, all!"

"The shoes were wrong," said Poirot dreamily, while I was still too stupefied to speak. "I have made my little observations of your English nation, and a lady, a born lady, is always particular about her shoes. She may have shabby clothes, but she will be well shod. Now, this Lady Millicent had smart, expensive clothes, and cheap shoes. It was not likely that either you or I should have seen the real Lady Millicent; she has been very little in London, and this girl had a certain superficial resemblance which would pass well enough. As I say, the shoes first awakened my suspicions, and then her story—and her veil—were a little melodramatic, eh? The Chinese box with a bogus compromising letter in the top must have been known to all the gang, but the log of wood was the late Mr. Lavington's own idea. *Eh, par exemple*, Hastings, I hope you will not again wound my feelings as you did yesterday by saying that I am unknown to the criminal classes. *Ma foi*, they even employ me when they themselves fail!"

# The Lost Mine

I LAID down my bankbook with a sigh.

"It is a curious thing," I observed, "but my overdraft never seems to grow any less."

"And it perturbs you not? Me, if I had an overdraft, never should I close my eyes all night," declared Poirot.

"You deal in comfortable balances, I suppose!" I retorted.

"Four hundred and forty-four pounds, four and fourpence," said Poirot with some complacency. "A neat figure, is it not?"

"It must be tact on the part of your bank manager. He is evidently acquainted with your passion for symmetrical details. What about investing, say three hundred of it, in the Porcupine oil fields? Their prospectus, which is advertised in the papers today, says that they will pay one hundred percent in dividends next year."

"Not for me," said Poirot, shaking his head. "I like not the sensational. For me the safe, the prudent investment—*les rentes,* the consols, the—how do you call it?—the conversion."

"Have you never made a speculative investment?"

"No, *mon ami,*" replied Poirot severely. "I have not. And the only shares I own which have not what you call the gilded edge are fourteen thousand shares in the Burma Mines, Ltd."

Poirot paused with an air of waiting to be encouraged to go on.

"Yes?" I prompted.

"And for them I paid no cash—no, they were the reward of the exercise of my little gray cells. You would like to hear the story? Yes?"

"Of course I would."

"These mines are situated in the interior of Burma about two hundred miles inland from Rangoon. They were discovered by the Chinese in the fifteenth century and worked down to the time of the Mohammedan Rebellion, being finally abandoned in the year 1868. The Chinese extracted the rich lead-silver ore from the upper part of the ore body, smelting it for the silver alone, and leaving large quantities of rich lead-bearing slag. This, of course, was soon discovered when prospecting work was carried out in Burma, but owing to the fact that the old workings had become full of loose filling and water, all attempts to find the source of the ore proved fruitless. Many parties were sent out by syndicates, and they dug over a large area, but this rich prize still eluded them. But a representative of one of the syndicates got on the track of a Chinese family who were supposed to have still kept a record of the situation of the mine. The present head of the family was one Wu Ling."

"What a fascinating page of commercial romance!" I exclaimed.

"Is it not? Ah, *mon ami*, one can have romance without golden-haired girls of matchless beauty—no, I am wrong; it is auburn hair that so excites you always. You remember—"

"Go on with the story," I said hastily.

"*Eh bien,* my friend, this Wu Ling was approached. He was an estimable merchant, much respected in the province where he lived. He admitted at once that he owned the documents in question, and was perfectly prepared to negotiate for this sale, but he objected to dealing with any other than principals. Finally it was arranged that he should journey to England and meet the directors of an important company.

"Wu Ling made the journey to England in the S.S. *Assunta,* and the *Assunta* duly docked at Southampton on a cold, foggy morning in November. One of the directors, Mr. Pearson, went down to Southampton to meet the boat, but owing to the fog, the train down was very much delayed, and by the time he arrived, Wu Ling had disembarked and left by special train for London. Mr. Pearson returned to town somewhat annoyed, as he had no idea where the Chinaman proposed to stay. Later in the day, however, the offices of the company were rung up on the telephone. Wu Ling was staying at the Russell Square Hotel. He was feeling somewhat unwell after the voyage, but declared himself perfectly able to attend the board meeting on the following day.

"The meeting of the board took place at eleven o'clock. When half-past eleven came, and Wu Ling had not put in an appearance, the secretary rang up the Russell Hotel. In answer to his inquiries, he was told that the Chinaman had gone out with a friend about half-past ten. It seemed clear that he had started out with the intention of coming to the meeting, but the morning wore away, and he did not appear. It was, of course, possible that he had lost his way, being unacquainted with London, but at a late hour that night, he had not returned to the hotel. Thoroughly alarmed now, Mr. Pearson put matters in the hands of the police. On the following day, there was still no trace of the missing man, but towards evening of the day after that again, a body was found in the Thames which proved to be that of the ill-fated Chinaman. Neither on the body, nor in the luggage at the hotel, was there any trace of the papers relating to the mine.

"At this juncture, *mon ami,* I was brought into the affair. Mr. Pearson called upon me. While profoundly shocked by the death of Wu Ling, his chief anxiety was to recover the papers which were the object of the Chinaman's visit to England. The main anxiety of the police, of course, would be to track down the murderer—the recovery of the papers would be a secondary consideration. What he wanted me to do was to coöperate with the police while acting in the interests of the company.

"I consented readily enough. It was clear that there were two fields of search open to me. On the one hand, I might look among the employees of the company who knew of the Chinaman's coming; on the other, among the passengers on the boat who might have been acquainted with his mission. I started with the second, as being a narrower field of search. In this I coincided with Inspector Miller, who was in charge of the case—a man altogether different to our friend Japp, conceited, ill-mannered and quite insufferable. Together we interviewed the officers of the ship. They had little to tell us. Wu Ling had kept much to himself on the voyage. He had been intimate with but two of the other passengers—one a broken-down European named Dyer who appeared to bear a somewhat unsavory reputation, the other a young bank clerk named Charles Lester, who was returning from Hong Kong. We were lucky enough to obtain snapshots of both these men. At the moment there seemed little doubt that if either of the two was implicated, Dyer was the man. He was known to be mixed up with a gang of Chinese crooks, and was altogether a most likely suspect.

"Our next step was to visit the Russell Square Hotel. Shown a snapshot of Wu Ling, they recognized him at once. We then showed them the snapshot of Dyer, but to our disappointment, the hall porter declared positively that that was not the man who had come to the hotel on the fatal morning. Almost as an afterthought, I produced the photograph of Lester, and to my surprise the man at once recognized it.

" 'Yes sir,' he asserted, 'that's the gentleman who came in at half-past ten and asked for Mr. Wu Ling, and afterwards went out with him.'

"The affair was progressing. Our next move was to interview Mr. Charles Lester. He met us with the utmost frankness, was desolated to hear of the Chinaman's untimely death, and put himself at our disposal in every way. His story was as follows: By arrangement with Wu Ling, he called for him at the hotel at ten-thirty. Wu Ling, however, did not appear. Instead, his servant came, explained that his master had had to go out, and offered to conduct the young man to where his master now was. Suspecting nothing, Lester agreed, and the China-man procured a taxi. They drove for some time in the direction of the docks. Suddenly becoming mistrustful, Lester stopped the taxi and got out, disregarding the servant's protests. That, he assured us, was all he knew.

"Apparently satisfied, we thanked him and took our leave. His story was soon proved to be a somewhat inaccurate one. To begin with, Wu Ling had had no servant with him, either on the boat or at the hotel. In the second place, the taxi driver who had driven the two men on that morning came forward. Far from Lester's having left the taxi en route, he and the Chinese gentleman had driven to a certain unsavory dwelling place in Limehouse, right in the heart of Chinatown. The place in question was more or less well known as an opium den of the lowest description. The two gentlemen had gone in—about an hour later the English gentleman, whom he identified from the photo-graph, came out alone. He looked very pale and ill, and directed the taximan to take him to the nearest underground station.

"Inquiries were made about Charles Lester's standing, and it was found that, though bearing an excellent character, he was heavily in debt, and had a secret passion for gambling. Dyer, of course, was not lost sight of. It seemed just faintly possible that he might have imperso-nated the other man, but that idea was proved utterly groundless. His alibi for the whole of the day in question was absolutely unimpeach-able. Of course, the proprietor of the opium den denied everything with Oriental stolidity. He had never seen Wu Ling; he had never seen Charles Lester. No two gentlemen had been to the place that morning. In any case, the police were wrong; no opium was ever smoked there.

"His denials, however well meant, did little to help Charles Lester. He was arrested for the murder of Wu Ling. A search of his effects was made, but no papers relating to the mine were discovered. The proprietor of the opium den was also taken into custody, but a cursory raid of his premises yielded nothing. Not even a stick of opium re-warded the zeal of the police.

"In the meantime my friend Mr. Pearson was in a great state of agitation. He strode up and down my room, uttering great lamenta-tions.

" 'But you must have some ideas, M. Poirot!' he kept urging. 'Surely you must have some ideas?'

" 'Certainly I have ideas,' I replied cautiously. 'That is the trouble—one has too many; therefore they all lead in different directions.'

" 'For instance?' he suggested.

" 'For instance—the taxi driver. We have only his word for it that he drove the two men to that house. That is one idea. Then—was it really that house they went to? Supposing that they left the taxi there, passed through the house and out by another entrance and went elsewhere?'

"Mr. Pearson seemed struck by that.

" 'But you do nothing but sit and think? Can't we *do* something?'

"He was of an impatient temperament, you comprehend.

" 'Monsieur,' I said with dignity, 'it is not for Hercule Poirot to run up and down the evil-smelling streets of Limehouse like a little dog of no breeding. Be calm. My agents are at work.'

"On the following day I had news for him. The two men had indeed passed through the house in question, but their real objective was a small eating house close to the river. They were seen to pass in there, and Lester came out alone.

"And then, figure to yourself, Hastings, an idea of the most unreasonable seized this Mr. Pearson! Nothing would suit him but that we should go ourselves to this eating house and make investigations. I argued and prayed, but he would not listen. He talked of disguising himself— he even suggested that I—*I* should—I hesitate to say it—should shave off my mustache! Yes, *rien que ça!* I pointed out to him that that was an idea ridiculous and absurd. One destroys not a thing of beauty wantonly. Besides, shall not a Belgian gentleman with a mustache desire to see life and smoke the opium just as readily as one without a mustache?

"*Eh bien,* he gave in on that, but he still insisted on his project. He turned up that evening—*mon Dieu,* what a figure! He wore what he called the 'pea jacket,' his chin, it was dirty and unshaved; he had a scarf of the vilest that offended the nose. And figure to yourself, he was enjoying himself! Truly, the English are mad! He made some changes in my own appearance. I permitted it. Can one argue with a maniac? We started out—after all, could I let him go alone, a child dressed up to act the charades?"

"Of course you couldn't," I replied.

"To continue—we arrived. Mr. Pearson talked English of the strangest. He represented himself to be a man of the sea. He talked of 'lubbers' and 'focselles' and I know not what. It was a low little room with many Chinese in it. We ate of peculiar dishes. *Ah, Dieu, mon estomac!*" Poirot clasped that portion of his anatomy tenderly before continuing. "Then there came to us the proprietor, a Chinaman with a face of evil smiles.

" 'You gentlemen no likee food here,' he said. 'You come for what you likee better. Piecee pipe, eh?'

"Mr. Pearson, he gave me the great kick under the table. (He had on the boots of the sea, too!) And he said: 'I don't mind if I do, John. Lead ahead.'

"The Chinaman smiled, and he took us through a door and to a cellar and through a trapdoor, and down some steps and up again into a room all full of divans and cushions of the most comfortable. We lay down and a Chinese boy took off our boots. It was the best moment of the evening. Then they brought us the opium pipes and cooked the opium pills, and we pretended to smoke and then to sleep and dream. But when we were alone, Mr. Pearson called softly to me, and immediately he began crawling along the floor. We went into another room where other people were asleep, and so on, until we heard two men talking. We stayed behind a curtain and listened. They were speaking of Wu Ling.

" 'What about the papers?' said one.

" 'Mr. Lester, he takee those,' answered the other, who was a Chinaman. 'He say, puttee them allee in safee place—where pleeceman no lookee.'

" 'Ah, but he's nabbed,' said the first one.

" 'He gettee free. Pleeceman not sure he done it.'

"There was more of the same kind of thing, then apparently the two men were coming our way, and we scuttled back to our beds.

" 'We'd better get out of here,' said Pearson, after a few minutes had elapsed. 'This place isn't healthy.'

" 'You are right, monsieur,' I agreed. 'We have played the farce long enough.'

"We succeeded in getting away, all right, paying handsomely for our smoke. Once clear of Limehouse, Pearson drew a long breath.

" 'I'm glad to get out of that,' he said. 'But it's something to be sure.'

" 'It is indeed,' I agreed. 'And I fancy that we shall not have much difficulty in finding what we want—after this evening's masquerade.'

"And there was no difficulty whatsoever," finished Poirot suddenly.

This abrupt ending seemed so extraordinary that I stared at him.

"But—but where were they?" I asked.

"In his pocket—*tout simplement.*"

"But in whose pocket?"

"Mr. Pearson's, *parbleu!*" Then, observing my look of bewilderment, he continued gently, "You do not yet see it? Mr. Pearson, like Charles Lester, was in debt. Mr. Pearson, like Charles Lester, was fond of gambling. And he conceived the idea of stealing the papers from the Chinaman. He met him all right at Southampton, came up to London with him, and took him straight to Limehouse. It was foggy that day; the Chinaman would not notice where he was going. I fancy Mr. Pearson smoked the opium fairly often down there and had some peculiar friends in consequence. I do not think he meant murder. His idea was that one of the Chinamen would impersonate Wu Ling and receive the money for the sale of the document. So far, so good! But, to the Oriental mind, it was infinitely simpler to kill Wu Ling and throw his body into the river, and Pearson's Chinese accomplices followed their own methods without consulting him. Imagine, then, what you would call the 'funk *bleu*' of M. Pearson. Someone may have seen him in the train with Wu Ling—murder is a very different thing to simple abduction.

"His salvation lies with the Chinaman who is personating Wu Ling at the Russell Square Hotel. If only the body is not discovered too soon! Probably Wu Ling had told him of the arrangement between him and Charles Lester whereby the latter was to call for him at the hotel. Pearson sees there an excellent way of diverting suspicion from himself. Charles Lester shall be the last person to be seen in company with Wu Ling. The impersonator has orders to represent himself to Lester as the servant of Wu Ling, and to bring him as speedily as possible to Limehouse. There, very likely, he was offered a drink. The drink would be suitably drugged, and when Lester emerged an hour later, he would have a very hazy impression of what had happened. So much was this the case, that as soon as Lester learned of Wu Ling's death, he loses his nerve, and denies that he ever reached Limehouse.

"By that, of course, he plays right into Pearson's hands. But is Pearson content? No—my manner disquiets him, and he determines to complete the case against Lester. So he arranges an elaborate masquerade. Me, I am to be gulled completely. Did I not say just now that he was as a child acting the charades? *Eh bien,* I play my part. He goes home rejoicing. But in the morning, Inspector Miller arrives on his doorstep. The papers are found on him; the game is up. Bitterly he regrets permitting himself to play the farce with Hercule Poirot! There was only one real difficulty in the affair."

"What was that?" I demanded curiously.

"Convincing Inspector Miller! What an animal, that! Both obstinate and imbecile. And in the end he took all the credit!"

"Too bad," I cried.

"Ah, well, I had my compensations. The other directors of the Burma Mines, Ltd., awarded me fourteen thousand shares as a small recompense for my services. Not so bad, eh? But when investing money, keep, I beg of you, Hastings, strictly to the conservative. The things you read in the paper, they may not be true. The directors of the Porcupine—they may be so many Mr. Pearsons!"

# The Chocolate Box

IT was a wild night. Outside, the wind howled malevolently, and the rain beat against the windows in great gusts.

Poirot and I sat facing the hearth, our legs stretched out to the cheerful blaze. Between us was a small table. On my side of it stood some carefully brewed hot toddy; on Poirot's was a cup of thick, rich chocolate which I would not have drunk for a hundred pounds! Poirot sipped the thick brown mess in the pink china cup, and sighed with contentment.

*"Quelle belle vie!"* he murmured.

"Yes, it's a good old world," I agreed. "Here am I with a job, and a good job too! And here are you, famous—"

"Oh, *mon ami!*" protested Poirot.

"But you are. And rightly so! When I think back on your long line of successes, I am positively amazed. I don't believe you know what failure is!"

"He would be a droll kind of original who could say that!"

"No, but seriously, *have* you ever failed?"

"Innumerable times, my friend. What would you? *La bonne chance,* it cannot always be on your side. I have been called in too late. Very often another, working toward the same goal, has arrived there first. Twice have I been stricken down with illness just as I was on the point of success. One must take the downs with the ups, my friend."

"I didn't quite mean that," I said. "I meant, had you ever been completely down and out over a case through your own fault?"

"Ah, I comprehend! You ask if I have ever made the complete prize ass of myself, as you say over here? Once, my friend—" A slow, reflective smile hovered over his face. "Yes, once I made a fool of myself."

He sat up suddenly in his chair.

"See here, my friend, you have, I know, kept a record of my little successes. You shall add one more story to the collection, the story of a failure!"

He leaned forward and placed a log on the fire. Then, after carefully wiping his hands on a little duster that hung on a nail by the fireplace, he leaned back and commenced his story.

That of which I tell you (said M. Poirot) took place in Belgium many years ago. It was at the time of the terrible struggle in France between church and state. M. Paul Déroulard was a French deputy of note. It was an open secret that the portfolio of a Minister awaited him. He was among the bitterest of the anti-Catholic party, and it was certain that on his accession to power, he would have to face violent enmity. He was in many ways a peculiar man. Though he neither drank nor smoked, he was nevertheless not so scrupulous in other ways. You comprehend, Hastings, *c'était des femmes—toujours des femmes!*

He had married some years earlier a young lady from Brussels who had brought him a substantial dot. Undoubtedly the money was useful to him in his career, as his family was not rich, though on the other hand he was entitled to call himself M. le Baron if he chose. There were no children of the marriage, and his wife died after two years— the result of a fall downstairs. Among the property which she bequeathed to him was a house on the Avenue Louise in Brussels.

It was in this house that his sudden death took place, the event coinciding with the resignation of the Minister whose portfolio he was to inherit. All the papers printed long notices of his career. His death, which had taken place quite suddenly in the evening after dinner, was attributed to heart failure.

At that time, *mon ami,* I was, as you know, a member of the Belgian detective force. The death of M. Paul Déroulard was not particularly interesting to me. I am, as you also know, *bon catholique,* and his demise seemed to me fortunate.

It was some three days afterward, when my vacation had just begun, that I received a visitor at my own apartments—a lady, heavily veiled, but evidently quite young; and I perceived at once that she was a *jeune fille tout à fait comme il faut.*

"You are Monsieur Hercule Poirot?" she asked in a low sweet voice. I bowed.

"Of the detective service?"

Again I bowed. "Be seated, I pray of you, mademoiselle," I said.

She accepted a chair and drew aside her veil. Her face was charming, though marred with tears, and haunted as though with some poignant anxiety.

"Monsieur," she said, "I understand that you are now taking a vacation. Therefore you will be free to take up a private case. You understand that I do not wish to call in the police."

I shook my head. "I fear what you ask is impossible, mademoiselle. Even though on vacation, I am still of the police."

She leaned forward. "*Écoutez, monsieur.* All that I ask of you is to investigate. The result of your investigations you are at perfect liberty to report to the police. If what I believe to be true *is* true, we shall need all the machinery of the law."

That placed a somewhat different complexion on the matter, and I placed myself at her service without more ado.

A slight color rose in her cheeks. "I thank you, monsieur. It is the death of M. Paul Déroulard that I ask you to investigate."

"*Comment?*" I exclaimed, surprised.

"Monsieur, I have nothing to go upon—nothing but my woman's instinct, but I am convinced—*convinced*, I tell you—that M. Déroulard did not die a natural death!"

"But surely the doctors—"

"Doctors may be mistaken. He was so robust, so strong. Ah, Monsieur Poirot, I beseech of you to help me—"

The poor child was almost beside herself. She would have knelt to me. I soothed her as best I could.

"I will help you, mademoiselle. I feel almost sure that your fears are unfounded, but we will see. First, I will ask you to describe to me the inmates of the house."

"There are the domestics, of course, Jeannette, Félicie, and Denise, the cook. She has been there many years; the others are simple country girls. Also there is François, but he too is an old servant. Then there is Monsieur Déroulard's mother who lived with him, and myself. My name is Virginie Mesnard. I am a poor cousin of the late Madame Déroulard, M. Paul's wife, and I have been a member of their ménage for over three years. I have now described to you the household. There were also two guests staying in the house."

"And they were?"

"M. de Saint Alard, a neighbor of M. Déroulard's in France. Also an English friend, Mr. John Wilson."

"Are they still with you?"

"Mr. Wilson, yes, but M. de Saint Alard departed yesterday."

"And what is your plan, Mademoiselle Mesnard?"

"If you will present yourself at the house in half an hour's time, I will have arranged some story to account for your presence. I had better represent you to be connected with journalism in some way. I shall say you have come from Paris, and that you have brought a card of introduction from M. de Saint Alard. Madame Déroulard is very feeble in health, and will pay little attention to details."

On mademoiselle's ingenious pretext I was admitted to the house, and after a brief interview with the dead deputy's mother, who was a wonderfully imposing and aristocratic figure though obviously in failing health, I was made free of the premises.

I wonder, my friend (continued Poirot), whether you can possibly figure to yourself the difficulties of my task? Here was a man whose death had taken place three days previously. If there *had* been foul play, only one possibility was admittable—*poison!* And I had had no chance of seeing the body, and there was no possibility of examining, or analyzing, any medium in which the poison could have been administered. There were no clues, false or otherwise, to consider. Had the man been poisoned? Had he died a natural death? I, Hercule Poirot, with nothing to help me, had to decide.

First, I interviewed the domestics, and with their aid, I recapitulated the evening. I paid especial notice to the food at dinner, and the method of serving it. The soup had been served by M. Déroulard himself from a tureen. Next a dish of cutlets, then a chicken. Finally a compote of fruits. And all placed on the table, and served by monsieur himself. The coffee was brought in a big pot to the dinner table. Nothing there, *mon ami*—impossible to poison one without poisoning all!

After dinner Madame Déroulard had retired to her own apartments and Mademoiselle Virginie had accompanied her. The three men had adjourned to M. Déroulard's study. Here they had chatted amicably for some time, when suddenly, without any warning, the deputy had fallen heavily to the ground. M. de Saint Alard had rushed out and told François to fetch a doctor immediately. He said it was without doubt an apoplexy, explained the man. But when the doctor arrived, the patient was past help.

Mr. John Wilson, to whom I was presented by Mademoiselle Virginie, was what was known in those days as a regular John Bull Englishman, middle-aged and burly. His account, delivered in very British French, was substantially the same.

"Déroulard went very red in the face, and down he fell."

There was nothing further to be found out there. Next I went to the scene of the tragedy, the study, and was left alone there at my own request. So far there was nothing to support Mademoiselle Mesnard's theory. I could not but believe that it was a delusion on her part. Evidently she had entertained a romantic passion for the dead man which had not permitted her to take a normal view of the case. Nevertheless, I searched the study with meticulous care. It was just possible that a hypodermic needle might have been introduced into the dead man's chair in such a way as to allow of a fatal injection. The minute puncture it would cause was likely to remain unnoticed. But I could discover no sign to support that theory. I flung myself down in the chair with a gesture of despair.

"*Enfin,* I abandon it!" I said aloud. "There is not a clue anywhere! Everything is perfectly normal."

As I said the words, my eyes fell on a large box of chocolates standing on a table near by, and my heart gave a leap. It might not be a clue to M. Déroulard's death, but here at least was something that was *not* normal. I lifted the lid. The box was full, untouched; not a chocolate was missing—but that only made the peculiarity that had caught my eye more striking. For, see you, Hastings, while the box itself was pink, the lid was *blue.* Now, one often sees a blue ribbon on a pink box, and vice versa, but a box of one color, and a lid of another—no, decidedly—*ça ne se voit jamais!*

I did not as yet see that this little incident was of any use to me, yet I determined to investigate it as being out of the ordinary. I rang the bell for François, and asked him if his late master had been fond of sweets. A faint melancholy smile came to his lips.

"Passionately fond of them, monsieur. He would always have a box of chocolates in the house. He did not drink wine of any kind, you see."

"Yet this box has not been touched?" I lifted the lid to show him.

"Pardon, monsieur, but that was a new box purchased on the day of his death, the other being nearly finished."

"Then the other box was finished on the day of his death," I said slowly.

"Yes, monsieur, I found it empty in the morning and threw it away."

"Did M. Déroulard eat sweets at all hours of the day?"

"Usually after dinner, monsieur."

I began to see light.

"François," I said, "you can be discreet?"

"If there is need, monsieur."

"*Bon!* Know, then, that I am of the police. Can you find me that other box?"

"Without doubt, monsieur. It will be in the dust bin."

He departed, and returned in a few minutes with a dust-covered object. It was the duplicate of the box I held, save for the fact that this time the box was *blue* and the lid was *pink.* I thanked François, recommended him once more to be discreet, and left the house in the Avenue Louise without more ado.

Next I called upon the doctor who had attended M. Déroulard. With him I had a difficult task. He entrenched himself prettily behind a wall of learned phraseology, but I fancied that he was not quite as sure about the case as he would like to be.

"There have been many curious occurrences of the kind," he observed, when I had managed to disarm him somewhat. "A sudden fit of anger, a violent emotion,—after a heavy dinner, *c'est entendu,*— then, with an access of rage, the blood flies to the head, and *pst!*— there you are!"

"But M. Déroulard had had no violent emotion."

"No? I made sure that he had been having a stormy altercation with M. de Saint Alard."

"Why should he?"

"*C'est évident!*" The doctor shrugged his shoulders. "Was not M. de Saint Alard a Catholic of the most fanatical? Their friendship was being ruined by this question of church and state. Not a day passed without discussions. To M. de Saint Alard, Déroulard appeared almost as Antichrist."

This was unexpected, and gave me food for thought.

"One more question, Doctor: would it be possible to introduce a fatal dose of poison into a chocolate?"

"It would be possible, I suppose," said the doctor slowly. "Pure prussic acid would meet the case if there were no chance of evaporation, and a tiny globule of anything might be swallowed unnoticed—but it does not seem a very likely supposition. A chocolate full of morphine or strychnine—" He made a wry face. "You comprehend, M. Poirot—one bite would be enough! The unwary one would not stand upon ceremony."

"Thank you, M. le Docteur."

I withdrew. Next I made inquiries of the chemists, especially those in the neighborhood of the Avenue Louise. It is good to be of the police. I got the information I wanted without any trouble. Only in one case could I hear of any poison having been supplied to the house in question. This was some eye drops of atropine sulphate for Madame Déroulard. Atropine is a potent poison, and for the moment I was elated, but the symptoms of atropine poisoning are closely allied to those of ptomaine, and bear no resemblance to those I was studying. Besides, the prescription was an old one. Madame Déroulard had suffered from cataract in both eyes for many years.

I was turning away discouraged when the chemist's voice called me back.

"*Un moment,* M. Poirot. I remember, the girl who brought that prescription, she said something about having to go on to the *English* chemist. You might try there."

I did. Once more enforcing my official status, I got the information I wanted. On the day before M. Déroulard's death they had made up a prescription for Mr. John Wilson. Not that there was any making up about it. They were simply little tablets of trinitrin. I asked if I might see some. He showed me them, and my heart beat faster—for the tiny tablets were of *chocolate*.

"It is a poison?" I asked.

"No, monsieur."

"Can you describe to me its effect?"

"It lowers the blood pressure. It is given for some forms of heart trouble—angina pectoris for instance. It relieves the arterial tension. In arteriosclerosis—"

I interrupted him. *"Ma foi!* This rigmarole says nothing to me. Does it cause the face to flush?"

"Certainly it does."

"And supposing I ate ten—twenty of your little tablets, what then?"

"I should not advise you to attempt it," he replied dryly.

"And yet you say it is not poison?"

"There are many things not called poison which can kill a man," he replied as before.

I left the shop elated. At last, things had begun to march!

I now knew that John Wilson held the means for the crime—but what about the motive? He had come to Belgium on business, and had asked M. Déroulard, whom he knew slightly, to put him up. There was apparently no way in which Déroulard's death could benefit him. Moreover, I discovered by inquiries in England that he had suffered for some years from that painful form of heart disease known as angina. Therefore he had a genuine right to have those tablets in his possession. Nevertheless, I was convinced that someone had gone to the chocolate box, opening the full one first by mistake, and had abstracted the contents of the last chocolate, cramming in instead as many little trinitrin tablets as it would hold. The chocolates were large ones. Between twenty or thirty tablets, I felt sure, could have been inserted. But who had done this?

There were two guests in the house. John Wilson had the means. Saint Alard had the motive. Remember, he was a fanatic, and there is no fanatic like a religious fanatic. Could he, by any means, have got hold of John Wilson's trinitrin?

Another little idea came to me. Ah! You smile at my little ideas! Why had Wilson run out of trinitrin? Surely he would bring an adequate supply from England. I called once more at the house in the Avenue Louise. Wilson was out, but I saw the girl who did his room, Félicie. I demanded of her immediately whether it was not true that M. Wilson had lost a bottle from his washstand some little time ago. The girl responded eagerly. It was quite true. She, Félicie, had been blamed for it. The English gentleman had evidently thought that she had broken it, and did not like to say so. Whereas she had never even touched it. Without doubt it was Jeannette—always nosing round where she had no business to be—

I calmed the flow of words, and took my leave. I knew now all that I wanted to know. It remained for me to prove my case. That, I felt, would not be easy. *I* might be sure that Saint Alard had removed the bottle of trinitrin from John Wilson's washstand, but to convince others, I would have to produce evidence. And I had none to produce!

Never mind. I *knew*—that was the great thing. You remember our difficulty in the Styles case, Hastings? There again, I *knew*—but it took me a long time to find the last link which made my chain of evidence against the murderer complete.

I asked for an interview with Mademoiselle Mesnard. She came at once. I demanded of her the address of M. de Saint Alard. A look of trouble came over her face.

"Why do you want it, monsieur?"

"Mademoiselle, it is necessary."

She seemed doubtful—troubled.

"He can tell you nothing. He is a man whose thoughts are not in this world. He hardly notices what goes on around him."

"Possibly, mademoiselle. Nevertheless, he was an old friend of M. Déroulard's. There may be things he can tell me—things of the past— old grudges—old love affairs."

The girl flushed and bit her lip. "As you please—but—but—I feel sure now that I have been mistaken. It was good of you to accede to my demand, but I was upset—almost distraught at the time. I see now that there is no mystery to solve. Leave it, I beg of you, monsieur."

I eyed her closely.

"Mademoiselle," I said, "it is sometimes difficult for a dog to find a scent, but once he *has* found it, nothing on earth will make him leave it! That is if he is a good dog! And I, mademoiselle, I, Hercule Poirot, am a very good dog."

Without a word she turned away. A few minutes later she returned with the address written on a sheet of paper. I left the house. François was waiting for me outside. He looked at me anxiously.

"There is no news, monsieur?"

"None as yet, my friend."

"Ah! *Pauvre* Monsieur Déroulard!" he sighed. "I too was of his way of thinking. I do not care for priests. Not that I would say so in the house. The women are all devout—a good thing perhaps. *Madame est très pieuse—et Mademoiselle Virginie aussi.*"

Mademoiselle Virginie? Was she *"très pieuse?"* Thinking of the tear-stained passionate face I had seen that first day, I wondered.

Having obtained the address of M. de Saint Alard, I wasted no time. I arrived in the neighborhood of his château in the Ardennes but it was some days before I could find a pretext for gaining admission to the house. In the end I did—how do you think—as a plumber, *mon ami!* It was the affair of a moment to arrange a neat little gas leak in his bedroom. I departed for my tools, and took care to return with them at an hour when I knew I should have the field pretty well to myself. What I was searching for, I hardly knew. The one thing needful,

I could not believe there was any chance of finding. He would never have run the risk of keeping it.

Still when I found a little cupboard above the washstand locked, I could not resist the temptation of seeing what was inside it. The lock was quite a simple one to pick. The door swung open. It was full of old bottles. I took them up one by one with a trembling hand. Suddenly, I uttered a cry. Figure to yourself, my friend, I held in my hand a little phial with an English chemist's label. On it were the words: *"Trinitrin Tablets. One to be taken when required. Mr. John Wilson."*

I controlled my emotion, closed the cupboard, slipped the bottle into my pocket, and continued to repair the gas leak! One must be methodical. Then I left the château, and took train for my own country as soon as possible. I arrived in Brussels late that night. I was writing out a report for the *préfet* in the morning, when a note was brought to me. It was from old Madame Déroulard, and it summoned me to the house in the Avenue Louise without delay.

François opened the door to me.

"Madame la Baronne is waiting for you."

He conducted me to her apartments. She sat in state in a large armchair. There was no sign of Mademoiselle Virginie.

"M. Poirot," said the old lady. "I have just learned that you are not what you pretended to be. You are a police officer."

"That is so, madame."

"You came here to inquire into the circumstances of my son's death?"

Again I replied, "That is so, madame."

"I should be glad if you would tell me what progress you have made."

I hesitated.

"First I would like to know how you have learned all this, madame."

"From one who is no longer of this world."

Her words, and the brooding way she uttered them, sent a chill to my heart. I was incapable of speech.

"Therefore, monsieur, I would beg of you most urgently to tell me exactly what progress you have made in your investigation."

"Madame, my investigation is finished."

"My son?"

"Was killed deliberately."

"You know by whom?"

"Yes, madame."

"Who, then?"

"M. de Saint Alard."

The old lady shook her head.

"You are wrong. M. de Saint Alard is incapable of such a crime."

"The proofs are in my hands."

"I beg of you once more to tell me all."

This time I obeyed, going over each step that had led me to the discovery of the truth. She listened attentively. At the end she nodded her head.

"Yes, yes, it is all as you say, all but one thing. It was not M. de Saint Alard who killed my son. It was I, his mother."

I stared at her. She continued to nod her head gently.

"It is well that I sent for you. It is the providence of the good God that Virginie told me before she departed for the convent, what she had done. Listen, M. Poirot! My son was an evil man. He persecuted the church. He led a life of mortal sin. He dragged down other souls beside his own. But there was worse than that. As I came out of my room in this house one morning, I saw my daughter-in-law standing at the head of the stairs. She was reading a letter. I saw my son steal up behind her. One swift push, and she fell, striking her head on the marble steps. When they picked her up she was dead. My son was a murderer, and only I, his mother, knew it."

She closed her eyes for a moment. "You cannot conceive, monsieur, of my agony, my despair. What was I to do? Denounce him to the police? I could not bring myself to do it. It was my duty, but my flesh was weak. Besides, would they believe me? My eyesight had been failing for some time—they would say I was mistaken. I kept silence. But my conscience gave me no peace. By keeping silence I too was a murderer. My son inherited his wife's money. He flourished as the green bay tree. And now he was to have a Minister's portfolio. His persecution of the church would be redoubled. And there was Virginie. She, poor child, beautiful, naturally pious, was fascinated by him. He had a strange and terrible power over women. I saw it coming. I was powerless to prevent it. He had no intention of marrying her. The time came when she was ready to yield everything to him.

"Then I saw my path clear. He was my son. I had given him life. I was responsible for him. He had killed one woman's body, now he would kill another's soul! I went to Mr. Wilson's room, and took the bottle of tablets. He had once said laughingly that there were enough in it to kill a man! I went into the study and opened the big box of chocolates that always stood on the table. I opened a new box by mistake. The other was on the table also. There was just one chocolate left in it. That simplified things. No one ate chocolates except my son and Virginie. I would keep her with me that night. All went as I had planned—"

She paused, closing her eyes a minute then opened them again.

"M. Poirot, I am in your hands. They tell me I have not many days to live. I am willing to answer for my action before the good God. Must I answer for it on earth also?"

I hesitated. "But the empty bottle, madame," I said to gain time. "How came that into M. de Saint Alard's possession?"

"When he came to say good-by to me, monsieur, I slipped it into his pocket. I did not know how to get rid of it. I am so infirm that I cannot move about much without help, and finding it empty in my rooms might have caused suspicion. You understand, monsieur,"—she drew herself up to her full height,—"it was with no idea of casting suspicion on M. de Saint Alard! I never dreamed of such a thing. I thought his valet would find an empty bottle and throw it away without question."

I bowed my head. "I comprehend, madame," I said.

"And your decision, monsieur?"

Her voice was firm and unfaltering, her head held as high as ever. I rose to my feet.

"Madame," I said, "I have the honor to wish you good day. I have made my investigations—and failed! The matter is closed."

He was silent for a moment, then said quietly: "She died just a week later. Mademoiselle Virginie passed through her novitiate, and duly took the veil. That, my friend, is the story. I must admit that I do not make a fine figure in it."

"But that was hardly a failure," I expostulated. "What else could you have thought under the circumstances?"

"*Ah, sacré, mon ami,*" cried Poirot, becoming suddenly animated. "Is it that you do not see? But I was thirty-six times an idiot! My gray cells, they functioned not at all. The whole time I had the true clue in my hands."

"What clue?"

"*The chocolate box!* Do you not see? Would anyone in possession of their full eyesight make such a mistake? I knew Madame Déroulard had cataracts—the atropine drops told me that. There was only one person in the household whose eyesight was such that she could not see which lid to replace. It was the chocolate box that started me on the track, and yet up to the end I failed consistently to perceive its real significance!

"Also my psychology was at fault. Had M. de Saint Alard been the criminal, he would never have kept an incriminating bottle. Finding it was a proof of his innocence. I had learned already from Mademoiselle Virginie that he was absent-minded. Altogether it was a miserable affair that I have recounted to you there! Only to you have I told the story. You comprehend, I do not figure well in it! An old lady commits a crime in such a simple and clever fashion that I, Hercule

Poirot, am completely deceived. *Sapristi!* it does not bear thinking of! Forget it. Or no—remember it, and if you think at any time that I am growing conceited—it is not likely, but it might arise."

I concealed a smile.

"*Eh bien,* my friend, you shall say to me, 'Chocolate box.' Is it agreed?"

"It's a bargain!"

"After all," said Poirot reflectively, "it was an experience! I, who have undoubtedly the finest brain in Europe at present, can afford to be magnanimous!"

"Chocolate box," I murmured gently.

"*Pardon, mon ami?*"

I looked at Poirot's innocent face, as he bent forward inquiringly, and my heart smote me. I had suffered often at his hands, but I, too, though not possessing the finest brain in Europe, could afford to be magnanimous!

"Nothing," I lied, and lit another pipe, smiling to myself.

# DEAD
# MAN'S
# MIRROR

# Dead Man's Mirror

## I

THE flat was a modern one. The furnishings of the room were modern, too. The armchairs were squarely built, the upright chairs were angular. A modern writing table was set squarely in front of the window and at it sat a small, elderly man. His head was practically the only thing in the room that was not square. It was egg-shaped.

M. Hercule Poirot was reading a letter:

Station: Whimperley.
Telegrams: Harborough
  St. John.

Hamborough Close,
Hamborough St. Mary,
Westshire.

September 24th, 1936.

M. Hercule Poirot,

Dear Sir,

    A matter has arisen which requires handling with great delicacy and discretion. I have heard good accounts of you and have decided to entrust the matter to you. I have reason to believe that I am the victim of fraud, but for family reasons I do not wish to call in the police. I am taking certain measures of my own to deal with the business, but you must be prepared to come down here immediately on receipt of a telegram. I should be obliged if you will not answer this letter.

Yours faithfully,

Gervase Chevenix-Gore.

The eyebrows of M. Hercule Poirot climbed slowly up his forehead until they nearly disappeared into his hair.

"And who, then," he demanded of space, "is this Gervase Chevenix-Gore?"

He crossed to a bookcase and took out a large, fat book.

He found what he wanted easily enough:

Chevenix-Gore, Sir Gervase Francis Xavier, 10th Bt. cr. 1694; formerly Captain 17th Lancer; b. 18th May 1878; e.s. of Sir Guy Chevenix-Gore, 9th Bt. and Lady Claudia Bretherton, 2nd d. of 8th Earl of Wallingford. S. father, 1911; m. 1912, Vanda Elizabeth, e.d. of Colonel Frederick Arbuthnot, q.v.; educ. Eton. Served European War 1914–18. Recreations: traveling, big game hunting. Address: Hamborough Close, Hamborough St. Mary, Westshire, and 218 Lowndes Square, S.W.1. Clubs: Cavalry, Travelers.

Poirot shook his head in a slightly dissatisfied manner. For a moment or two he remained lost in thought, then he went to the desk, pulled open a drawer, and took out a little pile of invitation cards.

His face brightened.

"*A la bonne heure!* Exactly my affair! He will certainly be there."

A Duchess greeted M. Hercule Poirot in fulsome tones:

"So you could manage to come after all, M. Poirot! Why, that's splendid."

"The pleasure is mine, madame," murmured Poirot, bowing.

He escaped from several important and splendid beings—a famous diplomat, an equally famous actress, and a well known sporting peer—and found at last the person he had come to seek, that invariably "also present" guest, Mr. Satterthwaite.

Mr. Satterthwaite twittered amiably:

"The dear Duchess—I always enjoy her parties. . . . Such a *personality*, if you know what I mean. I saw a lot of her in Corsica some years ago. . . ."

Mr. Satterthwaite's conversation was apt to be unduly burdened by mentions of his titled acquaintances. It is possible that he *may* sometimes have found pleasure in the company of Messrs. Jones, Brown, or Robinson, but if so, he did not mention the fact. And yet, to describe Mr. Satterthwaite as a mere snob and leave it at that would have been to do him an injustice. He was a keen observer of human nature, and if it is true that the looker-on knows most of the game, Mr. Satterthwaite knew a good deal.

"You know, my dear fellow, it is really ages since I saw you. I always feel myself privileged to have seen you work at close quarters in the crow's-nest business. I feel since then that I am in the know, so to speak. I saw Lady Mary only last week, by the way. A charming creature—potpourri and lavender!"

After passing lightly on one or two scandals of the moment—the indiscretions of an earl's daughter and the lamentable conduct of a viscount—Poirot succeeded in introducing the name of Gervase Chevenix-Gore.

Mr. Satterthwaite responded immediately:

"Ah! Now, there *is* a character, if you like! The Last of the Baronets—that's his nickname."

*"Pardon,* I do not quite comprehend—?"

Mr. Satterthwaite unbent indulgently to the lower comprehension of a foreigner.

"It's a joke, you know—a *joke.* Naturally, he's not *really* the last Baronet in England—but he *does* represent the end of an era. The Bold Bad Baronet—the mad harum-scarum Baronet so popular in the novels of the last century—the kind of fellow who laid impossible wagers and won 'em."

He went on to expound what he meant in more detail. In younger years, Gervase Chevenix-Gore had sailed round the world in a windjammer. He had been on an expedition to the Pole; he had challenged a racing peer to a duel. For a wager he had ridden his favorite mare up the staircase of a ducal house. He had once leapt from a box to the stage and carried off a well-known actress in the middle of her rôle. The anecdotes of him were innumerable.

"It's an old family," went on Mr. Satterthwaite. "Sir Guy Chevenix-Gore went on the first crusade. Now, alas, the line looks like coming to an end. Old Gervase is the last Chevenix-Gore."

"The estate, it is impoverished?"

"Not a bit of it. Gervase is fabulously wealthy. Owns valuable house property—coal fields—and in addition, he staked out a claim to some mine in Peru or somewhere in South America, when he was a young man, which has yielded him a fortune. An amazing man. Always fortunate in everything he's undertaken."

"He is now an elderly man, of course?"

"Yes, poor old Gervase." Mr. Satterthwaite sighed, shook his head. "Most people would describe him to you as mad as a hatter. It's true, in a way. He *is* mad—not in the sense of being certifiable or having delusions—but mad in the sense of being abnormal. He's always been a man of great originality of character."

"And originality becomes eccentricity as the years go by?" suggested Poirot.

"Very true. That's exactly what's happened to poor old Gervase."

"He has, perhaps, a swollen idea of his own importance?"

"Absolutely. I should imagine that, in Gervase's mind, the world has always been divided into two parts—the Chevenix-Gores—and the other people!"

"An exaggerated sense of family!"

"Yes. The Chevenix-Gores are all arrogant as the devil—a law unto themselves. Gervase, being the last of them, has got it badly. He is— well, really, you know, to hear him talk, you might imagine him to be—er, the Almighty!"

Poirot nodded his head slowly and thoughtfully.

"Yes, I imagined that. I have had, you see, a letter from him. It was an unusual letter. It did not demand. It summoned!"

"A royal command," said Mr. Satterthwaite, tittering a little.

"Precisely. It did not seem to occur to this Sir Gervase that I, Hercule Poirot, am a man of importance, a man of infinite affairs! That it was extremely unlikely that I should be able to fling everything aside and come hastening like an obedient dog—like a mere nobody, gratified to receive a commission!"

Mr. Satterthwaite bit his lip in an effort to suppress a smile. It may have occurred to him that where egoism was concerned, there was not much to choose between Hercule Poirot and Gervase Chevenix-Gore.

He murmured:

"Of course, if the cause of the summons was urgent—?"

"It was not!" Poirot's hands rose in the air in an emphatic gesture. "I was to hold myself at his disposition, that was all, *in case* he should require me! *Enfin, je vous demande!*"

Again the hands rose eloquently, expressing better than words could do M. Hercule Poirot's sense of utter outrage.

"I take it," said Mr. Satterthwaite, "that you refused?"

"I have not yet had the opportunity," said Poirot slowly.

"But you will refuse?"

A new expression passed over the little man's face. His brow furrowed itself perplexedly.

He said:

"How can I express myself? To refuse—yes, that was my first instinct. But I do not know. . . . One has, sometimes, a feeling. Faintly, I seem to smell the fish. . . ."

Mr. Satterthwaite received this last statement without any sign of amusement.

"Oh?" he said. "That is interesting. . . ."

"It seems to me," went on Hercule Poirot, "that a man such as you have described might be very vulnerable—"

"Vulnerable?" queried Mr. Satterthwaite. For the moment he was surprised. The word was not one that he would naturally have associ- ated with Gervase Chevenix-Gore. But he was a man of perception, quick in observation. He said slowly,

"I think—I see what you mean."

"Such a one is encased, is he not, in an armor—such an armor! The armor of the crusaders was nothing to it—an armor of arrogance, of pride, of complete self-esteem. This armor, it is in some ways a protection, the arrows, the everyday arrows of life glance off it. But there is this danger. *Sometimes a man in armor might not even know he was being attacked.* He will be slow to see, slow to hear—slower still to feel."

He paused, then asked with a change of manner:

"Of what does the family of this Sir Gervase consist?"

"There's Vanda—his wife. She was an Arbuthnot—very handsome girl. She's still quite a handsome woman. Frightfully vague, though. Devoted to Gervase. She's got a leaning towards the occult, I believe. Wears amulets and scarabs and gives out that she's the reincarnation of an Egyptian Queen. . . . Then there's Ruth—she's their adopted daughter. They've no children of their own. Very attractive girl in the modern style. That's all the family. Except, of course, for Hugo Trent. He's Gervase's nephew. Pamela Chevenix-Gore married Reggie Trent and Hugo was their only child. He's an orphan. He can't inherit the title, of course, but I imagine he'll come in for most of Gervase's money in the end. Good-looking lad; he's in the Blues."

Poirot nodded his head thoughtfully. Then he asked:

"It is a grief to Sir Gervase, yes, that he has no son to inherit his name?"

"I should imagine that it cuts pretty deep."

"The family name, it is a passion with him?"

"Yes."

Mr. Satterthwaite was silent a moment or two. He was very intrigued. Finally he ventured:

"You see a definite reason for going down to Hamborough Close?"

Slowly, Poirot shook his head.

"No," he said. "As far as I can see, there is no reason at all. But all the same, I fancy I shall go."


# II

Hercule Poirot sat in the corner of a first-class carriage speeding through the English countryside.

Meditatively he took from his pocket a neatly folded telegram, which he opened and re-read.

Take 4.30 from St. Pancras instruct guard have express stopped at Whimperley. Chevenix-Gore.

He folded up the telegram again and put it back in his pocket.

The guard on the train had been obsequious. The gentleman was going to Hamborough Close? Oh, yes, Sir Gervase Chevenix-Gore's guests always had the express stopped at Whimperley. "A special kind of prerogative I think it is, sir."

Since then the guard had paid two visits to the carriage: the first in order to assure the traveler that everything would be done to keep the carriage for himself, the second to announce that the express was running ten minutes late.

The train was due to arrive at 7.50, but it was exactly two minutes past eight when Hercule Poirot descended onto the platform of the little country station and pressed the expected half-crown in the attentive guard's hand.

There was a whistle from the engine and the Northern Express began to move once more. A tall chauffeur in a dark green uniform stepped up to Poirot.

"Mr. Poirot? For Hamborough Close?"

He picked up the detective's neat valise and led the way out of the station. A big Rolls was waiting. The chauffeur held the door open for Poirot to get in, arranged a sumptuous fur rug over his knees and they drove off.

After some ten minutes of cross-country driving, round sharp corners and down country lanes, the car turned in at a wide gateway flanked with huge stone griffons.

They drove through a park and up to the house. The door of it was opened as they drew up, and a butler of imposing proportions showed himself upon the front step.

"Mr. Poirot? This way, sir."

He led the way along the hall and threw open a door halfway along it on the right.

"Mr. Hercule Poirot," he announced.

The room contained a number of people in evening dress, and as Poirot walked in, his quick eyes perceived at once that his appearance was not expected. The eyes of all present rested on him in unfeigned surprise.

Then a tall woman, whose dark hair was threaded with gray, made an uncertain advance towards him.

Poirot bowed over her hand.

"My apologies, madame," he said. "I fear that my train was late."

"Not at all," said Lady Chevenix-Gore vaguely. Her eyes still stared at him in a puzzled fashion. "Not at all, Mr.—er—I didn't quite hear—"

"Hercule Poirot."

He said the name clearly and distinctly.

Somewhere behind him he heard a sudden sharp intake of breath.

At the same time he realized clearly that his host could not be in the room. He murmured gently:

"You knew I was coming, madame?"

"Oh—oh, yes. . . ." Her manner was not convincing. "I think—I mean I suppose so, but I am so terribly impractical, M. Poirot. I forget everything." Her tone held a melancholy pleasure in the fact. "I am told things. I appear to take them in—but they just pass through my brain and are gone! Vanished! As though they had never been."

Then, with a slight air of performing a duty long overdue, she glanced round her vaguely and murmured:

"I expect you know everybody."

Though this was patently not the case, the phrase was clearly a well-worn formula by means of which Lady Chevenix-Gore spared herself the trouble of introduction and the strain of remembering people's right names.

Making a supreme effort to meet the difficulties of this particular case, she added:

"My daughter—Ruth."

The girl who stood before him was also tall and dark, but she was of a very different type. Instead of the flattish, indeterminate features of Lady Chevenix-Gore, she had a well-chiseled nose, slightly aquiline, and a clear, sharp line of jaw. Her black hair swept back from her face into a mass of little tight curls. Her coloring was of carnation clearness and brilliance and owed little to make-up. She was, so Hercule Poirot thought, one of the loveliest girls he had seen.

He recognized, too, that she had brains as well as beauty, and guessed at certain qualities of pride and temper. Her voice, when she spoke, came with a slight drawl that struck him as deliberately put on.

"How exciting," she said, "to entertain M. Hercule Poirot! The Old Man arranged a little surprise for us, I suppose."

"So you did not know I was coming, mademoiselle?" he said quickly.

"I hadn't an idea of it. As it is, I must postpone getting my autograph book until after dinner."

The notes of a gong sounded from the hall, then the butler opened the door and announced:

"Dinner is served."

And then, almost before the last word, "served," had been uttered, something very curious happened. The pontifical domestic figure became, just for one moment, a highly astonished human being. . . .

The metamorphosis was so quick, and the mask of the well-trained servant was back again so soon, that anyone who had not happened to be looking would not have noticed the change. Poirot, however, *had* happened to be looking. He wondered.

The butler hesitated in the doorway. Though his face was again correctly expressionless, an air of tension hung about his figure.

Lady Chevenix-Gore said uncertainly:

"Oh, dear—this is most extraordinary—really, I—one hardly knows what to do."

Ruth said to Poirot:

"This singular consternation, M. Poirot, is occasioned by the fact that my father, for the first time for at least twenty years, is late for dinner."

"It is most extraordinary—" wailed Lady Chevenix-Gore. "Gervase never—"

An elderly man of upright soldierly carriage came to her side. He laughed genially.

"Good old Gervase! Late at last! Upon my word, we'll rag him over this. Elusive collar-stud, d'you think? Or is Gervase immune from our common weaknesses?"

Lady Chevenix-Gore said in a low, puzzled voice:

"But Gervase is *never* late."

It was almost ludicrous, the consternation caused by this simple *contretemps*. And yet, to Hercule Poirot, it was *not* ludicrous. . . . Behind the consternation he felt uneasiness—perhaps even apprehension. And he, too, found it strange that Gervase Chevenix-Gore should not appear to greet the guest he had summoned in such a mysterious manner.

In the meantime, it was clear that nobody knew quite what to do. An unprecedented situation had arisen with which nobody knew how to deal.

Lady Chevenix-Gore at last took the initiative, if initiative it could be called. Certainly her manner was vague in the extreme.

"Snell," she said, "is your master—?"

She did not finish the sentence, merely looked at the butler expectantly.

Snell, who was clearly used to his mistress's methods of seeking information, replied promptly to the unspecified question.

"Sir Gervase came downstairs at five minutes to eight, m'lady, and went straight to the study."

"Oh, I see—" Her mouth remained open, her eyes seemed far away. "You don't think—I mean—he heard the gong?"

"I think he must have done so, m'lady, the gong being immediately outside the study door. I did not, of course, know that Sir Gervase was still in the study, otherwise I should have announced to him that dinner was ready. Shall I do so now, m'lady?"

Lady Chevenix-Gore seized on the suggestion with manifest relief.

"Oh, thank you, Snell. Yes, please do. Yes, certainly."

She said, as the butler left the room:

"Snell is such a treasure. I rely on him absolutely. I really don't know what I should *do* without Snell."

Somebody murmured a sympathetic assent, but nobody spoke. Hercule Poirot, watching that room full of people with suddenly sharpened attention, had an idea that one and all were in a state of tension. His eyes ran quickly over them, tabulating them roughly. Two elderly men, the soldierly one who had spoken just now, and a thin, spare, gray-haired man with closely pinched legal lips. Two youngish men—very different in type from each other. One with a mustache and an air of modest arrogance, he guessed to be possibly Sir Gervase's nephew, the one in the Blues. The other, with sleek brushed-back hair and a rather obvious style of good looks, he put down as of a definitely inferior social class. There was a small middle-aged woman with pince-nez and intelligent eyes, and there was a girl with flaming red hair.

Snell appeared at the door. His manner was perfect, but once again the veneer of the impersonal butler showed signs of the perturbed human being beneath the surface.

"Excuse me, m'lady, the study door is locked."

"Locked?"

It was a man's voice—young, alert, with a ring of excitement in it. It was the good-looking young man with the slicked-back hair who had spoken. He went on, hurrying forward:

"Shall I go and see —?"

But very quietly, Hercule Poirot took command. He did it so naturally that no one thought it odd that this stranger, who had just arrived, should suddenly assume charge of the situation.

"Come," he said. "Let us go to the study."

He continued, speaking to Snell:

"Lead the way, if you please."

Snell obeyed. Poirot followed close behind him and, like a flock of sheep, everyone else followed.

Snell led the way through the big hall, past the great branching curve of the staircase, past an enormous grandfather clock and a recess in which stood a gong, along a narrow passage which ended in a door.

Here Poirot passed Snell and gently tried the handle. It turned, but the door did not open. Poirot rapped gently with his knuckles on the panel of the door. He rapped louder and louder. Then, suddenly desisting, he dropped to his knees and applied his eye to the keyhole.

Slowly he rose to his feet and looked round. His face was stern.

"Gentlemen," he said, "this door must be broken open immediately!"

Under his direction the two young men, who were both tall and powerfully built, attacked the door. It was no easy matter. The doors of Hamborough Close were solidly built.

At last, however, the lock gave, and the door swung inwards with a noise of splintering, rending wood.

And then, for a moment, everyone stood still, huddled in the doorway looking at the scene inside. The lights were on. Along the left-hand wall was a big writing table, a massive affair of solid mahogany. Sitting, not at the table, but sideways to it, so that his back was directly towards them, was a big man slouched down in a chair. His head and the upper part of his body hung down over the right side of the chair, and his right hand and arm hung limply down. Just below it on the carpet was a small, gleaming pistol. . . .

There was no need of speculation. The picture was clear. Sir Gervase Chevenix-Gore had shot himself.

# III

For a moment or two, the group in the doorway stood motionless, staring at the scene. Then Poirot strode forward.

At the same moment Hugo Trent said crisply:

"My God, the Old Man's shot himself!"

And there was a long, shuddering moan from Lady Chevenix-Gore. "Oh, Gervase—Gervase!"

Over his shoulder Poirot said sharply:

"Take Lady Chevenix-Gore away. She can do nothing here."

The elderly, soldierly man obeyed. He said:

"Come, Vanda. Come, my dear. You can do nothing. It's all over. Ruth, come and look after your mother."

But Ruth Chevenix-Gore had pressed into the room and stood close by Poirot's side as he bent over the dreadful sprawled figure in the chair—the figure of a man of Herculean build with a Viking beard.

She said in a low, tense voice, curiously restrained and muffled:

"You're quite sure he's—dead?"

Poirot looked up.

The girl's face was alive with some emotion—an emotion sternly checked and repressed—that he did not quite understand. It was not grief—it seemed more like a kind of half-fearful excitement.

The little woman with the pince-nez murmured:

"Your mother, my dear—Don't you think—?"

In a high, hysterical voice the girl with the red hair cried out:

"Then it *wasn't* a car or a champagne cork! It was a *shot* we heard. . . ."

Poirot turned and faced them all.

He said:

"Somebody must communicate with the police—"

Ruth Chevenix-Gore cried out violently:

"No!"

The elderly man with the legal face said:

"Unavoidable, I am afraid. Will you see to that, Burrows? Hugo—"

Poirot said:

"You are Mr. Hugo Trent?" to the tall young man with the mustache. "It would be well, I think, if everyone except you and I were to leave this room."

Again his authority was not questioned. The lawyer shepherded the others away. Poirot and Hugo Trent were left alone.

The latter said, staring:

"Look here—who *are* you? I mean, I haven't the foggiest idea. What are you doing here?"

Poirot took a card case from his pocket and selected a card.

Hugo Trent said, staring at it:

"Private detective—eh? Of course, I've heard of you. . . . But I still don't see what you are doing *here?*"

"You did not know that your uncle—he was your uncle, was he not—?"

Hugo's eyes dropped for a fleeting moment to the dead man.

"The Old Man? Yes, he was my uncle all right."

"You did not know that he had sent for me?"

Hugo shook his head. He said slowly:

"I'd no idea of it."

There was an emotion in his voice that was rather hard to classify. His face looked wooden and stupid—the kind of expression, Poirot thought, that made a useful mask in times of stress.

Poirot said quietly:

"We are in Westshire, are we not? I know your Chief Constable, Major Riddle, very well."

Hugo said:

"Riddle lives about half a mile away. He'll probably come over himself."

"That," said Poirot, "will be very convenient."

He began prowling gently round the room. He twitched aside the window curtains and examined the French windows, trying them gently. They were closed.

On the wall behind the desk there hung a round mirror. The mirror was shivered. Poirot bent and picked up a small object.

"What's that?" asked Hugo Trent.

"The bullet."

"It passed straight through his head and struck the mirror?"

"It seems so."

Poirot replaced the bullet meticulously where he had found it. He came up to the desk. Some papers were arranged neatly stacked in heaps. On the blotting pad itself there was a loose sheet of paper with the word SORRY printed across it in large, shaky handwriting.

Hugo said: "He must have written that just before he—did it."

Poirot nodded thoughtfully.

He looked again at the smashed mirror, then at the dead man. His brow creased itself a little as though in perplexity. He went over to the door, where it hung crookedly with its splintered lock. There was no key in the door, as he knew—otherwise he would not have been able to see through the keyhole. There was no sign of it on the floor. Poirot leaned over the dead man and ran his fingers over him.

"Yes," he said. "The key is in his pocket."

Hugo drew out a cigarette case and lighted a cigarette. He spoke rather hoarsely.

"It seems all quite clear," he said. "My uncle shut himself up in here, scrawled that message on a piece of paper, and then shot himself."

Poirot nodded meditatively. Hugo went on:

"But I don't understand why he sent for you? What was it all about?"

"That is rather more difficult to explain. While we are waiting, Mr. Trent, for the authorities to arrive, perhaps you will tell me exactly who all the people are whom I saw tonight when I arrived?"

"Who they are?" Hugo spoke almost absently. "Oh, yes, of course. Sorry. Shall we sit down?" He indicated a settee in the farthest corner of the room from the body. He went on, speaking jerkily, "Well, there's Vanda—my aunt, you know. And Ruth, my cousin. But you know them. Then the other girl is Susan Cardwell. She's just staying here. And there's Colonel Bury. He's an old friend of the family. And Ogilvie Forbes. He's an old friend, too, besides being the family lawyer and all that. Both the old boys had a passion for Vanda when she was young, and they still hang round in a faithful, devoted sort of way. Ridiculous, but rather touching. Then there's Godfrey Burrows, the Old Man's—I mean my uncle's—secretary, and Miss Lingard, who's here to help him write a history of the Chevenix-Gores. She mugs up historical stuff for writers. That's the lot, I think."

Poirot nodded. Then he said:

"And I understand you actually heard the shot that killed your uncle?"

"Yes, we did. Thought it was a champagne cork—at least, I did.

Susan and Miss Lingard thought it was a car backfiring outside—the road runs quite near, you know."

"When was this?"

"Oh! About ten past eight. Snell had just sounded the first gong."

"And where were you when you heard it?"

"In the hall. We—we were laughing about it—arguing, you know, as to where the sound came from. I said it came from the dining room, and Susan said it came from the direction of the drawing room, and Miss Lingard said it sounded like upstairs, and Snell said it came from the road outside, only it came through the upstairs windows. And Susan said, any more theories? And I laughed and said there was always murder! Seems pretty rotten to think of now."

His face twitched nervously.

"It did not occur to anyone that Sir Gervase might have shot himself?"

"No, of course not."

"You have, in fact, no idea why he should have shot himself?"

Hugo said slowly:

"Oh, well, I shouldn't say that—"

"You *have* an idea?"

"Yes—well—it's difficult to explain. Naturally I didn't expect him to commit suicide, but all the same, I'm not frightfully surprised. The truth of it is that my uncle was as mad as a hatter, M. Poirot. Everyone knew that."

"That strikes you as a sufficient explanation?"

"Well, people do shoot themselves when they're a bit balmy."

"An explanation of an admirable simplicity."

Hugo stared.

Poirot got up again and wandered aimlessly round the room. It was comfortably furnished, mainly in a rather heavy Victorian style. There were massive bookcases, huge armchairs, and some upright chairs of genuine Chippendale. There were not many ornaments, but some bronzes on the mantelpiece attracted Poirot's attention and apparently stirred his admiration. He picked them up one by one, carefully examining them before replacing them with care. From the one on the extreme left he detached something with a fingernail.

"What's that?" asked Hugo, without much interest.

"Nothing very much. A tiny sliver of looking glass."

Hugo said:

"Funny the way that mirror was smashed by the shot. A broken mirror means bad luck. Poor old Gervase. . . . I suppose his luck had held a bit too long."

"Your uncle was a lucky man?"

Hugo gave a short laugh.

"Why, his luck was proverbial! Everything he touched turned to gold! If he backed an outsider, it romped home! If he invested in a doubtful mine, they struck a vein of ore at once! He's had the most amazing escapes from the tightest of tight places. His life's been saved by a kind of miracle more than once. He was rather a fine old boy, in his way, you know. He'd certainly 'been places and seen things'— more than most of his generation."

Poirot murmured in a conversational tone:

"You were attached to your uncle, Mr. Trent?"

Hugo Trent seemed a little startled by the question.

"Oh—er—yes, of course," he said rather vaguely. "You know, he was a bit difficult at times. Frightful strain to live with, and all that. Fortunately I didn't have to see much of him."

*"He* was fond of *you?"*

"Not so that you'd notice it! As a matter of fact, he rather resented my existence, so to speak."

"How was that, Mr. Trent?"

"Well, you see, he had no son of his own—and he was pretty sore about it. He was mad about family and all that sort of thing. I believe it cut him to the quick to know that when he died the Chevenix-Gores would cease to exist. They've been going ever since the Norman Conquest, you know. The Old Man was the last of them. I suppose it *was* rather rotten from his point of view."

"You yourself do not share that sentiment?"

Hugo shrugged his shoulders.

"All that sort of thing seems to me rather out of date."

"What will happen to the estate?"

"Don't really know. I might get it. Or he may have left it to Ruth. Probably Vanda has it for her lifetime."

"Your uncle did not definitely declare his intentions?"

"Well, he had his pet idea."

"And what was that?"

"His idea was that Ruth and I should make a match of it."

"That would doubtless have been very suitable."

"Eminently suitable. But Ruth—well, Ruth has very decided views of her own about life. Mind you, she's an extremely attractive young woman, and she knows it. She's in no hurry to marry and settle down."

Poirot leaned forward.

"But you yourself would have been willing, M. Trent?"

Hugo said in a bored tone of voice:

"I really can't see it makes a ha'p'orth of difference who you marry nowadays. Divorce is so easy. If you're not hitting it off, nothing is easier than to cut the tangle and start again."

The door opened and Ogilvie Forbes entered with a tall, spruce-looking man.

The latter nodded to Trent.

"Hullo, Hugo. I'm extremely sorry about this. Very rough on all of you."

Hercule Poirot came forward.

"How do you do, Major Riddle? You remember me?"

"Yes, indeed." The Chief Constable shook hands. "So *you*'re down here?"

There was a meditative note in his voice. He glanced curiously at Hercule Poirot.

# IV

"Well?" said Major Riddle.

It was twenty minutes later. The Chief Constable's interrogative "Well" was addressed to the police surgeon, a lank elderly man with grizzled hair.

The latter shrugged his shoulders.

"He's been dead over half an hour—but not more than an hour. You don't want technicalities, I know, so I'll spare you them. The man was shot through the head, the pistol being held a few inches from the right temple. Bullet passed right through the brain and out again."

"Perfectly compatible with suicide?"

"Oh, perfectly. The body then slumped down in the chair and the pistol dropped from his hand."

"You've got the bullet?"

"Yes." The doctor held it up.

"Good," said Major Riddle. "We'll keep it for comparison with the pistol. Glad it's a clear case and no difficulties."

Hercule Poirot asked gently:

"You are sure there *are* no difficulties, doctor?"

"Well, I suppose you might call one thing a little odd. When he shot himself he must have been leaning slightly over to the right. Otherwise the bullet would have hit the wall *below* the mirror, instead of plumb in the middle."

"An uncomfortable position in which to commit suicide," said Poirot.

The doctor shrugged his shoulders.

"Oh, well—comfort—if you're going to end it all . . . " He left the sentence unfinished.

Major Riddle said:

"The body can be moved now?"

"Oh, yes. I've done with it until the post mortem."

"What about you, Inspector?" Major Riddle spoke to a tall impassive-faced man in plain clothes.

"O.K., sir, we've got all we want. Only the deceased's fingerprints on the pistol."

"Then you can get on with it."

The mortal remains of Gervase Chevenix-Gore were removed. The Chief Constable and Poirot were left together.

"Well," said Riddle. "Everything seems quite clear and above board. Door locked, window fastened, key of door in dead man's pocket. Everything according to Cocker—but for one circumstance."

"And what is that, my friend?" inquired Poirot.

"*You!*" said Riddle bluntly. "What are *you* doing down here?"

By way of reply, Poirot handed to him the letter he had received from the dead man a week ago, and the telegram which had finally brought him there.

"Humph!" said the Chief Constable. "Interesting. We'll have to get to the bottom of this. I should say it had a direct bearing upon his suicide."

"I agree."

"We must check up on who is in the house."

"I can tell you their names. I have just been making inquiries of Mr. Trent."

He repeated the list of names.

"Perhaps you, Major Riddle, know something about these people?"

"I know something of them, naturally. Lady Chevenix-Gore is quite as mad in her own way as old Sir Gervase. They were devoted to each other—and both quite mad. She's the vaguest creature that ever lived, with an occasional uncanny shrewdness that strikes the nail on the head in the most surprising fashion. People laugh at her a good deal. I think she knows it, but she doesn't care. She's absolutely no sense of humor."

"Miss Chevenix-Gore is only their adopted daughter, I understand?"

"A very handsome young lady."

"She's a devilishly attractive girl. Has played havoc with most of the young fellows around here. Leads them all on and then turns round and laughs at them. Good seat on a horse, and wonderful hands."

"That, for the moment, does not concern us."

"Er—no, perhaps not. . . . Well, about the other people; I know old Bury, of course. He's here most of the time. Almost a tame cat about the house. Kind of A.D.C. to Lady Chevenix-Gore. He's a very old friend. They've known him all their lives. I think he and Sir Gervase were both interested in some company of which Bury was a director."

"Ogilvie Forbes; do you know anything of him?"

"I rather believe I've met him once."

"Miss Lingard?"

"Never heard of her."

"Miss Susan Cardwell?"

"Rather a good-looking girl with red hair? I've seen her about with Ruth Chevenix-Gore the last few days."

"Mr. Burrows?"

"Yes, I know him. Chevenix-Gore's secretary. Between you and me I don't take to him much. He's good-looking and knows it. Not quite out of the top drawer."

"Had he been with Sir Gervase long?"

"About two years, I fancy."

"And there is no one else—?"

Poirot broke off.

A tall, fair-haired man in a lounge suit came hurrying in. He was out of breath and looked disturbed.

"Good evening, Major Riddle. I heard a rumor that Sir Gervase had shot himself and I hurried up here. Snell tells me it's true. It's incredible! I can't believe it!"

"It's true enough, Lake. Let me introduce you. This is Captain Lake, Sir Gervase's agent for the estate. M. Hercule Poirot, of whom you may have heard."

Lake's face lit up with what seemed a kind of delighted incredulity.

"M. Hercule Poirot? I'm most awfully pleased to meet you. At least—" He broke off, the quick charming smile vanished—he looked disturbed and upset. "There isn't anything—fishy—about this suicide, is there, sir?"

"Why should there be anything 'fishy,' as you call it?" asked the Chief Constable sharply.

"I mean, because M. Poirot is here. Oh! And because the whole business seems so incredible!"

"No, no," said Poirot quickly. "I am not here on account of the death of Sir Gervase. I was already in the house—as a guest."

"Oh, I see. Funny, he never told me you were coming when I was going over accounts with him this afternoon."

Poirot said quietly:

"You have twice used the word 'incredible,' Captain Lake. Are you then so surprised to hear of Sir Gervase committing suicide?"

"Indeed I am. Of course, he was mad as a hatter, everyone would agree about that. But all the same, I simply can't imagine his thinking the world would be able to get on without him."

"Yes," said Poirot. "It is a point, that." And he looked with appreciation at the frank, intelligent countenance of the young man.

Major Riddle cleared his throat.

"Since you are here, Captain Lake, perhaps you will sit down and answer a few questions."

"Certainly, sir."

Lake took a chair opposite the other two.

"When did you last see Sir Gervase?"

"This afternoon, just before three o'clock. There were some accounts to be checked and the question of a new tenant for one of the farms."

"How long were you with him?"

"Perhaps half an hour."

"Think carefully, and tell me whether you noticed anything unusual in his manner?"

The young man considered.

"No, I hardly think so. He was, perhaps, a trifle excited—but that wasn't unusual with him."

"He was not depressed in any way?"

"Oh, no, he seemed in good spirits. He was enjoying himself very much just now, writing up a history of the family."

"How long had he been doing this?"

"He began it about six months ago."

"Is that when Miss Lingard came here?"

"No. She arrived about two months ago when he had discovered that he could not manage the necessary research work by himself."

"And you consider he was enjoying himself?"

"Oh, simply enormously! He really didn't think that anything else mattered in the world except his family."

There was a momentary bitterness in the young man's tone.

"Then, as far as you know, Sir Gervase had no worries of any kind?"

There was a slight—a very slight—pause, before Captain Lake answered:

"No."

Poirot suddenly interposed a question:

"Sir Gervase was not, as far as you know, worried about his daughter in any way?"

"His daughter?"

"That is what I said."

"Not as far as I know," said the young man, stiffly.

Poirot said nothing further. Major Riddle said:

"Well, thank you, Lake. Perhaps you'd stay around in case I might want to ask you anything?"

"Certainly, sir." He rose. "Anything I can do?"

"Yes, you might send the butler here. And perhaps you'd find out for me how Lady Chevenix-Gore is, and if I could have a few words with her presently, or if she's too upset."

The young man nodded and left the room with a quick, decisive step.

"An attractive personality," said Hercule Poirot.

"Yes, nice fellow, and good at his job. Everyone likes him."

# V

"Sit down, Snell," said Major Riddle in a friendly tone. "I've a good many questions to ask you, and I expect this has been a shock to you."

"Oh, it has indeed, sir. Thank you, sir." Snell sat down with such a discreet air that it was practically the same as though he had remained on his feet.

"Been here a good long time, haven't you?"

"Sixteen years, sir, ever since Sir Gervase—er—settled down, so to speak."

"Ah, yes, of course, your master was a great traveler in his day."

"Yes, sir. He went on an expedition to the Pole and many other interesting places."

"Now, Snell, can you tell me when you last saw your master this evening?"

"I was in the dining room, sir, seeing that the table arrangements were all complete. The door into the hall was open and I saw Sir Gervase come down the stairs, cross the hall, and go along the passage to the study."

"That was at what time?"

"Just before eight o'clock. It might have been as much as five minutes before eight."

"And that was the last you saw of him?"

"Yes, sir."

"Did you hear a shot?"

"Oh, yes, indeed, sir, but of course I had no idea at the time—how should I have had?"

"What did you think it was?"

"I thought it was a car, sir. The road runs quite near the Park wall. Or it might have been a shot in the woods—a poacher perhaps. I never dreamed—"

Major Riddle cut him short.

"What time was that?"

"It was exactly eight minutes past eight, sir."

The Chief Constable said sharply:

"How is it you can fix the time to a minute?"

"That's easy, sir. I had just sounded the first gong."

"The first gong?"

"Yes, sir. By Sir Gervase's orders a gong was always to be sounded seven minutes before the actual dinner gong. Very particular he was, sir, that everyone should be assembled ready in the drawing room when the second gong went. As soon as I had sounded the second gong, I went to the drawing room and announced dinner and everyone went in."

"I begin to understand," said Hercule Poirot, "why you looked so surprised when you announced dinner this evening. It was usual for Sir Gervase to be in the drawing room?"

"I'd never known him not to be there before, sir. It was quite a shock. I little thought—"

Again Major Riddle interrupted adroitly:

"And were the others also usually there?"

Snell coughed.

"Anyone who was late for dinner, sir, was never asked to the house again."

"H'm, very drastic."

"Sir Gervase, sir, employed a chef who was formerly with the Emperor of Moravia. He used to say, sir, that dinner was as important as a religious ritual."

"And what about his own family?"

"Lady Chevenix-Gore was always very particular not to upset him, sir, and even Miss Ruth dared not be late for dinner."

"Interesting," murmured Hercule Poirot.

"I see," said Riddle. "So, dinner being at a quarter past eight, you sounded the first gong at eight minutes past, as usual?"

"That is so, sir—but it wasn't as usual. Dinner was usually at eight. Sir Gervase gave orders that dinner was to be a quarter of an hour later this evening as he was expecting a gentleman by the late train."

Snell made a little bow towards Poirot as he spoke.

"When your master went to the study, did he look upset or worried in any way?"

"I could not say, sir. It was too far for me to judge of 'is expression. I just noticed him, that was all."

"Was he alone when he went to the study?"

"Yes, sir."

"Did anyone go to the study after that?"

"I could not say, sir. I went to the butler's pantry after that and was there until I sounded the first gong at eight minutes past eight."

"That was when you heard the shot?"

"Yes, sir."

Poirot gently interposed a question.

"There were others, I think, who also heard the shot?"

"Yes, sir. Mr. Hugo and Miss Cardwell. And Miss Lingard."

"These people were also in the hall?"

"Miss Lingard came out from the drawing room and Miss Cardwell and Mr. Hugo were just coming down the stairs."

Poirot asked:

"Was there any conversation about the matter?"

"Well, sir, Mr. Hugo asked if there was champagne for dinner. I told him that sherry, hock, and burgundy were being served."

"He thought it was a champagne cork?"

"Yes, sir."

"But nobody took it seriously?"

"Oh, no, sir. They all went into the drawing room talking and laughing."

"Where were the other members of the household?"

"I could not say, sir."

Major Riddle said:

"Do you know anything about this pistol?" He held it out as he spoke.

"Oh, yes, sir. That belonged to Sir Gervase. He always kept it in the drawer of his desk in here."

"Was it usually loaded?"

"I couldn't say, sir."

Major Riddle laid down the pistol and cleared his throat.

"Now, Snell, I'm going to ask you a rather important question. I hope you will answer it as truthfully as you can. *Do you know of any reason which might lead your master to commit suicide?*"

"No, sir. I know of nothing."

"Sir Gervase had not been odd in his manner of late? Not depressed? Or worried?"

Snell coughed apologetically.

"You'll excuse my saying it, sir, but Sir Gervase was always what might have seemed to strangers a little odd in his manner. He was a highly original gentleman, sir."

"Yes, yes, I am quite aware of that."

"Outsiders, sir, did not always understand Sir Gervase."

Snell gave the phrase a definite value of capital letter.

"I know. I know. But there was nothing that *you* would have called unusual?"

The butler hesitated.

"I think, sir, that Sir Gervase was worried about something," he said at last.

"Worried and depressed?"

"I shouldn't say depressed, sir. But worried, yes."

"Have you any idea of the cause of that worry?"

"No, sir."

"Was it connected with any particular person, for instance?"

"I could not say at all, sir. In any case, it is only an impression of mine."

Poirot spoke again.

"You were surprised at his suicide?"

"Very surprised, sir. It has been a terrible shock to me. I never dreamed of such a thing."

Poirot nodded thoughtfully.

Riddle glanced at him, then said:

"Well, Snell, I think that is all we want to ask you. You are quite sure that there is nothing else you can tell us—no unusual incident, for instance, that has happened in the last few days?"

The butler, rising to his feet, shook his head.

"There is nothing, sir, nothing whatever."

"Then you can go."

"Thank you, sir."

Moving towards the doorway, Snell drew back and stood aside. Lady Chevenix-Gore floated into the room.

She was wearing an oriental-looking garment of purple and orange silk wound tightly round her body. Her face was serene and her manner collected and calm.

"Lady Chevenix-Gore." Major Riddle sprang to his feet.

She said:

"They told me you would like to talk to me, so I came."

"Shall we go into another room? This must be painful for you in the extreme."

Lady Chevenix-Gore shook her head and sat down on one of the Chippendale chairs. She murmured:

"Oh, no, what does it matter?"

"It is very good of you, Lady Chevenix-Gore, to put your feelings aside. I know what a frightful shock this must have been and—"

She interrupted him.

"It was rather a shock at first," she admitted. Her tone was easy and conversational. "But there is no such thing as Death, really, you know, only Change." She added, "As a matter of fact, Gervase is standing just behind your left shoulder now. I can see him distinctly."

Major Riddle's left shoulder twitched slightly. He looked at Lady Chevenix-Gore rather doubtfully.

She smiled at him, a vague, happy smile.

"You don't believe, of course! So few people will. To me, the spirit world is quite as real as this one. But please ask me anything you like and don't worry about distressing me. I'm not in the least distressed. Everything, you see, is Fate. One cannot escape one's Karma. It all fits in—the mirror—everything."

"The mirror, madame?" asked Poirot.

She nodded her head towards it vaguely.

"Yes. It's splintered, you see. A symbol! You know Tennyson's poem? I used to read it as a girl—though, of course, I didn't realize then the esoteric side of it. *'The mirror cracked from side to side; "The curse is come upon me!" cried the Lady of Shalott.'* That's what happened to Gervase. The Curse came upon him suddenly. I think, you know, most very old families have a curse. . . . The mirror cracked. He knew that he was doomed! *The Curse had come!*"

"But, madame, it was not a curse that cracked the mirror—it was a bullet!"

Lady Chevenix-Gore said, still in the same sweet vague manner:

"It's all the same thing really. . . . It was Fate."

"But your husband shot himself."

Lady Chevenix-Gore smiled indulgently.

"He shouldn't have done that, of course. But Gervase was always impatient. He could never wait. His hour had come—he went forward to meet it. It's all so simple, really."

Major Riddle, clearing his throat in exasperation, said sharply:

"Then you weren't surprised at your husband's taking his own life? Had you been expecting such a thing to happen?"

"Oh, no." Her eyes opened wide. "One can't always foresee the future. Gervase, of course, was a very strange man, a very unusual man. He was quite unlike anyone else. He was one of the Great Ones born again. I've known that for some time. I think he knew it himself. He found it very hard to conform to the silly little standards of the everyday world." She added, looking over Major Riddle's shoulder: "He's smiling now. He's thinking how foolish we all are. So we are really. Just like children. Pretending that life is real and that it matters. . . . Life is only one of the Great Illusions."

Feeling that he was fighting a losing battle, Major Riddle asked desperately:

"You can't help us at all as to *why* your husband should have taken his life?"

She shrugged her thin shoulders.

"Forces move us—they move us. . . . You cannot understand. You move only on the material plane."

Poirot coughed.

"Talking of the material plane, have you any idea, madame, as to how your husband has left his money?"

"Money?" She stared at him. "I never think of money."

Her tone was disdainful.

Poirot switched to another point.

"At what time did you come downstairs to dinner tonight?"

"Time? What is Time? Infinite, that is the answer. Time is infinite."

Poirot murmured:

"But your husband, Madame, was rather particular about time—especially, so I have been told, as regards the dinner hour."

"Dear Gervase," she smiled indulgently. "He was very foolish about that. But it made him happy. So we were never late."

"Were you in the drawing room, madame, when the first gong went?"

"No, I was in my room then."

"Do you remember who was in the drawing room when you did come down?"

"Nearly everybody, I think," said Lady Chevenix-Gore vaguely. "Does it matter?"

"Possibly not," admitted Poirot. "Then there is something else. Did your husband ever tell you that he suspected he was being robbed?"

Lady Chevenix-Gore did not seem much interested in the question. "Robbed? No, I don't think so."

"Robbed, swindled—victimized in some way—?"

"No—no—I don't think so. . . . Gervase would have been very angry if anybody had dared to do anything like that."

"At any rate he said nothing about it to you?"

"No—no." Lady Chevenix-Gore shook her head, still without much real interest. "I should have remembered. . . ."

"When did you last see your husband alive?"

"He looked in, as usual, on his way downstairs before dinner. My maid was there. He just said he was going down."

"What has he talked about most in the last few weeks?"

"Oh, the family history. He was getting on so well with it. He found that funny old thing, Miss Lingard, quite invaluable. She looked up things for him in the British Museum—all that sort of thing. She worked with Lord Mulcaster on his book, you know. And she was tactful—I mean, she didn't look up the wrong things. After all, there are ancestors one doesn't want raked up. Gervase was very sensitive. She helped me, too. She got a lot of information for me about Hatshepsut. I am a reincarnation of Hatshepsut, you know."

Lady Chevenix-Gore made this announcement in a calm voice.

"Before that," she went on, "I was a Priestess in Atlantis."

Major Riddle shifted a little in his chair.

"Er—er—very interesting," he said. "Well, really, Lady Chevenix-Gore, I think that will be all. Very kind of you—"

Lady Chevenix-Gore rose, clasping her oriental robes about her.

"Good night," she said. And then, her eyes shifting to a point behind Major Riddle, "Good night, Gervase dear. I wish you could come, but I know you have to stay here." She added in an explanatory fashion: "You have to stay in the place where you've passed over for at least twenty-four hours. It's some time before you can move about freely and communicate."

She trailed out of the room.

Major Riddle wiped his brow.

"Phew," he murmured. "She's a great deal madder than I ever thought. Does she really believe all that nonsense?"

Poirot shook his head thoughtfully.

"It is possible that she finds it helpful," he said. "She needs, at this moment, to create for herself a world of illusion so that she can escape the stark reality of her husband's death."

"She seems almost certifiable to me," said Major Riddle. "A long farrago of nonsense without one word of sense in it."

"No, no, my friend. The interesting thing is, as Mr. Hugo Trent casually remarked to me, that amidst all the vaporing there is an occasional shrewd thrust. She showed it by her remark about Miss Lingard's tact in not stressing undesirable ancestors. Believe me, Lady Chevenix-Gore is no fool."

He got up and paced up and down the room.

"There are things in this affair that I do not like. No, I do not like them at all."

Riddle looked at him curiously.

"You mean the motive for his suicide?"

"Suicide—suicide! It is all wrong, I tell you. *It is wrong psychologically.* How did Chevenix-Gore think of himself? As a Colossus, as an immensely important person, as the center of the Universe! Does such a man destroy himself? Surely not. He is far more likely to destroy someone else—some miserable, crawling ant of a human being who has dared to cause him annoyance. . . . Such an act he might regard as necessary—as sanctified! But self-destruction? The destruction of such a Self?"

"It's all very well, Poirot. But the evidence is clear enough. Door locked, key in his own pocket. Window closed and fastened. I know these things happen in books—but I've never come across them in real life. Anything else?"

"But, yes, there is something else." Poirot sat down in the chair. "Here I am. I am Chevenix-Gore. I am sitting at my desk. I am determined to kill myself because—because, let us say, I have made a discovery concerning some terrific dishonor to the family name. It is not very convincing, that, but it must suffice.

"*Eh bien*, what do I do? I scrawl on a piece of paper the word SORRY. Yes, that is quite possible. Then I open the drawer of the desk, take out the pistol which I keep there, load it, if it is not loaded, and then—do I proceed to shoot myself? No, I first turn my chair round—so, and I lean over a little to the right—so—and then—*then* I put the pistol to my temple and fire!"

Poirot sprang up from his chair, and wheeling round demanded:

"I ask you, does that make sense? *Why* turn the chair round? If, for instance, there had been a picture on the wall there, then, yes, there might be an explanation. Some portrait which a dying man might wish to be the last thing on earth his eyes would see, but a window curtain—*ah non*, that does not make sense."

"He might have wished to look out of the window. Last view out over the estate."

"My dear friend, you do not suggest that with any conviction. In fact, you know it is nonsense. At eight minutes past eight it was dark, and in any case the curtains are drawn. No, there must be some other explanation. . . ."

"There's only one as far as I can see. Gervase Chevenix-Gore was mad."

Poirot shook his head in a dissatisfied manner.

Major Riddle rose.

"Come," he said. "Let us go and interview the rest of the party. We may get at something that way."

# VI

After the difficulties of getting a direct statement from Lady Chevenix-Gore, Major Riddle found considerable relief in dealing with a shrewd lawyer like Ogilvie Forbes.

Mr. Forbes was extremely guarded and cautious in his statements, but his replies were all directly to the point.

He admitted that Sir Gervase's suicide had been a great shock to him. He should never have considered Sir Gervase the kind of man who would take his own life. He knew nothing of any cause for such an act.

"Sir Gervase was not only my client, but was a very old friend. I have known him since boyhood. I should say that he had always enjoyed life."

"In the circumstances, Mr. Forbes, I must ask you to speak quite candidly. You did not know of any secret anxiety or sorrow in Sir Gervase's life?"

"No. He had minor worries, like most men, but there was nothing of a serious nature."

"No illness? No trouble between him and his wife?"

"No. Sir Gervase and Lady Chevenix-Gore were devoted to each other."

Major Riddle said cautiously:

"Lady Chevenix-Gore appears to hold somewhat curious views."

Mr. Forbes smiled—an indulgent, manly smile.

"Ladies," he said, "must be allowed their fancies."

The Chief Constable went on:

"You managed all Sir Gervase's legal affairs?"

"Yes, my firm, Forbes, Ogilvie and Spence, have acted for the Chevenix-Gore family for well over a hundred years."

"Were there any—scandals in the Chevenix-Gore family?"

Mr. Forbes' eyebrows rose.

"Really, I fail to understand you?"

"M. Poirot, will you show Mr. Forbes the letter you showed me?"

In silence Poirot rose and handed the letter to Mr. Forbes with a little bow.

Mr. Forbes read it and his eyebrows rose still more.

"A most remarkable letter," he said. "I appreciate your question now. No, so far as my knowledge went, there was nothing to justify the writing of such a letter."

"Sir Gervase said nothing of this matter to you?"

"Nothing at all. I must say I find it very curious that he should not have done so."

"He was accustomed to confide in you?"

"I think he relied on my judgment."

"And you have no idea as to what this letter refers?"

"I should not like to make any rash speculations."

Major Riddle appreciated the subtlety of this reply.

"Now, Mr. Forbes, perhaps you can tell us how Sir Gervase has left his property?"

"Certainly. I see no objection to such a course. To his wife Sir Gervase left an annual income of six thousand pounds chargeable on the estate, and the choice of the Dower House or the town house in Lowndes Square, whichever she should prefer. There were, of course, several legacies and bequests, but nothing of an outstanding nature. The residue of his property was left to his adopted daughter, Ruth, on condition that, if she married, her husband should take the name of Chevenix-Gore."

"Was nothing left to his nephew, Mr. Hugo Trent?"

"Yes. A legacy of five thousand pounds."

"And I take it that Sir Gervase was a rich man?"

"He was extremely wealthy. He had a vast private fortune apart from the estate. Of course, he was not quite so well off as in the past. Practically all invested incomes have felt the strain. Also, Sir Gervase had dropped a good deal of money over a certain company—The Paragon Synthetic Rubberine Company in which Colonel Bury persuaded him to invest a good deal of money."

"Not very wise advice."

Mr. Forbes sighed.

"Retired soldiers are the worst sufferers when they engage in financial operations. I have found that their credulity far exceeds that of widows—and that is saying a good deal."

"But these unfortunate investments did not seriously affect Sir Gervase's income?"

"Oh, no, not seriously. He was still an extremely rich man."

"When was this will made?"

"Two years ago."

Poirot murmured:

"This arrangement, was it not possibly a little unfair to Mr. Hugo Trent, Sir Gervase's nephew? He is, after all, Sir Gervase's nearest blood relation."

Mr. Forbes shrugged his shoulders.

"One has to take a certain amount of family history into account."

"Such as—?"

Mr. Forbes seemed slightly unwilling to proceed.

Major Riddle said:

"You mustn't think we're unduly concerned with raking up old scandals or anything of that sort. But this letter of Sir Gervase's to M. Poirot has got to be explained."

"There is certainly nothing scandalous in the explanation of Sir Gervase's attitude to his nephew," said Mr. Forbes quickly. "It was simply that Sir Gervase always took his position as head of the family very seriously. He had a younger brother and sister. The brother, Anthony Chevenix-Gore, was killed in the War. The sister, Pamela, married, and Sir Gervase disapproved of the marriage. That is to say, he considered that she ought to have obtained his consent and approval before marrying. He thought that Captain Trent's family was not of sufficient prominence to be allied with a Chevenix-Gore. His sister was merely amused by his attitude. As a result, Sir Gervase has always been inclined to dislike his nephew. I think that dislike may have influenced him in deciding to adopt a child."

"There was no hope of his having children of his own?"

"No. There was a stillborn child about a year after his marriage. The doctors told Lady Chevenix-Gore that she would never be able to have another child. About two years later he adopted Ruth."

Poirot asked:

"And who *was* Mademoiselle Ruth? How did they come to settle upon her?"

"She was, I believe, the child of a distant connection."

"That I had guessed," said Poirot. He looked up at the wall which was hung with family portraits. "One can see that she was of the same blood—the nose, the line of the chin. It repeats itself on these walls many times."

"She inherits the temper, too," said Mr. Forbes, drily.

"So I should imagine. How did she and her adopted father get on?"

"Much as you might imagine. There was a fierce clash of wills more than once. But, in spite of these quarrels, I believe there was also an underlying harmony."

"Nevertheless, she caused him a good deal of anxiety?"

"Incessant anxiety. But I can assure you not to the point of causing him to take his own life."

"Ah, that, no," agreed Poirot. "One does not blow one's brains out because one has a headstrong daughter! And so mademoiselle inherits! Sir Gervase, he never thought of altering his will?"

"Ahem!" Mr. Forbes coughed to hide a little discomposure. "As a matter of fact, I took instructions from Sir Gervase on my arrival here (two days ago, that is to say) as to the drafting of a new will."

"What's this?" Major Riddle hitched his chair a little closer. "You didn't tell us this."

Mr. Forbes said quickly:

"You merely asked me what the terms of Sir Gervase's will were. I gave you the information for which you asked. The new will was not even properly drawn up—much less signed."

"What were its provisions? They may be some guide to Sir Gervase's state of mind."

"In the main, they were the same as before, but Miss Chevenix-Gore was only to inherit on condition that she married Mr. Hugo Trent."

"Aha," said Poirot. "But there is a very decided difference there."

"I did not approve of the clause," said Mr. Forbes. "And I felt bound to point out that it was quite possible it might be contested successfully. The Court does not look upon conditional bequests with approval. Sir Gervase, however, was quite decided."

"And if Miss Chevenix-Gore (or, incidentally, Mr. Trent) refused to comply?"

"If Mr. Trent was not willing to marry Miss Chevenix-Gore, then the money went to her unconditionally. But if *he* was willing and *she* refused, then the money went to him instead."

"Odd business," said Major Riddle.

Poirot leaned forward. He tapped the lawyer on the knee.

"But what is behind it? What was in the mind of Sir Gervase when he made that stipulation? There must have been something very definite. . . . There must, I think, have been the image of another man . . . a man of whom he disapproved. I think, M. Forbes, that *you* must know who that man was?"

"Really, M. Poirot, I have no information."

"But you could make a guess?"

"I never guess," said Mr. Forbes, and his tone was scandalized.

Removing his pince-nez, he wiped them with a silk handkerchief and inquired:

"Is there anything else that you desire to know?"

"At the moment, no," said Poirot. "Not, that is, as far as I am concerned."

Mr. Forbes looked as though, in his opinion, that was not very far, and bent his attention on the Chief Constable.

"Thank you, Mr. Forbes. I think that's all. I should like, if I may, to speak to Miss Chevenix-Gore."

"Certainly. I think she is upstairs with Lady Chevenix-Gore."

"Oh, well, perhaps I'll have a word with—what's his name?—Burrows, first, and the family history woman."

"They're both in the library. I will tell them."

# VII

"Hard work, that," said Major Riddle as the lawyer left the room. "Extracting information from these old-fashioned legal wallahs takes a bit of doing. The whole business seems to me to center about the girl."

"It would seem so—yes."

"Ah, here comes Burrows."

Godfrey Burrows came in with a pleasant eagerness to be of use. His smile was discreetly tempered with gloom and showed only a fraction too much teeth. It seemed more mechanical than spontaneous.

"Now, Mr. Burrows, we want to ask you a few questions."

"Certainly, Major Riddle. Anything you like."

"Well, first and foremost, to put it quite simply, have you any ideas of your own about Sir Gervase's suicide?"

"Absolutely none. It was the greatest shock to me."

"You heard the shot?"

"No; I must have been in the library at the time, as far as I can make out. I came down rather early and went to the library to look up a reference I wanted. The library's right the other side of the house from the study, so I shouldn't hear anything."

"Was anyone with you in the library?" asked Poirot.

"No one at all."

"You've no idea where the other members of the household were at the time?"

"Mostly upstairs dressing, I should imagine."

"When did you come to the drawing room?"

"Just before M. Poirot arrived. Everybody was there then—except Sir Gervase, of course."

"Did it strike you as strange that he wasn't there?"

"Yes, it did, as a matter of fact. As a rule he was always in the drawing room before the first gong sounded."

"Have you noticed any difference in Sir Gervase's manner lately? Has he been worried? Or anxious? Depressed?"

Godfrey Burrows considered.

"No—I don't think so. A little—well, preoccupied, perhaps."

"But he did not appear to be worried about any one definite matter?"

"Oh, no."

"No—financial worries of any kind?"

"He was rather perturbed about the affairs of one particular company—the Paragon Synthetic Rubberine Company, to be exact."

"What did he actually say about it?"

Again Godfrey Burrows' mechanical smile flashed out, and again it seemed slightly unreal.

"Well—as a matter of fact—what he said was: 'Old Bury's either a fool or a knave. A fool, I suppose. I must go easy with him for Vanda's sake.'"

"And why did he say that—*for Vanda's sake?*" inquired Poirot.

"Well, you see, Lady Chevenix-Gore was very fond of Colonel Bury, and he worshiped her. Followed her about like a dog."

"Sir Gervase was not—jealous at all?"

"Jealous?" Burrows stared and then laughed. "Sir Gervase jealous? He wouldn't know how to set about it. Why, it would never have entered his head that anyone could ever prefer another man to him. Such a thing just couldn't be, you understand."

Poirot said gently:

"You did not, I think, like Sir Gervase Chevenix-Gore very much?"

Burrows flushed.

"Oh, yes, I did. At least—well, all that sort of thing strikes one as rather ridiculous nowadays."

"All what sort of thing?" asked Poirot.

"Well, the feudal motif, if you like. This worship of ancestry and personal arrogance. Sir Gervase was a very able man in many ways, and had led an interesting life, but he would have been more interesting if he hadn't been so entirely wrapped up in himself and his own egoism."

"Did his daughter agree with you there?"

Burrows flushed again—this time a deep purple.

He said:

"I should imagine Miss Chevenix-Gore is quite one of the moderns! Naturally, I shouldn't discuss her father with her."

"But the moderns *do* discuss their fathers a good deal!" said Poirot. "It is entirely in the modern spirit to criticize your parents!"

Burrows shrugged his shoulders.

Major Riddle asked:

"And there was nothing else—no other financial anxiety? Sir Gervase never spoke of having been *victimized?*"

"Victimized?" Burrows sounded very astonished. "Oh, no."

"And you yourself were on quite good terms with him?"

"Certainly I was. Why not?"

"I am asking you, Mr. Burrows."

The young man looked sulky.

"We were on the best of terms."

"Did you know that Sir Gervase had written to M. Poirot asking him to come down here?"

"No."

"Did Sir Gervase usually write his own letters?"

"No, he nearly always dictated them to me."

"But he did not do so in this case?"

"No."

"Why was that, do you think?"

"I can't imagine."

"You can suggest no reason why he should have written this particular letter himself?"

"No, I can't."

"Ah!" said Major Riddle, adding smoothly, "Rather curious. When did you last see Sir Gervase?"

"Just before I went to dress for dinner. I took him some letters to sign."

"What was his manner then?"

"Quite normal. In fact, I should say he was feeling rather pleased with himself about something."

Poirot stirred a little in his chair.

"Ah!" he said. "So that was your impression, was it? That he was pleased about something. And yet, not so very long afterwards, he shoots himself. It is odd, that!"

Godfrey Burrows shrugged his shoulders.

"I'm only telling you my impressions."

"Yes, yes, they are very valuable. After all, you are probably one of the last people who saw Sir Gervase alive."

"Snell was the last person to see him."

"To see him, yes, but not to speak to him."

Burrows did not reply.

Major Riddle said:

"What time was it when you went up to dress for dinner?"

"About five minutes past seven."

"What did Sir Gervase do?"

"I left him in the study."

"How long did he usually take to change?"

"He usually gave himself a full three-quarters of an hour."

"Then, if dinner was at a quarter-past eight, he would probably have gone up at half-past seven at the latest?"

"Very likely."

"You yourself went to change early?"

"Yes, I thought I would change and then go to the library and look up the references I wanted."

Poirot nodded thoughtfully. Major Riddle said:

"Well, I think that's all for the moment. Will you send Miss What's-her-name along?"

Little Miss Lingard tripped in almost immediately. She was wearing several chains which tinkled a little as she sat down and looked inquiringly from one to the other of the two men.

"This is all very—er—sad, Miss Lingard," began Major Riddle.

"Very sad, indeed," said Miss Lingard decorously.

"You came to this house—when?"

"About two months ago. Sir Gervase wrote to a friend of his in the Museum—Colonel Fotheringay it was—and Colonel Fotheringay recommended me. I have done a good deal of historical research work."

"Did you find Sir Gervase difficult to work for?"

"Oh, not really. One had to humor him a little, of course. But then I always find one has to do that with men."

With an uneasy feeling that Miss Lingard was probably humoring him at this moment, Major Riddle went on.

"Your work here was to help Sir Gervase with the book he was writing?"

"Yes."

"What did that involve?"

For a moment, Miss Lingard looked quite human. Her eyes twinkled as she replied:

"Well, actually, you know, it involved writing the book! I looked up all the information and made notes, and arranged the material. And then, later, I revised what Sir Gervase had written."

"You must have had to exercise a good deal of tact, mademoiselle," said Poirot.

"Tact and firmness. One needs them both," said Miss Lingard.

"Sir Gervase did not resent your—er—firmness?"

"Oh, not at all. Of course I put it to him that he mustn't be bothered with all the petty detail."

"Oh, yes, I see."

"It was quite simple, really," said Miss Lingard. "Sir Gervase was perfectly easy to manage if one took him the right way."

"Now, Miss Lingard, I wonder if you know anything that can throw light on this tragedy?"

Miss Lingard shook her head.

"I'm afraid I don't. You see, naturally he wouldn't confide in me at all. I was practically a stranger. In any case, I think he was far too proud to speak to anyone of family troubles."

"But you think it *was* family troubles that caused him to take his life?"

Miss Lingard looked rather surprised.

"But, of course! Is there any other suggestion?"

"You feel sure that there were family troubles worrying him?"

"I know that he was in great distress of mind."

"Oh, you know that?"

"Why, of course."

"Tell me, mademoiselle, did he speak to you of the matter?"

"Not explicitly."

"What did he say?"

"Let me see. I found that he didn't seem to be taking in what I was saying—"

"One moment. *Pardon.* When was this?"

"This afternoon. We usually worked from three to five."

"Pray go on."

"As I say, Sir Gervase seemed to be finding it hard to concentrate—in fact, he said as much, adding that he had several grave matters preying on his mind. And he said—let me see—something like this—(of course, I can't be sure of the exact words): '*It's a terrible thing, Miss Lingard, when a family has been one of the proudest in the land, that dishonor should be brought on it.*'"

"And what did you say to that?"

"Oh, just something soothing. I think I said that every generation
had its weaklings—that that was one of the penalties of greatness—
but that their failings were seldom remembered by posterity."

"And did that have the soothing effect you hoped?"

"More or less. We got back to Sir Roger Chevenix-Gore. I had found
a most interesting mention of him in a contemporary manuscript. But
Sir Gervase's attention wandered again. In the end he said he would
not do any more work that afternoon. He said he had had a shock."

"A shock?"

"That is what he said. Of course, I didn't ask any questions. I just
said: 'I am sorry to hear it, Sir Gervase.' And then he asked me to
tell Snell that M. Poirot would be arriving and to put off dinner until
8:15, and send the car to meet the 7:50 train."

"Did he usually ask you to make these arrangements?"

"Well—no—that was really Mr. Burrows' business. I did nothing
but my own literary work. I wasn't a secretary in any sense of the
word."

Poirot asked:

"Do you think Sir Gervase had a definite reason for asking you to
make these arrangements, instead of asking Mr. Burrows to do so?"

Miss Lingard considered.

"Well, he may have had. . . . I did not think of it at the time. I
thought it was just a matter of convenience. Still, it's true now I come
to think of it, that he *did* ask me not to tell anyone that M. Poirot
was coming. It was to be a surprise, he said."

"Ah! he said that, did he? Very curious, very interesting. And *did*
you tell anyone?"

"Certainly not, M. Poirot. I told Snell about dinner and to send
the chauffeur to meet the 7:50 as a gentleman was arriving by it. I
didn't mention your name at all."

"Did Sir Gervase say anything else that may have had a bearing
on the situation?"

Miss Lingard thought.

"No—I don't think so—he was very much strung-up—I do remember
that just as I was leaving the room, he said: '*Not that it's any good
his coming now. It's too late.*'"

"And you have no idea at all what he meant by that?"

"N-no."

Just the faintest suspicion of indecision about the simple negative.
Poirot repeated with a frown:

"'*Too late.*' That is what he said, is it? '*Too late.*'"

Major Riddle said:

"You can give us no idea, Miss Lingard, as to the nature of the
circumstance that so distressed Sir Gervase?"

Miss Lingard said slowly:

"I have an idea that it was in some way connected with Mr. Hugo Trent."

"With Hugo Trent? Why do you think that?"

"Well, it was nothing definite, but yesterday afternoon we were just touching on Sir Hugo de Chevenix (who, I'm afraid, didn't bear too good a character in the War of the Roses) and Sir Gervase said, 'My sister *would* choose the family name of Hugo for her son! It's always been an unsatisfactory name in our family. She might have known no Hugo would turn out well.' "

"What you tell us there is suggestive," said Poirot. "Yes, it suggests a new idea to me."

"Sir Gervase said nothing more definite than that?" asked Major Riddle.

Miss Lingard shook her head.

"No, and of course it wouldn't have done for me to say anything. Sir Gervase was really just talking to himself. He wasn't really speaking to me."

"Quite so."

Poirot said:

"Mademoiselle, you, a stranger, have been here for two months. It would be, I think, very valuable if you were to tell us quite frankly your impressions of the family and household."

Miss Lingard took off her pince-nez and blinked reflectively.

"Well, at first, quite frankly, I felt as though I'd walked straight into a madhouse! What with Lady Chevenix-Gore continually seeing things that weren't there, and Sir Gervase behaving like—like a King—and dramatizing himself in the most extraordinary way—well, I really did think they were the queerest people I had ever come across. Of course, Miss Chevenix-Gore was perfectly normal, and I soon found that Lady Chevenix-Gore was really an extremely kind, nice woman. Nobody could be kinder or nicer to me than she has been. Sir Gervase—well, I really think he *was* mad. His egomania—isn't that what you call it?—was getting worse and worse every day."

"And the others?"

"Mr. Burrows had rather a difficult time with Sir Gervase, I should imagine. I think he was glad that our work on the book gave him a little more breathing space. Colonel Bury was always charming. He was devoted to Lady Chevenix-Gore and he managed Sir Gervase quite well. Mr. Trent, Mr. Forbes, and Miss Cardwell have only been here a few days, so of course I don't know much about them."

"Thank you, mademoiselle. And what about Captain Lake, the agent?"

"Oh, he's very nice. Everybody likes him."

"Including Sir Gervase?"

"Oh, yes. I've heard him say Lake was much the best agent he'd had. Of course, Captain Lake had his difficulties with Sir Gervase, too—but he managed pretty well, on the whole. It wasn't easy."

Poirot nodded thoughtfully. He murmured: "There was something— something—that I had in mind to ask you—some little thing. . . .What was it now?"

Miss Lingard turned a patient face towards him.

Poirot shook his head vexedly.

"Tchah! It is on the tip of my tongue."

Major Riddle waited a minute or two, then as Poirot continued to frown perplexedly, he took up the interrogation once more.

"When was the last time you saw Sir Gervase?"

"At tea time, in this room."

"What was his manner then? Normal?"

"As normal as it ever was."

"Was there any sense of strain among the party?"

"No, I think everybody seemed quite ordinary."

"Where did Sir Gervase go after tea?"

"He took Mr. Burrows with him into the study, as usual."

"That was the last time you saw him?"

"Yes. I went to the small morning room where I worked, and typed a chapter of the book from the notes I had gone over with Sir Gervase, until seven o'clock, when I went upstairs to rest and dress for dinner."

"You actually heard the shot, I understand?"

"Yes, I was in this room. I heard what sounded like a shot and I went out into the hall. Mr. Trent was there, and Miss Cardwell. Mr. Trent asked Snell if there was champagne for dinner, and made rather a joke of it. It never entered our heads to take the matter seriously, I'm afraid. We made sure it must have been a car backfiring."

Poirot said:

"Did you hear Mr. Trent say: *'There's always murder'*?"

"I believe he did say something like that—joking, of course."

"What happened next?"

"We all came in here."

"Can you remember the order in which the others came down to dinner?"

"Miss Chevenix-Gore was the first, I think, and then Mr. Forbes. Then Colonel Bury and Lady Chevenix-Gore together, and Mr. Burrows immediately after them. I think that was the order, but I can't be quite sure because they more or less came in all together."

"Gathered by the sound of the first gong?"

"Yes. Everyone always hustled when they heard that gong. Sir Gervase was a terrible stickler for punctuality in the evening."

"What time did he himself usually come down?"

"He was nearly always in the room before the first gong went."

"Did it surprise you that he was not down on this occasion?"

"Very much."

"Ah, I have it!" cried Poirot.

As the other two looked inquiringly at him, he went on:

"I have remembered what I wanted to ask. This evening, mademoiselle, as we all went along to the study on Snell's reporting it to be locked, you stooped and picked something up."

"I did?" Miss Lingard seemed very surprised.

"Yes, just as we turned into the straight passage to the study. Something small and bright."

"How extraordinary—I don't remember. Wait a minute—yes, I do. Only I wasn't thinking. Let me see—it must be in here."

Opening her black satin bag, she poured the contents on a table.

Poirot and Major Riddle surveyed the collection with interest. There were two handkerchiefs, a powder compact, a small bunch of keys, a spectacle case, and one other object on which Poirot pounced eagerly.

"A bullet, by Jove!" said Major Riddle.

The thing was indeed shaped like a bullet, but it proved to be a small pencil.

"That's what I picked up," said Miss Lingard. "I'd forgotten all about it."

"Do you know who this belongs to, Miss Lingard?"

"Oh, yes, it's Colonel Bury's. He had it made out of a bullet that hit him—or rather, didn't hit him, if you know what I mean—in the South African War."

"Do you know when he had it last?"

"Well, he had it this afternoon when they were playing bridge, because I noticed him writing with it on the score when I came in to tea."

"Who was playing bridge?"

"Colonel Bury, Lady Chevenix-Gore, Mr. Trent and Miss Cardwell."

"I think," said Poirot gently, "we will keep this and return it to the Colonel ourselves."

"Oh, please do. I am so forgetful, I might not remember to do so."

"Perhaps, mademoiselle, you would be so good as to ask Colonel Bury to come here now?"

"Certainly. I will go and find him at once."

She hurried away. Poirot got up and began walking aimlessly round the room.

"We begin," he said, "to reconstruct the afternoon. It is interesting. At half-past two Sir Gervase goes over accounts with Captain Lake.

*He is slightly preoccupied.* At three, he discusses the book he is writing with Miss Lingard. *He is in great distress of mind.* Miss Lingard associates that distress of mind with Hugo Trent on the strength of a chance remark. At tea time *his behavior is normal.* After tea, Godfrey Burrows tells us *he was in good spirits over something.* At five minutes to eight he comes downstairs, goes to his study, scrawls 'Sorry' on a sheet of paper, and shoots himself!"

Riddle said slowly:

"I see what you mean. It isn't consistent."

"Strange alternations of moods in Sir Gervase Chevenix-Gore! He is preoccupied—he is seriously upset—he is normal—he is in high spirits! There is something very curious here! And then that phrase he used: 'Too late.' That I should get here. 'Too late.' Well, it is true, that. I *did* get here too late—*to see him alive.*"

"I see. You really think—?"

"I shall never know now why Sir Gervase sent for me! That is certain!"

Poirot was still wandering round the room. He straightened one or two objects on the mantelpiece; he examined a card table that stood against a wall, he opened the drawer of it and took out the bridge markers. Then he wandered over to the writing-table and peered into the wastepaper basket. There was nothing in it but a paper bag. Poirot took it out, smelt it, murmured "Oranges" and flattened it out, reading the name on it. "Carpenter and Sons, Fruiterers, Hamborough St. Mary." He was just folding it neatly into squares when Colonel Bury entered the room.

# VIII

The Colonel dropped into the chair, shook his head, sighed and said:

"Terrible business, this, Riddle. Lady Chevenix-Gore is being wonderful—wonderful. Grand woman! Full of courage!"

Coming softly back to his chair, Poirot said:

"You have known her very many years, I think?"

"Yes, indeed. I was at her coming-out dance. Wore rosebuds in her hair, I remember. And a white fluffy dress. . . .Wasn't anyone to touch her in the room!"

His voice was full of enthusiasm. Poirot held out the pencil to him.

"This is yours, I think?"

"Eh? What? Oh, thank you; had it this afternoon when we were playing bridge. Amazing, you know, I held a hundred honors in spades three times running. Never done such a thing before."

"You were playing bridge before tea, I understand?" said Poirot. "What was Sir Gervase's frame of mind when he came in to tea?"

"Usual—quite usual. Never dreamed he was thinking of making away with himself. Perhaps he was a little more excitable than usual, now I come to think of it."

"When was the last time you saw him?"

"Why, then! Tea time! Never saw the poor chap alive again."

"You didn't go to the study at all after tea?"

"No, never saw him again."

"What time did you come down to dinner?"

"After the first gong went."

"You and Lady Chevenix-Gore came down together?"

"No, we—er—met in the hall. I think she'd been into the dining room to see to the flowers—something like that."

Major Riddle said:

"I hope you won't mind, Colonel Bury, if I ask you a somewhat personal question. Was there any trouble between you and Sir Gervase over the question of the Synthetic Paragon Rubberine Company?"

Colonel Bury's face became suddenly purple. He spluttered a little.

"Not at all. Not at all. Old Gervase was an unreasonable sort of fellow. You've got to remember that. He always expected everything he touched to turn out trumps! Didn't seem to realize that the whole world was going through a period of crisis. All stocks and shares bound to be affected."

"So there *was* a certain amount of trouble between you?"

"No trouble. Just damned unreasonable of Gervase!"

"He blamed you for certain losses he had sustained?"

"Gervase wasn't normal! Vanda knew that. But she could always handle him. I was content to leave it all in her hands."

Poirot coughed and Major Riddle, after glancing at him, changed the subject.

"You are a very old friend of the family, I know, Colonel Bury. Had you any knowledge as to how Sir Gervase had left his money?"

"Well, I should imagine the bulk of it would go to Ruth. That's what I gathered from what Gervase let fall."

"You don't think that was at all unfair to Hugo Trent?"

"Gervase didn't like Hugo. Never could stick him."

"But he had a great sense of family. Miss Chevenix-Gore was, after all, only his adopted daughter."

Colonel Bury hesitated, then after humming and hawing a moment, he said:

"Look here, I think I'd better tell you something. Strict confidence, and all that."

"Of course—of course."

"Ruth's illegitimate, but she's a Chevenix-Gore all right. Daughter of Gervase's brother, Anthony, who was killed in the War. Seemed he'd had an affair with a typist. When he was killed, the girl wrote to Vanda. Vanda went to see her, girl was expecting a baby. Vanda took it up with Gervase, she'd just been told that she herself could never have another child. Result was they took over the child when it was born, adopted it legally. The mother renounced all rights in it. They've brought Ruth up as their own daughter and to all intents and purposes, she *is* their own daughter, and you've only got to look at her to realize she's a Chevenix-Gore all right!"

"Aha!" said Poirot. "I see. That makes Sir Gervase's attitude very much clearer. But if he did not like Mr. Hugo Trent, why was he so anxious to arrange a marriage between him and Mademoiselle Ruth?"

"To regularize the family position. It pleased his sense of fitness."

"Even though he did not like or trust the young man?"

Colonel Bury snorted.

"You don't understand old Gervase. He couldn't regard people as human beings. He arranged alliances as though the parties were Royal Personages! He considered it fitting that Ruth and Hugo should marry, Hugo taking the name of Chevenix-Gore. What Hugo and Ruth thought about it didn't matter."

"And was Mademoiselle Ruth willing to fall in with this arrangement?"

Colonel Bury chuckled.

"Not she! She's a Tartar!"

"Did you know that shortly before his death Sir Gervase was drafting a new will by which Miss Chevenix-Gore would inherit only on condition that she should marry Mr. Trent?"

Colonel Bury whistled.

"Then he really *had* got the wind up about her and Burrows—"

As soon as he had spoken, he bit the words off, but it was too late. Poirot had pounced upon the admission.

"There was something between Mademoiselle Ruth and young Monsieur Burrows?"

"Probably nothing in it—nothing in it at all."

Major Riddle coughed and said:

"I think, Colonel Bury, that you must tell us all you know. It might have a direct bearing on Sir Gervase's state of mind."

"I suppose it might," said Colonel Bury, doubtfully. "Well, the truth of it is, young Burrows is not a bad-looking chap—at least, women seem to think so. He and Ruth seem to have got as thick as thieves just lately, and Gervase didn't like it—didn't like it at all. Didn't like to sack Burrows for fear of precipitating matters. He knows what Ruth's like. She won't be dictated to in any way. So I suppose he hit on this scheme. Ruth's not the sort of girl to sacrifice everything for love. She's fond of the fleshpots and she likes money."

"Do you yourself approve of Mr. Burrows?"

The Colonel delivered himself of the opinion that Godfrey Burrows was slightly hairy at the heel, a pronouncement which baffled Poirot completely, but made Major Riddle smile into his mustache.

A few more questions were asked and answered, and then Colonel Bury departed.

Riddle glanced over at Poirot who was sitting absorbed in thought.

"What do you make of it all, M. Poirot?"

The little man raised his hands.

"I seem to see a pattern—a purposeful design."

Riddle said: "It's difficult."

"Yes, it is difficult. . . . But more and more one phrase, lightly uttered, strikes me as significant."

"What was that?"

"That laughing sentence spoken by Hugo Trent: 'There's always murder'. . ."

Riddle said sharply:

"Yes, I can see that you've been leaning that way all along."

"Do you not agree, my friend, that the more we learn, the less and less motive we find for suicide? But for murder, we begin to have a surprising collection of motives!"

"Still, you've got to remember the facts—door locked, key in dead man's pocket. Oh, I know there are ways and means. Bent pins, strings—all sorts of devices. It would, I suppose, be *possible*. . . . But do those things really work? That's what I very much doubt."

"At all events, let us examine the position from the point of view of murder, not of suicide."

"Oh, all right. As *you* are on the scene, it probably *would* be murder!"

For a moment Poirot smiled.

"I hardly like that remark."

Then he became grave once more.

"Yes, let us examine the case from the standpoint of murder. The shot is heard, four people are in the hall, Miss Lingard, Hugo Trent, Miss Cardwell and Snell. Where are all the others?"

"Burrows was in the library, according to his own story. No one to check that statement. The others were presumably in their rooms, but who is to know if they were really there? Everybody seems to have come down separately. Even Lady Chevenix-Gore and Bury only met in the hall. Lady Chevenix-Gore came from the dining room.

Where did Bury come from? Isn't it possible that he came, not from upstairs, but *from the study?* There's that pencil."

"Yes, the pencil is interesting. He showed no emotion when I produced it, but that might be because he did not know where I found it and was unaware himself of having dropped it. Let us see, who else was playing bridge when the pencil was in use? Hugo Trent and Miss Cardwell. They're out of it. Miss Lingard and the butler can vouch for their alibis. The fourth was Lady Chevenix-Gore."

"You can't seriously suspect her."

"Why not, my friend? I tell you, me, I can suspect everybody! Supposing that, in spite of her apparent devotion to her husband, it is the faithful Bury she really loves?"

"H'm," said Riddle. "In a way it has been a kind of *ménage à trois* for years."

"And there is some trouble about this company between Sir Gervase and Colonel Bury."

"It's true that Sir Gervase might have been meaning to turn really nasty. We don't know the ins-and-outs of it. It might fit in with that summons to you. Say Sir Gervase suspects that Bury has deliberately fleeced him, but he doesn't want publicity because of a suspicion that his wife may be mixed up in it. Yes, that's possible. That gives either of those two a possible motive. And it *is* a bit odd really that Lady Chevenix-Gore should take her husband's death so calmly. All this spirit business may be acting!"

"Then there is the other complication," said Poirot. "Miss Chevenix-Gore and Burrows. It is very much to their interest that Sir Gervase should not sign the new will. As it is, she gets everything on condition that her husband takes the family name—"

"Yes, and Burrows' account of Sir Gervase's attitude this evening is a bit fishy. High spirits, pleased about something! That doesn't fit with anything else we've been told."

"There is, too, Mr. Ogilvie Forbes. Most correct, most severe, of an old and well-established firm. But lawyers, even the most respectable, have been known to embezzle their clients' money when they themselves are in a hole."

"You're getting a bit too sensational, I think, Poirot."

"You think what I suggest is too like the pictures? But life, Major Riddle, is often amazingly like the pictures."

"It hasn't been, so far, in Westshire," said the Chief Constable. "We'd better finish interviewing the rest of them, don't you think? It's getting late. We haven't seen Ruth Chevenix-Gore yet, and she's probably the most important of the lot."

"I agree. There is Miss Cardwell, too. Perhaps we might see her first, since that will not take long, and interview Miss Chevenix-Gore last."

"Quite a good idea."


# IX

Earlier that evening Poirot had only given Susan Cardwell a fleeting glance. He examined her now more attentively. An intelligent face, he thought, not strictly good-looking, but possessing an attraction that a merely pretty girl might envy. Her hair was magnificent, her face skillfully made up. Her eyes, he thought, were watchful.

After a few preliminary questions, Major Riddle said:

"I don't know how close a friend you are of the family, Miss Cardwell."

"I don't know them at all. Hugo arranged that I should be asked down here."

"You are, then, a friend of Hugo Trent's?"

"Yes, that's my position; Hugo's girl friend." Susan Cardwell smiled as she drawled out the words.

"You have known him a long time?"

"Oh, no, just a month or so."

She paused and then added:

"I'm by way of being engaged to him."

"And he brought you down here to introduce you to his people?"

"Oh, dear no, nothing like that. We were keeping it very hush-hush. I just came down to spy out the land. Hugo told me the place was just like a madhouse. I thought I'd better come and see for myself. Hugo, poor sweet, is a perfect pet, but he's got absolutely no brains. The position, you see, was rather critical. Neither Hugo nor I have any money, and old Sir Gervase, who was Hugo's main hope, had set his heart on Hugo making a match of it with Ruth. Hugo's a bit weak, you know. He might agree to this marriage and count on being able to get out of it later."

"That idea did not commend itself to you, mademoiselle?" inquired Poirot gently.

"Definitely not. Ruth might have gone all peculiar and refused to divorce him or something. I put my foot down. No trotting off to St. Paul's, Knightsbridge, until I could be there dithering with a sheaf of lilies."

"So you came down to study the situation for yourself?"

"Yes."

*"Eh bien!"* said Poirot.

"Well, of course, Hugo was right! The whole family was bughouse! Except Ruth, who seems perfectly sensible. She'd got her own boy friend and wasn't any keener on the marriage idea than I was."

"You refer to M. Burrows?"

"Burrows? Of course not. Ruth wouldn't fall for a bogus person like that."

"Then who was the object of her affection?"

Susan Cardwell paused, stretched for a cigarette, lit it, and remarked: "You'd better ask her that. After all, it isn't my business."

Major Riddle asked:

"When was the last time you saw Sir Gervase?"

"At tea."

"Did his manner strike you as peculiar in any way?"

The girl shrugged her shoulders.

"Not more than usual."

"What did you do after tea?"

"Played billiards with Hugo."

"You didn't see Sir Gervase again?"

"No."

"What about the shot?"

"That was rather odd. You see, I thought the first gong had gone, so I hurried up with my dressing, came dashing out of my room, heard, as I thought, the second gong and fairly raced down the stairs. I'd been one minute late for dinner the first night I was here and Hugo told me it had about wrecked our chances with the Old Man, so I fairly hared down. Hugo was just ahead of me and then there was a queer kind of pop-bang and Hugo said it was a champagne cork, but Snell said 'No' to that and, anyway, I didn't think it had come from the dining room. Miss Lingard thought it came from upstairs, but anyway we agreed it was a backfire and we trooped into the drawing-room and forgot about it."

"It did not occur to you for one moment that Sir Gervase might have shot himself?" asked Poirot.

"I ask you, should I be likely to think of such a thing? The Old Man seemed to enjoy himself throwing his weight about. I never imagined he'd do such a thing. I can't think why he did it. I suppose just because he was nuts."

"An unfortunate occurrence."

"Very—for Hugo and me. I gather he's left Hugo nothing at all, or practically nothing."

"Who told you that?"

"Hugo got it out of old Forbes."

"Well, Miss Cardwell—" Major Riddle paused a moment—"I think

that's all. Do you think Miss Chevenix-Gore is feeling well enough
to come down and talk to us?"

"Oh, I should think so. I'll tell her."

Poirot intervened.

"A little moment, mademoiselle. Have you seen this before?"

He held out the bullet pencil.

"Oh, yes, we had it at bridge this afternoon. Belongs to old Colonel
Bury, I think."

"Did he take it when the rubber was over?"

"I haven't the faintest idea."

"Thank you, mademoiselle. That is all."

"Right, I'll tell Ruth."

Ruth Chevenix-Gore came into the room like a queen. Her color
was vivid, her head held high. But her eyes, like the eyes of Susan
Cardwell, were watchful. She wore the same frock she had on when
Poirot arrived. It was a pale shade of apricot. On her shoulder was
pinned a deep salmon-pink rose. It had been fresh and blooming an
hour earlier, now it drooped.

"Well?" said Ruth.

"I'm extremely sorry to bother you . . ." began Major Riddle.

She interrupted him:

"Of course you have to bother me. You have to bother everyone.
I can save you time, though. I haven't the faintest idea why the Old
Man killed himself. All I can tell you is that it wasn't a bit like him."

"Did you notice anything amiss in his manner today? Was he depressed, or unduly excited—was there anything at all abnormal?"

"I don't think so. I wasn't noticing—"

"When did you see him last?"

"Tea time."

Poirot spoke:

"You did not go to the study—later?"

"No. The last I saw of him was in this room. Sitting there."

She indicated a chair.

"I see. Do you know this pencil, mademoiselle?"

"It's Colonel Bury's."

"Have you seen it lately?"

"I don't really remember."

"Do you know anything of a—disagreement between Sir Gervase
and Colonel Bury?"

"Over The Paragon Rubberine Company, you mean?"

"Yes."

"I should think so. The Old Man was rabid about it!"

"He considered, perhaps, that he had been swindled?"

Ruth shrugged her shoulders.

"He didn't understand the first thing about finance."

Poirot said:

"May I ask you a question, mademoiselle—a somewhat impertinent question?"

"Certainly, if you like."

"It is this—are you sorry that your—father is dead?"

She stared at him.

"Of course I'm sorry. I don't indulge in sob stuff. But I shall miss him. . . . I was fond of the Old Man. That's what we called him, Hugo and I, always. The 'Old Man'—you know—something of the primitive-anthropoid-ape-original-Patriarch-of-the-tribe business. It sounds disrespectful, but there's really a lot of affection behind it. Of course, he was really the most complete muddle-headed old ass that ever lived!"

"You interest me, mademoiselle."

"The Old Man had the brains of a louse! Sorry to have to say it, but it's true. He was incapable of any kind of headwork. Mind you, he was a character. Fantastically brave and all that! Could go careering off to the Pole, or fighting duels. I always think that he blustered such a lot because he really knew that his brains weren't up to much. Anyone could have got the better of him."

Poirot took the letter from his pocket.

"Read this, mademoiselle."

She read it through and handed it back to him.

"So that's what brought you here!"

"Does it suggest anything to you, that letter?"

She shook her head.

"No. It's possibly quite true. Anyone could have robbed the poor old pet. John says the last agent before him swindled him right and left. You see, the Old Man was so grand and so pompous that he never really condescended to look into details! He was an invitation to crooks."

"You paint a different picture of him, mademoiselle, from the accepted one."

"Oh, well—he put up a pretty good camouflage. Vanda (my mother) backed him for all she was worth. He was so happy stalking round pretending he was God Almighty. That's why, in a way, I'm glad he's dead. It's the best thing for him."

"I do not quite follow you, mademoiselle."

Ruth said broodingly:

"It was growing on him. One of these days he would have had to be locked up. . . . People were beginning to talk as it was."

"Did you know, mademoiselle, that he was contemplating a will whereby you could only inherit his money if you married Mr. Trent?"

She cried:

"How absurd! Anyway, I'm sure that could be set aside by law.
. . . I'm sure you can't dictate to people about whom they shall marry."

"If he had actually signed such a will, would you have complied
with its provisions, mademoiselle?"

She stared.

"I—I—"

She broke off. For two or three minutes she sat irresolute, looking
down at her dangling slipper. A little piece of earth detached itself
from the heel and fell on the carpet.

Suddenly Ruth Chevenix-Gore said:

"Wait!"

She got up and ran out of the room. She returned almost immediately
with Captain Lake by her side.

"It's got to come out," she said rather breathlessly. "You might as
well know now. John and I were married in London three weeks ago."

# X

Of the two of them, Captain Lake looked far the more embarrassed.

"This is a great surprise, Miss Chevenix-Gore—Mrs. Lake, I should
say," said Major Riddle. "Did no one know of this marriage of yours?"

"No, we kept it quite dark. John didn't like that part of it much."

Lake said, stammering a little:

"I—I know that it seems rather a rotten way to set about things. I
ought to have gone straight to Sir Gervase—"

Ruth interrupted:

"And told him you wanted to marry his daughter, and have been
kicked out on your head, and he'd probably have disinherited me,
raised hell generally in the house, and we could have told each other
how beautifully we'd behaved! Believe me, my way was better! If a
thing's done, it's done. There would still have been a row—but he'd
have come round."

Lake still looked unhappy. Poirot asked:

"When did you intend to break the news to Sir Gervase?"

Ruth answered:

"I was preparing the ground. He'd been rather suspicious about
me and John, so I pretended to turn my attentions to Godfrey. Naturally, he was ready to go quite off the deep end about that. I figured

it out that the news I was married to John would come almost as a relief!"

"Did anybody at all know of this marriage?"

"Yes, I told Vanda in the end. I wanted to get her on my side."

"And you succeeded in doing so?"

"Yes. You see, she wasn't very keen about my marrying Hugo—because he was a cousin, I think. She seemed to think the family was so batty already that we'd probably have completely batty children. That was probably rather absurd, because I'm only adopted, you know. I believe I'm some quite distant cousin's child."

"You are sure Sir Gervase had no suspicion of the truth?"

"Oh, no."

Poirot said:

"Is that true, Captain Lake? In your interview with Sir Gervase this afternoon, are you quite sure the matter was not mentioned?"

"No, sir. It was not."

"Because, you see, Captain Lake, there is certain evidence to show that Sir Gervase was in a highly excitable condition after the time he spent with you, and that he spoke once or twice of family dishonor."

"The matter was not mentioned," Lake repeated. His face had gone very white.

"Was that the last time you saw Sir Gervase?"

"Yes, I have already told you so."

"Where were you at eight minutes past eight this evening?"

"Where was I? In my house. At the end of the village, about half a mile away."

"You did not come up to Hamborough Close round about that time?"

"No."

Poirot turned to the girl.

"Where were you, mademoiselle, when your father shot himself?"

"In the garden."

"In the garden? You heard the shot?"

"Oh, yes. But I didn't think about it particularly. I thought it was someone out shooting rabbits, although now I remember I did think it sounded quite close at hand."

"You returned to the house—which way?"

"I came in through this window."

Ruth indicated with a turn of her head the window behind her.

"Was anyone in here?"

"No. But Hugo and Susan and Miss Lingard came in from the hall almost immediately. They were talking about shooting and murders and things."

"I see," said Poirot. "Yes, I think I see now. . . ."

Major Riddle said rather doubtfully:

"Well—er—thank you. I think that's all for the moment."

Ruth and her husband turned and left the room.

"What the devil—" began Major Riddle, and ended rather hopelessly: "It gets more and more difficult to keep track of this business."

Poirot nodded. He had picked up the little piece of earth that had fallen from Ruth's shoe and was holding it thoughtfully in his hand.

"It is like the mirror smashed on the wall," he said. "The dead man's mirror. Every new fact we come across shows us some different angle of the dead man. He is reflected from every conceivable point of view. We shall have soon a complete picture. . . ."

He rose and put the little piece of earth tidily in the wastepaper basket.

"I will tell you one thing, my friend. The clue to the whole mystery is the mirror. Go into the study and look for yourself, if you do not believe me."

Major Riddle said decisively:

"If it's murder, it's up to you to prove it. If you ask me, I say it's definitely suicide. Did you notice what the girl said about a former agent having swindled old Gervase? I bet Lake told that tale for his own purposes. He was probably helping himself a bit, Sir Gervase suspected it, and sent for you because he didn't know how far things had gone between Lake and Ruth. Then this afternoon Lake told him they were married. That broke Gervase up. It was 'too late' now for anything to be done. He determined to get out of it all. In fact, his brain, never very well-balanced at the best of times, gave way. In my opinion, that's what happened. What have you got to say against it?"

Poirot stood still in the middle of the room.

"What have I to say? This. I have nothing to say against your theory—but it does not go far enough. There are certain things it does not take into account."

"Such as?"

"The discrepancies in Sir Gervase's moods today, the finding of Colonel Bury's pencil, the evidence of Miss Cardwell (which is very important), the evidence of Miss Lingard as to the order in which people came down to dinner, the position of Sir Gervase's chair when he was found, the paper bag which had held oranges and, finally, the all-important clue of the broken mirror."

Major Riddle stared.

"Are you going to tell me that that rigmarole makes *sense?*" he asked.

Hercule Poirot replied softly:

"I hope to make it do so—by tomorrow."

# XI

It was just after dawn when Hercule Poirot awoke on the following morning. He had been given a bedroom on the east side of the house.

Getting out of bed, he drew aside the window blind and satisfied himself that the sun had risen and that it was a fine morning.

He began to dress with his usual meticulous care. Having finished his toilet, he wrapped himself up in a thick overcoat and wound a muffler round his neck.

Then he tiptoed out of his room and through the silent house down to the drawing room. He opened the French windows noiselessly and passed out into the garden.

The sun was just showing now. The air was misty, with the mist of a fine morning. Hercule Poirot followed the terraced walk round the side of the house until he came to the windows of Sir Gervase's study. Here he stopped and surveyed the scene.

Immediately outside the window was a strip of grass that ran parallel with the house. In front of that was a wide herbaceous border. The Michaelmas daisies still made a fine show. In front of the border was the flagged walk where Poirot was standing. A strip of grass ran from the grass walk behind the border to the terrace. Poirot examined it carefully, then shook his head. He turned his attention to the border on either side of it.

Very slowly he nodded his head. In the right-hand bed, distinct in the soft mold, there were footprints.

As he stared down at them, frowning, a sound caught his ears and he lifted his head sharply.

Above him a window had been pushed up. He saw a red head of hair. Framed in an aureole of golden red he saw the intelligent face of Susan Cardwell.

"What on earth are you doing at this hour, M. Poirot? A spot of sleuthing?"

Poirot bowed with the utmost correctitude.

"Good morning, mademoiselle. Yes, it is as you say. You now behold a detective—a great detective, I may say—in the act of detecting!"

The remark was a little flamboyant. Susan put her head on one side.

"I must remember this in my memoirs," she remarked. "Shall I come down and help?"

"I should be enchanted."

"I thought you were a burglar at first. Which way did you get out?"

"Through the drawing-room window."

"Just a minute and I'll be with you."

She was as good as her word. To all appearances Poirot was exactly in the same position as when she had first seen him.

"You are awake very early, mademoiselle?"

"I haven't been to sleep really properly. I was just getting that desperate feeling that one does get at five in the morning."

"It is not quite so early as that!"

"It feels like it! Now then, my super-sleuth, what are we looking at?"

"But observe, mademoiselle, footprints."

"So they are."

"Four of them," continued Poirot. "See, I will point them out to you. Two going towards the window, two coming from it."

"Whose are they? The gardener's?"

"Mademoiselle, mademoiselle. Those footmarks are made by the small dainty high-heeled shoes of a woman. See, convince yourself. Step, I beg of you, in the earth here beside them."

Susan hesitated a minute, then placed a foot gingerly onto the mold in the place indicated by Poirot. She was wearing small high-heeled slippers of dark brown leather.

"You see, yours are nearly the same size. Nearly, but not quite. These others are made by a rather longer foot than yours. Perhaps Miss Chevenix-Gore's—or Miss Lingard's—or even Lady Chevenix-Gore's."

"Not Lady Chevenix-Gore—she's got tiny feet. People did in those days—manage to have small feet, I mean. And Miss Lingard wears queer, flat-heeled things."

"Then they are the marks of Miss Chevenix-Gore. Ah, yes, I remember she mentioned having been out in the garden yesterday evening."

He led the way back round the house.

"Are we still sleuthing?" asked Susan.

"But, certainly. We will go now to Sir Gervase's study."

He led the way. Susan Cardwell followed him.

The door still hung in a melancholy fashion. Inside, the room was as it had been last night. Poirot pulled the curtain and admitted the daylight.

He stood there looking out a minute or two, then he said:

"You have not, I presume, mademoiselle, much acquaintance with burglars?"

Susan Cardwell shook her red head regretfully.

"I'm afraid not, M. Poirot."

"The Chief Constable, he, too, has not had the advantages of a friendly relationship with them. His connection with the criminal classes has always been strictly official. With me that is not so. I had a very pleasant chat with a burglar once. He told me an interesting thing about French windows—a trick that could sometimes be employed if the fastening was sufficiently loose."

He turned the handle as he spoke, the middle shaft came up out of the hole in the ground and Poirot was able to pull the two doors of the window towards him. Having opened them wide, he closed them again—closed them without turning the handle, so as not to send the shaft down into its socket. He let go of the handle, waited a moment, then struck a quick, jarring blow high up on the center of the shaft. The jar of the blow sent the shaft down into the socket in the ground—the handle turned of its own accord.

"You see, mademoiselle?"

"I think I do."

Susan had gone rather pale.

"The window is now closed. It is impossible to *enter* a room when the window is closed, but it *is* possible to *leave* a room, pull the doors to from outside, then hit it as I did, and the bolt goes down into the ground, turning the handle. The window then is firmly closed and anyone looking at it would say it had been closed from the *inside.*"

"Is that—" Susan's voice shook a little—"is that what happened last night?"

"I think so, yes, mademoiselle."

Susan said violently:

"I don't believe a word of it."

Poirot did not answer. He walked over to the mantelpiece. He wheeled sharply round.

"Mademoiselle, I have need of you as a witness. I have already one witness, Mr. Trent. He saw me find this tiny sliver of looking glass last night. I spoke of it to him. I left it where it was for the police. I even told the Chief Constable that a valuable clue was the broken mirror. But he did not avail himself of my hint. Now, you are a witness that I place this sliver of looking glass (to which, remember, I have already called Mr. Trent's attention) into a little envelope— so." He suited the action to the word. "And I write on it—so—and seal it up. You are a witness, mademoiselle?"

"Yes—but—but I don't know what it means."

Poirot walked over to the other side of the room. He stood in front of the desk and stared at the shattered mirror on the wall in front of him.

"I will tell you what it means, mademoiselle. If you had been standing here last night, looking into this mirror, you could have seen in it *murder being committed. . . .*"

# XII

For once in her life Ruth Chevenix-Gore—now Ruth Lake—came down to breakfast in good time. Hercule Poirot was in the hall and drew her aside before she went into the dining room.

"I have a question to ask you, madame."

"Yes?"

"You were in the garden last night. Did you at any time step in the flowerbed outside Sir Gervase's study window?"

Ruth stared at him.

"Yes, twice."

"Ah! *Twice.* How twice?"

"The first time I was picking Michaelmas daisies. That was about seven o'clock."

"Was it not rather an odd time of day to pick flowers?"

"Yes, it was, as a matter of fact. I'd done the flowers yesterday morning, but Vanda said after tea that the flowers on the dinner table weren't good enough. I had thought they would be all right, so I hadn't done them fresh."

"But your mother requested you to do them? Is that right?"

"Yes; so I went out just before seven. I took them from that part of the border because hardly anyone goes round there, and so it didn't matter spoiling the effect."

"Yes, yes, but the *second* time. You went there a *second* time, you said?"

"That was just before dinner. I had dropped a spot of brilliantine on my dress—just by the shoulder. I didn't want to bother to change and none of my artificial flowers went with the yellow of that dress. I remembered I'd seen a late rose when I was picking the Michaelmas daisies, so I hurried out and got it and pinned it on my shoulder."

Poirot nodded his head slowly.

"Yes, I remember that you wore a rose last night. What time was it, madame, when you picked that rose?"

"I don't really know."

"But it is *essential,* madame. Consider—reflect—"

Ruth frowned. She looked swiftly at Poirot and then away again.

"I can't say exactly," she said at last. "It must have been—oh, of course—it must have been about five minutes past eight. It was when I was on my way back round the house that I heard the gong go, and then that funny bang. I was hurrying because I thought it was the second gong and not the first."

"Ah! so you thought that—and did you not try the study window when you stood there in the flowerbed?"

"As a matter of fact, I did. I thought it might be open and it would be quicker to come in that way. But it was fastened."

"So everything is explained. I congratulate you, madame."

She stared at him.

"What do you mean?"

"That you have an explanation for everything, for the mold on your shoes, for your footprints in the flowerbed, for your fingerprints on the outside of the window. It is very convenient, that."

Before Ruth could answer, Miss Lingard came hurrying down the stairs. There was a queer purple flush on her cheeks and she looked a little startled at seeing Poirot and Ruth standing together.

"I beg your pardon," she said. "Is anything the matter?"

Ruth said angrily:

"I think M. Poirot has gone mad!"

She swept by them and into the dining room. Miss Lingard turned an astonished face on Poirot.

He shook his head.

"After breakfast," he said, "I will explain. I should like everyone to assemble in Sir Gervase's study at ten o'clock."

He repeated this request on entering the dining-room.

Susan Cardwell gave him a quick glance, then transferred her gaze to Ruth. When Hugo said:

"Eh? What's the idea?" she gave him a sharp nudge in the side, and he shut up obediently.

When he had finished his breakfast, Poirot rose and walked to the door. He turned and drew out a large old-fashioned watch.

"It is five minutes to ten. In five minutes—in the study."

Poirot looked round him. A circle of interested faces stared back at him. Everyone was there, he noted, with one exception, and at that very moment the exception swept into the room. Lady Chevenix-Gore came in with a soft, gliding step. She looked haggard and ill.

Poirot drew forward a big chair for her, and she sat down.

She looked up at the broken mirror, shivered, and pulled her chair a little way round.

"Gervase is still here," she remarked in a matter-of-fact tone. "Poor Gervase. . . . He will soon be free now."

Poirot cleared his throat and announced:

"I have asked you all to come here so that you may hear the true facts of Sir Gervase's suicide."

"It was Fate," said Lady Chevenix-Gore. "Gervase was strong, but his Fate was stronger."

Colonel Bury moved forward a little.

"Vanda—my dear."

She smiled up at him, then put up her hand. He took it in his. She said softly, "You are such a comfort, Ned."

Ruth said sharply:

"Are we to understand, M. Poirot, that you have definitely ascertained the cause of my father's suicide?"

Poirot shook his head.

"No, madame."

"Then what is all this rigmarole about?"

Poirot said quietly:

"I do not know the cause of Sir Gervase Chevenix-Gore's suicide, *because Sir Gervase Chevenix-Gore did not commit suicide*. He did not kill himself. *He was killed. . . .*"

"Killed?" Several voices echoed the word. Startled faces were turned in Poirot's direction. Lady Chevenix-Gore looked up, said, "Killed? Oh, no!" and gently shook her head.

"Killed, did you say?" It was Hugo who spoke now. "Impossible. There was no one in the room when we broke in. The window was fastened. The door was locked on the inside and the key was in my uncle's pocket. How could he have been killed?"

"Nevertheless, he was killed."

"And the murderer escaped through the keyhole, I suppose?" said Colonel Bury skeptically. "Or flew up the chimney?"

"The murderer," said Poirot, "went out through the window. I will show you how."

He repeated his maneuvers with the window.

"You see?" he said. "That was how it was done! From the first I could not consider it likely that Sir Gervase had committed suicide. He had a pronounced egomania and such a man does not kill himself.

"And there were other things! Apparently, just before his death, Sir Gervase had sat down at his desk, scrawled the word SORRY on a sheet of notepaper and had then shot himself. But before this last action he had, for some reason or other, altered the position of his chair, turning it so that it was sideways to the desk. Why? There must be some reason. I began to see light when I found, sticking to the base of a heavy bronze statuette, a tiny sliver of looking glass. . . .

"I asked myself, how does a sliver of broken looking glass come to be there?—and an answer suggested itself to me. The mirror had been broken, not by a bullet, *but by being struck with the heavy bronze figure*. That mirror had been broken *deliberately*.

"But why? I returned to the desk and looked down at the chair. Yes, I saw now. It was all wrong. No suicide would turn his chair round, lean over the edge of it, and then shoot himself. The whole thing was arranged. The suicide was a fake!

"And now I come to something very important. The evidence of

Miss Cardwell. Miss Cardwell said that she hurried downstairs last night because she thought that the *second* gong had sounded. That is to say, she thought that she had already heard the *first* gong.

"Now observe, *if* Sir Gervase is sitting at his desk in the normal fashion when he was shot, where would the bullet go? Traveling in a straight line, it would pass through the door, if the door were open, and finally *hit the gong!*

"You see now the importance of Miss Cardwell's statement? No one else heard that first gong, but then her room is situated immediately above this one, and she was in the best position for hearing it. It would consist of only one single note, remember.

"There could be no question of Sir Gervase's shooting himself. A dead man cannot get up, shut the door, lock it and arrange himself in a convenient position! Somebody else was concerned, and therefore it was not suicide, but murder. Someone whose presence was easily accepted by Sir Gervase, stood by his side talking to him. Sir Gervase was busy writing perhaps. The murderer brings the pistol up to the right side of his head and fires. The deed is done! Then quick, to work! The murderer slips on gloves. The door is locked, the key put in Sir Gervase's pocket. But supposing that one loud note of the gong has been heard? Then it will be realized that the door was *open,* not *shut,* when the shot was fired. So the chair is turned, the body rearranged, the dead man's fingers pressed on the pistol, the mirror deliberately smashed. Then the murderer goes out through the window, jars it shut, steps, not on the grass, but in the flowerbed where footprints can be smoothed out afterwards; then round the side of the house and into the drawing room."

He paused and said:

*"There was only one person who was out in the garden when the shot was fired.* That same person left her footprints in the flowerbed and her fingerprints on the outside of the window."

He came towards Ruth.

"And there was a motive, wasn't there? Your father had learnt of your secret marriage. He was preparing to disinherit you."

"It's a lie!" Ruth's voice came scornful and clear. "There's not a word of truth in your story. It's a lie from start to finish!"

"The proofs against you are very strong, madame. A jury *may* believe you. It may *not!*"

"She won't have to face a jury."

The others turned—startled. Miss Lingard was on her feet. Her face had altered. She was trembling all over.

*"I* shot him. I admit it! I had my reasons. I—I've been waiting for some time. M. Poirot is quite right. I followed him in here. I had taken the pistol out of the drawer earlier. I stood beside him talking

about the book—and I shot him. That was just after eight. The bullet struck the gong. I never dreamt it would pass right through his head like that. There wasn't time to go out and look for it. I locked the door and put the key in his pocket. Then I swung the chair round, smashed the mirror and, after scrawling 'sorry' on a piece of paper, I went out through the window and shut it the way M. Poirot showed you. I stepped in the flowerbed, but I smoothed out the footprints with a little rake I had put there ready. Then I went round to the drawing room. I had left the window open. I didn't know Ruth had gone out through it. She must have come round the front of the house while I went round the back. I had to put the rake away, you see, in a shed. I waited in the drawing room till I heard someone coming downstairs and Snell going to the gong, and then—"

She looked at Poirot.

"You don't know what I did then?"

"Oh, yes, I do. I found the bag in the wastepaper basket. It was very clever, that idea of yours. You did what children love to do. You blew up the bag and then hit it. It made a satisfactory big bang. You threw the bag into the wastepaper basket and rushed out into the hall. You had established the time of the suicide—and an alibi for yourself. But there was still one thing that worried you. You had not had time to pick up the bullet. It must be somewhere near the gong. It was essential that the bullet should be found in the study somewhere near the mirror. I don't know when you had the idea of taking Colonel Bury's pencil—"

"It was just then," said Miss Lingard. "When we all came in from the hall. I was surprised to see Ruth in the room. I realized she must have come from the garden through the window. Then I noticed Colonel Bury's pencil lying on the bridge table. I slipped it into my bag. If, later, anyone saw me pick up the bullet, I could pretend it was the pencil. As a matter of fact, I didn't think anyone saw me pick up the bullet. I dropped it by the mirror while you were looking at the body. When you tackled me on the subject, I was very glad I had thought of the pencil."

"Yes, that was clever. It confused me completely."

"I was afraid someone must hear the real shot, but I knew everyone was dressing for dinner and would be shut away in their rooms. The servants were in their quarters. Miss Cardwell was the only one at all likely to hear it, and she would probably think it was a backfire. What she did hear was the gong. I thought—I thought everything had gone without a hitch. . . ."

Mr. Forbes said slowly in his precise tones:

"This is a most extraordinary story. There seems no motive—"

Miss Lingard said clearly: "There *was* a motive. . . ."

She added fiercely:

"Go on, ring up the police! What are you waiting for?"

Poirot said gently:

"Will you all please leave the room? Mr. Forbes, ring up Major Riddle. I will stay here till he comes."

Slowly, one by one, the family filed out of the room. Puzzled, uncomprehending, shocked, they cast abashed glances at the trim upright figure with its neatly-parted gray hair.

Ruth was the last to go. She stood, hesitating in the doorway.

"I don't understand." She spoke angrily, defiantly, accusing Poirot. "Just now, you thought *I* had done it."

"No, no." Poirot shook his head. "No, I never thought that."

Ruth went out slowly.

Poirot was left with the prim little middle-aged woman who had just confessed to a cleverly-planned and cold-blooded murder.

"No," said Miss Lingard. "You didn't think she had done it. You accused *her* to make *me* speak. That's right, isn't it?"

Poirot bowed his head.

"While we're waiting," said Miss Lingard in a conversational tone, "you might tell me what made you suspect *me?*"

"Several things. To begin with, your account of Sir Gervase. A proud man like Sir Gervase would never speak disparagingly of his nephew to an outsider, especially someone in your position. You wanted to strengthen the theory of suicide. You also went out of your way to suggest that the cause of the suicide was some dishonorable trouble connected with Hugo Trent. That, again, was a thing Sir Gervase would never have admitted to a stranger. Then, there was the object you picked up in the hall, and the very significant fact that you did not mention that Ruth, when she entered the drawing room, did so *from the garden*. And then I found the paper bag—a most unlikely object to find in the wastepaper basket in the drawing room of a house like Hamborough Close! You were the only person who had been in the drawing room when the 'shot' was heard. The paper bag trick was one that would suggest itself to a woman—an ingenious homemade device. So everything fitted in. The endeavor to throw suspicion on Hugo, and to keep it away from Ruth. The mechanism of crime—and its motive."

The little gray-haired woman stirred.

"You know the motive?"

"I think so. Ruth's happiness—that was the motive! I fancy that you had seen her with John Lake—you knew how it was with them. And then with your easy access to Sir Gervase's papers, you came across the draft of his new will—Ruth disinherited unless she married Hugo Trent. That decided you to take the law into your own hands, using the fact that Sir Gervase had previously written to me. You probably saw a copy of that letter. What muddled feeling of suspicion and fear had caused him to write originally, I do not know. He must have suspected either Burrows or Lake of systematically robbing him. His uncertainty regarding Ruth's feelings made him seek a private investigation. You used that fact and deliberately set the stage for suicide, backing it up by your account of his being very distressed over something connected with Hugo Trent. You sent a telegram to me and reported Sir Gervase as having said I should arrive 'too late.' "

Miss Lingard said fiercely:

"Gervase Chevenix-Gore was a bully, a snob, and a windbag! I wasn't going to have him ruin Ruth's happiness."

Poirot said gently:

"Ruth is your daughter?"

"Yes—she is my daughter. I've often—thought about her. When I heard Sir Gervase Chevenix-Gore wanted someone to help him with a family history, I jumped at the chance. I was curious to see my— my girl. I knew Lady Chevenix-Gore wouldn't recognize me. It was years ago—I was young and pretty then, and I changed my name after that time. Besides, Lady Chevenix-Gore is too vague to know anything definitely. I liked her, but I hated the Chevenix-Gore family. They treated me like dirt. And there was Gervase going to ruin Ruth's life with his pride and snobbery. But I determined that she should be happy. And she *will* be happy—*if she never knows about me!*"

It was a plea—not a question.

Poirot bent his head gently.

"No one shall know from me."

Miss Lingard said quietly:

"Thank you."

Later, when the police had come and gone, Poirot found Ruth Lake with her husband in the garden.

She said challengingly:

"Did you really think that I had done it, M. Poirot?"

"I knew, madame, that you could *not* have done it—because of the Michaelmas daisies."

"The Michaelmas daisies? I don't understand."

"Madame, there were four footprints and four footprints *only* in the border. But if you had been picking flowers there would have been many more. That meant that between your first visit and your second, *someone had smoothed all those footsteps away.* That could only have been done by the guilty person, and since your footprints had *not* been removed, you were *not* the guilty person. You were automatically cleared."

Ruth's face lightened.

"Oh, I see. You know—I suppose it's dreadful, but I feel rather sorry for that poor woman. After all, she did confess rather than let me be arrested—or at any rate, that is what she thought. That was—rather noble in a way. I hate to think of her going through a trial for murder."

Poirot said gently:

"Do not distress yourself. It will not come to that. The doctor, he tells me that she has serious heart trouble. She will not live many weeks."

"I'm glad of that." Ruth picked an autumn crocus and pressed it idly against her cheek.

"Poor woman. I wonder why she did it. . . ."

# The Incredible Theft

## I

AS the butler handed round the soufflé Lord Mayfield leaned confidentially towards his neighbor on the right, Lady Julia Carrington. Known as a perfect host, Lord Mayfield took trouble to live up to his reputation. Although unmarried, he was always charming to women.

Lady Julia Carrington was a woman of forty, tall, dark and vivacious. She was very thin but still beautiful. Her hands and feet in particular were exquisite. Her manner was abrupt and restless, that of a woman who lived on her nerves.

About opposite to her at the round table sat her husband, Air Marshal Sir George Carrington. His career had begun in the Navy and he still retained the bluff breeziness of the ex-Naval man. He was laughing and chaffing the beautiful Mrs. Vanderlyn who was sitting on the other side of her host.

Mrs. Vanderlyn was an extremely good-looking blonde. Her voice held a soupçon of American accent, just enough to be pleasant without undue exaggeration.

On the other side of Sir George Carrington sat Mrs. Macatta, M.P. Mrs. Macatta was a great authority on Housing and Infant Welfare. She barked out short sentences rather than spoke them and was generally of a somewhat alarming aspect. It was perhaps natural that the Air Marshal would find his right-hand neighbor the pleasanter to talk to.

Mrs. Macatta, who always talked shop wherever she was, barked out short spates of information on her special subjects to her left-hand neighbor, young Reggie Carrington.

Reggie Carrington was twenty-one and completely uninterested in Housing, Infant Welfare and indeed any political subject. He said at interval, "How frightful!" and "I absolutely agree with you," and his mind was clearly elsewhere. Mr. Carlile, Lord Mayfield's private secretary, sat between young Reggie and his mother. A pale young man with pince-nez and an air of intelligent reserve, he talked little but was always ready to fling himself into any conversational breach. Noticing that Reggie Carrington was struggling with a yawn, he leaned forward and adroitly asked Mrs. Macatta a question about her "Fitness for Children" scheme.

Round the table, moving silently in the subdued amber light, a butler and two footmen offered dishes and filled up wine glasses. Lord Mayfield paid a very high salary to his chef, and was noted as a connoisseur of wines.

The table was a round one, but there was no mistaking who was the host. Where Lord Mayfield sat was so very decidedly the head of the table. A big man, square-shouldered, with thick silvery hair, a big straight nose and a slightly prominent chin. It was a face that lent itself easily to caricature. As Sir Charles McLaughlin, Lord Mayfield had combined a political career with being the head of a big engineering firm. He was himself a first-class engineer. His peerage had come a year ago and at the same time he had been created first Minister of Armaments, a new Ministry which had only just come into being.

The dessert had been placed on the table. The port had circulated once. Catching Mrs. Vanderlyn's eye, Lady Julia rose. The three women left the room.

The port passed round once more, and Lord Mayfield referred lightly to pheasants. The conversation for five minutes or so was sporting. Then Sir George said:

"Expect you'd like to join the others in the drawing room, Reggie, my boy. Lord Mayfield won't mind."

The boy took the hint easily enough.

"Thanks, Lord Mayfield, I think I will."

Mr. Carlile murmured:

"If you'll excuse me, Lord Mayfield—certain memoranda and other work to get through—"

Lord Mayfield nodded. The two young men left the room. The servants had retired some time before. The Minister for Armaments and the head of the Air Force were alone.

After a minute or two, Carrington said:

"Well—O.K.?"

"Absolutely! There's nothing to touch this new bomber in any country in Europe."

"Makes rings round 'em, eh? That's what I thought."

"Supremacy of the Air," said Lord Mayfield decisively.

Sir George Carrington gave a deep sigh.

"About time! You know, Charles, we've been through a ticklish spell. Lots of gunpowder everywhere all over Europe. And we weren't ready, damn it! We've had a narrow squeak. And we're not out of the woods yet, however much we hurry on construction."

Lord Mayfield murmured:

"Nevertheless, George, there are some advantages in starting late. A lot of the European stuff is out of date already—and they're perilously near bankruptcy."

"I don't believe that means anything," said Sir George gloomily. "One's always hearing this nation and that is bankrupt! But they carry on just the same. You know, finance is an absolute mystery to me."

Lord Mayfield's eyes twinkled a little. Sir George Carrington was always so very much the old-fashioned "bluff honest old sea dog." There were people who said that it was a pose he deliberately adopted.

Changing the subject Carrington said in a slightly over-casual manner:

"Attractive woman, Mrs. Vanderlyn—eh?"

Lord Mayfield said:

"Are you wondering what she's doing here?"

His eyes were amused.

Carrington looked a little confused.

"Not at all—not at all."

"Oh, yes, you were! Don't be an old humbug, George. You were wondering, in a slightly dismayed fashion, whether I was the latest victim!"

Carrington said slowly:

"I'll admit that it *did* seem a trifle odd to me that she should be here—well, this particular weekend."

Lord Mayfield nodded.

"Where the carcass is, there are the vultures gathered together. We've got a very definite carcass, and Mrs. Vanderlyn might be described as Vulture No. 1."

The Air Marshal said abruptly:

"Know anything about this Vanderlyn woman?"

Lord Mayfield clipped off the end of a cigar, lit it with precision and throwing his head back dropped out his words with careful deliberation.

"What do I know about Mrs. Vanderlyn? I know that she's an American subject. I know that she's had three husbands, one Italian, one German, and one Russian, and that in consequence she has made useful what I think are called 'contacts' in three countries. I know that she manages to buy very expensive clothes and live in a very luxurious manner and that there is some slight uncertainty as to where the income comes from which permits her to do so."

With a grin, Sir George Carrington murmured:

"Your spies have not been inactive, Charles, I see."

"I know," Lord Mayfield continued, "that in addition to having a seductive type of beauty, Mrs. Vanderlyn is also a very good listener and that she can display a fascinating interest in what we call 'shop.' That is to say, a man can tell her all about his job and feel that he is being intensely interesting to the lady! Sundry young officers have gone a little too far in their zeal to be interesting and their careers have suffered in consequence. They have told Mrs. Vanderlyn a little more than they should have done. Nearly all the lady's friends are in the Services—but last winter she was hunting in a certain county near one of our largest armament firms and she formed various friendships not at all sporting in character. To put it briefly, Mrs. Vanderlyn is a very useful person to—" He described a circle in the air with his cigar. "Perhaps we had better not say to whom! We will just say to a European power—and perhaps to more than one European power."

Carrington drew a deep breath.

"You take a great load off my mind, Charles."

"You thought I had fallen for the siren? My dear George! Mrs. Vanderlyn is just a little too obvious in her methods for a wary old bird like me. Besides she is, as they say, not quite so young as she once was. Your young Squadron Leaders wouldn't notice that. But I am fifty-six, my boy. In another four years I shall probably be a nasty old man continually haunting the society of unwilling débutantes."

"I was a fool," said Carrington apologetically, "but it seemed a bit odd—"

"It seemed to you odd that she should be here, in a somewhat intimate family party, just at the moment when you and I were to hold an unofficial conference over a discovery that will probably revolutionize the whole problem of Air Defense."

Sir George Carrington nodded.

Lord Mayfield said smiling;

"That's exactly it. That's the bait."

"The bait?"

"You see, George, to use the language of the movies, we've nothing actually 'on' the woman. And we want something! She's got away with rather more than she should in the past. But she's been careful, damnably careful. We know what she's been up to, but we've got no definite proof of it. We've got to tempt her with something big."

"Something big being the specifications of the new bomber."

"Exactly. It's got to be something big enough to induce her to take a risk—to come out into the open. And then—we've got her!"

Sir George grunted.

"Oh, well," he said. "I daresay it's all right. But suppose she won't take the risk?"

"That would be a pity," said Lord Mayfield. Then he added, "But I think she will. . . ."

He rose.

"Shall we join the ladies in the drawing room? We mustn't deprive your wife of her bridge."

Sir George grunted:

"Julia's a damned sight too fond of her bridge. Drops a packet over it. She can't afford to play as high as she does and I've told her so. The trouble is, Julia's a born gambler."

Coming round the table to join his host, he said:

"Well, I hope your plan comes off, Charles."

## II

In the drawing room conversation had flagged more than once. Mrs. Vanderlyn was usually at a disadvantage when left alone with members of her own sex. That charming sympathetic manner of hers, so much appreciated by members of the male sex, did not for some reason or other commend itself to women. Lady Julia was a woman whose manners were either very good or very bad. On this occasion she disliked Mrs. Vanderlyn and was bored by Mrs. Macatta and made no secret of her feelings. Conversation languished and might have ceased altogether but for the latter.

Mrs. Macatta was a woman of great earnestness of purpose. Mrs. Vanderlyn she dismissed immediately as a useless and parasitic type. Lady Julia she tried to interest in a forthcoming Charity entertainment which she was organizing. Lady Julia answered vaguely, stifled a yawn or two and retired into her own inner preoccupation. Why didn't Charles and George come? How tiresome men were. Her comments became even more perfunctory as she became absorbed in her own thoughts and worries.

The three women were sitting in silence when the men finally entered the room.

Lord Mayfield thought to himself:

"Julia looks ill tonight. What a mass of nerves the woman is."

Aloud he said:

"What about a rubber—eh?"

Lady Julia brightened at once. Bridge was as the breath of life to her.

Reggie Carrington entered the room at that minute and a four was arranged. Lady Julia, Mrs. Vanderlyn, Sir George and young Reggie sat down to the card table. Lord Mayfield devoted himself to the task of entertaining Mrs. Macatta.

When two rubbers had been played, Sir George looked ostentatiously at the clock on the mantelpiece.

"Hardly worthwhile beginning another," he remarked.

His wife looked annoyed.

"It's only a quarter to eleven. A short one."

"They never are, my dear," said Sir George good-temperedly. "Anyway, Charles and I have some work to do."

Mrs. Vanderlyn murmured:

"How important that sounds! I suppose you clever men who are at the top of things never get a real rest."

"No forty-eight hour week for us," said Sir George.

Mrs. Vanderlyn murmured:

"You know I feel rather ashamed of myself as a raw American, but I do get so *thrilled* at meeting people who control the destinies of a country. I expect that seems a very crude point of view to you, Sir George."

"My dear Mrs. Vanderlyn, I should never think of you as 'crude' or 'raw.'"

He smiled into her eyes. There was, perhaps, a hint of irony in the voice which she did not miss. Adroitly she turned to Reggie, smiling sweetly into his eyes.

"I'm sorry we're not continuing our partnership. That was a frightfully clever four no trump call of yours."

Flushed and pleased, Reggie mumbled:

"Bit of a fluke that it came off."

"Oh, no, it was really a clever bit of deduction on your part. You'd deduced from the bidding exactly where the cards must be, and you played accordingly. I thought it was brilliant."

Lady Julia rose abruptly.

"The woman lays it on with a palette knife," she thought disgustedly.

Then her eyes softened as they rested on her son. He believed it all. How pathetically young and pleased he looked. How incredibly naïve he was. No wonder he got into scrapes. He was too trusting— the truth of it was he had too sweet a nature. George didn't understand him in the least. Men were so unsympathetic in their judgments. They forgot that they had even been young themselves. George was much too harsh with Reggie.

Mrs. Macatta had risen. Good-nights were said.

The three women went out of the room. Lord Mayfield helped himself to a drink, after giving one to Sir George, then he looked up as Mr. Carlile appeared at the door.

"Get out the files and all the papers, will you, Carlile? Including the plans and the prints. The Air Marshal and I will be along shortly. We'll just take a turn outside first, eh, George? It's stopped raining."

Mr. Carlile, turning to depart, murmured an apology as he almost collided with Mrs. Vanderlyn.

She drifted towards the men, murmuring:

"My book. I was reading it before dinner."

Reggie sprang forward and held up a book.

"Is this it? On the sofa?"

"Oh, yes. Thank you *so* much."

She smiled sweetly, said good-night again and went out of the room.

Sir George had opened one of the French windows.

"Beautiful night now," he announced. "Good idea of yours to take a turn."

Reggie said:

"Well, good-night, sir. I'll be toddling off to bed."

"Good-night, my boy," said Lord Mayfield.

Reggie picked up a detective story which he had begun earlier in the evening and left the room.

Lord Mayfield and Sir George stepped out upon the terrace.

It was now a beautiful night with a clear sky studded with stars.

Sir George drew a deep breath.

"Phew, that woman uses a lot of scent," he remarked.

Lord Mayfield laughed.

"Anyway, it's not cheap scent. One of the most expensive brands in the market, I should say."

Sir George gave a grimace.

"I suppose one should be thankful for that."

"You should, indeed. I think a woman smothered in cheap scent is one of the greatest abominations known to mankind."

Sir George glanced up at the sky.

"Extraordinary the way it's cleared. I heard the rain beating down when we were at dinner."

The two men strolled slowly along the terrace.

The terrace ran the whole length of the house. Below it the ground sloped gently away permitting a magnificent view over the Sussex weald.

Sir George lit a cigar.

"About this metal alloy—" he began.

The talk became technical.

As they approached the far end of the terrace for the fifth time, Lord Mayfield said with a sigh:

"Oh, well, I suppose we'd better get down to it."

"Yes, good bit of work to get through."

The two men turned and Lord Mayfield uttered a surprised ejaculation.

"Hullo! See that?"

"See what?" asked Sir George.

"Thought I saw someone slip across the terrace from my study window."

"Nonsense, old boy. I didn't see anything."

"Well, I did—or I thought I did."

"Your eyes are playing tricks on you. I was looking straight down the terrace and I'd have seen anything there was to be seen. There's precious little *I* don't see—even if I do have to hold a newspaper at arm's length."

Lord Mayfield chuckled.

"I can put one over on you there, George. I read easily without glasses."

"But you can't always distinguish the fellow on the other side of the House. Or is that eyeglass gesture of yours sheer intimidation?"

Laughing, the two men entered Lord Mayfield's study, the French window of which was open.

Mr. Carlile was busy arranging some papers in a file by the safe.

He looked up as they entered.

"Ha, Carlile, everything ready?"

"Yes, Lord Mayfield, all the papers are on your desk."

The desk in question was a big important looking writing-table of mahogany set across a corner by the window. Lord Mayfield went over to it, and began sorting through the various documents laid out.

"Lovely night now," said Sir George.

Mr. Carlile agreed.

"Yes, indeed. Remarkable the way it's cleared up after the rain."

Putting away his file, Mr. Carlile asked:

"Will you want me any more tonight, Lord Mayfield?"

"No, I don't think so, Carlile. I'll put all these away myself. We shall probably be late. You'd better turn in."

"Thank you. Good-night, Lord Mayfield. Good-night, Sir George."

"Good-night, Carlile."

As the secretary was about to leave the room, Lord Mayfield said sharply:

"Just a minute, Carlile. You've forgotten the most important of the lot."

"I beg your pardon, Lord Mayfield."

"The actual plans of the bomber, man."

The secretary stared.

"They're right on the top, sir."

"They're nothing of the sort."

"But I've just put them there."

"Look for yourself, man."

With a bewildered expression, the young man came forward and joined Lord Mayfield at the desk.

Somewhat impatiently, the Minister indicated the pile of papers. Carlile sorted through them, his expression of bewilderment growing.

"You see? They're not there."

The secretary stammered:

"But—but it's incredible. I laid them there not three minutes ago."

Lord Mayfield said good-humoredly:

"You must have made a mistake; they must be still in the safe."

"I don't see how—I *know* I put them there!"

Lord Mayfield brushed past him to the open safe. Sir George joined them. A very few minutes sufficed to show that the plans of the bomber were not there.

Dazed and unbelieving, the three men returned to the desk and once more turned over the papers.

"My God!" said Mayfield. "They're gone!"

Mr. Carlile cried:

"But it's impossible!"

"Who's been in this room?" snapped out the Minister.

"No one. No one at all."

"Look here, Carlile, those plans haven't just vanished into thin air. Someone has taken them. Has Mrs. Vanderlyn been in here?"

"Mrs. Vanderlyn? Oh, no, sir."

"I'll back that," said Carrington. He sniffed the air. "You'd soon smell if she had. That scent of hers."

"Nobody has been in here," insisted Carlile. "I can't understand it."

"Look here, Carlile," said Lord Mayfield. "Pull yourself together. We've got to get to the bottom of this. You're absolutely sure the plans were in the safe?"

"Absolutely."

"You actually saw them? You didn't just assume they were among the others?"

"No, no, Lord Mayfield. I saw them. I put them on top of the others on the desk."

"And since then, you say, nobody has been in the room. Have you been out of the room?"

"No—at least—yes."

"Ah!" cried Sir George. "Now we're getting at it!"

Lord Mayfield said sharply:

"What on earth—" when Carlile interrupted.

"In the normal course of events, Lord Mayfield, I should not, of course, have dreamed of leaving the room when important papers were lying about, but hearing a woman scream—"

"A woman scream!" ejaculated Lord Mayfield in a surprised voice.

"Yes, Lord Mayfield. It startled me more than I can say. I was just laying the papers on the desk when I heard it and naturally I ran out into the hall."

"Who screamed?"

"Mrs. Vanderlyn's French maid. She was standing halfway up the stairs, looking very white and upset and shaking all over. She said she had seen a ghost."

"Seen a ghost?"

"Yes, a tall woman dressed all in white who moved without a sound and floated in the air."

"What a ridiculous story!"

"Yes, Lord Mayfield, that is what I told her. I must say she seemed rather ashamed of herself. She went off upstairs and I came back in here."

"How long ago was this?"

"Just a minute or two before you and Sir George came in."

"And you were out of the room—how long?"

The secretary considered.

"Two minutes—at the most three."

"Long enough," groaned Lord Mayfield. Suddenly he clutched his friend's arm.

"George, that shadow I saw—slinking away from this window. That was it! As soon as Carlile left the room, he nipped in, seized the plans and made off."

"Dirty work," said Sir George.

Then he seized his friend by the arm.

"Look here, Charles, this is the devil of a business. What the hell are we going to do about it?"


# III

"At any rate give it a trial, Charles."

It was half an hour later. The two men were in Lord Mayfield's study and Sir George had been expending a considerable amount of persuasion to induce his friend to adopt a certain course.

Lord Mayfield, at first most unwilling, was gradually becoming less averse to the idea.

Sir George went on:

"Don't be so damned pig-headed, Charles."

Lord Mayfield said slowly:

"Why drag in a wretched foreigner we know nothing about?"

"But I happen to know a lot about him. The man's a marvel."

"Humph."

"Look here, Charles. It's a chance! Discretion is the essence of this business. If it leaks out—"

"*When* it leaks out is what you mean!"

"Not necessarily. This man, Hercule Poirot—"

"Will come down here and produce the plans like a conjurer taking rabbits out of his hat, I suppose?"

"He'll get at the truth. And the truth is what we want. Look here, Charles, I take all responsibility on myself."

Lord Mayfield said slowly:

"Oh, well, have it your own way, but I don't see what the fellow can do. . . ."

Sir George picked up the phone.

"I'm going to get through to him—now."

"He'll be in bed."

"He can get up. Dash it all, Charles, you can't let that woman get away with it."

"Mrs. Vanderlyn, you mean?"

"Yes. You don't doubt, do you, that she's at the bottom of this?"

"No, I don't. She's turned the tables on me with a vengeance. I don't like admitting, George, that a woman's been too clever for us. It goes against the grain. But it's true. We shan't be able to prove anything against her and yet we both know that she's been the prime mover in the affair."

"Women are the devil," said Carrington with feeling.

"Nothing to connect her with it, damn it all! We may believe that she put the girl up to that screaming trick and that the man lurking outside was her accomplice, but the devil of it is, we can't prove it."

"Perhaps Hercule Poirot can."

Suddenly Lord Mayfield laughed.

"By the Lord, George, I thought you were too much of an old John Bull to put your trust in a Frenchman, however clever."

"He's not even a Frenchman, he's a Belgian," said Sir George in a rather shamefaced manner.

"Well, have your Belgian down. Let him try his wits on this business. I'll bet he can't make more of it than we can."

Without replying, Sir George stretched a hand to the telephone.

# IV

Blinking a little, Hercule Poirot turned his head from one man to the other. Very delicately he smothered a yawn.

It was half-past two in the morning. He had been roused from sleep and rushed down through the darkness in a big Rolls-Royce. Now he had just finished hearing what the two men had to tell him.

"Those are the facts, M. Poirot," said Lord Mayfield.

He leaned back in his chair, and slowly fixed his monocle in one eye. Through it a shrewd pale blue eye watched Poirot attentively. Besides being shrewd, the eye was definitely skeptical. Poirot cast a swift glance at Sir George Carrington.

That gentleman was leaning forward with an expression of almost childlike hopefulness on his face.

Poirot said slowly:

"I have the facts, yes. The maid screams, the secretary goes out, the nameless watcher comes in, the plans are there on top of the desk, he snatches them up and goes. The facts—they are all very convenient."

Something in the way he uttered the last phrase seemed to attract Lord Mayfield's attention. He sat up a little straighter, his monocle dropped. It was as though a new alertness came to him.

"I beg your pardon, M. Poirot?"

"I said, Lord Mayfield, that the facts were all very convenient—for the thief. By the way, you are sure it was a *man* you saw?"

Lord Mayfield shook his head.

"That I couldn't say. It was just a—shadow. In fact, I was almost doubtful if I had seen anyone."

Poirot transferred his gaze to the Air Marshal.

"And you, Sir George? Could you say if it was a man or a woman?"

"I didn't see anyone myself."

Poirot nodded thoughtfully. Then he skipped suddenly to his feet and went over to the writing table.

"I can assure you that the plans are not there," said Lord Mayfield. "We have all three been through those papers half a dozen times."

"All three? You mean, your secretary also?"

"Yes, Carlile."

Poirot turned suddenly.

"Tell me, Lord Mayfield, which paper was on top when you went over to the desk?"

Mayfield frowned a little in the effort of remembrance.

"Let me see—yes, it was a rough memorandum of some of our air defense positions."

Deftly, Poirot nipped out a paper and brought it over.

"Is this the one, Lord Mayfield?"

Lord Mayfield took it and glanced over it.

"Yes, that's the one."

Poirot took it over to Carrington.

"Did you notice this paper on the desk?"

Sir George took it, held it away from him, then slipped on his pince-nez.

"Yes, that's right. I looked through them too, with Carlile and Mayfield. This was on top."

Poirot nodded thoughtfully. He replaced the paper on the desk. Mayfield looked at him in a slightly puzzled manner.

"If there are any other questions—" he began.

"But yes, certainly there is a question. *Carlile*. Carlile is the question!"

Lord Mayfield's color rose a little.

"Carlile, M. Poirot, is quite above suspicion! He has been my confidential secretary for nine years. He has access to all my private papers, and I may point out to you that he could have made a copy of the plans and a tracing of the specifications quite easily without anyone being the wiser."

"I appreciate your point," said Poirot. "If he had been guilty there would be no need for him to stage a clumsy robbery."

"In any case," said Lord Mayfield, "I am sure of Carlile. I will guarantee him."

"Carlile," said Carrington gruffly, "is all right."

Poirot spread out his hands gracefully.

"And this Mrs. Vanderlyn—she is all wrong?"

"She's a wrong 'un all right," said Sir George.

Lord Mayfield said in more measured tones:

"I think, M. Poirot, that there can be no doubt of Mrs. Vanderlyn's—well—activities. The Foreign Office can give you more precise data as to that."

"And the maid, you take it, is in with her mistress?"

"Not a doubt of it," said Sir George.

"It seems to me a plausible assumption," said Lord Mayfield more cautiously.

There was a pause. Poirot sighed, and absent-mindedly rearranged one or two articles on a table at his right hand. Then he said:

"I take it that these papers represented money? That is, the stolen papers would be definitely worth a large sum in cash."

"If presented in a certain quarter—yes."

"Such as?"

Sir George mentioned the names of two European powers.

Poirot nodded.

"That fact would be known to anyone, I take it?"

"Mrs. Vanderlyn would know it all right."

"I said to *anyone?*"

"I suppose so, yes."

"Anyone with a minimum of intelligence would appreciate the cash value of the plans?"

"Yes, but, M. Poirot—" Lord Mayfield was looking rather uncomfortable.

Poirot held up a hand.

"I do what you call explore all the avenues."

Suddenly he rose again, stepped nimbly out of the window and with a flashlight examined the edge of the grass at the further side of the terrace.

The two men watched him.

He came in again, sat down and said:

"Tell me, Lord Mayfield, this malefactor, this skulker in the shadows, you do not have him pursued?"

Lord Mayfield shrugged his shoulders.

"At the bottom of the garden he could make his way out to a main road. If he had a car waiting there, he would soon be out of reach—"

"But there are the police—the A.A. scouts—"

Sir George interrupted.

"You forget, M. Poirot. *We cannot risk publicity.* If it were to get out that these plans had been stolen, the result would be extremely unfavorable to the Party."

"Ah, yes," said Poirot. "One must remember *La Politique.* The great discretion must be observed. You send instead for me. Ah, well, perhaps it is simpler."

"You are hopeful of success, M. Poirot?" Lord Mayfield sounded a trifle incredulous.

The little man shrugged his shoulders.

"Why not? One has only to reason—to reflect."

He paused a moment and then said:

"I would like now to speak to Mr. Carlile."

"Certainly." Lord Mayfield rose. "I asked him to wait up. He will be somewhere near at hand."

He went out of the room.

Poirot looked at Sir George.

*"Eh bien,"* he said. "What about this man on the terrace?"

"My dear M. Poirot. Don't ask me! I didn't see him, and I can't describe him."

Poirot leaned forward.

"So you have already said. But it is a little different from that, is it not?"

"What d'you mean?" asked Sir George abruptly.

"How shall I say it? Your disbelief, it is more profound."

Sir George started to speak, then stopped.

"But, yes," said Poirot encouragingly. "Tell me. You are both at the end of the terrace. Lord Mayfield sees a shadow slip from the window and across the grass. Why do you not see that shadow?"

Carrington stared at him.

"You've hit it, M. Poirot. I've been worrying about that ever since. You see, I'd swear that no one did leave this window. I thought Mayfield had imagined it—branch of a tree waving—something of that kind. And then when we came in here and found there had been a robbery, it seemed as though Mayfield must have been right and I'd been wrong. And yet—"

Poirot smiled.

"And yet you still in your heart of hearts believe in the evidence (the negative evidence) of your own eyes?"

"You're right, M. Poirot, I do."

Poirot gave a sudden smile.

"How wise you are."

Sir George said sharply:

"There were no footprints on the grass edge?"

Poirot nodded.

"Exactly. Lord Mayfield, he fancies he sees a shadow. Then there comes the robbery and he is sure—but sure! It is no longer a fancy—he actually *saw* the man. But that is not so. Me, I do not concern myself much with footprints and such things, but for what it is worth we have that negative evidence. *There were no footprints on the grass.* It had rained heavily this evening. If a man had crossed the terrace to the grass this evening his footprints would have shown."

Sir George said staring, "But then—but then—"

"It brings us back to the house. To the people in the house."

He broke off as the door opened and Lord Mayfield entered with Mr. Carlile.

Though still looking very pale and worried, the secretary had regained a certain composure of manner. Adjusting his pince-nez he sat down and looked at Poirot inquiringly.

"How long had you been in this room when you heard the scream, Monsieur?"

Carlile considered.

"Between five and ten minutes I should say."

"And before that there had been no disturbance of any kind?"

"No."

"I understand that the house party had been in one room for the greater part of the evening."

"Yes, the drawing room."

Poirot consulted his notebook.

"Sir George Carrington and his wife. Mrs. Macatta. Mrs. Vanderlyn. Mr. Reggie Carrington. Lord Mayfield and yourself. Is that right?"

"I myself was not in the drawing room. I was working here the greater part of the evening."

Poirot turned to Lord Mayfield.

"Who went up to bed first?"

"Lady Julia Carrington, I think. As a matter of fact, the three ladies went out together."

"And then?"

"Mr. Carlile came in and I told him to get out the papers as Sir George and I would be along in a minute."

"It was then that you decided to take a turn on the terrace?"

"It was."

"Was anything said in Mrs. Vanderlyn's hearing as to your working in the study?"

"The matter was mentioned, yes."

"But she was not in the room when you instructed Mr. Carlile to get out the papers?"

"No."

"Excuse me, Lord Mayfield," said Carlile. "Just after you had said that, I collided with her in the doorway. She had come back for a book."

"So that she might have overheard?"

"I think it is quite possible, yes."

"She came back for a book," mused Poirot. "Did you find her her book, Lord Mayfield?"

"Yes, Reggie gave it to her."

"Ah, yes, it is what you call the old gasp—no, pardon, the old wheeze—that—to come back for a book. It is often useful!"

"You think it was deliberate?"

Poirot shrugged his shoulders.

"And after that, you two gentlemen go out on the terrace. And Mrs. Vanderlyn?"

"She went off with her book."

"And the young M. Reggie. He went to bed also?"

"Yes."

"And Mr. Carlile he comes here and sometimes between five and ten minutes later he hears a scream. Continue, M. Carlile. You heard a scream and you went out into the hall. Ah, perhaps it would be simplest if you reproduced exactly your actions."

Mr. Carlile got up a little awkwardly.

"Here I scream," said Poirot helpfully. He opened his mouth and emitted a shrill bleat. Lord Mayfield turned his head away to hide a smile and Mr. Carlile looked extremely uncomfortable.

"*Allez!* Forward! March!" cried Poirot. "It is your cue that I give you there."

Mr. Carlile walked stiffly to the door, opened it and went out. Poirot followed him. The other two came behind.

"The door, did you close it after you or leave it open?"

"I can't really remember. I think I must have left it open."

"No matter. Proceed."

Still with extreme stiffness, Mr. Carlile walked to the bottom of the staircase and stood there looking up.

Poirot said:

"The maid, you say, was on the stairs. Whereabouts?"

"About halfway up."

"And she was looking upset?"

"Definitely so."

"*Eh bien,* me, I am the maid." Poirot ran nimbly up the stairs. "About here?"

"A step or two higher."

"Like this?"

Poirot struck an attitude.

"Well—er—not quite like that."

"How then?"

"Well, she had her hands to her head."

"Ah, her hands to her *head.* That is very interesting. Like this?" Poirot raised his arms, his hands rested on his head just above each ear.

"Yes, that's it."

"Aha! And tell me, M. Carlile, she was a pretty girl—yes?"

"Really, I didn't notice."

Carlile's voice was repressive.

"Aha, you did not notice? But you are a young man. Does not a young man notice when a girl is pretty?"

"Really, M. Poirot, I can only repeat that *I* did not do so."

Carlile cast an agonized glance at his employer. Sir George Carrington gave a sudden chuckle.

"M. Poirot seems determined to make you out a gay dog, Carlile," he remarked.

Mr. Carlile gave him a cold glance.

"Me, I always notice when a girl is pretty," announced Poirot as he descended the stairs.

The silence with which Mr. Carlile greeted this remark was somewhat pointed. Poirot went on:

"And it was then she told you this tale of having seen a ghost?"

"Yes."

"Did you believe the story?"

"Well, hardly, M. Poirot!"

"I do not mean, do you believe in ghosts. I mean did it strike you that the girl herself really thought she had seen something?"

"Oh, as to that, I couldn't say. She was certainly breathing fast, as I say, and seemed upset."

"You did not see or hear anything of her mistress?"

"Yes, as a matter of fact, I did. She came out of her room in the gallery above and called 'Leonie.' "

"And then?"

"The girl ran up to her and I went back to the study."

"Whilst you were standing at the foot of the stairs here could anyone have entered the study by the door you had left open?"

Carlile shook his head.

"Not without passing me. The study door is at the end of the passage, as you see."

Poirot nodded thoughtfully. Mr. Carlile went on in his careful precise voice.

"I may say that I am very thankful that Lord Mayfield actually saw the thief leaving the window. Otherwise I myself should be in a very unpleasant position."

"Nonsense, my dear Carlile," broke in Lord Mayfield impatiently. "No suspicion could possibly attach to you."

"It is very kind of you to say so, Lord Mayfield, but facts are facts, and I can quite see that it looks badly for me. In any case I hope that my belongings and myself may be searched."

"Nonsense, my dear fellow," said Mayfield.

Poirot murmured:

"You are serious in wishing that?"

"I should infinitely prefer it."

Poirot looked at him thoughtfully for a minute or two and murmured: "I see."

Then he asked:

"Where is Mrs. Vanderlyn's room situated in regard to the study?"

"It is directly over it."

"With a window giving on the terrace?"

"Yes."

Again Poirot nodded. Then he said:

"Let us go to the drawing room."

Here he wandered round the room, examined the fastenings of the windows, glanced at the scorers on the bridge table and then finally addressed Lord Mayfield:

"This affair," he said, "is more complicated than it appears. But one thing is quite certain. The stolen plans have not left this house."

Lord Mayfield stared at him.

"But, my dear M. Poirot, the man I saw leaving the study—"

"There was no man."

"But I *saw* him—"

"With the greatest respect, Lord Mayfield, you imagined you saw him. The shadow cast by the branch of a tree deceived you. The fact that a robbery occurred naturally seemed a proof that what you had imagined was true."

"Really, M. Poirot, the evidence of my own eyes—"

"Back my eyes against yours any day, old boy," put in Sir George.

"You must permit me, Lord Mayfield, to be very definite on that point. *No one crossed the terrace to the grass.*"

Looking very pale and speaking stiffly, Mr. Carlile said:

"In that case, if M. Poirot is correct, suspicion automatically attaches itself to me. I am the only person who could possibly have committed the robbery."

Lord Mayfield sprang up.

"Nonsense! Whatever M. Poirot thinks about it, I don't agree with him. I am convinced of your innocence, my dear Carlile. In fact, I'm willing to guarantee it."

Poirot murmured mildly:

"But I have not said that I suspect M. Carlile."

Carlile answered:

"No, but you've made it perfectly clear that no one else had a chance to commit the robbery."

"*Du tout! Du tout!*"

"But I have told you nobody passed me in the hall to get to the study door."

"I agree. But someone might have come in through the study *window.*"

"But that is just what you said did not happen."

"I said that no one from *outside* could have come and left without leaving marks on the grass. But it could have been managed from *inside* the house. Someone could have gone out from this room by one of these windows, slipped along the terrace, in at the study window, and back again in here."

Mr. Carlile objected:

"But Lord Mayfield and Sir George Carrington were on the terrace."

"They were on the terrace, yes, but they were *en promenade.* Sir George Carrington's eyes may be of the most reliable—" Poirot made a little bow—"but he does not keep them in the back of his head! The study window is at the extreme left of the terrace, the windows of this room come next, but the terrace continues to the right past one, two, three, perhaps four rooms?"

"Dining room, billiard room, morning room and library," said Lord Mayfield.

"And you walked up and down the terrace, how many times?"

"At least five or six."

"You see, it is easy enough; the thief has only to watch for the right moment!"

Carlile said slowly:

"You mean that when I was in the hall, talking to the French girl, the thief was waiting in the drawing room?"

"That is my suggestion. It is, of course, only a suggestion."

"It doesn't sound very probable to me," said Lord Mayfield. "Too risky."

The Air Marshal demurred.

"I don't agree with you, Charles. It's perfectly possible. Wonder I hadn't the wits to think of it for myself."

"So you see," said Poirot, "why I believe that the plans are still in the house. The problem now is to find them!"

Sir George snorted.

"That's simple enough. Search everybody."

Lord Mayfield made a movement of dissent, but Poirot spoke before he could:

"No, no, it is not so simple as that. The person who took those plans will anticipate that a search will be made and will make quite sure that they are not found amongst his or her belongings. They will have been hidden in neutral ground."

"Do you suggest that we've got to go playing hide and seek all over the bally house?"

Poirot smiled.

"No, no, we need not be so crude as that. We can arrive at the hiding place (or alternatively at the identity of the guilty person) by reflection. That will simplify matters. In the morning I would like an interview with every person in the house. It would, I think, be unwise to seek those interviews now."

Lord Mayfield nodded.

"Cause too much comment," he said, "if we dragged everybody out of their beds at three in the morning. In any case, you'll have to proceed with a good deal of camouflage, M. Poirot. This matter has got to be kept dark."

Poirot waved an airy hand.

"Leave it to Hercule Poirot. The lies I invent are always most delicate and most convincing. Tomorrow, then, I conduct my investigations. But tonight, I should like to begin by interviewing you, Sir George, and you, Lord Mayfield."

He bowed to them both.

"You mean—alone?"

"That was my meaning."

Lord Mayfield raised his eyes slightly, then he said:

"Certainly. I'll leave you alone with Sir George. When you want me, you'll find me in my study. Come, Carlile."

He and the secretary went out, shutting the door behind them.

Sir George sat down, reaching mechanically for a cigarette. He turned a puzzled face to Poirot.

"You know," he said slowly, "I don't quite get this."

"That is very simply explained," said Poirot with a smile. "In two words, to be accurate. Mrs. Vanderlyn!"

"Oh," said Carrington. "I think I see. Mrs. Vanderlyn?"

"Precisely. It might be, you see, that it would not be very delicate to ask Lord Mayfield the question I want to ask. *Why* Mrs. Vanderlyn? This lady, she is known to be a suspicious character. Why, then, should she be here? I say to myself there are three explanations. One, that Lord Mayfield has a *penchant* for the lady (and that is why I seek to talk to you alone. I do not wish to embarrass him); two, that Mrs. Vanderlyn is perhaps the dear friend of someone else in the house?"

"You can count me out!" said Sir George with a grin.

"Then, if neither of those cases is true, the question returns in redoubled force. *Why Mrs. Vanderlyn?* And it seems to me I perceive a shadowy answer. There was a *reason.* Her presence at this particular juncture was definitely desired by Lord Mayfield for a special reason. Am I right?"

Sir George nodded.

"You're quite right," he said. "Mayfield is too old a bird to fall for her wiles. He wanted her here for quite another reason. It was like this."

He retailed the conversation that had taken place at the dinner table. Poirot listened attentively.

"Ah," he said. "I comprehend now. Nevertheless, it seems that the lady has turned the tables on you both rather neatly!"

Sir George swore freely.

Poirot watched him with some slight amusement, then he said:

"You do not doubt that this theft is her doing—I mean that she is responsible for it, whether or no she played an active part?"

Sir George stared.

"Of course not! There isn't the least doubt of that. Why, who else would have any interest in stealing those plans?"

"Ah!" said Hercule Poirot. He leaned back and looked at the ceiling. "And yet, Sir George, we agreed not a quarter of an hour ago that these papers represented very definitely, money. Not perhaps, in quite so obvious a form as bank notes, or gold, or jewelry, but nevertheless they were potential money. If there were anyone here who was hard up—"

The other interrupted him with a snort.

"Who isn't in these days? I suppose I can say it without incriminating myself."

He smiled and Poirot smiled politely back at him and murmured:

"*Mais oui,* you can say what you like, for you, Sir George, have the one unimpeachable alibi in this affair."

"But I'm damned hard up myself!"

Poirot shook his head sadly.

"Yes, indeed, a man in your position has heavy living expenses. Then you have a young son at a most expensive age—"

Sir George groaned.

"Education's bad enough, then debts on top of it. Mind you, the lad's not a bad lad."

Poirot listened sympathetically. He heard a lot of the Air Marshal's accumulated grievances. The lack of grit and stamina in the younger generation, the fantastic way in which mothers spoilt their children and always took their side, the curse of gambling once it got hold of a woman, the folly of playing for higher stakes than you could afford. It was all couched in general terms, Sir George did not allude directly to either his wife or his son, but his natural transparency made his generalizations very easy to see through.

He broke off suddenly.

"Sorry, mustn't take up your time with something that's right off the subject, especially at this hour of the night—or rather morning."

He stifled a yawn.

"I suggest, Sir George, that you should go to bed. You have been most kind and helpful."

"Right; think I will turn in. You really think there is a chance of getting the plans back?"

Poirot shrugged his shoulders.

"I mean to try. I do not see why not."

"Well, I'll be off. Good-night."

He left the room.

Poirot remained in his chair staring thoughtfully at the ceiling, then he took out a little notebook and turning to a clean page he wrote:

*Mrs. Vanderlyn?*
*Lady Julia Carrington?*
*Mrs. Macatta?*
*Reggie Carrington?*
*Mr. Carlile?*

Underneath he wrote:

*Mrs. Vanderlyn and Mr. Reggie Carrington?*
*Mrs. Vanderlyn and Lady Julia?*
*Mrs. Vanderlyn and Mr. Carlile?*

He shook his head in a dissatisfied manner, murmuring:
*"C'est plus simple que ça."*
Then he added a few short sentences:
*Did Lord Mayfield see a "shadow?" If not, why did he say he did?*
*Did Sir George see anything? He was positive he had seen nothing*
*AFTER I examined flower-bed.* Note: *Lord Mayfield is near-sighted,*
*can read without glasses but has to use a monocle to look across a*
*room. Sir George is long-sighted. Therefore, from the far end of terrace,*
*his sight is more to be depended upon than Lord Mayfield's. Yet Lord*
*Mayfield is very positive that he DID see something and is quite un-*
*shaken by his friend's denial.*
*Can anyone be quite as above suspicion as Mr. Carlile appears to*
*be? Lord Mayfield is very emphatic as to his innocence. Too much*
*so. Why? Because he secretly suspects him and is ashamed of his suspi-*
*cions? Or because he definitely suspects some other person? That is*
*to say, some person OTHER than Mrs. Vanderlyn?*
He put the notebook away.
Then, getting up, he went along to the study.

# V

Lord Mayfield was seated at his desk when Poirot entered the study.
He swung round, laid down his pen, and looked up inquiringly.
"Well, M. Poirot, had your interview with Carrington?"
Poirot smiled and sat down.
"Yes, Lord Mayfield. He cleared up a point that had puzzled me."
"What was that?"
"The reason for Mrs. Vanderlyn's presence here. You comprehend,
I thought it possible—"

Mayfield was quick to realize the cause of Poirot's somewhat exaggerated embarrassment.

"You thought I had a weakness for the lady? Not at all! Far from it. Funnily enough, Carrington thought the same."

"Yes, he has told me of the conversation he held with you on the subject."

Lord Mayfield looked rather rueful.

"My little scheme didn't come off. Always annoying to have to admit that a woman has got the better of you."

"Ah, but she hasn't got the better of you *yet*, Lord Mayfield."

"You think we may yet win? Well, I'm glad to hear you say so. I'd like to think it was true."

He sighed.

"I feel that I've acted like a complete fool—so pleased with my stratagem for entrapping the lady."

Hercule Poirot said as he lit one of his tiny cigarettes:

"What *was* your stratagem exactly, Lord Mayfield?"

"Well," Lord Mayfield hesitated, "I hadn't exactly got down to details."

"You didn't discuss it with anyone?"

"No."

"Not even with Mr. Carlile?"

"No."

Poirot smiled.

"You prefer to play a lone hand, Lord Mayfield."

"I have usually found it the best way," said the other a little grimly.

"Yes, you are wise. *Trust no one*. But you *did* mention the matter to Sir George Carrington?"

"Simply because I realized that the dear fellow was seriously perturbed about me."

Lord Mayfield smiled at the remembrance.

"He is an old friend of yours?"

"Yes. I have known him for over twenty years."

"And his wife?"

"I have known his wife also, of course."

"But (pardon me if I am impertinent) you are not on the same terms of intimacy with her?"

"I don't really see what my personal relationship to people has to do with the matter in hand, M. Poirot."

"But I think, Lord Mayfield, that they may have a good deal to do with it. You agreed, did you not, that my theory of someone in the drawing room was a possible one?"

"Yes. In fact I agree with you that that is what must have happened."

"We will not say 'must.' That is too self-confident a word. But if that theory of mine is true, who do you think the person in the drawing room could have been?"

"Obviously Mrs. Vanderlyn. She had been back there once for a book. She could have come back for another book, or a handbag, or a dropped handkerchief—one of a dozen feminine excuses. She arranges with her maid to scream and get Carlile away from the study. Then she slips in and out by the windows, as you said."

"You forget, it could not have been Mrs. Vanderlyn. Carlile heard her call the maid from *upstairs* while he was talking to the girl."

Lord Mayfield bit his lip.

"True. I forgot that." He looked thoroughly annoyed.

"You see," said Poirot gently. "We progress. We have first the simple explanation of a thief who comes from *outside* and makes off with the booty. A very convenient theory as I said at the time, too convenient to be readily accepted. We have disposed of that. Then we come to the theory of the foreign agent, Mrs. Vanderlyn, and that again seems to fit together beautifully up to a certain point. But now it looks as though that, too, was too easy—too convenient—to be accepted."

"You'd wash Mrs. Vanderlyn out of it altogether?"

"It was not Mrs. Vanderlyn in the drawing room. It may have been an ally of Mrs. Vanderlyn's who committed the theft, but it is just possible that it was committed by another person altogether. If so, we have to consider the question of motive."

"Isn't this rather far-fetched, M. Poirot?"

"I do not think so. Now what motives could there be? There is the motive of money. The papers were stolen with the object of turning them into cash. That is the simplest motive to consider. But the motive might possibly be something quite different."

"Such as—"

Poirot said slowly:

"It might have been done definitely with the idea of damaging someone."

"Who?"

"Possibly Mr. Carlile. He would be the obvious suspect. But there might be more to it than that. The men who control the destiny of a country, Lord Mayfield, are particularly vulnerable to displays of popular feeling."

"Meaning that the theft was aimed at damaging *me?*"

Poirot nodded.

"I think I am correct in saying, Lord Mayfield, that about five years ago you passed through a somewhat trying time. You were suspected of friendship with a European Power at that time bitterly unpopular with the electorate of this country."

"Quite true, M. Poirot."

"A statesman in these days has a difficult task. He has to pursue the policy he deems advantageous to his country, but he has at the same time to recognize the force of popular feeling. Popular feeling is very often sentimental, muddle-headed, and eminently unsound, but it cannot be disregarded for all that."

"How well you express it! That is exactly the curse of a politician's life. He has to bow to the country's feeling, however dangerous and foolhardy he knows it to be."

"That was your dilemma, I think. There were rumors that you had concluded an agreement with the country in question. The country and the newspapers were up in arms about it. Fortunately, the Prime Minister was able categorically to deny the story, and you repudiated it, though still making no secret of the way your sympathies lay."

"All this is quite true, M. Poirot, but why rake up past history?"

"Because I consider it possible that an enemy, disappointed in the way you surmounted that crisis, might endeavor to stage a further dilemma. You soon regained public confidence. Those particular circumstances have passed away, you are now, deservedly, one of the most popular figures in political life. You are spoken of freely as the next Prime Minister when Mr. Hunberly retires."

"You think this is an attempt to discredit me? Nonsense!"

"*Tout de même,* Lord Mayfield, it would not look well if it were known that the plans of Britain's new bomber had been stolen during a weekend when a certain very charming lady had been your guest. Little hints in the newspapers as to your relationship with that lady would create a feeling of distrust in you."

"Such a thing could not really be taken seriously."

"My dear Lord Mayfield, you know perfectly well it could! It takes so little to undermine public confidence in a man."

"Yes, that's true," said Lord Mayfield. He looked suddenly very worried. "God! How desperately complicated this business is becoming. Do you really think—but it's impossible—impossible."

"You know of nobody who is—jealous of you?"

"Absurd!"

"At any rate you will admit that my questions about your personal relationships with the members of this house-party are not totally irrelevant."

"Oh, perhaps—perhaps. You asked me about Julia Carrington. There's really not very much to say. I've never taken to her very much, and I don't think she cares for me. She's one of these restless nervy women, recklessly extravagant, and mad about cards. She's old-fashioned enough, I think, to despise me as being a self-made man."

Poirot said:

"I looked you up in *Who's Who* before I came down. You were

the head of a famous engineering firm and you are yourself a first-
class engineer."

"There's certainly nothing I don't know about the practical side.
I've worked my way up from the bottom."

Lord Mayfield spoke rather grimly.

"Oh, la, la!" cried Poirot. "I have been a fool—but a fool!"

The other stared at him.

"I beg your pardon, M. Poirot?"

"It is that a portion of the puzzle has become clear to me. Something
I did not see before. . . . But it all fits in. Yes—it fits in with beautiful
precision."

Lord Mayfield looked at him in somewhat astonished inquiry.

But with a slight smile Poirot shook his head.

"No, no, not now. I must arrange my ideas a little more clearly."

He rose.

"Good-night, Lord Mayfield. I think I know where those plans are."

Lord Mayfield cried out:

"You know? Then let us get hold of them at once!"

Poirot shook his head.

"No, no, that would not do. Precipitancy would be fatal. But leave
it all to Hercule Poirot."

He went out of the room. Lord Mayfield raised his shoulders in
contempt.

"Man's a mountebank," he muttered. Then, putting away his papers
and turning out the lights, he, too, made his way up to bed.

# VI

"If there's been a burglary, why the devil doesn't old Mayfield send
for the police?" demanded Reggie Carrington.

He pushed his chair slightly back from the breakfast table.

He was the last down. His host, Mrs. Macatta, and Sir George had
finished their breakfasts some time before. His mother and Mrs. Vanderlyn were breakfasting in bed.

Sir George, repeating his statement on the lines agreed upon between Lord Mayfield and Hercule Poirot, had a sensation that he was
not managing it as well as he might have done.

"To send for a queer foreigner like this seems very odd to me,"
said Reggie. "What was taken, Father?"

"I don't know exactly, my boy."

Reggie got up. He looked rather nervy and on edge this morning.

"Nothing—important? No—papers or anything like that?"

"To tell you the truth, Reggie, I can't tell you exactly."

"Very hush, hush, is it? I see."

Reggie ran up the stairs, paused for a moment half-way with a frown on his face, and then continued his ascent and tapped on his mother's door. Her voice bade him enter.

Lady Julia was sitting up in bed, scribbling figures on the back of an envelope.

"Good morning, darling." She looked up, then said sharply:

"Reggie, is anything the matter?"

"Nothing much, but it seems there was a burglary last night."

"A burglary? What was taken?"

"Oh, I don't know. It's all very hush, hush. There's some odd kind of private inquiry agent downstairs asking everybody questions."

"How extraordinary!"

"It's rather unpleasant," said Reggie slowly, "staying in a house when that kind of thing happens."

"What did happen exactly?"

"Don't know. It was some time after we all went to bed. Look out, Mother, you'll have that tray off."

He rescued the breakfast tray and carried it to a table by the window.

"Was money taken?"

"I tell you I don't know."

Lady Julia said slowly:

"I suppose this inquiry man is asking everybody questions?"

"I suppose so."

"Where they were last night? All that kind of thing?"

"Probably. Well, I can't tell him much. I went straight up to bed and was asleep in next to no time."

Lady Julia did not answer.

"I say, Mother, I suppose you couldn't let me have a spot of cash. I'm absolutely broke."

"No, I couldn't," his mother replied decisively. "I've got the most frightful overdraft myself. I don't know what your father will say when he hears about it."

There was a tap at the door and Sir George entered.

"Ah, there you are, Reggie. Will you go down to the library? M. Hercule Poirot wants to see you."

Poirot had just concluded an interview with the redoubtable Mrs. Macatta.

A few brief questions had elicited the information that Mrs. Macatta had gone up to bed just before eleven, and had heard or seen nothing helpful.

Poirot slid gently from the topic of the burglary to more personal matters. He himself had a great admiration for Lord Mayfield. As a member of the general public he felt that Lord Mayfield was a truly great man. Of course Mrs. Macatta, being in the know, would have a far better means of estimating that than himself.

"Lord Mayfield has brains," allowed Mrs. Macatta. "And he has carved his career out entirely for himself. He owes nothing to hereditary influence. He has a certain lack of vision, perhaps. In that I find all men sadly alike. They lack the breadth of a woman's imagination. Women, M. Poirot, are going to be the great force in Government in ten years' time."

Poirot said that he was sure of it.

He slid to the topic of Mrs. Vanderlyn. Was it true, as he had heard hinted, that she and Lord Mayfield were very close friends?

"Not in the least. To tell you the truth, I was very surprised to meet her here. Very surprised, indeed."

Poirot invited Mrs. Macatta's opinion of Mrs. Vanderlyn—and got it.

"One of those absolutely *useless* women, M. Poirot. Women that make one despair of one's own sex! A parasite, first and last, a parasite."

"Men admire her?"

"Men!" Mrs. Macatta spoke the word with contempt. "Men are always taken in by those very obvious good looks. That boy, now, young Reggie Carrington, flushing up every time she spoke to him, absurdly flattered by being taken notice of by her. And the silly way she flattered him, too! Praising his bridge—which actually was far from brilliant."

"He is not a good player?"

"He made all sorts of mistakes last night."

"Lady Julia is a good player, is she not?"

"Much *too* good in my opinion," said Mrs. Macatta. "It's almost a profession with her. She plays morning, noon, and night."

"For high stakes?"

"Yes, indeed, much higher than I would care to play. Indeed, I shouldn't consider it *right.*"

"She makes a good deal of money at the game?"

Mrs. Macatta gave a loud and virtuous snort.

"She reckons on paying her debts that way. But she's been having a bad run of luck lately, so I've heard. She looked last night as though she had something on her mind. The evils of gambling, M. Poirot, are only slightly less than the evils caused by drink. If I had my way this country should be purified—"

Poirot was forced to listen to a somewhat lengthy disquisition on the purification of England's morals. Then he closed the conversation adroitly and sent for Reggie Carrington.

He summed the young man up carefully as he entered the room;

the weak mouth camouflaged by the rather charming smile, the indecisive chin, the eyes set far apart, the rather narrow head. He thought that he knew Reggie Carrington's type fairly well.

"Mr. Reggie Carrington?"

"Yes. Anything I can do?"

"Just tell me what you can about last night?"

"Well, let me see, we played bridge—in the drawing room. After that I went up to bed."

"That was at what time?"

"Just before eleven. I suppose the robbery took place after that?"

"Yes, after that. You did not hear or see anything?"

Reggie shook his head regretfully.

"I'm afraid not. I went straight to bed and I sleep pretty soundly."

"You went straight up from the drawing room to your bedroom and remained there until the morning?"

"That's right."

"Curious," said Poirot.

Reggie said sharply:

"What do you mean, curious?"

"You did not, for instance, hear a scream?"

"No, I didn't."

"Ah, very curious."

"Look here, I don't know what you mean."

"You are, perhaps, slightly deaf?"

"Certainly not."

Poirot's lips moved. It was possible that he was repeating the word "curious" for the third time. Then he said:

"Well, thank you, Mr. Carrington, that is all."

Reggie got up and stood rather irresolutely.

"You know," he said, "now you come to mention it, I believe I did hear something of the kind."

"Ah, you did hear something?"

"Yes, but you see, I was reading a book—a detective story as a matter of fact—and I—well, I didn't really quite take it in."

"Ah," said Poirot, "a most satisfying explanation."

His face was quite impassive.

Reggie still hesitated, then he turned and walked slowly to the door. There he paused and asked:

"I say, what was stolen?"

"Something of great value, Mr. Carrington. That is all I am at liberty to say."

"Oh," said Reggie rather blankly.

He went out.

Poirot nodded his head.

"It fits," he murmured. "It fits very nicely."

He touched a bell and inquired courteously if Mrs. Vanderlyn was up yet.

# VII

Mrs. Vanderlyn swept into the room looking very handsome. She was wearing an artfully cut russet sports suit that showed up the warm lights in her hair. She swept to a chair and smiled in a dazzling fashion at the little man in front of her.

For a moment something showed through the smile. It might have been triumph, it might almost have been mockery. It was gone almost immediately but it had been there. Poirot found the suggestion of it interesting.

"Burglars? Last night? But how dreadful! Why, no, I never heard a *thing*. What about the police? Can't they *do* anything?" (Again, just for a moment, the mockery showed in her eyes.)

Hercule Poirot thought:

"It is very clear that *you* are not afraid of the police, my lady. You know very well that they are not going to be called in."

And from that followed—what?

He said soberly:

"You comprehend, madame, it is an affair of the most discreet."

"Why, naturally, M. Poirot—isn't it?—I shouldn't dream of breathing a word. I'm much too great an admirer of dear Lord Mayfield's to do anything to cause him the least little bit of worry."

She crossed her knees. A highly polished slipper of brown leather dangled on the tip of her silk-shod foot.

She smiled, a warm compelling smile of perfect health and deep satisfaction.

"Do tell me if there's anything at all I can do?"

"I thank you, madame. You played bridge in the drawing room last night?"

"Yes."

"I understand that then all the ladies went up to bed?"

"That is right."

"But someone came back to fetch a book. That was you, was it not, Mrs. Vanderlyn?"

"I was the first one to come back—yes."

"What do you mean—the *first* one?" said Poirot sharply.

"I came back right away," explained Mrs. Vanderlyn. "Then I went up and rang for my maid. She was a long time coming. I rang again. Then I went out on the landing. I heard her voice and I called her. After she had brushed my hair I sent her away; she was in a nervous upset state and tangled the brush in my hair once or twice. It was then, just as I sent her away, that I saw Lady Julia coming up the stairs. She told me she had been down again for a book, too. Curious, wasn't it?"

Mrs. Vanderlyn smiled as she finished, a wide, rather feline smile. Hercule Poirot thought to himself that Mrs. Vanderlyn did not like Lady Julia Carrington.

"As you say, madame. Tell me, did you hear your maid scream?"

"Why, yes, I did hear something of the kind."

"Did you ask her about it?"

"Yes. She told me she thought she had seen a floating figure in white—such nonsense!"

"What was Lady Julia wearing last night?"

"Oh, you think perhaps—Yes, I see. She *was* wearing a white evening dress. Of course, that explains it. Leonie must have caught sight of her in the darkness just as a white figure. These girls are so superstitious."

"Your maid has been with you a long time, madame?"

"Oh, no." Mrs. Vanderlyn opened her eyes rather wide. "Only about five months."

"I should like to see her presently, if you do not mind, madame."

Mrs. Vanderlyn raised her eyebrows.

"Oh, certainly," she said rather coldly.

"I should like, you understand, to question her."

"Oh, yes."

Again a flicker of amusement.

Poirot rose and bowed.

"Madame," he said, "you have my complete admiration."

Mrs. Vanderlyn for once seemed a trifle taken aback.

"Oh, M. Poirot, how nice of you, but why?"

"You are, madame, so perfectly armored, so completely sure of yourself."

Mrs. Vanderlyn laughed a little uncertainly.

"Now I wonder," she said, "if I am to take that as a compliment?"

Poirot said:

"It is, perhaps, a warning—not to treat life with arrogance."

Mrs. Vanderlyn laughed with more assurance. She got up and held out a hand.

"Dear M. Poirot, I do wish you all success. Thank you for all the charming things you have said to me."

She went out. Poirot murmured to himself:

"You wish me success, do you? Ah, but you are very sure I am not going to meet with success! Yes, you are very sure indeed. That, it annoys me very much."

With a certain petulance, he pulled the bell and asked that Mademoiselle Leonie might be sent to him.

His eyes roamed over her appreciatively as she stood hesitating in the doorway, demure in her black dress with her neatly parted black waves of hair and her modestly dropped eyelids. He nodded slow approval.

"Come in, Mademoiselle Leonie," he said. "Do not be afraid."

She came in and stood demurely before him.

"Do you know," said Poirot with a sudden change of tone, "that I find you very good to look at?"

Leonie responded promptly. She flashed him a glance out of the corner of her eyes and murmured softly:

"Monsieur is very kind."

"Figure to yourself," said Poirot. "I demand of M. Carlile whether you are or are not good-looking and he replies that he does not know!"

Leonie cocked her chin up contemptuously.

"That image!"

"That describes him very well."

"I do not believe he has ever looked at a girl in his life, that one."

"Probably not. A pity. He has missed a lot. But there are others in this house who are more appreciative, is it not so?"

"Really, I do not know what monsieur means."

"Oh, yes, Mademoiselle Leonie, you know very well. A pretty history that you recount last night about a ghost that you have seen. As soon as I hear that you are standing there with your hands to your head, I know very well that there is no question of ghosts. If a girl is frightened she clasps her heart, or she raises her hands to her mouth to stifle a cry, but if her hands are on her hair it means something very different. *It means that her hair has been ruffled and that she is hastily patting it into shape again!* Now, then, mademoiselle, let us have the truth. Why did you scream on the stairs?"

"But, monsieur, it is true, I saw a tall figure all in white—"

"Mademoiselle, do not insult my intelligence. That story, it may have been good enough for M. Carlile, but it is not good enough for Hercule Poirot. The truth is that you had just been kissed, is it not so? And I will make a guess that it was M. Reggie Carrington who kissed you."

Leonie twinkled an unabashed eye at him.

*"Eh bien,"* she demanded, "after all, what is a kiss?"

"What, indeed?" said Poirot gallantly.

"You see, the young gentleman he came up behind me and caught me round the waist—and so naturally he startled me and I screamed. If I had known—well, then naturally I would not have screamed."

"Naturally," agreed Poirot.

"But he came upon me like a cat. Then the study door opened and out came M. le secrétaire and the young gentleman slipped away upstairs and there I was looking like a fool. Naturally I had to say something—especially to—" she broke into French—"*un jeune homme comme ça, tellement comme il faut!*"

"So you invent a ghost?"

"Indeed, monsieur, it was all I could think of. A tall figure all in white that floated. It is ridiculous but what else could I do?"

"Nothing. So now, all is explained. I had my suspicions from the first."

Leonie shot him a provocative glance.

"Monsieur is very clever, and very sympathetic."

"And since I am not going to make you any embarrassments over the affair you will do something for me in return?"

"Most willingly, monsieur."

"How much do you know of your mistress's affairs?"

The girl shrugged her shoulders.

"Not very much, monsieur. I have my ideas, of course."

"And those ideas?"

"Well, it does not escape me that the friends of madame are always soldiers or sailors or airmen. And then there are other friends—foreign gentlemen who come to see her very quietly sometimes. Madame is very handsome, though I do not think she will be so much longer. The young men, they find her very attractive. Sometimes, I think, they say too much. But it is only my idea, that. Madame does not confide in me."

"What you would have me understand is that madame plays a lone hand?"

"That is right, monsieur."

"In other words, you cannot help me?"

"I fear not, monsieur. I would do so if I could."

"Tell me, your mistress is in a good mood today?"

"Decidedly, monsieur."

"Something has happened to please her?"

"She has been in good spirits ever since she came here."

"Well, Leonie, you should know."

The girl answered confidently:

"Yes, monsieur. I could not be mistaken there. I know all madame's moods. She is in high spirits."

"Positively triumphant?"

"That is exactly the word, monsieur."

Poirot nodded gloomily.

"I find that—a little hard to bear. Yet I perceive that it is inevitable. Thank you, mademoiselle, that is all."

Leonie threw him a coquettish glance.

"Thank you, monsieur. If I meet monsieur on the stairs, be well assured that I shall not scream."

"My child," said Poirot with dignity, "I am of advanced years. What have I to do with such frivolities?"

But with a little twitter of laughter Leonie took herself off.

Poirot paced slowly up and down the room. His face became grave and anxious.

"And now," he said at last, "for Lady Julia. What will she say, I wonder?"

Lady Julia came into the room with a quiet air of assurance. She bent her head graciously, accepted the chair that Poirot drew forward and spoke in a low, well-bred voice.

"Lord Mayfield says that you wish to ask me some questions?"

"Yes, madame. It is about last night."

"About last night, yes?"

"What happened after you had finished your game of bridge?"

"My husband thought it was too late to begin another. I went up to bed."

"And then?"

"I went to sleep."

"That is all?"

"Yes. I'm afraid I can't tell you anything of much interest. When did this"—she hesitated—"burglary occur?"

"Very soon after you went upstairs."

"I see. And what exactly was taken?"

"Some private papers, madame."

"Important papers?"

"Very important."

She frowned a little and then said:

"They were—valuable?"

"Yes, madame, they were worth a good deal of money."

"I see."

There was a pause and then Poirot said:

"What about your book, madame?"

"My book?" She raised bewildered eyes to him.

"Yes, I understood Mrs. Vanderlyn to say that some time after you three ladies had retired you came down again to fetch a book."

"Yes, of course, so I did."

"So that, as a matter of fact, you did *not* go straight to bed when you went upstairs? You returned to the drawing room?"

"Yes, that is true. I had forgotten."

"While you were in the drawing room, did you hear someone scream?"

"No—yes—I don't think so."

"Surely, madame. You could not have failed to hear it in the drawing room."

Lady Julia flung her head back and said firmly:

"I heard nothing."

Poirot raised his eyebrows, but did not reply.

The silence grew uncomfortable. Lady Julia asked abruptly:

"What is being done?"

"Being done? I do not understand you, madame."

"I mean about the robbery. Surely the police must be doing something."

Poirot shook his head.

"The police have not been called in. I am in charge."

She stared at him, her restless haggard face sharpened and tense. Her eyes, dark and searching, sought to pierce his impassivity.

They fell at last—defeated.

"You cannot tell me what is being done?"

"I can only assure you, madame, that I am leaving no stone unturned."

"To catch the thief—or to—recover the papers?"

"The recovery of the papers is the main thing, madame."

Her manner changed. It became bored, listless.

"Yes," she said indifferently. "I suppose it is."

There was another pause.

"Is there anything else, M. Poirot?"

"No, madame, I will not detain you further."

"Thank you."

He opened the door for her. She passed out without glancing at him.

Poirot went back to the fireplace and carefully rearranged the ornaments on the mantelpiece. He was still at it when Lord Mayfield came in through the window.

"Well?" said the latter.

"Very well, I think. Events are shaping themselves as they should."

Lord Mayfield said, staring at him:

"You are pleased?"

"No, I am not pleased. But I am content."

"Really, M. Poirot, I cannot make you out."

"I am not such a charlatan as you think."

"I never said—"

"No, but you *thought!* No matter. I am not offended. It is sometimes necessary for me to adopt a certain pose."

Lord Mayfield looked at him doubtfully with a certain amount of distrust. Hercule Poirot was a man he did not understand. He wanted to despise him, but something warned him that this ridiculous little man was not so futile as he appeared. Charles McLaughlin had always been able to recognize capability when he saw it.

"Well," he said, "we are in your hands. What do you advise next?"

"Can you get rid of your guests?"

"I think it might be arranged. . . . I could explain that I have to go to London over this affair. They will then probably offer to leave."

"Very good. Try and arrange it like that."

Lord Mayfield hesitated.

"You don't think—"

"I am quite sure that that would be the wise course to take."

Lord Mayfield shrugged his shoulders.

"Well, if you say so."

He went out.

# VIII

The guests left after lunch. Mrs. Vanderlyn and Mrs. Macatta went by train, the Carringtons had their car. Poirot was standing in the hall as Mrs. Vanderlyn bade her host a charming farewell.

"So terribly sorry for you having this bother and anxiety. I do hope it will turn out all right for you. I shan't breathe a word of anything."

She pressed his hand and went out to where the Rolls was waiting to take her to the station. Mrs. Macatta was already inside. Her adieus had been curt and unsympathetic.

Suddenly Leonie, who had been getting in front with the chauffeur, came running back into the hall.

"The dressing case of madame, it is not in the car," she exclaimed.

There was a hurried search. At last Lord Mayfield discovered it where it had been put down in the shadow of an old oak chest. Leonie uttered a glad little cry as she seized the elegant affair of green morocco, and hurried out with it.

Then Mrs. Vanderlyn leaned out of the car.

"Lord Mayfield! Lord Mayfield!" She handed him a letter. "Would you mind? If you'd put it in your post box. If I keep it meaning to post it in town, I'm sure to forget. Letters just stay in my bag for days."

Sir George Carrington was fidgeting with his watch, opening and shutting it. He was a maniac for punctuality.

"They're cutting it fine," he murmured. "Very fine. Unless they're careful, they'll miss the train—"

His wife said irritably:

"Oh, don't fuss, George. After all it's their train, not ours!"

He looked at her reproachfully.

The Rolls drove off.

Reggie drew up at the front door in the Carringtons' Morris.

"All ready, Father," he said.

The servants began bringing out the Carringtons' luggage. Reggie supervised its disposal in the dickey.

Poirot moved out of the front door, watching the proceeding.

Suddenly he felt a hand on his arm. Lady Julia's voice spoke in an agitated whisper.

"M. Poirot. I must speak to you—at once."

He yielded to her insistent hand. She drew him into a small morning room and closed the door. She came close to him.

"Is it true what you said—that the recovery of the papers is what matters most to Lord Mayfield?"

Poirot looked at her curiously.

"It is quite true, madame."

"If—if those papers were returned to you, would you undertake that they should be given back to Lord Mayfield and no questions asked?"

"I am not sure that I understand you."

"You must! I am sure that you do! I am suggesting that the—the thief should remain anonymous if the papers are returned."

Poirot asked:

"How soon would that be, madame?"

"Definitely within twelve hours."

"You can promise that?"

"I can promise it."

As he did not answer, she repeated urgently:

"Will you guarantee that there will be no publicity?"

He answered then—very gravely:

"Yes, madame, I will guarantee that."

"Then everything can be arranged."

She passed abruptly from the room. A moment later Poirot heard the car drive away.

He crossed the hall and went along the passage to the study. Lord Mayfield was there. He looked up as Poirot entered.

"Well?" he said.

Poirot spread out his hands.

"The case is ended, Lord Mayfield."

"What?"

Poirot repeated word for word the scene between himself and Lady Julia.

Lord Mayfield looked at him with a stupefied expression.

"But what does it mean? I don't understand."

"It is very clear, is it not? Lady Julia knows who stole the plans."

"You don't mean she took them herself!"

"Certainly not. Lady Julia may be a gambler. She is certainly not a thief. But if she offers to return them, it means that they were taken by her husband or her son. Now Sir George Carrington was out on the terrace with you. That leaves us the son. I think I can reconstruct the happenings of last night fairly accurately. Lady Julia went to her son's room last night and found it empty. She came downstairs to look for him but did not find him. This morning she hears of the theft and she also hears that her son declares that he went straight to his room *and never left it.* That, she knows, is not true. And she knows something else about her son. She knows that he is weak, that he is desperately hard up for money. She has observed his infatuation for Mrs. Vanderlyn. The whole thing is clear to her. Mrs. Vanderlyn has persuaded Reggie to steal the plans. But Lady Julia determines to play her part also. She will tackle Reggie, get hold of the papers, and return them."

"But the whole thing is quite impossible," cried Lord Mayfield.

"Yes, it is impossible, but Lady Julia does not know that. She does not know what I, Hercule Poirot, know, that young Reggie Carrington was not stealing papers last night, but instead was philandering with Mrs. Vanderlyn's French maid."

"The whole thing is a mare's nest!"

"Exactly."

"And the case is not ended at all!"

"Yes, it is ended. *I, Hercule Poirot, know the truth.* You do not believe me? You did not believe me yesterday when I said I knew where the plans were. But I did know. They were very close at hand."

"Where?"

"They were in your pocket, my lord."

There was a pause, then Lord Mayfield said:

"Do you really know what you are saying, M. Poirot?"

"Yes, I know. I know that I am speaking to a very clever man. From the first it worried me that you, who were admittedly short-sighted, should be so positive about the figure you had seen leaving the window. You wanted that solution—the convenient solution—to be accepted. Why? Later, one by one, I eliminated everyone else. Mrs. Vanderlyn was upstairs, Sir George was with you on the terrace,

Reggie Carrington was with the French girl on the stairs, Mrs. Macatta was blamelessly in her bedroom. (It is next to the housekeeper's room and Mrs. Macatta snores!) Lady Julia, it is true, was in the drawing room, but Lady Julia clearly believes her son guilty. So there remained only two possibilities. Either Carlile did not put the papers on the desk but into his own pocket (and that is not reasonable because, as you pointed out, he could have taken a tracing of them) or else—or else the plans were there when you walked over to the desk and the only place they could have gone was into *your* pocket. In that case everything was clear. Your insistence on the figure you had seen, your insistence on Carlile's innocence, your disinclination to have me summoned.

"One thing did puzzle me—the motive. You were, I was convinced, an honest man, a man of integrity. That showed in your anxiety that no innocent person should be suspected. It was also obvious that the theft of the plans might easily affect your career unfavorably. Why, then, this wholly unreasonable theft? And at last the answer came to me. The crisis in your career, some years ago, the assurances given to the world by the Prime Minister that you had had no negotiations with the Power in question. Suppose that that was not strictly true, that there remained some record—a letter perhaps—showing that in actual fact you *had* done what you had publicly denied. Such a denial was necessary in the interests of public policy. But it is doubtful if the man in the street would see it that way. It might mean that at the moment when supreme power might be given into your hands, some stupid echo from the past would undo everything.

"I suspect that that letter has been preserved in the hands of a certain government, that that government offered to trade with you—the letter in exchange for the plans of the new bomber. Some men would have refused. You—did not! You agreed. Mrs. Vanderlyn was the agent in the matter. She came here by arrangement to make the exchange. You gave yourself away when you admitted that you had formed no definite stratagem for entrapping her. That admission made your reason for inviting her here incredibly weak.

"You arranged the robbery. Pretended to see the thief on the terrace—thereby clearing Carlile of suspicion. Even if he had not left the room, the desk was so near the window that a thief might have taken the plans while Carlile was busy at the safe with his back turned. You walked over to the desk, took the plans and kept them on your own person until the moment, when by prearranged plan, you slipped them into Mrs. Vanderlyn's dressing-case. In return, she handed you the fatal letter disguised as an unposted letter of her own."

Poirot stopped.

Lord Mayfield said:

"Your knowledge is very complete, M. Poirot. You must think me an unutterable skunk."

Poirot made a quick gesture.

"No, no, Lord Mayfield. I think, as I said, that you are a very clever man. It came to me suddenly as we talked here last night. You are a first-class engineer. There will be, I think, some subtle alterations in the specifications of that bomber, alterations done so skillfully that it will be difficult to grasp why the machine is not the success it ought to be. A certain foreign power will find the type a failure. . . . It will be a disappointment to them, I am sure. . . ."

Again there was a silence—then Lord Mayfield said:

"You are much too clever, M. Poirot. I will only ask you to believe one thing. I have faith in myself. I believe that I am the man needed to guide England through the days of crisis that I see coming. If I did not honestly believe that I am needed by my country to steer the ship of state, I would not have done what I have done—made the best of both worlds—saved myself from disaster by a clever trick."

"My Lord," said Poirot, "if you could not make the best of both worlds, you could not be a politician!"

# Murder in the Mews

## I

"PENNY for the guy, sir?"

A small boy with a grimy face grinned ingratiatingly.

"Certainly not!" said Chief Inspector Japp. "And, look here, my lad—"

A short homily followed. The dismayed urchin beat a precipitate retreat, remarking briefly and succinctly to his youthful friends:

"Blimy if it ain't a cop all togged up!"

The band took to its heels chanting the incantation,

> *"Remember, remember*
> *The fifth of November*
> *Gunpowder treason and plot;*
> *We see no reason*
> *Why gunpowder treason*
> *Should ever be forgot."*

The Chief Inspector's companion, a small elderly man with an egg-shaped head and large military-looking mustaches, was smiling to himself.

"*Très bien*, Japp," he observed. "You preach the sermon very well! I congratulate you!"

"Rank excuse for begging, that's what Guy Fawkes Day is!" said Japp.

"An interesting survival," mused Hercule Poirot. "The fireworks go up—crack—crack—long after the man they commemorate and his deed are forgotten."

The Scotland Yard man agreed.

"Don't suppose many of those kids really know who Guy Fawkes was."

"And soon doubtless there will be confusion of thought. Is it in

263

honor or in execration that on the 5th of November the *feu d'artifice* are sent up? To blow up an English parliament, was it a sin or a noble deed?"

Japp chuckled.

"Some people would say undoubtedly the latter."

Turning off the main road, the two men passed into the comparative quiet of a Mews. They had been dining together and were now taking a short cut to Hercule Poirot's flat.

As they walked along the sound of squibs was still heard periodically. An occasional shower of golden rain illuminated the sky.

"Good night for a murder," remarked Japp with professional interest. "Nobody would hear a shot, for instance, on a night like this."

"It has always seemed odd to me that more criminals do not take advantage of the fact," said Hercule Poirot.

"Do you know, Poirot, I almost wish sometimes that *you* would commit a murder."

*"Mon cher!"*

"Yes, I'd like to see just how you'd set about it."

"My dear Japp, *if* I committed a murder you would not have the least chance of seeing—how I set about it! You would not even be aware, probably, that a murder had been committed."

Japp laughed good-humoredly and affectionately.

"Cocky little devil, aren't you?" he said indulgently.

At half-past ten the following morning, Hercule Poirot's telephone rang.

" 'Allo? 'Allo?"

"Hullo, that you, Poirot?"

*"Oui, c'est moi."*

"Japp speaking here. Remember we came home last night through Bardsley Gardens Mews?"

"Yes?"

"And that we talked about how easy it would be to shoot a person with all those squibs and crackers and the rest of it going off?"

"Certainly."

"Well, there was a suicide in that Mews. No. 14. A young widow—Mrs. Allen. I'm going round there now. Like to come?"

"Excuse me, but does someone of your eminence, my dear friend, usually get sent to a case of suicide?"

"Sharp fellow. No—he doesn't. As a matter of fact, our doctor seems to think there's something funny about this. Will you come? I kind of feel you ought to be in on it."

"Certainly I will come. No. 14, you say?"

"That's right."

Poirot arrived at No. 14 Bardsley Gardens Mews almost at the same moment as a car drew up containing Japp and three other men.

No. 14 was clearly marked out as the center of interest. A big circle of people: chauffeurs, their wives, errand boys, loafers, well-dressed passers-by, and innumerable children were drawn up, all gazing at No. 14 with open mouths and fascinated stares.

A police constable in uniform stood on the step and did his best to keep back the curious. Alert-looking young men with cameras were busy and surged forward as Japp alighted.

"Nothing for you now," said Japp, brushing them aside. He nodded to Poirot. "So here you are. Let's get inside."

They passed in quickly, the door shut behind them and they found themselves squeezed together at the foot of a ladderlike flight of stairs.

A man came to the top of the staircase, recognized Japp and said: "Up here, sir."

Japp and Poirot mounted the stairs.

The man at the stairhead opened a door on the left and they found themselves in a small bedroom.

"Thought you'd like me to run over the chief points, sir."

"Quite right, Jameson," said Japp. "What about it?"

Divisional Inspector Jameson took up the tale.

"Deceased's a Mrs. Allen, sir. Lived here with a friend—a Miss Plenderleith. Miss Plenderleith was away staying in the country and returned this morning. She let herself in with her key, was surprised to find no one about. A woman usually comes in at nine o'clock to do for them. She went upstairs first into her friend's room. Door was locked on the inside. She rattled the handle. Knocked and called, but couldn't get any answer. In the end, getting alarmed, she rang up the police station. That was at 10:45. We came along at once and forced the door open. Mrs. Allen was lying in a heap on the floor, shot through the head. There was an automatic in her hand—a Webley .25—and it looked a clear case of suicide."

"Where is Miss Plenderleith now?"

"She's downstairs in the sitting room, sir. A very cool, efficient young lady, I should say. Got a head on her."

"I'll talk to her presently. I'd better see Brett now."

Accompanied by Poirot he crossed the landing and entered the opposite room. A tall elderly man looked up and nodded.

"Hullo, Japp, glad you've got here. Funny business, this."

Japp advanced towards him. Hercule Poirot sent a quick searching glance round the room.

It was much larger than the room they had just quitted. It had a built-out bay window, and whereas the other room had been a bedroom pure and simple, this was emphatically a bedroom disguised as a sitting room.

The walls were silver and the ceiling emerald green. There were curtains of a modernistic pattern in silver and green. There was a divan covered with a shimmering emerald green silk quilt and numbers of gold and silver cushions. There was a tall antique walnut bureau, a walnut tallboy and several modern chairs of gleaming chromium. On a low glass table there was a big ashtray full of cigarette stubs.

Delicately Hercule Poirot sniffed the air. Then he joined Japp where the latter stood looking down at the body.

In a heap on the floor, lying as she had fallen from one of the chromium chairs, was the body of a young woman of perhaps twenty-seven. She had fair hair and delicate features. There was very little make-up on the face. It was a pretty, wistful, perhaps slightly stupid face. On the left side of the head was a mass of congealed blood. The fingers of the right hand were clasped round a small pistol. The woman was dressed in a simple frock of dark green high to the neck.

"Well, Brett, what's the trouble?"

Japp was looking down also at the huddled figure.

"Position's all right," said the doctor. "If she shot herself she'd probably have slipped from the chair into just that position. The door was locked and the window was fastened on the inside."

"That's all right, you say. Then what's wrong?"

"Take a look at the pistol. I haven't handled it—waiting for the fingerprint men. But you can see quite well what I mean."

Together Poirot and Japp knelt down and examined the pistol closely.

"I see what you mean," said Japp, rising. "It's in the curve of her hand. It *looks* as though she's holding it—but as a matter of fact she *isn't* holding it. Anything else?"

"Plenty. She's got the pistol in her *right* hand. Now take a look at the wound. The pistol was held close to the head just above the *left* ear—the *left* ear, mark you."

"H'm," said Japp. "That does seem to settle it. She couldn't hold a pistol and fire it in that position with her right hand."

"Plumb impossible, I should say. You might get your arm round but I doubt if you could fire the shot."

"That seems pretty obvious, then. Someone else shot her and tried to make it look like suicide. What about the locked door and window, though?"

Inspector Jameson answered this.

"Window was closed and bolted, sir, but although the door was locked, *we haven't been able to find the key.*"

Japp nodded.

"Yes, that was a bad break. Whoever did it locked the door when he left and hoped the absence of the key wouldn't be noticed."

Poirot murmured:

"*C'est bête, ça!*"

"Oh, come now, Poirot, old man, you mustn't judge everybody else by the light of your shining intellect! As a matter of fact that's the sort of little detail that's quite apt to be overlooked. Door's locked. People break in. Woman found dead—pistol in her hand—clear case of suicide—she locked herself in to do it. They don't go hunting for keys. As a matter of fact Miss Plenderleith's sending for the police was lucky. She might have got one or two of the chauffeurs to come and burst in the door—and then the key question would have been overlooked altogether."

"Yes, I suppose that is true," said Hercule Poirot. "It would have been many people's natural reaction. The police, they are the last resource, are they not?"

He was still staring down at the body.

"Anything strike you?" Japp asked.

The question was careless but his eyes were keen and attentive.

Hercule Poirot shook his head slowly.

"I was looking at her wristwatch."

He bent over and just touched it with a fingertip. It was a dainty jeweled affair on a black moiré strap on the wrist of the hand that held the pistol.

"Rather a swell piece, that," observed Japp. "Must have cost money!" He cocked his head inquiringly at Poirot. "Something in that maybe?"

"It is possible—yes."

Poirot strayed across to the writing bureau. It was the kind that has a front flap that lets down. This was daintily set out to match the general color scheme.

There was a somewhat massive silver inkstand in the center, in front of it a handsome green lacquer blotter. To the left of the blotter was an emerald glass pen tray containing a silver pen holder—a stick of green sealing wax, a pencil and two stamps. On the right of the blotter was a movable calendar giving the day of the week, date and month. There was also a little glass jar of shot and standing in it a flamboyant green quill pen. Poirot seemed interested in the pen. He took it out and looked at it but the quill was innocent of ink. It was clearly a decoration—nothing more. The silver penholder with the ink-stained nib was the one in use. His eyes strayed to the calendar.

"Tuesday, November 5th," said Japp. "Yesterday. That's all correct."

He turned to Brett.

"How long has she been dead?"

"She was killed at eleven-thirty-three yesterday morning," said Brett promptly.

Then he grinned as he saw Japp's surprised face.

"Sorry, old boy," he said. "Had to do the super-doctor of fiction! As a matter of fact eleven is about as near as I can put it—with a margin of about an hour either way."

"Oh! I thought the wristwatch might have stopped—or something."

"It's stopped all right, but it's stopped at a quarter past four."

"And I suppose she couldn't have been killed possibly at a quarter past four?"

"You can put that right out of your mind."

Poirot had turned back the cover of the blotter.

"Good idea," said Japp. "But no luck."

The blotter showed an innocent white sheet of blotting-paper; Poirot turned over the leaves but they were all the same.

He turned his attention to the wastepaper basket.

It contained two or three torn up letters and circulars. They were only torn once and were easily reconstructed. An appeal for money from some Society for assisting ex-service men, an invitation to a cocktail party on November 3rd, an appointment with a dressmaker. The circulars were an announcement of a furriers' sale and a catalogue from a department store.

"Nothing there," said Japp.

"No, it is odd . . ." said Poirot.

"You mean they usually leave a letter when it's suicide?"

"Exactly."

"In fact, one more proof that it *isn't* suicide!"

He moved away.

"I'll have my men get to work now. We'd better go down and interview this Miss Plenderleith. Coming, Poirot?"

Poirot still seemed fascinated by the writing bureau and its appointments.

He left the room, but at the door his eyes went back once more to the flaunting emerald quill pen.

# II

At the foot of the narrow flight of stairs a door gave admission to a large-sized living room—actually the converted stables. In this room, the walls of which were finished in a roughened plaster effect and on which hung etchings and woodcuts, two people were sitting.

One, in a chair near the fireplace, her hand stretched out to the blaze, was a dark efficient-looking young woman of twenty-seven or eight. The other, an elderly woman of ample proportions who carried a string bag, was panting and talking when the two men entered the room.

"—and as I said, miss, such a turn it gave me I nearly dropped down where I stood. And to think that this morning of all mornings—"

The other cut her short.

"That will do, Mrs. Pierce. These gentlemen are police officers, I think."

"Miss Plenderleith?" asked Japp, advancing.

The girl nodded.

"That is my name. This is Mrs. Pierce who comes in to work for us every day."

The irrepressible Mrs. Pierce broke out again.

"And as I was saying to Miss Plenderleith, to think that this morning, of all mornings, my sister's Louisa Maud should have been took with a fit and me the only one handy and, as I say, flesh and blood is flesh and blood, and I didn't think Mrs. Allen would mind, though I never likes to disappoint my ladies—"

Japp broke in with some dexterity.

"Quite so, Mrs. Pierce. Now perhaps you would take Inspector Jameson into the kitchen and give him a brief statement."

Having then got rid of the voluble Mrs. Pierce, who departed with Jameson, talking thirteen to the dozen, Japp turned his attention once more to the girl.

"I am Chief Inspector Japp. Now, Miss Plenderleith, I should like to know all you can tell me about this business."

"Certainly. Where shall I begin?"

Her self-possession was admirable. There were no signs of grief or shock save for an almost unnatural rigidity of manner.

"You arrived this morning at what time?"

"I think it was just before half-past ten. Mrs. Pierce, the old liar, wasn't here, I found—"

"Is that a frequent occurrence?"

Jane Plenderleith shrugged her shoulders.

"About twice a week she turns up at twelve—or not at all. She's supposed to come at nine. Actually, as I say, twice a week she either 'comes over queer' or else some member of her family is overtaken by sickness. All these daily women are like that—fail you now and again. She's not bad as they go."

"You've had her long?"

"Just over a month. Our last one pinched things."

"Please go on, Miss Plenderleith."

"I paid off the taxi, carried in my suitcase, looked round for Mrs. P., couldn't see her and went upstairs to my room. I tidied up a bit, then I went across to Barbara—Mrs. Allen—and found the door locked. I rattled the handle and knocked but could get no reply. I came downstairs and rang up the police station."

"*Pardon!*" Poirot interposed a quick deft question. "It did not occur to you to try and break down the door—with the help of one of the chauffeurs in the Mews, say?"

Her eyes turned to him—cool gray-green eyes. Her glance seemed to sweep over him quickly and appraisingly.

"No, I don't think I thought of that. If anything was wrong, it seemed to me that the police were the people to send for."

"Then you thought—*pardon, mademoiselle*—that there was something wrong?"

"Naturally."

"Because you could not get a reply to your knocks? But possibly your friend might have taken a sleeping draught or something of that kind—"

"She didn't take sleeping draughts."

The reply came sharply.

"Or she might have gone away and locked her door before going?"

"Why should she lock it? In any case she would have left a note for me."

"And she did not—leave a note for you? You are quite sure of that?"

"Of course I am sure of it. I should have seen it at once."

The sharpness of her tone was accentuated.

Japp said:

"You didn't try and look through the keyhole, Miss Plenderleith?"

"No," said Jane Plenderleith thoughtfully. "I never thought of that. But I couldn't have seen anything, could I? Because the key would have been in it."

Her inquiring gaze, innocent, wide-eyed, met Japp's. Poirot smiled suddenly to himself.

"You did quite right, of course, Miss Plenderleith," said Japp. "I suppose you'd no reason to believe that your friend was likely to commit suicide?"

"Oh, no."

"She hadn't seemed worried—or distressed in any way?"

There was a pause—an appreciable pause before the girl answered.

"No."

"Did you know she had a pistol?"

Jane Plenderleith nodded.

"Yes, she had it out in India. She always kept it in a drawer in her room."

"H'm. Got a license for it?"

"I imagine so. I don't know for certain."

"Now, Miss Plenderleith, will you tell me all you can about Mrs. Allen, how long you've known her, where her relations are—everything in fact."

Jane Plenderleith nodded.

"I've known Barbara about five years. I met her first traveling abroad—in Egypt to be exact. She was on her way home from India. I'd been at the British School in Athens for a bit and was having a few weeks in Egypt before going home. We were on a Nile cruise together. We made friends, decided we liked each other; I was looking at the time for someone to share a flat or a tiny house with me. Barbara was alone in the world. We thought we'd get on well together."

"And you did get on well together?" asked Poirot.

"Very well. We each had our own friends—Barbara was more social in her likings—my friends were more of the artistic kind. It probably worked better that way."

Poirot nodded. Japp went on:

"What do you know about Mrs. Allen's family and her life before she met you?"

Jane Plenderleith shrugged her shoulders.

"Not very much really. Her maiden name was Armitage, I believe."

"Her husband?"

"I don't fancy that he was anything to write home about. He drank, I think. I gather he died a year or two after the marriage. There was one child, a little girl, but that died when it was three years old. Barbara didn't talk much about her husband. I believe she married him in India when she was about seventeen. Then they went off to Borneo or one of the God-forsaken spots you send ne'er-do-wells to— but as it was obviously a painful subject I didn't refer to it."

"Do you know if Mrs. Allen was in any financial difficulties?"

"No, I'm sure she wasn't."

"Not in debt? Anything of that kind?"

"Oh, no! I'm sure she wasn't in that kind of a jam."

"Now there's another question I must ask—and I hope you won't be upset about it, Miss Plenderleith. Had Mrs. Allen any particular man friend or men friends?"

Jane Plenderleith answered coolly:

"Well, she was engaged to be married if that answers your question."

"What is the name of the man she was engaged to?"

"Charles Laverton-West. He's M.P. for some place in Hampshire."

"Had she known him long?"

"A little over a year."

"And she has been engaged to him—how long?"

"Two—no—nearer three months."

"As far as you know there has not been any quarrel?"

Miss Plenderleith shook her head.

"No. I should be surprised if there had been anything of the sort. Barbara wasn't the quarreling kind."

"How long is it since you last saw Mrs. Allen?"

"Friday last, just before I went away for the weekend."

"Mrs. Allen was remaining in town?"

"Yes. She was going out with her fiancé on the Sunday I believe."

"And you, yourself, where did you spend the weekend?"

"At Laidells Hall, Laidells, Essex."

"And the name of the people with whom you were staying?"

"Mr. and Mrs. Bentinck."

"You only left them this morning?"

"Yes."

"You must have left very early?"

"Mr. Bentinck motored me up. He starts early because he has to get to the city by ten."

"I see."

Japp nodded comprehendingly. Miss Plenderleith's replies had all been crisp and convincing.

Poirot in his turn put a question.

"What is your own opinion of Mr. Laverton-West?"

The girl shrugged her shoulders.

"Does that matter?"

"No, it does not matter, perhaps, but I should like to have your opinion."

"I don't know that I've thought about him one way or the other. He's young—not more than thirty-one or two—ambitious—a good public speaker—means to get on in the world."

"That is on the credit side—and on the debit?"

"Well." Miss Plenderleith considered for a moment or two. "In my opinion, he's commonplace—his ideas are not particularly original— and he's slightly pompous."

"Those are not very serious faults, mademoiselle," said Poirot, smiling.

"Don't you think so?"

Her tone was slightly ironic.

"They might be to you."

He was watching her, saw her look a little disconcerted. He pursued his advantage.

"But to Mrs. Allen—no, she would not notice them."

"You're perfectly right. Barbara thought he was wonderful—took him entirely at his own valuation."

Poirot said gently:

"You were fond of your friend?"

He saw the hand clench on her knee, the tightening of the line of the jaw, yet the answer came in a matter-of-fact voice free from emotion.

"You are quite right. I was."

Japp said:

"Just one other thing, Miss Plenderleith. You and she didn't have a quarrel? There was no upset between you?"

"None whatever."

"Not over this engagement business?"

"Certainly not. I was glad she was able to be so happy about it."

There was a momentary pause, then Japp said:

"As far as you know, did Mrs. Allen have any enemies?"

This time there was a definite interval before Jane Plenderleith replied. When she did so, her tone had altered very slightly.

"I don't know quite what you mean by enemies?"

"Anyone, for instance, who would profit by her death?"

"Oh, no, that would be ridiculous. She had a very small income anyway."

"And who inherits that income?"

Jane Plenderleith's voice sounded mildly surprised as she said:

"Do you know, I really don't know. I shouldn't be surprised if I did. That is, if she ever made a will."

"And no enemies in any other sense?" Japp slid off to another aspect quickly. "People with a grudge against her?"

"I don't think anyone had a grudge against her. She was a very gentle creature, always anxious to please. She had a really sweet lovable nature."

For the first time that hard matter-of-fact voice broke a little. Poirot nodded gently.

Japp said:

"So it amounts to this: Mrs. Allen has been in good spirits lately, she wasn't in any financial difficulty, she was engaged to be married and was happy in her engagement. There was nothing in the world to make her commit suicide. That's right, isn't it?"

There was a momentary silence before Jane said:

"Yes."

Japp rose.

"Excuse me; I must have a word with Inspector Jameson."

He left the room.

Hercule Poirot remained tête-à-tête with Jane Plenderleith.

# III

For a few minutes there was silence.

Jane Plenderleith shot a swift appraising glance at the little man but after that she stared in front of her and did not speak. Yet a consciousness of his presence showed itself in a certain nervous tension. Her body was still but not relaxed. When at last Poirot did break the silence the mere sound of his voice seemed to give her a certain relief. In an agreeable everyday voice he asked a question.

"When did you light the fire, mademoiselle?"

"The fire?" Her voice sounded vague and rather absent-minded. "Oh! As soon as I arrived this morning."

"Before you went upstairs or afterwards?"

"Before."

"I see. Yes, naturally. . . . And it was already laid—or did you have to lay it?"

"It was laid. I only had to put a match to it."

There was a slight impatience in her voice. Clearly she suspected him of making conversation. Possibly that was what he was doing. At any rate he went on in quiet conversational tones.

"But your friend—in her room I noticed there was a gas fire only?"

Jane Plenderleith answered mechanically.

"This is the only coal fire we have—the others are all gas fires."

"And you cook with gas, too?"

"I think everyone does nowadays."

"True. It is much more labor-saving."

The little interchange died down. Jane Plenderleith tapped on the ground with her shoe. Then she said abruptly:

"That man—Chief Inspector Japp—is he considered clever?"

"He is very sound. Yes, he is well thought of. He works hard and painstakingly and very little escapes him."

"I wonder—" muttered the girl.

Poirot watched her. His eyes looked very green in the firelight. He asked quietly:

"It was a great shock to you, your friend's death?"

"Terrible."

She spoke with abrupt sincerity.

"You did not expect it—no?"

"Of course not."

"So that it seemed to you at first, perhaps, that it was impossible— that it could not be?"

The quiet sympathy of his tone seemed to break down Jane Plenderleith's defenses. She replied eagerly, naturally, without stiffness.

"That's just it. Even if Barbara *did* kill herself, I can't imagine her *killing herself that way.*"

"Yet she had a pistol?"

Jane Plenderleith made an impatient gesture.

"Yes, but that pistol was a—Oh! A hang-over. She'd been in out of the way places. She kept it out of habit—not with any other idea. I'm sure of that."

"Ah! And why are you sure of that?"

"Oh, because of the things she said."

"Such as—?"

His voice was very gentle and friendly. It led her on subtly.

"Well, for instance, we were discussing suicide once and she said much the easiest way would be to turn the gas on and stuff up all the cracks and just go to bed. I said I thought that would be impossible— to lie there waiting. I said I'd far rather shoot myself. And she said no, she could never shoot herself. She'd be too frightened in case it didn't come off and anyway she said she'd hate the bang."

"I see," said Poirot. "As you say it is odd. Because, as you have just told me, *there was a gas fire in her room.*"

Jane Plenderleith looked at him, slightly startled.

"Yes, there was . . . I can't understand—no, I can't understand why she didn't do it that way."

Poirot shook his head.

"Yes, it seems—odd—not natural somehow."

"The whole thing doesn't seem natural. I still can't believe she killed herself. I suppose it *must* be suicide?"

"Well—there is one other possibility."

"What do you mean?"

Poirot looked straight at her.

"It might be—murder."

"Oh, no!" Jane Plenderleith shrank back. "Oh, no! What a horrible suggestion."

"Horrible, perhaps, but does it strike you as an impossible one?"

"But the door was locked on the inside. So was the window."

"The door was locked—yes. But there is nothing to show if it were locked from the inside or the outside. You see, *the key was missing.*"

"But then—if it is missing . . ." She took a minute or two. "Then it must have been locked from the *outside*. Otherwise it would be somewhere in the room."

"Ah, but it may be. The room has not been thoroughly searched yet, remember. Or it may have been thrown out of the window and somebody may have picked it up."

"Murder!" said Jane Plenderleith. She turned over the possibility, her dark clever face eager on the scent. "I believe—I believe you're right."

"But if it were murder there would have to be a motive. Do you know of a motive, mademoiselle?"

Slowly she shook her head. And yet, in spite of the denial, Poirot got the impression that Jane Plenderleith was deliberately keeping something back. The door opened and Japp came in.

Poirot rose.

"I have been suggesting to Miss Plenderleith," he said, "that her friend's death was not suicide."

Japp looked momentarily put out. He cast a glance of reproach at Poirot.

"It's a bit early on to say anything definite," he remarked. "We've always got to take all possibilities into account, you understand. That's all there is to it at the moment."

Jane Plenderleith replied quietly:

"I see."

Japp came towards her.

"Now then, Miss Plenderleith, have you ever seen this before?"

On the palm of his hand he held out a small oval of dark blue enamel.

Jane Plenderleith shook her head.

"No, never."

"It's not yours nor Mrs. Allen's?"

"No. It's not the kind of thing usually worn by our sex, is it?"

"Oh! So you recognize it."

"Well, it's pretty obvious, isn't it? That's half of a man's cuff link."

# IV

"That young woman's too cocky by half," Japp complained.

The two men were once more in Mrs. Allen's bedroom. The body had been photographed and removed and the fingerprint man had done his work and departed.

"It would be inadvisable to treat her as a fool," agreed Poirot. "She most emphatically is *not* a fool. She is, in fact, a particularly clever and competent young woman."

"Think she did it?" asked Japp with a momentary ray of hope. "She might have, you know. We'll have to get her alibi looked in to. Some quarrel over this young man—this budding M.P. She's rather *too* scathing about him, I think! Sounds fishy. Rather as though she were sweet on him herself and he'd turned her down. She's the kind that would bump anyone off if she felt like it, and keep her head while she was doing it, too. Yes, we'll have to look into that alibi. She had it very pat and after all Essex isn't very far away. Plenty of trains. Or a fast car. It's worthwhile finding out if she went to bed with a headache for instance last night."

"You are right," agreed Poirot.

"In any case," continued Japp, "she's holding out on us. Eh? Didn't you feel that, too? That young woman knows something."

Poirot nodded thoughtfully.

"Yes, that could be clearly seen."

"That's always a difficulty in these cases," Japp complained. "People will hold their tongues, sometimes out of the most honorable motives."

"For which one can hardly blame them, my friend."

"No, but it makes it much harder for *us*," Japp grumbled.

"It merely displays to its full advantage your ingenuity," Poirot consoled him. "What about fingerprints, by the way?"

"Well, it's murder all right. No prints whatever on the pistol. Wiped clean before being placed in her hand. Even if she managed to wind her arm around her head in some marvelous acrobatic fashion she could hardly fire off a pistol without hanging on to it and she couldn't wipe it after she was dead."

"No, no, an outside agency is clearly indicated."

"Otherwise the prints are disappointing. None on the door handle. None on the window. Suggestive, eh? Plenty of Mrs. Allen's all over the place."

"Did Jameson get anything?"

"Out of that daily woman? No. She talked a lot but she didn't really know much. Confirmed the fact that Allen and Plenderleith were on good terms. I've sent Jameson out to make inquiries in the Mews. We'll have to have a word with Mr. Laverton-West, too. Find out where he was and what he was doing last night. In the meantime, we'll have a look through her papers."

He set to without more ado. Occasionally he grunted and tossed something over to Poirot. The search did not take long. There were not many papers in the desk and what were there were neatly arranged and docketed.

Finally Japp leaned back and uttered a sigh.

"Not very much, is there?"

"As you say."

"Most of it quite straightforward—receipted bills, a few bills as yet unpaid—nothing particularly outstanding. Social stuff—invitations. Notes from friends. These—" he laid his hand on a pile of seven or eight letters—"and her checkbook and passbook. Anything strike you there?"

"Yes, she was overdrawn."

"Anything else?"

Poirot smiled.

"Is it an examination that you put me through? But yes, I noticed what you are thinking of. Two hundred pounds drawn to self three months ago—and two hundred pounds drawn out yesterday—"

"And nothing on the counterfoil of the checkbook. No other checks to self except small sums—fifteen pounds the highest. And I'll tell you this—there's no such sum of money in the house. Four pounds ten in a handbag and an odd shilling or two in another bag. That's pretty clear, I think."

"Meaning that she paid that sum away yesterday."

"Yes. Now who did she pay it to?"

The door opened and Inspector Jameson entered.

"Well, Jameson, get anything?"

"Yes, sir, several things. To begin with, nobody actually heard the shot. Two or three women say they did because they want to think they did—but that's all there is to it. With all those fireworks going off there wasn't a dog's chance."

Japp grunted.

"Don't suppose there is. Go on."

"Mrs. Allen was at home most of yesterday afternoon and evening. Came in about five o'clock. Then she went out again about six but only to the post box at the end of the Mews. At about nine-thirty a car drove up—Standard Swallow saloon—a man got out. Description about forty-five, well set up military-looking gent, dark blue overcoat, bowler hat, toothbrush mustache. James Hogg, chauffeur from No. 18, says he's seen him calling on Mrs. Allen before."

"Forty-five," said Japp. "Can't very well be Laverton-West."

"This man, whoever he was, stayed here for just under an hour. Left at about ten-twenty. Stopped in the doorway to speak to Mrs. Allen. Small boy, Frederick Hogg, was hanging about quite near and heard what he said."

"And what did he say?"

" '*Well, think it over and let me know.*' And then she said something and he answered: '*All right. So long.*' After that he got in his car and drove away."

"That was at ten-twenty," said Poirot thoughtfully.

Japp rubbed his nose.

"Then at ten-twenty Mrs. Allen was still alive," he said.

"What next?" asked Poirot.

"Nothing more, sir, as far as I can learn. The chauffeur at No. 22 got in at half-past ten and he'd promised his kids to let off some fireworks for them. They'd been waiting for him—and all the other kids in the Mews, too. He let 'em off and everybody round about was busy watching them. After that everyone went to bed."

"And nobody else was seen to enter No. 14?"

"No—but that's not saying they didn't. Nobody would have noticed."

"H'm," said Japp. "That's true. Well, we'll have to get hold of this 'military gentleman with the toothbrush mustache.' It's pretty clear that he was the last person to see her alive. I wonder who he was?"

"Miss Plenderleith might tell us," suggested Poirot.

"She might," said Japp gloomily. "On the other hand she might not. I've no doubt she could tell us a good deal if she liked. What about you, Poirot, old boy? You were alone with her for a bit. Didn't you trot out that Father Confessor manner of yours that sometimes makes such a hit?"

Poirot spread out his hands.

"Alas, we talked only of gas fires."

"Gas fires—gas fires!" Japp sounded disgusted. "What's the matter with you, old cock? Ever since you've been here the only things you've taken interest in are quill pens and wastepaper baskets. Oh, yes, I saw you having a quiet look into the one downstairs. Anything in it?"

Poirot sighed.

"A catalogue of bulbs and an old magazine."

"What's the idea anyway? If anyone wants to throw away an incriminating document or whatever it is you have in mind they're not likely just to pitch it into a wastepaper basket."

"That is very true what you say there. Only something quite unimportant would be thrown away like that."

Poirot spoke meekly. Nevertheless Japp looked at him suspiciously.

"Well," he said. "I know what I'm going to do next. What about you?"

"Eh bien," said Poirot. "I shall complete my search for the unimportant. There is still the dustbin."

He skipped nimbly out of the room. Japp looked after him with an air of disgust.

"Potty," he said. "Absolutely potty."

Inspector Jameson preserved a respectful silence. His face said with British superiority, "Foreigners!"

Aloud he said:

"So that's Mr. Hercule Poirot! I've heard of him."

"Old friend of mine," explained Japp. "Not half as balmy as he looks, mind you. All the same he's getting on now."

"Gone a bit gaga, as they say, sir," suggested Inspector Jameson. "Ah, well, age will tell."

"All the same," said Japp, "I wish I knew what he was up to."

He walked over to the writing bureau and stared uneasily at an emerald-green quill pen.

# V

Japp was just engaging his third chauffeur's wife in conversation when Poirot, walking noiselessly as a cat, suddenly appeared at his elbow.

"Whew, you made me jump!" said Japp. "Got anything?"

"Not what I was looking for."

Japp turned back to Mrs. James Hogg.

"And you say you've seen this gentleman before?"

"Oh, yes, sir. And my husband, too. We knew him at once."

"Now look here, Mrs. Hogg, you're a shrewd woman, I can see. I've no doubt that you know all about everyone in the Mews. And you're a woman of judgment—unusually good judgment, I can tell that—" Unblushingly he repeated this remark for the third time. Mrs. Hogg bridled slightly and assumed an expression of almost superhuman intelligence. "Give me a line on those two young women—Mrs. Allen and Miss Plenderleith. What were they like? Gay? Lots of parties? That sort of thing?"

"Oh, no, sir, nothing of the kind. They went out a good bit—Mrs. Allen especially—but they're *class*, if you know what I mean. Not like some as I could name down the other end. I'm sure the way that Mrs. Stevens goes on—if she *is* a Mrs. at all, which I doubt—well, I shouldn't like to tell you what goes on there—I—"

"Quite so," said Japp, dexterously stopping the flow.

"Now that's very important what you've told me. Mrs. Allen and Miss Plenderleith were well liked, then?"

"Oh, yes, sir, very nice ladies, both of them—especially Mrs. Allen. Always spoke a nice word to the children, she did. Lost her own little girl, I believe, poor dear. Ah, well, I've buried three myself. And what I say is—"

"Yes, yes, very sad. And Miss Plenderleith?"

"Well, of course she was a nice lady too, but much more abrupt if you know what I mean. Just go by with a nod, she would, and not stop to pass the time of day. But I've nothing against her—nothing at all."

"She and Mrs. Allen got on well together?"

"Oh, yes, sir. No quarreling—nothing like that. Very happy and contented they were—and I'm sure Mrs. Pierce will bear me out."

"Yes, we've talked to her. Do you know Mrs. Allen's fiancé by sight?"

"The gentleman she's going to marry? Oh, yes. He's been here quite a bit off and on. Member of Parliament, they do say."

"It wasn't he who came last night?"

"No, sir, it was *not.*" Mrs. Hogg drew herself up. A note of excitement disguised beneath intense primness came into her voice. "And if you ask me, sir, what you are thinking is all *wrong.* Mrs. Allen wasn't *that* kind of lady, I'm sure. It's true that there was no one in the house, but I do *not* believe anything of the kind—I said so to Hogg only this morning. 'No, Hogg,' I said. 'Mrs. Allen was a lady—a real lady—so don't go suggesting things'—knowing what a man's mind is, if you'll excuse my mentioning it. Always coarse in their ideas."

Passing this insult by, Japp proceeded:

"You saw him arrive and you saw him leave—that's so, isn't it?"

"That's so, sir."

"And you didn't hear anything else? Any sounds of a quarrel?"

"No, sir, nor likely to. Not, that is to say, that such things couldn't be heard—because the contrary to that is well known—and down the other end the way Mrs. Stevens goes for that poor frightened maid of hers is common talk—and one and all we've advised her not to stand it, but there, the wages is good—temper of the devil she may have but pays for it—thirty shillings a week—"

Japp said quickly:

"But you didn't hear anything of the kind at No. 14?"

"No, sir. Nor likely to with fireworks popping off here, there and everywhere and my Eddie with his eyebrows singed off as near as nothing."

"This man left at ten-twenty—that's right, is it?"

"It might be, sir. I couldn't say myself. But Hogg says so and he's a very reliable steady man."

"You actually saw him leave. Did you hear what he said?"

"No, sir. I wasn't near enough for that. Just saw him from my window standing in the doorway talking to Mrs. Allen."

"See her, too?"

"Yes, sir, she was standing just inside the doorway."

"Notice what she was wearing?"

"Now, really, sir, I couldn't say. Not noticing particularly, as it were."

Poirot said:

"You did not even notice if she was wearing day dress or evening dress?"

"No, sir. I can't say I did."

Poirot looked thoughtfully up at the window above and then across to No. 14. He smiled and for a moment his eye caught Japp's.

"And the gentleman?"

"He was in a dark blue overcoat and a bowler hat. Very smart and well set up."

Japp asked a few more questions and then proceeded to his next interview. This was with Master Frederick Hogg, an impish-faced bright-eyed lad, considerably swollen with self-importance.

"Yes, sir. I heard them talking. *'Think it over and let me know,'* the gent said. Pleasant-like, you know. And then she said something and he answered, *'All right. So long.'* And he got into the car—I was holding the door open but he didn't give me nothing," said Master Hogg, with a slight tinge of depression in his tone. "And he drove away."

"You didn't hear what Mrs. Allen said?"

"No, sir, I can't say I did."

"Can you tell me what she was wearing? What color, for instance?"

"Couldn't say, sir. You see, I didn't really see her. She must have been round behind the door."

"Just so," said Japp. "Now look here, my boy, I want you to think and answer my next question very carefully. If you don't know and can't remember, say so. Is that clear?"

"Yes, sir."

Master Hogg looked at him eagerly.

"Which of 'em closed the door, Mrs. Allen or the gentleman?"

"The front door?"

"The front door naturally."

The child reflected. His eyes screwed themselves up in an effort of remembrance.

"Think the lady probably did—No, she didn't. He did. Pulled it to with a bit of a bang and jumped into the car quick. Looked as though he had a date somewhere."

"Right. Well, young man, you seem a bright kind of shaver. Here's sixpence for you."

Dismissing Master Hogg, Japp turned to his friend. Slowly with one accord they nodded.

"Could be!" said Japp.

"There are possibilities," agreed Poirot.

His eyes shone with a green light. They looked like a cat's.

# VI

On reentering the sitting-room of No. 14, Japp wasted no time in beating about the bush. He came straight to the point.

"Now look here, Miss Plenderleith, don't you think it's better to spill the beans here and now? It's going to come to that in the end."

Jane Plenderleith raised her eyebrows. She was standing by the mantelpiece, gently warming one foot at the fire.

"I really don't know what you mean."

"Is that quite true, Miss Plenderleith?"

She shrugged her shoulders.

"I've answered all your questions. I don't see what more I can do."

"Well, it's my opinion you could do a lot more—if you chose."

"That's only an opinion, though, isn't it, Chief Inspector?"

Japp grew rather red in the face.

"I think," said Poirot, "that mademoiselle would appreciate better the reason for your questions if you told her just how the case stands."

"That's very simple. Now then, Miss Plenderleith, the facts are as follows: Your friend was found shot through the head with a pistol in her hand and the door and the window fastened. That looked like a plain case of suicide. *But it wasn't suicide.* The medical evidence alone proves that."

"How?"

All her ironic coolness had disappeared. She leaned forward—intent—watching his face.

"The pistol was in her hand—*but the fingers weren't grasping it.* Moreover there were *no fingerprints at all* on the pistol. And the angle of the wound makes it impossible that the wound should have been self-inflicted. Then again she left no letter—rather an unusual thing for a suicide. And though the door was locked, the key has not been found."

Jane Plenderleith turned slowly and sat down in a chair facing them.

"So that's it!" she said. "All along I've felt it was *impossible* that she should have killed herself! I was right! She *didn't* kill herself. Someone else killed her."

For a minute or two she remained lost in thought. Then she raised her head brusquely.

"Ask me any questions you like," she said. "I will answer them to the best of my ability."

Japp began:

"Last night Mrs. Allen had a visitor. He is described as a man of forty-five, military bearing, toothbrush mustache, smartly dressed and driving a Standard Swallow saloon car. Do you know who that is?"

"I can't be sure, of course, but it sounds like Major Eustace."

"Who is Major Eustace? Tell me all you can about him."

"He was a man Barbara had known abroad—in India. He turned up about a year ago and we've seen him on and off since."

"He was a friend of Mrs. Allen's?"

"He behaved like one," said Jane drily.

"What was her attitude to him?"

"I don't think she really liked him—in fact I'm sure she didn't."

"But she treated him with outward friendliness?"

"Yes."

"Did she ever seem—think carefully, Miss Plenderleith—afraid of him?"

Jane Plenderleith considered this thoughtfully for a minute or two. Then she said:

"Yes—I think she was. She was always nervous when he was about."

"Did he and Mr. Laverton-West meet at all?"

"Only once, I think. They didn't take to each other much. That is to say, Major Eustace made himself as agreeable as he could to Charles, but Charles wasn't having any. Charles has got a very good nose for anybody who isn't well—quite—quite."

"And Major Eustace was not—what you call—quite—quite?" asked Poirot.

The girl said drily:

"No, he wasn't. Bit hairy at the heel. Definitely not out of the top drawer."

"Alas—I do not know those two expressions. You mean to say he was not the *pukka sahib?*"

A fleeting smile passed across Jane Plenderleith's face, but she replied gravely, "No."

"Would it come as a great surprise to you, Miss Plenderleith, if I suggested that this man was blackmailing Mrs. Allen?"

Japp sat forward to observe the result of his suggestion.

He was well satisfied. The girl started forward, the color rose in her cheeks, she brought down her hand sharply on the arm of her chair.

"So that was it! What a fool I was not to have guessed. Of course!"

"You think the suggestion feasible, mademoiselle?" asked Poirot.

"I was a fool not to have thought of it! Barbara's borrowed small sums off me several times during the last six months. And I've seen her sitting poring over her passbook. I knew she was living well within her income, so I didn't bother, but of course if she was paying out sums of money—"

"And it would accord with her general demeanor—yes?" asked Poirot.

"Absolutely. She was nervous. Quite jumpy sometimes. Altogether different from what she used to be."

Poirot said gently:

"Excuse me, but that is not just what you told us before."

"That was different." Jane Plenderleith waved an impatient hand. "She wasn't *depressed*. I mean she wasn't feeling suicidal or anything like that. But blackmail—yes. I wish she'd told *me*. I'd have sent him to the devil."

"But he might have gone—not to the devil, but to Mr. Charles Laverton-West?" observed Poirot.

"Yes," said Jane Plenderleith slowly. "Yes . . . that's true. . . ."

"You've no idea of what this man's hold over her may have been?" asked Japp.

The girl shook her head.

"I haven't the faintest idea. I can't believe, knowing Barbara, that it could have been anything really serious. On the other hand—" she paused, then went on—"what I mean is, Barbara was a bit of a simpleton in some ways. She'd be very easily frightened. In fact, she was the kind of girl who would be a positive gift to a blackmailer! The nasty brute!"

She snapped out the last three words with real venom.

"Unfortunately," said Poirot, "the crime seems to have taken place the wrong way round. It is the victim who should kill the blackmailer, not the blackmailer his victim."

Jane Plenderleith frowned a little.

"No—that is true—but I can imagine circumstances—"

"Such as?"

"Supposing Barbara got desperate. She may have threatened him with that silly little pistol of hers. He tries to wrench it away from her and in the struggle he fires it and kills her. Then he's horrified at what he's done and tries to pretend it was suicide."

"Might be," said Japp. "But there's a difficulty."

She looked at him inquiringly.

"Major Eustace (if it was he) left here last night at ten-twenty and said good-by to Mrs. Allen on the doorstep."

"Oh!" The girl's face fell. "I see." She paused a minute or two. "But he might have come back later," she said slowly.

"Yes, that is possible," said Poirot.

Japp continued:

"Tell me, Miss Plenderleith, where was Mrs. Allen in the habit of receiving guests? Here or in the room upstairs?"

"Both. But this room was used more for communal parties or for my own special friends. You see, the arrangement was that Barbara had the big bedroom and used it as a sitting room as well, and I had the little bedroom and used this room."

"If Major Eustace came by appointment last night, in which room do you think Mrs. Allen would have received him?"

"I think she would probably bring him in here." The girl sounded a little doubtful. "It would be less intimate. On the other hand, if she wanted to write a check or anything of that kind, she would probably take him upstairs. There are no writing materials down here."

Japp shook his head.

"There was no question of a check. Mrs. Allen drew out two hundred pounds in cash yesterday. And so far we've not been able to find any trace of it in the house."

"And she gave it to that brute? Oh, poor Barbara! Poor, poor Barbara!"

Poirot coughed.

"Unless, as you suggest, it was more or less of an accident, it still seems a remarkable fact that he should kill an apparently regular source of income."

"Accident? It wasn't an accident. He lost his temper and saw red and shot her."

"That is how you think it happened?"

"Yes." She added vehemently, "It was murder—*murder!*"

Poirot said gravely:

"I will not say that you are wrong, mademoiselle."

Japp said:

"What cigarettes did Mrs. Allen smoke?"

"Gaspers. There are some in that box."

Japp opened the box, took out a cigarette and nodded. He slipped the cigarette into his pocket.

"And you, mademoiselle?" asked Poirot.

"The same."

"You do not smoke Turkish?"

"Never."

"Nor Mrs. Allen?"

"No, she didn't like them."

Poirot asked:

"And Mr. Laverton-West? What did he smoke?"

She stared hard at him.

"Charles? What does it matter what he smoked? You're not going to pretend that *he* killed her?"

Poirot shrugged his shoulders.

"A man has killed the woman he loved before now, mademoiselle."

Jane shook her head impatiently.

"Charles wouldn't kill anybody. He's a very careful man."

"All the same, mademoiselle, it is the careful men who commit the cleverest murders."

She stared at him.

"But not for the motive you have just advanced, M. Poirot."

He bowed his head.

"No, that is true."

Japp rose.

"Well, I don't think that there's much more I can do here. I'd like to have one more look round."

"In case that money should be tucked away somewhere? Certainly. Look anywhere you like. And in my room, too—although it isn't likely Barbara would hide it there."

Japp's search was quick but efficient. The living-room had given up all its secrets in a very few minutes. Then he went upstairs. Jane Plenderleith sat on the arm of a chair, smoking a cigarette and frowning into the fire. Poirot watched her.

After some minutes, he said quietly:

"Do you know if Mr. Laverton-West is in London at present?"

"I don't know at all. I rather fancy he's in Hampshire with his people. I suppose I ought to have wired him. How dreadful. I forgot."

"It is not easy to remember everything, mademoiselle, when a catastrophe occurs. And after all, the bad news, it will keep. One hears it only too soon."

"Yes, that's true," the girl said absently.

Japp's footsteps were heard descending the stairs. Jane went out to meet him.

"Well?"

Japp shook his head.

"Nothing helpful, I'm afraid, Miss Plenderleith. I've been over the whole house now. Oh, I suppose I'd better just have a look in this cupboard under the stairs."

He caught hold of the handle as he spoke, and pulled.

Jane Plenderleith said:

"It's locked."

Something in her voice made both men look at her sharply.

"Yes," said Japp pleasantly. "I can see it's locked. Perhaps you'll get the key."

The girl was standing as though carved in stone.

"I—I'm not sure where it is."

Japp shot a quick glance at her. His voice continued resolutely pleasant and offhand.

"Dear me, that's too bad. Don't want to splinter the wood opening it by force. I'll send Jameson out to get an assortment of keys."

She moved forward stiffly.

"Oh," she said. "One minute. It might be—"

She went back into the living room and reappeared a moment later holding a fair-sized key in her hand.

"We keep it locked," she explained, "because one's umbrellas and things have a habit of getting pinched."

"Very wise precaution," said Japp, cheerfully accepting the key.

He turned it in the lock and threw the door open. It was dark inside the cupboard. Japp took out his pocket flashlight and let it play round the inside.

Poirot felt the girl at his side stiffen and stop breathing for a second. His eyes followed the sweep of Japp's torch.

There was not very much in the cupboard. Three umbrellas (one broken), four walking sticks, a set of golf clubs, two tennis racquets, a neatly folded rug, and several sofa cushions in various stages of dilapidation. On the top of these last reposed a small smart-looking briefcase.

As Japp stretched out a hand toward it, Jane Plenderleith said quickly:

"That's mine. I—it came back with me this morning. So there can't be anything there."

"Just as well to make quite sure," said Japp, his cheery friendliness increasing slightly.

The case was unlocked. Inside it was fitted with shagreen brushes and toilet bottles. There were two magazines in it but nothing else.

Japp examined the whole outfit with meticulous attention. When at last he shut the lid and began a cursory examination of the cushions, the girl gave an audible sigh of relief.

There was nothing else in the cupboard beyond what was plainly to be seen. Japp's examination was soon finished.

He relocked the door and handed the key to Jane Plenderleith.

"Well," he said "that concludes matters. Can you give me Mr. Laverton-West's address?"

"Farlescombe Hall, Little Ledbury, Hampshire."

"Thank you, Miss Plenderleith. That's all for the present. I may be round again later. By the way, mum's the word. Leave it at suicide as far as the general public's concerned."

"Of course; I quite understand."

She shook hands with them both.

As they walked away down the Mews, Japp exploded:

"What the—the hell was there in that cupboard? There was *something*."

"Yes, there was something."

"And I'll bet ten to one it was something to do with the briefcase! But like the double-dyed mutt I must be, I couldn't find anything.

Looked in all the bottles—felt the lining—what the devil could it be?"

Poirot shook his head thoughtfully.

"That girl's in it somehow," Japp went on. "Brought that case back this morning? Not on your life, she didn't! Notice that there were two magazines in it?"

"Yes."

"Well, one of them was for *last July!*"

# VII

It was the following day when Japp walked into Poirot's flat, flung his hat onto the table in deep disgust and dropped into a chair.

"Well," he growled, *"she's* out of it!"

"Who's out of it?"

"Plenderleith. Was playing bridge up to midnight. Host, hostess, naval commander guest, and two servants can all swear to that. No doubt about it we've got to give up any idea of her being concerned in the business. All the same I'd like to know *why* she went all hot and bothered about that little briefcase under the stairs. That's something in *your* line, Poirot. You like solving the kind of triviality that leads nowhere. 'The Mystery of the Small Briefcase.' Sounds quite promising!"

"I will give you yet another suggestion for a title: 'The Mystery of the Smell of Cigarette Smoke.' "

"A bit clumsy for a title. Smell—eh? Was *that* why you were sniffing so when we first examined the body? I saw you—*and* heard you! Sniff—sniff—sniff. Thought you had a cold in your head."

"You were entirely in error."

Japp sighed.

"I always thought it was the little gray cells of the brain. Don't tell me the cells of your nose are equally superior to anyone else's."

"No, no, calm yourself."

"*I* didn't smell any cigarette smoke," went on Japp suspiciously.

"No more did I, my friend."

Japp looked at him doubtfully. Then he extracted a cigarette from his pocket.

"That's the kind Mrs. Allen smoked—gaspers. Six of those stubs were hers. *The other three were Turkish.*"

"Exactly."

"Your wonderful nose knew that without looking at them, I suppose!"

"I assure you my nose does not enter into the matter. My nose registered nothing."

"But the brain cells registered a lot?"

"Well—there were certain indications—do you not think so?"

Japp looked at him sideways.

"Such as?"

"*Eh bien,* there was very definitely something missing from the room. Also something added, I think. . . . And then, on the writing bureau—"

"I knew it! We're coming to that damned quill pen!"

"*Du tout.* The quill pen plays a purely negative rôle."

Japp retreated to safer ground.

"I've got Charles Laverton-West coming to see me at Scotland Yard in half an hour. I thought you might like to be there."

"I should very much."

"And you'll be glad to hear we've tracked down Major Eustace. Got a service flat in the Cromwell Road."

"Excellent."

"And we've got a little to go on there. Not at all a nice person, Major Eustace. After I've seen Laverton-West, we'll go and see him. That suit you?"

"Perfectly."

"Well, come along then."

At half-past eleven Charles Laverton-West was ushered into Chief Inspector Japp's room. Japp rose and shook hands.

The M.P. was a man of medium height with a very definite personality. He was clean-shaven with the mobile mouth of an actor, and the slightly prominent eyes that so often go with the gift of oratory. He was good-looking in a quiet well-bred way.

Though looking pale and somewhat distressed, his manner was perfectly formal and composed.

He took a seat, laid his gloves and hat on the table and looked towards Japp.

"I'd like to say, first of all, Mr. Laverton-West, that I fully appreciate how distressing this must be to you."

Laverton-West waved this aside.

"Do not let us discuss my feelings. Tell me, Chief Inspector, have you any idea what caused my—Mrs. Allen to take her own life?"

"You, yourself, cannot help us in any way?"

"No, indeed."

"There was no quarrel? No estrangement of any kind between you?"

"Nothing of the kind. It has been the greatest shock to me."

"Perhaps it will be more understandable, sir, if I tell you that it was *not* suicide—but murder!"

"Murder?" Charles Laverton-West's eyes popped nearly out of his head. "You say *murder?*"

"Quite correct. Now, Mr. Laverton-West, have you any idea who might be likely to make away with Mrs. Allen?"

Laverton-West fairly spluttered out his answer.

"No—no, indeed—nothing of the sort! The mere idea is—is *unimaginable!*"

"She never mentioned any enemies? Anyone who might have a grudge against her?"

"Never."

"Did you know that she had a pistol?"

"I was not aware of the fact, no."

He looked a little startled.

"Miss Plenderleith says that Mrs. Allen brought this pistol back from abroad with her some years ago."

"Really?"

"Of course we have only Miss Plenderleith's word for that. It is quite possible that Mrs. Allen felt herself to be in danger from some source and kept the pistol handy for reasons of her own."

Charles Laverton-West shook his head doubtfully. He seemed quite bewildered and dazed.

"What is your opinion of Miss Plenderleith, Mr. Laverton-West? I mean, does she strike you as a reliable, truthful person?"

The other pondered a minute.

"I think so—yes, I should say so."

"You don't like her?" suggested Japp, who had been watching him closely.

"I wouldn't say that. She is not the type of young woman I admire. That sarcastic independent type is not attractive to me, but I should say she was quite truthful."

"H'm," said Japp. "Do you know a Major Eustace?"

"Eustace? Eustace? Ah, yes, I remember the name. I met him once at Barbara's—Mrs. Allen's. Rather a doubtful customer in my opinion. I said as much to my—to Mrs. Allen. He wasn't the type of man I should have encouraged to come to the house after we were married."

"And what did Mrs. Allen say?"

"Oh, she quite agreed. She trusted my judgment implicitly. A man knows other men better than a woman can do. She explained that she couldn't very well be rude to a man whom she had not seen for some time—I think she felt especially a horror of being snobbish! Naturally, as my wife, she would find a good many of her old associates well—unsuitable, shall we say?"

"Meaning that in marrying you she was bettering her position?" Japp asked bluntly.

Laverton-West held up a well-manicured hand.

"No, no, not quite that. As a matter of fact, Mrs. Allen's mother was a distant relation of my own family. She was fully my equal in birth. But, of course, in my position, I have to be especially careful in choosing my friends—and my wife in choosing hers. One is to a certain extent in the limelight."

"Oh, quite," said Japp drily. He went on: "So you can't help us in any way?"

"No, indeed. I am utterly at sea. Barbara! Murdered! It seems incredible."

"Now, Mr. Laverton-West, can you tell me what your own movements were on the night of November 5th?"

"My movements? *My* movements?"

Laverton-West's voice rose in shrill protest.

"Purely a matter of routine," explained Japp. "We—er—have to ask everybody."

Charles Laverton-West looked at him with dignity.

"I should hope that a man in my position might be exempt."

Japp merely waited.

"I was—now let me see . . . Ah, yes, I was at the House. Left at half-past ten. Went for a walk along the Embankment. Watched some of the fireworks."

"Nice to think there aren't any plots of that kind nowadays," said Japp cheerily.

Laverton-West gave him a fishlike stare.

"Then I—er—walked home."

"Reaching home—your London address is Onslow Square, I think—at what time?"

"I hardly know exactly."

"Eleven? Half-past?"

"Somewhere about then."

"Perhaps someone let you in."

"No, I have my key."

"Meet anybody whilst you were walking?"

"No—er—really, Chief Inspector, I *resent* these questions very much!"

"I assure you it's just a matter of routine, Mr. Laverton-West. They aren't personal, you know."

The reply seemed to soothe the irate M.P.

"If that is all—"

"That is all for the present, Mr. Laverton-West."

"You will keep me informed—"

"Naturally, sir. By the way, let me introduce M. Hercule Poirot. You may have heard of him."

Mr. Laverton-West's eye fastened itself interestedly on the little Belgian.

"Yes—yes—I have heard the name."

"Monsieur," said Poirot, his manner suddenly very foreign, "believe me, my heart bleeds for you. Such a loss! Such agony as you must be enduring! Ah, but I will say no more. How magnificently the English hide their emotions." He whipped out his cigarette case. "Permit me— Ah, it is empty. Japp?"

Japp slapped his pockets and shook his head.

Laverton-West produced his own cigarette case, murmured, "Er— have one of mine, M. Poirot."

"Thank you—thank you." The little man helped himself.

"As you say, M. Poirot," resumed the other, "we English do not parade our emotions. A stiff upper lip—that is our motto."

He bowed to the two men and went out.

"Bit of a stuffed fish," said Japp disgustedly. "*And* a boiled owl! The Plenderleith girl was quite right about him. Yet he's a good-looking sort of chap—might go down well with some woman who had no sense of humor. What about that cigarette?"

Poirot handed it over shaking his head.

"Egyptian. An expensive variety."

"No, that's no good. A pity, for I've never heard a weaker alibi! In fact it wasn't an alibi at all. . . . You know, Poirot, it's a pity the boot wasn't on the other leg. If *she'd* been blackmailing him . . . He's a lovely type for blackmail—would pay out like a lamb! Anything to avoid a scandal."

"My friend, it is very pretty to reconstruct the case as you would like it to be, but that is not strictly our affair."

"No, Eustace is our affair. I've got a few lines on him. Definitely a nasty fellow."

"By the way, did you do as I suggested about Miss Plenderleith?"

"Yes. Wait a sec, I'll ring through and get the latest."

He picked up the telephone receiver and spoke through it.

After a brief interchange he replaced it and looked up at Poirot.

"Pretty heartless piece of goods. Gone off to play golf. That's a nice thing to do when your friend's been murdered only the day before."

Poirot uttered an exclamation.

"What's the matter now?" asked Japp.

But Poirot was murmuring to himself.

"Of course . . . of course . . . but naturally . . . What an imbecile I am—why it leapt to the eye!"

Japp said rudely:

"Stop jabbering to yourself and let's go and tackle Eustace."

He was amazed to see the radiant smile that spread over Poirot's face.

"But yes—most certainly let us tackle him. For now, see you, I know everything—but everything!"

# VIII

Major Eustace received the two men with the easy assurance of a man of the world.

His flat was small, a mere *pied à terre,* as he explained. He offered the two men drinks and when they refused he took out his cigarette case.

Both Japp and Poirot accepted a cigarette. A quick glance passed between them.

"You smoke Turkish, I see," said Japp, as he twirled the cigarette between his fingers.

"Yes. I'm sorry, do you prefer a gasper. I've got one somewhere about."

"No, no, this will do me very well." Then he leaned forward—his tone changed. "Perhaps you can guess, Major Eustace, what it was I came to see you about?"

The other shook his head. His manner was nonchalant. Major Eustace was a tall man, good-looking in a somewhat coarse fashion. There was a puffiness round the eyes—small crafty eyes that belied the good-humored geniality of his manner.

He said:

"No—I've no idea what brings such a big gun as a Chief Inspector to see me. Anything to do with my car?"

"No, it is not your car. I think you knew a Mrs. Barbara Allen, Major Eustace?"

The Major leaned back, puffed out a cloud of smoke, and said in an enlightened voice:

"Oh, so that's it! Of course, I might have guessed. Very sad business."

"You know about it?"

"Saw it in the paper last night. Too bad."

"You knew Mrs. Allen out in India, I think."

"Yes, that's some years ago now."

"Did you also know her husband?"

There was a pause—a mere fraction of a second—but during that fraction the little pig eyes flashed a quick look at the faces of the two men. Then he answered:

"No, as a matter of fact I never came across Allen."

"But you know something about him?"

"Heard he was by way of being a bad hat. Of course that was only rumor."

"Mrs. Allen did not say anything?"

"Never talked about him."

"You were on intimate terms with her?"

Major Eustace shrugged his shoulders.

"We were old friends, you know, old friends. But we didn't see each other very often."

"But you did see her that last evening? The evening of November 5th?"

"Yes, as a matter of fact, I did."

"You called at her house, I think."

Major Eustace nodded. His voice took on a gentle regretful note.

"Yes, she asked me to advise her about some investments. Of course I can see what you're driving at—her state of mind—all that sort of thing. Well, really, it's very difficult to say. Her manner seemed normal enough and yet she *was* a bit jumpy, come to think of it."

"But she gave you no hint as to what she contemplated doing?"

"Not the least in the world. As a matter of fact when I said good-bye I said I'd ring her up soon and we'd do a show together."

"You said you'd ring her up? Those were your last words?"

"Yes."

"Curious. I have information that you said something quite different."

Eustace changed color.

"Well, of course, I can't remember the exact words."

"My information is that what you actually said was: *'Well, think it over and let me know.'* "

"Let me see; yes, I believe you're right. Not exactly that. I think I was suggesting she should let me know when she was free."

"Not quite the same thing, is it?" said Japp.

Major Eustace shrugged his shoulders.

"My dear fellow, you can't expect a man to remember word for word what he said on any given occasion."

"And what did Mrs. Allen reply?"

"She said she'd give me a ring. That is, as near as I can remember."

"And then you said, *'All right. So long.'* "

"Probably. Something of the kind anyway."

Japp said quietly:

"You say that Mrs. Allen asked you to advise her about her investments. *Did she, by any chance, entrust you with the sum of two hundred pounds in cash to invest for her?*"

Eustace's face flushed a dark purple. He leaned forward and growled out:

"What the devil do you mean by that?"

"Did she or did she not?"

"That's my business, Mr. Chief Inspector."

Japp said quietly:

"Mrs. Allen drew out the sum of two hundred pounds in cash from her bank. Some of the money was in five-pound notes. The numbers of these can, of course, be traced."

"What if she did?"

"*Was* the money for investment—or was it—blackmail, Major Eustace?"

"That's a preposterous suggestion. What next will you suggest?"

Japp said in his most official manner:

"I think, Major Eustace, that at this point I must ask you if you are willing to come to Scotland Yard and make a statement. There is, of course, no compulsion and you can, if you prefer it, have your solicitor present."

"Solicitor? What the devil should I want with a solicitor? And what are you cautioning me for?"

"I am inquiring into the circumstances of the death of Mrs. Allen."

"Good God, man, you don't suppose— Why, that's nonsense! Look here, what happened was this: I called round to see Barbara by appointment—"

"That was at what time?"

"At about half-past nine, I should say. We sat and talked—"

"And smoked?"

"Yes, and smoked. Anything damaging in that?" demanded the Major belligerently.

"Where did this conversation take place?"

"In the sitting room. Left of the door as you go in. We talked together quite amicably, as I say. I left a little before half-past ten. I stayed for a minute on the doorstep for a few last words—"

"Last words—precisely," murmured Poirot.

"Who are *you,* I'd like to know?" Eustace turned and spat the words at him. "Some kind of damned dago! What are *you* butting in for?"

"I am Hercule Poirot," said the little man with dignity.

"I don't care if you are the Achilles statue. As I say, Barbara and I parted quite amicably. I drove straight to the Far East Club. Got there at five and twenty to eleven and went straight up to the card room. Stayed there playing bridge until 1:30. Now then, put that in your pipe and smoke it."

"I do not smoke the pipe," said Poirot. "It is a pretty *alibi* you have there."

"It should be a pretty cast iron one anyway! Now then, sir." He looked at Japp. "Are you satisfied?"

"You remained in the sitting room throughout your visit?"

"Yes."

"You did not go upstairs to Mrs. Allen's own boudoir?"

"No, I tell you. We stayed in the one room and didn't leave it."

Japp looked at him thoughtfully for a minute or two. Then he said: "How many sets of cuff links have you?"

"Cuff links? Cuff links? What's that got to do with it?"

"You are not bound to answer the question, of course."

"Answer it? I don't mind answering it. I've got nothing to hide. And I shall demand an apology. There are these—" He stretched out his arms.

Japp noted the gold and platinum with a nod.

"And I've got these."

He rose, opened a drawer and taking out a case he opened it and shoved it rudely almost under Japp's nose.

"Very nice design," said the Chief Inspector. "I see one is broken— bit of enamel chipped off."

"What of it?"

"You don't remember when that happened, I suppose?"

"A day or two ago, not longer."

"Would you be surprised to hear that it happened *when you were visiting Mrs. Allen?*"

"Why shouldn't it? I've not denied that I was there." The Major spoke haughtily. He continued to bluster, to act the part of the justly indignant man, but his hands were trembling.

Japp leaned forward and said with emphasis:

"Yes, but that bit of cuff link *wasn't found in the sitting room.* It was found *upstairs* in Mrs. Allen's boudoir—there in the room where she was killed, and where a man sat smoking *the same kind of cigarettes as you smoke.*"

The shot told. Eustace fell back into his chair. His eyes went from side to side. The collapse of the bully and the appearance of the craven was not a pretty sight.

"You've got nothing on me." His voice was almost a whine. "You're trying to frame me. . . . But you can't do it. I've got an alibi. . . . I never came near the house again that night. . . ."

Poirot in his turn spoke.

"No, you did not come near the house again. . . . *You did not need to.* . . . For perhaps Mrs. Allen was *already dead when you left it.*"

"That's impossible—impossible—She was just inside the door—she spoke to me. . . . People must have heard her—seen her. . . ."

Poirot said softly:

"They heard *you* speak to her . . . and pretending to wait for her answer and then speaking again. . . . It is an old trick that. . . . People may have *assumed* she was there, but they did not *see* her, because *they could not even say whether she was wearing evening dress or not—nor even mention what color she was wearing.* . . ."

"My God—it isn't true—it isn't true—"

He was shaking now—collapsed. . . .

Japp looked at him with disgust. He spoke crisply:

"I'll have to ask you, sir, to come with me."

"You're arresting me?"

"Detained for inquiry—we'll put it that way."

The silence was broken with a long shuddering sigh. The despairing voice of the erstwhile blustering Major Eustace said:

"I'm sunk. . . ."

Hercule Poirot rubbed his hands together and smiled cheerfully. He seemed to be enjoying himself.

# IX

"Pretty the way he went all to pieces," said Japp with professional appreciation later that day.

He and Poirot were driving in a car along the Brompton Road.

"He knew the game was up," said Poirot absently.

"We've got plenty on him," said Japp. "Two or three different aliases, a tricky business over a check, and a very nice affair when he stayed at the Ritz and called himself Colonel de Bathe. Swindled half a dozen Piccadilly tradesmen. We're holding him on that charge for the moment—until we get this affair finally squared up. What's the idea of this rush to the country, old man?"

"My friend, an affair must be rounded off properly. Everything must be explained. I am on the quest of the mystery you suggested. 'The Mystery of the Missing Briefcase.'"

"'The Mystery of the Missing Briefcase'—that's what I called it—it isn't missing that I know of."

"Wait, *mon ami.*"

The car turned into the Mews. At the door of No. 14 Jane Plenderleith was just alighting from a small Austin 7. She was in golfing clothes.

She looked from one to the other of the two men, then produced a key and opened the door.

"Come in, won't you?"

She led the way. Japp followed her into the sitting room. Poirot remained for a minute or two in the hall, muttering something about:

"*C'est embêtant*—how difficult to get out of these sleeves."

In a moment or two he also entered the sitting room minus his overcoat, but Japp's lips twitched under his mustache. He had heard the very faint squeak of an opening cupboard door.

Japp threw Poirot an inquiring glance and the other gave a hardly perceptible nod.

"We won't detain you, Miss Plenderleith," said Japp briskly. "Only came to ask you if you could tell us the name of Mrs. Allen's solicitor."

"Her solicitor?" The girl shook her head. "I don't even know that she had once."

"Well, when she rented this house with you, someone must have drawn up the agreement?"

"No, I don't think so. You see, I took the house; the lease is in my name. Barbara paid me half the rent. It was quite informal."

"I see. Oh! well, I suppose there's nothing doing, then."

"I'm sorry I can't help you," said Jane politely.

"It doesn't really matter very much." Japp turned towards the door. "Been playing golf?"

"Yes." She flushed. "I suppose it seems rather heartless to you. But as a matter of fact it got me down rather, being here in this house. I felt I must go out and *do* something—tire myself—or I'd choke!"

She spoke with intensity.

Poirot said quickly:

"I comprehend, mademoiselle. It is most understandable—most natural. To sit in this house and think—no, it would not be pleasant."

"So long as you understand," said Jane shortly.

"You belong to a club?"

"Yes, I play at Wentworth."

"It has been a pleasant day," said Poirot. "Alas, there are few leaves left on the trees now! A week ago the woods were magnificent."

"It was quite lovely today."

"Good afternoon, Miss Plenderleith," said Japp formally. "I'll let you know when there's anything definite. As a matter of fact we have got a man detained on suspicion."

"What man?"

She looked at them eagerly.

"Major Eustace."

She nodded and turned away, stooping down to put a match to the fire.

"Well?" said Japp as the car turned the corner of the Mews.

Poirot grinned.

"It was quite simple. The key was in the door this time."

"And—?"

Poirot smiled.

"*Eh bien*, the golf clubs had gone—"

"Naturally. The girl isn't a fool, whatever else she is. *Anything else gone?*"

Poirot nodded his head.

"Yes, my friend—*the little briefcase!*"

The accelerator leaped under Japp's foot.

"Damnation!" he said. "I knew there was *something*. But what the devil is it? I searched that case pretty thoroughly."

"My poor Japp—but it is—how do you say 'obvious, my dear Watson.' "

Japp threw him an exasperated look.

"Where are we going?" he asked.

Poirot consulted his watch.

"It is not yet four o'clock. We could get to Wentworth, I think, before it is dark."

"Do you think she really went there?"

"I think so—yes. She would know that we might make inquiries. Oh, yes, I think we will find that she has been there."

Japp grunted.

"Oh, well, come on." He threaded his way dexterously through the traffic. "Though what this briefcase business has to do with the crime I can't imagine. I can't see that it's got anything at all to do with it."

"Precisely, my friend, I agree with you—it has nothing to do with it."

"Then why—No, don't tell me! Order and method and everything nicely rounded off! Oh, well, it's a fine day."

The car was a fast one. They arrived at Wentworth Golf Club a little after half-past four. There was no great congestion there on a week day.

Poirot went straight to the caddie master and asked for Miss Plenderleith's clubs. She would be playing on a different course tomorrow, he explained.

The caddie master raised his voice and a boy sorted through some golf clubs standing in a corner. He finally produced a bag bearing the initials J.P.

"Thank you," said Poirot. He moved away, then turned carelessly and asked, "She did not leave with you a small briefcase also, did she?"

"Not today, sir. May have left it in the clubhouse."

"She was down here today?"

"Oh, yes, I saw her."

"Which caddie did she have, do you know? She's mislaid a briefcase and can't remember where she had it last."

"She didn't take a caddie. She came in here and bought a couple of balls. Just took out a couple of irons. I rather fancy she had a little case in her hand then."

Poirot turned away with a word of thanks. The two men walked round the clubhouse. Poirot stood a moment admiring the view.

"It is beautiful, is it not, the dark pine trees—and then the lake. Yes, the lake—"

Japp gave him a quick glance.

"That's the idea, is it?"

Poirot smiled.

"I think it possible that someone may have seen something. I should set the inquiries in motion if I were you."

# X

Poirot stepped back, his head a little on one side as he surveyed the arrangement of the room. A chair here—another chair there. Yes, that was very nice. And now a ring at the bell—that would be Japp.

The Scotland Yard man came in alertly.

"Quite right, old cock! Straight from the horse's mouth. A young woman was seen to throw something into the lake at Wentworth yesterday. Description of her answers to Jane Plenderleith. We managed to fish it up without much difficulty. A lot of reeds just there."

"And it was?"

"It was the briefcase all right! But *why*, in Heaven's name? Well, it beats me! Nothing inside it—not even the magazines. Why a presumably sane young woman should want to fling an expensively fitted dressing case into a lake—d'you know I worried all night because I couldn't get the hang of it."

"*Mon pauvre Japp!* But you need worry no longer. Here is the answer coming. The bell has just rung."

George, Poirot's immaculate manservant, opened the door and announced:

"Miss Plenderleith."

The girl came into the room with her usual air of complete self-assurance. She greeted the two men.

"I asked you to come here—" explained Poirot. "Sit here, will you not, and you here, Japp—because I have certain news to give you."

The girl sat down. She looked from one to the other, pushing aside her hat. She took it off and laid it aside impatiently.

"Well," she said. "Major Eustace has been arrested."

"You saw that, I expect, in the morning paper?"

"Yes."

"He is at the moment charged with a minor offense," went on Poirot. "In the meantime we are gathering evidence in connection with the murder."

"It *was* murder, then?"

The girl asked it eagerly.

Poirot nodded his head.

"Yes," he said. "It was murder. The willful destruction of one human being by another human being."

She shivered a little.

"Don't," she murmured. "It sounds horrible when you say it like that."

"Yes—but it is horrible!"

He paused—then he said:

"Now, Miss Plenderleith, I am going to tell you just how I arrived at the truth in this matter."

She looked from Poirot to Japp. The latter was smiling.

"He has his methods, Miss Plenderleith," he said. "I humor him, you know. I think we'll listen to what he has to say."

Poirot began.

"As you know, mademoiselle, I arrived with my friend on the scene of the crime on the morning of November the 6th. We went into the room where the body of Mrs. Allen had been found and I was struck at once by several significant details. There were things, you see, in that room that were decidedly odd."

"Go on," said the girl.

"To begin with," said Poirot "there was the smell of cigarette smoke."

"I think you're exaggerating there, Poirot," said Japp. "*I* didn't smell anything."

Poirot turned on him in a flash.

"Precisely. *You did not smell any stale smoke. No more did I.* And that was very, very strange—for the door and the window were both closed and on an ashtray there were the stubs of no fewer than ten cigarettes. It was odd, very odd, that the room should smell—as it did, perfectly fresh."

"So that's what you were getting at!" Japp sighed. "Always have to get at things in such a tortuous way."

"Your Sherlock Holmes did the same. He drew attention, remember, to the curious incident of the dog in the nighttime—and the answer to that was there was no curious incident. The dog did nothing in the nighttime. To proceed:

"The next thing that attracted my attention was a wristwatch worn by the dead woman."

"What about it?"

"Nothing particular about it, but it was worn on the *right* wrist. Now in my experience it is more usual for a watch to be worn on the left wrist."

Japp shrugged his shoulders. Before he could speak, Poirot hurried on:

"But, as you say, there is nothing very definite about *that.* Some people *prefer* to wear one on the right hand. And now I come to something really interesting—I come, my friends, to the writing bureau."

"Yes, I guessed that," said Japp.

"That was really *very* odd—*very* remarkable! For two reasons. The first reason was that something was missing from that writing table."

Jane Plenderleith spoke:

"What was missing?"

Poirot turned to her.

"*A sheet of blotting paper, mademoiselle.* The blotting book had on the top a clean untouched piece of blotting paper."

Jane shrugged her shoulders.

"Really, M. Poirot. People do occasionally tear off a very much used sheet!"

"Yes, but what do they do with it? Throw it into the wastepaper basket, do they not? *But it was not in the wastepaper basket. I looked.*"

Jane Plenderleith seemed impatient.

"Because it had probably been already thrown away the day before. The sheet was clean because Barbara hadn't written any letters that day."

"That could hardly be the case, mademoiselle. *For Mrs. Allen was seen going to the post box that evening. Therefore she must have been writing letters.* She could not write downstairs—there were no writing materials. She would be hardly likely to go to *your* room to write. So, then, what had happened to the sheet of paper on which she had blotted her letters? It is true that people sometimes throw things in the fire instead of the wastepaper basket, but there was only a gas fire in the room. *And the fire downstairs had not been alight the previous day since you told me it was all laid ready when you set a match to it.*"

He paused.

"A curious little problem. I looked everywhere, in the wastepaper baskets, in the dustbin, but I could not find a sheet of used blotting paper—and that seemed to me very important. It looked as though someone had deliberately taken that sheet of blotting paper away. Why? Because there was writing on it that could easily have been read by holding it up to a mirror.

"But there was a second curious point about the writing bureau. Perhaps, Japp, you remember roughly the arrangement of it? Blotter and inkstand in the center, pen tray to the left, calendar and quill pen to the right. *Eh bien?* You do not see? The quill pen, remember, I examined, it was for show only—it had not been used. Ah! *Still* you do not see? I will say it again. Blotter in the center, pen tray to the left—to the *left*, Japp. But is it not usual to find a pen tray *on the right*, convenient to *the right hand!*

"Ah, now it comes to you, does it not? The pen tray on the *left*— the wristwatch on the *right* wrist—the blotting paper removed—and something else brought *into* the room—the ashtray with the cigarette ends!

"That room was fresh and pure smelling, Japp, a room in which the window had been *open*, not closed all night. . . . And I made to myself a picture."

He spun round and faced Jane.

"A picture of you, mademoiselle, driving up in your taxi, paying it off, running up the stairs, calling perhaps, 'Barbara'—and you open the door and you find your friend there lying dead with the pistol clasped in her hand—the left hand, naturally, *since she is left-handed*— and, therefore, too, the bullet has entered on the *left side of the head*. There is a note there addressed to you. It tells you what it is that has driven her to take her own life. It was, I fancy, a very moving letter. . . . A young, gentle, unhappy woman driven by blackmail to take her life. . . .

"I think that, almost at once, the idea flashed into your head. This was a certain man's doing. Let him be punished—fully and adequately punished! You take the pistol, wipe it, and place it in the *right* hand. You take the note and you tear off the top sheet of the blotting paper on which the note has been blotted. You go down, light the fire, and put them both on the flames. Then you carry up the ashtray—to further the illusion that two people sat up there talking—and you also take up a fragment of enamel cuff link that is on the floor. That is a lucky find and you expect it to clinch matters. Then you close the window and lock the door. There must be no suspicion that you have tampered with the room. The police must see it exactly as it is—so you do not seek help in the Mews but ring up the police straightaway.

"And so it goes on. You play your chosen rôle with judgment and coolness. You refuse at first to say anything but cleverly you suggest doubts of suicide. Later you are quite ready to set us on the trail of Major Eustace. . . .

"Yes, mademoiselle, it was clever—a very clever murder—for that is what it is. The attempted murder of Major Eustace."

Jane Plenderleith sprang to her feet.

"It wasn't murder—it was justice. That man *hounded* poor Barbara to her death! She was so sweet and so helpless. You see, poor kid, she got involved with a man in India when she first went out. She was only seventeen and he was a married man years older than she. Then she had a baby. She could have put it in a Home but she wouldn't hear of that. She went off to some out of the way spot and came back calling herself Mrs. Allen. Later the child died. She came back here and she fell in love with Charles—that pompous stuffed owl! She adored him—and he took her adoration very complacently. If he had been a different kind of man I'd have advised her to tell him everything. But as it was, I urged her to hold her tongue. After all, nobody knew anything about that business except me.

"And then that devil Eustace turned up! You know the rest. He began to bleed her systematically, but it wasn't till that last evening that she realized that she was exposing Charles, too, to the risk of scandal. Once married to Charles, Eustace had got her where he wanted her—married to a rich man with a horror of any scandal! When Eustace had gone with the money she had got for him she sat thinking it over. Then she came up and wrote a letter to me. She said she loved Charles and couldn't live without him, but that for his own sake she mustn't marry him. She was taking the best way out, she said."

Jane flung her head back.

"Do you wonder I did what I did? And you stand there calling it *murder!*"

"Because it is murder." Poirot's voice was stern. "Murder can sometimes seem justified, *but it is murder all the same.* You are truthful and clear-minded—face the truth, mademoiselle! Your friend died, in the last resort, *because she had not the courage to live.* We may sympathize with her. We may pity her. But the fact remains—the act was *hers*—not another's."

He paused.

"And you? That man is now in prison, he will serve a long sentence for other matters. Do you really wish, of your own volition to destroy the life—the *life*, mind—of *any* human being?"

She stared at him. Her eyes darkened. Suddenly she muttered:

"No. You're right. I don't."

Then, turning on her heel, she went swiftly from the room. The outer door banged. . . .

Japp gave a long—a very prolonged—whistle.

"Well, I'm damned!" he said.

Poirot sat down and smiled at him amiably. It was quite a long time before the silence was broken. Then Japp said:

"Not murder disguised as suicide, but suicide made to look like murder."

"Yes, and very cleverly done, too. Nothing over-emphasized."

Japp said suddenly:

"But the briefcase? Where did that come in?"

"But, my dear, my very dear friend, I have already told you that *it did not come in.*"

"Then why—?"

"The golf clubs. The golf clubs, Japp. *They were the golf clubs of a left-handed person.* Jane Plenderleith kept her clubs at Wentworth. They were Barbara Allen's clubs. No wonder the girl got, as you say, the wind up when we opened that cupboard. Her whole plan might have been ruined. But she is quick, she realized that she had, for one short moment, given herself away. *She* saw that *we* saw. So she does the best thing she can think of on the spur of the moment. She tries to focus our attention on the *wrong object.* She says of the brief-case, 'That's mine. I—it came back with me this morning. So there can't be anything there.' And, as she hoped, away you go on the false trail. For the same reason, when she sets out the following day to get rid of the golf clubs, she continues to use the briefcase as a—what is it—kippered herring?"

"Red herring. Do you mean that her real object was—?"

"Consider, my friend. Where is the best place to get rid of a bag of golf clubs? One cannot burn them or put them in a dustbin. If one leaves them somewhere they may be returned to you. Miss Plen-derleith took them to a golf course. She leaves them in the clubhouse while she gets a couple of irons from her own bag and then she goes round with a caddie. Doubtless at judicious intervals she breaks a club in half and throws it into some deep undergrowth and ends by throwing the empty bag away. If anyone should find a broken golf club here and there it will not create surprise. People have been known to break and throw away *all* their clubs in a mood of intense exasperation over the game! It is, in fact, that kind of game!

"But since she realizes that her actions may still be a matter of interest, she throws that useful red herring, the briefcase in a somewhat spectacular manner into the lake—and that, my friend, is the truth of 'The Mystery of the Small Briefcase.' "

Japp looked at his friend for some moments in silence. Then he rose, clapped him on the shoulder, and burst out laughing.

"Not so bad for an old dog! Upon my word, you take the cake! Come out and have a spot of lunch?"

"With pleasure, my friend, but we will not have the cake. Indeed, an *Omelette aux Champignons, Blanquette de Veau, Petits pois à la française* and—to follow—a *Baba au Rhum*."

"Lead me to it," said Japp.

# Triangle at Rhodes

HERCULE Poirot sat on the white sand and looked out across the sparkling blue water. He was carefully dressed in a dandified fashion in white flannels, and a large panama hat protected his head. He belonged to the old-fashioned generation which believed in covering itself carefully from the sun. Miss Pamela Lyall, who sat beside him and talked ceaselessly, represented the modern school of thought in that she was wearing the barest minimum of clothing on her sun-browned person.

Occasionally her flow of conversation stopped whilst she reanointed herself from a bottle of oily fluid which stood beside her.

On the further side of Miss Pamela Lyall her great friend, Miss Susan Blake, lay face downwards on a gaudily striped towel. Miss Blake's tanning was as perfect as possible and her friend cast dissatisfied glances at her more than once.

"I'm so patchy still," she murmured regretfully. "M. Poirot—*would* you mind? Just below the right shoulder blade—I can't reach to rub it in properly."

M. Poirot obliged and then wiped his oily hand carefully on his handkerchief. Miss Lyall, whose principal interests in life were the observation of people round her and the sound of her own voice, continued to talk,

"I was right about that woman—the one in the Chanel model—it *is* Valentine Dacres—Chantry, I mean. I thought it was. I recognized her at once. She's really rather marvelous, isn't she? I mean I can understand how people go quite crazy about her. She just obviously *expects* them to! That's half the battle. Those other people who came last night are called Gold. He's terribly good-looking."

"Honeymooners?" murmured Susan in a stifled voice.

Miss Lyall shook her head in an experienced manner.

"Oh, no—her clothes aren't *new* enough. You can always tell brides!

Don't you think it's the most fascinating thing in the world to watch people, M. Poirot, and see what you can find out about them by just looking?"

"Not just looking, darling," said Susan sweetly. "You ask a lot of questions, too."

"I haven't even spoken to the Golds yet," said Miss Lyall with dignity. "And anyway I don't see why one shouldn't be interested in one's fellow creatures. Human nature is simply fascinating. Don't you think so, M. Poirot?"

This time she paused long enough to allow her companion to reply.

Without taking his eyes off the blue water, M. Poirot replied:

*"Ça depend."*

Pamela was shocked.

"Oh, M. Poirot! I don't think *anything's* so interesting—so *incalculable* as a human being!"

"Incalculable? That, no."

"Oh, but they *are*. Just as you think you've got them beautifully taped—they do something completely unexpected."

Hercule Poirot shook his head.

"No, no, that is not true. It is most rare that anyone does an action that is not *dans son caractère*. It is in the end monotonous."

"I don't agree with you at all!" said Miss Pamela Lyall.

She was silent for quite a minute and a half before returning to the attack.

"As soon as I see people I begin wondering about them—what they're like—what relations they are to each other—what they're thinking and feeling. It's—oh, it's quite thrilling."

"Hardly that," said Hercule Poirot. "Nature repeats herself more than one would imagine. The sea," he added thoughtfully, "has infinitely more variety."

Susan turned her head sideways and asked:

"You think that human beings tend to reproduce certain patterns? Stereotyped patterns?"

*"Précisément,"* said Poirot, and traced a design in the sand with his finger.

"What's that you're drawing?" asked Pamela curiously.

"A triangle," said Poirot.

But Pamela's attention had been diverted elsewhere.

"Here are the Chantrys," she said.

A woman was coming down the beach—a tall woman very conscious of herself and her body. She gave a half nod and a smile and sat down a little distance away on the beach. The scarlet and gold silk wrap slipped down from her shoulders. She was wearing a white bathing dress.

Pamela sighed.

"Hasn't she got a lovely figure?"

But Poirot was looking at her face—the face of a woman of thirty-nine who had been famous since sixteen for her beauty.

He knew, as everyone knew, all about Valentine Chantry. She had been famous for many things—for her caprices, for her wealth, for her enormous sapphire-blue eyes, for her matrimonial ventures and adventures. She had had five husbands and innumerable lovers. She had in turn been the wife of an Italian Count, of an American steel magnate, of a tennis professional, of a racing motorist; of these four the American had died, but the others had been shed negligently in the divorce court. Six months ago she had married a fifth time—a Commander in the Navy.

He it was who came striding down the beach behind her. Silent, dark—with a pugnacious jaw and a sullen manner. A touch of the primeval ape about him.

She said:

"Tony, darling—my cigarette case. . . ."

He had it ready for her—lighted her cigarette—helped her to slip the straps of the white bathing dress from her shoulders. She lay, arms outstretched in the sun. He sat by her like some wild beast that guards its prey.

Pamela said, her voice just lowered sufficiently:

"You know they interest me *frightfully*. . . . He's such a brute! So silent and—sort of *glowering*. I suppose a woman of her kind likes that. It must be like controlling a tiger! I wonder how long it will last. She gets tired of them very soon, I believe—especially nowadays. All the same, if she tries to get rid of him, I think he might be dangerous."

Another couple came down the beach—rather shyly. They were the newcomers of the night before. Mr. and Mrs. Douglas Gold, as Miss Lyall knew from her inspection of the hotel visitors' book. She knew too, for such were the Italian regulations—their Christian names and their ages as set down from their passports.

Mr. Douglas Cameron Gold was thirty-one and Mrs. Marjorie Emma Gold was thirty-five.

Miss Lyall's hobby in life, as has been said, was the study of human beings. Unlike most English people, she was capable of speaking to strangers on sight instead of allowing from four days to a week to elapse before making the first cautious advance, as is the customary British habit. She, therefore, noting the slight hesitancy and shyness of Mrs. Gold's advance, called out:

"Good morning! Isn't it a lovely day?"

Mrs. Gold was a small woman—rather like a mouse. She was not bad-looking, indeed her features were regular and her complexion good, but she had a certain air of diffidence and dowdiness that made her liable to be overlooked. Her husband, on the other hand, was extremely good-looking in an almost theatrical manner. Very fair crisply curling hair, blue eyes, broad shoulders, narrow hips. He looked more like a young man on the stage than a young man in real life, but the moment he opened his mouth that impression faded. He was quite natural and unaffected, even, perhaps, a little stupid.

Mrs. Gold looked gratefully at Pamela and sat down near her.

"What a lovely shade of brown you are. I feel terribly underdone!"

"One has to take a frightful lot of trouble to brown evenly," sighed Miss Lyall.

She paused a minute and then went on:

"You've only just arrived, haven't you?"

"Yes. Last night. We came on the Vapo d'Italia boat."

"Have you ever been to Rhodes before?"

"No. It is lovely, isn't it?"

Her husband said:

"Pity it's such a long way to come."

"Yes, if it were only nearer England—"

In a muffled voice Susan said:

"Yes, but then it would be awful. Rows and rows of people laid out like fish on a slab. Bodies everywhere!"

"That's true, of course," said Douglas Gold. "It's a nuisance the Italian exchange is so absolutely ruinous at present."

"It does make a difference, doesn't it?"

The conversation was running on strictly stereotyped lines. It could hardly have been called brilliant.

A little way along the beach Valentine Chantry stirred and sat up. With one hand she held her bathing dress in position across her breast.

She yawned, a wide yet delicate catlike yawn. She glanced casually down the beach. Her eyes slanted past Marjorie Gold—and stayed thoughtfully on the crisp golden head of Douglas Gold.

She moved her shoulders sinuously. She spoke and her voice was raised a little higher than it need have been.

"Tony, darling—isn't it divine—this sun? I simply *must* have been a sun worshiper once—don't you think so?"

Her husband grunted something in reply that failed to reach the others. Valentine Chantry went on in that high drawling voice:

"Just pull that towel a little flatter, will you, darling?"

She took infinite pains in the resettling of her beautiful body. Douglas Gold was looking now. His eyes were frankly interested.

Mrs. Gold chirped happily in a subdued key to Miss Lyall:

"What a beautiful woman!"

Pamela, as delighted to give as to receive information, replied in a lower voice:

"That's Valentine Chantry—you know, who used to be Valentine Dacres—she *is* rather marvelous, isn't she? He's simply crazy about her—won't let her out of his sight!"

Mrs. Gold looked once more along the beach. Then she said:

"The sea really is lovely—so blue. I think we ought to go in now, don't you, Douglas?"

He was still watching Valentine Chantry and took a minute or two to answer. Then he said, rather absently:

"Go in? Oh, yes, rather, in a minute."

Marjorie Gold got up and strolled down to the water's edge.

Valentine Chantry rolled over a little on one side. Her eyes looked along at Douglas Gold. Her scarlet mouth curved faintly into a smile.

The neck of Mr. Douglas Gold became slightly red.

Valentine Chantry said:

"Tony, darling—would you mind? I want a little pot of face cream—it's up on the dressing table. I meant to bring it down. Do get it for me—there's an angel."

The Commander rose obediently. He stalked off into the hotel.

Marjorie Gold plunged into the sea, calling out:

"It's lovely, Douglas—so warm. Do come."

Pamela Lyall said to him:

"Aren't you going in?"

He answered vaguely:

"Oh! I like to get well hotted up first."

Valentine Chantry stirred. Her head was lifted for a moment as though to recall her husband—but he was just passing inside the wall of the hotel garden.

"I like my dip the last thing," explained Mr. Gold.

Mrs. Chantry sat up again. She picked up a flask of sunbathing oil. She had some difficulty with it—the screw top seemed to resist her efforts.

She spoke loudly and petulantly:

"Oh, dear—I *can't* get this thing undone!"

She looked towards the other group:

"I wonder—"

Always gallant, Poirot rose to his feet, but Douglas Gold had the advantage of youth and suppleness. He was by her side in a moment.

"Can I do it for you?"

"Oh, thank you—" It was the sweet empty drawl again. "You *are* kind. I'm such a *fool* at undoing things—I always seem to screw them the wrong way. Oh! you've done it! Thank you ever so much—"

Hercule Poirot smiled to himself.

He wandered along the beach in the opposite direction. He did not go very far but his progress was leisurely. As he was on his way back Mrs. Gold came out of the sea and joined him. She had been swimming. Her face, under a singularly unbecoming bathing cap, was radiant.

She said breathlessly; "I do love the sea. And it's so warm and lovely here."

She was, he perceived, an enthusiastic bather.

She said, "Douglas and I are simply mad on bathing. He can stay in for hours."

And at that Hercule Poirot's eyes slid over her shoulder to the shore where that enthusiastic bather, Mr. Douglas Gold, was sitting talking to Valentine Chantry.

His wife said:

"I can't think why he doesn't come. . . ."

Her voice held a kind of childish bewilderment.

Poirot's eyes rested thoughtfully on Valentine Chantry. He thought that other women in their time had made that same remark.

Beside him, he heard Mrs. Gold draw in her breath sharply.

She said—and her voice was cold:

"She's supposed to be very attractive, I believe. But Douglas doesn't like that type of woman."

Hercule Poirot did not reply.

Mrs. Gold plunged into the sea again.

She swam away from the shore with slow steady strokes. You could see that she loved the water.

Poirot retraced his steps to the group on the beach.

It had been augmented by the arrival of old General Barnes, a veteran who was usually in the company of the young. He was sitting now between Pamela and Susan, and he and Pamela were engaged in dishing up various scandals with appropriate embellishments.

Commander Chantry had returned from his errand. He and Douglas Gold were sitting on either side of Valentine.

Valentine was sitting up very straight between the two men and talking. She talked easily and lightly in her sweet drawling voice, turning her head to take first one man and then the other in the conversation.

She was just finishing an anecdote.

"—and what do you think the foolish man said? 'It may have been only a minute, but I'd remember you *anywhere*, Mum!' Didn't he, Tony? And you know, I thought it was so *sweet* of him. I do think it's such a kind world—I mean everybody is so frightfully kind to *me* always—I don't know why—they just are. But I said to Tony—d'you remember, darling—'Tony, if you want to be a teeny weeny bit jealous, you can be jealous of that Commissionaire.' Because he really was too adorable. . . ."

There was a pause and Douglas Gold said:

"Good fellows—some of those Commissionaires."

"Oh, yes—but he took such trouble—really an immense amount of trouble—and seemed just pleased to be able to help me."

Douglas Gold said:

"Nothing odd about that. Anyone would for you, I'm sure."

She cried delightedly:

"How nice of you! Tony, did you hear that?"

Commander Chantry grunted.

His wife sighed:

"Tony never makes pretty speeches—do you, my lamb?"

Her white hand with its long red nails ruffled up his dark head.

He gave her a sudden sidelong look. She murmured:

"I don't really know how he puts up with me. He's simply frightfully clever—absolutely frantic with brains—and I just go on talking nonsense the whole time, but he doesn't seem to mind. Nobody minds what I do or say—everybody spoils me. I'm sure it's frightfully bad for me."

Commander Chantry said across her to the other man: "That your Missus in the sea?"

"Yes. Expect it's about time I joined her."

Valentine murmured:

"But it's so lovely here in the sun. You mustn't go into the sea yet. Tony, darling, I don't think I shall actually *bathe* today—not my first day. I might get a chill or something. But why don't you go in now, Tony, darling. Mr.—Mr. Gold will stay and keep me company while you're in."

Chantry said rather grimly:

"No, thanks. Shan't go in just yet. Your wife seems to be waving to you, Gold."

Valentine said:

"How well your wife swims. I'm sure she's one of those terribly efficient women who do everything well. They always frighten me so because I feel they despise me. I'm so frightfully bad at everything— an absolute duffer, aren't I, Tony, darling?"

But again Commander Chantry only grunted.

His wife murmured affectionately:

"You're too sweet to admit it. Men are so wonderfully loyal—that's what I like about them. I do think men are so much more loyal than women—and they never say nasty things. Women, I always think, are rather *petty*."

Susan Blake rolled over on her side towards Poirot.

She murmured between her teeth:

"Examples of pettiness, to suggest that dear Mrs. Chantry is in any way not absolute perfection! What a complete idiot the woman is! I really do think Valentine Chantry is very nearly the most idiotic woman I ever met. She can't do anything but say, 'Tony, darling,' and roll her eyes. I should fancy she'd got cottonwool padding instead of brains."

Poirot raised his expressive eyebrows.

*"Un peu sévère!"*

"Oh, yes. Put it down as pure 'Cat,' if you like. She certainly has her methods! Can't she leave *any* man alone? Her husband's looking like thunder."

Looking out to sea, Poirot remarked:

"Mrs. Gold swims well."

"Yes, she isn't like us who find it a nuisance to get wet. I wonder if Mrs. Chantry will ever go into the sea at all while she's out here."

"Not she," said General Barnes huskily. "She won't risk that make-up of hers coming off. Not that she isn't a fine-looking woman, although perhaps a bit long in the tooth."

"She's looking your way, General," said Susan wickedly. "And you're wrong about the make-up. We're all waterproof and kissproof nowadays."

"Mrs. Gold's coming out," announced Pamela.

"Here we come gathering nuts and may," hummed Susan. "Here comes his wife to fetch him away—fetch him away—fetch him away. . . ."

Mrs. Gold came straight up the beach. She had quite a pretty figure but her plain waterproof cap was rather too serviceable to be attractive.

"Aren't you coming, Douglas?" she demanded impatiently. "The sea is lovely and warm."

"Rather."

Douglas Gold rose hastily to his feet. He paused a moment and as he did so Valentine Chantry looked up at him with a sweet smile.

*"Au revoir,"* she said.

Gold and his wife went down the beach.

As soon as they were out of earshot, Pamela said critically:

"I don't think, you know, that that was wise. To snatch your husband away from another woman is always bad policy. It makes you seem so possessive. And husbands hate that."

"You seem to know a lot about husbands, Miss Pamela," said General Barnes.

"Other people's—not my own!"

"Ah! that's where the difference comes in."

"Yes, but, General, I shall have learnt a lot of 'Do Nots.' "

'Well, darling," said Susan. "I shouldn't wear a cap like that for one thing. . . ."

"Seems very sensible to me," said the General. "Seems a nice sensible little woman altogether."

"You've hit it exactly, General," said Susan. "But you know there's a limit to the sensibleness of sensible women. I have a feeling she won't be so sensible when it's a case of Valentine Chantry."

She turned her head and exclaimed in a low, excited whisper:

"Look at him now. Just like thunder. That man looks as though he had got the most frightful temper. . . ."

Commander Chantry was indeed scowling after the retreating husband and wife in a singularly unpleasant fashion.

Susan looked up at Poirot.

"Well?" she said. "What do you make of all this?"

Hercule Poirot did not reply in words, but once again his forefinger traced a design in the sand. The same design—a triangle.

"The Eternal Triangle," mused Susan. "Perhaps you're right. If so we're in for an exciting time in the next few weeks."

# II

M. Hercule Poirot was disappointed with Rhodes. He had come to Rhodes for a rest and for a holiday. A holiday, especially, from crime. In late October, so he had been told, Rhodes would be nearly empty. A peaceful secluded spot.

That, in itself, was true enough. The Chantrys, the Golds, Pamela and Susan, the General and himself and two Italian couples were the only guests. But within that restricted circle the intelligent brain of M. Poirot perceived the inevitable shaping of events to come.

"It is that I am crime-minded," he told himself reproachfully. "I have the indigestion! I imagine things."

But he still worried.

One morning he came down to find Mrs. Gold sitting on the terrace doing needlework.

As he came up to her he had the impression that there was the flicker of a cambric handkerchief swiftly whisked out of sight.

Mrs. Gold's eyes were dry, but they were suspiciously bright. Her manner, too, struck him as being a shade too cheerful. The brightness of it was a shade overdone.

She said:

"Good morning, M. Poirot," with such enthusiasm as to arouse his doubts.

He felt that she could not possibly be quite as pleased to see him as she appeared to be. For she did not, after all, know him very well. And though Hercule Poirot was a conceited little man where his profession was concerned, he was quite modest in his estimate of his personal attractions.

"Good morning, madame," he responded. "Another beautiful day."

"Yes, isn't it fortunate? But Douglas and I are always lucky in our weather."

"Indeed?"

"Yes. We're really very lucky altogether. You know, M. Poirot, when one sees so much trouble and unhappiness, and so many couples divorcing each other and all that sort of thing, well, one does feel very grateful for one's own happiness."

"It is pleasant to hear you say so, madame."

"Yes. Douglas and I are so wonderfully happy together. We've been married five years, you know, and, after all, five years is quite a long time nowadays—"

"I have no doubt that in some cases it can seem an eternity, madame," said Poirot drily.

"—but I really believe that we're happier now than when we were first married. You see, we're so absolutely suited to each other."

"That, of course, is everything."

"That's why I feel so sorry for people who aren't happy."

"You mean—"

"Oh! I was speaking generally, M. Poirot."

"I see. I see."

Mrs. Gold picked up a strand of silk, held it to the light, approved of it, and went on:

"Mrs. Chantry, for instance—"

"Yes, Mrs. Chantry?"

"I don't think she's at all a nice woman."

"No. No, perhaps not."

"In fact I'm quite sure she's not a nice woman. But in a way one feels sorry for her. Because in spite of her money and her good looks and all that—" Mrs. Gold's fingers were trembling and she was quite unable to thread her needle—"she's not the sort of woman men really stick to. She's the sort of woman, I think, that men would get tired of very easily. Don't you think so?"

"I myself should certainly get tired of her conversation before any great space of time had passed," said Poirot cautiously.

"Yes, that's what I mean. She has, of course, a kind of appeal. . . ." Mrs. Gold hesitated, her lips trembled, she stabbed uncertainly at her work. A less acute observer than Hercule Poirot could not have failed to notice her distress. She went on inconsequently:

"Men are just like children! They believe *anything*. . . ."

She bent over her work. The tiny wisp of cambric came out again unobtrusively.

Perhaps Hercule Poirot thought it well to change the subject.

He said:

"You do not bathe this morning? And monsieur, your husband, is he down on the beach?"

Mrs. Gold looked up, blinked, resumed her almost defiantly bright manner and replied:

"No, not this morning. We arranged to go round the walls of the old city. But somehow or other we—we missed each other. They started without me."

The pronoun was revealing, but before Poirot could say anything, General Barnes came up from the beach below and dropped into a chair beside them.

"Good morning, Mrs. Gold. Good morning, Poirot. Both deserters this morning? A lot of absentees. You two, and your husband, Mrs. Gold—and Mrs. Chantry."

"And Commander Chantry?" inquired Poirot casually.

"Oh, no, he's down there. Miss Pamela's got him in hand." The General chuckled. "She's finding him a little bit difficult! One of the strong silent men you hear about in books."

Marjorie Gold said with a little shiver:

"He frightens me a little, that man. He—he looks so black sometimes. As though he might do—anything!"

She shivered again.

"Just indigestion, I expect," said the General cheerfully. "Dyspepsia is responsible for many a reputation for romantic melancholy or ungovernable rages."

Marjorie Gold smiled a polite little smile.

"And where's your good man?" inquired the General.

Her reply came without hesitation—in a natural cheerful voice:

"Douglas? Oh, he and Mrs. Chantry have gone into the town. I believe they've gone to have a look at the walls of the old city."

"Ha, yes—very interesting. Time of the knights and all that. . . . You ought to have gone too, little lady."

Mrs. Gold said:

"I'm afraid I came down rather late."

She got up suddenly with a murmured excuse and went into the hotel.

General Barnes looked after her with a concerned expression, shaking his head gently.

"Nice little woman, that. Worth a dozen painted trollops like someone whose name we won't mention. Ha! Husband's a fool! Doesn't know when he's well off."

He shook his head again. Then, rising, he went indoors.

Susan Blake had just come up from the beach and had heard the General's last speech.

Making a face at the departing warrior's back, she remarked as she flung herself into a chair:

"Nice little woman—nice little woman! Men always approve of dowdy women—but when it comes to brass tacks, the dressed-up trollops win hands down! Sad, but there it is."

"Mademoiselle," said Poirot and his voice was abrupt, "I do not like all this!"

"Don't you? Nor do I. No, let's be honest, I suppose I *do* like it really. There is a horrid side of one that enjoys accidents and public calamities and the unpleasant things that happen to one's friends."

Poirot asked:

"Where is Commander Chantry?"

"On the beach being dissected by Pamela (*she's* enjoying herself, if you like!) and not being improved in temper by the proceeding. He was looking like a thundercloud when I came up. There are squalls ahead, believe me."

Poirot murmured:

"There is something I do not understand—"

"It's easy enough to *understand*," said Susan. "But what's going to *happen*—that's the question."

Poirot shook his head and murmured:

"As you say, mademoiselle—it is the future that causes one inquietude."

"What a nice way of putting it," said Susan and went into the hotel.

In the doorway she almost collided with Douglas Gold. The young man came out looking rather pleased with himself but at the same time slightly guilty. He said:

"Hullo, M. Poirot," and added rather self-consciously, "been showing Mrs. Chantry the Crusaders' walls. Marjorie didn't feel up to going."

Poirot's eyebrows rose slightly, but even had he wished he would have had no time to make a comment for Valentine Chantry came sweeping out crying in her high voice:

"Douglas—a pink gin—positively I must have a pink gin."

Douglas Gold went off to order the drink. Valentine sank into a chair by Poirot. She was looking radiant this morning.

She saw her husband and Pamela coming up towards them and waved a hand, crying out:

"Have a nice bathe, Tony, darling? Isn't it a divine morning?"

Commander Chantry did not answer. He swung up the steps, passed her without a word or a look and vanished into the bar.

His hands were clenched by his sides and that faint likeness to a gorilla was accentuated.

Valentine Chantry's perfect but rather foolish mouth fell open.

She said, "Oh," rather blankly.

Pamela Lyall's face expressed keen enjoyment of the situation. Masking it as far as was possible to one of her ingenuous disposition she sat down by Valentine Chantry and inquired:

"Have you had a nice morning?"

As Valentine began, "Simply marvelous. We—" Poirot got up and in his turn strolled gently towards the bar. He found young Gold waiting for the pink gin with a flushed face. He looked disturbed and angry.

He said to Poirot, "That man's a brute!" and he nodded his head in the direction of the retreating figure of Commander Chantry.

"It is possible," said Poirot. "Yes, it is quite possible. But *les femmes,* they like brutes, remember that!"

Douglas muttered:

"I shouldn't be surprised if he ill-treats her!"

"She probably likes that too."

Douglas Gold looked at him in a puzzled way, took up the pink gin and went out with it.

Hercule Poirot sat on a stool and ordered a *sirop de cassis.* While he was sipping it with long sighs of enjoyment, Chantry came in and drank several pink gins in rapid succession.

He said suddenly and violently to the world at large rather than to Poirot:

"If Valentine thinks she can get rid of me like she's got rid of a lot of other damned fools, she's mistaken! I've got her and I mean to keep her. No other fellow's going to get her except over my dead body."

He flung down some money, turned on his heel and went out.

# III

It was three days later that Hercule Poirot went to the Mount of the Prophet. It was a cool agreeable drive through the golden green fir trees, winding higher and higher, far above the petty wrangling and squabbling of human beings. The car stopped at the restaurant. Poirot got out and wandered into the woods. He came out at last on a spot that seemed truly on top of the world. Far below, deeply and dazzlingly blue, was the sea.

Here at last he was at peace—removed from cares—above the world. Carefully placing his folded overcoat on a tree stump, Hercule Poirot sat down.

"Doubtless *le bon Dieu* knows what he does. But it is odd that he should have permitted himself to fashion certain human beings. *Eh bien,* here for a while at least I am away from these vexing problems."

He looked up with a start. A little woman in a brown coat and skirt was hurrying towards him. It was Marjorie Gold and this time she had abandoned all pretense. Her face was wet with tears.

Poirot could not escape. She was upon him.

"M. Poirot! You've got to help me. I'm so miserable I don't know what to do! Oh, what shall I do? What shall I do?"

She looked up at him with a distracted face. Her fingers fastened on his coat sleeve. Then, as something she saw in his face alarmed her, she drew back a little.

"What—what is it?" she faltered.

"You want my advice, madame? It is that you ask?"

She stammered: "Yes. . . . Yes. . . ."

*"Eh bien*—here it is." He spoke curtly—trenchantly. "Leave this place at once—*before it is too late.*"

"What?" She stared at him.

"You heard me. Leave this island."

She stared at him stupefied.

"That is what I say."

"But why—why?"

"It is my advice to you—*if you value your life.*"

She gave a gasp.

"Oh! what do you mean? You're frightening me—you're frightening me."

"Yes," said Poirot gravely, "that is my intention."

She sank down, her face in her hands.

"But I can't! He wouldn't come! Douglas wouldn't, I mean. She wouldn't let him. She's got hold of him—body and soul. He won't listen to anything against her. . . . He's crazy about her. . . . He believes everything she tells him—that her husband ill-treats her—that she's an injured innocent—that nobody has ever understood her. . . . He doesn't even think about me anymore—I don't count—I'm not real to him. He wants me to give him his freedom—to divorce him. He believes that she'll divorce her husband and marry him. But I'm afraid. . . . Chantry won't give her up. He's not that kind of man. Last night she showed Douglas bruises on her arm—said her husband had done it. It made Douglas wild. He's so chivalrous. . . . Oh! I'm *afraid!* What will come of it all? Tell me what to do!"

Hercule Poirot stood looking straight across the water to the blue line of hills on the mainland. He said:

"I have told you. Leave this island *before it is too late. . . .*"

She shook her head.

"I can't—I can't—unless Douglas . . ."

Poirot sighed.

He shrugged his shoulders.


# IV

Hercule Poirot sat with Pamela Lyall on the beach.

She said with a certain amount of gusto, "The Triangle's going strong! They sat one each side of her last night—glowering at each other! Chantry had had too much to drink. He was positively insulting to Douglas Gold. Gold behaved very well. Kept his temper. The Valentine woman enjoyed it, of course. Purred like the man-eating tiger she is. What do you think will happen?"

Poirot shook his head.

"I am afraid. I am very much afraid. . . ."

"Oh, we all are," said Miss Lyall hypocritically. She added, "This business is rather in *your* line. Or it may come to be. Can't you do anything?"

"I have done what I could."

Miss Lyall leaned forward eagerly.

"What *have* you done?" she asked with pleasurable excitement.

"I advised Mrs. Gold to leave the island before it was too late."

"Oo-er—so you think—" She stopped.

"Yes, mademoiselle."

"So *that's* what you think is going to happen!" said Pamela slowly. "But he couldn't—he'd never do a thing like that. . . . He's so *nice* really. It's all that Chantry woman. He wouldn't—He wouldn't—do—"

She stopped—then she said softly:

"*Murder?* Is that—is that really the word that's in your mind?"

"It is in someone's mind, mademoiselle. I will tell you that."

Pamela gave a sudden shiver.

"I don't believe it," she declared.

# V

The sequence of events on the night of October the 29th was perfectly clear.

To begin with, there was a scene between the two men—Gold and Chantry. Chantry's voice rose louder and louder and his last words were overheard by four persons—the cashier at the desk, the manager, General Barnes, and Pamela Lyall.

"You damn swine! If you and my wife think you can put this over on me, you're mistaken! *As long as I'm alive,* Valentine will remain my wife."

Then he had flung out of the hotel, his face livid with rage.

That was before dinner. After dinner (how arranged no one knew) a reconciliation took place. Valentine asked Marjorie Gold to come for a moonlight drive. Pamela and Susan went with them.

Gold and Chantry played billiards together. Afterwards they found Hercule Poirot and General Barnes in the lounge.

For the first time, almost, Chantry's face was smiling and good-tempered.

"Have a good game?" asked the General.

The Commander said:

"This fellow's too good for me! Ran out with a break of forty-six."

Douglas Gold deprecated this modestly.

"Pure fluke. I assure you it was. What'll you have? I'll go and get hold of a waiter."

"Pink gin for me, thanks."

"Right. General?"

"Thanks. I'll have a whisky and soda."

"Same for me. What about you, M. Poirot?"

"You are most amiable. I should like a *sirop de cassis.*"

"A *sirop*—excuse me?"

"*Sirop de cassis.* The syrup of the black currants."

"Oh, a liqueur! I see. I suppose they have it here? I never heard of it."

"They have it, yes. But it is not a liqueur."

Douglas Gold said, laughing:

"Sounds a funny taste to me—but for every man his own poison! I'll go and order them."

Commander Chantry sat down. Though not by nature a talkative nor a social man, he was clearly doing his best to be genial.

"Odd how one gets used to doing without any news," he remarked.

The General grunted.

"Can't say the *Continental Daily Mail* four days old is much use to *me*. Of course I get the *Times* sent to me and *Punch* every week, but they're a devilish long time in coming."

"Wonder if we'll have a General Election over this Palestine business?"

"Whole thing's been badly mismanaged," declared the General just as Douglas Gold reappeared, followed by a waiter with the drinks.

The General had just begun on an anecdote of his military career in India in the year 1905. The two Englishmen were listening politely, if without great interest. Hercule Poirot was sipping his *sirop de cassis*.

The General reached the point of his narrative and there was dutiful laughter all round.

Then the women appeared at the doorway of the lounge. They all four seemed in the best of spirits and were talking and laughing.

"Tony, darling, it was too divine," cried Valentine as she dropped into a chair by his side. "The most marvelous idea of Mrs. Gold's. You all ought to have come!"

Her husband said:

"What about a drink?"

He looked inquiringly at the others.

"Pink gin for me, darling," said Valentine.

"Gin and ginger beer," said Pamela.

"Sidecar," said Susan.

"Right." Chantry stood up. He pushed his own untouched pink gin over to his wife. "You have this. I'll order another for myself. What's yours, Mrs. Gold?"

Mrs. Gold was being helped out of her coat by her husband. She turned, smiling.

"Can I have an orangeade, please?"

"Right you are. Orangeade."

He went towards the door. Mrs. Gold smiled up in her husband's face.

"It was so lovely, Douglas. I wish you had come."

"I wish I had too. We'll go another night, shall we?"

They smiled at each other.

Valentine Chantry picked up the pink gin and drained it.

"Oo! I needed that," she sighed.

Douglas Gold took Marjorie's coat and laid it on a settee.

As he strolled back to the others he said sharply:

"Hullo, what's the matter?"

Valentine Chantry was leaning back in her chair. Her lips were blue and her hand had gone to her heart.

"I feel—rather queer. . . ."

She gasped, fighting for breath.

Chantry came back into the room. He quickened his step.

"Hullo, Val, what's the matter?"

"I—I don't know. . . . That drink—it tasted queer. . . ."

"The pink gin?"

Chantry swung round, his face worked. He caught Douglas Gold by the shoulder.

"That was *my* drink . . . Gold, what the hell did you put in it?"

Douglas Gold was staring at the convulsed face of the woman in the chair. He had gone dead white.

"I—I—never—"

Valentine Chantry slipped down in her chair.

General Barnes cried out:

"Get a doctor—quick. . . ."

Five minutes later Valentine Chantry died. . . .

# VI

There was no bathing the next morning.

Pamela Lyall, white-faced, clad in a simple dark dress, clutched at Hercule Poirot in the hall and drew him into the little writing room.

"It's horrible!" she said. "Horrible! You said so! You foresaw it! Murder!"

He bent his head gravely.

"Oh!" she cried out. She stamped her foot on the floor. "You should have stopped it! Somehow! It *could* have been stopped!"

"How?" asked Hercule Poirot.

That brought her up short for the moment.

"Couldn't you go to someone—to the police—?"

"And say what? What is there to say—*before the event?* That someone has murder in their heart. I tell you, *mon enfant,* if one human being is determined to kill another human being—"

"You could warn the victim," insisted Pamela.

"Sometimes," said Hercule Poirot, "warnings are useless."

Pamela said slowly: "You could warn the murderer—show him that you knew what was intended. . . ."

Poirot nodded appreciatively.

"Yes—a better plan, that. But even then you have to reckon with a criminal's chief vice."

"What is that?"

"Conceit! A criminal never believes that his crime can fail."

"But it's absurd—stupid," cried Pamela. "The whole crime was childish! Why, the police arrested Douglas Gold at once last night."

"Yes." He added thoughtfully, "Douglas Gold is a very stupid young man."

"Incredibly stupid! I hear that they found the rest of the poison—whatever it was—?"

"A form of stropanthin. A heart poison."

"That they actually found the rest of it in his dinner jacket pocket?"

"Quite true."

"Incredibly stupid!" said Pamela again. "Perhaps he meant to get rid of it—and the shock of the wrong person being poisoned paralyzed him. What a scene it would make on the stage. The lover putting the stropanthin in the husband's glass and then, just when his attention is elsewhere, the wife drinks it instead. . . . Think of the ghastly moment when Douglas Gold turned round and realized he had killed the woman he loved. . . ."

She gave a little shiver.

"Your triangle. *The Eternal Triangle!* Who would have thought it would end like this?"

"I was afraid of it," murmured Poirot.

Pamela turned on him.

"You warned *her*—Mrs. Gold. Then why didn't you warn him as well?"

"You mean, why didn't I warn Douglas Gold?"

"No. I mean Commander Chantry. You could have told him that he was in danger—after all *he* was the real obstacle! I've no doubt Douglas Gold relied on being able to bully his wife into giving him a divorce—she's a meek-spirited little woman and terribly fond of him. But Chantry is a mulish sort of devil. He was determined not to give Valentine her freedom."

Poirot shrugged his shoulders.

"It would have been no good my speaking to Chantry," he said.

"Perhaps not," Pamela admitted. "He'd probably have said he could look after himself and told you to go to the devil. But I do feel there ought to have been *something* one could have done."

"I did think," said Poirot slowly, "of trying to persuade Valentine Chantry to leave the island, but she would not have believed what I had to tell her. She was far too stupid a woman to take in a thing like that. *Pauvre femme,* her stupidity killed her."

"I don't believe it would have been any good if she *had* left the island," said Pamela. "He would simply have followed her."

"He?"

"Douglas Gold."

"You think Douglas Gold would have followed her? Oh, no, made-moiselle, you are wrong—you are completely wrong. You have not yet appreciated the truth of this matter. If Valentine Chantry had left the island, her husband would have gone with her."

Pamela looked puzzled.

"Well, naturally."

"And then, you see, the crime would simply have taken place somewhere else."

"I don't understand you."

"I am saying to you that the same crime would have occurred somewhere else—*that crime being the murder of Valentine Chantry by her husband.*"

Pamela stared.

"Are you trying to say that it was Commander Chantry—Tony Chantry—who murdered Valentine?"

"Yes. You saw him do it! Douglas Gold brought him his drink. He sat with it in front of him. When the women came in we all looked across the room, he had the stropanthin ready, he dropped it into the pink gin and presently, courteously, he passed it along to his wife and she drank it."

"But the packet of stropanthin was found in Douglas Gold's pocket!"

"A very simple matter to slip it there when we were all crowding round the dying woman."

It was quite two minutes before Pamela got her breath.

"But I don't understand a word! The triangle—you said yourself—"

Hercule Poirot nodded his head vigorously.

"I said there was a triangle—yes. But you, you imagined *the wrong one.* You were deceived by some very clever acting! You thought, as you were meant to think, that both Tony Chantry and Douglas Gold were in love with Valentine Chantry. You believed, as you were meant to believe, that Douglas Gold, being in love with Valentine Chantry (whose husband refused to divorce her), took the desperate step of administering a powerful heart poison to Chantry and that, by a fatal mistake, Valentine Chantry drank that poison instead. All that is illusion. Chantry has been meaning to do away with his wife for some time. He was bored to death with her, I could see that from the first. He married her for her money. Now he wants to marry another woman—so he planned to get rid of Valentine and keep her money. That entailed murder."

"Another *woman?*"

Poirot said slowly:

"Yes, yes—*the little Marjorie Gold.* It was the eternal triangle all right! But you saw it the wrong way round. Neither of those two men cared in the least for Valentine Chantry. It was her vanity *and Marjorie Gold's very clever stage managing* that made you think they did! A very clever woman, Mrs. Gold, and amazingly attractive in her demure

Madonna, poor little thing way! I have known four women criminals of the same type. There was Mrs. Adams who was acquitted of murdering her husband, but everybody knows she did it. Mary Parker did away with an aunt, a sweetheart, and two brothers before she got a little careless and was caught. Then there was Mrs. Rowden, she was hanged all right. Mrs. Lecray escaped by the skin of her teeth. This woman is exactly the same type. I recognized it as soon as I saw her! That type takes to crime like a duck to water! And a very pretty bit of well-planned work it was. Tell me, what evidence did you ever have that Douglas Gold was in love with Valentine Chantry? When you come to think it out, you realize that there was only Mrs. Gold's confidences and Chantry's jealous bluster. Yes? You see?"

"It's horrible," cried Pamela.

"They were a clever pair," said Poirot with professional detachment. "They planned to 'meet' here and stage their crime. That Marjorie Gold, she is a cold-blooded devil. She would have sent her poor innocent fool of a husband to the scaffold without the least remorse."

Pamela cried out:

"But he was arrested and taken away by the police last night."

"Ah," said Hercule Poirot, "but after that, me, I had a few little words with the police. It is true that I did not see Chantry put the stropanthin in the glass. I, like everyone else, looked up when the ladies came in. But the moment I realized that Valentine Chantry had been poisoned, I watched her husband without taking my eyes off him. And so, you see, I actually saw him slip the packet of stropanthin in Douglas Gold's coat pocket. . . ."

He added with a grim expression on his face:

"I am a good witness. My name is well known. The moment the police heard my story they realized that it put an entirely different complexion on the matter."

"And then?" demanded Pamela, fascinated.

"*Eh bien,* then they asked Commander Chantry a few questions. He tried to bluster it out, but he is not really clever, he soon broke down."

"So Douglas Gold was set at liberty?"

"Yes."

"And—Marjorie Gold?"

Poirot's face grew stern.

"I warned her," he said.

"Yes, I warned her. . . . Up on the Mount of the Prophet. . . . It was the only chance of averting the crime. I as good as told her that I suspected her. She understood. But she believed herself too clever. . . . I told her to leave the island *if* she valued her life. She chose— to remain. . . ."

# THE
# REGATTA
# MYSTERY

# The Mystery of the Bagdad Chest

T HE words made a catchy headline, and I said as much to my friend, Hercule Poirot. I knew none of the parties. My interest was merely the dispassionate one of the man in the street. Poirot agreed.

"Yes, it has a flavor of the Oriental, of the mysterious. The chest may very well have been a sham Jacobean one from the Tottenham Court Road; nonetheless the reporter who thought of naming it the Bagdad Chest was happily inspired. The word 'Mystery' is also thoughtfully placed in juxtaposition, though I understand there is very little mystery about the case."

"Exactly. It is all rather horrible and macabre, but it is not mysterious."

"Horrible and macabre," repeated Poirot thoughtfully.

"The whole idea is revolting," I said, rising to my feet and pacing up and down the room. "The murderer kills this man—his friend—shoves him into the chest, and half an hour later is dancing in that same room with the wife of his victim. Think! If she had imagined for one moment—"

"True," said Poirot thoughtfully. "That much-vaunted possession, a woman's intuition—it does not seem to have been working."

"The party seems to have gone off very merrily," I said with a slight shiver. "And all that time, as they danced and played poker, there was a dead man in the room with them. One could write a play about such an idea."

"It has been done," said Poirot. "But console yourself, Hastings," he added kindly. "Because a theme has been used once, there is no reason why it should not be used again. Compose your drama."

I had picked up the paper and was studying the rather blurred reproduction of a photograph.

"She must be a beautiful woman," I said slowly. "Even from this, one gets an idea."

Below the picture ran the inscription:

## A Recent Portrait of Mrs. Clayton, the Wife of the Murdered Man

Poirot took the paper from me.

"Yes," he said. "She is beautiful. Doubtless she is of those born to trouble the souls of men."

He handed the paper back to me with a sigh.

*"Dieu merci,* I am not of an ardent temperament. It has saved me from many embarrassments. I am duly thankful."

I do not remember that we discussed the case further. Poirot displayed no special interest in it at the time. The facts were so clear, and there was so little ambiguity about them, that discussion seemed merely futile.

Mr. and Mrs. Clayton and Major Rich were friends of fairly long standing. On the day in question, the tenth of March, the Claytons had accepted an invitation to spend the evening with Major Rich. At about seven-thirty, however, Clayton explained to another friend, a Major Curtiss, with whom he was having a drink, that he had been unexpectedly called to Scotland and was leaving by the eight o'clock train.

"I'll just have time to drop in and explain to old Jack," went on Clayton. "Marguerita is going, of course. I'm sorry about it, but Jack will understand how it is."

Mr. Clayton was as good as his word. He arrived at Major Rich's rooms about twenty to eight. The major was out at the time, but his manservant, who knew Mr. Clayton well, suggested that he come in and wait. Mr. Clayton said that he had not time, but that he would come in and write a note. He added that he was on his way to catch a train.

The valet accordingly showed him into the sitting room.

About five minutes later Major Rich, who must have let himself in without the valet hearing him, opened the door of the sitting room, called his man and told him to go out and get some cigarettes. On his return the man brought them to his master, who was then alone in the sitting room. The man naturally concluded that Mr. Clayton had left.

The guests arrived shortly afterwards. They comprised Mrs. Clayton, Major Curtiss and a Mr. and Mrs. Spence. The evening was spent dancing to the phonograph and playing poker. The guests left shortly after midnight.

The following morning, on coming to do the sitting room, the valet was startled to find a deep stain discoloring the carpet below and in front of a piece of furniture which Major Rich had brought from the East and which was called the Bagdad Chest.

Instinctively the valet lifted the lid of the chest and was horrified to find inside the doubled-up body of a man who had been stabbed to the heart.

Terrified, the man ran out of the flat and fetched the nearest policeman. The dead man proved to be Mr. Clayton. The arrest of Major Rich followed very shortly afterward. The major's defense, it was understood, consisted of a sturdy denial of everything. He had not seen Mr. Clayton the preceding evening and the first he had heard of his going to Scotland had been from Mrs. Clayton.

Such were the bald facts of the case. Innuendoes and suggestions naturally abounded. The close friendship and intimacy of Major Rich and Mrs. Clayton were so stressed that only a fool could fail to read between the lines. The motive for the crime was plainly indicated.

Long experience has taught me to make allowance for baseless calumny. The motive suggested might, for all the evidence, be entirely nonexistent. Some quite other reason might have precipitated the issue. But one thing did stand out clearly—that Rich was the murderer.

As I say, the matter might have rested there, had it not happened that Poirot and I were due at a party given by Lady Chatterton that night.

Poirot, while bemoaning social engagements and declaring a passion for solitude, really enjoyed these affairs enormously. To be made a fuss of and treated as a lion suited him down to the ground.

On occasions he positively purred! I have seen him blandly receiving the most outrageous compliments as no more than his due, and uttering the most blatantly conceited remarks, such as I can hardly bear to set down.

Sometimes he would argue with me on the subject.

"But, my friend, I am not an Anglo-Saxon. Why should I play the hypocrite? *Si, si,* that is what you do, all of you. The airman who has made a difficult flight, the tennis champion—they look down their noses, they mutter inaudibly that 'it is nothing.' But do they really think that themselves? Not for a moment. They would admire the exploit in someone else. So, being reasonable men, they admire it in themselves. But their training prevents them from saying so. Me, I am not like that. The talents that I possess—I would salute them in another. As it happens, in my own particular line, there is no one to touch me. *C'est dommage!* As it is, I admit freely and without the hypocrisy that I am a great man. I have the order, the method, and the psychology in an unusual degree. I am, in fact, Hercule Poirot! Why should I turn red and stammer and mutter into my chin that really I am very stupid? It would not be true."

"There is certainly only one Hercule Poirot," I agreed—not without a spice of malice, of which, fortunately, Poirot remained quite oblivious.

Lady Chatterton was one of Poirot's most ardent admirers. Starting from the mysterious conduct of a Pekingese, he had unraveled a chain which led to a noted burglar and housebreaker. Lady Chatterton had been loud in his praises ever since.

To see Poirot at a party was a great sight. His faultless evening clothes, the exquisite set of his white tie, the exact symmetry of his hair parting, the sheen of pomade on his hair, and the tortured splendor of his famous mustaches—all combined to paint the perfect picture of an inveterate dandy. It was hard, at these moments, to take the little man seriously.

It was about half-past eleven when Lady Chatterton, bearing down upon us, whisked Poirot neatly out of an admiring group, and carried him off—I need hardly say, with myself in tow.

"I want you to go into my little room upstairs," said Lady Chatterton rather breathlessly as soon as she was out of earshot of her other guests. "You know where it is, M. Poirot. You'll find someone there who needs your help very badly—and you will help her, I know. She's one of my dearest friends—so don't say no."

Energetically leading the way as she talked, Lady Chatterton flung open a door, exclaiming as she did so, "I've got him, Marguerita darling. And he'll do anything you want. You *will* help Mrs. Clayton, won't you, M. Poirot?"

And taking the answer for granted, she withdrew with the same energy that characterized all her movements.

Mrs. Clayton had been sitting in a chair by the window. She rose now and came toward us. Dressed in deep mourning, the dull black showed up her fair coloring. She was a singularly lovely woman, and there was about her a simple childlike candor which made her charm quite irresistible.

"Alice Chatterton is so kind," she said. "She arranged this. She said you would help me, M. Poirot. Of course I don't know whether you will or not—but I hope you will."

She had held out her hand and Poirot had taken it. He held it now for a moment or two while he stood scrutinizing her closely. There was nothing ill-bred in his manner of doing it. It was more the kind but searching look that a famous consultant gives a new patient as the latter is ushered into his presence.

"Are you sure, madame," he said at last, "that I can help you?"

"Alice says so."

"Yes, but I am asking you, madame."

A little flush rose to her cheeks.

"I don't know what you mean."

"What is it, madame, that you want me to do?"

"You—you—know who I am?" she asked.

"Assuredly."

"Then you can guess what it is I am asking you to do, M. Poirot—Captain Hastings"—I was gratified that she realized my identity—"Major Rich did *not* kill my husband."

"Why not?"

"I beg your pardon?"

Poirot smiled at her slight discomfiture.

"I said, 'Why not?' " he repeated.

"I'm not sure that I understand."

"Yet it is very simple. The police—the lawyers—they will all ask the same question: Why did Major Rich kill M. Clayton? I ask the opposite. I ask you, madame, why did Major Rich *not* kill Major Clayton?"

"You mean—why I'm so sure? Well, but I *know*. I know Major Rich so well."

"You know Major Rich so well," repeated Poirot tonelessly.

The color flamed into her cheeks.

"Yes, that's what they'll say—what they'll think! Oh, I know!"

*"C'est vrai.* That is what they will ask you about—how well you knew Major Rich. Perhaps you will speak the truth, perhaps you will lie. It is very necessary for a woman to lie sometimes. Women must defend themselves—and the lie, it is a good weapon. But there are three people, madame, to whom a woman should speak the truth. To her father confessor, to her hairdresser, and to her private detective—if she trusts him. Do you trust me, madame?"

Marguerita Clayton drew a deep breath. "Yes," she said. "I do. I must," she added rather childishly.

"Then, how well do you know Major Rich?"

She looked at him for a moment in silence, then she raised her chin defiantly.

"I will answer your question. I loved Jack from the first moment I saw him—two years ago. Lately I think—I believe—he has come to love me. But he has never said so."

*"Épatant!"* said Poirot. "You have saved me a good quarter of an hour by coming to the point without beating the bush. You have the good sense. Now your husband—did he suspect your feelings?"

"I don't know," said Marguerita slowly. "I thought—lately—that he might. His manner has been different. . . . But that may have been merely my fancy."

"Nobody else knew?"

"I do not think so."

"And—pardon me, madame—you did not love your husband?"

There were, I think, very few women who would have answered that question as simply as this woman did. They would have tried to explain their feelings.

Marguerita Clayton said quite simply, "No."

"*Bien*. Now we know where we are. According to you, madame, Major Rich did not kill your husband, but you realize that all the evidence points to his having done so. Are you aware, privately, of any flaw in that evidence?"

"No. I know nothing."

"When did your husband first inform you of his visit to Scotland?"

"Just after lunch. He said it was a bore, but he'd have to go. Something to do with land values, he said it was."

"And after that?"

"He went out—to his club, I think. I—I didn't see him again."

"Now as to Major Rich—what was his manner that evening? Just as usual?"

"Yes, I think so."

"You are not sure?"

Marguerita wrinkled her brows.

"He was—a little constrained. With me—not with the others. But I thought I knew why that was. You understand? I am sure the constraint or—or—absentmindedness perhaps describes it better—had nothing to do with Edward. He was surprised to hear that Edward had gone to Scotland, but not unduly so."

"And nothing else unusual occurs to you in connection with that evening?"

Marguerita thought.

"No, nothing whatever."

"You—noticed the chest?"

She shook her head with a little shiver.

"I don't even remember it—or what it was like. We played poker most of the evening."

"Who won?"

"Major Rich. I had very bad luck, and so did Major Curtiss. The Spences won a little, but Major Rich was the chief winner."

"The party broke up—when?"

"About half-past twelve, I think. We all left together."

"Ah!"

Poirot remained silent, lost in thought.

"I wish I could be more helpful to you," said Mrs. Clayton. "I seem to be able to tell you so little."

"About the present—yes. What about the past, madame?"

"The past?"

"Yes. Have there not been incidents?"

She flushed.

"You mean that dreadful little man who shot himself. It wasn't my fault, M. Poirot. Indeed it wasn't."

"It was not precisely of that incident that I was thinking."

"That ridiculous duel? But Italians do fight duels. I was so thankful the man wasn't killed."

"It must have been a relief to you," agreed Poirot gravely.

She was looking at him doubtfully. He rose and took her hand in his.

"I shall not fight a duel for you, madame," he said. "But I will do what you have asked me. I will discover the truth. And let us hope that your instincts are correct—that the truth will help and not harm you."

Our first interview was with Major Curtiss. He was a man of about forty, of soldierly build, with very dark hair and a bronzed face. He had known the Claytons for some years and Major Rich also. He confirmed the press reports.

Clayton and he had had a drink together at the club just before half-past seven, and Clayton had then announced his intention of looking in on Major Rich on his way to Euston.

"What was Mr. Clayton's manner? Was he depressed or cheerful?"

The major considered. He was a slow-spoken man.

"Seemed in fairly good spirits," he said at last.

"He said nothing about being on bad terms with Major Rich?"

"Good Lord, no. They were pals."

"He didn't object to—his wife's friendship with Major Rich?"

The major became very red in the face.

"You've been reading those damned newspapers, with their hints and lies. Of course he didn't object. Why, he said to me, 'Marguerita's going, of course.' "

"I see. Now during the evening—the manner of Major Rich—was that much as usual?"

"I didn't notice any difference."

"And madame? She, too, was as usual."

"Well," he reflected, "now I come to think of it, she was a bit quiet. You know, thoughtful and faraway."

"Who arrived first?"

"The Spences. They were there when I got there. As a matter of fact, I'd called round for Mrs. Clayton, but found she'd already started. So I got there a bit late."

"And how did you amuse yourselves? You danced? You played the cards?"

"A bit of both. Danced first of all."

"There were five of you?"

"Yes, but that's all right, because I don't dance. I put on the records and the others danced."

"Who danced most with whom?"

"Well, as a matter of fact the Spences like dancing together. They've got a sort of craze on it—fancy steps and all that."

"So that Mrs. Clayton danced mostly with Major Rich?"

"That's about it."

"And then you played poker?"

"Yes."

"And when did you leave?"

"Oh, quite early. A little after midnight."

"Did you all leave together?"

"Yes. As a matter of fact, we shared a taxi, dropped Mrs. Clayton first, then me, and the Spences took it on to Kensington."

Our next visit was to Mr. and Mrs. Spence. Only Mrs. Spence was at home, but her account of the evening tallied with that of Major Curtiss except that she displayed a slight acidity concerning Major Rich's luck at cards.

Earlier in the morning Poirot had had a telephone conversation with Inspector Japp, of Scotland Yard. As a result we arrived at Major Rich's rooms and found his manservant, Burgoyne, expecting us.

The valet's evidence was very precise and clear.

Mr. Clayton had arrived at twenty minutes to eight. Unluckily Major Rich had just that very minute gone out. Mr. Clayton had said that he couldn't wait, as he had to catch a train, but he would just scrawl a note. He accordingly went into the sitting room to do so. Burgoyne had not actually heard his master come in, as he was running the bath, and Major Rich, of course, let himself in with his own key. In his opinion it was about ten minutes later that Major Rich called him and sent him out for cigarettes. No, he had not gone into the sitting room. Major Rich had stood in the doorway. He had returned with the cigarettes five minutes later and on this occasion he had gone into the sitting room, which was then empty, save for his master, who was standing by the window smoking. His master had inquired if his bath were ready and on being told it was had proceeded to take it. He, Burgoyne, had not mentioned Mr. Clayton, as he assumed that his master had found Mr. Clayton there and let him out himself. His master's manner had been precisely the same as usual. He had taken his bath, changed, and shortly after, Mr. and Mrs. Spence had arrived, to be followed by Major Curtiss and Mrs. Clayton.

It had not occurred to him, Burgoyne explained, that Mr. Clayton might have left before his master's return. To do so, Mr. Clayton would have had to bang the front door behind him and that the valet was sure he would have heard.

Still in the same impersonal manner, Burgoyne proceeded to his finding of the body. For the first time my attention was directed to the fatal chest. It was a good-sized piece of furniture standing against the wall next to the phonograph cabinet. It was made of some dark wood and plentifully studded with brass nails. The lid opened simply enough. I looked in and shivered. Though well scrubbed, ominous stains remained.

Suddenly Poirot uttered an exclamation. "Those holes there—they are curious. One would say that they had been newly made."

The holes in question were at the back of the chest against the wall. There were three or four of them. They were about a quarter of an inch in diameter and certainly had the effect of having been freshly made.

Poirot bent down to examine them, looking inquiringly at the valet.

"It's certainly curious, sir. I don't remember ever seeing those holes in the past, though maybe I wouldn't notice them."

"It makes no matter," said Poirot.

Closing the lid of the chest, he stepped back into the room until he was standing with his back against the window. Then he suddenly asked a question.

"Tell me," he said. "When you brought the cigarettes into your master that night, was there not something out of place in the room?"

Burgoyne hesitated for a minute, then with some slight reluctance he replied,

"It's odd your saying that, sir. Now you come to mention it, there was. That screen there that cuts off the draft from the bedroom door— it was moved a bit more to the left."

"Like this?"

Poirot darted nimbly forward and pulled at the screen. It was a handsome affair of painted leather. It already slightly obscured the view of the chest, and as Poirot adjusted it, it hid the chest altogether.

"That's right, sir," said the valet. "It was like that."

"And the next morning?"

"It was still like that. I remember. I moved it away and it was then I saw the stain. The carpet's gone to be cleaned, sir. That's why the boards are bare."

Poirot nodded.

"I see," he said. "I thank you."

He placed a crisp piece of paper in the valet's palm.

"Thank you, sir."

"Poirot," I said when we were out in the street, "that point about the screen—is that a point helpful to Rich?"

"It is a further point against him," said Poirot ruefully. "The screen hid the chest from the room. It also hid the stain on the carpet. Sooner or later the blood was bound to soak through the wood and stain the carpet. The screen would prevent discovery for the moment. Yes—but there is something there that I do not understand. The valet, Hastings, the valet."

"What about the valet? He seemed a most intelligent fellow."

"As you say, most intelligent. Is it credible, then, that Major Rich failed to realize that the valet would certainly discover the body in the morning? Immediately after the deed he had no time for anything—granted. He shoves the body into the chest, pulls the screen in front of it and goes through the evening hoping for the best. But after the guests are gone? Surely, then is the time to dispose of the body."

"Perhaps he hoped the valet wouldn't notice the stain?"

"That, *mon ami*, is absurd. A stained carpet is the first thing a good servant would be bound to notice. And Major Rich, he goes to bed and snores there comfortably and does nothing at all about the matter. Very remarkable and interesting, that."

"Curtiss might have seen the stains when he was changing the records the night before?" I suggested.

"That is unlikely. The screen would throw a deep shadow just there. No, but I begin to see. Yes, dimly I begin to see."

"See what?" I asked eagerly.

"The possibilities, shall we say, of an alternative explanation. Our next visit may throw light on things."

Our next visit was to the doctor who had examined the body. His evidence was a mere recapitulation of what he had already given at the inquest. Deceased had been stabbed to the heart with a long thin knife something like a stiletto. The knife had been left in the wound. Death had been instantaneous. The knife was the property of Major Rich and usually lay on his writing table. There were no fingerprints on it, the doctor understood. It had been either wiped or held in a handkerchief. As regards time, any time between seven and nine seemed indicated.

"He could not, for instance, have been killed after midnight?" asked Poirot.

"No. That I can say. Ten o'clock at the outside—but seven-thirty to eight seems clearly indicated."

"There *is* a second hypothesis possible," Poirot said when we were back home. "I wonder if you see it, Hastings. To me it is very plain, and I only need one point to clear up the matter for good and all."

"It's no good," I said. "I'm not there."

"But make an effort, Hastings. Make an effort."

"Very well," I said. "At seven-forty Clayton is alive and well. The last person to see him alive is Rich—"

"So we assume."

"Well, isn't it so?"

"You forget, *mon ami,* that Major Rich denies that. He states explicitly that Clayton had gone when he came in."

"But the valet says that he would have heard Clayton leave because
of the bang of the door. And also, if Clayton had left, when did he
return? He couldn't have returned after midnight because the doctor
says positively that he was dead at least two hours before that. That
only leaves one alternative."

"Yes, *mon ami?*" said Poirot.

"That in the five minutes Clayton was alone in the sitting room,
someone else came in and killed him. But there we have the same
objection. Only someone with a key could come in without the valet's
knowing, and in the same way the murderer on leaving would have
had to bang the door, and that again the valet would have heard."

"Exactly," said Poirot. "And therefore—"

"And therefore—nothing," I said. "I can see no other solution."

"It is a pity," murmured Poirot. "And it is really so exceedingly
simple—as the clear blue eyes of Madame Clayton."

"You really believe—"

"I believe nothing—until I have got proof. One little proof will convince me."

He took up the telephone and called Japp at Scotland Yard.

Twenty minutes later we were standing before a little heap of assorted objects laid out on a table. They were the contents of the dead
man's pockets.

There was a handkerchief, a handful of loose change, a pocketbook
containing three pounds ten shillings, a couple of bills, and a worn
snapshot of Marguerita Clayton. There was also a pocketknife, a gold
pencil, and a cumbersome wooden tool.

It was on this latter that Poirot swooped. He unscrewed it and several
small blades fell out.

"You see, Hastings, a gimlet and all the rest of it. Ah! it would be
a matter of a very few minutes to bore a few holes in the chest with
this."

"Those holes we saw?"

"Precisely."

"You mean it was Clayton who bored them himself?"

"*Mais, oui—mais, oui!* What did they suggest to you, those holes?
They were not to *see* through, because they were at the back of the
chest. What were they for, then? Clearly for air? But you do not make
air holes for a dead body, so clearly they were *not* made by the murderer. They suggest one thing—and one thing only—that a man was
going to *hide* in that chest. And at once, on that hypothesis, things

become intelligible. Mr. Clayton is jealous of his wife and Rich. He plays the old, old trick of pretending to go away. He watches Rich go out, then he gains admission, is left alone to write a note, quickly bores those holes and hides inside the chest. His wife is coming there that night. Possibly Rich will put the others off, possibly she will remain after the others have gone, or pretend to go and return. Whatever it is, Clayton will *know*. Anything is preferable to the ghastly torment of suspicion he is enduring."

"Then you mean that Rich killed him *after* the others had gone? But the doctor said that was impossible."

"Exactly. So you see, Hastings, he must have been killed *during* the evening."

"But everyone was in the room!"

"Precisely," said Poirot gravely. "You see the beauty of that? 'Everyone was in the room.' What an alibi! What sangfroid—what nerve—what audacity!"

"I still don't understand."

"Who went behind that screen to wind up the phonograph and change the records? The phonograph and the chest were side by side, remember. The others are dancing—the phonograph is playing. And the man who does not dance lifts the lid of the chest and thrusts the knife he has just slipped into his sleeve deep into the body of the man who was hiding there."

"Impossible! The man would cry out."

"Not if he were drugged first?"

"Drugged?"

"Yes. Who did Clayton have a drink with at seven-thirty? Ah! Now you see. Curtiss! Curtiss has inflamed Clayton's mind with suspicions against his wife and Rich. Curtiss suggests this plan—the visit to Scotland, the concealment in the chest, the final touch of moving the screen. Not so that Clayton can raise the lid a little and get relief—no, so that he, Curtiss, can raise that lid unobserved. The plan is Curtiss', and observe the beauty of it, Hastings. If Rich had observed the screen was out of place and moved it back—well, no harm is done. He can make another plan. Clayton hides in the chest, the mild narcotic that Curtiss had administered takes effect. He sinks into unconsciousness. Curtiss lifts up the lid and strikes—and the phonograph goes on playing 'Walking My Baby Back Home.' "

I found my voice. "Why? But why?"

Poirot shrugged his shoulders.

"Why did a man shoot himself? Why did two Italians fight a duel? Curtiss is of a dark passionate temperament. He wanted Marguerita Clayton. With her husband and Rich out of the way, she would, or so he thought, turn to him."

He added musingly:

"These simple childlike women . . . they are very dangerous. But *mon Dieu!* what an artistic masterpiece! It goes to my heart to hang a man like that. I may be a genius myself, but I am capable of recognizing genius in other people. A perfect murder, *mon ami.* I, Hercule Poirot, say it to you. A perfect murder. *Épatant!*"

# How Does Your Garden Grow?

**H**ERCULE POIROT arranged his letters in a neat pile in front of him. He picked up the topmost letter, studied the address for a moment, then neatly slit the back of the envelope with a little paperknife that he kept on the breakfast table for that express purpose and extracted the contents. Inside was yet another envelope, carefully sealed with purple wax and marked "Private and Confidential."

Hercule Poirot's eyebrows rose a little on his egg-shaped head. He murmured, *"Patience! Nous allons arriver!"* and once more brought the little paperknife into play. This time the envelope yielded a letter— written in a rather shaky and spiky handwriting. Several words were heavily underlined.

Hercule Poirot unfolded it and read. The letter was headed once again "Private and Confidential." On the right-hand side was the address—Rosebank, Charman's Green, Bucks—and the date—March twenty-first.

> *Dear M. Poirot:* I have been recommended to you by an old and valued friend of mine who knows the *worry* and *distress* I have been in lately. Not that this friend knows the actual *circumstances*—those I have kept *entirely* to myself—the matter being strictly private. My friend assures me that you are *discretion* itself—and that there will be no fear of my being involved in a *police* matter which, if my suspicions should prove correct, I should *very much dislike*. But it is of course possible that I am *entirely* mistaken. I do not feel myself clear-headed enough nowadays—suffering as I do from insomnia and the result of a severe illness last winter—to investigate things for myself. I have neither the *means* nor the *ability*. On the other hand, I must reiterate once more that this is a very delicate family matter and that for many reasons I may want the *whole thing hushed up*. If I am once assured of the *facts*, I can deal with the matter myself

344

and should prefer to do so. I hope that I have made myself clear on this point. If you will undertake this investigation, perhaps you will let me know to the above address?

Yours very truly,

AMELIA BARROWBY.

Poirot read the letter through twice. Again his eyebrows rose slightly. Then he placed it on one side and proceeded to the next envelope in the pile.

At ten o'clock precisely he entered the room where Miss Lemon, his confidential secretary, sat awaiting her instructions for the day. Miss Lemon was forty-eight and of unprepossessing appearance. Her general effect was that of a lot of bones flung together at random. She had a passion for order almost equaling that of Poirot himself; and though capable of thinking, she never thought unless told to do so.

Poirot handed her the morning correspondence. "Have the goodness, mademoiselle, to write refusals couched in correct terms to all of these."

Miss Lemon ran an eye over the various letters, scribbling in turn a hieroglyphic on each of them. These marks were legible to her alone and were in a code of her own: "Soft soap"; "slap in the face"; "purr purr"; "curt"; and so on. Having done this, she nodded and looked up for further instructions.

Poirot handed her Amelia Barrowby's letter. She extracted it from its double envelope, read it through and looked up inquiringly.

"Yes, M. Poirot?" Her pencil hovered—ready—over her shorthand pad.

"What is your opinion of that letter, Miss Lemon?"

With a slight frown Miss Lemon put down the pencil and read through the letter again.

The contents of a letter meant nothing to Miss Lemon except from the point of view of composing an adequate reply. Very occasionally her employer appealed to her human, as opposed to her official, capacities. It slightly annoyed Miss Lemon when he did so—she was very nearly the perfect machine, completely and gloriously uninterested in all human affairs. Her real passion in life was the perfection of a filing system beside which all other filing systems should sink into oblivion. She dreamed of such a system at night. Nevertheless, Miss Lemon was perfectly capable of intelligence on purely human matters, as Hercule Poirot well knew.

"Well?" he demanded.

"Old lady," said Miss Lemon. "Got the wind up pretty badly."

"Ah! The wind rises in her, you think?"

Miss Lemon, who considered that Poirot had been long enough in Great Britain to understand its slang terms, did not reply. She took a brief look at the double envelope.

"Very hush-hush," she said. "And tells you nothing at all."

"Yes," said Hercule Poirot. "I observed that."

Miss Lemon's hand hung once more hopefully over the shorthand pad. This time Hercule Poirot responded.

"Tell her I will do myself the honor to call upon her at any time she suggests, unless she prefers to consult me here. Do not type the letter—write it by hand."

"Yes, M. Poirot."

Poirot produced more correspondence. "These are bills."

Miss Lemon's efficient hands sorted them quickly. "I'll pay all but these two."

"Why those two? There is no error in them."

"They are firms you've only just begun to deal with. It looks bad to pay too promptly when you've just opened an account—looks as though you were working up to get some credit later on."

"Ah!" murmured Poirot. "I bow to your superior knowledge of the British tradesman."

"There's nothing much I don't know about them," said Miss Lemon grimly.

The letter to Miss Amelia Barrowby was duly written and sent, but no reply was forthcoming. Perhaps, thought Hercule Poirot, the old lady had unraveled her mystery herself. Yet he felt a shade of surprise that in that case she should not have written a courteous word to say that his services were no longer required.

It was five days later when Miss Lemon, after receiving her morning's instructions, said, "That Miss Barrowby we wrote to—no wonder there's been no answer. She's dead."

Hercule Poirot said very softly, "Ah—dead." It sounded not so much like a question as an answer.

Opening her handbag, Miss Lemon produced a newspaper cutting. "I saw it in the tube and tore it out."

Just registering in his mind approval of the fact that, though Miss Lemon used the word "tore," she had neatly cut the entry out with scissors, Poirot read the announcement taken from the Births, Deaths and Marriages in the *Morning Post*: "On March 26th—suddenly—at Rosebank, Charman's Green, Amelia Jane Barrowby, in her seventy-third year. No flowers, by request."

Poirot read it over. He murmured under his breath, "Suddenly."

Then he said briskly, "If you will be so obliging as to take a letter, Miss Lemon?"

The pencil hovered. Miss Lemon, her mind dwelling on the intricacies of the filing system, took down in rapid and correct shorthand:

*Dear Miss Barrowby:* I have received no reply from you, but as I shall be in the neighborhood of Charman's Green on Friday, I will call upon you on that day and discuss more fully the matter you mentioned to me in your letter.

Yours, etc.

"Type this letter, please; and if it is posted at once, it should get to Charman's Green tonight."

On the following morning a letter in a black-edged envelope arrived by the second post:

*Dear Sir:* In reply to your letter my aunt, Miss Barrowby, passed away on the twenty-sixth, so the matter you speak of is no longer of importance.

Yours truly,

MARY DELAFONTAINE.

Poirot smiled to himself. "No longer of importance. . . . Ah—that is what we shall see. *En avant*—to Charman's Green."

Rosebank was a house that seemed likely to live up to its name, which is more than can be said for most houses of its class and character.

Hercule Poirot paused as he walked up the path to the front door and looked approvingly at the neatly planned beds on either side of him. Rose trees that promised a good harvest later in the year, and at present daffodils, early tulips, blue hyacinths—the last bed was partly edged with shells.

Poirot murmured to himself, "How does it go, the English rhyme the children sing?

> *Mistress Mary, quite contrary,*
> *How does your garden grow?*
> *With cockle-shells, and silver bells,*
> *And pretty maids all in a row.*

"Not a row, perhaps," he considered, "but here is at least one pretty maid to make the little rhyme come right."

The front door had opened and a neat little maid in cap and apron was looking somewhat dubiously at the spectacle of a heavily mustached foreign gentleman talking aloud to himself in the front garden. She was, as Poirot had noted, a very pretty little maid, with round blue eyes and rosy cheeks.

Poirot raised his hat with courtesy and addressed her: "Pardon, but does a Miss Amelia Barrowby live here?"

The little maid gasped and her eyes grew rounder.

"Oh, sir, didn't you know? She's dead. Ever so sudden it was. Tuesday night."

She hesitated, divided between two strong instincts: the first, distrust of a foreigner; the second, the pleasurable enjoyment of her class in dwelling on the subject of illness and death.

"You amaze me," said Hercule Poirot, not very truthfully. "I had an appointment with the lady for today. However, I can perhaps see the other lady who lives here."

The little maid seemed slightly doubtful. "The mistress? Well, you could see her, perhaps, but I don't know whether she'll be seeing anyone or not."

"She will see me," said Poirot, and handed her a card.

The authority of his tone had its effect. The rosy-cheeked maid fell back and ushered Poirot into a sitting room on the right of the hall. Then, card in hand, she departed to summon her mistress.

Hercule Poirot looked round him. The room was a perfectly conventional drawing room—oatmeal-colored paper with a frieze round the top, indeterminate cretonnes, rose-colored cushions and curtains, a good many china knickknacks and ornaments. There was nothing in the room that stood out, that announced a definite personality.

Suddenly Poirot, who was very sensitive, felt eyes watching him. He wheeled round. A girl was standing in the entrance of the French window—a small, sallow girl, with very black hair and suspicious eyes.

She came in, and as Poirot made a little bow she burst out abruptly, "Why have you come?"

Poirot did not reply. He merely raised his eyebrows.

"You are not a lawyer—no?" Her English was good, but not for a minute would anyone have taken her to be English.

"Why should I be a lawyer, mademoiselle?"

The girl stared at him sullenly. "I thought you might be. I thought you had come perhaps to say that she did not know what she was doing. I have heard of such things—the not due influence; that is what they call it, no? But that is not right. She wanted me to have the money, and I shall have it. If it is needful I shall have a lawyer of my own. The money is mine. She wrote it down so, and so it shall be." She looked ugly, her chin thrust out, her eyes gleaming.

The door opened and a tall woman entered and said, "Katrina."

The girl shrank, flushed, muttered something and went out through the window.

Poirot turned to face the newcomer who had so effectually dealt with the situation by uttering a single word. There had been authority in her voice, and contempt and a shade of well-bred irony. He realized at once that this was the owner of the house, Mary Delafontaine.

"M. Poirot? I wrote to you. You cannot have received my letter."

"Alas, I have been away from London."

"Oh, I see; that explains it. I must introduce myself. My name is Delafontaine. This is my husband. Miss Barrowby was my aunt."

Mr. Delafontaine had entered so quietly that his arrival had passed unnoticed. He was a tall man with grizzled hair and an indeterminate manner. He had a nervous way of fingering his chin. He looked often toward his wife, and it was plain that he expected her to take the lead in any conversation.

"I much regret that I intrude in the midst of your bereavement," said Hercule Poirot.

"I quite realize that it is not your fault," said Mrs. Delafontaine. "My aunt died on Tuesday evening. It was quite unexpected."

"Most unexpected," said Mr. Delafontaine. "Great blow." His eyes watched the window where the foreign girl had disappeared.

"I apologize," said Hercule Poirot. "And I withdraw." He moved a step toward the door.

"Half a sec," said Mr. Delafontaine. "You—er—had an appointment with Aunt Amelia, you say?"

*"Parfaitement."*

"Perhaps you will tell us about it," said his wife. "If there is anything we can do—"

"It was of a private nature," said Poirot. "I am a detective," he added simply.

Mr. Delafontaine knocked over a little china figure he was handling. His wife looked puzzled.

"A detective? And you had an appointment with auntie? But how extraordinary!" She stared at him. "Can't you tell us a little more, M. Poirot? It—it seems quite fantastic."

Poirot was silent for a moment. He chose his words with care.

"It is difficult for me, madame, to know what to do."

"Look here," said Mr. Delafontaine. "She didn't mention Russians, did she?"

"Russians?"

"Yes, you know—Bolshies, Reds, all that sort of thing."

"Don't be absurd, Henry," said his wife.

Mr. Delafontaine collapsed. "Sorry—sorry—I just wondered."

Mary Delafontaine looked frankly at Poirot. Her eyes were very blue—the color of forget-me-nots. "If you can tell us anything, M. Poirot, I should be glad if you would do so. I can assure you that I have a—a reason for asking."

Mr. Delafontaine looked alarmed. "Be careful, old girl—you know there may be nothing in it."

Again his wife quelled him with a glance. "Well, M. Poirot?"

Slowly, gravely, Hercule Poirot shook his head. He shook it with visible regret, but he shook it. "At present, madame," he said, "I fear I must say nothing."

He bowed, picked up his hat and moved to the door. Mary Delafontaine came with him into the hall. On the doorstep he paused and looked at her.

"You are fond of your garden, I think, madame?"

"I? Yes, I spend a lot of time gardening."

*"Je vous fait mes compliments."*

He bowed once more and strode down to the gate. As he passed out of it and turned to the right he glanced back and registered two impressions—a sallow face watching him from a first-floor window, and a man of erect and soldierly carriage pacing up and down on the opposite side of the street.

Hercule Poirot nodded to himself. *"Definitivement,"* he said. "There is a mouse in this hole! What move must the cat make now?"

His decision took him to the nearest post office. Here he put through a couple of telephone calls. The result seemed to be satisfactory. He bent his steps to Charman's Green police station, where he inquired for Inspector Sims.

Inspector Sims was a big, burly man with a hearty manner. "M. Poirot?" he inquired. "I thought so. I've just this minute had a telephone call through from the chief constable about you. He said you'd be dropping in. Come into my office."

The door shut, the inspector waved Poirot to one chair, settled himself in another, and turned a gaze of acute inquiry upon his visitor.

"You're very quick onto the mark, M. Poirot. Come to see us about this Rosebank case almost before we know it is a case. What put you onto it?"

Poirot drew out the letter he had received and handed it to the inspector. The latter read it with some interest.

"Interesting," he said. "The trouble is, it might mean so many things. Pity she couldn't have been a little more explicit. It would have helped us now."

"Or there might have been no need for help."

"You mean?"

"She might have been alive."

"You go as far as that, do you? H'm—I'm not sure you're wrong."

"I pray of you, inspector, recount to me the facts. I know nothing at all."

"That's easily done. Old lady was taken bad after dinner on Tuesday night. Very alarming. Convulsions—spasms—what not. They sent for the doctor. By the time he arrived she was dead. Idea was she'd died of a fit. Well, he didn't much like the look of things. He hemmed and hawed and put it with a bit of soft sawder, but he made it clear that he couldn't give a death certificate. And as far as the family go, that's where the matter stands. They're awaiting the result of the post-mortem. We've got a bit farther. The doctor gave us the tip right away—he and the police surgeon did the autopsy together—and the result is in no doubt whatever. The old lady died of a large dose of strychnine."

"Aha!"

"That's right. Very nasty bit of work. Point is, who gave it to her? It must have been administered very shortly before death. First idea was it was given to her in her food at dinner—but, frankly, that seems to be a washout. They had artichoke soup, served from a tureen, fish pie and apple tart."

" 'They' being?"

"Miss Barrowby, Mr. Delafontaine and Mrs. Delafontaine. Miss Barrowby had a kind of nurse-attendant—a half-Russian girl—but she didn't eat with the family. She had the remains as they came out from the dining room. There's a maid, but it was her night out. She left the soup on the stove and the fish pie in the oven, and the apple tart was cold. All three of them ate the same thing—and, apart from that, I don't think you could get strychnine down anyone's throat that way. Stuff's as bitter as gall. The doctor told me you could taste it in a solution of one in a thousand, or something like that."

"Coffee?"

"Coffee's more like it, but the old lady never took coffee."

"I see your point. Yes, it seems an insuperable difficulty. What did she drink at the meal?"

"Water."

"Worse and worse."

"Bit of a teaser, isn't it?"

"She had money, the old lady?"

"Very well to do, I imagine. Of course, we haven't got exact details yet. The Delafontaines are pretty badly off, from what I can make out. The old lady helped with the upkeep of the house."

Poirot smiled a little. He said, "So you suspect the Delafontaines. Which of them?"

"I don't exactly say I suspect either of them in particular. But there it is; they're her only near relations, and her death brings them a tidy sum of money, I've no doubt. We all know what human nature is!"

"Sometimes inhuman—yes, that is very true. And there was nothing else the old lady ate or drank?"

"Well, as a matter of fact—"

"Ah, *voilà!* I felt that you had something, as you say, up your sleeve—the soup, the fish pie, the apple tart—a *bêtise!* Now we come to the hub of the affair."

"I don't know about that. But as a matter of fact, the old girl took a cachet before meals. You know, not a pill or a tablet; one of those rice-paper things with a powder inside. Some perfectly harmless thing for the digestion."

"Admirable. Nothing is easier than to fill a cachet with strychnine and substitute it for one of the others. It slips down the throat with a drink of water and is not tasted."

"That's all right. The trouble is, the girl gave it to her."

"The Russian girl?"

"Yes. Katrina Rieger. She was a kind of lady-help, nurse-companion to Miss Barrowby. Fairly ordered about by her, too, I gather. Fetch this, fetch that, fetch the other, rub my back, pour out my medicine, run round to the chemist—all that sort of business. You know how it is with these old women—they mean to be kind, but what they need is a sort of slave!"

Poirot smiled.

"And there you are, you see," continued Inspector Sims. "It doesn't fit in what you might call nicely. Why should the girl poison her? Miss Barrowby dies and now the girl will be out of a job, and jobs aren't so easy to find—she's not trained or anything."

"Still," suggested Poirot, "if the box of cachets was left about, anyone in the house might have the opportunity."

"Naturally we're onto that, M. Poirot. I don't mind telling you we're making our inquiries—quiet like, if you understand me. When the prescription was last made up, where it was usually kept; patience and a lot of spade work—that's what will do the trick in the end. And then there's Miss Barrowby's solicitor. I'm having an interview with him tomorrow. And the bank manager. There's a lot to be done still."

Poirot rose. "A little favor, Inspector Sims; you will send me a little word how the affair marches. I would esteem it a great favor. Here is my telephone number."

"Why, certainly, M. Poirot. Two heads are better than one; and, besides, you ought to be in on this, having had that letter and all."

"You are too amiable, inspector." Politely, Poirot shook hands and took his leave.

He was called to the telephone on the following afternoon. "Is that M. Poirot? Inspector Sims here. Things are beginning to sit up and look pretty in that little matter you and I know of."

"In verity? Tell me, I pray of you."

"Well, here's item No. 1—and a pretty big item. Miss B. left a small legacy to her niece and everything else to K. In consideration of her great kindness and attention—that's the way it was put. That alters the complexion of things."

A picture rose swiftly in Poirot's mind. A sullen face and a passionate voice saying, "The money is mine. She wrote it down and so it shall be." The legacy would not come as a surprise to Katrina—she knew about it beforehand.

"Item No. 2," continued the voice of Inspector Sims. "Nobody but K. handled that cachet."

"You can be sure of that?"

"The girl herself doesn't deny it. What do you think of that?"

"Extremely interesting."

"We only want one thing more—evidence of how the strychnine came into her possession. That oughtn't to be difficult."

"But so far you haven't been successful?"

"I've barely started. The inquest was only this morning."

"What happened at it?"

"Adjourned for a week."

"And the young lady—K.?"

"I'm detaining her on suspicion. Don't want to run any risks. She might have some funny friends in the country who'd try to get her out of it."

"No," said Poirot. "I do not think she has any friends."

"Really? What makes you say that, M. Poirot?"

"It is just an idea of mine. There were no other 'items,' as you call them?"

"Nothing that's strictly relevant. Miss B. seems to have been monkeying about a bit with her shares lately—must have dropped quite a tidy sum. It's rather a funny business, one way and another, but I don't see how it affects the main issue—not at present, that is."

"No, perhaps you are right. Well, my best thanks to you. It was most amiable of you to ring me up."

"Not at all. I'm a man of my word. I could see you were interested. Who knows, you may be able to give me a helping hand before the end."

"That would give me great pleasure. It might help you, for instance, if I could lay my hand on a friend of the girl Katrina."

"I thought you said she hadn't got any friends?" said Inspector Sims, surprised.

"I was wrong," said Hercule Poirot. "She has one."

Before the inspector could ask a further question, Poirot had rung off.

With a serious face he wandered into the room where Miss Lemon sat at her typewriter. She raised her hands from the keys at her employer's approach and looked at him inquiringly.

"I want you," said Poirot, "to figure to yourself a little history."

Miss Lemon dropped her hands into her lap in a resigned manner. She enjoyed typing, paying bills, filing papers, and entering up engagements. To be asked to imagine herself in hypothetical situations bored her very much, but she accepted it as a disagreeable part of a duty.

"You are a Russian girl," began Poirot.

"Yes," said Miss Lemon, looking intensely British.

"You are alone and friendless in this country. You have reasons for not wishing to return to Russia. You are employed as a kind of drudge, nurse-attendant and companion to an old lady. You are meek and uncomplaining."

"Yes," said Miss Lemon obediently, but entirely failing to see herself being meek to any old lady under the sun.

"The old lady takes a fancy to you. She decides to leave her money to you. She tells you so." Poirot paused.

Miss Lemon said "Yes" again.

"And then the old lady finds out something; perhaps it is a matter of money—she may find that you have not been honest with her. Or it might be more grave still—a medicine that tasted different, some food that disagreed. Anyway, she begins to suspect you of something and she writes to a very famous detective—*enfin*, to the most famous detective—me! I am to call upon her shortly. And then, as you say, the dripping will be in the fire. The great thing is to act quickly. And so—before the great detective arrives—the old lady is dead. And the money comes to you. . . . Tell me, does that seem to you reasonable?"

"Quite reasonable," said Miss Lemon. "Quite reasonable for a Russian, that is. Personally, I should never take a post as a companion. I like my duties clearly defined. And of course I should not dream of murdering anyone."

Poirot sighed. "How I miss my friend Hastings. He had such an imagination. Such a romantic mind! It is true that he always imagined wrong—but that in itself was a guide."

Miss Lemon was silent. She had heard about Captain Hastings before, and was not interested. She looked longingly at the typewritten sheet in front of her.

"So it seems to you reasonable," mused Poirot.

"Doesn't it to you?"

"I am almost afraid it does," sighed Poirot.

The telephone rang and Miss Lemon went out of the room to answer it. She came back to say, "It's Inspector Sims again."

Poirot hurried to the instrument. " 'Allo, 'allo. What is that you say?"

Sims repeated his statement. "We've found a packet of strychnine in the girl's bedroom—tucked underneath the mattress. The sergeant's just come in with the news. That about clinches it, I think."

"Yes," said Poirot, "I think that clinches it." His voice had changed. It rang with sudden confidence.

When he had rung off, he sat down at his writing table and arranged the objects on it in a mechanical manner. He murmured to himself, "There was something wrong. I felt it—no, not felt. It must have been something I saw. *En avant*, the little gray cells. Ponder—reflect. Was everything logical and in order? The girl—her anxiety about the money; Mme. Delafontaine; her husband—his suggestion of Russians— imbecile, but he is an imbecile; the room; the garden—ah! Yes, the garden."

He sat up very stiff. The green light shone in his eyes. He sprang up and went into the adjoining room.

"Miss Lemon, will you have the kindness to leave what you are doing and make an investigation for me?"

"An investigation, M. Poirot? I'm afraid I'm not very good—"

Poirot interrupted her. "You said one day that you knew all about tradesmen."

"Certainly I do," said Miss Lemon with confidence.

"Then the matter is simple. You are to go to Charman's Green and you are to discover a fishmonger."

"A fishmonger?" asked Miss Lemon, surprised.

"Precisely. The fishmonger who supplied Rosebank with fish. When you have found him you will ask him a certain question."

He handed her a slip of paper. Miss Lemon took it, noted its contents without interest, then nodded and slipped the lid on her typewriter.

"We will go to Charman's Green together," said Poirot. "You to the fishmonger and I to the police station. It will take us but half an hour from Baker Street."

On arrival at his destination, he was greeted by the surprised Inspector Sims. "Well, this is quick work, M. Poirot. I was talking to you on the phone only an hour ago."

"I have a request to make to you; that you allow me to see this girl Katrina—what is her name?"

"Katrina Rieger. Well, I don't suppose there's any objection to that."
The girl Katrina looked even more sallow and sullen than ever.

Poirot spoke to her very gently. "Mademoiselle, I want you to believe that I am not your enemy. I want you to tell me the truth."

Her eyes snapped defiantly. "I have told the truth. To everyone I have told the truth! If the old lady was poisoned, it was not I who poisoned her. It is all a mistake. You wish to prevent me having the money." Her voice was rasping. She looked, he thought, like a miserable little cornered rat.

"Tell me about this cachet, mademoiselle," M. Poirot went on. "Did no one handle it but you?"

"I have said so, have I not? They were made up at the chemist's that afternoon. I brought them back with me in my bag—that was just before supper. I opened the box and gave Miss Barrowby one with a glass of water."

"No one touched them but you?"

"No." A cornered rat—with courage!

"And Miss Barrowby had for supper only what we have been told. The soup, the fish pie, the tart?"

"Yes." A hopeless "yes"—dark, smoldering eyes that saw no light anywhere.

Poirot patted her shoulder. "Be of good courage, mademoiselle. There may yet be freedom—yes, and money—a life of ease."

She looked at him suspiciously.

As he went out Sims said to him, "I didn't quite get what you said through the telephone—something about the girl having a friend."

"She has one. Me!" said Hercule Poirot, and had left the police station before the inspector could pull his wits together.

At the Green Cat tearooms, Miss Lemon did not keep her employer waiting. She went straight to the point.

"The man's name is Rudge, in the High Street, and you were quite right. A dozen and a half exactly. I've made a note of what he said." She handed it to him.

"Arrr." It was a deep, rich sound like the purr of a cat.

Hercule Poirot betook himself to Rosebank. As he stood in the front garden, the sun setting behind him, Mary Delafontaine came out to him.

"M. Poirot?" Her voice sounded surprised. "You have come back?"

"Yes, I have come back." He paused and then said, "When I first came here, madame, the children's nursery rhyme came into my head:

> *Mistress Mary, quite contrary,*
> *How does your garden grow?*
> *With cockle-shells, and silver bells,*
> *And pretty maids all in a row.*

Only they are not *cockle* shells, are they, madame? They are *oyster* shells." His hand pointed.

He heard her catch her breath and then stay very still. Her eyes asked a question.

He nodded. *"Mais, oui,* I know! The maid left the dinner ready—she will swear and Katrina will swear that that is all you had. Only you and your husband know that you brought back a dozen and a half oysters—a little treat *pour la bonne tante.* So easy to put the strychnine in an oyster. It is swallowed—*comme ça!* But there remain the shells—they must not go in the bucket. The maid would see them. And so you thought of making an edging of them to a bed. But there were not enough—the edging is not complete. The effect is bad—it spoils the symmetry of the otherwise charming garden. Those few oyster shells struck an alien note—they displeased my eye on my first visit."

Mary Delafontaine said, "I suppose you guessed from the letter. I knew she had written—but I didn't know how much she'd said."

Poirot answered evasively, "I knew at least that it was a family matter. If it had been a question of Katrina there would have been no point in hushing things up. I understand that you or your husband handled Miss Barrowby's securities to your own profit, and that she found out—"

Mary Delafontaine nodded. "We've done it for years—a little here and there. I never realized she was sharp enough to find out. And then I learned she had sent for a detective; and I found out, too, that she was leaving her money to Katrina—that miserable little creature!"

"And so the strychnine was put in Katrina's bedroom? I comprehend. You save yourself and your husband from what I may discover, and you saddle an innocent child with murder. Had you no pity, madame?"

Mary Delafontaine shrugged her shoulders—her blue forget-me-not eyes looked into Poirot's. He remembered the perfection of her acting the first day he had come and the bungling attempts of her husband. A woman above the average—but inhuman.

She said, "Pity? For that miserable intriguing little rat?" Her contempt rang out.

Hercule Poirot said slowly, "I think, madame, that you have cared in your life for two things only. One is your husband."

He saw her lips tremble.

"And the other—is your garden."

He looked round him. His glance seemed to apologize to the flowers for that which he had done and was about to do.

# Yellow Iris

HERCULE Poirot stretched out his feet towards the electric radiator set in the wall. Its neat arrangement of red-hot bars pleased his orderly mind.

"A coal fire," he mused to himself, "was always shapeless and haphazard! Never did it achieve the symmetry."

The telephone bell rang. Poirot rose, glancing at his watch as he did so. The time was close on half-past eleven. He wondered who was ringing him up at this hour. It might, of course, be a wrong number.

"And it might," he murmured to himself with a whimsical smile, "be a millionaire newspaper proprietor, found dead in the library of his country house, with a spotted orchid clasped in his left hand and a page torn from a cookery book pinned to his breast."

Smiling at the pleasing conceit, he lifted the receiver.

Immediately a voice spoke—a soft husky woman's voice with a kind of desperate urgency about it.

*"Is that M. Hercule Poirot? Is that M. Hercule Poirot?"*

"Hercule Poirot speaks."

*"M. Poirot—can you come at once—at once—I'm in danger—in great danger—I know it. . . ."*

Poirot said sharply:

"Who are you? Where are you speaking from?"

The voice came more faintly but with an even greater urgency.

*"At once . . . it's life or death. . . . The Jardin des Cygnes . . . at once . . . table with yellow irises. . . ."*

There was a pause—a queer kind of gasp—the line went dead.

Hercule Poirot hung up. His face was puzzled. He murmured between his teeth:

"There is something here very curious."

In the doorway of the Jardin des Cygnes, fat Luigi hurried forward.

"Buona sera, M. Poirot. You desire a table—yes?"

"No, no, my good Luigi. I seek here for some friends. I will look

359

round—perhaps they are not here yet. Ah, let me see, that table there in the corner with the yellow irises—a little question by the way, if it is not indiscreet. On all the other tables there are tulips—pink tulips—why on that one table do you have yellow iris?"

Luigi shrugged his expressive shoulders.

"A command, Monsieur! A special order! Without doubt, the favorite flowers of one of the ladies. That table, it is the table of Mr. Barton Russell—an American—immensely rich."

"Aha, one must study the whims of the ladies, must one not, Luigi?"

"Monsieur has said it," said Luigi.

"I see at that table an acquaintance of mine. I must go and speak to him."

Poirot skirted his way delicately round the dancing floor on which couples were revolving. The table in question was set for six, but it had at the moment only one occupant, a young man who was thoughtfully, and it seemed pessimistically, drinking champagne.

He was not at all the person that Poirot had expected to see. It seemed impossible to associate the idea of danger or melodrama with any party of which Tony Chapell was a member.

Poirot paused delicately by the table.

"Ah, it is, is it not, my friend Anthony Chapell?"

"By all that's wonderful—Poirot the police hound!" cried the young man. "Not Anthony, my dear fellow—Tony to friends!"

He drew out a chair.

"Come, sit with me. Let us discourse of crime! Let us go further and drink to crime." He poured champagne into an empty glass. "But what are you doing in this haunt of song and dance and merriment, my dear Poirot? We have no bodies here, positively not a single body to offer you."

Poirot sipped the champagne.

"You seem very gay, *mon cher?*"

"Gay? I am steeped in misery—wallowing in gloom. Tell me, you hear this tune they are playing. You recognize it?"

Poirot hazarded cautiously:

"Something perhaps to do with your baby having left you?"

"Not a bad guess," said the young man, "but wrong for once. 'There's nothing like love for making you miserable!' That's what it's called."

"Aha?"

"My favorite tune," said Tony Chapell mournfully. "And my favorite restaurant and my favorite band—and my favorite girl's here and she's dancing it with somebody else."

"Hence the melancholy?" said Poirot.

"Exactly. Pauline and I, you see, have had what the vulgar call words. That is to say, she's had ninety-five words to five of mine out of every hundred. My five are: *'But, darling—I can explain.'*—Then she starts in on her ninety-five again and we get no further. I think," added Tony sadly, "that I shall poison myself."

"Pauline?" murmured Poirot.

"Pauline Weatherby. Barton Russell's young sister-in-law. Young, lovely, disgustingly rich. Tonight Barton Russell gives a party. You know him? Big Business, clean-shaven American—full of pep and personality. His wife was Pauline's sister."

"And who else is there at this party?"

"You'll meet 'em in a minute when the music stops. There's Lola Valdez—you know, the South American dancer in the new show at the Metropole, and there's Stephen Carter. D'you know Carter—he's in the diplomatic service. Very hush-hush. Known as silent Stephen. Sort of man who says, 'I am not at liberty to state, etc., etc.' Hullo, here they come."

Poirot rose. He was introduced to Barton Russell, to Stephen Carter, to Señora Lola Valdez, a dark and luscious creature, and to Pauline Weatherby, very young, very fair, with eyes like cornflowers.

Barton Russell said:

"What, is this the great M. Hercule Poirot? I am indeed pleased to meet you, sir. Won't you sit down and join us? That is, unless—"

Tony Chapell broke in.

"He's got an appointment with a body, I believe, or is it an absconding financier, or the Rajah of Borrioboolagah's great ruby?"

"Ah, my friend, do you think I am never off duty? Can I not, for once, seek only to amuse myself?"

"Perhaps you've got an appointment with Carter here. The latest from Geneva. International situation now acute. The stolen plans *must* be found or war will be declared tomorrow!"

Pauline Weatherby said cuttingly:

"Must you be so *completely* idiotic, Tony?"

"Sorry, Pauline."

Tony Chapell relapsed into crestfallen silence.

"How severe you are, mademoiselle."

"I hate people who play the fool all the time!"

"I must be careful, I see. I must converse only of serious matters."

"Oh, no, M. Poirot. I didn't mean you."

She turned a smiling face to him and asked:

"Are you really a kind of Sherlock Holmes and do wonderful deductions?"

"Ah, the deductions—they are not so easy in real life. But shall I try? Now then, I deduce—that yellow irises are your favorite flowers?"

"Quite wrong, M. Poirot. Lilies of the valley or roses."

Poirot sighed.

"A failure. I will try once more. This evening, not very long ago, you telephoned to someone."

Pauline laughed and clapped her hands.

"Quite right."

"It was not long after you arrived here?"

"Right again. I telephoned the minute I got inside the doors."

"Ah—that is not so good. You telephoned *before* you came to this table?"

"Yes."

"Decidedly very bad."

"Oh, no, I think it was very clever of you. How did you know I had telephoned?"

"That, mademoiselle, is the great detective's secret. And the person to whom you telephoned—does the name begin with a P—or perhaps with an H?"

Pauline laughed.

"Quite wrong. I telephoned to my maid to post some frightfully important letters that I'd never sent off. Her name's Louise."

"I am confused—quite confused."

The music began again.

"What about it, Pauline?" asked Tony.

"I don't think I want to dance again so soon, Tony."

"Isn't that too bad?" said Tony bitterly to the world at large.

Poirot murmured to the South American girl on his other side:

"Señora, I would not dare to ask you to dance with me. I am too much of the antique."

Lola Valdez said:

"Ah, it ees nonsense that you talk there! You are steel young. Your hair, eet is still black!"

Poirot winced slightly.

"Pauline, as your brother-in-law and your guardian," Barton Russell spoke heavily, "I'm just going to force you onto the floor! This one's a waltz and a waltz is about the only dance I really can do."

"Why, of course, Barton, we'll take the floor right away."

"Good girl, Pauline, that's swell of you."

They went off together. Tony tipped back his chair. Then he looked at Stephen Carter.

"Talkative little fellow, aren't you, Carter?" he remarked. "Help to make a party go with your merry chatter, eh, what?"

"Really, Chapell, I don't know what you mean?"

"Oh, you don't—don't you?" Tony mimicked him.

"My dear fellow."

"Drink, man, drink, if you won't talk."

"No, thanks."

"Then I will."

Stephen Carter shrugged his shoulders.

"Excuse me, must just speak to a fellow I know over there. Fellow I was with at Eton."

Stephen Carter got up and walked to a table a few places away.

Tony said gloomily:

"Somebody ought to drown old Etonians at birth."

Hercule Poirot was still being gallant to the dark beauty beside him.

He murmured:

"I wonder, may I ask, what are the favorite flowers of mademoiselle?"

"Ah, now, why ees eet you want to know?"

Lola was arch.

"Mademoiselle, if I send flowers to a lady, I am particular that they should be flowers she likes."

"'That ees very charming of you, M. Poirot. I weel tell you—I adore the big dark red carnations—or the dark red roses."

"Superb—yes, superb! You do not, then, like yellow flowers—yellow irises?"

"Yellow flowers—no—they do not accord with my temperament."

"How wise. . . . Tell me, mademoiselle, did you ring up a friend tonight, since you arrived here?"

"I? Ring up a friend? No, what a curious question!"

"Ah, but I, I am a very curious man."

"I'm sure you are." She rolled her dark eyes at him. "A vairy *dan*gerous man."

"No, no, not dangerous; say, a man who may be useful—in danger! You understand?"

Lola giggled. She showed white even teeth.

"No, no," she laughed. "You are dangerous."

Hercule Poirot sighed.

"I see that you do not understand. All this is very strange."

Tony came out of a fit of abstraction and said suddenly:

"Lola, what about a spot of swoop and dip? Come along."

"I weel come—yes. Since M. Poirot ees not brave enough!"

Tony put an arm round her and remarked over his shoulder to Poirot as they glided off:

"You can meditate on crime yet to come, old boy!"

Poirot said, "It is profound what you say there. Yes, it is profound. . . ."

He sat meditatively for a minute or two, then he raised a finger. Luigi came promptly, his wide Italian face wreathed in smiles.

*"Mon vieux,"* said Poirot. "I need some information."

"Always at your service, monsieur."

"I desire to know how many of these people at this table here have used the telephone tonight?"

"I can tell you, monsieur. The young lady, the one in white, she telephoned at once when she got here. Then she went to leave her cloak and while she was doing that the other lady came out of the cloakroom and went into the telephone box."

"So the señora *did* telephone! Was that *before* she came into the restaurant?"

"Yes, monsieur."

"Anyone else?"

"No, monsieur."

"All this, Luigi, gives me furiously to think!"

"Indeed, monsieur."

"Yes. I think, Luigi, that *tonight of all nights,* I must have my wits about me! *Something* is going to happen, Luigi, and I am not at all sure what it is."

"Anything I can do, monsieur—"

Poirot made a sign. Luigi slipped discreetly away. Stephen Carter was returning to the table.

"We are still deserted, Mr. Carter," said Poirot.

"Oh—er—quite," said the other.

"You know Mr. Barton Russell well?"

"Yes, known him a good while."

"His sister-in-law, little Miss Weatherby, is very charming."

"Yes, pretty girl."

"You know her well, too?"

"Quite."

"Oh, quite, quite," said Poirot.

Carter stared at him.

The music stopped and the others returned.

Barton Russell said to a waiter:

"Another bottle of champagne—quickly."

Then he raised his glass.

"See here, folks. I'm going to ask you to drink a toast. To tell you the truth, there's an idea back of this little party tonight. As you know, I'd ordered a table for six. There were only five of us. That gave us an empty place. Then, by a very strange coincidence, M. Hercule Poirot happened to pass by and I asked him to join our party.

"You don't know yet what an apt coincidence that was. You see that empty seat tonight represents a lady—the lady in whose memory this party is being given. This party, ladies and gentlemen, is being held in memory of my dear wife—Iris—who died exactly four years ago on this very date!"

There was a startled movement round the table. Barton Russell, his face quietly impassive, raised his glass.

"I'll ask you to drink to her memory. *Iris!*"

"Iris?" said Poirot sharply.

He looked at the flowers. Barton Russell caught his glance and gently nodded his head.

There were little murmurs round the table.

"Iris—Iris. . . ."

Everyone looked startled and uncomfortable.

Barton Russell went on, speaking with his slow, monotonous American intonation, each word coming out weightily.

"It may seem odd to you all that I should celebrate the anniversary of a death in this way—by a supper party in a fashionable restaurant. But I have a reason—yes, I have a reason. For M. Poirot's benefit, I'll explain."

He turned his head towards Poirot.

"Four years ago tonight, M. Poirot, there was a supper party held in New York. At it were my wife and myself, Mr. Stephen Carter who was attached to the Embassy in Washington, Mr. Anthony Chapell who had been a guest in our house for some weeks, and Señora Valdez who was at that time enchanting New York City with her dancing. Little Pauline here"—he patted her shoulder—"was only sixteen but she came to the supper party as a special treat. You remember, Pauline?"

"I remember—yes." Her voice shook a little.

"M. Poirot, on that night a tragedy happened. There was a roll of drums and the cabaret started. The lights went down—all but a spotlight in the middle of the floor. When the lights went up again, M. Poirot, my wife was seen to have fallen forward on the table. She was dead—stone dead. There was potassium cyanide found in the dregs of her wine glass, and the remains of the packet was discovered in her handbag."

"She had committed suicide?" said Poirot.

"That was the accepted verdict. . . . It broke me up, M. Poirot. There was, perhaps, a possible reason for such an action—the police thought so. I accepted their decision."

He pounded suddenly on the table.

"But I was not satisfied. . . . No, for four years I've been thinking and brooding—and I'm not satisfied: I don't believe Iris killed herself. I believe, M. Poirot, that she was murdered—by one of those people at the table."

"Look here, sir—"

Tony Chapell half sprung to his feet.

"Be quiet, Tony," said Russell. "I haven't finished. One of them did it—I'm sure of that now. Someone who, under cover of the darkness, slipped the half emptied packet of cyanide into her handbag. I think I know which of them it was. I mean to know the truth—"

Lola's voice rose sharply.

"You are mad—crazee—who would have harmed her? No, you are mad. Me, I will not stay—"

She broke off. There was a roll of drums.

Barton Russell said:

"The cabaret. Afterwards we will go on with this. Stay where you are, all of you. I've got to go and speak to the dance band. Little arrangement I've made with them."

He got up and left the table.

"Extraordinary business," commented Carter. "Man's mad."

"He ees crazee, yes," said Lola.

The lights were lowered.

"For two pins I'd clear out," said Tony.

"No!" Pauline spoke sharply. Then she murmured, "Oh, dear—oh, dear—"

"What is it, mademoiselle?" murmured Poirot.

She answered almost in a whisper.

"It's horrible! It's just like it was that night—"

"Sh! Sh!" said several people.

Poirot lowered his voice.

"A little word in your ear." He whispered, then patted her shoulder. "All will be well," he assured her.

"My God, listen," cried Lola.

"What is it, señora?"

"It's the same tune—the same song that they played that night in New York. Barton Russell must have fixed it. I don't like this."

"Courage—courage—"

There was a fresh hush.

A girl walked out into the middle of the floor, a coal black girl with rolling eyeballs and white glistening teeth. She began to sing in a deep hoarse voice—a voice that was curiously moving.

> *I've forgotten you*
> *I never think of you*
> *The way you walked*
> *The way you talked*
> *The things you used to say*
> *I've forgotten you*
> *I never think of you*
> *I couldn't say*
> *For sure today*

*Whether your eyes were blue or gray*
*I've forgotten you*
*I never think of you.*

*I'm through*
*Thinking of you*
*I tell you I'm through*
*Thinking of you . . .*
*You . . . you . . . you. . . .*

The sobbing tune, the deep golden Negro voice had a powerful effect. It hypnotized—cast a spell. Even the waiters felt it. The whole room stared at her, hypnotized by the thick cloying emotion she distilled.

A waiter passed softly round the table filling up glasses, murmuring "champagne" in an undertone but all attention was on the one glowing spot of light—the black woman whose ancestors came from Africa, singing in her deep voice:

*I've forgotten you*
*I never think of you*

*Oh, what a lie*
*I shall think of you, think of you, think of you*

*Till I die. . . .*

The applause broke out frenziedly. The lights went up. Barton Russell came back and slipped into his seat.

"She's great, that girl—" cried Tony.

But his words were cut short by a low cry from Lola.

*"Look—look. . . ."*

And then they all saw. Pauline Weatherby dropped forward onto the table.

Lola cried:

"She's dead—just like Iris—like Iris in New York."

Poirot sprang from his seat, signing to the others to keep back. He bent over the huddled form, very gently lifted a limp hand and felt for a pulse.

His face was white and stern. The others watched him. They were paralyzed, held in a trance.

Slowly, Poirot nodded his head.

"Yes, she is dead—*la pauvre petite*. And I sitting by her! Ah! but this time the murderer shall not escape."

Barton Russell, his face gray, muttered:

"Just like Iris. . . . She saw something—Pauline saw something that night—Only she wasn't sure—she told me she wasn't sure. . . . We must get the police. . . . Oh, God, little Pauline."

Poirot said:

"Where is her glass?" He raised it to his nose. "Yes, I can smell the cyanide. A smell of bitter almonds . . . the same method, the same poison. . . ."

He picked up her handbag.

"Let us look in her handbag."

Barton Russell cried out:

"You don't believe this is suicide, too? Not on your life."

"Wait," Poirot commanded. "No, there is nothing here. The lights went up, you see, too quickly, the murderer had not time. Therefore, the poison is still on him."

"Or her," said Carter.

He was looking at Lola Valdez.

She spat out:

"What do you mean—what do you say? That I killed her—eet is not true—not true—why should I do such a thing!"

"You had rather a fancy for Barton Russell yourself in New York. That's the gossip I heard. Argentine beauties are notoriously jealous."

"That ees a pack of lies. And I do not come from the Argentine. I come from Peru. Ah—I spit upon you. I—" She relapsed into Spanish.

"I demand silence," cried Poirot. "It is for me to speak."

Barton Russell said heavily:

"Everyone must be searched."

Poirot said calmly:

"*Non, non,* it is not necessary."

"What d'you mean, not necessary?"

"I, Hercule Poirot, know. I see with the eyes of the mind. And I will speak! M. Carter, *will you show us the packet in your breast pocket?*"

"There's nothing in my pocket. What the hell—"

"Tony, my good friend, if you will be so obliging."

Carter cried out:

"Damn you—"

Tony flipped the packet neatly out before Carter could defend himself.

"There you are, M. Poirot, just as you said!"

"It's a damned lie," cried Carter.

Poirot picked up the packet, read the label.

"Cyanide of potassium. The case is complete."

Barton Russell's voice came thickly.

"Carter! I always thought so. Iris was in love with you. She wanted to go away with you. You didn't want a scandal for the sake of your precious career so you poisoned her. You'll hang for this, you dirty dog."

"Silence!" Poirot's voice rang out, firm and authoritative. "This is not finished yet. I, Hercule Poirot, have something to say. My friend here, Tony Chapell, he says to me when I arrive, that I have come in search of crime. That, it is partly true. There *was* crime in my mind—but it was to prevent a crime that I came. And I have prevented it. The murderer, he planned well—but Hercule Poirot he was one move ahead. He had to think fast, and to whisper quickly in mademoiselle's ear when the lights went down. She is very quick and clever, Mademoiselle Pauline, she played her part well. Mademoiselle, will you be so kind as to show us that you are not dead after all?"

Pauline sat up. She gave an unsteady laugh.

"Resurrection of Pauline," she said.

"Pauline—darling."

"Tony!"

"My sweet."

"Angel."

Barton Russell gasped.

"I—I don't understand. . . ."

"I will help you to understand, Mr. Barton Russell. Your plan has miscarried."

"My plan?"

"Yes, your plan. Who was the only man who had an alibi during the darkness? The man who left the table—you, Mr. Barton Russell. But you returned to it under cover of the darkness, circling round it, with a champagne bottle, filling up glasses, putting cyanide in Pauline's glass and dropping the half empty packet in Carter's pocket as you bent over him to remove a glass. Oh, yes, it is easy to play the part of a waiter in darkness when the attention of everyone is elsewhere. That was the real reason for your party tonight. The safest place to commit a murder is in the middle of a crowd."

"What the—why the hell should I want to kill Pauline?"

"It might be, perhaps, a question of money. Your wife left you guardian to her sister. You mentioned that fact tonight. Pauline is twenty. At twenty-one or on her marriage you would have to render an account of your stewardship. I suggest that you could not do that. You have speculated with it. I do not know, Mr. Barton Russell, whether you killed your wife in the same way, or whether her suicide suggested the idea of this crime to you, but I do know that tonight you have been guilty of attempted murder. It rests with Miss Pauline whether you are prosecuted for that."

"No," said Pauline. "He can get out of my sight and out of this country. I don't want a scandal."

"You had better go quickly, Mr. Barton Russell, and I advise you to be careful in future."

Barton Russell got up, his face working.

"To hell with you, you interfering little Belgian jackanapes."

He strode out angrily.

Pauline sighed.

"M. Poirot, you've been wonderful. . . ."

"You, mademoiselle, you have been the marvelous one. To pour away the champagne, to act the dead body so prettily."

"Ugh," she shivered, "you give me the creeps."

He said gently:

"It was you who telephoned me, was it not?"

"Yes."

"Why?"

"I don't know. I was worried and—frightened without knowing quite why I was frightened. Barton told me he was having this party to commemorate Iris's death. I realized he had some scheme on—but he wouldn't tell me what it was. He looked so—so queer and so excited that I felt something terrible might happen—only of course I never dreamed that he meant to—to get rid of *me.*"

"And so, mademoiselle?"

"I'd heard people talking about you. I thought if I could only get you here perhaps it would stop anything happening. I thought that being a—a foreigner—if I rang up and pretended to be in danger and—and made it sound mysterious—"

"You thought the melodrama, it would attract me? That is what puzzled me. The message itself—definitely it was what you call 'bogus'—it did not ring true. But the fear in the voice—that was real. Then I came—and you denied very categorically having sent me a message."

"I had to. Besides, I didn't want you to know it was me."

"Ah, but I was fairly sure of that! Not at first. But I soon realized that the only two people who could know about the yellow irises on the table were you or Mr. Barton Russell."

Pauline nodded.

"I heard him ordering them to be put on the table," she explained. "That, and his ordering a table for six when I knew only five were coming, made me suspect—"

She stopped, biting her lip.

"What did you suspect, mademoiselle?"

She said slowly:

"I was afraid—of something happening—to Mr. Carter."

Stephen Carter cleared his throat. Unhurriedly but quite decisively he rose from the table.

"Er—h'm—I have to—er—thank you, Mr. Poirot. I owe you a great deal. You'll excuse me, I'm sure, if I leave you. Tonight's happenings have been—rather upsetting."

Looking after his retreating figure, Pauline said violently:

"I hate him. I've always thought it was—because of him that Iris killed herself. Or perhaps—Barton killed her. Oh, it's all so hateful. . . ."

Poirot said gently:

"Forget, mademoiselle . . . forget. . . . Let the past go. . . . Think only of the present. . . ."

Pauline murmured, "Yes—you're right. . . ."

Poirot turned to Lola Valdez.

"Señora, as the evening advances I become more brave. If you would dance with me now—"

"Oh, yes, indeed. You are—you arc ze cat's whiskers, M. Poirot. I inseest on dancing with you."

"You are too kind, señora."

Tony and Pauline were left. They leant towards each other across the table.

"Darling Pauline."

"Oh, Tony, I've been such a nasty, spiteful, spitfiring little cat to you all day. Can you ever forgive me?"

"Angel! This is Our Tune again. Let's dance."

They danced off, smiling at each other and humming softly:

> *There's nothing like Love for making you miserable*
> *There's nothing like Love for making you blue*
> *Depressed*
> *Possessed*
> *Sentimental*
> *Temperamental*
> *There's nothing like Love*
> *For getting you down.*
>
> *There's nothing like Love for driving you crazy*
> *There's nothing like Love for making you mad*
> *Abusive*
> *Allusive*
> *Suicidal*
> *Homicidal*
> *There's nothing like Love*
> *There's nothing like Love. . . .*

# The Dream

**H**ERCULE Poirot gave the house a steady appraising glance. His eyes wandered a moment to its surroundings, the shops, the big factory building on the right, the blocks of cheap mansion flats opposite.

Then once more his eyes returned to Northway House, relic of an earlier age—an age of space and leisure, when green fields had surrounded its well-bred arrogance. Now it was an anachronism, submerged and forgotten in the hectic sea of modern London, and not one man in fifty could have told you where it stood.

Furthermore, very few people could have told you to whom it belonged, though its owner's name would have been recognized as one of the world's richest men. But money can quench publicity as well as flaunt it. Benedict Farley, that eccentric millionaire, chose not to advertise his choice of residence. He himself was rarely seen, seldom making a public appearance. From time to time he appeared at board meetings, his lean figure, beaked nose, and rasping voice easily dominating the assembled directors. Apart from that, he was just a well-known figure of legend. There were his strange meannesses, his incredible generosities, as well as more personal details—his famous patchwork dressing gown, now reputed to be twenty-eight years old, his invariable diet of cabbage soup and caviar, his hatred of cats. All these things the public knew.

Hercule Poirot knew them also. It was all he did know of the man he was about to visit. The letter which was in his coat pocket told him little more.

After surveying this melancholy landmark of a past age for a minute or two in silence, he walked up the steps to the front door and pressed the bell, glancing as he did so at the neat wristwatch which had at last replaced an earlier favorite—the large turnip-faced watch of earlier days. Yes, it was exactly nine-thirty. As ever, Hercule Poirot was exact to the minute.

The door opened after just the right interval. A perfect specimen of the genus butler stood outlined against the lighted hall.

"Mr. Benedict Farley?" asked Hercule Poirot.

The impersonal glance surveyed him from head to foot, inoffensively but effectively.

*"En gros et en détail,"* thought Hercule Poirot to himself with appreciation.

"You have an appointment, sir?" asked the suave voice.

"Yes."

"Your name, sir?"

"M. Hercule Poirot."

The butler bowed and drew back. Hercule Poirot entered the house. The butler closed the door behind him.

But there was yet one more formality before the deft hands took hat and stick from the visitor.

"You will excuse me, sir. I was to ask for a letter."

With deliberation Poirot took from his pocket the folded letter and handed it to the butler. The latter gave it a mere glance, then returned it with a bow. Hercule Poirot returned it to his pocket. Its contents were simple.

Northway House, W.8.

M. HERCULE POIROT.

DEAR SIR,

Mr. Benedict Farley would like to have the benefit of your advice. If convenient to yourself he would be glad if you would call upon him at the above address at 9:30 tomorrow (Thursday) evening.

Yours truly,

HUGO CORNWORTHY
(Secretary).

P.S.—Please bring this letter with you.

Deftly the butler relieved Poirot of hat, stick, and overcoat. He said:

"Will you please come up to Mr. Cornworthy's room?"

He led the way up the broad staircase. Poirot followed him, looking with appreciation at such *objets d'art* as were of an opulent and florid nature! His taste in art was always somewhat bourgeois.

On the first floor the butler knocked on a door.

Hercule Poirot's eyebrows rose very slightly. It was the first jarring note. For the best butlers do not knock at doors—and yet indubitably this was a first-class butler!

It was, so to speak, the first intimation of contact with the eccentricity of a millionaire.

A voice from within called out something. The butler threw open the door. He announced (and again Poirot sensed the deliberate departure from orthodoxy):

"The gentleman you are expecting, sir."

Poirot passed into the room. It was a fair-sized room, very plainly furnished in a workmanlike fashion. Filing cabinets, books of reference, a couple of easy chairs, and a large and imposing desk covered with neatly docketed papers. The corners of the room were dim, for the only light came from a big green-shaded reading lamp which stood on a small table by the arm of one of the easy chairs. It was placed so as to cast its full light on anyone approaching from the door. Hercule Poirot blinked a little, realizing that the lamp bulb was at least 150 watts. In the armchair sat a thin figure in a patchwork dressing gown—Benedict Farley. His head was stuck forward in a characteristic attitude, his beaked nose projecting like that of a bird. A crest of white hair like that of a cockatoo rose above his forehead. His eyes glittered behind thick lenses as he peered suspiciously at his visitor.

"Hey," he said at last—and his voice was shrill and harsh, with a rasping note in it. "So you're Hercule Poirot, hey?"

"At your service," said Poirot politely and bowed, one hand on the back of the chair.

"Sit down—sit down," said the old man testily.

Hercule Poirot sat down—in the full glare of the lamp. From behind it the old man seemed to be studying him attentively.

"How do I know you're Hercule Poirot—hey?" he demanded fretfully. "Tell me that—hey?"

Once more Poirot drew the letter from his pocket and handed it to Farley.

"Yes," admitted the millionaire grudgingly. "That's it. That's what I got Cornworthy to write." He folded it up and tossed it back. "So you're the fellow, are you?"

With a little wave of his hand Poirot said:

"I assure you there is no deception!"

Benedict Farley chuckled suddenly.

"That's what the conjuror says before he takes the goldfish out of the hat! Saying that is part of the trick, you know."

Poirot did not reply. Farley said suddenly:

"Think I'm a suspicious old man, hey? So I am. Don't trust anybody! That's my motto. Can't trust anybody when you're rich. No, no, it doesn't do."

"You wished," Poirot hinted gently, "to consult me?"

The old man nodded.

"That's right. Always buy the best. That's my motto. Go to the expert and don't count the cost. You'll notice, M. Poirot, I haven't asked you your fee. I'm not going to! Send me in the bill later—*I* shan't cut up rough over it. Damned fools at the dairy thought they could charge me two and nine for eggs when two and seven's the market price— lot of swindlers! I won't be swindled. But the man at the top's different. He's worth the money. I'm at the top myself—I know."

Hercule Poirot made no reply. He listened attentively, his head poised a little on one side.

Behind his impassive exterior he was conscious of a feeling of disappointment. He could not exactly put his finger on it. So far Benedict Farley had run true to type—that is, he had conformed to the popular idea of himself; and yet—Poirot was disappointed.

"The man," he said disgustedly to himself, "is a mountebank—nothing but a mountebank!"

He had known other millionaires, eccentric men too, but in nearly every case he had been conscious of a certain force, an inner energy that had commanded his respect. If they had worn a patchwork dressing gown, it would have been because they liked wearing such a dressing gown. But the dressing-gown of Benedict Farley, or so it seemed to Poirot, was essentially a stage property. And the man himself was essentially stagey. Every word he spoke was uttered, so Poirot felt assured, sheerly for effect.

He repeated again unemotionally, "You wished to consult me, Mr. Farley?"

Abruptly the millionaire's manner changed.

He leaned forward. His voice dropped to a croak.

"Yes. Yes . . . I want to hear what you've got to say—what you think. . . . Go to the top! That's my way! The best doctor—the best detective—it's between the two of them."

"As yet, monsieur, I do not understand."

"Naturally," snapped Farley. "I haven't begun to tell you."

He leaned forward once more and shot out an abrupt question.

"What do you know, M. Poirot, about dreams?"

The little man's eyebrows rose. Whatever he had expected, it was not this.

"For that, Monsieur Farley, I should recommend Napoleon's *Book of Dreams*—or the latest practicing psychologist from Harley Street."

Benedict Farley said soberly, "I've tried both. . . ."

There was a pause, then the millionaire spoke, at first almost in a whisper, then with a voice growing higher and higher.

"It's the same dream—night after night. And I'm afraid, I tell you—

I'm afraid. . . . It's always the same. I'm sitting in my room next door to this. Sitting at my desk, writing. There's a clock there and I glance at it and see the time—exactly twenty-eight minutes past three. Always the same time, you understand.

*"And when I see the time, M. Poirot, I know I've got to do it.* I don't want to do it—I loathe doing it—but I've got to. . . ."

His voice had risen shrilly.

Unperturbed, Poirot said, "And what is it that you have to do?"

"At twenty-eight minutes past three," Benedict Farley said hoarsely, "I open the second drawer down on the right of my desk, take out the revolver that I keep there, load it and walk over to the window. And then—and then—"

"Yes?"

Benedict Farley said in a whisper:

*"Then I shoot myself. . . ."*

There was silence.

Then Poirot said, "That is your dream?"

"Yes."

"The same every night?"

"Yes."

"What happens after you shoot yourself?"

"I wake up."

Poirot nodded his head slowly and thoughtfully. "As a matter of interest, do you keep a revolver in that particular drawer?"

"Yes."

"Why?"

"I have always done so. It is as well to be prepared."

"Prepared for what?"

Farley said irritably, "A man in my position has to be on his guard. All rich men have enemies."

Poirot did not pursue the subject. He remained silent for a moment or two, then he said:

"Why exactly did you send for me?"

"I will tell you. First of all I consulted a doctor—three doctors to be exact."

"Yes?"

"The first told me it was all a question of diet. He was an elderly man. The second was a young man of the modern school. He assured me that it all hinged on a certain event that took place in infancy at that particular time of day—three twenty-eight. I am so determined, he says, not to remember that event, that I symbolize it by destroying myself. That is his explanation."

"And the third doctor?" asked Poirot.

Benedict Farley's voice rose in shrill anger.

"He's a young man too. He has a preposterous theory! He asserts that I, myself, am tired of life, that my life is so unbearable to me that I deliberately want to end it! But since to acknowledge that fact would be to acknowledge that essentially I am a failure, I refuse in my waking moments to face the truth. But when I am asleep, all inhibitions are removed, and I proceed to do that *which I really wish to do*. I put an end to myself."

"His view is that you really wish, unknown to yourself, to commit suicide?" said Poirot.

Benedict Farley cried shrilly:

"And that's impossible—impossible! I'm perfectly happy! I've got everything I want—everything money can buy! It's fantastic—unbelievable even to suggest a thing like that!"

Poirot looked at him with interest. Perhaps something in the shaking hands, the trembling shrillness of the voice, warned him that the denial was *too* vehement, that its very insistence was in itself suspect. He contented himself with saying:

"And where do I come in, monsieur?"

Benedict Farley calmed down suddenly. He tapped with an emphatic finger on the table beside him.

"There's another possibility. And if it's right, you're the man to know about it! You're famous, you've had hundreds of cases—fantastic, improbable cases! You'd know if anyone does."

"Know what?"

Farley's voice dropped to a whisper.

"Supposing someone wants to kill me. . . . Could they do it this way? Could they make me dream that dream night after night?"

"Hypnotism, you mean?"

"Yes."

Hercule Poirot considered the question.

"It would be possible, I suppose," he said at last. "It is more a question for a doctor."

"You don't know of such a case in your experience?"

"Not precisely on those lines, no."

"You see what I'm driving at? I'm made to dream the same dream, night after night, night after night—and then—one day the suggestion is too much for me—*and I act upon it*. I do what I've dreamed of so often—kill myself!"

Slowly Hercule Poirot shook his head.

"You don't think that is possible?" asked Farley.

*"Possible?"* Poirot shook his head. "That is not a word I care to meddle with."

"But you think it improbable?"

"Most improbable."

Benedict Farley murmured, "The doctor said so too. . . ." Then his voice rising shrilly again, he cried out, "But why do I have this dream? Why? Why?"

Hercule Poirot shook his head. Benedict Farley said abruptly, "You're sure you've never come across anything like this in your experience?"

"Never."

"That's what I wanted to know."

Delicately, Poirot cleared his throat.

"You permit," he said, "a question?"

"What is it? What is it? Say what you like."

"Who is it you suspect of wanting to kill you?"

Farley snapped out, "Nobody. Nobody at all."

"But the idea presented itself to your mind?" Poirot persisted.

"I wanted to know—if it was a possibility."

"Speaking from my own experience, I should say No. Have you ever been hypnotized, by the way?"

"Of course not. D'you think I'd lend myself to such tomfoolery?"

"Then I think one can say that your theory is definitely improbable."

"But the dream, you fool, the dream."

"The dream is certainly remarkable," said Poirot thoughtfully. He paused and then went on. "I should like to see the scene of this drama—the table, the clock, and the revolver."

"Of course, I'll take you next door."

Wrapping the folds of his dressing gown round him, the old man half rose from his chair. Then suddenly, as though a thought had struck him, he resumed his seat.

"No," he said. "There's nothing to see there. I've told you all there is to tell."

"But I should like to see for myself—"

"There's no need," Farley snapped. "You've given me your opinion. That's the end."

Poirot shrugged his shoulders. "As you please." He rose to his feet. "I am sorry, Mr. Farley, that I have not been able to be of assistance to you."

Benedict Farley was staring straight ahead of him.

"Don't want a lot of hanky-pankying around," he growled out. "I've told you the facts—you can't make anything of them. That closes the matter. You can send me in a bill for a consultation fee."

"I shall not fail to do so," said the detective drily. He walked towards the door.

"Stop a minute." The millionaire called him back. "That letter—I want it."

"The letter from your secretary?"

"Yes."

Poirot's eyebrows rose. He put his hand into his pocket, drew out a folded sheet, and handed it to the old man. The latter scrutinized it, then put it down on the table beside him with a nod.

Once more Hercule Poirot walked to the door. He was puzzled. His busy mind was going over and over the story he had been told. Yet in the midst of his mental preoccupation, a nagging sense of something wrong obtruded itself. And that something had to do with himself—not with Benedict Farley.

With his hand on the door knob, his mind cleared. He, Hercule Poirot, had been guilty of an error! He turned back into the room once more.

"A thousand pardons! In the interest of your problem I have committed a folly! That letter I handed to you—by mischance I put my hand into my right-hand pocket instead of the left—"

"What's all this? What's all this?"

"The letter that I handed you just now—an apology from my laundress concerning the treatment of my collars." Poirot was smiling, apologetic. He dipped into his left-hand pocket. "This is *your* letter."

Benedict Farley snatched at it—grunted, "Why the devil can't you mind what you're doing?"

Poirot retrieved his laundress's communication, apologized gracefully once more, and left the room.

He paused for a moment outside on the landing. It was a spacious one. Directly facing him was a big old oak settle with a refectory table in front of it. On the table were magazines. There were also two armchairs and a table with flowers. It reminded him a little of a dentist's waiting-room.

The butler was in the hall below waiting to let him out.

"Can I get you a taxi, sir?"

"No, I thank you. The night is fine. I will walk."

Hercule Poirot paused a moment on the pavement waiting for a lull in the traffic before crossing the busy street.

A frown creased his forehead.

"No," he said to himself. "I do not understand at all. Nothing makes sense. Regrettable to have to admit it, but I, Hercule Poirot, am completely baffled."

That was what might be termed the first act of the drama. The second act followed a week later. It opened with a telephone call from one John Stillingfleet, M.D.

He said with a remarkable lack of medical decorum:

"That you, Poirot, old horse? Stillingfleet here."

"Yes, my friend. What is it?"

"I'm speaking from Northway House—Benedict Farley's."

"Ah, yes?" Poirot's voice quickened with interest. "What of—Mr. Farley?"

"Farley's dead. Shot himself this afternoon."

There was a pause, then Poirot said:

"Yes. . . ."

"I notice you're not overcome with surprise. Know something about it, old horse?"

"Why should you think that?"

"Well, it isn't brilliant deduction or telepathy or anything like that. We found a note from Farley to you making an appointment about a week ago."

"I see."

"We've got a tame police inspector here—got to be careful, you know, when one of these millionaire blokes bumps himself off. Wondered whether you could throw any light on the case. If so, perhaps you'd come round?"

"I will come immediately."

"Good for you, old boy. Some dirty work at the crossroads—eh?"

Poirot merely repeated that he would set forth immediately.

"Don't want to spill the beans over the telephone? Quite right. So long."

A quarter of an hour later Poirot was sitting in the library, a low, long room at the back of Northway House on the ground floor. There were five other persons in the room. Inspector Barnett, Dr. Stillingfleet, Mrs. Farley, the widow of the millionaire, Joanna Farley, his only daughter, and Hugo Cornworthy, his private secretary.

Of these, Inspector Barnett was a discreet soldierly looking man. Dr. Stillingfleet, whose professional manner was entirely different from his telephonic style, was a tall, long-faced young man of thirty. Mrs. Farley was obviously very much younger than her husband. She was a handsome dark-haired woman. Her mouth was hard and her black eyes gave absolutely no clue to her emotions. She appeared perfectly self-possessed. Joanna Farley had fair hair and a freckled face. The prominence of her nose and chin was clearly inherited from her father. Her eyes were intelligent and shrewd. Hugo Cornworthy was a somewhat colorless young man, very correctly dressed. He seemed intelligent and efficient.

After greetings and introductions, Poirot narrated simply and clearly the circumstances of his visit and the story told him by Benedict Farley. He could not complain of any lack of interest.

"Most extraordinary story I've ever heard!" said the inspector. "A dream, eh? Did you know anything about this, Mrs. Farley?"

She bowed her head.

"My husband mentioned it to me. It upset him very much. I—I

told him it was indigestion—his diet, you know, was very peculiar—and suggested his calling in Dr. Stillingfleet."

That young man shook his head.

"He didn't consult me. From M. Poirot's story, I gather he went to Harley Street."

"I would like your advice on that point, doctor," said Poirot. "Mr. Farley told me that he consulted three specialists. What do you think of the theories they advanced?"

Stillingfleet frowned.

"It's difficult to say. You've got to take into account that what he passed on to you wasn't exactly what had been said to him. It was a layman's interpretation."

"You mean he had got the phraseology wrong?"

"Not exactly. I mean they would put a thing to him in professional terms, he'd get the meaning a little distorted, and then recast it in his own language."

"So that what he told me was not really what the doctors said."

"That's what it amounts to. He's just got it all a little wrong, if you know what I mean."

Poirot nodded thoughtfully. "Is it known whom he consulted?" he asked.

Mrs. Farley shook her head, and Joanna Farley remarked:

"None of us had any idea he had consulted anyone."

"Did he speak to *you* about his dream?" asked Poirot.

The girl shook her head.

"And you, Mr. Cornworthy?"

"No, he said nothing at all. I took down a letter to you at his dictation, but I had no idea why he wished to consult you. I thought it might possibly have something to do with some business irregularity."

Poirot asked, "And now as to the actual facts of Mr. Farley's death?"

Inspector Barnett looked interrogatively at Mrs. Farley and at Dr. Stillingfleet and then took upon himself the rôle of spokesman.

"Mr. Farley was in the habit of working in his own room on the first floor every afternoon. I understand that there was a big amalgamation of businesses in prospect—"

He looked at Hugo Cornworthy who said, "Consolidated Coachlines."

"In connection with that," continued Inspector Barnett, "Mr. Farley had agreed to give an interview to two members of the Press. He very seldom did anything of the kind—only about once in five years, I understand. Accordingly two reporters, one from the Associated Newsgroups, and one from Amalgamated Press-sheets, arrived at a quarter past three by appointment. They waited on the first floor outside Mr. Farley's door—which was the customary place for people to wait who had an appointment with Mr. Farley. At twenty past three a messenger arrived from the office of Consolidated Coachlines with some urgent papers. He was shown into Mr. Farley's room where he handed over the documents. Mr. Farley accompanied him to the door of the room, and from there spoke to the two members of the Press. He said:

" 'I am sorry, gentlemen, to have to keep you waiting, but I have some urgent business to attend to. I will be as quick as I can.'

"The two gentlemen, Mr. Adams and Mr. Stoddart, assured Mr. Farley that they would await his convenience. He went back into his room, shut the door—and was never seen alive again!"

"Continue," said Poirot.

"At a little after four o'clock," went on the inspector, "Mr. Cornworthy here came out of his room which is next door to Mr. Farley's, and was surprised to see the two reporters still waiting. He wanted Mr. Farley's signature to some letters and thought he had also better remind him that these two gentlemen were waiting. He accordingly went into Mr. Farley's room. To his surprise he could not at first see Mr. Farley and thought the room was empty. Then he caught sight of a boot sticking out behind the desk (which is placed in front of the window). He went quickly across and discovered Mr. Farley lying there dead, with a revolver beside him.

"Mr. Cornworthy hurried out of the room and directed the butler to ring up Dr. Stillingfleet. By the latter's advice, Mr. Cornworthy also informed the police."

"Was the shot heard?" asked Poirot.

"No. The traffic is very noisy here, the landing window was open. What with lorries and motor horns it would be most unlikely if it had been noticed."

Poirot nodded thoughtfully. "What time is it supposed he died?" he asked.

Stillingfleet said:

"I examined the body as soon as I got here—that is, at thirty-two minutes past four. Mr. Farley had been dead at least an hour."

Poirot's face was very grave.

"So then, it seems possible that his death could have occurred at the time he mentioned to me—that is, at twenty-eight minutes past three."

"Exactly," said Stillingfleet.

"Any finger-marks on the revolver?"

"Yes, his own."

"And the revolver itself?"

The inspector took up the tale.

"Was one which he kept in the second right-hand drawer of his desk, just as he told you. Mrs. Farley has identified it positively. More-over, you understand, there is only one entrance to the room, the door giving on to the landing. The two reporters were sitting exactly opposite that door and they swear that no one entered the room from the time Mr. Farley spoke to them, until Mr. Cornworthy entered it at a little after four o'clock."

"So that there is every reason to suppose that Mr. Farley committed suicide?"

Inspector Barnett smiled a little.

"There would have been no doubt at all but for one point."

"And that?"

"The letter written to you."

Poirot smiled too.

"I see! Where Hercule Poirot is concerned—immediately the suspi-cion of murder arises!"

"Precisely," said the inspector drily. "However, after your clearing up of the situation—"

Poirot interrupted him. "One little minute." He turned to Mrs. Far-ley. "Had your husband ever been hypnotized?"

"Never."

"Had he studied the question of hypnotism? Was he interested in the subject?"

She shook her head. "I don't think so."

Suddenly her self-control seemed to break down. "That horrible dream! It's uncanny! That he should have dreamed that—night after night—and then—and then—it's as though he were—*hounded* to death!"

Poirot remembered Benedict Farley saying—*"I proceed to do that which I really wish to do. I put an end to myself."*

He said, "Had it ever occurred to you that your husband might be tempted to do away with himself?"

"No—at least—sometimes he was very queer. . . ."

Joanna Farley's voice broke in clear and scornful. "Father would never have killed himself. He was far too careful of himself."

Dr. Stillingfleet said, "It isn't the people who threaten to commit suicide who usually do it, you know, Miss Farley. That's why suicides sometimes seem unaccountable."

Poirot rose to his feet. "Is it permitted," he asked, "that I see the room where the tragedy occurred?"

"Certainly. Dr. Stillingfleet—"

The doctor accompanied Poirot upstairs.

Benedict Farley's room was a much larger one than the secretary's next door. It was luxuriously furnished with deep leather-covered arm-chairs, a thick pile carpet, and a superb outsize writing-desk.

Poirot passed behind the latter to where a dark stain on the carpet showed just before the window. He remembered the millionaire saying, *"At twenty-eight minutes past three I open the second drawer down on the right of my desk, take out the revolver that I keep there, load it, and walk over to the window. And then—and then I shoot myself."*

He nodded slowly. Then he said:

"The window was open like this?"

"Yes. But nobody could have got in that way."

Poirot put his head out. There was no sill or parapet and no pipes near. Not even a cat could have gained access that way. Opposite rose the blank wall of the factory, a dead wall with no windows in it.

Stillingfleet said, "Funny room for a rich man to choose as his own sanctum with that outlook. It's like looking out on to a prison wall."

"Yes," said Poirot. He drew his head in and stared at the expanse of solid brick. "I think," he said, "that that wall is important."

Stillingfleet looked at him curiously. "You mean—psychologically?"

Poirot had moved to the desk. Idly, or so it seemed, he picked up a pair of what are usually called lazy tongs. He pressed the handles; the tongs shot out to their full length. Delicately, Poirot picked up a burnt match stump with them from beside a chair some feet away and conveyed it carefully to the waste-paper basket.

"When you've finished playing with those things . . ." said Stillingfleet irritably.

Hercule Poirot murmured, "An ingenious invention," and replaced the tongs neatly on the writing-table. Then he asked:

"Where were Mrs. Farley and Miss Farley at the time of the—death?"

"Mrs. Farley was resting in her room on the floor above this. Miss Farley was painting in her studio at the top of the house."

Hercule Poirot drummed idly with his fingers on the table for a minute or two. Then he said:

"I should like to see Miss Farley. Do you think you could ask her to come here for a minute or two?"

"If you like."

Stillingfleet glanced at him curiously, then left the room. In another minute or two the door opened and Joanna Farley came in.

"You do not mind, mademoiselle, if I ask you a few questions?"

She returned his glance coolly. "Please ask anything you choose."

"Did you know that your father kept a revolver in his desk?"

"No."

"Where were you and your mother—that is to say your stepmother—that is right?"

"Yes, Louise is my father's second wife. She is only eight years older than I am. You were about to say—?"

"Where were you and she on Thursday of last week? That is to say, on Thursday night."

She reflected for a minute or two.

"Thursday? Let me see. Oh, yes, we had gone to the theater. To see *Little Dog Laughed.*"

"Your father did not suggest accompanying you?"

"He never went out to theaters."

"What did he usually do in the evenings?"

"He sat in here and read."

"He was not a very sociable man?"

The girl looked at him directly. "My father," she said, "had a singularly unpleasant personality. No one who lived in close association with him could possibly be fond of him."

"That, mademoiselle, is a very candid statement."

"I am saving you time, M. Poirot. I realize quite well what you are getting at. My stepmother married my father for his money. I live here because I have no money to live elsewhere. There is a man I wish to marry—a poor man; my father saw to it that he lost his job. He wanted me, you see, to marry well—an easy matter since I was to be his heiress!"

"Your father's fortune passes to you?"

"Yes. That is, he left Louise, my stepmother, a quarter of a million free of tax, and there are other legacies, but the residue goes to me." She smiled suddenly. "So you see, M. Poirot, I had every reason to desire my father's death!"

"I see, mademoiselle, that you have inherited your father's intelligence."

She said thoughtfully, "Father was clever. . . . One felt that with him—that he had force—driving power—but it had all turned sour—bitter—there was no humanity left. . . ."

Hercule Poirot said softly, *"Grand Dieu,* but what an imbecile I am. . . ."

Joanna Farley turned towards the door. "Is there anything more?"

"Two little questions. These tongs here," he picked up the lazy tongs, "were they always on the table?"

"Yes. Father used them for picking up things. He didn't like stooping."

"One other question. Was your father's eyesight good?"

She stared at him.

"Oh, no—he couldn't see at all—I mean he couldn't see without his glasses. His sight had always been bad from a boy."

"But with his glasses?"

"Oh, he could see all right then, of course."

"He could read newspapers and fine print?"

"Oh, yes."

"That is all, mademoiselle."

She went out of the room.

Poirot murmured, "I was stupid. It was there, all the time, under my nose. And because it was so near I could not see it."

He leaned out of the window once more. Down below, in the narrow way between the house and the factory, he saw a small dark object.

Hercule Poirot nodded, satisfied, and went downstairs again.

The others were still in the library. Poirot addressed himself to the secretary:

"I want you, Mr. Cornworthy, to recount to me in detail the exact circumstances of Mr. Farley's summons to me. When, for instance, did Mr. Farley dictate that letter?"

"On Wednesday afternoon—at five-thirty, as far as I can remember."

"Were there any special directions about posting it?"

"He told me to post it myself."

"And you did so?"

"Yes."

"Did he give any special instructions to the butler about admitting me?"

"Yes. He told me to tell Holmes (Holmes is the butler) that a gentleman would be calling at 9:30. He was to ask the gentleman's name. He was also to ask to see the letter."

"Rather peculiar precautions to take, don't you think?"

Cornworthy shrugged his shoulders.

"Mr. Farley," he said carefully, "was rather a peculiar man."

"Any other instructions?"

"Yes. He told me to take the evening off."

"Did you do so?"

"Yes, immediately after dinner I went to the cinema."

"When did you return?"

"I let myself in about a quarter past eleven."

"Did you see Mr. Farley again that evening?"

"No."

"And he did not mention the matter the next morning?"

"No."

Poirot paused a moment, then resumed, "When I arrived I was not shown into Mr. Farley's own room."

"No. He told me that I was to tell Holmes to show you into my room."

"Why was that? Do you know?"

Cornworthy shook his head. "I never questioned any of Mr. Farley's orders," he said drily. "He would have resented it if I had."

"Did he usually receive visitors in his own room?"

"Usually, but not always. Sometimes he saw them in my room."

"Was there any reason for that?"

Hugo Cornworthy considered.

"No—I hardly think so—I've never really thought about it."

Turning to Mrs. Farley, Poirot asked:

"You permit that I ring for your butler?"

"Certainly, M. Poirot."

Very correct, very urbane, Holmes answered the bell.

"You rang, madam?"

Mrs. Farley indicated Poirot with a gesture. Holmes turned politely. "Yes, sir?"

"What were your instructions, Holmes, on the Thursday night when I came here?"

Holmes cleared his throat, then said:

"After dinner Mr. Cornworthy told me that Mr. Farley expected a Mr. Hercule Poirot at 9:30. I was to ascertain the gentleman's name, and I was to verify the information by glancing at a letter. Then I was to show him up to Mr. Cornworthy's room."

"Were you also told to knock on the door?"

An expression of distaste crossed the butler's countenance.

"That was one of Mr. Farley's orders. I was always to knock when introducing visitors—business visitors, that is," he added.

"Ah, that puzzled me! Were you given any other instructions concerning me?"

"No, sir. When Mr. Cornworthy had told me what I have just repeated to you he went out."

"What time was that?"

"Ten minutes to nine, sir."

"Did you see Mr. Farley after that?"

"Yes, sir, I took him up a glass of hot water as usual at nine o'clock."

"Was he then in his own room or in Mr. Cornworthy's?"

"He was in his own room, sir."

"You noticed nothing unusual about that room?"

"Unusual? No, sir."

"Where were Mrs. Farley and Miss Farley?"

"They had gone to the theater, sir."

"Thank you, Holmes, that will do."

Holmes bowed and left the room. Poirot turned to the millionaire's widow.

"One more question, Mrs. Farley. Had your husband good sight?"

"No. Not without his glasses."

"He was very short-sighted?"

"Oh, yes, he was quite helpless without his spectacles."

"He had several pairs of glasses?"

"Yes."

"Ah," said Poirot. He leaned back. "I think that that concludes the case. . . ."

There was silence in the room. They were all looking at the little man who sat there complacently stroking his mustache. On the inspector's face was perplexity, Dr. Stillingfleet was frowning, Cornworthy merely stared uncomprehendingly, Mrs. Farley gazed in blank astonishment, Joanna Farley looked eager.

Mrs. Farley broke the silence.

"I don't understand, M. Poirot." Her voice was fretful. "The dream—"

"Yes," said Poirot. "That dream was very important."

Mrs. Farley shivered. She said:

"I've never believed in anything supernatural before—but now— to dream it night after night beforehand—"

"It's extraordinary," said Stillingfleet. "Extraordinary! If we hadn't got your word for it, Poirot, and if you hadn't had it straight from the horse's mouth—" he coughed in embarrassment, and readopting his professional manner, "I beg your pardon, Mrs. Farley. If Mr. Farley himself had not told that story—"

"Exactly," said Poirot. His eyes, which had been half-closed, opened suddenly. They were very green. *"If Benedict Farley hadn't told me—"*

He paused a minute, looking round at a circle of blank faces.

"There are certain things, you comprehend, that happened that evening which I was quite at a loss to explain. First, why make such a point of my bringing that letter with me?"

"Identification," suggested Cornworthy.

"No, no, my dear young man. Really, that idea is too ridiculous. There must be some much more valid reason. For not only did Mr. Farley require to see that letter produced, but he definitely demanded that I should leave it behind me. And moreover even then he did not destroy it! It was found among his papers this afternoon. *Why did he keep it?"*

Joanna Farley's voice broke in. "He wanted, in case anything happened to him, that the facts of his strange dream should be made known."

Poirot nodded approvingly.

"You are astute, mademoiselle. That must be—that can only be— the point of the keeping of the letter. When Mr. Farley was dead, the story of that strange dream was to be told! That dream was very important. That dream, mademoiselle, was *vital!*

"I will come now," he went on, "to the second point. After hearing his story I ask Mr. Farley to show me the desk and the revolver. He seems about to get up to do so, then suddenly refuses. Why did he refuse?"

This time no one advanced an answer.

"I will put that question differently. *What was there in that next room that Mr. Farley did not want me to see?*"

There was still silence.

"Yes," said Poirot, "it is difficult, that. And yet there was some reason—some *urgent* reason why Mr. Farley received me in his secretary's room and refused point-blank to take me into his own room. *There was something in that room he could not afford to have me see.*

"And now I come to the third inexplicable thing that happened on that evening. Mr. Farley, just as I was leaving, requested me to hand him the letter I had received. By inadvertence I handed him a communication from my laundress. He glanced at it and laid it down beside him. Just before I left the room I discovered my error—and rectified it! After that I left the house and—I admit it—I was completely at sea! The whole affair and especially that last incident seemed to me quite inexplicable."

He looked round from one to the other.

"You do not see?"

Stillingfleet said, "I don't really see how your laundress comes into it, Poirot."

"My laundress," said Poirot, "was very important. That miserable woman who ruins my collars, was, for the first time in her life, useful to somebody. Surely you see—it is so obvious. Mr. Farley glanced at that communication—*one glance* would have told him that it was the wrong letter—and yet he knew nothing. Why? *Because he could not see it properly!*"

Inspector Barnett said sharply, "Didn't he have his glasses on?"

Hercule Poirot smiled. "Yes," he said. "He had his glasses on. That is what makes it so very interesting."

He leaned forward.

"Mr. Farley's dream was very important. He dreamed, you see, that he committed suicide. And a little later on, he did commit suicide. That is to say he was alone in a room and was found there with a revolver by him, and no one entered or left the room at the time that he was shot. What does that mean? It means, does it not, that it *must* be suicide!"

"Yes," said Stillingfleet.

Hercule Poirot shook his head.

"On the contrary," he said. "It was murder. An unusual and a very cleverly planned murder."

Again he leaned forward, tapping the table, his eyes green and shining.

"Why did Mr. Farley not allow me to go into his own room that evening? What was there in there that I must not be allowed to see? I think, my friends, that there was—Benedict Farley himself!"

He smiled at the blank faces.

"Yes, yes, it is not nonsense what I say. Why could the Mr. Farley to whom I had been talking not realize the difference between two totally dissimilar letters? Because, *mes amis,* he was a man of *normal sight* wearing a pair of very powerful glasses. Those glasses would render a man of normal eyesight practically blind. Isn't that so, doctor?"

Stillingfleet murmured, "That's so—of course."

"Why did I feel that in talking to Mr. Farley I was talking to a mountebank, to an actor playing a part? Because he *was* playing a part! Consider the setting. The dim room, the green shaded light turned blindingly away from the figure in the chair. What did I see—the famous patchwork dressing-gown, the beaked nose (faked with that useful substance, nose putty) the white crest of hair, the powerful lenses concealing the eyes. What evidence is there that Mr. Farley ever had a dream? Only the story I was told and the evidence of *Mrs. Farley.* What evidence is there that Benedict Farley kept a revolver in his desk? Again only the story told me and the word of Mrs. Farley. Two people carried this fraud through—Mrs. Farley and Hugo Cornworthy. Cornworthy wrote the letter to me, gave instructions to the butler, went out ostensibly to the cinema, but let himself in again immediately with a key, went to his room, made himself up, and played the part of Benedict Farley.

"And so we come to this afternoon. The opportunity for which Mr. Cornworthy has been waiting arrives. There are two witnesses on the landing to swear that no one goes in or out of Benedict Farley's room. Cornworthy waits until a particularly heavy batch of traffic is about to pass. Then he leans out of his window, and with the lazy tongs which he has purloined from the desk next door he holds an object against the window of that room. Benedict Farley comes to the window. Cornworthy snatches back the tongs and as Farley leans out, and the lorries are passing outside, Cornworthy shoots him with the revolver that he has ready. There is a blank wall opposite, remember. There can be no witness of the crime. Cornworthy waits for over half an hour, then gathers up some papers, conceals the lazy tongs and the revolver between them and goes out on to the landing and into the next room. He replaces the tongs on the desk, lays down the revolver after pressing the dead man's fingers on it, and hurries out with the news of Mr. Farley's 'suicide.'

"He arranges that the letter to me shall be found and that I shall arrive with my story—the story I heard *from Mr. Farley's own lips*— of his extraordinary 'dream'—the strange compulsion he felt to kill

himself! A few credulous people will discuss the hypnotism theory—
but the main result will be to confirm without a doubt that the actual
hand that held the revolver was Benedict Farley's own."

Hercule Poirot's eyes went to the widow's face—the dismay—the
ashy pallor—the blind fear.

"And in due course," he finished gently, "the happy ending would
have been achieved. A quarter of a million and two hearts that beat
as one. . . ."

John Stillingfleet, M.D., and Hercule Poirot walked along the side
of Northway House. On their right was the towering wall of the factory.
Above them, on their left, were the windows of Benedict Farley's
and Hugo Cornworthy's rooms. Hercule Poirot stopped and picked
up a small object—a black stuffed cat.

"*Voilà*," he said. "That is what Cornworthy held in the lazy tongs
against Farley's window. You remember, he hated cats? Naturally he
rushed to the window."

"Why on earth didn't Cornworthy come out and pick it up after
he'd dropped it?"

"How could he? To do so would have been definitely suspicious.
After all, if this object were found what would anyone think—that
some child had wandered round here and dropped it."

"Yes," said Stillingfleet with a sigh. "That's probably what the ordinary person *would* have thought. But not good old Hercule! D'you
know, old horse, up to the very last minute I thought you were leading
up to some subtle theory of highfalutin psychological 'suggested' murder? I bet those two thought so too! Nasty bit of goods, the Farleys.
Goodness, how she cracked! Cornworthy might have got away with
it if she hadn't had hysterics and tried to spoil your beauty by going
for you with her nails. I only got her off you just in time."

He paused a minute and then said:

"I rather like the girl. Grit, you know, and brains. I suppose I'd
be thought to be a fortune hunter if I had a shot at her . . . ?"

"You are too late, my friend. There is already someone *sur le tapis*.
Her father's death has opened the way to happiness."

"Take it all round, *she* had a pretty good motive for bumping off
the unpleasant parent."

"Motive and opportunity are not enough," said Poirot. "There must
also be the criminal temperament!"

"I wonder if you'll ever commit a crime, Poirot?" said Stillingfleet.
"I bet you could get away with it all right. As a matter of fact, it
would be *too* easy for you—I mean the thing would be off as definitely
too unsporting."

"That," said Poirot, "is a typically English idea."

# Problem at Sea

"COLONEL Clapperton!" said General Forbes.

He said it with an effect midway between a snort and a sniff.

Miss Ellie Henderson leaned forward, a strand of her soft gray hair blowing across her face. Her eyes, dark and snapping, gleamed with a wicked pleasure.

"Such a *soldierly*-looking man!" she said with malicious intent, and smoothed back the lock of hair to await the result.

"Soldierly!" exploded General Forbes. He tugged at his military mustache and his face became bright red.

"In the Guards, wasn't he?" murmured Miss Henderson, completing her work.

"Guards? Guards? Pack of nonsense. Fellow was on the music hall stage! Fact! Joined up and was out in France counting tins of plum and apple. Huns dropped a stray bomb and he went home with a flesh wound in the arm. Somehow or other got into Lady Carrington's hospital."

"So that's how they met."

"Fact! Fellow played the wounded hero. Lady Carrington had no sense and oceans of money. Old Carrington had been in munitions. She'd been a widow only six months. This fellow snaps her up in no time. She wangled him a job at the War Office. *Colonel* Clapperton! Pah!" he snorted.

"And before the war he was on the music hall stage," mused Miss Henderson, trying to reconcile the distinguished gray-haired Colonel Clapperton with a red-nosed comedian singing mirth-provoking songs.

"Fact!" said General Forbes. "Heard it from old Bassington-ffrench. And he heard it from old Badger Cotterill who'd got it from Snooks Parker."

Miss Henderson nodded brightly. "That does seem to settle it!" she said.

A fleeting smile showed for a minute on the face of a small man sitting near them. Miss Henderson noticed the smile. She was observant. It had shown appreciation of the irony underlying her last remark—irony which the General never for a moment suspected.

The General himself did not notice the smiles. He glanced at his watch, rose and remarked, "Exercise. Got to keep oneself fit on a boat," and passed out through the open door onto the deck.

Miss Henderson glanced at the man who had smiled. It was a well-bred glance indicating that she was ready to enter into conversation with a fellow traveler.

"He is energetic—yes?" said the little man.

"He goes round the deck forty-eight times exactly," said Miss Henderson. "What an old gossip! And they say *we* are the scandal-loving sex."

"What an impoliteness!"

"Frenchmen are always polite," said Miss Henderson—there was the nuance of a question in her voice.

The little man responded promptly. "Belgian, mademoiselle."

"Oh! Belgian."

"Hercule Poirot. At your service."

The name aroused some memory. Surely she had heard it before—? "Are you enjoying this trip, M. Poirot?"

"Frankly, no. It was an imbecility to allow myself to be persuaded to come. I detest *la mer*. Never does it remain tranquil—no, not for a little minute."

"Well, you admit it's quite calm now."

M. Poirot admitted this grudgingly. "*À ce moment*, yes. That is why I revive. I once more interest myself in what passes around me—your very adept handling of the General Forbes, for instance."

"You mean—" Miss Henderson paused.

Hercule Poirot bowed. "Your methods of extracting the scandalous matter. Admirable!"

Miss Henderson laughed in an unashamed manner. "That touch about the Guards? I knew that would bring the old boy up spluttering and gasping." She leaned forward confidentially. "I admit I *like* scandal—the more ill-natured, the better!"

Poirot looked thoughtfully at her—her slim well-preserved figure, her keen dark eyes, her gray hair; a woman of forty-five who was content to look her age.

Ellie said abruptly, "I have it! Aren't you the great detective?"

Poirot bowed. "You are too amiable, mademoiselle." But he made no disclaimer.

"How thrilling," said Miss Henderson. "Are you 'hot on the trail' as they say in books? Have we a criminal secretly in our midst? Or am I being indiscreet?"

"Not at all. Not at all. It pains me to disappoint your expectations, but I am simply here, like everyone else, to amuse myself."

He said it in such a gloomy voice that Miss Henderson laughed.

"Oh! Well, you will be able to get ashore tomorrow at Alexandria. You have been to Egypt before?"

"Never, mademoiselle."

Miss Henderson rose somewhat abruptly.

"I think I shall join the General on his constitutional," she announced.

Poirot sprang politely to his feet.

She gave him a little nod and passed out onto the deck.

A faint puzzled look showed for a moment in Poirot's eyes then, a little smile creasing his lips, he rose, put his head through the door and glanced down the deck. Miss Henderson was leaning against the rail talking to a tall, soldierly looking man.

Poirot's smile deepened. He drew himself back into the smoking room with the same exaggerated care with which a tortoise withdraws itself into its shell. For the moment he had the smoking room to himself, though he rightly conjectured that that would not last long.

It did not. Mrs. Clapperton, her carefully waved platinum head protected with a net, her massaged and dieted form dressed in a smart sports suit, came through the door from the bar with the purposeful air of a woman who has always been able to pay top price for anything she needed.

She said: "John—? Oh! Good morning, M. Poirot—have you seen John?"

"He's on the starboard deck, madame. Shall I—?"

She arrested him with a gesture. "I'll sit here a minute." She sat down in a regal fashion in the chair opposite him. From the distance she had looked a possible twenty-eight. Now, in spite of her exquisitely made-up face, her delicately plucked eyebrows, she looked not her actual forty-nine years, but a possible fifty-five. Her eyes were a hard pale blue with tiny pupils.

"I was sorry not to have seen you at dinner last night," she said. "It was just a shade choppy, of course—"

"*Précisément,*" said Poirot with feeling.

"Luckily, I am an excellent sailor," said Mrs. Clapperton. "I say luckily, because, with my weak heart, seasickness would probably be the death of me."

"You have the weak heart, madame?"

"Yes, I have to be *most* careful. I must *not* overtire myself! *All* the specialists say so!" Mrs. Clapperton had embarked on the—to her—ever-fascinating topic of her health. "John, poor darling, wears himself out trying to prevent me from doing too much. I live so intensely, if you know what I mean, M. Poirot?"

"Yes, yes."

"He always says to me: 'Try to be more of a vegetable, Adeline.' But I can't. Life was meant to be *lived,* I feel. As a matter of fact I wore myself out as a girl in the war. My hospital—you've heard of my hospital? Of course I had nurses and matrons and all that—but *I* actually ran it." She sighed.

"Your vitality is marvelous, dear lady," said Poirot, with the slightly mechanical air of one responding to his cue.

Mrs. Clapperton gave a girlish laugh.

"Everyone tells me how young I am! It's absurd. I never try to pretend I'm a day less than forty-three," she continued with slightly mendacious candor, "but a lot of people find it hard to believe. 'You're so *alive*, Adeline,' they say to me. But really, M. Poirot, what would one *be* if one wasn't alive?"

"Dead," said Poirot.

Mrs. Clapperton frowned. The reply was not to her liking. The man, she decided, was trying to be funny. She got up and said coldly, "I must find John."

As she stepped through the door she dropped her handbag. It opened and the contents flew far and wide. Poirot rushed gallantly to the rescue. It was some few minutes before the lipsticks, vanity boxes, cigarette case and lighter and other odds and ends were collected. Mrs. Clapperton thanked him politely, then she swept down the deck and said, "John—"

Colonel Clapperton was still deep in conversation with Miss Henderson. He swung round and came quickly to meet his wife. He bent over her protectively. Her deck chair—was it in the right place? Wouldn't it be better—? His manner was courteous—full of gentle consideration. Clearly an adored wife spoilt by an adoring husband.

Miss Ellie Henderson looked out at the horizon as though something about it rather disgusted her.

Standing in the smoking room door, Poirot looked on.

A hoarse quavering voice behind him said:

"I'd take a hatchet to that woman if I were her husband." The old gentleman known disrespectfully among the Younger Set on board as the Grandfather of All the Tea Planters, had just shuffled in. "Boy!" he called. "Get me a whisky peg."

Poirot stooped to retrieve a torn scrap of notepaper, an overlooked item from the contents of Mrs. Clapperton's bag. Part of a prescription, he noted, containing digitalin. He put it in his pocket, meaning to restore it to Mrs. Clapperton later.

"Yes," went on the aged passenger. "Poisonous woman. I remember a woman like that in Poona. In '87 that was."

"Did anyone take a hatchet to her?" inquired Poirot.

The old gentleman shook his head sadly.

"Worried her husband into his grave within the year. Clapperton ought to assert himself. Gives his wife her head too much."

"She holds the purse strings," said Poirot gravely.

"Ha ha!" chuckled the old gentleman. "You've put the matter in a nutshell. Holds the purse strings. Ha ha!"

Two girls burst into the smoking room. One had a round face with freckles and dark hair streaming out in a windswept confusion, the other had freckles and curly chestnut hair.

"A rescue—a rescue!" cried Kitty Mooney. "Pam and I are going to rescue Colonel Clapperton."

"From his wife," gasped Pamela Cregan.

"We think he's a *pet*. . . ."

"And she's just awful—she won't let him do *anything*," the two girls exclaimed.

"And if he isn't with her, he's usually grabbed by the Henderson woman. . . ."

"Who's quite nice. But terribly *old*. . . ."

They ran out, gasping in between giggles:

"A rescue—a rescue . . ."

That the rescue of Colonel Clapperton was no isolated sally, but a fixed project was made clear that same evening when the eighteen-year-old Pam Cregan came up to Hercule Poirot, and murmured, "Watch us, M. Poirot. He's going to be cut out from under her nose and taken to walk in the moonlight on the boat deck."

It was just at that moment that Colonel Clapperton was saying, "I grant you the price of a Rolls-Royce. But it's practically good for a lifetime. Now my car—"

"*My* car, I think, John." Mrs. Clapperton's voice was shrill and penetrating.

He showed no annoyance at her ungraciousness. Either he was used to it by this time, or else—

"Or else?" thought Poirot and let himself speculate.

"Certainly, my dear, *your* car," Clapperton bowed to his wife and finished what he had been saying, perfectly unruffled.

"*Voilà ce qu'on appelle le pukka sahib*," thought Poirot. "But the General Forbes says that Clapperton is no gentleman at all. I wonder now."

There was a suggestion of bridge. Mrs. Clapperton, General Forbes and a hawk-eyed couple sat down to it. Miss Henderson had excused herself and gone out on deck.

"What about your husband?" asked General Forbes, hesitating.

"John won't play," said Mrs. Clapperton. "Most tiresome of him."

The four bridge players began shuffling the cards.

Pam and Kitty advanced on Colonel Clapperton. Each one took an arm.

"You're coming with us!" said Pam. "To the boat deck. There's a moon."

"Don't be foolish, John," said Mrs. Clapperton. "You'll catch a chill."

"Not with us, he won't," said Kitty. "We're hot stuff!"

He went with them, laughing.

Poirot noticed that Mrs. Clapperton said No Bid to her initial bid of Two Clubs.

He strolled out onto the promenade deck. Miss Henderson was standing by the rail. She looked round expectantly as he came to stand beside her and he saw the drop in her expression.

They chatted for a while. Then presently as he fell silent she asked, "What are you thinking about?"

Poirot replied, "I am wondering about my knowledge of English. Mrs. Clapperton said, 'John won't play bridge.' Is not 'can't play' the usual term?"

"She takes it as a personal insult that he doesn't, I suppose," said Ellie drily. "The man was a fool ever to have married her."

In the darkness Poirot smiled. "You don't think it's just possible that the marriage may be a success?" he asked diffidently.

"With a woman like that?"

Poirot shrugged his shoulders. "Many odious women have devoted husbands. An enigma of Nature. You will admit that nothing she says or does appears to gall him."

Miss Henderson was considering her reply when Mrs. Clapperton's voice floated out through the smoking-room window.

"No—I don't think I will play another rubber. So stuffy. I think I'll go up and get some air on the boat deck."

"Good night," said Miss Henderson. "I'm going to bed." She disappeared abruptly.

Poirot strolled forward to the lounge—deserted save for Colonel Clapperton and the two girls. He was doing card tricks for them, and noting the dexterity of his shuffling and handling of the cards, Poirot remembered the General's story of a career on the music hall stage.

"I see you enjoy the cards even though you do not play bridge," he remarked.

"I've my reasons for not playing bridge," said Clapperton, his charming smile breaking out. "I'll show you. We'll play one hand."

He dealt the cards rapidly. "Pick up your hands. Well, what about it?" He laughed at the bewildered expression on Kitty's face. He laid down his hand and the others followed suit. Kitty held the entire club suit, M. Poirot the hearts, Pam the diamonds and Colonel Clapperton the spades.

"You see?" he said. "A man who can deal his partner and his adversaries any hand he pleases had better stand aloof from a friendly game! If the luck goes too much his way, ill-natured things might be said."

"Oh!" gasped Kitty. "How *could* you do that? It all looked perfectly ordinary."

"The quickness of the hand deceives the eye," said Poirot sententiously—and caught the sudden change in the Colonel's expression.

It was as though he realized that he had been off his guard for a moment or two.

Poirot smiled. The conjuror had shown himself through the mask of the *pukka sahib.*

The ship reached Alexandria at dawn the following morning.

As Poirot came up from breakfast he found the two girls all ready to go on shore. They were talking to Colonel Clapperton.

"We ought to get off now," urged Kitty. "The passport people will be going off the ship presently. You'll come with us, won't you? You wouldn't let us go ashore all by ourselves? Awful things might happen to us."

"I certainly don't think you ought to go by yourselves," said Clapperton, smiling. "But I'm not sure my wife feels up to it."

"That's too bad," said Pam. "But she can have a nice long rest."

Colonel Clapperton looked a little irresolute. Evidently the desire to play truant was strong upon him. He noticed Poirot.

"Hullo, M. Poirot—you going ashore?"

"No, I think not," M. Poirot replied.

"I'll—I'll—just have a word with Adeline," decided Colonel Clapperton.

"We'll come with you," said Pam. She flashed a wink at Poirot. "Perhaps we can persuade her to come too," she added gravely.

Colonel Clapperton seemed to welcome this suggestion. He looked decidedly relieved.

"Come along then, the pair of you," he said lightly. They all three went along the passage of B deck together.

Poirot, whose cabin was just opposite the Clappertons, followed them out of curiosity.

Colonel Clapperton rapped a little nervously at the cabin door.

"Adeline, my dear, are you up?"

The sleepy voice of Mrs. Clapperton from within replied, "Oh, bother—what is it?"

"It's John. What about going ashore?"

"Certainly not." The voice was shrill and decisive. "I've had a very bad night. I shall stay in bed most of the day."

Pam nipped in quickly, "Oh, Mrs. Clapperton, I'm so sorry. We did so want you to come with us. Are you sure you're not up to it?"

"I'm quite certain." Mrs. Clapperton's voice sounded even shriller.

The Colonel was turning the door handle without result.

"What is it, John? The door's locked. I don't want to be disturbed by the stewards."

"Sorry, my dear, sorry. Just wanted my Baedeker."

"Well, you can't have it," snapped Mrs. Clapperton. "I'm not going to get out of bed. Do go away, John, and let me have a little peace."

"Certainly, certainly, my dear." The Colonel backed away from the door. Pam and Kitty closed in on him.

"Let's start at once. Thank goodness your hat's on your head. Oh! gracious—your passport isn't in the cabin, is it?"

"As a matter of fact it's in my pocket—" began the Colonel.

Kitty squeezed his arm. "Glory be!" she exclaimed. "Now, come on."

Leaning over the rail, Poirot watched the three of them leave the ship. He heard a faint intake of breath beside him and turned his head to see Miss Henderson. Her eyes were fastened on the three retreating figures.

"So they've gone ashore," she said flatly.

"Yes. Are you going?"

She had a shade hat, he noticed, and a smart bag and shoes. There was a shore-going appearance about her. Nevertheless, after the most infinitesimal of pauses, she shook her head.

"No," she said. "I think I'll stay on board. I have a lot of letters to write."

She turned and left him.

Puffing after his morning tour of forty-eight rounds of the deck, General Forbes took her place. "Aha!" he exclaimed as his eyes noted the retreating figures of the Colonel and the two girls. "So *that's* the game! Where's the Madam?"

Poirot explained that Mrs. Clapperton was having a quiet day in bed.

"Don't you believe it!" The old warrior closed one knowing eye. "She'll be up for tiffin—and if the poor devil's found to be absent without leave, there'll be ructions."

But the General's prognostications were not fulfilled. Mrs. Clapperton did not appear at lunch and by the time the Colonel and his attendant damsels returned to the ship at four o'clock, she had not shown herself.

Poirot was in his cabin and heard the husband's slightly guilty knock on his cabin door. Heard the knock repeated, the cabin door tried, and finally heard the Colonel's call to a steward.

"Look here, I can't get an answer. Have you a key?"

Poirot rose quickly from his bunk and came out into the passage.

The news went like wildfire round the ship. With horrified incredulity people heard that Mrs. Clapperton had been found dead in her bunk—a native dagger driven through her heart. A string of amber beads was found on the floor of her cabin.

Rumor succeeded rumor. All bead sellers who had been allowed on board that day were being rounded up and questioned! A large sum in cash had disappeared from a drawer in the cabin! The notes had been traced! They had not been traced! Jewelry worth a fortune had been taken! No jewelry had been taken at all! A steward had been arrested and had confessed to the murder!

"What is the truth of it all?" demanded Miss Ellie Henderson, waylaying Poirot. Her face was pale and troubled.

"My dear lady, how should I know?"

"Of course you know," said Miss Henderson.

It was late in the evening. Most people had retired to their cabins. Miss Henderson led Poirot to a couple of deck chairs on the sheltered side of the ship. "Now tell me," she commanded.

Poirot surveyed her thoughtfully. "It's an interesting case," he said.

"Is it true that she had some very valuable jewelry stolen?"

Poirot shook his head. "No. No jewelry was taken. A small amount of loose cash that was in a drawer has disappeared, though."

"I'll never feel safe on a ship again," said Miss Henderson with a shiver. "Any clue as to which of those coffee-colored brutes did it?"

"No," said Hercule Poirot. "The whole thing is rather—strange."

"What do you mean?" asked Ellie sharply.

Poirot spread out his hands. *"Eh bien*—take the facts. Mrs. Clapperton had been dead at least five hours when she was found. Some money had disappeared. A string of beads was on the floor by her bed. The door was locked and the key was missing. The window—*window*, not porthole—gives on the deck and was open."

"Well?" asked the woman impatiently.

"Do you not think it is curious for a murder to be committed under those particular circumstances? Remember that the postcard sellers, money changers, and bead sellers who are allowed on board are all well known to the police."

"The stewards usually lock your cabin, all the same," Ellie pointed out.

"Yes, to prevent any chance of petty pilfering. But this—was murder."

"What exactly are you thinking of, M. Poirot?" Her voice sounded a little breathless.

"I am thinking of the *locked door.*"

Miss Henderson considered this. "I don't see anything in that. The man left by the door, locked it, and took the key with him so as to avoid having the murder discovered too soon. Quite intelligent of him, for it wasn't discovered until four o'clock in the afternoon."

"No, no, mademoiselle, you don't appreciate the point I'm trying to make. I'm not worried as to how he got *out,* but as to how he got *in.*"

"The window of course."

"*C'est possible.* But it would be a very narrow fit—and there were people passing up and down the deck all the time, remember."

"Then through the door," said Miss Henderson impatiently.

"But you forget, mademoiselle. *Mrs. Clapperton had locked the door on the inside.* She had done so before Colonel Clapperton left the boat this morning. He actually tried it—so we *know* that is so."

"Nonsense. It probably stuck—or he didn't turn the handle properly."

"But it does not rest on his word. We actually heard *Mrs. Clapperton herself say so.*"

"We?"

"Miss Mooney, Miss Cregan, Colonel Clapperton, and myself."

Ellie Henderson tapped a neatly shod foot. She did not speak for a moment or two. Then she said in a slightly irritable tone:

"Well—what exactly do you deduce from that? If Mrs. Clapperton could lock the door she could unlock it too, I suppose."

"Precisely, precisely." Poirot turned a beaming face upon her. "And you see where that leads us. *Mrs. Clapperton unlocked the door and let the murderer in.* Now would she be likely to do that for a bead seller?"

Ellie objected, "She might not have known who it was. He may have knocked—she got up and opened the door—and he forced his way in and killed her."

Poirot shook his head. "*Au contraire.* She was lying peacefully in bed when she was stabbed."

Miss Henderson stared at him. "What's your idea?" she asked abruptly.

Poirot smiled. "Well, it looks, does it not, as though she *knew* the person she admitted. . . ."

"You mean," said Miss Henderson and her voice sounded a little harsh, *"that the murderer is a passenger on the ship?"*

Poirot nodded. "It seems indicated."

"And the string of beads left on the floor was a blind?"

"Precisely."

"The theft of the money also?"

"Exactly."

There was a pause, then Miss Henderson said slowly, "I thought Mrs. Clapperton a very unpleasant woman and I don't think anyone on board really liked her—but there wasn't anyone who had any reason to kill her."

"Except her husband, perhaps," said Poirot.

"You don't really think—" She stopped.

"It is the opinion of every person on this ship that Colonel Clapperton would have been quite justified in 'taking a hatchet to her.' That was, I think, the expression used."

Ellie Henderson looked at him—waiting.

"But I am bound to say," went on Poirot, "that I myself have not noted any signs of exasperation on the good Colonel's part. Also, what is more important, he had an alibi. He was with those two girls all day and did not return to the ship till four o'clock. By then, Mrs. Clapperton had been dead many hours."

There was another minute of silence. Ellie Henderson said softly: "But you still think—a passenger on the ship?"

Poirot bowed his head.

Ellie Henderson laughed suddenly—a reckless defiant laugh. "Your theory may be difficult to prove, M. Poirot. There are a good many passengers on this ship."

Poirot bowed to her. "I will use a phrase from one of your detective story writers. 'I have my methods, Watson.' "

The following evening, at dinner, every passenger found a typewritten slip by his plate requesting him to be in the main lounge at 8:39. When the company were assembled, the Captain stepped onto the raised platform where the orchestra usually played and addressed them.

"Ladies and Gentlemen, you all know of the tragedy which took place yesterday. I am sure you all wish to cooperate in bringing the perpetrator of that foul crime to justice." He paused and cleared his throat. "We have on board with us M. Hercule Poirot who is probably known to you all as a man who has had wide experience in—er—such matters. I hope you will listen carefully to what he has to say."

It was at this minute that Colonel Clapperton who had not been at dinner came in and sat down next to General Forbes. He looked like a man bewildered by sorrow—not at all like a man conscious of great relief. Either he was a very good actor or else he had been genuinely fond of his disagreeable wife.

"M. Hercule Poirot," said the Captain and stepped down. Poirot took his place. He looked comically self-important as he beamed on his audience.

*"Messieurs, Mesdames,"* he began. "It is most kind of you to be so indulgent as to listen to me. *M. le Capitaine* has told you that I have had a certain experience in these matters. I have, it is true, a little idea of my own about how to get to the bottom of this particular case." He made a sign and a steward pushed forward and passed up to him a bulky, shapeless object wrapped in a sheet.

"What I am about to do may surprise you a little," Poirot warned them. "It may occur to you that I am eccentric, perhaps mad. Nevertheless I assure you that behind my madness there is—as you English say—a method."

His eyes met those of Miss Henderson for just a minute. He began unwrapping the bulky object.

"I have here, *Messieurs* and *Mesdames,* an important witness to the truth of who killed Mrs. Clapperton." With a deft hand he whisked away the last enveloping cloth, and the object it concealed was revealed—an almost life-sized wooden doll, dressed in a velvet suit and lace collar.

"Now, Arthur," said Poirot and his voice changed subtly—it was no longer foreign—it had instead a confident English, a slightly Cockney inflection. "Can you tell me—I repeat—can you tell me—anything at all about the death of Mrs. Clapperton?"

The doll's neck oscillated a little, its wooden lower jaw dropped and wavered and a shrill high-pitched woman's voice spoke:

*"What is it, John? The door's locked. I don't want to be disturbed by the stewards. . . ."*

There was a cry—an overturned chair—a man stood swaying, his hand to his throat—trying to speak—trying . . . Then suddenly, his figure seemed to crumple up. He pitched headlong.

It was Colonel Clapperton.

Poirot and the ship's doctor rose from their knees by the prostrate figure.

"All over, I'm afraid. Heart," said the doctor briefly.

Poirot nodded. "The shock of having his trick seen through," he said.

He turned to General Forbes. "It was you, General, who gave me a valuable hint with your mention of the music hall stage. I puzzle—I think—and then it comes to me. Supposing that before the war Clapperton was a *ventriloquist.* In that case, it would be perfectly possible for three people to hear Mrs. Clapperton speak from inside her cabin *when she was already dead. . . ."*

Ellie Henderson was beside him. Her eyes were dark and full of pain. "Did you know his heart was weak?" she asked.

"I guessed it. . . . Mrs. Clapperton talked of her own heart being affected, but she struck me as the type of woman who likes to be thought ill. Then I picked up a torn prescription with a very strong dose of digitalin in it. Digitalin is a heart medicine but it couldn't be Mrs. Clapperton's because digitalin dilates the pupils of the eyes. I had never noticed such a phenomenon with her—but when I looked at his eyes I saw the signs at once."

Ellie murmured, "So you thought—it might end—this way?"

"The best way, don't you think, mademoiselle?" he said gently.

He saw the tears rise in her eyes. She said: "You've known. You've known all along. . . . That I cared. . . . But he didn't do it for *me*. . . . It was those girls—youth—it made him feel his slavery. He wanted to be free before it was too late. . . . Yes, I'm sure that's how it was. . . . When did you guess—that it was he?"

"His self-control was too perfect," said Poirot simply. "No matter how galling his wife's conduct, it never seemed to touch him. That meant either that he was so used to it that it no longer stung him, or else—*eh bien*—I decided on the latter alternative. . . . And I was right. . . .

"And then there was his insistence on his conjuring ability—the evening before the crime. He pretended to give himself away. But a man like Clapperton doesn't give himself away. There must be a reason. So long as people thought he had been a *conjuror* they weren't likely to think of his having been a *ventriloquist.*"

"And the voice we heard—Mrs. Clapperton's voice?"

"One of the stewardesses had a voice not unlike hers. I induced her to hide behind the stage and taught her the words to say."

"It was a trick—a cruel trick," cried out Ellie.

"I do not approve of murder," said Hercule Poirot.

# THE
# LABORS
# OF
# HERCULES

# Foreword

HERCULE Poirot's flat was essentially modern in its furnishings. It gleamed with chromium. Its easy chairs, though comfortably padded, were square and uncompromising in outline.

On one of these chairs sat Hercule Poirot, neatly—in the middle of the chair. Opposite him, in another chair, sat Dr. Burton, Fellow of All Souls, sipping appreciatively at a glass of Poirot's Château Mouton Rothschild. There was no neatness about Dr. Burton. He was plump, untidy, and beneath his thatch of white hair beamed a rubicund and benign countenance. He had a deep, wheezy chuckle and the habit of covering himself and everything round him with tobacco ash. In vain did Poirot surround him with ashtrays.

Dr. Burton was asking a question.

"Tell me," he said. "Why Hercule?"

"You mean, my Christian name?" "Hardly a *Christian* name," the other demurred. "Definitely pagan. But why? That's what I want to know. Father's fancy? Mother's whim? Family reasons? If I remember rightly—though my memory isn't what it was—you also had a brother called Achille, did you not?"

Poirot's mind raced back over the details of Achille Poirot's career. Had all that really happened?

"Only for a short space of time," he replied.

Dr. Burton passed tactfully from the subject of Achille Poirot.

"People should be more careful how they name their children," he ruminated. "I've got godchildren. I know. Blanche, one of 'em is called—dark as a gypsy! Then there's Deirdre, Deirdre of the Sorrows—she's turned out merry as a grig. As for young Patience, she might as well have been named Impatience and be done with it! And Diana—well, Diana—" the old classical scholar shuddered. "Weighs twelve stone *now*—and she's only fifteen! They *say* it's puppy fat—but it doesn't look that way to me. *Diana!* They wanted to call her Helen, but I did put my foot down there. Knowing what her father and mother looked like! And her grandmother for that matter! I tried hard for

Martha or Dorcas or something sensible—but it was no good—waste of breath. Rum people, parents. . . ."

He began to wheeze gently—his small fat face crinkled up.

Poirot looked at him inquiringly.

"Thinking of an imaginary conversation. Your mother and the late Mrs. Holmes, sitting sewing little garments or knitting: 'Achille, Hercule, Sherlock, Mycroft. . . .' "

Poirot failed to share his friend's amusement.

"What I understand you to mean is that in physical appearance *I* do not resemble a Hercules?"

Dr. Burton's eyes swept over Hercule Poirot, over his small neat person attired in striped trousers, correct black jacket and natty bow tie, swept up from his patent leather shoes to his eggshaped head and the immense moustache that adorned his upper lip.

"Frankly, Poirot," said Dr. Burton, "you don't! I gather," he added, "that you've never had much time to study the classics?"

"That is so."

"Pity. Pity. You've missed a lot. Everyone should be made to study the classics if I had my way."

Poirot shrugged his shoulders.

"*Eh bien,* I have got on very well without them."

"Got on! *Got on?* It's not a question of getting on. That's the wrong view altogether. The classics aren't a ladder leading to quick success, like a modern correspondence course! It's not a man's working hours that are important—it's his leisure hours. That's the mistake we all make. Take yourself now, you're getting on, you'll be wanting to get out of things, to take things easy—what are you going to do then with *your* leisure hours?"

Poirot was ready with his reply.

"I am going to attend—seriously—to the cultivation of vegetable marrows."

Dr. Burton was taken aback.

"Vegetable marrows? What d'yer mean? Those great swollen green things that taste of water?"

"Ah," Poirot spoke enthusiastically. "But that is the whole point of it. They need *not* taste of water."

"Oh! I know—sprinkle 'em with cheese, or minced onion or white sauce."

"No, no—you are in error. It is my idea that the actual flavour of the marrow itself can be improved. It can be given," he screwed up his eyes, "a bouquet—"

"Good God, man, it's not a claret." The word *bouquet* reminded Dr. Burton of the glass at his elbow. He sipped and savoured. "Very good wine, this. Very sound. Yes." His head nodded in approbation.

"But this vegetable marrow business—you're not *serious?* You don't mean—" he spoke in lively horror—"that you're actually going to *stoop*—" his hands descended in sympathetic horror on his own plump stomach—"stoop, and fork dung on the things, and feed 'em with strands of wool dipped in water and all the rest of it?"

"You seem," Poirot said, "to be well acquainted with the culture of the marrow?"

"Seen gardeners doing it when I've been staying in the country. But seriously, Poirot, what a hobby! Compare that to—" his voice sank to an appreciative purr—"an easy chair in front of a wood fire in a long, low room lined with books—must be a *long* room—not a square one. Books all round one. A glass of port—and a book open in your hand. Time rolls back as you read." He quoted sonorously:

$$\text{Μήτι δ' αὖυτε κυβερνήτης ἐνὶ οἴνοπι πόοντωι}$$
$$\text{νῆα θοὴν ἰθύνει ἐρεχθυμένην ἀνέμοισι}$$

He translated:

> *"By skill again, the pilot on the wine-dark sea straightens*
> *The swift ship buffeted by the winds.*

"Of course you can never really get the spirit of the original."

For the moment, in his enthusiasm, he had forgotten Poirot. And Poirot, watching him, felt suddenly a doubt—an uncomfortable twinge. Was there, here, something that he had missed? Some richness of the spirit? Sadness crept over him. Yes, he should have become acquainted with the classics. . . . Long ago. . . . Now, alas, it was too late. . . .

Dr. Burton interrupted his melancholy.

"Do you mean that you really are thinking of retiring?"

"Yes."

The other chuckled.

"You won't!"

"But I assure you—"

"You won't be able to do it, man. You're too interested in your work."

"No—indeed—I make all the arrangements. A few more cases—specially selected ones—not, you understand, everything that presents itself—just problems that have a personal appeal."

Dr. Burton grinned.

"That's the way of it. Just a case or two, just one case more—and so on. The prima donna's farewell performance won't be in it with yours, Poirot!"

He chuckled and rose slowly to his feet, an amiable white-haired gnome.

"Yours aren't the Labors of Hercules," he said. "Yours are labors of love. You'll see if I'm not right. Bet you that in twelve months' time you'll still be here, and vegetable marrows will still be—" he shuddered—"merely marrows."

Taking leave of his host, Dr. Burton left the severe rectangular room.

He passes out of these pages not to return to them. We are concerned only with what he left behind him which was an Idea.

For after his departure Hercule Poirot sat down again slowly like a man in a dream and murmured:

"The Labors of Hercules. . . . *Mais oui, c'est une idée, ça.* . . ."

The following day saw Hercule Poirot perusing a large calf-bound volume, with occasional harried glances at various typewritten slips of paper, and other slimmer works.

His secretary, Miss Lemon, had been detailed to collect information on the subject of Hercules and to place same before him.

Without interest (hers not the type to wonder why!) but with perfect efficiency, Miss Lemon had fulfilled her task.

Hercule Poirot was plunged head first in a bewildering sea of classical lore with particular reference to "Hercules, a celebrated hero who, after death, was ranked among the gods, and received divine honours."

So far, so good—but thereafter it was far from plain sailing. For two hours Poirot read diligently, making notes, frowning, consulting his slips of paper and his other books of reference. Finally, he sank back in his chair and shook his head. His mood of the previous evening was dispelled. What people!

Take this Hercules—this hero! Hero indeed? What was he but a large muscular creature of low intelligence and criminal tendencies! Poirot was reminded of one Adolfe Durand, a butcher, who had been tried at Lyon in 1895—a creature of oxlike strength who had killed several children. The defence had been epilepsy—from which he undoubtedly suffered—though whether *grand mal* or *petit mal* had been an argument of several days' discussion. This ancient Hercules probably suffered from *grand mal.* No, Poirot shook his head, if *that* was the Greeks' idea of a hero, then measured by modern standards it certainly would not do. The whole classical pattern shocked him. These gods and goddesses—they seemed to have as many different aliases as a modern criminal. Indeed they seemed to be definitely criminal types. Drink, debauchery, incest, rape, loot, homicide and chicanery—enough to keep a *juge d'Instruction* constantly busy. No decent family life. No order, no method. Even in their crimes, no order or method!

"Hercules indeed!" said Hercule Poirot, rising to his feet, disillusioned.

He looked round him with approval. A square room, with good

square modern furniture—even a piece of good modern sculpture representing one cube placed on another cube and above it a geometrical arrangement of copper wire. And in the midst of this shining and orderly room, *himself.* He looked at himself in the glass. Here, then, was a *modern* Hercules—very distinct from that unpleasant sketch of a naked figure with bulging muscles, brandishing a club. Instead, a small compact figure attired in correct urban wear with a moustache—such a moustache as Hercules never dreamed of cultivating— a moustache magnificent yet sophisticated.

Yet there was between this Hercule Poirot and the Hercules of classical lore one point of resemblance. Both of them, undoubtedly, had been instrumental in ridding the world of certain pests. . . . Each of them could be described as a benefactor to the society he lived in. . . .

What had Dr. Burton said last night as he left? "Yours are not the Labors of Hercules. . . ."

Ah, but there he was wrong, the old fossil. There should be, once again, the Labors of Hercules—a modern Hercules. An ingenious and amusing conceit! In the period before his final retirement he would accept twelve cases, no more, no less. And those twelve cases should be selected with special reference to the twelve labors of ancient Hercules. Yes, that would not only be amusing, it would be artistic, it would be *spiritual.*

Poirot picked up the Classical Dictionary and immersed himself once more in classical lore. He did not intend to follow his prototype too closely. There should be no women, no Shirt of Nessus. . . . The Labors and the Labors only.

The first Labor, then, would be that of the Nemean Lion.

"The Nemean Lion," he repeated, trying it over on his tongue.

Naturally he did not expect a case to present itself actually involving a flesh and blood lion. It would be too much of a coincidence should he be approached by the Directors of the Zoological Gardens to solve a problem for them involving a real lion.

No, here symbolism must be involved. The first case must concern some celebrated public figure, it must be sensational and of the first importance! Some master criminal—or, alternatively, someone who was a lion in the public eye. Some well-known writer, or politician, or painter—or even royalty?

He liked the idea of royalty. . . .

He would not be in a hurry. He would wait—wait for that case of high importance that should be the first of his self-imposed Labors.

# I

# The Nemean Lion

"ANYTHING of interest this morning, Miss Lemon?" He asked as he entered the room the following morning.

He trusted Miss Lemon. She was a woman without imagination, but she had an instinct. Anything that she mentioned as worth consideration usually was worth consideration. She was a born secretary.

"Nothing much, M. Poirot. There is just one letter that I thought might interest you. I have put it on the top of the pile."

"And what is that?" He took an interested step forward.

"It's from a man who wants you to investigate the disappearance of his wife's Pekinese dog."

Poirot paused with his foot still in the air. He threw a glance of deep reproach at Miss Lemon. She did not notice it. She had begun to type. She typed with the speed and precision of a quick firing tank.

Poirot was shaken; shaken and embittered. Miss Lemon, the efficient Miss Lemon, had let him down! A Pekinese *dog*. A *Pekinese* dog! And after the dream he had had last night. He had been leaving Buckingham Palace after being personally thanked when his valet had come in with his morning chocolate!

Words trembled on his lips—witty, caustic words. He did not utter them because Miss Lemon, owing to the speed and efficiency of her typing, would not have heard them.

With a grunt of disgust he picked up the topmost letter from the little pile on the side of his desk.

Yes, it was exactly as Miss Lemon had said. A city address—a curt, businesslike, unrefined demand. The subject—the kidnapping of a Pekinese dog. One of those bulging-eyed, overpampered pets of a rich woman. Hercule Poirot's lip curled as he read it.

Nothing unusual about this. Nothing out of the way or— But yes,

yes, in one small detail, Miss Lemon was right. In one small detail there *was* something unusual.

Hercule Poirot sat down. He read the letter slowly and carefully. It was not the kind of case he wanted, it was not the kind of case he had promised himself. It was not in any sense an important case, it was supremely unimportant. It was not—and here was the crux of his objection—it was not a proper Labor of Hercules.

But unfortunately he was curious. . . .

Yes, he was curious. . . .

He raised his voice so as to be heard by Miss Lemon above the noise of her typing.

"Ring up this Sir Joseph Hoggin," he ordered, "and make an appointment for me to see him at his office as he suggests."

As usual, Miss Lemon had been right.

"I'm a plain man, M. Poirot," said Sir Joseph Hoggin.

Hercule Poirot made a noncommittal gesture with his right hand. It expressed (if you chose to take it so) admiration for the solid worth of Sir Joseph's career and an appreciation of his modesty in so describing himself. It could also have conveyed a graceful deprecation of the statement. In any case it gave no clue to the thought then uppermost in Hercule Poirot's mind which was that Sir Joseph certainly was (using the term in its more colloquial sense) a very plain man indeed. Hercule Poirot's eyes rested critically on the swelling jowl, the small pig eyes, the bulbous nose, and the close-lipped mouth. The whole general effect reminded him of someone or something—but for the moment he could not recollect who or what it was. A memory stirred dimly. A long time ago . . . in Belgium . . . something, surely, to do with *soap*. . . .

Sir Joseph was continuing.

"No frills about me. I don't beat about the bush. Most people, M. Poirot, would let this business go. Write it off as a bad debt and forget about it. But that's not Joseph Hoggin's way. I'm a rich man—and in a manner of speaking £200 is neither here nor there to me—"

Poirot interpolated swiftly:

"I congratulate you."

"Eh?"

Sir Joseph paused a minute. His small eyes narrowed themselves still more. He said sharply:

"That's not to say that I'm in the habit of throwing my money about. What I want I pay for. But I pay the market price—no more."

Hercule Poirot said:

"You realise that my fees are high?"

"Yes, yes. But this," Sir Joseph looked at him cunningly, "is a very small matter."

Hercule Poirot shrugged his shoulders. He said:

"I do not bargain. I am an expert. For the services of an expert you have to pay."

Sir Joseph said frankly:

"I know you're a tiptop man at this sort of thing. I made inquiries and I was told that you were the best man available. I mean to get to the bottom of this business and I don't grudge the expense. That's why I got you to come here."

"You were fortunate," said Hercule Poirot.

Sir Joseph said "Eh?" again.

"Exceedingly fortunate," said Hercule Poirot firmly. "I am, I may say so without undue modesty, at the apex of my career. Very shortly I intend to retire—to live in the country, to travel occasionally to see the world—also, it may be, to cultivate my garden—with particular attention to improving the strain of vegetable marrows. Magnificent vegetables—but they lack flavor. That, however, is not the point. I wished merely to explain that before retiring I had imposed upon myself a certain task. I have decided to accept twelve cases—no more, no less. A self-imposed 'Labors of Hercules' if I may so describe it. Your case, Sir Joseph, is the first of the twelve. I was attracted to it," he sighed, "by its striking unimportance."

"Importance?" said Sir Joseph.

"*Un*importance was what I said. I have been called in for varying causes—to investigate murders, unexplained deaths, robberies, thefts of jewelry. This is the first time that I have been asked to turn my talents to elucidate the kidnapping of a Pekinese dog."

Sir Joseph grunted. He said:

"You surprise me! I should have said you'd have had no end of women pestering you about their pet dogs."

"That, certainly. But it is the first time that I am summoned by the husband in the case."

Sir Joseph's little eyes narrowed appreciatively.

He said:

"I begin to see why they recommended you to me. You're a shrewd fellow, M. Poirot."

Poirot murmured:

"If you will now tell me the facts of the case. The dog disappeared, when?"

"Exactly a week ago."

"And your wife is by now quite frantic, I presume?"

Sir Joseph stared. He said:

"You don't understand. The dog has been returned."

"Returned? Then, permit me to ask, where do *I* enter the matter?"
Sir Joseph went crimson in the face.

"Because I'm damned if I'll be swindled! Now then, M. Poirot, I'm
going to tell you the whole thing. The dog was stolen a week ago—
nipped in Kensington Gardens where he was out with my wife's companion. The next day my wife got a demand for £200. I ask you—
£*200!* For a damned yapping little brute that's always getting under
your feet anyway!"

Poirot murmured:

"You did not approve of paying such a sum, naturally?"

"Of course I didn't—or wouldn't have if I'd known anything about
it! Milly (my wife) knew that well enough. She didn't say anything to
*me*. Just sent off the money—in one-pound notes as stipulated—to
the address given."

"And the dog was returned?"

"Yes. That evening the bell rang and there was the little brute
sitting on the doorstep. And not a soul to be seen."

"Perfectly. Continue."

"Then, of course, Milly confessed what she'd done and I lost my
temper a bit. However, I calmed down after a while—after all, the
thing was done and you can't expect a woman to behave with any
sense—and I daresay I should have let the whole thing go if it hadn't
been for meeting old Samuelson at the Club."

"Yes?"

"Damn it all, this thing must be a positive racket! Exactly the same
thing had happened to him. Three hundred pounds they'd rooked
his wife of! Well, that was a bit too much. I decided the thing had
got to be stopped. I sent for you."

"But surely, Sir Joseph, the proper thing (and a very much more
inexpensive thing) would have been to send for the police?"

Sir Joseph rubbed his nose.

He said:

"Are you married, M. Poirot?"

"Alas," said Poirot, "I have not that felicity."

"Hm," said Sir Joseph. "Don't know about felicity, but if you were,
you'd know that women are funny creatures. My wife went into hysterics at the mere mention of the police—she'd got it into her head that
something would happen to her precious Shan Tung if I went to them.
She wouldn't hear of the idea—and I may say she doesn't take very
kindly to the idea of your being called in. But I stood firm there and
at last she gave way. But, mind you, she doesn't like it."

Hercule Poirot murmured:

"The position is, I perceive, a delicate one. It would be as well,
perhaps, if I were to interview madame your wife and gain further

particulars from her while at the same time reassuring her as to the future safety of her dog."

Sir Joseph nodded and rose to his feet. He said:

"I'll take you along in the car right away."

## 2

In a large, hot, ornately furnished drawing room two women were sitting.

As Sir Joseph and Hercule Poirot entered, a small Pekinese dog rushed forward, barking furiously, and circling dangerously round Poirot's ankles.

"Shan—Shan, come here. Come here to mother, lovey— Pick him up, Miss Carnaby."

The second woman hurried forward and Hercule Poirot murmured:

"A veritable lion, indeed."

Rather breathlessly Shan Tung's captor agreed.

"Yes, indeed, he's such a *good* watch dog. He's not frightened of anything or anyone. There's a lovely boy, then."

Having performed the necessary introduction, Sir Joseph said:

"Well, M. Poirot, I'll leave you to get on with it," and with a short nod he left the room.

Lady Hoggin was a stout, petulant-looking woman with dyed henna-red hair. Her companion, the fluttering Miss Carnaby, was a plump, amiable-looking creature between forty and fifty. She treated Lady Hoggin with great deference and was clearly frightened to death of her.

Poirot said:

"Now tell me, Lady Hoggin, the full circumstances of this abominable crime."

Lady Hoggin flushed.

"I'm very glad to hear you say that, M. Poirot. For it was a crime. Pekinese are terribly sensitive—just as sensitive as children. Poor Shan Tung might have died of fright if of nothing else."

Miss Carnaby chimed in breathlessly:

"Yes, it was wicked—wicked!"

"Please tell me the facts."

"Well, it was like this. Shan Tung was out for his walk in the park with Miss Carnaby—"

"Oh, dear me, yes, it was all my fault," chimed in the companion. "How could I have been so stupid—so careless—"

Lady Hoggin said acidly:

"I don't want to reproach you, Miss Carnaby, but I do think you might have been more alert."

Poirot transferred his gaze to the companion.

"What happened?"

Miss Carnaby burst into voluble and slightly flustered speech.

"Well, it was the most extraordinary thing! We had just been along the flower walk—Shan Tung was on the lead, of course—he'd had his little run on the grass—and I was just about to turn and go home when my attention was caught by a baby in a pram—such a lovely baby—it smiled at me—lovely rosy cheeks and such curls. I couldn't just resist speaking to the nurse in charge and asking how old it was— seventeen months, she said—and I'm sure I was only speaking to her for about a minute or two, and then suddenly I looked down and Shan wasn't there any more. The lead had been cut right through—"

Lady Hoggin said:

"If you'd been paying proper attention to your duties, nobody could have sneaked up and cut that lead."

Miss Carnaby seemed inclined to burst into tears. Poirot said hastily:

"And what happened next?"

"Well, of course I looked everywhere. And called! And I asked the park attendant if he'd seen a man carrying a Pekinese dog but he hadn't noticed anything of the kind—and I didn't know what to do— and I went on searching, but at last, of course, I had to come home—"

Miss Carnaby stopped dead. Poirot could imagine the scene that followed well enough. He asked:

"And then you received a letter?"

Lady Hoggin took up the tale.

"By the first post the following morning. It said that if I wanted to see Shan Tung alive I was to send £200 in one-pound notes in an unregistered packet to Captain Curtis, 38 Bloomsbury Road Square. It said that if the money were marked or the police informed then— then—Shan Tung's ears and tail would be—cut off!"

Miss Carnaby began to sniff.

"So awful," she murmured. "How people can be such fiends!"

Lady Hoggin went on:

"It said that if I sent the money at once, Shan Tung would be returned the same evening alive and well but that if—if afterwards I went to the police, it would be Shan Tung who would suffer for it—"

Miss Carnaby murmured tearfully:

"Oh, dear, I'm so afraid that even now—of course, M. Poirot isn't exactly the police—"

Lady Hoggin said anxiously:

"So you see, M. Poirot, you will have to be very careful—"

Hercule Poirot was quick to allay her anxiety.

"But I, I am not of the police. My inquiries, they will be conducted very discreetly, very quietly. You can be assured, Lady Hoggin, that Shan Tung will be perfectly safe. That I will guarantee."

Both ladies seemed relieved by the magic word. Poirot went on:

"You have here the letter?"

Lady Hoggin shook her head.

"No, I was instructed to enclose it with the money."

"And you did so?"

"Yes."

"Hm, that is a pity."

Miss Carnaby said brightly:

"But I have the dog lead still. Shall I get it?"

She left the room. Hercule Poirot profited by her absence to ask a few pertinent questions.

"Amy Carnaby? Oh! she's quite all right. A good soul, though foolish, of course. I have had several companions and they have all been complete fools. But Amy was devoted to Shan Tung and she was terribly upset over the whole thing—as well she might be—hanging over perambulators and neglecting my little sweetheart! These old maids are all the same, idiotic over babies! No, I'm quite sure she had nothing whatever to do with it."

"It does not seem likely," Poirot agreed. "But as the dog disappeared when in her charge one must make quite certain of her honesty. She has been with you long?"

"Nearly a year. I had excellent references with her. She was with old Lady Hartingfield until she died—ten years, I believe. After that she looked after an invalid sister for a while. She is really an excellent creature—but a complete fool, as I said."

Amy Carnaby returned at this minute, slightly more out of breath, and produced the cut dog lead which she handed to Poirot with the utmost solemnity, looking at him with hopeful expectancy.

Poirot surveyed it carefully.

"*Mais oui,*" he said. "This has undoubtedly been cut."

The two women still waited expectantly. He said:

"I will keep this."

Solemnly he put it in his pocket. The two women breathed a sigh of relief. He had clearly done what was expected of him.

## 3

It was the habit of Hercule Poirot to leave nothing untested.

Though on the face of it it seemed unlikely that Miss Carnaby was anything but the foolish and rather muddle-headed woman that she appeared to be, Poirot nevertheless managed to interview a somewhat forbidding lady who was the niece of the late Lady Hartingfield.

"Amy Carnaby?" said Miss Maltravers. "Of course, remember her perfectly. She was a good soul and suited Aunt Julia down to the ground. Devoted to dogs and excellent at reading aloud. Tactful, too, never contradicted an invalid. What's happened to her? Not in distress of any kind, I hope. I gave her a reference about a year ago to some woman—name began with H—"

Poirot explained hastily that Miss Carnaby was still in her post. There had been, he said, a little trouble over a lost dog.

"Amy Carnaby is devoted to dogs. My aunt had a Pekinese. She left it to Miss Carnaby when she died and Miss Carnaby was devoted to it. I believe she was quite heartbroken when it died. Oh, yes, she's a good soul. Not, of course, precisely intellectual."

Hercule Poirot agreed that Miss Carnaby could not, perhaps, be described as intellectual.

His next proceeding was to discover the park keeper to whom Miss Carnaby had spoken on the fateful afternoon. This he did without much difficulty. The man remembered the incident in question.

"Middle-aged lady, rather stout—in a regular state she was—lost her Pekinese dog. I knew her well by sight—brings the dog along most afternoons. I saw her come in with it. She was in a rare taking when she lost it. Came running to me to know if I'd seen anyone with a Pekinese dog! Well, I ask you! I can tell you, the Gardens is full of dogs—every kind—terriers, Pekes, German sausage dogs—even them Borzoys—all kinds we have. Not likely as I'd notice one Peke more than another."

Hercule Poirot nodded his head thoughtfully.

He went to 38 Bloomsbury Road Square.

Nos. 38, 39 and 40 were incorporated together as the Balaclava Private Hotel. Poirot walked up the steps and pushed open the door. He was greeted inside by gloom and a smell of cooking cabbage with a reminiscence of breakfast kippers. On his left was a mahogany table with a sad-looking chrysanthemum plant on it. Above the table was a big baize-covered rack into which letters were stuck. Poirot stared at the board thoughtfully for some minutes. He pushed open a door on his right. It led into a kind of lounge with small tables and some so-called easy chairs covered with a depressing pattern of cretonne.

Three old ladies and one fierce-looking old gentleman raised their heads and gazed at the intruder with deadly venom. Hercule Poirot blushed and withdrew.

He walked further along the passage and came to a staircase. On his right a passage branched at right angles to what was evidently the dining room.

A little way along this passage was a door marked OFFICE.

On this Poirot tapped. Receiving no response, he opened the door and looked in. There was a large desk in the room, covered with papers, but there was no one to be seen. He withdrew, closing the door again. He penetrated to the dining room.

A sad-looking girl in a dirty apron was shuffling about with a basket of knives and forks with which she was laying the tables.

Hercule Poirot said apologetically:

"Excuse me, but could I see the manageress?"

The girl looked at him with lacklustre eyes.

She said:

"I don't know, I'm sure."

Hercule Poirot said:

"There is no one in the office."

"Well, I don't know where she'd be, I'm sure."

"Perhaps," Hercule Poirot said, patient and persistent, "you could find out?"

The girl sighed. Dreary as her day's round was, it had now been made additionally so by this new burden laid upon her. She said sadly:

"Well, I'll see what I can do."

Poirot thanked her and removed himself once more to the hall, not daring to face the malevolent glare of the occupants of the lounge. He was staring up at the baize-covered letter rack when a rustle and a strong smell of Devonshire violets proclaimed the arrival of the manageress.

Mrs. Harte was full of graciousness. She exclaimed:

"So sorry I was not in my office. You were requiring rooms?"

Hercule Poirot murmured:

"Not precisely. I was wondering if a friend of mine had been staying here lately. A Captain Curtis."

"Curtis," exclaimed Mrs. Harte. "Captain Curtis? Now where have I heard that name?"

Poirot did not help her. She shook her head vexedly.

He said:

"You have not, then, had a Captain Curtis staying here?"

"Well, not lately, certainly. And yet, you know, the name is certainly familiar to me. Can you describe your friend at all?"

"That," said Hercule Poirot, "would be difficult." He went on, "I suppose it sometimes happens that letters arrive for people when in actual fact no one of that name is staying here?"

"That does happen, of course."

"What do you do with such letters?"

"Well, we keep them for a time. You see, it probably means that the person in question will arrive shortly. Of course, if letters or parcels are a long time here unclaimed, they are returned to the post office."

Hercule Poirot nodded thoughtfully.

He said:

"I comprehend." He added, "It is like this, you see. I wrote a letter to my friend here."

Mrs. Harte's face cleared.

"That explains it. I must have noticed the name on an envelope. But really we have so many ex-Army gentlemen staying here or passing through— Let me see now."

She peered up at the board.

Hercule Poirot said:

"It is not there now."

"It must have been returned to the postman, I suppose. I am so sorry. Nothing important, I hope?"

"No, no, it was of no importance."

As he moved towards the door, Mrs. Harte, enveloped in her pungent odour of violets, pursued him.

"If your friend should come—"

"It is most unlikely. I must have made a mistake. . . ."

"Our terms," said Mrs. Harte, "are very moderate. Coffee after dinner is included. I would like you to see one or two of our bed-sitting rooms. . . ."

With difficulty Hercule Poirot escaped.

# 4

The drawing room of Mrs. Samuelson was larger, more lavishly furnished, and enjoyed an even more stifling amount of central heating than that of Lady Hoggin. Hercule Poirot picked his way giddily among gilded console tables and large groups of statuary.

Mrs. Samuelson was taller than Lady Hoggin and her hair was dyed with peroxide. Her Pekinese was called Nanki Poo. His bulging eyes surveyed Hercule Poirot with arrogance. Miss Keble, Mrs. Samuelson's companion, was thin and scraggy where Miss Carnaby had been plump, but she also was voluble and slightly breathless. She, too, had been blamed for Nanki Poo's disappearance.

"But, really, M. Poirot, it was the most amazing thing. It all happened in a second. Outside Harrods it was. A nurse there asked me the time—"

Poirot interrupted her.

"A nurse? A hospital nurse?"

"No, no—a children's nurse. Such a sweet baby it was, too! A dear little mite. Such lovely rosy cheeks. They say children don't look healthy in London, but I'm sure—"

"Ellen," said Mrs. Samuelson.

Miss Keble blushed, stammered, and subsided into silence.

Mrs. Samuelson said acidly:

"And while Miss Keble was bending over a perambulator that had nothing to do with her, this audacious villain cut Nanki Poo's lead and made off with him."

Miss Keble murmured tearfully:

"It all happened in a second. I looked round and the darling boy was gone—there was just the dangling lead in my hand. Perhaps you'd like to see the lead, M. Poirot?"

"By no means," said Poirot hastily. He had no wish to make a collection of cut dog leads. "I understand," he went on, "that shortly afterwards you received a letter?"

The story followed the same course exactly—the letter—the threats of violence to Nanki Poo's ears and tail. Only two things were different—the sum of money demanded—£300—and the address to which it was to be sent; this time it was to Commander Blackleigh, Harrington Hotel, 76 Clonmel Gardens, Kensington.

Mrs. Samuelson went on:

"When Nanki Poo was safely back again, I went to the place myself, M. Poirot. After all, three hundred pounds is three hundred pounds."

"Certainly it is."

"The very first thing I saw was my letter enclosing the money in a kind of rack in the hall. Whilst I was waiting for the proprietress I slipped it into my bag. Unfortunately—"

Poirot said:

"Unfortunately, when you opened it it contained only blank sheets of paper."

"How did you know?" Mrs. Samuelson turned on him with awe.

Poirot shrugged his shoulders.

"Obviously, *chère madame,* the thief would take care to recover the money before he returned the dog. He would then replace the notes with blank paper and return the letter to the rack in case its absence should be noticed."

"No such person as Commander Blackleigh had ever stayed there."

Poirot smiled.

"And, of course, my husband was extremely annoyed about the whole thing. In fact, he was livid—absolutely livid!"

Poirot murmured cautiously:

"You did not—er—consult him before despatching the money?"

"Certainly not," said Mrs. Samuelson, with decision.

Poirot looked a question. The lady explained.

"I wouldn't have risked it for a moment. Men are so extraordinary when it's a question of money. Jacob would have insisted on going to the police. I couldn't risk that. My poor darling Nanki Poo. Anything might have happened to him! Of course, I *had* to tell my husband afterwards, because I had to explain why I was overdrawn at the bank."

Poirot murmured:

"Quite so—quite so."

"And I have really never seen him so angry. Men," said Mrs. Samuelson, rearranging her handsome diamond bracelet and turning her rings on her fingers, "think of nothing but money."

# 5

Hercule Poirot went up in the lift to Sir Joseph Hoggin's office. He sent in his card and was told that Sir Joseph was engaged at the moment but would see him presently. A haughty blonde sailed out of Sir Joseph's room at last with her hands full of papers. She gave the quaint little man a disdainful glance in passing.

Sir Joseph was seated behind his immense mahogany desk. There was a trace of lipstick on his chin.

"Well, M. Poirot? Sit down. Got any news for me?"

Hercule Poirot said:

"The whole affair is of a pleasing simplicity. In each case the money was sent to one of those boarding houses or private hotels where there is no porter or hall attendant and where a large number of guests are always coming and going, including a fairly large preponderance of ex-Service men. Nothing would be easier than for anyone to walk in, abstract a letter from the rack, either take it away, or else remove the money and replace it with blank paper. Therefore, in every case, the trail ends abruptly in a blank wall."

"You mean you've no idea who the fellow is?"

"I have certain ideas, yes. It will take a few days to follow them up."

Sir Joseph looked at him curiously.

"Good work. Then, when you've got anything to report—"

"I will report to you at your house."

Sir Joseph said:

"If you get to the bottom of this business, it will be a pretty good piece of work."

Hercule Poirot said:

"There is no question of failure. Hercule Poirot does not fail."

Sir Joseph Hoggin looked at the little man and grinned.

"Sure of yourself, aren't you?" he demanded.

"Entirely with reason."

"Oh, well," Sir Joseph Hoggin leaned back in his chair. "Pride goes before a fall, you know."


# 6

Hercule Poirot, sitting in front of his electric radiator (and feeling a quiet satisfaction in its neat geometrical pattern) was giving instructions to his valet and general factotum.

"You understand, Georges?"

"Perfectly, sir."

"More probably a flat or maisonette. And it will definitely be within certain limits. South of the Park, east of Kensington Church, west of Knightsbridge Barracks, and north of Fulham Road."

"I understand perfectly, sir."

Poirot murmured:

"A curious little case. There is evidence here of a very definite talent for organization. And there is, of course, the surprising invisibility of the star performer—the Nemean Lion himself, if I may so style him. Yes, an interesting little case. I could wish that I felt more attracted to my client—but he bears an unfortunate resemblance to a soap manufacturer of Liège who poisoned his wife in order to marry a blond secretary. One of my early successes."

Georges shook his head. He said gravely:

"These blondes, sir, they're responsible for a lot of trouble."


# 7

It was three days later when the invaluable Georges said:

"This is the address, sir."

Hercule Poirot took the piece of paper handed to him.

"Excellent, my good Georges. And what day of the week?"

"Thursdays, sir."

"Thursdays. And today, most fortunately, is a Thursday. So there need be no delay."

Twenty minutes later Hercule Poirot was climbing the stairs of an obscure block of flats tucked away in a little street leading off a more fashionable one. No. 10 Rosholm Mansions was on the third and top floor and there was no lift. Poirot toiled upwards round and round the narrow corkscrew staircase.

He paused to regain his breath on the top landing and from behind the door of No. 10 a new sound broke the silence—the sharp bark of a dog.

Hercule Poirot nodded his head with a slight smile. He pressed the bell of No. 10.

The barking redoubled—footsteps came to the door, it was opened. . . .

Miss Amy Carnaby fell back, her hand went to her ample breast.

"You permit that I enter?" said Hercule Poirot, and entered without waiting for the reply.

There was a sitting room door open on the right and he walked in. Behind him Miss Carnaby followed as though in a dream.

The room was very small and much overcrowded. Among the furniture a human being could be discovered, an elderly woman lying on a sofa drawn up to the gas fire. As Poirot came in, a Pekinese dog jumped off the sofa and came forward, uttering a few sharp suspicious barks.

"Aha," said Poirot. "The chief actor! I salute you, my little friend."

He bent forward, extending his hand. The dog sniffed at it, his intelligent eyes fixed on the man's face.

Miss Carnaby murmured faintly:

"So you know?"

Hercule Poirot nodded.

"Yes, I know." He looked at the woman on the sofa. "Your sister, I think?"

Miss Carnaby said mechanically: "Yes, Emily, this—this is M. Poirot."

Emily Carnaby gave a gasp. She said: "Oh!"

Amy Carnaby said:

"Augustus . . ."

The Pekinese looked towards her—his tail moved—then he resumed his scrutiny of Poirot's hand. Again his tail moved faintly.

Gently, Poirot picked the little dog up and sat down with Augustus on his knee. He said:

"So I have captured the Nemean Lion. My task is completed."

Amy Carnaby said in a hard, dry voice:

"Do you really know everything?"

Poirot nodded.

"I think so. You organized this business—with Augustus to help you. You took your employer's dog out for his usual walk, brought him here and went on to the Park with Augustus. The park keeper saw you with a Pekinese as usual. The nurse girl, if we had ever found her, would also have agreed that you had a Pekinese with you when you spoke to her. Then, while you were talking, you cut the lead and Augustus, trained by you, slipped off at once and made a beeline back home. A few minutes later you gave the alarm that the dog had been stolen."

There was a pause. Then Miss Carnaby drew herself up with a certain pathetic dignity. She said:

"Yes. It is all quite true. I—I have nothing to say."

The invalid woman on the sofa began to cry softly.

Poirot said:

"Nothing at all, mademoiselle?"

Miss Carnaby said:

"Nothing. I have been a thief—and now I am found out."

Poirot murmured:

"You have nothing to say—in your own defence?"

A spot of red showed suddenly in Amy Carnaby's white cheeks. She said:

"I—I don't regret what I did. I think that you are a kind man, M. Poirot, and that possibly you might understand. You see, I've been so terribly afraid."

"Afraid?"

"Yes, it's difficult for a gentleman to understand, I expect. But you see, I'm not a clever woman at all, and I've no training and I'm getting older—and I'm so terrified for the future. I've not been able to save anything—how could I, with Emily to be cared for?—and as I get older and more incompetent there won't be anyone who wants me. They'll want somebody young and brisk. I've—I've known so many people like I am—nobody wants you and you live in one room and you can't have a fire or any warmth and not very much to eat, and at last you can't even pay the rent of your room. . . . There are institutions, of course, but it's not very easy to get into them unless you have influential friends, and I haven't. There are a good many others situated like I am—poor companions—untrained, useless women with nothing to look forward to but a deadly fear. . . ."

Her voice shook. She said:

"And so—some of us—got together and—and I thought of this. It was really having Augustus that put it into my mind. You see, to most people, one Pekinese is very much like another. (Just as we think the Chinese are.) Really, of course, it's ridiculous. No one who knew could mistake Augustus for Nanki Poo or Shan Tung or any of the other Pekes. He's far more intelligent for one thing, and he's much handsomer, but, as I say, to most people a Peke is just a Peke. Augustus put it into my head—that, combined with the fact that so many rich women have Pekinese dogs."

Poirot said with a faint smile:

"It must have been a profitable—racket! How many are there in the—the gang? Or perhaps I had better ask how often operations have been successfully carried out?"

Miss Carnaby said simply:

"Shan Tung was the sixteenth."

Hercule Poirot raised his eyebrows.

"I congratulate you. Your organization must have been indeed excellent."

Emily Carnaby said:

"Amy was always good at organization. Our father—he was the vicar of Kellington in Essex—always said that Amy had quite a genius for planning. She always made all the arrangements for the socials and the bazaars and all that."

Poirot said with a little bow:

"I agree. As a criminal, mademoiselle, you are quite in the first rank."

Amy Carnaby cried:

"A criminal. Oh, dear, I suppose I am. But—but it never felt like that."

"How did it feel?"

"Of course, you are quite right. It was breaking the law. But you see—how can I explain it? Nearly all these women who employ us are so very rude and unpleasant. Lady Hoggin, for instance, doesn't mind what she says to me. She said her tonic tasted unpleasant the other day and practically accused me of tampering with it. All that sort of thing." Miss Carnaby flushed. "It's really very unpleasant. And not being able to say anything or answer back makes it rankle more, if you know what I mean."

"I know what you mean," said Hercule Poirot.

"And then seeing money frittered away so wastefully—that is upsetting. And Sir Joseph, occasionally he used to describe a coup he had made in the city—sometimes something that seemed to me (of course, I know I've only got a woman's brain and don't understand finance) downright dishonest. Well, you know, M. Poirot, it all—it all unsettled me, and I felt that to take a little money away from these people who really wouldn't miss it and hadn't been too scrupulous in acquiring it—well, really it hardly seemed wrong at all."

Poirot murmured:

"A modern Robin Hood! Tell me, Miss Carnaby, did you ever have to carry out the threats you used in your letters?"

"Threats?"

"Were you ever compelled to mutilate the animals in the way you specified?"

Miss Carnaby regarded him in horror.

"Of course, I would never have dreamed of doing such a thing! That was just—just an artistic touch."

"Very artistic. It worked."

"Well, of course I knew it would. I know how I should have felt about Augustus, and of course I had to make sure these women never told their husbands until afterwards. The plan worked beautifully every time. In nine cases out of ten the companion was given the letter with the money to post. We usually steamed it open, took out the notes, and replaced them with paper. Once or twice the woman posted it herself. Then, of course, the companion had to go to the hotel and take the letter out of the rack. But that was quite easy, too."

"And the nursemaid touch? Was it always a nursemaid?"

"Well, you see, M. Poirot, old maids are known to be foolishly sentimental about babies. So it seemed quite natural that they should be absorbed over a baby and not notice anything."

Hercule Poirot sighed. He said:

"Your psychology is excellent, your organization is first-class, and you are also a very fine actress. Your performance the other day when I interviewed Lady Hoggin was irreproachable. Never think of yourself disparagingly, Miss Carnaby. You may be what is termed an untrained woman but there is nothing wrong with your brains or with your courage."

Miss Carnaby said with a faint smile:

"And yet I have been found out, M. Poirot."

"Only by me. That was inevitable! When I had interviewed Mrs. Samuelson I realised that the kidnapping of Shan Tung was one of a series. I had already learned that you had once been left a Pekinese dog and had an invalid sister. I had only to ask my invaluable servant to look for a small flat within a certain radius occupied by an invalid lady who had a Pekinese dog and a sister who visited her once a week on her day out. It was simple."

Amy Carnaby drew herself up. She said:

"You have been very kind. It emboldens me to ask you a favor. I cannot, I know, escape the penalty for what I have done. I shall be sent to prison, I suppose. But if you could, M. Poirot, avert some of the publicity. So distressing for Emily—and for those few who knew us in the old days. I could not, I suppose, go to prison under a false name? Or is that a very wrong thing to ask?"

Hercule Poirot said:

"I think I can do more than that. But first of all I must make one thing quite clear. This racket has got to stop. There must be no more disappearing dogs. All that is finished!"

"Yes! Oh, yes!"

"And the money you extracted from Lady Hoggin must be returned."

Amy Carnaby crossed the room, opened the drawer of a bureau and returned with a packet of notes which she handed to Poirot.

"I was going to pay it into the pool today."

Poirot took the notes and counted them. He got up.

"I think it possible, Miss Carnaby, that I may be able to persuade Sir Joseph not to prosecute."

"Oh, M. Poirot!"

Amy Carnaby clasped her hands. Emily gave a cry of joy. Augustus barked and wagged his tail.

"As for you, *mon ami*," said Poirot addressing him, "there is one thing that I wish you would give me. It is your mantle of invisibility that I need. In all these cases nobody for a moment suspected that there was a *second* dog involved. Augustus possessed the lion's skin of invisibility."

"Of course, M. Poirot, according to the legend, Pekinese were lions once. And they still have the hearts of lions!"

"Augustus is, I suppose, the dog that was left to you by Lady Hartingfield and who is reported to have died? Were you never afraid of him coming home alone through the traffic?"

"Oh, no, M. Poirot, Augustus is very clever about traffic. I have trained him most carefully. He has even grasped the principle of one-way streets."

"In that case," said Hercule Poirot, "he is superior to most human beings!"

# 8

Sir Joseph received Hercule Poirot in his study. He said:

"Well, M. Poirot? Made your boast good?"

"Let me first ask you a question," said Poirot as he seated himself. "I know who the criminal is and I think it possible that I can produce sufficient evidence to convict this person. But in that case I doubt if you will ever recover your money."

"Not get back my money?"

Sir Joseph turned purple.

Hercule Poirot went on:

"But I am not a policeman. I am acting in this case solely in your interests. I could, I think, recover your money intact, if no proceedings were taken."

"Eh?" said Sir Joseph. "That needs a bit of thinking about."

"It is entirely for you to decide. Strictly speaking, I suppose you ought to prosecute in the public interest. Most people would say so."

"I daresay they would," said Sir Joseph drily. "It wouldn't be their money that had gone west. If there's one thing I hate it's to be swindled. Nobody's ever swindled me and got away with it."

"Well, then, what do you decide?"

Sir Joseph hit the table with his fist.

"I'll have the brass! Nobody's going to say they got away with two hundred pounds of my money."

Hercule Poirot rose, crossed to the writing table, wrote out a cheque for two hundred pounds and handed it to the other man.

Sir Joseph said in a weak voice:

"Well, I'm damned! Who the devil is this fellow?"

Poirot shook his head.

"If you accept the money, there must be no questions asked."

Sir Joseph folded up the cheque and put it in his pocket.

"That's a pity. But the money's the thing. And what do I owe you, M. Poirot?"

"My fees will not be high. This was, as I said, a very unimportant matter." He paused—and added, "Nowadays nearly all my cases are murder cases. . . ."

Sir Joseph started slightly.

"Must be interesting?" he said.

"Sometimes. Curiously enough, you recall to me one of my early cases in Belgium, many years ago—the chief protagonist was very like you in appearance. He was a wealthy soap manufacturer. He poisoned his wife in order to be free to marry his secretary. . . .Yes—the resemblance is very remarkable. . . ."

A faint sound came from Sir Joseph's lips—they had gone a queer blue colour. All the ruddy hue had faded from his cheeks. His eyes, starting out of his head, stared at Poirot. He slipped down a little in his chair.

Then, with a shaking hand, he fumbled in his pocket. He drew out the cheque and tore it into pieces.

"That's washed out—see? Consider it as your fee."

"Oh, but, Sir Joseph, my fee would not have been as large as that."

"That's all right. You keep it."

"I shall send it to a deserving charity."

"Send it anywhere you damn well like."

Poirot leaned forward. He said:

"I think I need hardly point out, Sir Joseph, that in your position, you would do well to be exceedingly careful."

Sir Joseph said, his voice almost inaudible:

"You needn't worry. I shall be careful all right."

Hercule Poirot left the house. As he went down the steps he said to himself:

"So—I was right."

## 9

Lady Hoggin said to her husband:

"Funny, this tonic tastes quite different. It hasn't got that bitter taste any more. I wonder why?"

Sir Joseph growled:

"Chemist. Careless fellows. Make things up differently different times."

Lady Hoggin said doubtfully:

"I suppose that must be it."

"Of course it is. What else could it be?"

"Has the man found out anything about Shan Tung?"

"Yes. He got me my money back all right."

"Who was it?"

"He didn't say. Very close fellow, Hercule Poirot. But you needn't worry."

"He's a funny little man, isn't he?"

Sir Joseph gave a slight shiver and threw a sideways glance upwards as though he felt the invisible presence of Hercule Poirot behind his right shoulder. He had an idea that he would always feel it there.

He said:

"He's a damned clever little devil!"

And he thought to himself, "Greta can go hang! *I*'m not going to risk my neck for any damned platinum blonde!"

## 10

"*Oh!*"

Amy Carnaby gazed down incredulously at the cheque for two hundred pounds. She cried:

"Emily! *Emily!* Listen to this:

Dear Miss Carnaby,

Allow me to enclose a contribution to your very deserving fund before it is finally wound up.

Yours very truly,

Hercule Poirot.

"Amy," said Emily Carnaby, "you've been incredibly lucky. Think where you might be now."

"Wormwood Scrubbs—or is it Holloway?" murmured Amy Carnaby. "But that's all over now—isn't it, Augustus? No more walks to the park with mother or mother's friends and a little pair of scissors."

A faraway wistfulness came into her eyes. She sighed.

"Dear Augustus! It seems a pity. He's so clever. . . . One can teach him anything. . . ."

# II

# The Lernean Hydra

## I

HERCULE Poirot looked encouragingly at the man seated opposite him.

Dr. Charles Oldfield was a man of perhaps forty. He had fair hair slightly grey at the temples and blue eyes that held a worried expression. He stooped a little and his manner was a trifle hesitant. Moreover, he seemed to find difficulty in coming to the point.

He said, stammering slightly:

"I've come to you, M. Poirot, with rather an odd request. And now that I'm here, I'm inclined to funk the whole thing. Because, as I see very well now, it's the sort of thing that no one can possibly do anything about."

Hercule Poirot murmured:

"As to that, you must let me judge."

Oldfield muttered:

"I don't know why I thought that perhaps—"

He broke off.

Hercule Poirot finished the sentence.

"That perhaps I could help you? *Eh bien,* perhaps I can. Tell me your problem."

Oldfield straightened himself. Poirot noted anew how haggard the man looked.

Oldfield said, and his voice had a note of hopelessness in it:

"You see, it isn't any good going to the police. . . . They can't do anything. And yet—every day it's getting worse and worse. I—I don't know what to do. . . ."

"What is getting worse?"

"The rumours . . . Oh, it's quite simple, M. Poirot. Just a little over a year ago, my wife died. She had been an invalid for some years. They are saying, everyone is saying, that I killed her—that I poisoned her!"

"Aha," said Poirot. "And did you poison her?"

"M. Poirot!" Dr. Oldfield sprang to his feet.

"Calm yourself," said Hercule Poirot. "And sit down again. We will take it, then, that you did not poison your wife. But your practice, I imagine, is situated in a country district—"

"Yes. Market Loughborough—in Berkshire. I have always realised that it was the kind of place where people gossiped a good deal, but I never imagined that it could reach the lengths it has done." He drew his chair a little forward. "M. Poirot, you have no idea of what I have gone through. At first I had no inkling of what was going on. I did notice that people seemed less friendly, that there was a tendency to avoid me—but I put it down to—to the fact of my recent bereavement. Then it became more marked. In the street, even, people will cross the road to avoid speaking to me. My practice is falling off. Wherever I go I am conscious of lowered voices, of unfriendly eyes that watch me while malicious tongues whisper their deadly poison. I have had one or two letters—vile things."

He paused—and then went on:

"And—and I don't know what to do about it. I don't know how to fight this—this vile network of lies and suspicion. How can you refute what is never said openly to your face? I am powerless—trapped— and slowly mercilessly being destroyed."

Poirot nodded his head thoughtfully. He said:

"Yes. Rumour is indeed the nine-headed Hydra of Lernea which cannot be exterminated because as fast as one head is cropped off two grow in its place."

Dr. Oldfield said:

"That's just it. There's nothing I can do—nothing! I came to you as a last resort—but I don't suppose for a minute that there is anything you can do either."

Hercule Poirot was silent for a minute or two. Then he said:

"I am not so sure. Your problem interests me, Dr. Oldfield. I should like to try my hand at destroying the many-headed monster. First of all, tell me a little more about the circumstances which gave rise to this malicious gossip. Your wife died, you say, just over a year ago. What was the cause of death?"

"Gastric ulcer."

"Was there an autopsy?"

"No. She had been suffering from gastric trouble over a considerable period."

Poirot nodded.

"And the symptoms of gastric inflammation and of arsenical poisoning are closely alike—a fact which everybody knows nowadays. Within the last ten years there have been at least four sensational murder cases in each of which the victim has been buried without suspicion with a certificate of gastric disorder. Was your wife older or younger than yourself?"

"She was five years older."

"How long had you been married?"

"Fifteen years."

"Did she leave any property?"

"Yes. She was a fairly well-to-do woman. She left, roughly, about thirty thousand pounds."

"A very useful sum. It was left to you?"

"Yes."

"Were you and your wife on good terms?"

"Certainly."

"No quarrels? No scenes?"

"Well—" Charles Oldfield hesitated. "My wife was what might be termed a difficult woman. She was an invalid and very concerned over her health and inclined, therefore, to be fretful and difficult to please. There were days when nothing I could do was right."

Poirot nodded. He said:

"Ah, yes, I know the type. She would complain, possibly, that she was neglected, unappreciated—that her husband was tired of her and would be glad when she was dead."

Oldfield's face registered the truth of Poirot's surmise. He said with a wry smile:

"You've got it exactly!"

Poirot went on:

"Did she have a hospital nurse to attend on her? Or a companion? Or a devoted maid?"

"A nurse companion. A very sensible and competent woman. I really don't think she would talk."

"Even the sensible and the competent have been given tongues by *le bon Dieu*—and they do not always employ their tongues wisely. I have no doubt that the nurse companion talked, that the servants talked, that everyone talked! You have all the materials there for the starting of a very enjoyable village scandal. Now I will ask you one thing more. Who is the lady?"

"I don't understand." Dr. Oldfield flushed angrily.

Poirot said gently:

"I think you do. I am asking you who the lady is with whom your name has been coupled."

Dr. Oldfield rose to his feet. His face was stiff and cold. He said:

"There is no 'lady in the case.' I'm sorry, M. Poirot, to have taken up so much of your time."

He went towards the door.

Hercule Poirot said:

"I regret it also. Your case interests me. I would like to have helped you. But I cannot do anything unless I am told the whole truth."

"I have told you the truth."

"No . . ."

Dr. Oldfield stopped. He wheeled round.

"Why do you insist that there is a woman concerned in this?"

"*Mon cher docteur!* Do you not think I know the female mentality? The village gossip, it is based always, always on the relations of the sexes. If a man poisons his wife in order to travel to the North Pole or to enjoy the peace of a bachelor existence—it would not interest his fellow villagers for a minute! It is because they are convinced that the murder has been committed in order that the man may marry another woman that the talk grows and spreads. That is elemental psychology."

Oldfield said irritably:

"I'm not responsible for what a pack of damned gossiping busybodies think!"

"Of course you are not."

Poirot went on:

"So you might as well come back and sit down and give me the answer to the question I asked you just now."

Slowly, almost reluctantly, Oldfield came back and resumed his seat.

He said, colouring up to his eyebrows:

"I suppose it's possible that they've been saying things about Miss Moncrieffe. Jean Moncrieffe is my dispenser, a very fine girl indeed."

"How long has she worked for you?"

"For three years."

"Did your wife like her?"

"Er—well, no, not exactly."

"She was jealous?"

"It was absurd!"

Poirot smiled.

He said:

"The jealousy of wives is proverbial. But I will tell you something. In my experience jealousy, however farfetched and extravagant it may seem, is nearly always based on reality. There is a saying, is there not, that the customer is always right? Well, the same is true of the jealous husband or wife. However little concrete evidence there may be, fundamentally they are always right."

Dr. Oldfield said robustly:

"Nonsense. I've never said anything to Jean Moncrieffe that my wife couldn't have overheard."

"That, perhaps. But it does not alter the truth of what I said." Hercule Poirot leaned forward. His voice was urgent, compelling. "Dr. Oldfield, I am going to do my utmost in this case. But I must have from you the most absolute frankness without regard to conventional appearances or to your own feelings. It is true, is it not, that you had ceased to care for your wife for some time before she died?"

Oldfield was silent for a minute or two. Then he said:

"This business is killing me. I must have hope. Somehow or other I feel that you will be able to do something for me. I will be honest with you, M. Poirot. I did not care deeply for my wife. I made her, I think, a good husband, but I was never really in love with her."

"And this girl, Jean?"

The perspiration came out in a fine dew on the doctor's forehead. He said:

"I—I should have asked her to marry me before now if it weren't for all this scandal and talk."

Poirot sat back in his chair. He said:

"Now at last we have come to the true facts! *Eh bien,* Dr. Oldfield, I will take up your case. But remember this—it is the truth that I shall seek out."

Oldfield said bitterly:

"It isn't the truth that's going to hurt me!"

He hesitated and said:

"You know, I've contemplated the possibility of an action for slander! If I could pin anyone down to a definite accusation—surely then I should be vindicated? At least, sometimes I think so. . . . At other times I think it would only make things worse—give bigger publicity to the whole thing and have people saying: 'It mayn't have been proved but there's no smoke without fire.' "

He looked at Poirot.

"Tell me, honestly, is there any way out of this nightmare?"

"There is always a way," said Hercule Poirot.

## 2

"We are going into the country, Georges," said Hercule Poirot to his valet.

"Indeed, sir?" said the imperturbable Georges.

"And the purpose of our journey is to destroy a monster with nine heads."

"Really, sir? Something after the style of the Loch Ness Monster?"

"Less tangible than that. I did not refer to a flesh-and-blood animal, Georges."

"I misunderstood you, sir."

"It would be easier if it were one. There is nothing so intangible, so difficult to pin down, as the source of a rumour."

"Oh, yes, indeed, sir. It's difficult to know how a thing starts sometimes."

"Exactly."

Hercule Poirot did not put up at Dr. Oldfield's house. He went instead to the local inn. The morning after his arrival, he had his first interview with Jean Moncrieffe.

She was a tall girl with copper-coloured hair and steady blue eyes. She had about her a watchful look, as of one who is upon her guard.

She said:

"So Dr. Oldfield did go to you. . . . I knew he was thinking about it."

There was a lack of enthusiasm in her tone.

Poirot said:

"And you did not approve?"

Her eyes met his. She said coldly:

"What can you do?"

Poirot said quietly:

"There might be a way of tackling the situation."

"What way?" She threw the words at him scornfully. "Do you mean to go round to all the whispering old women and say, 'Really, please, you must stop talking like this. It's so bad for poor Dr. Oldfield.' And they'd answer you and say, 'Of course, I have never believed the story!' That's the worst of the whole thing—they don't say, 'My dear, has it ever occurred to you that perhaps Mrs. Oldfield's death wasn't quite what it seemed?' No, they say, 'My dear, of course I don't believe that story about Dr. Oldfield and his wife. I'm sure he wouldn't do such a thing, though it's true that he did neglect her just a little perhaps and I don't think, really, it's quite wise to have quite a young girl as his dispenser—of course, I'm not saying for a minute that there was anything wrong between them. Oh, no, I'm sure it was quite all right. . . .'" She stopped. Her face was flushed and her breath came rather fast.

Hercule Poirot said:

"You seem to know very well just what is being said."

Her mouth closed sharply. She said bitterly:

"I know, all right!"

"And what is your solution?"

Jean Moncrieffe said:

"The best thing for him to do is to sell his practice and start again somewhere else."

"Don't you think the story might follow him?"

She shrugged her shoulders.

"He must risk that."

Poirot was silent for a minute or two. Then he said:

"Are you going to marry Dr. Oldfield, Miss Moncrieffe?"

She displayed no surprise at the question. She said shortly:

"He hasn't asked me to marry him."

"Why not?"

Her blue eyes met his and flickered for a second. Then she said:

"Because I've choked him off."

"Ah, what a blessing to find someone who can be frank!"

"I will be as frank as you please. When I realized that people were saying that Charles had got rid of his wife in order to marry me, it seemed to me that if we did marry it would just put the lid on things. I hoped that if there appeared to be no question of marriage between us, the silly scandal might die down."

"But it hasn't?"

"No, it hasn't."

"Surely," said Hercule Poirot, "that is a little odd?"

Jean said bitterly:

"They haven't got much to amuse them down here."

Poirot asked:

"Do you want to marry Charles Oldfield?"

The girl answered coolly enough.

"Yes, I do. I wanted to almost as soon as I met him."

"Then his wife's death was very convenient for you?"

Jean Moncrieffe said:

"Mrs. Oldfield was a singularly unpleasant woman. Frankly, I was delighted when she died."

"Yes," said Poirot. "You are certainly frank!"

She gave the same scornful smile.

Poirot said:

"I have a suggestion to make."

"Yes?"

"Drastic means are required here. I suggest that somebody—possibly yourself—might write to the Home Office."

"What on earth do you mean?"

"I mean that the best way of disposing of this story once and for all is to get the body exhumed and an autopsy performed."

She took a step back from him. Her lips opened, then shut again. Poirot watched her.

"Well, mademoiselle?" he said at last.

Jean Moncrieffe said quietly:

"I don't agree with you."

"But why not? Surely a verdict of death from natural causes would silence all tongues?"

"If you got that verdict, yes."

"Do you know what you are suggesting, mademoiselle?"

Jean Moncrieffe said impatiently:

"I know what I'm talking about. You're thinking of arsenic poisoning—you could prove that she was not poisoned by arsenic. But there are other poisons—the vegetable alkaloids. After a year, I doubt if you'd find any traces of them even if they had been used. And I know what these official analyst people are like. They might return a noncommittal verdict saying that there was nothing to show what caused death—and then the tongues would wag faster than ever!"

Hercule Poirot was silent for a minute or two, then he said:

"Who in your opinion is the most inveterate talker in the village?"

The girl considered. She said at last:

"I really think old Miss Leatheran is the worst cat of the lot."

"Ah! Would it be possible for you to introduce me to Miss Leatheran—in a casual manner if possible?"

"Nothing would be easier. All the old tabbies are prowling about doing their shopping at this time of the morning. We've only got to walk down the main street."

As Jean had said, there was no difficulty about the procedure. Outside the post office, Jean stopped and spoke to a tall, thin, middle-aged woman with a long nose and sharp inquisitive eyes.

"Good morning, Miss Leatheran."

"Good morning, Jean. Such a lovely day, is it not?"

The sharp eyes ranged inquisitively over Jean Moncrieffe's companion. Jean said:

"Let me introduce M. Poirot who is staying down here for a few days."

## 3

Nibbling delicately at a scone and balancing a cup of tea on his knee, Hercule Poirot allowed himself to become confidential with his hostess. Miss Leatheran had been kind enough to ask him to tea and had thereupon made it her business to find out exactly what this exotic little foreigner was doing in their midst.

For some time he parried her thrusts with dexterity—thereby whetting her appetite. Then, when he judged the moment ripe, he leant forward:

"Ah, Miss Leatheran," he said. "I can see that you are too clever for me! You have guessed my secret. I am down here at the request of the Home Office. But, please," he lowered his voice, "keep this information to yourself."

"Of course—of course—" Miss Leatheran was fluttered—thrilled to the core. "The Home Office—you don't mean—not poor Mrs. Oldfield?"

Poirot nodded his head slowly several times.

"We-ell!" Miss Leatheran breathed into that one word a whole gamut of pleasurable emotion.

Poirot said:

"It is a delicate matter, you understand. I have been ordered to report whether there is or is not a sufficient case for exhumation."

Miss Leatheran exclaimed:

"You are going to dig the poor thing up. How terrible!"

If she had said "how splendid" instead of "how terrible" the words would have suited her tone of voice better.

"What is your opinion, Miss Leatheran?"

"Well, of course, M. Poirot, there has been a lot of talk. But I never listen to talk. There is always so much unreliable gossip going about. There is no doubt that Dr. Oldfield has been very odd in his manner ever since it happened, but as I have said repeatedly we surely need not put that down to a guilty conscience. It might be just grief. Not, of course, that he and his wife were on really affectionate terms. That I *do* know—on first-hand authority. Nurse Harrison, who was with Mrs. Oldfield for three or four years up to the time of her death, has admitted that much. And I have always felt, you know, that Nurse Harrison had her suspicions—not that she ever said anything, but one can tell, can't one, from a person's manner?"

Poirot said sadly:

"One has so little to go upon."

"Yes, I know, but of course, M. Poirot, if the body is exhumed then you will know."

"Yes," said Poirot, "then we will know."

"There have been cases like it before, of course," said Miss Leatheran, her nose twitching with pleasurable excitement. "Armstrong, for instance, and that other man—I can't remember his name—and then Crippen, of course. I've always wondered if Ethel Le Neve was in it with him or not. Of course, Jean Moncrieffe is a very nice girl, I'm sure. . . . I wouldn't like to say she led him on exactly—but men do get rather silly about girls, don't they? And, of course, they were thrown very much together!"

Poirot did not speak. He looked at her with an innocent expression of inquiry calculated to produce a further spate of conversation. Inwardly he amused himself by counting the number of times the words "of course" occurred.

"And, of course, with a post-mortem and all that, so much would be bound to come out, wouldn't it? Servants and all that. Servants always know so much, don't they? And, of course, it's quite impossible to keep them from gossiping, isn't it? The Oldfields' Beatrice was dismissed almost immediately after the funeral—and I've always thought that was odd—especially with the difficulty of getting maids nowadays. It looks as though Dr. Oldfield was afraid she might know something."

"It certainly seems as though there were grounds for an inquiry," said Poirot solemnly.

Miss Leatheran gave a little shiver of reluctance.

"One does so shrink from the idea," she said. "Our dear, quiet little village—dragged into the newspapers—all the publicity!"

"It appalls you?" asked Poirot.

"It does a little. I'm old-fashioned, you know."

"And, as you say, it is probably nothing but gossip!"

"Well—I wouldn't like conscientiously to say that. You know, I do think it's so true—the saying that there's no smoke without fire."

"I myself was thinking exactly the same thing," said Poirot.

He rose.

"I can trust your discretion, mademoiselle?"

"Oh, of course! I shall not say a word to anybody."

Poirot smiled and took his leave.

On the doorstep he said to the little maid who handed him his hat and coat:

"I am down here to inquire into the circumstances of Mrs. Oldfield's death, but I shall be obliged if you will keep that strictly to yourself."

Miss Leatheran's Gladys nearly fell backward into the umbrella stand. She breathed excitedly:

"Oh, sir, then the doctor did do her in?"

"You've thought so for some time, haven't you?"

"Well, sir, it wasn't me. It was Beatrice. She was up there when Mrs. Oldfield died."

"And she thought there had been—" Poirot selected the melodramatic words deliberately—"'foul play'?"

Gladys nodded excitedly.

"Yes, she did. And she said so did Nurse that was up there, Nurse Harrison. Ever so fond of Mrs. Oldfield Nurse was, and ever so distressed when she died, and Gladys always said as how Nurse Harrison knew something about it because she turned right round against the doctor afterwards and she wouldn't of done that unless there was something wrong, would she?"

"Where is Nurse Harrison now?"

"She looks after old Miss Bristow—down at the end of the village. You can't miss it. It's got pillars and a porch."

# 4

It was a very short time afterwards that Hercule Poirot found himself sitting opposite to the woman who certainly must know more about the circumstances that had given rise to the rumours than anyone else.

Nurse Harrison was a still handsome woman nearing forty. She had the calm serene features of a madonna with big sympathetic dark eyes. She listened to him patiently and attentively. Then she said slowly:

"Yes, I know that there are these unpleasant stories going about. I have done what I could to stop them, but it's hopeless. People like the excitement, you know."

Poirot said:

"But there must have been something to give rise to these rumours?"

He noted that her expression of distress deepened. But she merely shook her head perplexedly.

"Perhaps," Poirot suggested, "Dr. Oldfield and his wife did not get on well together and it was that that started the rumour?"

Nurse Harrison shook her head decidedly.

"Oh, no, Dr. Oldfield was always extremely kind and patient with his wife."

"He was really very fond of her?"

She hesitated.

"No—I would not quite say that. Mrs. Oldfield was a very difficult woman, not easy to please and making constant demands for sympathy and attention which were not always justified."

"You mean," said Poirot, "that she exaggerated her condition?"

The nurse nodded.

"Yes—her bad health was largely a matter of her own imagination."

"And yet," said Poirot gravely, "she died. . . ."

"Oh, I know—I know. . . ."

He watched her for a minute or two; her troubled perplexity—her palpable uncertainty.

He said:

"I think—I am sure—that you do know what first gave rise to all these stories."

Nurse Harrison flushed.

She said:

"Well—I could, perhaps, make a guess. I believe it was the maid, Beatrice, who started all these rumours and I think I know what put it into her head."

"Yes?"

Nurse Harrison said rather incoherently:

"You see, it was something I happened to overhear—a scrap of conversation between Dr. Oldfield and Miss Moncrieffe—and I'm pretty certain Beatrice overheard it, too, only I don't suppose she'd ever admit it."

"What was this conversation?"

Nurse Harrison paused for a minute as though to test the accuracy of her own memory, then she said:

"It was about three weeks before the last attack that killed Mrs. Oldfield. They were in the dining room. I was coming down the stairs when I heard Jean Moncrieffe say:

" 'How much longer will it be? I can't bear to wait much longer.'

"And the doctor answered her:

" 'Not much longer now, darling, I swear it.' And she said again:

" 'I can't bear this waiting. You do think it will be all right, don't you?' And he said, 'Of course. Nothing can go wrong. This time next year we'll be married.' "

She paused.

"That was the very first inkling I'd had, M. Poirot, that there was anything between the doctor and Miss Moncrieffe. Of course I knew he admired her and that they were very good friends, but nothing more. I went back up the stairs again—it had given me quite a shock—but I did notice that the kitchen door was open and I've thought since that Beatrice must have been listening. And you can see, can't you, that the way they were talking could be taken two ways? It might just mean that the doctor knew his wife was very ill and couldn't live much longer—and I've no doubt that that was the way he meant it—but to anyone like Beatrice it might sound differently—it might look as though the doctor and Jean Moncrieffe were—well—were definitely planning to do away with Mrs. Oldfield."

"But *you* don't think so, yourself?"

"No—no, of course not . . . ."

Poirot looked at her searchingly. He said:

"Nurse Harrison, is there something more that you know? Something that you haven't told me?"

She flushed and said violently:

"No. No. Certainly not. What could there be?"

"I do not know. But I thought that there might be—something?"

She shook her head. The old troubled look had come back.

Hercule Poirot said:

"It is possible that the Home Office may order an exhumation of Mrs. Oldfield's body!"

"Oh, no!" Nurse Harrison was horrified. "What a horrible thing!"

"You think it would be a pity?"

"I think it would be dreadful! Think of the talk it would create! It would be terrible—quite terrible for poor Dr. Oldfield."

"You don't think that it might really be a good thing for him?"

"How do you mean?"

Poirot said, "If he is innocent—his innocence will be proved."

He broke off. He watched the thought take root in Nurse Harrison's mind, saw her frown perplexedly, and then saw her brow clear.

She took a deep breath and looked at him.

"I hadn't thought of that," she said simply. "Of course, it is the only thing to be done."

There were a series of thumps on the floor overhead. Nurse Harrison jumped up.

"It's my old lady, Miss Bristow. She's woken up from her rest. I must go and get her comfortable before her tea is brought to her and I go out for my walk. Yes, M. Poirot, I think you are quite right. An autopsy will settle the business once for all. It will scotch the whole thing and all these dreadful rumours against poor Dr. Oldfield will die down."

She shook hands and hurried out of the room.

# 5

Hercule Poirot walked along to the post office and put through a call to London.

The voice at the other end was petulant.

"Must you go nosing out these things, my dear Poirot? Are you sure it's a case for us? You know what these country town rumours usually amount to—just nothing at all."

"This," said Hercule Poirot, "is a special case."

"Oh, well—if you say so. You have such a tiresome habit of being right. But if it's all a mare's nest we shan't be pleased with you, you know."

Hercule Poirot smiled to himself. He murmured:

"No, I shall be the one who is pleased."

"What's that you say? Can't hear."

"Nothing. Nothing at all."

He rang off.

Emerging into the post office he leaned across the counter. He said in his most engaging tones:

"Can you by any chance tell me, Madame, where the maid who was formerly with Dr. Oldfield—Beatrice, her Christian name was—now resides?"

"Beatrice King? She's had two places since then. She's with Mrs. Marley over the Bank now."

Poirot thanked her, bought two postcards, a book of stamps and a piece of local pottery. During the purchase, he contrived to bring the death of the late Mrs. Oldfield into the conversation. He was quick to note the peculiar furtive expression that stole across the postmistress's face. She said:

"Very sudden, wasn't it? It's made a lot of talk as you may have heard."

A gleam of interest came into her eyes as she asked:

"Maybe that's what you'd be wanting to see Beatrice King for? We all thought it odd the way she was got out of there all of a sudden. Somebody thought she knew something—and maybe she did. She's dropped some pretty broad hints."

Beatrice King was a short, rather sly-looking girl with adenoids. She presented an appearance of stolid stupidity but her eyes were more intelligent than her manner would have led one to expect. It seemed, however, that there was nothing to be got out of Beatrice King. She repeated:

"I don't know nothing about anything. . . . It's not for me to say what went on up there. . . . I don't know what you mean by overhearing a conversation between the doctor and Miss Moncrieffe. I'm not one to go listening to doors, and you've no right to say I did. I don't know nothing."

Poirot said:

"Have you ever heard of poisoning by arsenic?"

A flicker of quick furtive interest came into the girl's sullen face. She said:

"So that's what it was in the medicine bottle?"

"What medicine bottle?"

Beatrice said:

"One of the bottles of medicine what that Miss Moncrieffe made up for the missus. Nurse was all upset—I could see that. Tasted it, she did, and smelt it, and then poured it away down the sink and filled up the bottle with plain water from the tap. It was white medicine like water, anyway. And once, when Miss Moncrieffe took up a pot of tea to the missus, Nurse brought it down again and made it fresh—said it hadn't been made with boiling water but that was just my eye, that was! I thought it was just the sort of fussing way nurses have at the time—but I dunno—it may have been more than that."

Poirot nodded. He said:

"Did you like Miss Moncrieffe, Beatrice?"

"I didn't mind her. . . . A bit standoffish. Of course, I always knew as she was sweet on the doctor. You'd only to see the way she looked at him."

Again Poirot nodded his head. He went back to the inn.

There he gave certain instructions to Georges.

# 6

Dr. Alan Garcia, the Home Office Analyst, rubbed his hands and twinkled at Hercule Poirot. He said:

"Well, this suits you, M. Poirot, I suppose? The man who's always right."

Poirot said:

"You are too kind."

"What put you onto it? Gossip?"

"As you say— Enter Rumour, painted full of tongues."

The following day Poirot once more took a train to Market Loughborough.

Market Loughborough was buzzing like a beehive. It had buzzed mildly ever since the exhumation proceedings.

Now that the findings of the autopsy had leaked out, excitement had reached fever heat.

Poirot had been at the inn for about an hour and had just finished a hearty lunch of steak and kidney pudding washed down by beer when word was brought to him that a lady was waiting to see him.

It was Nurse Harrison. Her face was white and haggard.

She came straight to Poirot.

"Is this true? Is this really true, M. Poirot?"

He put her gently into a chair.

"Yes. More than sufficient arsenic to cause death has been found."

Nurse Harrison cried:

"I never thought—I never for one moment thought—" and burst into tears.

Poirot said gently:

"The truth had to come out, you know."

She sobbed.

"Will they hang him?"

Poirot said:

"A lot has to be proved still. Opportunity—access to poison—the vehicle in which it was administered."

"But supposing, M. Poirot, that he had nothing to do with it—nothing at all."

"In that case," Poirot shrugged his shoulders, "he will be acquitted."

Nurse Harrison said slowly:

"There is something—something that, I suppose, I ought to have told you before—but I didn't think that there was really anything in it. It was just queer."

"I knew there was something," said Poirot. "You had better tell it to me now."

"It isn't much. It's just that one day when I went down to the dispensary for something, Jean Moncrieffe was doing something rather—odd."

"Yes?"

"It sounds so silly. It's only that she was filling up her powder compact—a pink enamel one—"

"Yes?"

"But she wasn't filling it up with powder—with face powder, I mean. She was tipping something into it from one of the bottles out of the poison cupboard. When she saw me she started and shut up the compact and whipped it into her bag—and put back the bottle quickly into the cupboard so that I couldn't see what it was. I daresay it doesn't mean anything—but now that I know that Mrs. Oldfield was really poisoned—" She broke off—

Poirot said: "You will excuse me?"

He went out and telephoned to Detective Sergeant Grey of the Berkshire Police.

Hercule Poirot came back and he and Nurse Harrison sat in silence.

Poirot was seeing the face of a girl with red hair and hearing a clear hard voice say, "I don't agree." Jean Moncrieffe had not wanted an autopsy. She had given a plausible enough excuse, but the fact remained. A competent girl—efficient—resolute. In love with a man who was tied to a complaining invalid wife, who might easily live for years since, according to Nurse Harrison, she had very little the matter with her.

Hercule Poirot sighed.

Nurse Harrison said:

"What are you thinking of?"

Poirot answered:

"The pity of things. . . ."

Nurse Harrison said:

"I don't believe for a minute he knew anything about it."

Poirot said:

"No. I am sure he did not."

The door opened and Detective Sergeant Grey came in. He had something in his hand, wrapped in a silk handkerchief. He unwrapped it and set it carefully down. It was a bright rose pink enamel compact.

Nurse Harrison said:

"That's the one I saw."

Grey said:

"Found it pushed right to the back of Miss Moncrieffe's bureau drawer. Inside a handkerchief sachet. As far as I can see there are no fingerprints on it, but I'll be careful."

With the handkerchief over his hand he pressed the spring. The case flew open. Grey said:

"This stuff isn't face powder."

He dipped a finger and tasted it gingerly on the tip of his tongue.

"No particular taste."

Poirot said:

"White arsenic does not taste."

Grey said:

"It will be analysed at once." He looked at Nurse Harrison. "You can swear to this being the same case?"

"Yes. I'm positive. That's the case I saw Miss Moncrieffe with in the dispensary about a week before Mrs. Oldfield's death."

Sergeant Grey sighed. He looked at Poirot and nodded. The latter rang the bell.

"Send my servant here, please."

Georges, the perfect valet, discreet, unobtrusive, entered and looked inquiringly at his master.

Hercule Poirot said:

"You have identified this powder compact, Miss Harrison, as one you saw in the possession of Miss Moncrieffe over a year ago. *Would you be surprised to learn that this particular case was sold by Messrs. Woolworth only a few weeks ago and that, moreover, it is of a pattern and colour that has only been manufactured for the last three months?*"

Nurse Harrison gasped. She stared at Poirot, her eyes round and dark. Poirot said:

"Have you seen this compact before, Georges?"

Georges stepped forward:

"Yes, sir. I observed this person, Nurse Harrison, purchase it at Woolworth's on Friday the 18th. Pursuant to your instructions I followed this lady whenever she went out. She took a bus over to Darnington on the day I have mentioned and purchased this compact. She took it home with her. Later, the same day, she came to the house in which Miss Moncrieffe lodges. Acting as by your instructions, I was already in the house. I observed her go into Miss Moncrieffe's bedroom and hide this in the back of the bureau drawer. I had a good view through

the crack of the door. She then left the house, believing herself unobserved. I may say that no one locks their front doors down here and
it was dusk."

Poirot said to Nurse Harrison, and his voice was hard and implacable:

"Can you explain these facts, Nurse Harrison? I think not. There
was no arsenic in that box when it left Messrs. Woolworth, but there
was when it left Miss Bristow's house." He added softly, "It was unwise
of you to keep a supply of arsenic in your possession."

Nurse Harrison buried her face in her hands. She said in a low,
dull voice:

"It's true—it's all true. . . . I killed her. And all for nothing—nothing . . . I was mad."

## 7

Jean Moncrieffe said:

"I must ask you to forgive me, M. Poirot. I have been so angry
with you—so terribly angry with you. It seemed to me that you were
making everything so much worse."

Poirot said with a smile:

"So I was to begin with. It is like in the old legend of the Lernean
Hydra. Every time a head was cut off, two heads grew in its place.
So, to begin with, the rumours grew and multiplied. But you see my
task, like that of my namesake Hercules, was to reach the first—the
original head. Who had started this rumour? It did not take me long
to discover that the originator of the story was Nurse Harrison. I went
to see her. She appeared to be a very nice woman—intelligent and
sympathetic. But almost at once she made a bad mistake—she repeated
to me a conversation which she had overheard taking place between
you and the doctor, and that conversation, you see, was all wrong. It
was psychologically most unlikely. If you and the doctor had planned
together to kill Mrs. Oldfield, you are both of you far too intelligent
and level-headed to hold such a conversation in a room with an open
door, easily overheard by someone on the stairs or someone in the
kitchen. Moreover, the words attributed to you did not fit in at all
with your mental makeup. They were the words of a much older
woman and of one of a quite different type. They were words such
as would be imagined by Nurse Harrison as being used by herself in
like circumstances.

"I had, up to then, regarded the whole matter as fairly simple. Nurse
Harrison, I realised, was a fairly young and still handsome woman—

she had been thrown closely with Dr. Oldfield for nearly three years—the doctor had been very fond of her and grateful to her for her tact and sympathy. She had formed the impression that if Mrs. Oldfield died, the doctor would probably ask her to marry him. Instead of that, after Mrs. Oldfield's death, she learns that Dr. Oldfield is in love with you. Straightaway, driven by anger and jealousy, she starts spreading the rumour that Dr. Oldfield has poisoned his wife.

"That, as I say, was how I had visualised the position at first. It was a case of a jealous woman and a lying rumour. But the old trite phrase 'no smoke without fire' recurred to me significantly. I wondered if Nurse Harrison had done more than spread a rumour. Certain things she said rang strangely. She told me that Mrs. Oldfield's illness was largely imaginary—that she did not really suffer much pain. But the doctor himself had been in no doubt about the reality of his wife's suffering. He had not been surprised by her death. He had called in another doctor shortly before her death and the other doctor had realised the gravity of her condition. Tentatively, I brought forward the suggestion of exhumation. . . . Nurse Harrison was at first frightened out of her wits by the idea. Then, almost at once, her jealousy and hatred took command of her. Let them find arsenic—no suspicion would attach to her. It would be the doctor and Jean Moncrieffe who would suffer.

"There was only one hope. To make Nurse Harrison overreach herself. If there were a chance that Jean Moncrieffe would escape, I fancied that Nurse Harrison would strain every nerve to involve her in the crime. I gave instructions to my faithful Georges—the most unobtrusive of men whom she did not know by sight. He was to follow her closely. And so—all ended well."

Jean Moncrieffe said:

"You've been wonderful."

Dr. Oldfield chimed in. He said:

"Yes, indeed. I can never thank you enough. What a blind fool I was!"

Poirot asked curiously:

"Were you as blind, mademoiselle?"

Jean Moncrieffe said slowly:

"I have been terribly worried. You see, the arsenic in the poison cupboard didn't tally. . . ."

Oldfield cried:

"Jean—you didn't think—?"

"No, no—not you. What I *did* think was that Mrs. Oldfield had somehow or other got hold of it—and that she was taking it so as to make herself ill and get sympathy and that she had inadvertently taken too much. But I was afraid that if there was an autopsy and arsenic was found, they would never consider that theory and would leap to the conclusion that you'd done it. That's why I never said anything about the missing arsenic. I even cooked the poison book! But the last person I would ever have suspected was Nurse Harrison."

Oldfield said:

"I, too. She was such a gentle, womanly creature. Like a madonna."

Poirot said sadly:

"Yes, she would have made, probably, a good wife and mother.
. . . Her emotions were just a little too strong for her." He sighed and murmured once more under his breath:

"The pity of it."

Then he smiled at the happy looking middle-aged man and the eager-faced girl opposite him. He said to himself:

"These two have come out of its shadow into the sun . . . and I—I have performed the second Labor of Hercules."

# III

# The Arcadian Deer

Hercule Poirot stamped his feet, seeking to warm them. He blew upon his fingers. Flakes of snow melted and dripped from the corners of his moustache.

There was a knock at the door and a chambermaid appeared. She was a slow-breathing, thickset country girl and she stared with a good deal of curiosity at Hercule Poirot. It was possible that she had never seen anything quite like him before.

She asked, "Did you ring?"

"I did. Will you be so good as to light the fire?"

She went out and came back again immediately with paper and sticks. She knelt down in front of the big Victorian grate and began to lay a fire.

Hercule Poirot continued to stamp his feet, swing his arms and blow on his fingers.

He was annoyed. His car—an expensive Messarro Gratz—had not behaved with that mechanical perfection which he expected of a car. His chauffeur, a young man who enjoyed a handsome salary, had not succeeded in putting things right. The car had staged a final refusal in a secondary road a mile and a half from anywhere with a fall of snow beginning. Hercule Poirot, wearing his usual smart patent leather shoes, had been forced to walk that mile and a half to reach the riverside village of Hartly Dene—a village which, though showing every sign of animation in summertime, was completely moribund in winter. The Black Swan had registered something like dismay at the arrival of a guest. The landlord had been almost eloquent as he pointed out that the local garage could supply a car in which the gentleman could continue his journey.

Hercule Poirot repudiated the suggestion. His Latin thrift was offended. Hire a car? He already had a car—a large car—an expensive car. In that car and no other he proposed to continue his journey

453

back to town. And in any case, even if repairs to it could be quickly effected, he was not going on in this snow until next morning. He demanded a room, a fire, and a meal. Sighing, the landlord showed him to the room, sent the maid to supply the fire, and then retired to discuss with his wife the problem of the meal.

An hour later, his feet stretched out towards the comforting blaze, Hercule Poirot reflected leniently on the dinner he had just eaten. True, the steak had been both tough and full of gristle, the Brussels sprouts had been large, pale, and definitely watery, the potatoes had had hearts of stone. Nor was there much to be said for the portion of stewed apple and custard which had followed. The cheese had been hard and the biscuits soft. Nevertheless, thought Hercule Poirot, looking graciously at the leaping flames, and sipping delicately at a cup of liquid mud euphemistically called coffee, it was better to be full than empty, and after tramping snowbound lanes in patent leather shoes, to sit in front of a fire was Paradise!

There was a knock on the door and the chambermaid appeared.

"Please, sir, the man from the garage is here and would like to see you."

Hercule Poirot replied amiably:

"Let him mount."

The girl giggled and retired. Poirot reflected kindly that her account of him to her friends would provide entertainment for many winter days to come.

There was another knock—a different knock—and Poirot called: "Come in."

He looked up with approval at the young man who entered and stood there looking ill at ease, twisting his cap in his hands.

Here, he thought, was one of the handsomest specimens of humanity he had ever seen, a simple young man with the outward semblance of a Greek god.

The young man said in a low, husky voice:

"About the car, sir, we've brought it in. And we've got at the trouble. It's a matter of an hour's work or so."

Poirot said:

"What is wrong with it?"

The young man plunged eagerly into technical details. Poirot nodded his head gently, but he was not listening. Perfect physique was a thing he admired greatly. There were, he considered, too many rats in spectacles about. He said to himself approvingly, "Yes, a Greek god—a young shepherd in Arcady."

The young man stopped abruptly. It was then that Hercule Poirot's brows knitted themselves for a second. His first reaction had been aesthetic, his second was mental. His eyes narrowed themselves curiously as he looked up.

He said:

"I comprehend. Yes, I comprehend." He paused and then added: "My chauffeur, he has already told me that which you have just said."

He saw the flush that came to the other's cheek, saw the fingers grip the cap nervously.

The young man stammered:

"Yes—er—yes, sir. I know."

Hercule Poirot went on smoothly:

"But you thought that you would also come and tell me yourself?"

"Er—yes, sir, I thought I'd better."

"That," said Hercule Poirot, "was very conscientious of you. Thank you."

There was a faint but unmistakable note of dismissal in the last words but he did not expect the other to go and he was right. The young man did not move.

His fingers moved convulsively, crushing the tweed cap, and he said in a still lower, embarrassed voice:

"Er—excuse me, sir—but it's true, isn't it, that you're the detective gentleman—you're Mr. Hercules Pwarrit?" He said the name carefully.

Poirot said:

"That is so."

Red crept up the young man's face. He said:

"I read a piece about you in the paper."

"Yes?"

The boy was now scarlet. There was distress in his eyes—distress and appeal. Hercule Poirot came to his aid. He said gently:

"Yes? What is it you want to ask me?"

The words came with a rush now.

"I'm afraid you may think it's awful cheek of me, sir. But your coming here by chance like this—well, it's too good to be missed. Having read about you and the clever things you've done. Anyway, I said as after all I might as well ask you. There's no harm in asking, is there?"

Hercule Poirot shook his head. He said:

"You want my help in some way?"

The other nodded. He said, his voice husky and embarrassed:

"It's—it's about a young lady. If—if you could find her for me."

"Find her? Has she disappeared, then?"

"That's right, sir."

Hercule Poirot sat up in his chair. He said sharply:

"I could help you, perhaps, yes. But the proper people for you to go to are the police. It is their job and they have far more resources at their disposal than I have."

The boy shuffled his feet. He said awkwardly:

"I couldn't do that, sir. It's not like that at all. It's all rather peculiar, so to speak."

Hercule Poirot stared at him. Then he indicated a chair.

*"Eh bien,* then, sit down—what is your name?"

"Williamson, sir, Ted Williamson."

"Sit down, Ted. And tell me all about it."

"Thank you, sir." He drew forward the chair and sat down carefully on the edge of it. His eyes had still that appealing doglike look.

Hercule Poirot said gently:

"Tell me."

Ted Williamson drew a deep breath.

"Well, you see, sir, it was like this. I never saw her but the once. And I don't know her right name nor anything. But it's queer like, the whole thing, and my letter coming back and everything."

"Start," said Hercule Poirot, "at the beginning. Do not hurry yourself. Just tell me everything that occurred."

"Yes, sir. Well, perhaps you know Grasslawn, sir, that big house down by the river past the bridge?"

"I know nothing at all."

"Belongs to Sir George Sanderfield, it does. He uses it in the summer time for weekends and parties—rather a gay lot he has down as a rule. Actresses and that. Well, it was in last June—and the wireless was out of order and they sent me up to see to it."

Poirot nodded.

"So I went along. The gentleman was out on the river with his guests and the cook was out and his manservant had gone along to serve the drinks and all that on the launch. There was only this girl in the house—she was the lady's maid to one of the guests. She let me in and showed me where the set was, and stayed there while I was working on it. And so we got to talking and all that. . . . Nita her name was, so she told me, and she was lady's maid to a Russian dancer who was staying there."

"What nationality was she, English?"

"No, sir, she'd be French, I think. She'd a funny sort of accent. But she spoke English all right. She—she was friendly and after a bit I asked her if she could come out that night and go to the pictures, but she said her lady would be needing her. But then she said as how she could get off early in the afternoon because as how they wasn't going to be back off the river till late. So the long and the short of it was that I took the afternoon off without asking (and nearly got the sack for it too) and we went for a walk along by the river."

He paused. A little smile hovered on his lips. His eyes were dreamy. Poirot said gently:

"And she was pretty, yes?"

"She was just the loveliest thing you ever saw. Her hair was like gold—it went up each side like wings—and she had a gay kind of way of tripping along. I—I—well, I fell for her right away, sir. I'm not pretending anything else."

Poirot nodded. The young man went on:

"She said as how her lady would be coming down again in a fortnight and we fixed up to meet again then." He paused. "But she never came. I waited for her at the spot she'd said, but not a sign of her, and at last I made bold to go up to the house and ask for her. The Russian lady was staying there all right and her maid, too, they said. Sent for her, they did, but when she came, why, it wasn't Nita at all! Just a dark, catty-looking girl—a bold lot if there ever was one. Marie, they called her. 'You want to see me?' she says, simpering all over. She must have seen I was took aback. I said was she the Russian lady's maid and something about her not being the one I'd seen before, and then she laughed and said that the last maid had been sent away sudden. 'Sent away?' I said. 'What for?' She sort of shrugged her shoulders and stretched out her hands. 'How should I know?' she said. 'I was not there.'

"Well, sir, it took me aback. At the moment I couldn't think of anything to say. But afterwards I plucked up courage and I got to see this Marie again and asked her to get me Nita's address. I didn't let on to her that I didn't even know Nita's last name. I promised her a present if she did what I asked—she was the kind as wouldn't do anything for you for nothing. Well, she got it all right for me—an address in North London, it was, and I wrote to Nita there—but the letter came back after a bit—sent back through the post office with *no longer at this address* scrawled on it."

Ted Williamson stopped. His eyes, those deep blue steady eyes, looked across at Poirot. He said:

"You see how it is, sir? It's not a case for the police. But I want to find her. And I don't know how to set about it. If—if you could find her for me." His colour deepened. "I've—I've a bit put by. I could manage five pounds—or even ten."

Poirot said gently:

"We need not discuss the financial side for the moment. First reflect on this point—this girl, this Nita—she knew your name and where you worked?"

"Oh, yes, sir."

"She could have communicated with you if she had wanted to?"

Ted said more slowly:

"Yes, sir."

"Then do you not think—perhaps—"

Ted Williamson interrupted him.

"What you're meaning, sir, is that I fell for her but she didn't fall for me? Maybe that's true in a way. . . . But she liked me—she did like me—it wasn't just a bit of fun to her. . . . And I've been thinking, sir, as there might be a reason for all this. You see, sir, it was a funny crowd she was mixed up in. She might be in a bit of trouble, if you know what I mean."

"You mean she might have been going to have a child? Your child?"

"Not mine, sir." Ted flushed. "There wasn't nothing wrong between us."

Poirot looked at him thoughtfully. He murmured:

"And if what you suggest is true—you still want to find her?"

The colour surged up in Ted Williamson's face. He said:

"Yes, I do, and that's flat! I want to marry her if she'll have me. And that's no matter what kind of a jam she's in! If you'll only try and find her for me, sir?"

Hercule Poirot smiled. He said, murmuring to himself:

" 'Hair like wings of gold.' Yes, I think this is the third Labor of Hercules. . . . If I remember rightly, that happened in Arcady. . . ."

## 2

Hercule Poirot looked thoughtfully at the sheet of paper on which Ted Williamson had laboriously inscribed a name and address.

Miss Valetta, 17 Upper Renfrew Lane, N.15.

He wondered if he would learn anything at that address. Somehow he fancied not. But it was the only help Ted could give him.

17 Upper Renfrew Lane was a dingy but respectable street. A stout woman with bleary eyes opened the door to Poirot's knock.

"Miss Valetta?"

"Gone away a long time ago, she has."

Poirot advanced a step into the doorway just as the door was about to close.

"You can give me, perhaps, her address?"

"Couldn't say, I'm sure. She didn't leave one."

"When did she go away?"

"Last summer it was."

"Can you tell me exactly when?"

A gentle clinking noise came from Poirot's right hand where two half crowns jostled each other in friendly fashion.

The bleary-eyed woman softened in an almost magical manner. She became graciousness itself.

"Well, I'm sure I'd like to help you, sir. Let me see now. August, no, before that—July—yes, July it must have been. About the third week in July. Went off in a hurry, she did. Back to Italy, I believe."

"She was an Italian, then?"

"That's right, sir."

"And she was at one time lady's maid to a Russian dancer, was she not?"

"That's right. Madame Semoulina or some such name. Danced at the Thespian in this Bally everyone's so wild about. One of the stars, she was."

Poirot said:

"Do you know why Miss Valetta left her post?"

The woman hesitated a moment before saying:

"I couldn't say, I'm sure."

"She was dismissed, was she not?"

"Well—I believe there was a bit of a dust up! But mind you, Miss Valetta didn't let on much about it. She wasn't one to give things away. But she looked wild about it. Wicked temper she had—real Eyetalian—her black eyes all snapping and looking as if she'd like to put a knife into you. I wouldn't have crossed her when she was in one of her moods!"

"And you are quite sure you do not know Miss Valetta's present address?"

The half crowns clinked again encouragingly.

The answer rang true enough:

"I wish I did, sir. I'd be only too glad to tell you. But there—she went off in a hurry and there it is!"

Poirot said to himself thoughtfully:

"Yes, there it is. . . ."


## 3

Ambrose Vandel, diverted from his enthusiastic account of the décor he was designing for a forthcoming ballet, supplied information easily enough.

"Sanderfield? George Sanderfield? Nasty fellow. Rolling in money but they say he's a crook. Dark horse! Affair with a dancer? But of course, my dear—he had an affair with Katrina. Katrina Samoushenka. You must have seen her? Oh, my dear—too delicious. Lovely technique. *The Swan of Tuolela*—you must have seen *that*? My décor! And that other thing of Debussy or is it Mannine, 'La Biche au Bois'? She danced it with Michael Novgin. He's so marvellous, isn't he?"

"And she was a friend of Sir George Sanderfield?"

"Yes, she used to weekend with him at his house on the river. Marvellous parties I believe he gives."

"Would it be possible, *mon cher,* for you to introduce me to Mademoiselle Samoushenka?"

"But, my dear, she isn't here any longer. She went to Paris or somewhere quite suddenly. You know, they do say that she was a Bolshevik spy or something—not that I believed it myself—you know people love saying things like that. Katrina always pretended that she was a White Russian—her father was a Prince or a Grand Duke—the usual thing! It goes down so much better." Vandel paused and returned to the absorbing subject of himself. "Now as I was saying, if you want to get the spirit of Bathsheba you've got to steep yourself in the Semitic tradition. I express it by—"

He continued happily.

# 4

The interview that Hercule Poirot managed to arrange with Sir George Sanderfield did not start too auspiciously.

The "dark horse," as Ambrose Vandel had called him, was slightly ill at ease. Sir George was a short square man with dark coarse hair and a roll of fat in his neck.

He said:

"Well, M. Poirot, what can I do for you? Er—we haven't met before, I think?"

"No, we have not met."

"Well, what is it? I confess, I'm quite curious."

"Oh, it is very simple—a mere matter of information."

The other gave an uneasy laugh.

"Want me to give you some inside dope, eh? Didn't know you were interested in finance."

"It is not a matter of *les affaires.* It is a question of a certain lady."

"Oh, a woman." Sir George Sanderfield leant back in his armchair. He seemed to relax. His voice held an easier note.

Poirot said:

"You were acquainted, I think, with Mademoiselle Katrina Samoushenka?"

Sanderfield laughed.

"Yes. An enchanting creature. Pity she's left London."

"Why did she leave London?"

"My dear fellow, I don't know. Row with the management, I believe. She was temperamental, you know—very Russian in her moods. I'm sorry that I can't help you but I haven't the least idea where she is now. I haven't kept up with her at all."

There was a note of dismissal in his voice as he rose to his feet.

Poirot said:

"But it is not Mademoiselle Samoushenka that I am anxious to trace."

"It isn't?"

"No, it is a question of her maid."

"Her maid?" Sanderfield stared at him.

Poirot said:

"Do you—perhaps—remember her maid?"

All Sanderfield's uneasiness had returned. He said awkwardly:

"Good Lord, no, how should I? I remember she had one, of course. . . . Bit of a bad lot, too, I should say. Sneaking, prying sort of girl. If I were you I shouldn't put any faith in a word that girl says. She's the kind of girl who's a born liar."

Poirot murmured:

"So actually, you remember quite a lot about her?"

Sanderfield said hastily:

"Just an impression, that's all. . . . Don't even remember her name. Let me see, Marie something or other—no, I'm afraid I can't help you to get hold of her. Sorry."

Poirot said gently:

"I have already got the name of Marie Hellin from the Thespian Theatre—and her address. But I am speaking, Sir George, of the maid who was with Mademoiselle Samoushenka before Marie Hellin. I am speaking of Nita Valetta."

Sanderfield stared. He said:

"Don't remember her at all. Marie's the only one *I* remember. Little dark girl with a nasty look in her eye."

Poirot said:

"The girl I mean was at your house, Grasslawn, last July."

Sanderfield said sulkily:

"Well, all I can say is I don't remember her. Don't believe she had a maid with her. I think you're making a mistake."

Hercule Poirot shook his head. He did not think he was making a mistake.

## 5

Marie Hellin looked swiftly at Poirot out of small, intelligent eyes and as swiftly looked away again. She said in smooth, even tones:

"But I remember perfectly, monsieur. I was engaged by Madame Samoushenka the last week in July. Her former maid had departed in a hurry."

"Did you ever hear why that maid left?"

"She went—suddenly—that is all I know! It may have been illness—something of that kind. Madame did not say."

Poirot said:

"Did you find your mistress easy to get on with?"

The girl shrugged her shoulders.

"She had great moods. She wept and laughed in turns. Sometimes she was so despondent she would not speak or eat. Sometimes she was wildly gay. They are like that, these dancers. It is temperament."

"And Sir George?"

The girl looked up alertly. An unpleasant gleam came into her eyes.

"Ah, Sir George Sanderfield? You would like to know about him? Perhaps it is that that you really want to know? The other was only an excuse, eh? Ah, Sir George, I could tell you some curious things about him. I could tell you—"

Poirot interrupted:

"It is not necessary."

She stared at him, her mouth open. Angry disappointment showed in her eyes.

## 6

"I always say you know everything, Alexis Pavlovitch."

Hercule Poirot murmured the words with his most flattering intonation.

He was reflecting to himself that this third Labor of Hercules had necessitated more travelling and more interviews than could have been imagined possible. This little matter of a missing lady's maid was proving one of the longest and most difficult problems he had ever tackled. Every clue, when examined, led exactly nowhere.

It had brought him this evening to the Samovar Restaurant in Paris whose proprietor, Count Alexis Pavlovitch, prided himself on knowing everything that went on in the artistic world.

He nodded now complacently:

"Yes, yes, my friend, *I* know—I always know. You ask me where she is gone—the little Samoushenka, the exquisite dancer? Ah! she was the real thing, that little one." He kissed his fingertips. "What fire—what abandon! She would have gone far—she would have been the première ballerina of her day—and then suddenly it all ends— she creeps away—to the end of the world—and soon, ah! so soon, they forget her."

"Where is she then?" demanded Poirot.

"In Switzerland. At Vagray les Alpes. It is there that they go, those who have the little dry cough and who grow thinner and thinner. She will die, yes, she will die! She has a fatalistic nature. She will surely die."

Poirot coughed to break the tragic spell. He wanted information.

"You do not, by chance, remember a maid she had? A maid called Nita Valetta?"

"Valetta? Valetta? I remember seeing a maid once—at the station when I was seeing Katrina off to London. She was an Italian from Pisa, was she not? Yes, I am sure she was an Italian who came from Pisa."

Hercule Poirot groaned.

"In that case," he said, "I must now journey to Pisa."

# 7

Hercule Poirot stood in the Campo Santo at Pisa and looked down on a grave.

So it was here that his quest had come to an end—here by this humble mound of earth. Underneath it lay the joyous creature who had stirred the heart and imagination of a simple English mechanic.

Was this perhaps the best end to that sudden, strange romance? Now the girl would live always in the young man's memory as he had seen her for those few enchanted hours of a July afternoon. The clash of opposing nationalities, of different standards, the pain of disillusionment, all that was ruled out for ever.

Hercule Poirot shook his head sadly. His mind went back to his conversation with the Valetta family. The mother, with her broad peasant face, the upright grief-stricken father, the dark hard-lipped sister.

"It was sudden, signor, it was very sudden. Though for many years she had had pains on and off. . . . The doctor gave us no choice—he said there must be an operation immediately for the appendicitis. He took her off to the hospital then and there. . . . *Si, si*, it was under the anaesthetic she died. She never recovered consciousness."

The mother sniffed, murmuring:

"Bianca was always such a clever girl. It is terrible that she should have died so young. . . ."

Hercule Poirot repeated to himself:

"She died young. . . ."

That was the message he must take back to the young man who had asked his help so confidingly.

"She is not for you, my friend. She died young."

His quest had ended—here where the leaning Tower was silhouetted against the sky and the first spring flowers were showing pale and creamy with their promise of life and joy to come.

Was it the stirring of spring that made him feel so rebelliously disinclined to accept this final verdict? Or was it something else? Something stirring at the back of his brain—words—a phrase—a name? Did not the whole thing finish too neatly—dovetail too obviously?

Hercule Poirot sighed. He must take one more journey to put things beyond any possible doubt. He must go to Vagray les Alpes.

# 8

Here, he thought, really was the world's end. This shelf of snow— these scattered huts and shelters in each of which lay a motionless human being fighting an insidious death.

So he came at last to Katrina Samoushenka. When he saw her, lying there with hollow cheeks in each of which was a vivid red stain, and long, thin, emaciated hands stretched out on the coverlet, a memory stirred in him. He had not remembered her name, but he had seen her dance—had been carried away and fascinated by the supreme art that can make you forget art.

He remembered Michael Novgin, the Hunter, leaping and twirling in that outrageous and fantastic forest that the brain of Ambrose Vandel had conceived. And he remembered the lovely flying Hind, eternally pursued, eternally desirable—a golden beautiful creature with horns on her head and twinkling bronze feet. He remembered her final collapse, shot and wounded, and Michael Novgin standing bewildered, with the body of the slain Deer in his arms.

Katrina Samoushenka was looking at him with faint curiosity. She said:

"I have never seen you before, have I? What is it you want of me?"

Hercule Poirot made her a little bow.

"First, I wish to thank you—for your art which made for me once an evening of beauty."

She smiled faintly.

"But also I am here on a matter of business. I have been looking, for a long time for a certain maid of yours—her name was Nita."

"Nita?"

She stared at him. Her eyes were large and startled. She said:

"What do you know about—Nita?"

"I will tell you."

He told her of the evening when his car had broken down and of Ted Williamson standing there twisting his cap between his fingers and stammering out his love and his pain. She listened with close attention.

She said when he had finished:

"It is touching, that—yes, it is touching. . . ."

Hercule Poirot nodded.

"Yes," he said. "It is a tale of Arcady, is it not? What can you tell me, madame, of this girl?"

Katrina Samoushenka sighed.

"I had a maid—Juanita. She was lovely, yes—gay, light of heart. It happened to her what happens so often to those the gods favour. She died young."

They had been Poirot's own words—final words—irrevocable words— Now he heard them again—and yet he persisted. He asked:

"She is dead?"

"Yes, she is dead."

Hercule Poirot was silent a minute, then he said:

"Yet there is one thing I do not quite understand. I asked Sir George Sanderfield about this maid of yours and he seemed afraid. Why was that?"

There was a faint expression of disgust on the dancer's face.

"You just said a maid of mine. He thought you meant Marie—the girl who came to me after Juanita left. She tried to blackmail him, I believe, over something that she found out about him. She was an odious girl—inquisitive, always prying into letters and locked drawers."

Poirot murmured:

"Then that explains that."

He paused a minute, then he went on, still persistent:

"Juanita's other name was Valetta and she died of an operation for appendicitis in Pisa. Is that correct?"

He noted the hesitation, hardly perceptible but nevertheless there, before the dancer bowed her head.

"Yes, that is right. . . ."

Poirot said meditatively:

"And yet—there is still a little point—her people spoke of her, not as Juanita but as *Bianca*."

Katrina shrugged her thin shoulders. She said: "Bianca—Juanita, does it matter? I suppose her real name was Bianca but she thought the name of Juanita was more romantic and so chose to call herself by it."

"Ah, you think that?" He paused and then, his voice changing, he said, "For me, there is another explanation."

"What is it?"

Poirot leaned forward. He said:

"The girl that Ted Williamson saw had hair that he described as being like wings of gold."

He leaned still a little further forward. His finger just touched the two springing waves of Katrina's hair.

"Wings of gold, horns of gold? It is as you look at it, it is whether one sees you as devil or as angel! You might be either. Or are they perhaps only the golden horns of the stricken deer?"

Katrina murmured:

*"The stricken deer . . ."* and her voice was the voice of one without hope.

Poirot said:

"All along Ted Williamson's description has worried me—it brought something to my mind—that something was you, dancing on your twinkling bronze feet through the forest. Shall I tell you what I think, mademoiselle? I think there was a week when you had no maid, when you went down alone to Grasslawn, for Bianca Valetta had returned to Italy and you had not yet engaged a new maid. Already you were feeling the illness which has since overtaken you, and you stayed in the house one day when the others went on an all-day excursion on the river. There was a ring at the door and you went to it and you saw—shall I tell you what you saw? You saw a young man who was as simple as a child and as handsome as a god! And you invented for him a girl—not Juanita—but Incognita—and for a few hours you walked with him in Arcady. . . ."

There was a long pause. Then Katrina said in a low hoarse voice:

"In one thing at least I have told you the truth. I have given you the right end to the story. Nita will die young."

*"Ah non!"* Hercule Poirot was transformed. He struck his hand on the table. He was suddenly prosaic, mundane, practical.

He said:

"It is quite unnecessary! You need not die. You can fight for your life, can you not, as well as another?"

She shook her head—sadly, hopelessly—

"What life is there for me?"

"Not the life of the stage, *bien entendu!* But think, there is another life. Come now, mademoiselle, be honest, was your father really a Prince or a Grand Duke, or even a General?"

She laughed suddenly. She said:

"He drove a lorry in Leningrad!"

"Very good! And why should you not be the wife of a garage hand in a country village? And have children as beautiful as gods, and with feet, perhaps, that will dance as you once danced."

Katrina caught her breath.

"But the whole idea is fantastic!"

"Nevertheless," said Hercule Poirot with great self-satisfaction, "I believe it is going to come true!"

# IV

# The Erymanthian Boar

## I

THE accomplishment of the third Labor of Hercules having brought him to Switzerland, Hercule Poirot decided that being there, he might take advantage of the fact and visit certain places which were up to now unknown to him.

He passed an agreeable couple of days at Chamonix, lingered a day or two at Montreux and then went on to Aldermatt, a spot which he had heard various friends praise highly.

Aldermatt, however, affected him unpleasantly. It was at the end of a valley with towering snow-peaked mountains shutting it in. He felt, unreasonably, that it was difficult to breathe.

"Impossible to remain here," said Hercule Poirot to himself. It was at that moment that he caught sight of a funicular railway. "Decidedly, I must mount."

The funicular, he discovered, ascended first to Les Avines, then to Caurouchet, and finally to Rochers Neiges, ten thousand feet above sea level.

Poirot did not propose mounting as high as all that. Les Avines, he thought, would be quite sufficiently his affair.

But here he reckoned without that element of chance which plays so large a part in life. The funicular had started when the conductor approached Poirot and demanded his ticket. After he had inspected it and punched it with a fearsome pair of clippers, he returned it with a bow. At the same time Poirot felt a small wad of paper pressed into his hand with the ticket.

The eyebrows of Hercule Poirot rose a little on his forehead. Presently, unostentatiously, without hurrying himself, he smoothed out the wad of paper. It proved to be a hurriedly scribbled note written in pencil.

*Impossible* (it ran) *to mistake those moustaches! I salute you, my dear colleague. If you are willing, you can be of great assistance to me. You have doubtless read of the affaire Salley? The killer—Marrascaud—is believed to have a rendezvous with some members of his gang at Rochers Neiges—of all places in the world! Of course the whole thing may be a blague—but our information is reliable—there is always someone who squeals, is there not? So keep your eyes open, my friend. Get in touch with Inspector Drouet who is on the spot. He is a sound man—but he cannot pretend to the brilliance of Hercule Poirot. It is important, my friend, that Marrascaud should be taken— and taken alive. He is not a man—he is a wild boar—one of the most dangerous killers alive today. I did not risk speaking to you at Aldermatt as I might have been observed and you will have a freer hand if you are thought to be a mere tourist. Good hunting! Your old friend— Lementeuil.*

Thoughtfully, Hercule Poirot caressed his moustaches. Yes, indeed, impossible to mistake the moustaches of Hercule Poirot. Now what was all this? He had read in the papers the details of *l'affaire Salley*— the cold-blooded murder of a well known Parisian bookmaker. The identity of the murderer was known. Marrascaud was a member of a well known race course gang. He had been suspected of many other killings—but this time his guilt was proved up to the hilt. He had got away, out of France, it was thought, and the police in every country in Europe were on the lookout for him.

So Marrascaud was said to have a rendezvous at Rochers Neiges. . . .

Hercule Poirot shook his head slowly. He was puzzled. For Rochers Neiges was above the snow line. There was a hotel there, but it communicated with the world only by the funicular, standing as it did on a long, narrow ledge overhanging the valley. The hotel opened in June, but there was seldom anyone there until July and August. It was a place ill supplied with entrances and exits—if a man were tracked there, he was caught in a trap. It seemed a fantastic place to choose as the rendezvous of a gang of criminals.

And yet, if Lementeuil said his information was reliable, then Lementeuil was probably right. Hercule Poirot respected the Swiss Commissaire of Police. He knew him as a sound and dependable man.

Some reason unknown was bringing Marrascaud to this meeting place far above civilisation.

Hercule Poirot sighed. To hunt down a ruthless killer was not his idea of a pleasant holiday. Brain work from an armchair, he reflected, was more in his line. Not to ensnare a wild boar upon a mountain side.

A *wild boar*—that was the term Lementeuil had used. It was certainly an odd coincidence. . . .

He murmured to himself, "The fourth Labor of Hercules. The Erymanthian Boar?"

Quietly, without ostentation, he took careful stock of his fellow passengers.

On the seat opposite him was an American tourist. The pattern of his clothes, of his overcoat, the grip he carried, down to his hopeful friendliness and his naïve absorption in the scenery, even the guide book in his hand, all gave him away and proclaimed him a small-town American seeing Europe for the first time. In another minute or two, Poirot judged, he would break into speech. His wistful dog-like expression could not be mistaken.

On the other side of the carriage, a tall, rather distinguished-looking man with greyish hair and a big curved nose was reading a German book. He had the strong mobile fingers of a musician or a surgeon.

Further away still were three men all of the same type. Men with bowed legs and an indescribable suggestion of horsiness about them. They were playing cards. Presently, perhaps, they would suggest a stranger cutting in on the game. At first the stranger would win. Afterwards, the luck would run the other way.

Nothing very unusual about the three men. The only thing that was unusual was the place where they were.

One might have seen them in any train on the way to a race meeting—or on an unimportant liner. But in an almost empty funicular—no!

There was one other occupant of the carriage—a woman. She was tall and dark. It was a beautiful face—a face that might have expressed a whole gamut of emotion—but which instead was frozen into a strange inexpressiveness. She looked at no one, staring out at the valley below.

Presently, as Poirot had expected, the American began to talk. His name, he said, was Schwartz. It was his first visit to Europe. The scenery, he said, was just grand. He'd been very deeply impressed by the Castle of Chillon. He didn't think much of Paris as a city—overrated—he'd been to the Folies Bergères and the Louvre and Notre Dame and he'd noticed that none of the restaurants and cafés could play hot jazz properly. The Champs Elysées, he thought, was pretty good, and he liked the fountains especially when they were floodlit.

Nobody got out at Les Avines or at Caurouchet. It was clear that everyone in the funicular was going up to Rochers Neiges.

Mr. Schwartz explained his own reasons. He had always wished, he said, to be high up among snow mountains. Ten thousand feet was pretty good—he'd heard that you couldn't boil an egg properly when you were as high up as that.

In the innocent friendliness of his heart, Mr. Schwartz endeavoured to draw the tall gray-haired man on the other side of the carriage into the conversation, but the latter merely stared at him coldly over his pince-nez and returned to the perusal of his book.

Mr. Schwartz then offered to exchange places with the dark lady—
she would get a better view, he explained.

It was doubtful whether she understood English. Anyway, she
merely shook her head and shrank closer into the fur collar of her
coat.

Mr. Schwartz murmured to Poirot:

"Seems kind of wrong to see a woman travelling about alone with
no one to see to things for her. A woman needs a lot of looking after
when she's travelling."

Remembering certain American women he had met on the Continent, Hercule Poirot agreed.

Mr. Schwartz sighed. He found the world unfriendly. And surely,
his brown eyes said expressively, there's no harm in a little friendliness
all round?

2

To be received by a hotel manager correctly garbed in frock coat
and patent leather shoes seemed somehow ludicrous in this out-of-
the-way, or rather above-the-world, spot.

The manager was a big handsome man, with an important manner.
He was very apologetic.

So early in the season . . . The hot water system was out of order
. . . things were hardly in running order. . . . Naturally, he would
do everything he could. . . . Not a full staff yet. . . . He was quite
confused by the unexpected number of visitors.

It all came rolling out with professional urbanity and yet it seemed
to Poirot that behind the urbane façade he caught a glimpse of some
poignant anxiety. This man, for all his easy manner, was not at ease.
He was worried about something.

Lunch was served in a long room overlooking the valley far below.
The solitary waiter, addressed as Gustave, was skillful and adroit. He
darted here and there, advising on the menu, whipping out his wine
list. The three horsy men sat at a table together. They laughed and
talked in French, their voices rising.

"Good old Joseph!—What about the little Denise, *mon vieux?*—Do
you remember that *sacré* pig of a horse that let us all down at Auteuil?"

It was all very hearty, very much in character—and incongruously
out of place!

The woman with the beautiful face sat alone at a table in the corner.
She looked at no one.

Afterwards, as Poirot was sitting in the lounge, the manager came to him and was confidential.

Monsieur must not judge the hotel too hardly. It was out of the season. No one came here till the end of July. That lady, monsieur had noticed her, perhaps? She came at this time every year. Her husband had been killed climbing three years ago. It was very sad. They had been very devoted. She came here always before the season commenced—so as to be quiet. It was a sacred pilgrimage. The elderly gentleman was a famous doctor, Dr. Karl Lutz, from Vienna. He had come here, so he said, for quiet and repose.

"It is peaceful, yes," agreed Hercule Poirot. "And *ces messieurs* there?" He indicated the three horsy men. "Do they also seek repose, do you think?"

The manager shrugged his shoulders. Again there appeared in his eyes that worried look. He said vaguely:

"Ah, the tourists, they wish always a new experience. . . . The altitude—that alone is a new sensation."

It was not, Poirot thought, a very pleasant sensation. He was conscious of his own rapidly beating heart. The lines of a nursery rhyme ran idiotically through his mind. *"Up above the world so high, Like a tea tray in the sky."*

Schwartz came into the lounge. His eyes brightened when he saw Poirot. He came over to him at once.

"I've been talking to that doctor. He speaks English after a fashion. He's a Jew—been turned out of Austria by the Nazis. Say, I guess those people are just crazy! This Dr. Lutz was quite a big man, I gather—nerve specialist—psychoanalysis—that kind of stuff."

His eyes went to where a tall woman was looking out of a window at remorseless mountains. He lowered his voice.

"I got her name from the waiter. She's a Madame Grandier. Her husband was killed climbing. That's why she comes here. I sort of feel, don't you, that we ought to do something about it—try to take her out of herself?"

Hercule Poirot said:

"If I were you I should not attempt it."

But the friendliness of Mr. Schwartz was indefatigable.

Poirot saw him make his overtures, saw the remorseless way in which they were rebuffed. The two stood together for a minute silhouetted against the light. The woman was taller than Schwartz. Her head was thrown back and her expression was cold and forbidding. He did not hear what she said, but Schwartz came back looking crestfallen.

"Nothing doing," he said. He added wistfully, "Seems to me that as we're all human beings together there's no reason we shouldn't be friendly to one another. Don't you agree, Mr.— You know, I don't know your name?"

"My name," said Poirot, "is Poirier." He added, "I am a silk merchant from Lyons."

"I'd like to give you my card, M. Poirier, and if ever you come to Fountain Springs you'll be sure of a welcome."

Poirot accepted the card, clapped his hand to his own pocket, murmured:

"Alas, I have not a card on me at the moment. . . ."

That night, when he went to bed, Poirot read through Lementeuil's letter carefully before replacing it, neatly folded, in his wallet. As he got into bed he said to himself:

"It is curious—I wonder if . . ."

# 3

Gustave, the waiter, brought Hercule Poirot his breakfast of coffee and rolls. He was apologetic over the coffee.

"Monsieur comprehends, does he not, that at this altitude it is impossible to have the coffee really hot? Lamentably, it boils too soon."

Poirot murmured:

"One must accept these vagaries of nature with fortitude."

Gustave murmured:

"Monsieur is a philosopher."

He went to the door, but instead of leaving the room, he took one quick look outside, then shut the door again and returned to the bedside. He said:

"M. Hercule Poirot? I am Drouet, Inspector of Police."

"Ah," said Poirot, "I had already suspected as much."

Drouet lowered his voice.

"M. Poirot, something very grave has occurred. There has been an accident to the funicular!"

"An accident?" Poirot sat up. "What kind of an accident?"

"Nobody has been injured. It happened in the night. It was occasioned, perhaps, by natural causes—a small avalanche that swept down boulders and rocks. But it is possible that there was human agency at work. One does not know. In any case the result is that it will take many days to repair and that in the meantime we are cut off up here. So early in the season, when the snow is still heavy, it is impossible to communicate with the valley below."

Hercule Poirot sat up in bed. He said softly:

"That is very interesting."

The Inspector nodded.

"Yes," he said. "It shows that our commissaire's information was correct. Marrascaud has a rendezvous here, and he has made sure that that rendezvous shall not be interrupted."

Hercule Poirot cried impatiently:

"But it is fantastic!"

"I agree." Inspector Drouet threw up his hands. "It does not make the common sense—but there it is. This Marrascaud, you know, is a fantastic creature! Myself," he nodded, "I think he is mad."

Poirot said:

"A madman and a murderer!"

Drouet said drily:

"It is not amusing. I agree."

Poirot said slowly:

"But if he has a rendezvous here, on this ledge of snow high above the world, then it also follows that Marrascaud himself is here already, since communications are now cut."

Drouet said quietly:

"I know."

Both men were silent for a minute or two. Then Poirot asked:

"Dr. Lutz? Can he be Marrascaud?"

Drouet shook his head.

"I do not think so. There is a real Dr. Lutz—I have seen his pictures in the papers—a distinguished and well-known man. This man resembles these photographs closely."

Poirot murmured:

"If Marrascaud is an artist in disguise, he might play the part successfully."

"Yes, but is he? I never heard of him as an expert in disguise. He has not the guile and cunning of the serpent. He is a wild boar, ferocious, terrible, who charges in blind fury."

Poirot said:

"All the same . . ."

Drouet agreed quickly.

"Ah, yes, he is a fugitive from justice. Therefore he is forced to dissemble. So he may—in fact he must be—more or less disguised."

"You have his description?"

The other shrugged his shoulders.

"Roughly only. The official Bertillon photograph and measurements were to have been sent up to me today. I know only that he is a man of thirty odd, of a little over medium height and of dark complexion. No distinguishing marks."

Poirot shrugged his shoulders.

"That could apply to anybody. What about the American, Schwartz?"

"I was going to ask you that. You have spoken with him, and you have lived, I think, much with the English and the Americans. To a casual glance he appears to be the normal travelling American. His passport is in order. It is perhaps strange that he should elect to come here—but Americans when travelling are quite incalculable. What do you think yourself?"

Hercule Poirot shook his head in perplexity.

He said:

"On the surface, at any rate, he appears to be a harmless, slightly over-friendly man. He might be a bore, but it seems difficult to regard him as a danger." He went on, "But there are three more visitors here."

The Inspector nodded, his face suddenly eager.

"Yes, and they *are* the type we are looking for. I'll take my oath, M. Poirot, that those three men at any rate, are members of Marrascaud's gang. They're race-course toughs if I ever saw them! And one of the three may be Marrascaud himself."

Hercule Poirot reflected. He recalled the three faces.

One was a broad face with overhanging brows and a fat jowl—a hoggish bestial face. One was lean and thin with a sharp, narrow face and cold eyes. The third man was a pasty-faced fellow with a slightly dandiacal air.

Yes, one of the three might well be Marrascaud but, if so, the question came insistently, why? Why should Marrascaud and two members of his gang journey together and ascend into a rat trap on a mountain side? A meeting surely could be arranged in safer and less fantastic surroundings—in a café—in a railway station—in a crowded cinema— in a public park—somewhere where there were exits in plenty—not here far above the world in a wilderness of snow.

Something of this he tried to convey to Inspector Drouet and the latter agreed readily enough.

"But yes, it is fantastic, it does not make sense."

"If it is a rendezvous, why do they travel together? No, indeed, it does not make sense."

Drouet said, his face worried:

"In that case, we have to examine a second supposition. These three men are members of Marrascaud's gang and they have come here to meet Marrascaud himself. Who then is Marrascaud?"

Poirot asked:

"What about the staff of the hotel?"

Drouet shrugged his shoulders.

"There is no staff to speak of. There is an old woman who cooks, there is her old husband Jacques—they have been here for fifty years I should think. There is the waiter whose place I have taken, that is all."

Poirot said:

"The manager, he knows of course who you are?"

"Naturally. It needed his cooperation."

"Has it struck you," said Hercule Poirot, "that he looks worried?"

The remark seemed to strike Drouet. He said thoughtfully:

"Yes, that is true."

"It may be that it is merely the anxiety of being involved in police proceedings."

"But you think it may be more than that? You think that he may—know something?"

"It occurred to me, that is all."

Drouet said somberly:

"I wonder."

He paused and then went on:

"Could one get it out of him, do you think?"

Poirot shook his head doubtfully. He said:

"It would be better, I think, not to let him know of our suspicions. Keep your eye on him, that is all."

Drouet nodded. He turned towards the door.

"You've no suggestions, M. Poirot? I—I know your reputation. We have heard of you in this country of ours."

Poirot said perplexedly:

"For the moment I can suggest nothing. It is the reason which escapes me—the reason for a rendezvous in this place. In fact, the reason for a rendezvous at all?"

"Money," said Drouet succinctly.

"He was robbed, then, as well as murdered, this poor fellow Salley?"

"Yes, he had a very large sum of money on him which has disappeared."

"And the rendezvous is for the purpose of sharing out, you think?"

"It is the most obvious idea."

Poirot shook his head in a dissatisfied manner.

"Yes, but why *here*?" He went on slowly, "The worst place possible for a rendezvous of criminals. But it is a place, this, where one might come to meet a woman. . . ."

Drouet took a step forward eagerly.

He said excitedly:

"You think—?"

"I think," said Poirot, "that Madame Grandier is a very beautiful woman. I think that anyone might well mount ten thousand feet for her sake—that is, if she had suggested such a thing."

"You know," said Drouet, "that's interesting. I never thought of her in connection with the case. After all, she's been to this place several years running."

Poirot said gently:

"Yes—and therefore her presence would not cause comment. It would be a reason, would it not, why Rochers Neiges should have been the spot selected?"

Drouet excitedly:

"You've had an idea, M. Poirot. I'll look into that angle."

# 4

The day passed without incident. Fortunately the hotel was well provisioned. The manager explained that there need be no anxiety. Supplies were assured.

Hercule Poirot endeavoured to get into conversation with Dr. Karl Lutz and was rebuffed. The doctor intimated plainly that psychology was his professional preoccupation and that he was not going to discuss it with amateurs. He sat in a corner, reading a large German tome on the subconscious and making copious notes and annotations.

Hercule Poirot went outside and wandered aimlessly round to the kitchen premises. There he entered into conversation with the old man Jacques, who was surly and suspicious. His wife, the cook, was more forthcoming. Fortunately, she explained to Poirot, there was a large reserve of tinned food—but she herself thought little of food in tins. It was wickedly expensive and what nourishment could there be in it? The good God had never intended people to live out of tins.

The conversation came round to the subject of the hotel staff. Early in July the chambermaids and the extra waiters arrived. But for the next three weeks, there would be nobody or next to nobody. Mostly people who came up and had lunch and then went back again. She and Jacques and one waiter could manage that easily.

Poirot asked:

"There was already a waiter here before Gustave came, was there not?"

"But yes, indeed, a poor kind of a waiter. No skill, no experience. No class at all."

"How long was he here before Gustave replaced him?"

"A few days only—the inside of a week. Naturally he was dismissed. We were not surprised. It was bound to come."

Poirot murmured:

"He did not complain unduly?"

"Ah, no, he went quietly enough. After all, what could he expect? This is a hotel of good class. One must have proper service here."

Poirot nodded. He asked:

"Where did he go?"

"That Robert, you mean?" She shrugged her shoulders. "Doubtless back to the obscure café he came from."

"He went down in the funicular?"

She looked at him curiously.

"Naturally, monsieur. What other way is there to go?"

Poirot asked:

"Did anyone see him go?"

They both stared at him.

"Ah! Do you think it likely that one goes to see off an animal like that—that one gives him the grand farewell? One has one's own affairs to occupy one."

"Precisely," said Hercule Poirot.

He walked slowly away, staring up as he did so at the building above him. A large hotel—with only one wing open at present. In the other wings were many rooms, closed and shuttered where no one was likely to enter. . . .

He came round the corner of the hotel and nearly ran into one of the three card playing men. It was the one with the pasty face and pale eyes. The eyes looked at Poirot without expression. Only the lips curled back a little showing the teeth like a vicious horse.

Poirot passed him and went on. There was a figure ahead of him— the tall, graceful figure of Madame Grandier.

He hastened his pace a little and caught her up. He said:

"This accident to the funicular, it is distressing. I hope, madame, that it has not inconvenienced you?"

She said:

"It is a matter of indifference to me."

Her voice was very deep—a full contralto. She did not look at Poirot. She swerved aside and went into the hotel by a small side door.

# 5

Hercule Poirot went to bed early. He was awakened some time after midnight.

Someone was fumbling with the lock of the door.

He sat up, putting on the light. At the same moment the lock yielded to manipulation and the door swung open. Three men stood there, the three card-playing men. They were, Poirot thought, slightly drunk. Their faces were foolish and yet malevolent. He saw the gleam of a razor blade.

The big thickset man advanced. He spoke in a growling voice.

"Sacred pig of a detective! Bah!"

He burst into a torrent of profanity. The three of them advanced purposefully on the defenceless man in the bed.

"We'll carve him up, boys. Eh, little horses? We'll slash Monsieur Detective's face open for him. He won't be the first one tonight."

They came on, steady, purposeful—the razor blades flashed. . . .

And then, startling in its crisp transatlantic tones, a voice said:

"Stick 'em up."

They swerved round. Schwartz, dressed in a peculiarly vivid set of striped pyjamas, stood in the doorway. In his hand he held an automatic.

"Stick 'em up, guys. I'm pretty good at shooting."

He pressed the trigger—and a bullet sang past the big man's ear and buried itself in the woodwork of the window.

Three pairs of hands were raised rapidly.

Schwartz said:

"Can I trouble you, M. Poirier?"

Hercule Poirot was out of bed in a flash. He collected the gleaming weapons and passed his hands over the three men's bodies to make sure that they were not armed.

Schwartz said:

"Now then, march! There's a big cupboard just along the corridor. No window in it. Just the thing."

He marched them into it and turned the key on them. He swung round to Poirot, his voice breaking with pleasurable emotion.

"If that doesn't just show? Do you know, M. Poirier, there were folks in Fountain Springs who laughed at me because I said I was going to take a gun abroad with me. 'Where do you think you're going?' they asked. 'Into the jungle?' Well, sir, I'd say the laugh is with me. Did you ever see such an ugly bunch of toughs?"

Poirot said:

"My dear Mr. Schwartz, you appeared in the nick of time. It might have been a drama on the stage! I am very much in your debt."

"That's nothing. Where do we go from here? We ought to turn these boys over to the police and that's just what we can't do! It's a knotty problem. Maybe we'd better consult the manager."

Hercule Poirot said:

"Ah, the manager. I think first we will consult the waiter—Gustave—

alias Inspector Drouet. But yes—the waiter Gustave is really a detective."

Schwartz stared at him.

"So that's why they did it!"

"That is why who did what?"

"This bunch of crooks got to you second on the list. They'd already carved up Gustave."

"What?"

"Come with me. The doc's busy on him now."

Drouet's room was a small one on the top floor. Dr. Lutz, in a dressing gown, was busy bandaging the injured man's face.

He turned his head as they entered.

"Ah! It is you, Mr. Schwartz? A nasty business, this. What butchers! What inhuman monsters!"

Drouet lay still, moaning faintly.

Schwartz asked:

"Is he in danger?"

"He will not die if that is what you mean. But he must not speak—there must be no excitement. I have dressed the wounds—there will be no risk of septicemia."

The three men left the room together. Schwartz said to Poirot:

"Did you say Gustave was a police officer?"

Hercule Poirot nodded.

"But what was he doing up at Rochers Neiges?"

"He was engaged in tracking down a very dangerous criminal."

In a few words Poirot explained the situation.

Dr. Lutz said:

"Marrascaud? I read about the case in the paper. I should much like to meet that man. There is some deep abnormality there! I should like to know the particulars of his childhood."

"For myself," said Hercule Poirot, "I should like to know exactly where he is at this minute."

Schwartz said:

"Isn't he one of those three we locked in the cupboard?"

Poirot said in a dissatisfied voice:

"It is possible—yes, but me, I am not sure. . . . I have an idea—"

He broke off, staring down at the carpet. It was of a light buff colour and there were marks on it of a deep rusty brown.

Hercule Poirot said:

"Footsteps—footsteps that have trodden, I think, in blood and they lead from the unused wing of the hotel. Come—we must be quick!"

They followed him, through a swing door and along a dim, dusty corridor. They turned the corner of it, still following the marks on the carpet until the tracks led them to a half open doorway.

Poirot pushed the door open and entered.

He uttered a sharp horrified exclamation.

The room was a bedroom. The bed had been slept in and there was a tray of food on the table.

In the middle of the floor lay the body of a man. He was of just over middle height and he had been attacked with savage and unbelievable ferocity. There were a dozen wounds on his arms and chest and his head and face had been battered almost to a pulp.

Schwartz gave a half-stifled exclamation and turned away, looking as though he might be sick.

Dr. Lutz uttered a horrified exclamation in German.

Schwartz said faintly:

"Who is this guy? Does anyone know?"

"I fancy," said Poirot, "that he was known here as Robert, a rather unskilful waiter. . . ."

Lutz had gone nearer, bending over the body. He pointed with a finger.

There was a paper pinned to the dead man's breast. It had some words scrawled on it in ink.

*Marrascaud will kill no more—nor will he rob his friends!*

Schwartz ejaculated:

"Marrascaud? So this is Marrascaud? But what brought him up here to this out-of-the-way spot? And why do you say his name is Robert?"

Poirot said:

"He was here masquerading as a waiter—and by all accounts he was a very bad waiter. So bad that no one was surprised when he was given the sack. He left—presumably to return to Andermatt. But nobody saw him go."

Lutz said in his slow, rumbling voice:

"So—and what do you think happened?"

Poirot replied:

"I think we have here the explanation of a certain worried expression on the hotel manager's face. Marrascaud must have offered him a big bribe to allow him to remain hidden in the unused part of the hotel—"

He added thoughtfully:

"But the manager was not happy about it. Oh, no, he was not happy at all."

"And Marrascaud continued to live in this unused wing with no one but the manager knowing about it?"

"So it seems. It would be quite possible, you know."

Dr. Lutz said:

"And why was he killed? And who killed him?"

Schwartz cried:

"That's easy. He was to share out the money with his gang. He didn't. He double-crossed them. He came here, to this out-of-the-way place, to lie low for a while. He thought it was the last place in the world they'd ever think of. He was wrong. Somehow or other they got wise to it and followed him." He touched the dead body with the tip of his shoe. "And they settled his account—like this."

Hercule Poirot murmured:

"Yes, it was not quite the kind of rendezvous we thought."

Dr. Lutz said irritably:

"These hows and whys may be very interesting, but I am concerned with our present position. Here we have a dead man. I have a sick man on my hands and a limited amount of medical supplies. And we are cut off from the world! For how long?"

Schwartz added:

"And we've got three murderers locked in a cupboard! It's what I'd call kind of an interesting situation."

Dr. Lutz said:

"What do we do?"

Poirot said:

"First, we get hold of the manager. He is not a criminal, that one, only a man who was greedy for money. He is a coward, too. He will do everything we tell him. My good friend Jacques, or his wife, will perhaps provide some cord. Our three miscreants must be placed where we can guard them in safety until the day when help comes. I think that Mr. Schwartz's automatic will be effective in carrying out any plans we may make."

Dr. Lutz said:

"And I? What do I do?"

"You, doctor," said Poirot gravely, "will do all you can for your patient. The rest of us will employ ceaseless vigilance—and wait. There is nothing else we can do."

# 6

It was three days later that a little party of men appeared in front of the hotel in the early hours of the morning.

It was Hercule Poirot who opened the front door to them with a flourish.

"Welcome, *mon vieux.*"

Monsieur Lementeuil, Commissaire of Police, seized Poirot by both hands.

"Ah, my friend, with what emotion I greet you! What stupendous events—what emotions you have passed through! And we below, our anxiety, our fears—knowing nothing—fearing everything. No wireless—no means of communication. To heliograph, that was indeed a stroke of genius on your part."

"No, no," Poirot endeavoured to look modest. "After all, when the inventions of man fail, one falls back upon nature. There is always the sun in the sky."

The little party filed into the hotel. Lementeuil said:

"We are not expected?" His smile was somewhat grim.

Poirot smiled also. He said:

"But, no! It is believed that the funicular is not nearly repaired yet."

Lementeuil said with emotion:

"Ah, this is a great day. There is no doubt, you think? It is really Marrascaud?"

"It is Marrascaud all right. Come with me."

They went up the stairs. A door opened and Schwartz came out in his dressing-gown. He stared when he saw the men.

"I heard voices," he explained. "Why, what's this?"

Hercule Poirot said grandiloquently:

"Help has come! Accompany us, monsieur. This is a great moment."

He started up the next flight of stairs.

Schwartz said:

"Are you going up to Drouet? How is he, by the way?"

"Dr. Lutz reported him going on well last night."

They came to the door of Drouet's room. Poirot flung it open. He announced:

"Here is your wild boar, gentleman. Take him alive and see to it that he does not cheat the guillotine."

The man in the bed, his face still bandaged, started up. But the police officers had him by the arms before he could move.

Schwartz cried bewildered:

"But that's Gustave the waiter—that's Inspector Drouet."

"It is Gustave, yes—but it is not Drouet. Drouet was the first waiter, the waiter Robert who was imprisoned in the unused part of the hotel and whom Marrascaud killed the same night as the attack was made on me."

7

Over breakfast, Poirot explained gently to the bewildered American.

"You comprehend, there are certain things one knows—knows quite certainly in the course of one's profession. One knows, for instance, the difference between a detective and a murderer! Gustave was no waiter—that I suspected at once—but equally he was not a policeman. I have dealt with policemen all my life and I know. He could pass as a detective to an outsider—but not to a man who was a policeman himself.

"And so, at once, I was suspicious. That evening, I did not drink my coffee. I poured it away. And I was wise. Late that evening a man came into my room, came in with the easy confidence of one who knows that the man whose room he is searching is drugged. He looked through my affairs and he found the letter in my wallet—where I had left it for him to find! The next morning Gustave comes into my room with my coffee. He greets me by name and acts his part with complete assurance. But he is anxious—horribly anxious—for somehow or other the police have got on his track! They have learnt where he is and that is for him a terrible disaster. It upsets all his plans. He is caught up here like a rat in a trap."

Schwartz said:

"The damn fool thing was ever to come here! Why did he?"

Poirot said gravely:

"It is not so foolish as you think. He had need, urgent need, of a retired spot, away from the world, where he could meet a certain person, and where a certain happening could take place."

"What person?"

"Dr. Lutz."

"Dr. Lutz? Is he a crook, too?"

"Dr. Lutz is really Dr. Lutz—but he is not a nerve specialist—not a psychoanalyst. He is a surgeon, my friend, a surgeon who specialises in facial surgery. That is why he was to meet Marrascaud here. He is poor now, turned out of his country. He was offered a huge fee to meet a man here and change that man's appearance by means of his surgical skill. He may have guessed that that man was a criminal, but if so, he shut his eyes to the fact. Realize this, they dared not risk a nursing home in some foreign country. No, up here, where no one ever comes so early in the season except for an odd visit, where the manager is a man in need of money who can be bribed, was an ideal spot.

"But, as I say, matters went wrong. Marrascaud was betrayed. The three men, his bodyguards, who were to meet him here and look after him had not yet arrived, but Marrascaud acts at once. The police officer who is pretending to be a waiter is kidnapped, and Marrascaud takes his place. The gang arrange for the funicular to be wrecked. It is a matter of time. The following evening Drouet is killed and a paper is pinned on the dead body. It is hoped that by the time that communications are established with the world Drouet's body may have been buried as that of Marrascaud. Dr. Lutz performs his operation without delay. But one man must be silenced—Hercule Poirot. So the gang are sent to attack me. Thanks to you, my friend—"

Hercule Poirot bowed gracefully to Schwartz who said:

"So you're really Hercule Poirot?"

"Precisely."

"And you were never fooled by that body for a minute? You knew all along that it wasn't Marrascaud?"

"Certainly."

"Why didn't you say so?"

Hercule Poirot's face was suddenly stern.

"Because I wanted to be quite sure of handing the real Marrascaud over to the police."

He murmured below his breath:

"To capture alive the wild boar of Erymanthea. . . ."

# V

# The Augean Stables

"THE situation is an extremely delicate one, M. Poirot."

A faint smile flitted across Hercule Poirot's lips. He almost replied:

"It always is!"

Instead, he composed his face and put on what might be described as a bedside manner of extreme discretion.

Sir George Conway proceeded weightily. Phrases fell easily from his lips—the extreme delicacy of the Government's position—the interests of the public—the solidarity of the party—the necessity of presenting a united front—the power of the press—the welfare of the country. . . .

It all sounded well—and meant nothing. Hercule Poirot felt that familiar aching of the jaw when one longs to yawn and politeness forbids. He had felt the same sometimes when reading parliamentary debates. But on those occasions there had been no need to restrain his yawns.

He steeled himself to endure patiently. He felt, at the same time, a sympathy for Sir George Conway. The man obviously wanted to tell him something—and as obviously had lost the art of simple narration. Words had become to him a means of obscuring facts—not of revealing them. He was an adept in the art of the useful phrase—that is to say the phrase that falls soothingly on the ear and is quite empty of meaning.

The words rolled on—poor Sir George became quite red in the face. He shot a desperate glance at the other man sitting at the head of the table, and that other man responded.

Edward Ferrier said:

"All right, George. I'll tell him."

Hercule Poirot shifted his gaze from the Home Secretary to the

486

Prime Minister. He felt a keen interest in Edward Ferrier—an interest aroused by a chance phrase from an old man of eighty-two. Professor Fergus MacLeod, after disposing of a chemical difficulty in the conviction of a murderer, had touched for a moment on politics. On the retirement of the famous and beloved John Hammett (now Lord Dittisham), his son-in-law, Edward Ferrier, had been asked to form a Cabinet. As politicians go, he was a young man—under fifty. Professor MacLeod had said, "Ferrier was once one of my students. He's a sound man."

That was all, but to Hercule Poirot it represented a good deal. If MacLeod called a man sound it was a testimonial to character compared with which no popular or press enthusiasm counted at all.

It coincided, it was true, with the popular estimate. Edward Ferrier was considered sound—just that—not brilliant, not great, not a particularly eloquent orator, not a man of deep learning. He was a sound man—a man bred in the tradition—a man who had married John Hammett's daughter—who had been John Hammett's right-hand man and who could be trusted to carry on the government of the country in the John Hammett traditions.

For John Hammett was particularly dear to the people and press of England. He represented every quality which was dear to Englishmen. People said of him, "One does feel that Hammett's honest." Anecdotes were told of his simple home life, of his fondness for gardening. Corresponding to Baldwin's pipe and Chamberlain's umbrella, there was John Hammett's raincoat. He always carried it—a weatherworn garment. It stood as a symbol—of the English climate, of the prudent forethought of the English race, of their attachment to old possessions. Moreover, in his bluff British way, John Hammett was an orator. His speeches, quietly and earnestly delivered, contained those simple sentimental clichés which are so deeply rooted in the English heart. Foreigners sometimes criticize them as being both hypocritical and unbearably noble. John Hammett did not in the least mind being noble—in a sporting, public school, deprecating fashion.

Moreover, he was a man of fine presence, tall, upstanding, with fair colouring and very bright blue eyes. His mother had been a Dane and he himself had been for many years First Lord of the Admiralty, which gave rise to his nickname of 'the Viking.' When at last ill health forced him to give up the reins of office, deep uneasiness was felt. Who would succeed him? The brilliant Lord Charles Delafield? (Too brilliant—England didn't need brilliance.) Evan Whittler? (Clever—but perhaps a little unscrupulous.) John Potter? (The sort of man who might fancy himself as dictator—and we didn't want any dictators in this country, thank you very much.) So a sigh of relief went up when the quiet Edward Ferrier assumed office. Ferrier was all right. He had been trained by the Old Man, he had married the Old Man's daughter. In the classic British phrase, Ferrier would "carry on."

Hercule Poirot studied the quiet, dark-faced man with the low pleasant voice. Lean and dark and tired-looking.

Edward Ferrier was saying:

"Perhaps, M. Poirot, you are acquainted with a weekly periodical called the *X-Ray News?*"

"I have glanced at it," admitted Poirot, blushing slightly.

The Prime Minister said:

"Then you know more or less of what it consists. Semi-libellous matter. Snappy paragraphs hinting at sensational secret history. Some of them true, some of them harmless—but all served up in a spicy manner. Occasionally—"

He paused and then said, his voice altering a little:

"Occasionally something more."

Hercule Poirot did not speak. Ferrier went on:

"For two weeks now there have been hints of impending disclosures of a first-class scandal in 'the highest political circles.' 'Astonishing revelations of corruption and jobbery.' "

Hercule Poirot said, shrugging his shoulders:

"A common trick. When the actual revelations come they usually badly disappoint the cravers after sensation."

Ferrier said drily:

"These will not disappoint them."

Hercule Poirot asked:

"You know, then, what these revelations are going to be?"

"With a fair amount of accuracy."

Edward Ferrier paused a minute, then he began speaking. Carefully, methodically, he outlined the story.

It was not an edifying story. Accusations of shameless chicanery, of share juggling, of a gross misuse of party funds. The charges were levelled against the former Prime Minister, John Hammett. They showed him to be a dishonest rascal, a gigantic confidence trickster, who had used his position to amass for himself a vast private fortune.

The Prime Minister's quiet voice stopped at last. The Home Secretary groaned. He spluttered out:

"It's monstrous—monstrous! This fellow, Perry, who edits the rag, ought to be shot!"

Hercule Poirot said:

"These so-called revelations are to appear in the *X-Ray News?*"

"Yes."

"What steps do you propose to take about them?"

Ferrier said slowly:

"They constitute a private attack on John Hammett. It is open to him to sue the paper for libel."

"Will he do that?"

"No."

"Why not?"

Ferrier said:

"It is probable that there is nothing the *X-Ray News* would like better. The publicity given them would be enormous. Their defense would be fair comment and that the statements complained of were true. The whole business would be exhaustively held up to view in a blaze of limelight."

"Still, if the case went against them, the damages would be extremely heavy."

Ferrier said slowly:

"It might not go against them."

"Why?"

Sir George said primly, "I really think that—"

But Edward Ferrier was already speaking.

"Because what they intend to print is—the truth."

A groan burst from Sir George Conway, outraged at such un-Parliamentary frankness. He cried out:

"Edward, my dear fellow. We don't admit, surely—"

The ghost of a smile passed over Edward Ferrier's tired face. He said:

"Unfortunately, George, there are times when the stark truth has got to be told. This is one of them."

Sir George exclaimed:

"You understand, M. Poirot, all this is strictly in confidence. Not one word—"

Ferrier interrupted him. He said:

"M. Poirot understands that." He went on slowly, "What he may not understand is this: the whole future of the People's Party is at stake. John Hammett, M. Poirot, was the People's Party. He stood for what it represents to the people of England— He stood for decency and honesty. No one has ever thought us brilliant. We have muddled and blundered. But we have stood for the tradition of doing one's best—and we have stood, too, for fundamental honesty. Our disaster is this—that the man who was our figurehead, the Honest Man of the People, *par excellence*—turns out to have been one of the worst crooks of this generation."

Another groan burst from Sir George.

Poirot asked:

"You knew nothing of all this?"

Again the smile flashed across the weary face. Ferrier said:

"You may not believe me, M. Poirot, but like everyone else I was completely deceived. I never understood my wife's curious attitude of reserve towards her father. I understand it now. She knew his essential character."

He paused and then said:

"When the truth began to leak out, I was horrified, incredulous. We insisted on my father-in-law's resignation on the grounds of ill health and we set to work to—to clean up the mess, shall I say?"

Sir George groaned.

"The Augean stables!"

Poirot started.

Ferrier said:

"It will prove, I fear, too Herculean a task for us. Once the facts become public, there will be a wave of reaction all over the country. The Government will fall. There will be a General Election and in all probability Everhard and his party will be returned to power. You know Everhard's policy."

Sir George spluttered.

"A firebrand—a complete firebrand."

Ferrier said gravely:

"Everhard has ability—but he is reckless, belligerent and utterly tactless. His supporters are inept and vacillating—it would be practically a dictatorship."

Hercule Poirot nodded.

Sir George bleated out:

"If only the whole thing can be hushed up. . . ."

Slowly, the Premier shook his head. It was a movement of defeat.

Poirot said:

"You do not believe that it can be hushed up?"

Ferrier said:

"I sent for you, M. Poirot, as a last hope. In my opinion, this business is too big, too many people know about it, for it to be successfully concealed. The only two methods open to us—which are, to put it bluntly, the use of force, or the adoption of bribery—cannot really hope to succeed. The Home Secretary compared our trouble with the cleansing of the Augean stables. It needs, M. Poirot, the violence of a river in spate, the disruption of the great natural forces of nature— nothing less, in fact, than a miracle."

"It needs, in fact, a Hercules," said Poirot, nodding his head with a pleased expression.

He added:

"My name, remember, is Hercule. . . ."

Edward Ferrier said:

"Can you perform miracles, M. Poirot?"

"It is why you sent for me, is it not? Because you thought that I might?"

"That is true. . . . I realised that if salvation were to be achieved, it could only come through some fantastic and completely unorthodox suggestion."

He paused a minute, then he said:

"But perhaps, M. Poirot, you take an ethical view of the situation? John Hammett was a crook, the legend of John Hammett must be exploded. Can one build an honest house on dishonest foundations? I do not know. But I do know that I want to try." He smiled with a sudden sharp bitterness. "The politician wants to remain in office—as usual from the highest motives."

Hercule Poirot rose. He said:

"Monsieur, my experience in the police force has not, perhaps, allowed me to think very highly of politicians. If John Hammett were in office—I would not lift a finger—no, not a little finger. But I know something about you. I have been told, by a man who is really great, one of the greatest scientists and brains of the day, that you are—a sound man. I will do what I can."

He bowed and left the room.

Sir George burst out:

"Well, of all the damned cheek—"

But Edward Ferrier, still smiling, said:

"It was a compliment."

## 2

On his way downstairs, Hercule Poirot was intercepted by a tall, fair-haired woman. She said:

"Please come into my sitting room, M. Poirot."

He bowed and followed her.

She shut the door, motioned him to a chair, and offered him a cigarette. She sat down opposite him. She said quietly:

"You have just seen my husband—and he has told you—about my father."

Poirot looked at her with attention. He saw a tall woman, still handsome, with character and intelligence in her face. Mrs. Ferrier was a popular figure. As the wife of the Prime Minister, she naturally came in for a good share of limelight. As the daughter of her father, her popularity was even greater. Dagmar Ferrier represented the popular ideal of English womanhood.

She was a devoted wife, a fond mother, she shared her husband's love of country life. She interested herself in just those aspects of public life which were generally felt to be proper spheres of womanly activity. She dressed well, but never in an ostentatiously fashionable manner. She devoted much of her time and activity to large-scale charities, she had inaugurated special schemes for the relief of the wives of unemployed men. She was looked up to by the whole nation and was a most valuable asset to the party.

Hercule Poirot said:

"You must be terribly worried, madame."

"Oh, I am—you don't know how much. For years I have been dreading—something."

Poirot said:

"You had no idea of what was actually going on?"

She shook her head.

"No—not in the least. I only knew that my father was not—was not what everyone thought him. I realised, from the time that I was a child, that he was a—a humbug."

Her voice was deep and bitter. She said:

"It is through marrying me that Edward—that Edward will lose everything."

Poirot said in a quiet voice:

"Have you any enemies, madame?"

She looked up at him, surprised.

"Enemies? I don't think so."

Poirot said thoughtfully:

"I think you have. . . ."

He went on:

"Have you courage, madame? There is a great campaign afoot— against your husband—and against yourself. You must prepare to defend yourself."

She cried:

"But it doesn't matter about me. Only about Edward!"

Poirot said:

"The one includes the other. Remember, madame, you are Caesar's wife."

He saw her colour ebb. She leaned forward. She said:

"What is it you are trying to tell me?"

## 3

Percy Perry, Editor of the *X-Ray News,* sat behind his desk smoking. He was a small man, with a face like a weasel.

He was saying in a soft oily voice:

"We'll give 'em the dirt, all right. Lovely—lovely! Oh, boy!"

His second-in-command, a thin, spectacled youth, said uneasily:

"You're not nervous?"

"Expecting strong-arm stuff? Not them. Haven't got the nerve. Wouldn't do them any good, either. Not the way we've got it farmed out—in this country and on the Continent and America."

The other said:

"They must be in a pretty good stew. Won't they do anything?"

"They'll send someone to talk pretty—"

A buzzer sounded. Percy Perry picked up a receiver. He said:

"Who do you say? Right, send him up."

He put the receiver down—grinned.

"They've got that high-toned Belgian dick onto it. He's coming up now to do his stuff. Wants to know if we'll play ball."

Hercule Poirot came in. He was immaculately dressed—a white camellia in his buttonhole.

Percy Perry said:

"Pleased to meet you, M. Poirot. On your way to the Royal Enclosure at Ascot? No? My mistake."

Hercule Poirot said:

"I am flattered. One hopes to present a good appearance. It is even more important," his eyes roamed innocently over the editor's face and somewhat slovenly attire, "when one has few natural advantages."

Perry said shortly:

"What do you want to see me about?"

Poirot leaned forward, tapped him on the knee, and said with a beaming smile:

"Blackmail."

"What the devil do you mean, blackmail?"

"I have heard—the little bird has told me—that on occasions you have been on the point of publishing certain very damaging statements in your so *spirituel* paper—then, there has been a pleasant little increase in your bank balance—and after all, those statements have not been published."

Poirot leaned back and nodded his head in a satisfied sort of way.

"Do you realise that what you're suggesting amounts to slander?"

Poirot smiled confidently.

"I am sure you will not take offense."

"I do take offense! As to blackmail, there is no evidence of my ever having blackmailed anybody."

"No, no, I am quite sure of that. You misunderstood me. I was not threatening you. I was leading up to a simple question. *How much?*"

"I don't know what you're talking about," said Percy Perry.

"A matter of national importance, M. Perry."

They exchanged a significant glance.

Percy Perry said:

"I'm a reformer, M. Poirot. I want to see politics cleaned up. I'm opposed to corruption. Do you know what the state of politics is in this country? The Augean stables, no more, no less."

*"Tiens!"* said Hercule Poirot. "You, too, use that phrase."

"And what is needed," went on the editor, "to cleanse those stables is the great purifying flood of public opinion."

Hercule Poirot got up. He said:

"I applaud your sentiments."

He added:

"It is a pity that you do not feel in need of money."

Percy Perry said hurriedly:

"Here, wait a sec—I didn't say that exactly. . . ."

But Hercule Poirot had gone through the door.

His excuse for later events is that he does not like blackmailers.


# 4

Everitt Dashwood, the cheery young man on the staff of *The Branch*, clapped Hercule Poirot affectionately on the back.

He said:

"There's dirt and dirt, my boy. My dirt's clean dirt—that's all."

"I was not suggesting that you were on a par with Percy Perry."

"Damned little bloodsucker. He's a blot on our profession. We'd all down him if we could."

"It happens," said Hercule Poirot, "that I am engaged at the moment on a little matter of clearing up a political scandal."

"Cleaning out the Augean stables, eh?" said Dashwood. "Too much for you, my boy. Only hope is to divert the Thames and wash away the Houses of Parliament."

"You are cynical," said Hercule Poirot, shaking his head.

"I know the world, that's all."

Poirot said:

"You, I think, are just the man I seek. You have a reckless disposition, you are the good sport, you like something that is out of the usual."

"And granting all that?"

"I have a little scheme to put into action. If my ideas are right, there is a sensational plot to unmask. That, my friend, shall be a scoop for your paper."

"Can do," said Dashwood, cheerfully.

"It will concern a scurrilous plot against a woman."

"Better and better. Sex stuff always goes."

"Then sit down and listen."

# 5

People were talking.

In the Goose and Feathers at Little Wimplington.

"Well, I don't believe it. John Hammett, he was always an honest man, he was. Not like some of these political folk."

"That's what they say about all swindlers before they're found out."

"Thousands, they say he made, out of that Palestine oil business. Just a crook deal, it was."

"Whole lot of 'em tarred with the same brush. Dirty crooks, every one of 'em."

"You wouldn't find Everhard doing that. He's one of the old school."

"Eh, but I can't believe as John Hammett was a wrong 'un. You can't believe all these papers say."

"Ferrier's wife was 'is daughter. Have you seen what it says about her?"

They pored over a much-thumbed copy of the *X-Ray News.*

*Caesar's wife? We hear that a certain highly placed political lady was seen in very strange surroundings the other day. Complete with her gigolo. Oh, Dagmar, Dagmar, how could you be so naughty?*

A rustic voice said slowly:

"Mrs. Ferrier's not that kind. Gigolo? That's one of these dago skunks."

Another voice said:

"You never can tell with women. The whole bunch of 'em wrong 'uns, if you ask me."

# 6

People were talking.

"But, darling, I believe it's absolutely true. Naomi had it from Paul and he had it from Andy. She's absolutely depraved."

"But she was always so terribly dowdy and proper and opening bazaars."

"Just camouflage, darling. They say she's a nymphomaniac. Well, I mean! It's all in the *X-Ray News*. Oh, not right out, but you can read between the lines. I don't know how they get hold of these things."

"What do you think of all this political scandal touch? They say her father embezzled the party funds."

# 7

People were talking.

"I don't like to think of it, and that's a fact, Mrs. Rogers. I mean, I always thought Mrs. Ferrier was a really nice woman."

"Do you think all these awful things are true?"

"As I say, I don't like to think it of her. Why, she opened a bazaar in Pelchester only last June. I was as near to her as I am to that sofa. And she had such a pleasant smile."

"Yes, but what I say is there's no smoke without fire."

"Well, of course that's true. Oh, dear, it seems as though you can't believe in anyone!"

# 8

Edward Ferrier, his face white and strained, said to Poirot:

"These attacks on my wife! They're scurrilous—absolutely scurrilous! I'm bringing an action against that vile rag."

Hercule Poirot said:

"I do not advise you to do so."

"But these damned lies have got to be stopped."

"Are you sure they are lies?"

"Damn you, yes!"

Poirot said, his head held a little on one side:

"What does your wife say?"

For a moment, Ferrier looked taken aback.

"She says it is best to take no notice. . . . But I can't do that— everybody is talking."

Hercule Poirot said:

"Yes, everybody is talking."

## 9

And then came the small bald announcement in all the papers.

*Mrs. Ferrier has had a slight nervous breakdown. She has gone to Scotland to recuperate.*

Conjectures, rumours—positive information that Mrs. Ferrier was not in Scotland, had never been to Scotland.

Stories, scandalous stories, of where Mrs. Ferrier really was. . . .

And, again, people talking.

"I tell you Andy saw her. At that frightful place! She was drunk or doped and with an awful Argentine gigolo—Ramón. *You* know!"

More talking.

Mrs. Ferrier had gone off with an Argentine dancer. She had been seen in Paris, doped. She had been taking drugs for years. She drank like a fish.

Slowly, the righteous mind of England, at first unbelieving, hardened against Mrs. Ferrier. "Seems as though there must be something in it!" "That isn't the sort of woman to be the Prime Minister's wife." "A Jezebel, that's what she is, nothing better than a Jezebel!"

And then came the camera records.

Mrs. Ferrier, photographed in Paris—lying back in a night club, her arm twined familiarly over the shoulder of a dark, olive-skinned, vicious-looking young man.

Other snapshots—half-naked on a beach—her head on the lounge lizard's shoulder.

And underneath:

*"Mrs. Ferrier has a good time. . . ."*

Two days later an action for libel was brought against the *X-Ray News*.

## IO

The case for the prosecution was opened by Sir Mortimer Inglewood, K.C. He was dignified and full of righteous indignation. Mrs. Ferrier was the victim of an infamous plot—a plot only to be equalled by the famous case of the Queen's Necklace, familiar to readers of Alexandre Dumas. That plot had been engineered to lower Queen Marie Antoinette in the eyes of the populace. This plot, also, had been engineered to discredit a noble and virtuous lady who was in this country in the position of Caesar's wife. Sir Mortimer spoke with bitter disparagement of Fascists and Communists, both of whom sought to undermine democracy by every unfair machination known. He then proceeded to call witnesses.

The first was the Bishop of Northumbria.

Dr. Henderson, the Bishop of Northumbria, was one of the best-known figures in the English church, a man of great saintliness and integrity of character. He was broadminded, tolerant, and a fine preacher. He was loved and revered by all who knew him.

He went into the box and swore that between the dates mentioned Mrs. Edward Ferrier had been staying in the Palace with himself and his wife. Worn out by her activities in good works, she had been recommended a thorough rest. Her visit had been kept a secret so as to obviate any worry from the press.

An eminent doctor followed the Bishop and deposed to having ordered Mrs. Ferrier rest and complete absence from worry.

A local general practitioner gave evidence to the effect that he had attended Mrs. Ferrier at the Palace.

The next witness called was Thelma Andersen.

A thrill went round the court when she entered the witness box. Everyone realised at once what a strong resemblance the woman bore to Mrs. Edward Ferrier.

"Your name is Thelma Andersen?"

"Yes."

"You are a Danish subject?"

"Yes. Copenhagen is my home."

"And you formerly worked at a café there?"

"Yes, sir."

"Please tell us in your own words what happened on the 18th of March last."

"There is a gentleman who comes to my table there—an English gentleman. He tells me he works for an English paper—the *X-Ray News.*"

"You are sure he mentioned that name—*X-Ray News?*"

"Yes, I am sure—because, you see, I think at first it must be a medical paper. But, no, it seems not so. Then he tell me there is an English film actress who wants to find a 'stand-in,' and that I am just the type. I do not go to the pictures much, and I do not recognise the name he says, but he tells me, yes, she is very famous, and she has not been well and so she wants someone to appear as her in public places, and for that she will pay very much money."

"How much money did this gentleman offer you?"

"Five hundred pounds in English money. I do not at first believe—I think it is some trick, but he pays me at once half the money. So, then, I give in my notice where I work."

The tale went on. She had been taken to Paris, supplied with smart clothes, and had been provided with an "escort." "A very nice Argentinian gentleman—very respectful, very polite."

It was clear that the woman had thoroughly enjoyed herself. She had flown over to London and had been taken there to certain "night clubs" by her olive-skinned cavalier. She had been photographed in Paris with him. Some of the places to which she had gone were not, she admitted, quite nice. . . . Indeed, they were not respectable! And some of the photographs taken, they too, had not been very nice. But these things, they had told her, were necessary for "advertisement"—and Señor Ramón himself had always been most respectful.

In answer to questioning, she declared that the name of Mrs. Ferrier had never been mentioned and that she had had no idea that it was that lady she was supposed to be understudying. She had meant no harm. She identified certain photographs which were shown to her as having been taken of her in Paris and on the Riviera.

There was the hallmark of absolute honesty about Thelma Andersen. She was quite clearly a pleasant, but slightly stupid woman. Her distress at the whole thing, now that she understood it, was patent to everyone.

The defense was unconvincing. A frenzied denial of having had any dealings with the woman Andersen. The photos in question had been brought to the London office and had been believed to be genuine. Sir Mortimer's closing speech roused enthusiasm. He described the whole thing as a dastardly political plot, formed to discredit the Prime Minister and his wife. All sympathy would be extended to the unfortunate Mrs. Ferrier.

The verdict, a foregone conclusion, was given amidst unparalleled scenes. Damages were assessed at an enormous figure. As Mrs. Ferrier and her husband and father left the court, they were greeted by the appreciative roars of a vast crowd.

## II

Edward Ferrier grasped Poirot warmly by the hand.

He said:

"I thank you, M. Poirot, a thousand times. Well, that finishes the *X-Ray News*. Dirty little rag. They're wiped out completely. Serves them right for cooking up such a scurrilous plot. Against Dagmar, too, the kindliest creature in the world. Thank goodness, you managed to expose the whole thing for the wicked romp it was. . . . What put you on to the idea that they might be using a double?"

"It is not a new idea," Poirot reminded him. "It was employed successfully in the case of Jeanne de la Motte when she impersonated Marie Antoinette."

"I know. I must re-read *The Queen's Necklace*. But how did you actually *find* the woman they were employing?"

"I looked for her in Denmark, and I found her there."

"But why Denmark?"

"Because Mrs. Ferrier's grandmother was a Dane, and she herself was a markedly Danish type. And there were other reasons."

"The resemblance was certainly quite striking. What a devilish idea! I wonder how the little rat came to think of it?"

Poirot smiled.

"But he did not."

He tapped himself on the chest.

"I thought of it!"

Edward Ferrier stared.

"I don't understand. What do you mean?"

Poirot said:

"We must go back to an older story than that of *The Queen's Necklace*—to the cleansing of the Augean Stables. What Hercules used was a river—that is to say, one of the great forces of nature. Modernise that! What is a great force of nature? Sex, is it not? It is the sex angle that sells stories, that makes news. Give people scandal allied to sex and it appeals far more than any mere political chicanery or fraud.

"*Eh bien, that* was my task! First, to put my own hands in the mud like Hercules, to build up a dam that should turn the course of that river. A journalistic friend of mine aided me. He searched Denmark until he found a suitable person to attempt the impersonation. He approached her, casually mentioned the *X-Ray News* to her, hoping she would remember it. She did.

"And so, what happened? *Mud*—a great deal of mud! Caesar's wife is bespattered with it. Far more interesting to everybody than any political scandal. And the result—the dénouement? Why? Reaction! Virtue vindicated! The pure woman cleared! A great tide of romance and sentiment sweeping through the Augean Stables.

"If all the newspapers in the country publish the news of John Hammett's defalcations now, no one will believe it. It will be put down as another political plot to discredit the Government."

Edward Ferrier took a deep breath. For a moment Hercule Poirot came nearer to being physically assaulted than at any other time in his career.

"My wife! You dared to use her—"

Fortunately, perhaps, Mrs. Ferrier herself entered the room at this moment.

"Well," she said, "that went off very well."

"Dagmar, did you—know all along?"

"Of course, dear," said Dagmar Ferrier.

And she smiled, the gentle maternal smile of a devoted wife.

"And you never told me!"

"But, Edward, you would never have let M. Poirot do it."

"Indeed, I would not!"

Dagmar smiled.

"That's what we thought."

"We?"

"I and M. Poirot."

She smiled at Hercule Poirot and at her husband.

She added:

"I had a very restful time with the dear Bishop—I feel full of energy now. They want me to christen the new battleship at Liverpool next month—I think it would be a popular thing to do."

# VI

# The Stymphalean Birds

I

**H**AROLD Waring noticed them first walking up the path from the lake. He was sitting outside the hotel on the terrace. The day was fine, the lake was blue, and the sun shone. Harold was smoking a pipe and feeling that the world was a pretty good place.

His political career was shaping well. An under-secretaryship at the age of thirty was something to be justly proud of. It had been reported that the Prime Minister had said to someone that "young Waring would go far." Harold was, not unnaturally, elated. Life presented itself to him in rosy colours. He was young, sufficiently good-looking, in first-class condition, and quite unencumbered with romantic ties.

He had decided to take a holiday in Herzoslovakia so as to get right off the beaten track and have a real rest from everyone and everything. The hotel at Lake Stempka, though small, was comfortable and not overcrowded. The few people there were mostly foreigners. So far the only other English people were an elderly woman, Mrs. Rice, and her married daughter, Mrs. Clayton. Harold liked them both. Elsie Clayton was pretty in a rather old-fashioned style. She made up very little, if at all, and was gentle and rather shy. Mrs. Rice was what is called a woman of character. She was tall, with a deep voice and a masterful manner, but she had a sense of humour and was good company. Her life was clearly bound up in that of her daughter.

Harold had spent some pleasant hours in the company of mother and daughter, but they did not attempt to monopolise him and relations remained friendly and unexacting between them.

The other people in the hotel had not aroused Harold's notice. Usually they were hikers, or members of a motor coach tour. They stayed a night or two and then went on. He had hardly noticed anyone else—until this afternoon.

They came up the path from the lake very slowly and it just happened that at the moment when Harold's attention was attracted to them, a cloud came over the sun. He shivered a little.

Then he stared. Surely there was something odd about these two women? They had long curved noses, like birds, and their faces, which were curiously alike, were quite immobile. Over their shoulders they wore loose cloaks that flapped in the wind like the wings of two big birds.

Harold thought to himself:

"They are like birds—" He added, almost without volition, "birds of ill omen."

The women came straight up on the terrace and passed close by him. They were not young—perhaps nearer fifty than forty—and the resemblance between them was so close that they were obviously sisters. Their expression was forbidding. As they passed Harold the eyes of both of them rested on him for a minute. It was a curious, appraising glance—almost inhuman.

Harold's impression of evil grew stronger. He noticed the hand of one of the two sisters, a long clawlike hand. . . . Although the sun had come out, he shivered once again. He thought:

"Horrible creatures. Like birds of prey. . . ."

He was distracted from these imaginings by the emergence of Mrs. Rice from the hotel. He jumped up and drew forward a chair. With a word of thanks she sat down and, as usual, began to knit vigorously.

Harold asked:

"Did you see those two women who just went into the hotel?"

"With cloaks on? Yes, I passed them."

"Extraordinary creatures, didn't you think?"

"Well—yes, perhaps they are rather odd. They only arrived yesterday, I think. Very alike—they must be twins."

Harold said:

"I may be fanciful, but I distinctly felt there was something evil about them."

"How curious. I must look at them more closely and see if I agree with you."

She added:

"We'll find out from the *concierge* who they are. Not English, I imagine?"

"Oh, no."

Mrs. Rice glanced at her watch. She said:

"Tea time. I wonder if you'd mind going in and ringing the bell, Mr. Waring?"

"Certainly, Mrs. Rice."

He did so and then as he returned to his seat he asked:

"Where's your daughter this afternoon?"

"Elsie? We went for a walk together. Part of the way round the lake and then back through the pinewoods. It really was lovely."

A waiter came out and received orders for tea. Mrs. Rice went on, her needles flying vigorously:

"Elsie had a letter from her husband. She mayn't come down to tea."

"Her husband?" Harold was surprised. "Do you know, I always thought she was a widow."

Mrs. Rice shot him a sharp glance. She said drily:

"Oh, no, Elsie isn't a widow." She added with emphasis: "Unfortunately!"

Harold was startled.

Mrs. Rice, nodding her head grimly, said:

"Drink is responsible for a lot of unhappiness, Mr. Waring."

"Does he drink?"

"Yes. And a good many other things as well. He's insanely jealous and has a singularly violent temper." She sighed. "It's a difficult world, Mr. Waring. I'm devoted to Elsie, she's my only child—and to see her unhappy isn't an easy thing to bear."

Harold said with real emotion:

"She's such a gentle creature."

"A little too gentle, perhaps."

"You mean—"

Mrs. Rice said slowly:

"A happy creature is more arrogant. Elsie's gentleness comes, I think, from a sense of defeat. Life has been too much for her."

Harold said with some slight hesitation:

"How—did she come to marry this husband of hers?"

Mrs. Rice answered:

"Philip Clayton was a very attractive person. He had, still has, great charm, a certain amount of money—and there was no one to advise us of his real character. I had been a widow for many years. Two women, living alone, are not the best judges of a man's character."

Harold said thoughtfully:

"No, that's true."

He felt a wave of indignation and pity sweep over him. Elsie Clayton could not be more than twenty-five at the most. He recalled the clear friendliness of her blue eyes, the soft droop of her mouth. He realised, suddenly, that his interest in her went a little beyond friendship.

And she was tied to a brute. . . .

## 2

That evening, Harold joined mother and daughter after dinner. Elsie Clayton was wearing a soft dull pink dress. Her eyelids, he noticed, were red. She had been crying.

Mrs. Rice said briskly:

"I've found out who your two harpies are, Mr. Waring. Polish ladies— of very good family—so the concierge says."

Harold looked across the room to where the Polish ladies were sitting. Elsie said with interest:

"Those two women over there? With the henna dyed hair? They look rather horrible somehow—I don't know why."

Harold said triumphantly:

"That's just what I thought."

Mrs. Rice said with a laugh:

"I think you are both being absurd. You can't possibly tell what people are like just by looking at them."

Elsie laughed.

She said:

"I suppose one can't. All the same *I* think they're vultures!"

"Picking out dead men's eyes!" said Harold.

"Oh, don't," cried Elsie.

Harold said quickly:

"Sorry."

Mrs. Rice said with a smile:

"Anyway they're not likely to cross *our* path."

Elsie said:

"*We* haven't got any guilty secrets!"

"Perhaps Mr. Waring has," said Mrs. Rice, with a twinkle. Harold laughed, throwing his head back. He said:

"Not a secret in the world. My life's an open book."

And it flashed across his mind:

"What fools people are who leave the straight path. A clear conscience—that's all one needs in life. With that you can face the world and tell everyone who interferes with you to go to the devil!"

He felt suddenly very much alive—very strong—very much master of his fate!

# 3

Harold Waring, like many other Englishmen, was a bad linguist. His French was halting and decidedly British in intonation. Of German and Italian he knew nothing.

Up to now, these linguistic disabilities had not worried him. In most hotels on the Continent, he had always found, everyone spoke English, so why worry?

But in this out-of-the-way spot, where the native language was a form of Slovak and even the concierge only spoke German, it was sometimes galling to Harold when one of his two women friends acted as interpreter for him. Mrs. Rice, who was fond of languages, could even speak a little Slovak.

Harold determined that he would set about learning German. He decided to buy some textbooks and spend a couple of hours each morning in mastering the language.

The morning was fine and after writing some letters, Harold looked at his watch and saw there was still time for an hour's stroll before lunch. He went down towards the lake and then turned aside into the pine woods. He had walked there for perhaps five minutes when he heard an unmistakable sound. Somewhere, not far away, a woman was sobbing her heart out.

Harold paused a minute, then went in the direction of the sound. The woman was Elsie Clayton and she was sitting on a fallen tree with her face buried in her hands and her shoulders quivering with the violence of her grief.

Harold hesitated a minute, then he came up to her. He said gently: "Mrs. Clayton—Elsie?"

She started violently and looked up at him. Harold sat down beside her.

He said with real sympathy:

"Is there anything I can do? Anything at all?"

She shook her head.

"No—no—you're very kind. But there's nothing that anyone can do for me."

Harold said rather diffidently:

"Is it to do with—your husband?"

She nodded. Then she wiped her eyes and took out her powder compact, struggling to regain command of herself. She said in a quavering voice:

"I didn't want Mother to worry. She's so upset when she sees me unhappy. So I came out here to have a good cry. It's silly, I know.

Crying doesn't help. But—sometimes—one just feels that life is quite unbearable."

Harold said:

"I'm terribly sorry."

She threw him a grateful glance. Then she said hurriedly:

"It's my own fault, of course. I married Philip of my own free will. It—it's turned out badly, I've only myself to blame."

Harold said:

"It's very plucky of you to put it like that."

Elsie shook her head.

"No, I'm not plucky. I'm not brave at all. I'm an awful coward. That's partly the trouble with Philip. I'm terrified of him—absolutely terrified—when he gets in one of his rages."

Harold said with feeling:

"You ought to leave him!"

"I daren't. He—he wouldn't let me."

"Nonsense! What about a divorce?"

She shook her head slowly.

"I've no grounds." She straightened her shoulders. "No, I've got to carry on. I spend a fair amount of time with Mother, you know. Philip doesn't mind that. Especially when we go somewhere off the beaten track like this." She added, the colour rising in her cheeks, "You see, part of the trouble is that he's insanely jealous. If—if I so much as speak to another man he makes the most frightful scenes."

Harold's indignation rose. He had heard many women complain of the jealousy of a husband, and while professing sympathy, had been secretly of the opinion that the husband was amply justified. But Elsie Clayton was not one of those women. She had never thrown him so much as a flirtatious glance.

Elsie drew away from him with a slight shiver. She glanced up at the sky.

"The sun's gone in. It's quite cold. We'd better get back to the hotel. It must be nearly lunch time."

They got up and turned in the direction of the hotel. They had walked for perhaps a minute when they overtook a figure going in the same direction. They recognised her by the flapping cloak she wore. It was one of the Polish sisters.

They passed her, Harold bowing slightly. She made no response but her eyes rested on them both for a minute and there was a certain appraising quality in the glance which made Harold feel suddenly hot. He wondered if the woman had seen him sitting by Elsie on the tree trunk. If so, she probably thought . . .

Well, she looked as though she thought . . . A wave of indignation overwhelmed him! What foul minds some women had!

Odd that the sun had gone in and that they should both have shivered—perhaps just at the moment that that woman was watching them. . . .

Somehow, Harold felt a little uneasy.

4

That evening, Harold went to his room a little after ten. The English mail had arrived and he had received a number of letters, some of which needed immediate answers.

He got into pajamas and a dressing gown and sat down at the desk to deal with his correspondence. He had written three letters and was just starting on the fourth when the door was suddenly flung open and Elsie Clayton staggered into the room.

Harold jumped up, startled. Elsie had pushed the door to behind her and was standing clutching at the chest of drawers. Her breath was coming in great gasps, her face was the colour of chalk. She looked frightened to death.

She gasped out:

"It's my husband! He arrived unexpectedly. I—I think he'll kill me. He's mad—quite mad. I came to you. Don't—don't let him find me."

She took a step or two forward, swaying so much that she almost fell. Harold put out an arm to support her.

As he did so, the door was flung open and a man stood in the doorway. He was of medium height with thick eyebrows and a sleek dark head. In his hand he carried a heavy car spanner. His voice rose high and shook with rage. He almost screamed the words.

"So that Polish woman was right! You are carrying on with this fellow!"

Elsie cried:

"No, no, Philip. It's not true. You're wrong."

Harold thrust the girl swiftly behind him, as Philip Clayton advanced on them both. The latter cried:

"Wrong, am I? When I find you here in his room? You she-devil, I'll kill you for this."

With a swift sideways movement he dodged Harold's arm. Elsie, with a cry, ran round the other side of Harold, who swung round to fend the other off.

But Philip Clayton had only one idea, to get at his wife. He swerved round again. Elsie, terrified, rushed out of the room. Philip Clayton dashed after her, and Harold, with not a moment's hesitation, followed him.

Elsie had darted back into her own bedroom at the end of the corridor. Harold could hear the sound of the key turning in the lock, but it did not turn in time. Before the lock could catch Philip Clayton wrenched the door open. He disappeared into the room and Harold heard Elsie's frightened cry. In another minute Harold burst in after them.

Elsie was standing at bay against the curtains of the window. As Harold entered Philip Clayton rushed at her, brandishing the spanner. She gave a terrified cry, then snatching up a heavy paperweight from the desk beside her, she flung it at him.

Clayton went down like a log. Elsie screamed. Harold stopped, petrified, in the doorway. The girl fell on her knees beside her husband. He lay quite still where he had fallen.

Outside in the passage, there was the sound of the bolt of one of the doors being drawn back. Elsie jumped up and ran to Harold.

"Please—please—" Her voice was low and breathless. "Go back to your room. They'll come—they'll find you here."

Harold nodded. He took in the situation like lightning. For the moment, Philip Clayton was *hors de combat*. But Elsie's scream might have been heard. If he were found in her room it could only cause embarrassment and misunderstanding. Both for her sake and his own there must be no scandal.

As noiselessly as possible, he sprinted down the passage and back into his room. Just as he reached it, he heard the sound of an opening door.

He sat in his room for nearly half an hour, waiting. He dared not go out. Sooner or later, he felt sure, Elsie would come.

There was a light tap on his door. Harold jumped up to open it.

It was not Elsie who came in but her mother and Harold was aghast at her appearance. She looked suddenly years older. Her grey hair was dishevelled and there were deep black circles under her eyes.

He sprang up and helped her to a chair. She sat down, her breath coming painfully. Harold said quickly:

"You look all in, Mrs. Rice. Can I get you something?"

She shook her head.

"No. Never mind me. I'm all right, really. It's only the shock. Mr. Waring, a terrible thing has happened."

Harold asked:

"Is Clayton seriously injured?"

She caught her breath.

"Worse than that. *He's dead.* . . ."

## 5

The room spun round.

A feeling as of icy water trickling down his spine rendered Harold incapable of speech for a moment or two.

He repeated dully:

"Dead?"

Mrs. Rice nodded.

She said, and her voice had the flat, level tones of complete exhaustion:

"The corner of that marble paperweight caught him right on the temple and he fell back with his head on the iron fender. I don't know which it was that killed him—but he is certainly dead. I have seen death often enough to know."

Disaster—that was the word that rang insistently in Harold's brain. Disaster, disaster, disaster. . . .

He said vehemently:

"It was an accident . . . I saw it happen."

Mrs. Rice said sharply:

"Of course it was an accident. *I* know that. But—but—is anyone else going to think so? I'm—frankly, I'm frightened, Harold! This isn't England."

Harold said slowly:

"I can confirm Elsie's story."

Mrs. Rice said:

"Yes, and she can confirm yours. That—that is just it!"

Harold's brain, naturally a keen and cautious one, saw her point. He reviewed the whole thing and appreciated the weakness of their position.

He and Elsie had spent a good deal of their time together. Then there was the fact that they had been seen together in the pine woods by one of the Polish women under rather compromising circumstances. The Polish ladies apparently spoke no English, but they might nevertheless understand it a little. The woman might have known the meaning of words like "jealousy" and "husband" if she had chanced to overhear their conversation. Anyway, it was clear that it was something she had said to Clayton that had aroused his jealousy. And now—his death. When Clayton had died, he, Harold, had been in Elsie Clayton's room. There was nothing to show that he had not deliberately assaulted Philip Clayton with the paperweight. Nothing to show that the jealous husband had not actually found them together. There was only his word and Elsie's. Would they be believed?

A cold fear gripped him.

He did not imagine—no, he really did *not* imagine—that either he or Elsie was in danger of being condemned to death for a murder they had not committed. Surely, in any case, it could be only a charge of manslaughter brought against them. (Did they have manslaughter in these foreign countries?) But even if they were acquitted of blame there would have to be an inquiry—it would be reported in all the papers. An English man and woman accused—jealous husband—rising politician. Yes, it would mean the end of his political career. It would never survive a scandal like that.

He said on an impulse:

"Can't we get rid of the body somehow? Plant it somewhere?"

Mrs. Rice's astonished and scornful look made him blush. She said incisively:

"My dear Harold, this isn't a detective story! To attempt a thing like that would be quite crazy."

"I suppose it would." He groaned. "What can we do? My God, what can we do?"

Mrs. Rice shook her head despairingly. She was frowning, her mind working painfully.

Harold demanded:

"Isn't there anything we can do? Anything to avoid this frightful disaster?"

There, it was out—disaster! Terrible—unforeseen—utterly damning.

They stared at each other. Mrs. Rice said hoarsely:

"Elsie—my little girl. I'd do anything. . . . It will kill her if she has to go through a thing like this." And she added: "You, too, your career—everything."

Harold managed to say:

"Never mind me."

But he did not really mean it.

Mrs. Rice went on bitterly:

"And all so unfair—so utterly untrue! It's not as though there had ever been anything between you. *I* know that well enough."

Harold suggested, catching at a straw:

"You'll be able to say that at least—That it was all perfectly all right."

Mrs. Rice said bitterly:

"Yes, if they believe me. But you know what these people out here are like!"

Harold agreed gloomily. To the Continental mind, there would undoubtedly be a guilty connection between himself and Elsie, and all Mrs. Rice's denials would be taken as a mother lying herself black in the face for her daughter.

Harold said gloomily:

"Yes, we're not in England, worse luck."

"Ah!" Mrs. Rice lifted her head. "That's true. . . . It's not England. I wonder now if something could be done—"

"Yes?" Harold looked at her eagerly.

Mrs. Rice said abruptly:

"How much money have you got?"

"Not much with me." He added: "I could wire for money, of course."

Mrs. Rice said grimly:

"We may need a good deal. But I think it's worth trying."

Harold felt a faint lifting of despair. He said:

"What is your idea?"

Mrs. Rice spoke decisively.

"We haven't a chance of concealing the death ourselves, but I do think there's just a chance of hushing it up officially!"

"You really think so?" Harold was hopeful but slightly incredulous.

"Yes, for one thing the manager of the hotel will be on our side. He'd much rather have the thing hushed up. It's my opinion that in these out-of-the-way curious little Balkan countries you can bribe anyone and everyone—and the police are probably more corrupt than anyone else!"

Harold said slowly:

"Do you know, I believe you're right."

Mrs. Rice went on:

"Fortunately, I don't think anyone in the hotel heard anything."

"Who has the room next to Elsie's on the other side from yours?"

"The two Polish ladies. They didn't hear anything. They'd have come out into the passage if they had. Philip arrived late, nobody saw him but the night porter. Do you know, Harold, I believe it will be possible to hush the whole thing up—and get Philip's death certified as due to natural causes! It's just a question of bribing high enough—and finding the right man—probably the Chief of Police!"

Harold smiled faintly. He said:

"It's rather Comic Opera, isn't it? Well, after all, we can but try."

## 6

Mrs. Rice was energy personified. First, the manager was summoned. Harold remained in his room, keeping out of it. He and Mrs. Rice had agreed that the story told had better be that of a quarrel between husband and wife. Elsie's youth and prettiness would command more sympathy.

On the following morning various police officials arrived and were shown up to Mrs. Rice's bedroom. They left at midday. Harold had wired for money but otherwise had taken no part in the proceedings— indeed he would have been unable to do so since none of these official personages spoke English.

At twelve o'clock Mrs. Rice came to his room. She looked white and tired, but the relief on her face told its own story. She said simply: "It's worked!"

"Thank heaven! You've really been marvellous! It seems incredible!" Mrs. Rice said thoughtfully:

"By the ease with which it went, you might almost think it was quite normal. They practically held out their hands right away. It's— it's rather disgusting, really!"

Harold said drily:

"This isn't the moment to quarrel with the corruption of the public services. How much?"

"The tariff's rather high."

She read out a list of figures.

> *The Chief of Police*
> *The Commissaire*
> *The Agent*
> *The Doctor*
> *The Hotel Manager*
> *The Night Porter*

Harold's comment was merely:

"The night porter doesn't get much, does he? I suppose it's mostly a question of gold lace."

Mrs. Rice explained:

"The manager stipulated that the death should not have taken place in his hotel at all. The official story will be that Philip had a heart attack in the train. He went along the corridor for air—you know how they always leave those doors open— And he fell out on the line. It's wonderful what the police can do when they try!"

"Well," said Harold. "Thank God, our police force isn't like that." And in a British and superior mood he went down to lunch.

## 7

After lunch Harold usually joined Mrs. Rice and her daughter for coffee. He decided to make no change in his usual behaviour.

This was the first time he had seen Elsie since the night before.

She was very pale and was obviously still suffering from shock, but she made a gallant endeavour to behave as usual, uttering small commonplaces about the weather and the scenery.

They commented on a new guest who had just arrived, trying to guess his nationality. Harold thought a moustache like that must be French—Elsie said German—and Mrs. Rice thought he might be Spanish.

There was no one else but themselves on the terrace with the exception of the two Polish ladies who were sitting at the extreme end, both doing fancy work.

As always when he saw them, Harold felt a queer shiver of apprehension pass over him. Those still faces, those curved beaks of noses, those long clawlike hands . . .

A page boy approached and told Mrs. Rice she was wanted. She rose and followed him. At the entrance to the hotel they saw her encounter a police official in full uniform.

Elsie caught her breath.

"You don't think—anything's gone wrong?"

Harold reassured her quickly:

"Oh, no, no, nothing of that kind."

But he himself knew a sudden pang of fear.

He said:

"Your mother's been wonderful!"

"I know. Mother is a great fighter. She'll never sit down under defeat." Elsie shivered. "But it is all horrible, isn't it?"

"Now, don't dwell on it. It's all over and done with."

Elsie said in a low voice:

"I can't forget that—that it was *I* who killed him."

Harold said urgently:

"Don't think of it that way. It was an accident. You know that really."

Her face grew a little happier. Harold added:

"And anyway it's past. The past is the past. Try never to think of it again."

Mrs. Rice came back. By the expression on her face they saw that all was well.

"It gave me quite a fright," she said almost gaily. "But it was only a formality about some papers. Everything's all right, my children. We're out of the shadow. I think we might order ourselves a liqueur on the strength of it."

The liqueur was ordered and came. They raised their glasses.

Mrs. Rice said:

"To the future!"

Harold smiled at Elsie and said:

"To your happiness!"

She smiled back at him and said as she lifted her glass:

"And to you—to your success! I'm sure you're going to be a very great man."

With the reaction from fear they felt gay, almost lightheaded. The shadow had lifted! All was well—

From the far end of the terrace the two birdlike women rose. They rolled up their work carefully. They came across the stone flags.

With little bows they sat down by Mrs. Rice. One of them began to speak. The other one let her eyes rest on Elsie and Harold. There was a little smile on her lips. It was not, Harold thought, a nice smile. . . .

He looked over at Mrs. Rice. She was listening to the Polish woman and though he couldn't understand a word, the expression on Mrs. Rice's face was clear enough. All the old anguish and despair came back. She listened and occasionally spoke a brief word.

Presently the two sisters rose, and with stiff little bows went into the hotel.

Harold leaned forward. He said hoarsely:

"What is it?"

Mrs. Rice answered him in the quiet hopeless tones of despair.

"Those women are going to blackmail us. They heard everything last night. And now we've tried to hush it up, it makes the whole thing a thousand times worse. . . ."


# 8

Harold Waring was down by the lake. He had been walking feverishly for over an hour, trying by sheer physical energy to still the clamour of despair that had attacked him.

He came at last to the spot where he had first noticed the two grim women who held his life and Elsie's in their evil talons. He said aloud:

"Curse them! Damn them for a pair of devilish blood-sucking harpies!"

A slight cough made him spin round. He found himself facing the luxuriantly moustached stranger who had just come out from the shade of the trees.

Harold found it difficult to know what to say. This little man must have almost certainly overheard what he had just said.

Harold, at a loss, said somewhat ridiculously:

"Oh—er—good afternoon."

In perfect English, the other replied:

"But for you, I fear, it is not a good afternoon?"

"Well, er—I—" Harold was in difficulties again.

The little man said:

"You are, I think, in trouble, Monsieur? Can I be of any assistance to you?"

"Oh, no, thanks—no, thanks! Just blowing off steam, you know."

The other said gently:

"But I think, you know, that I could help you. I am correct, am I not, in connecting your troubles with two ladies who were sitting on the terrace just now?"

Harold stared at him.

"Do you know anything about them?" He added: "Who are you, anyway?"

As though confessing to royal birth the little man said modestly:

"I am Hercule Poirot. Shall we walk a little way into the wood and you shall tell me your story? As I say, I think I can aid you."

To this day, Harold is not quite certain what made him suddenly pour out the whole story to a man to whom he had only spoken a few minutes before. Perhaps it was overstrain. Anyway, it happened. He told Hercule Poirot the whole story.

The latter listened in silence. Once or twice he nodded his head gravely. When Harold came to a stop the other spoke dreamily.

"The Stymphalean Birds, with iron beaks, who feed on human flesh and who dwell by the Stymphalean Lake. . . . Yes, it accords very well."

"I beg your pardon," said Harold staring.

Perhaps, he thought, this curious-looking little man was mad!

Hercule Poirot smiled.

"I reflect, that is all. I have my own way of looking at things, you understand. Now as to this business of yours. You are very unpleasantly placed."

Harold said impatiently:

"I don't need you to tell me that!"

Hercule Poirot went on:

"It is a serious business, blackmail. These harpies will force you to pay—and pay—and pay again! And if you defy them, well, what happens?"

Harold said bitterly:

"The whole thing comes out. My career's ruined, and a wretched girl who's never done anyone any harm will be put through hell, and God knows what the end of it all will be!"

"Therefore," said Hercule Poirot, "something must be done!"

Harold said baldly:

"What?"

Hercule Poirot leaned back, half closing his eyes. He said (and again a doubt of his sanity crossed Harold's mind):

"It is the moment for the castanets of bronze."

Harold said:

"Are you quite mad?"

The other shook his head. He said.

"*Mais non!* I strive only to follow the example of my great predecessor, Hercules. Have a few hours' patience, my friend. By tomorrow I may be able to deliver you from your persecutors."

# 9

Harold Waring came down the following morning to find Hercule Poirot sitting alone on the terrace. In spite of himself Harold had been impressed by Hercule Poirot's promises.

He came up to him now and asked anxiously:

"Well?"

Hercule Poirot beamed upon him.

"It is well."

"What do you mean?"

"Everything has settled itself satisfactorily."

"But what has happened?"

Hercule Poirot replied dreamily:

"I have employed the castanets of bronze. Or, in modern parlance, I have caused metal wires to hum—in short I have employed the telegraph! Your Stymphalean Birds, Monsieur, have been removed to where they will be unable to exercise their ingenuity for some time to come."

"They were wanted by the police? They have been arrested?"

"Precisely."

Harold drew a deep breath.

"How marvellous! I never thought of that." He got up. "I must find Mrs. Rice and Elsie and tell them."

"They know."

"Oh, good." Harold sat down again. "Tell me just what—"

He broke off.

Coming up the path from the lake were two figures with flapping cloaks and profiles like birds.

He exclaimed:

"I thought you said they had been taken away!"

Hercule Poirot followed his glance.

"Oh, those ladies? They are very harmless; Polish ladies of good family, as the porter told you. Their appearance is, perhaps, not very pleasing but that is all."

"But I don't *understand!*"

"No, you do not understand! It is the other ladies who were wanted by the police—the resourceful Mrs. Rice and the lachrymose Mrs. Clayton! It is they who are well-known birds of prey. Those two, they make their living by blackmail, *mon cher.*"

Harold had a sensation of the world spinning round him. He said faintly:

"But the man—the man who was killed?"

"No one was killed. There was no man!"

"But I *saw* him!"

"Oh, no. The tall, deep-voiced Mrs. Rice is a very successful male impersonator. It was she who played the part of the husband—without her grey wig and suitably made up for the part."

He leaned forward and tapped the other on the knee.

"You must not go through life being too credulous, my friend. The police of a country are not so easily bribed—they are probably not to be bribed at all—certainly not when it is a question of murder! These women trade on the average Englishman's ignorance of foreign languages. Because she speaks French or German, it is always this Mrs. Rice who interviews the manager and takes charge of the affair. The police arrive and go to her room, yes! But what actually passes? *You* do not know. Perhaps she says she has lost a brooch—something of that kind. Any excuse to arrange for the police to come so that you shall see them. For the rest, what actually happens? You wire for money, a lot of money, and you hand it over to Mrs. Rice who is in charge of all the negotiations! And that is that! But they are greedy, these birds of prey. They have seen that you have taken an unreasonable aversion to these two unfortunate Polish ladies. The ladies in question come and hold a perfectly innocent conversation with Mrs. Rice and she cannot resist repeating the game. She knows you cannot understand what is being said.

"So you will have to send for more money which Mrs. Rice will pretend to distribute to a fresh set of people."

Harold drew a deep breath. He said:

"And Elsie—Elsie?"

Hercule Poirot averted his eyes.

"She played her part very well. She always does. A most accomplished little actress. Everything is very pure—very innocent. She appeals, not to sex, but to chivalry."

Hercule Poirot added dreamily:

"That is always successful with Englishmen."

Harold Waring drew a deep breath. He said crisply:

"I'm going to set to work and learn every European language there is! Nobody's going to make a fool of me a second time!"

# VII

# The Cretan Bull

## I

HERCULE Poirot looked thoughtfully at his visitor.

He saw a pale face with a determined-looking chin, eyes that were more grey than blue, and hair that was of that real blue-black shade so seldom seen—the hyacinthine locks of ancient Greece.

He noted the well-cut but also well-worn country tweeds, the shabby handbag, and the unconscious arrogance of manner that lay behind the girl's obvious nervousness. He thought to himself:

"Ah, yes, she is 'the County'—but no money! And it must be something quite out of the way that would bring her to me."

Diana Maberly said, and her voice shook a little:

"I—I don't know whether you can help me or not, M. Poirot. It's—it's a very extraordinary position."

Poirot said:

"But yes? Tell me?"

Diana Maberly said:

"I've come to you because I don't know what to do! I don't even know if there is anything to do!"

"Will you let me judge of that?"

The colour surged suddenly into the girl's face. She said rapidly and breathlessly:

"I've come to you because the man I've been engaged to for over a year has broken off our engagement."

She stopped and eyed him defiantly.

"You must think," she said, "that I'm completely mental."

Slowly, Hercule Poirot shook his head.

"On the contrary, mademoiselle, I have no doubt whatever but that you are extremely intelligent. It is certainly not my *métier* in life to patch up the lovers' quarrels, and I know very well that you are quite aware of that. It is, therefore, that there is something unusual about the breaking of this engagement. That is so, is it not?"

The girl nodded. She said in a clear, precise voice:

"Hugh broke off our engagement because he thinks he is going mad. He thinks people who are mad should not marry."

Hercule Poirot's eyebrows rose a little.

"And do you not agree?"

"I don't know. . . . What is being mad, after all? Everyone is a little mad."

"It has been said so," Poirot agreed cautiously.

"It's only when you begin thinking you're a poached egg or something that they have to shut you up."

"And your fiancé has not reached that stage?"

Diana Maberly said:

"I can't see that there's anything wrong with Hugh at all. He's, oh, he's the sanest person I know. Sound—dependable—"

"Then why does he think he is mad?"

Poirot paused a moment before going on.

"Is there, perhaps, madness in his family?"

Reluctantly Diana jerked her head in assent. She said:

"His grandfather was mental, I believe—and some great-aunt or other. But what I say is, that every family has got someone queer in it. You know, a bit half-witted or extra clever or something!"

Her eyes were appealing.

Hercule Poirot shook his head sadly. He said:

"I am very sorry for you, mademoiselle."

Her chin shot out. She cried:

"I don't want you to be sorry for me! I want you to do something!"

"What do you want me to do?"

"I don't know—but there's something wrong."

"Will you tell me, mademoiselle, all about your fiancé?"

Diana spoke rapidly:

"His name's Hugh Chandler. He's twenty-four. His father is Admiral Chandler. They live at Lyde Manor. It's been in the Chandler family since the time of Elizabeth. Hugh's the only son. He went into the Navy—all the Chandlers are sailors—it's a sort of tradition—ever since Sir Gilbert Chandler sailed with Sir Walter Raleigh in 15-something or other. Hugh went into the Navy as a matter of course. His father wouldn't have heard of anything else. And yet—and yet, it was his father who insisted on getting him out of it!"

"When was that?"

"Nearly a year ago. Quite suddenly."

"Was Hugh Chandler happy in his profession?"

"Absolutely."

"There was no scandal of any kind?"

"About Hugh? Absolutely nothing. He was getting on splendidly. He—he couldn't understand his father."

"What reason did Admiral Chandler himself give?"

Diana said slowly:

"He never really gave a reason. Oh, he said it was necessary Hugh should learn to manage the estate—but—but that was only a pretext. Even George Frobisher realised that."

"Who is George Frobisher?"

"Colonel Frobisher. He's Admiral Chandler's oldest friend and Hugh's godfather. He spends most of his time down at the Manor."

"And what did Colonel Frobisher think of Admiral Chandler's determination that his son should leave the Navy?"

"He was dumbfounded. He couldn't understand it at all. Nobody could."

"Not even Hugh Chandler himself?"

Diana did not answer at once. Poirot waited a minute, then he went on:

"At the time, perhaps, he too was astonished. But now? Has he said nothing—nothing at all?"

Diana murmured reluctantly:

"He said—about a week ago—that—that his father was right—that it was the only thing to be done."

"Did you ask him why?"

"Of course. But he wouldn't tell me."

Hercule Poirot reflected for a minute or two. Then he said:

"Have there been any unusual occurrences in your part of the world? Starting, perhaps, about a year ago? Something that has given rise to a lot of local talk and surmise?"

She flashed out:

"I don't know what you mean!"

Poirot said quietly, but with authority in his voice:

"You had better tell me."

"There wasn't anything—nothing of the kind you mean."

"Of what kind then?"

"I think you're simply odious! Queer things often happen on farms. It's revenge—or the village idiot or somebody."

"What happened?"

She said reluctantly:

"There was a fuss about some sheep. . . . Their throats were cut. Oh! it was horrid! But they all belonged to one farmer and he's a very hard man. The police thought it was some kind of spite against him."

"But they didn't catch the person who had done it?"

"No."

She added fiercely. "But if you think—"

Poirot held up his hand. He said:

"You do not know in the least what I think. Tell me this, has your fiancé consulted a doctor?"

"No, I'm sure he hasn't."

"Wouldn't that be the simplest thing for him to do?"

Diana said slowly:

"He won't. He—he hates doctors."

"And his father?"

"I don't think the Admiral believes much in doctors either. Says they're a lot of humbug merchants."

"How does the Admiral seem himself? Is he well? Happy?"

Diana said in a low voice:

"He's aged terribly in—in—"

"In the last year?"

"Yes. He's a wreck—a sort of shadow of what he used to be."

Poirot nodded thoughtfully. Then he said:

"Did he approve of his son's engagement?"

"Oh, yes. You see, my people's land adjoins his. We've been there for generations. He was frightfully pleased when Hugh and I fixed it up."

"And now? What does he say to your engagement being broken off?"

The girl's voice shook a little. She said:

"I met him yesterday morning. He was looking ghastly. He took my hand in both of his. He said: 'It's hard on you, my girl. But the boy's doing the right thing—the only thing he can do.' "

"And so," said Hercule Poirot, "you came to me?"

She nodded. She asked:

"Can you do anything?"

Hercule Poirot replied:

"I do not know. But I can at least come down and see for myself."

## 2

It was Hugh Chandler's magnificent physique that impressed Hercule Poirot more than anything else. Tall, magnificently proportioned, with a terrific chest and shoulders, and a tawny head of hair. There was a tremendous air of strength and virility about him.

On their arrival at Diana's house, she had at once rung up Admiral Chandler, and they had forthwith gone over to Lyde Manor where they had found tea waiting on the long terrace. And with the tea, three men. There was Admiral Chandler, white-haired, looking older than his years, his shoulders bowed as though by an over-heavy burden, and his eyes dark and brooding. A contrast to him was his friend Colonel Frobisher, a dried-up, tough little man with reddish hair turning grey at the temples. A restless, irascible, snappy little man, rather like a terrier—but the possessor of a pair of extremely shrewd eyes. He had a habit of drawing down his brows over his eyes and lowering his head, thrusting it forward, whilst those same shrewd little eyes studied you piercingly. The third man was Hugh.

"Fine specimen, eh?" said Colonel Frobisher.

He spoke in a low voice, having noted Poirot's close scrutiny of the young man.

Hercule Poirot nodded his head. He and Frobisher were sitting close together. The other three had their chairs on the far side of the tea table and were chatting together in an animated but slightly artificial manner.

Poirot murmured: "Yes, he is magnificent—magnificent. He is the young Bull—yes, one might say the Bull dedicated to Poseidon. . . . A perfect specimen of healthy manhood."

"Looks fit enough, doesn't he?"

Frobisher sighed. His shrewd little eyes stole sideways, considering Hercule Poirot. Presently he said:

"I know who you are, you know."

"Ah, that, it is no secret!"

Poirot waved a royal hand. He was not incognito, the gesture seemed to say. He was travelling as Himself.

After a minute or two, Frobisher asked: "Did the girl get you down—over this business?"

"The business—?"

"The business of young Hugh. . . . Yes, I see you know all about it. But I can't quite see why she went to you. . . . Shouldn't have thought this sort of thing was in your line—meantersay, it's more a medical show."

"All kinds of things are in my line. . . . You would be surprised."

"I mean I can't see quite what she expected you could *do.*"

"Miss Maberly," said Poirot, "is a fighter."

Colonel Frobisher nodded a warm assent.

"Yes, she's a fighter all right. She's a fine kid. She won't give up. All the same, you know, there are some things that you can't fight. . . ."

His face looked suddenly old and tired.

Poirot dropped his voice still lower. He murmured discreetly:

"There is—insanity, I understand, in the family?"

Frobisher nodded.

"Only crops up now and again," he murmured. "Skips a generation or two. Hugh's grandfather was the last."

Poirot threw a quick glance in the direction of the other three. Diana was holding the conversation well, laughing and bantering Hugh. You would have said that the three of them had not a care in the world.

"What form did the madness take?" Poirot asked softly.

"The old boy became pretty violent in the end. He was perfectly all right up to thirty—normal as could be. Then he began to go a bit queer. It was some time before people noticed it. Then a lot of rumours began going around. People started talking properly. Things happened that were hushed up. But—well," he raised his shoulders "ended up as mad as a hatter, poor devil! Homicidal! Had to be certified."

He paused for a moment and then added:

"He lived to be quite an old man, I believe. . . . That's what Hugh is afraid of, of course. That's why he doesn't want to see a doctor. He's afraid of being shut up and living shut up for years. Can't say I blame him. I'd feel the same."

"And Admiral Chandler, how does he feel?"

"It's broken him up completely," Frobisher spoke shortly.

"He is very fond of his son?"

"Wrapped up in the boy. You see, his wife was drowned in a boating accident when the boy was only ten years old. Since then he's lived for nothing but the child."

"Was he very devoted to his wife?"

"Worshipped her. Everybody worshipped her. She was—she was one of the loveliest women I've ever known." He paused a moment and then said jerkily, "Care to see her portrait?"

"I should like to see it very much."

Frobisher pushed back his chair and rose. Aloud he said:

"Going to show M. Poirot one or two things, Charles. He's a bit of a connoisseur."

The Admiral raised a vague hand. Frobisher tramped along the terrace and Poirot followed him. For a moment Diana's face dropped its mask of gaiety and looked an agonised question. Hugh, too, raised his head, and looked steadily at the small man with the big black moustache.

Poirot followed Frobisher into the house. It was so dim at first coming in out of the sunlight that he could hardly distinguish one article from another. But he realised that the house was full of old and beautiful things.

Colonel Frobisher led the way to the picture gallery. On the panelled walls hung portraits of dead and gone Chandlers. Faces stern and gay, men in court dress or in naval uniform, women in satin and pearls.

Finally Frobisher stopped under a portrait at the end of the gallery.

"Painted by Orpen," he said gruffly.

They stood looking up at a tall woman, her hand on a greyhound's collar. A woman with auburn hair and an expression of radiant vitality.

"Boy's the spitting image of her," said Frobisher. "Don't you think so?"

"In some things, yes."

"He hasn't got her delicacy—her femininity, of course. He's a masculine edition—but in all the essential things—" He broke off. "Pity he inherited from the Chandlers the one thing he could well have done without. . . ."

They were silent. There was melancholy in the air all around them—as though dead and gone Chandlers sighed for the taint that lay in their blood and which, remorselessly, from time to time they passed on. . . .

Hercule Poirot turned his head to look at his companion. George Frobisher was still gazing up at the beautiful woman on the wall above him. And Poirot said softly:

"You knew her well. . . ."

Frobisher spoke jerkily.

"We were boy and girl together. I went off as a subaltern to India when she was sixteen. . . . When I got back—she was married to Charles Chandler."

"You knew him well also?"

"Charles is one of my oldest friends. He's my best friend—always has been."

"Did you see much of them—after the marriage?"

"Used to spend most of my leaves here. Like a second home to me, this place. Charles and Caroline always kept my room here—ready and waiting. . . ." He squared his shoulders, suddenly thrust his head forward pugnaciously. "That's why I'm here now—to stand by in case I'm wanted. If Charles needs me—I'm here."

Again the shadow of tragedy crept over them.

"And what do you think—about all this?" Poirot asked.

Frobisher stood stiffly. His brows came down over his eyes.

"What I think is, the least said the better. And to be frank, I don't see what you're doing in the business, M. Poirot. I don't see why Diana roped you in and got you down here."

"You are aware that Diana Maberly's engagement to Hugh Chandler has been broken off?"

"Yes, I know that."

"And you know the reason for it?"

Frobisher replied stiffly:

"I don't know anything about that. Young people manage these things between them. Not my business to butt in."

Poirot said:

"Hugh Chandler told Diana that it was not right that they should marry, because he was going out of his mind."

He saw the beads of perspiration break out on Frobisher's forehead. He said:

"Have you got to talk about the damned thing? What do you think you can do? Hugh's done the right thing, poor devil. It's not his fault, it's heredity—germ plasm—brain cells. . . . But once he knew, well, what else could he do but break the engagement? It's one of those things that just has to be done."

"If I could be convinced of that—"

"You can take it from me."

"But you have told me nothing."

"I tell you I don't want to talk about it."

"Why did Admiral Chandler force his son to leave the Navy?"

"Because it was the only thing to be done."

"Why?"

Frobisher shook an obstinate head.

Poirot murmured softly:

"Was it to do with some sheep being killed?"

The other man said angrily:

"So you've heard about that?"

"Diana told me."

"That girl had far better keep her mouth shut."

"She did not think it was conclusive."

"She doesn't know."

"What doesn't she know?"

Unwillingly, jerkily, angrily, Frobisher spoke:

"Oh, well, if you must have it. . . . Chandler heard a noise that night. Thought it might be someone got in the house. Went out to investigate. Light in the boy's room. Chandler went in. Hugh asleep on bed—dead asleep—in his clothes. Blood on the clothes. Basin in the room full of blood. His father couldn't wake him. Next morning heard about sheep being found with their throats cut. Questioned Hugh. Boy didn't know anything about it. Didn't remember going out—and his shoes found by the side door caked in mud. Couldn't explain the blood in the basin. Couldn't explain anything. Poor devil didn't *know*, you understand.

"Charles came to me, talked it over. What was the best thing to be done? Then it happened again—three nights later. After that— well, you can see for yourself. The boy had got to leave the service. If he was here, under Charles' eye, Charles could watch over him.

Couldn't afford to have a scandal in the Navy. Yes, it was the only thing to be done."

Poirot asked:

"And since then?"

Frobisher said fiercely: "I'm not answering any more questions. Don't you think Hugh knows his own business best?"

Hercule Poirot did not answer. He was always loath to admit that anyone could know better than Hercule Poirot.

# 3

As they came into the hall, they met Admiral Chandler coming in. He stood for a moment, a dark figure silhouetted against the bright light outside.

He said in a low, gruff voice:

"Oh, there you both are. M. Poirot, I would like a word with you. Come into my study."

Frobisher went out through the open door, and Poirot followed the Admiral. He had rather the feeling of having been summoned to the quarter-deck to give an account of himself.

The Admiral motioned Poirot to take one of the big easy chairs and himself sat down in the other. Poirot, while with Frobisher, had been impressed by the other's restlessness, nervousness and irritability—all the signs of intense mental strain. With Admiral Chandler he felt a sense of hopelessness, of quiet, deep despair. . . .

With a deep sigh, Chandler said: "I can't help being sorry Diana has brought you into this. . . . Poor child, I know how hard it is for her. But—well—it is our own private tragedy, and I think you understand, M. Poirot, that we don't want outsiders."

"I can understand your feeling, certainly."

"Diana, poor child, can't believe it. . . . *I* couldn't at first. Probably wouldn't believe it now if I didn't know—"

He paused.

"Know what?"

"That it's in the blood. The taint, I mean."

"And yet you agreed to the engagement?"

Admiral Chandler flushed.

"You mean, I should have put my foot down then? But at the time I'd no idea. Hugh takes after his mother—nothing about him to remind you of the Chandlers. I hoped he'd taken after her in every way. From his childhood upwards, there's never been a trace of abnormality about him until now. I couldn't know that— Dash it all, there's a trace of insanity in nearly every old family!"

Poirot said softly:

"You have not consulted a doctor?"

Chandler roared: "No, and I'm not going to! The boy's safe enough here with me to look after him. They shan't shut him up between four walls like a wild beast. . . ."

"He is safe here, you say. But are others safe?"

"What do you mean by that?"

Poirot did not reply. He looked steadily into Admiral Chandler's sad dark eyes.

The Admiral said bitterly:

"Each man to his trade. You're looking for a criminal! My boy's *not* a criminal, M. Poirot."

"Not yet."

"What do you mean by 'not yet'?"

"These things increase. Those sheep—"

"Who told you about the sheep?"

"Diana Maberly. And also your friend, Colonel Frobisher."

"George would have done better to keep his mouth shut."

"He is a very old friend of yours, is he not?"

"My best friend," the Admiral said, gruffly.

"And he was a friend of—your wife's, too?"

Chandler smiled.

"Yes. George was in love with Caroline, I believe. When she was very young. He's never married. I believe that's the reason. Ah, well, I was the lucky one—or so I thought. I carried her off—only to lose her."

He sighed and his shoulders sagged.

Poirot said: "Colonel Frobisher was with you when your wife was— drowned?"

Chandler nodded.

"Yes, he was with us down in Cornwall when it happened. She and I were out in the boat together—he happened to stay at home that day. I've never understood how that boat came to capsize. . . . Must have sprung a sudden leak. We were right out in the bay—strong tide running. I held her up as long as I could. . . ." His voice broke. "Her body was washed up two days later. Thank the Lord we hadn't taken little Hugh out with us! At least, that's what I thought at the time. Now—well—better for Hugh, poor devil, perhaps, if he *had* been with us. If it had all been finished and done for then. . . ."

Again there came that deep, hopeless sigh.

"We're the last of the Chandlers, M. Poirot. There will be no more Chandlers at Lyde after we're gone. When Hugh got engaged to Diana,

I hoped—well, it's no good talking of that. Thank God, they didn't marry. That's all I can say!"

# 4

Hercule Poirot sat on a seat in the rose garden. Beside him sat Hugh Chandler. Diana Maberly had just left them.

The young man turned a handsome, tortured face towards his companion.

He said:

"You've got to make her understand, M. Poirot."

He paused for a minute and then went on:

"You see, Di's a fighter. She won't give in. She won't accept what she's darned well got to accept. She—she *will* go on believing that I'm—sane."

"While you yourself are quite certain that you are—pardon me—insane?"

The young man winced. He said:

"I'm not actually hopelessly off my head yet—but it's getting worse. Diana doesn't know, bless her. She's only seen me when I am—all right."

"And when you are—all wrong, what happens?"

Hugh Chandler took a long breath. Then he said:

"For one thing—I *dream*. And when I dream, I *am* mad. Last night, for instance—I wasn't a man any longer. I was first of all a bull—a mad bull—racing about in blazing sunlight—tasting dust and blood in my mouth—dust and blood. . . . And then I was a dog—a great slavering dog. I had hydrophobia—children scattered and fled as I came—men tried to shoot me—someone set down a great bowl of water for me and I couldn't drink. I couldn't drink. . . ."

He paused. "I woke up. And I knew it was true. I went over to the washstand. My mouth was parched—horribly parched—and dry. I was thirsty. But I couldn't drink, M. Poirot. . . . I couldn't swallow. . . . Oh, my God, I wasn't able to drink. . . ."

Hercule Poirot made a gentle murmur. Hugh Chandler went on. His hands were clenched on his knees. His face was thrust forward, his eyes were half closed as though he saw something coming towards him.

"And there are things that aren't dreams. Things that I see when I'm wide awake. Spectres, frightful shapes. They leer at me. And sometimes I'm able to fly, to leave my bed, and fly through the air, to ride the winds—and fiends bear me company!"

"Tcha, tcha," said Hercule Poirot.

It was a gentle, deprecating little noise.

Hugh Chandler turned to him.

"Oh, there isn't any doubt. It's in my blood. It's my family heritage. I can't escape. Thank God, I found it out in time! Before I'd married Diana. Suppose we'd had a child and handed on this frightful thing to him!"

He laid a hand on Poirot's arm.

"You must make her understand. You must tell her. She's got to forget. She's *got* to. There will be someone else some day. There's young Steve Graham—he's crazy about her and he's an awfully good chap. She'd be happy with him—and safe. I want her—to be happy. Graham's hard up, of course, and so are her people, but when I'm gone they'll be all right."

Hercule's voice interrupted him.

"Why will they be 'all right' when you are gone?"

Hugh Chandler smiled. It was a gentle, lovable smile. He said:

"There's my mother's money. She was an heiress, you know. It came to me. I've left it all to Diana."

Hercule Poirot sat back in his chair. He said: "Ah!"

Then he said:

"But you may live to be quite an old man, Mr. Chandler."

Hugh Chandler shook his head. He said sharply:

"No, M. Poirot. I am not going to live to be an old man."

Then he drew back with a sudden shudder.

"My God! Look!" He stared over Poirot's shoulder. "There—standing by you . . . it's a skeleton—its bones are shaking. It's calling to me—beckoning—"

His eyes, the pupils widely dilated, stared into the sunshine. He leaned suddenly sideways as though collapsing.

Then, turning to Poirot, he said in an almost childlike voice:

"You didn't see—anything?"

Slowly, Hercule Poirot shook his head.

Hugh Chandler said hoarsely:

"I don't mind this so much—seeing things. It's the blood I'm frightened of. The blood in my room—on my clothes. . . . We had a parrot. One morning it was there in my room with its throat cut—and I was lying on the bed with the razor in my hand wet with its blood!"

He leant closer to Poirot.

"Even just lately things have been killed," he whispered. "All around—in the village—out on the downs. Sheep, young lambs—a collie dog. Father locks me in at night, but sometimes—sometimes—the door's open in the morning. I must have a key hidden somewhere but I don't know where I've hidden it. I don't know. It isn't *I* who do these things—it's someone else who comes into me—who takes possession of me—who turns me from a man into a raving monster who wants blood and who can't drink water. . . ."

Suddenly he buried his face in his hands.

After a minute or two, Poirot asked:

"I still do not understand why you have not seen a doctor?"

Hugh Chandler shook his head. He said:

"Don't you really understand? Physically I'm strong. I'm as strong as a bull. I might live for years—years—shut up between four walls! That I can't face! It would be better to go out altogether. . . . There are ways, you know. An accident, cleaning a gun . . . that sort of thing. Diana will understand. . . . I'd rather take my own way out!"

He looked defiantly at Poirot, but Poirot did not respond to the challenge. Instead he asked mildly:

"What do you eat and drink?"

Hugh Chandler flung his head back. He roared with laughter.

"Nightmares after indigestion? Is that your idea?"

Poirot merely repeated gently:

"What do you eat and drink?"

"Just what everybody else eats and drinks."

"No special medicine? Cachets? Pills?"

"Good Lord, no. Do you really think patent pills would cure my trouble?" He quoted derisively: " 'Canst thou then minister to a mind diseased?' "

Hercule Poirot said drily:

"I am trying to. Does anyone in this house suffer with eye trouble?"

Hugh Chandler stared at him. He said:

"Father's eyes give him a good deal of trouble. He has to go to an oculist fairly often."

"Ah!" Poirot meditated for a moment or two. Then he said:

"Colonel Frobisher, I suppose, has spent much of his life in India?"

"Yes, he was in the Indian Army. He's very keen on India—talks about it a lot—native traditions—and all that."

Poirot murmured "Ah!" again.

Then he remarked:

"I see that you have cut your chin."

Hugh put his hand up.

"Yes, quite a nasty gash. Father startled me one day when I was shaving. I'm a bit nervy these days, you know. And I've had a bit of a rash over my chin and neck. Makes shaving difficult."

Poirot said:

"You should use a soothing cream."

"Oh, I do. Uncle George gave me one."

He gave a sudden laugh.

"We're talking like a woman's beauty parlour. Lotions, soothing creams, patent pills, eye trouble. What does it all amount to? What are you getting at, M. Poirot?"

Poirot said quietly:

"I am trying to do the best I can for Diana Maberly."

Hugh's mood changed. His face sobered. He laid a hand on Poirot's arm.

"Yes, do what you can for her. Tell her she's got to forget. Tell her that it's no good hoping. . . . Tell her some of the things I've told you. . . . Tell her—oh, tell her for God's sake to keep away from me! That's the only thing she can do for me now. Keep away—and try to forget!"

## 5

"Have you courage, mademoiselle? Great courage? You will need it."

Diana cried sharply:

"Then it's true. It's true? He *is* mad?"

Hercule Poirot said:

"I am not an alienist, mademoiselle. It is not I who can say, 'This man is mad.' 'This man is sane.' "

She came closer to him.

"Admiral Chandler thinks Hugh is mad. George Frobisher thinks he is mad. Hugh himself thinks he is mad—"

Poirot was watching her.

"And you, mademoiselle?"

"I? I say he isn't mad! That's why—"

She stopped.

"That is why you came to me?"

"Yes. I couldn't have had any other reason for coming to you, could I?"

"That," said Hercule Poirot, "is exactly what I have been asking myself, mademoiselle!"

"I don't understand you."

"Who is Stephen Graham?"

She stared.

"Stephen Graham? Oh, he's—he's just someone."

She caught him by the arm.

"What's in your mind? What are you thinking about? You just stand there—behind that great moustache of yours—blinking your eyes in the sunlight, and you don't tell me anything. You're making me afraid—horribly afraid. Why are you making me afraid?"

"Perhaps," said Poirot, "because I am afraid myself."

The deep grey eyes opened wide, stared up at him. She said in a whisper:

"What are you afraid of?"

Hercule Poirot sighed—a deep sigh. He said:

"It is much easier to catch a murderer than it is to prevent a murder."

She cried out:

"Murder? Don't use that word."

"Nevertheless," said Hercule Poirot, "I do use it."

He altered his tone, speaking quickly and authoritatively.

"Mademoiselle, it is necessary that both you and I should pass the night at Lyde Manor. I look to you to arrange the matter. You can do that?"

"I—yes—I suppose so. But why—?"

"Because there is no time to lose. You have told me that you have courage. Prove that courage now. Do what I ask and make no questions about it."

She nodded without a word and turned away.

Poirot followed her into the house after the lapse of a moment or two. He heard her voice in the library and the voices of three men. He passed up the broad staircase. There was no one on the upper floor.

He found Hugh Chandler's room easily enough. In the corner of the room was a fitted washbasin with hot and cold water. Over it, on a glass shelf, were various tubes and pots and bottles.

Hercule Poirot went quickly and dexterously to work. . . .

What he had to do did not take him long. He was downstairs again in the hall when Diana came out of the library, looking flushed and rebellious.

"It's all right," she said.

Admiral Chandler drew Poirot into the library and closed the door. He said, "Look here, M. Poirot. I don't like this."

"What don't you like, Admiral Chandler?"

"Diana has been insisting that you and she should both spend the night here. I don't want to be inhospitable—"

"It is not a question of hospitality."

"As I say, I don't like being inhospitable—but, frankly, I don't like it, M. Poirot. I—I don't want it. And I don't understand the reason for it. What good can it possibly do?"

"Shall we say that it is an experiment I am trying?"

"What kind of an experiment?"

"That, you will pardon me, is my business. . . ."

"Now, look here, M. Poirot, I didn't ask you to come here in the first place—"

Poirot interrupted.

"Believe me, Admiral, I quite understand and appreciate your point of view. I am here simply and solely because of the obstinacy of a girl in love. You have told me certain things. Colonel Frobisher has told me certain things. Hugh himself has told me certain things. Now—I want to see for myself."

"Yes, but see *what?* I tell you, there's nothing to see! I lock Hugh into his room every night and that's that."

"And yet—sometimes—he tells me that the door is not locked in the morning?"

"What's that?"

"Have you not found the door unlocked yourself?"

Chandler was frowning.

"I always imagined George had unlocked—what do you mean?"

"Where do you leave the key—in the lock?"

"No, I lay it on the chest outside. I, or George, or Withers, the valet, take it from there in the morning. We've told Withers it's because Hugh walks in his sleep. . . . I daresay he knows more—but he's a faithful fellow, been with me for years."

"Is there another key?"

"Not that I know of."

"One could have been made."

"But who—"

"Your son thinks that he himself has one hidden somewhere, although he is unaware of it in his waking state."

Colonel Frobisher, speaking from the far end of the room, said:

"I don't like it, Charles. . . . The girl—"

Admiral Chandler said quickly: "Just what I was thinking. The girl mustn't come back with you. Come back yourself, if you like."

Poirot said: "Why don't you want Miss Maberly here tonight?"

Frobisher said in a low voice:

"It's too risky. In these cases—"

He stopped.

Poirot said, "Hugh is devoted to her. . . ."

Chandler cried, "That's just why! Damn it all, man, everything's topsy-turvy where a madman's concerned. Hugh knows that himself. Diana mustn't come here."

"As to that," said Poirot, "Diana must decide for herself."

He went out of the library. Diana was waiting outside in the car. She called out, "We'll get what we want for the night and be back in time for dinner."

As they drove down the long drive, Poirot repeated to her the con-

versation he had just held with the Admiral and Colonel Frobisher.
She laughed scornfully.

"Do they think Hugh would hurt me?"

By way of reply, Poirot asked her if she would mind stopping at
the chemist's in the village. He had forgotten, he said, to pack a toothbrush.

The chemist's shop was in the middle of the peaceful village street.
Diana waited outside in the car. It struck her that Hercule Poirot
was a long time choosing a toothbrush. . . .

# 6

In the big bedroom with the heavy Elizabethan oak furniture, Hercule Poirot sat and waited. There was nothing to do but wait. All his
arrangements were made.

It was towards early morning that the summons came.

At the sound of footsteps outside Poirot drew back the bolt and
opened the door. There were two men in the passage outside—two
middle-aged men who looked older than their years. The Admiral
was stern-faced and grim, Colonel Frobisher twitched and trembled.

Chandler said simply:

"Will you come with us, M. Poirot?"

There was a huddled figure lying outside Diana Maberly's bedroom
door. The light fell on a rumpled, tawny head. Hugh Chandler lay
there, breathing stertorously. He was in his dressing gown and slippers.
In his right hand was a sharply curved shining knife. Not all of it
was shining—here and there it was obscured by red glistening patches.

Hercule Poirot exclaimed softly:

*"Mon Dieu!"*

Frobisher said sharply:

"She's all right. He hasn't touched her." He raised his voice and
called: "Diana! It's us! Let us in!"

Poirot heard the Admiral groan and mutter under his breath:

"My boy. My poor boy."

There was a sound of bolts being drawn. The door opened and
Diana stood there. Her face was dead white.

She faltered out:

*"What's happened?"* There was someone—trying to get in—I heard
them—feeling the door—the handle—scratching on the panels— Oh!
it was awful. . . . like an animal. . . ."

Frobisher said sharply:

"Thank God your door was locked!"

"M. Poirot told me to lock it."

Poirot said:

"Lift him up and bring him inside."

The two men stooped and raised the unconscious man. Diana caught her breath with a little gasp as they passed her.

"Hugh? Is it Hugh? What's that—on his hands?"

Hugh Chandler's hands were sticky and wet with a brownish red stain.

Diana breathed:

"Is that blood?"

Poirot looked inquiringly at the two men. The Admiral nodded. He said:

"Not human, thank God! A cat! I found it downstairs in the hall. Throat cut. Afterwards he must have come up here—"

"Here?" Diana's voice was low with horror. "To me?"

The man on the chair stirred—muttered. They watched him, fascinated. Hugh Chandler sat up. He blinked.

"Hullo," his voice was dazed—hoarse. "What's happened? Why am I—?"

He stopped. He was staring at the knife which he held still clasped in his hand.

He said in a slow, thick voice:

"What have I done?"

His eyes went from one to the other. They rested last on Diana, shrinking back against the wall. He said quietly:

"Did I attack Diana?"

His father shook his head. Hugh said:

"Tell me what has happened? I've got to know!"

They told him—told him unwillingly—haltingly. His quiet perseverance drew it out of them.

Outside the window the sun was coming up. Hercule Poirot drew a curtain aside. The radiance of dawn came into the room.

Hugh Chandler's face was composed, his voice was steady.

He said:

"I see."

Then he got up. He smiled and stretched himself. His voice was quite natural as he said:

"Beautiful morning, what? Think I'll go out in the woods and try to get a rabbit."

He went out of the room and left them staring after him.

Then the Admiral started forward. Frobisher caught him by the arm.

"No, Charles, no. It's the best way—for him, poor devil, if for nobody else."

Diana had thrown herself sobbing on the bed.

Admiral Chandler said, his voice coming unevenly:

"You're right, George—you're right, I know. The boy's got guts. . . ."

Frobisher said, and his voice too was broken:

*"He's a man. . . ."*

There was a moment's silence and then Chandler said:

"Damn it, where's that cursed foreigner?"

## 7

In the gun room, Hugh Chandler had lifted his gun from the rack and was in the act of loading it when Hercule Poirot's hand fell on his shoulder.

Hercule Poirot's voice said one word and said it with a strange authority. He said:

"No!"

Hugh Chandler stared at him. He said in a thick, angry voice:

"Take your hands off me. Don't interfere. There's going to be an accident, I tell you. It's the only way out."

Again Hercule Poirot repeated that one word:

*"No."*

"Don't you realise that if it hadn't been for the accident of her door being locked, I should have cut Diana's throat—Diana's!—with that knife?"

"I realise nothing of the kind. You would not have killed Miss Maberly."

"I killed the cat, didn't I?"

"No, you did not kill the cat. You did not kill the parrot. You did not kill the sheep."

Hugh stared at him. He demanded:

"Are you mad, or am I?"

Hercule Poirot replied:

"Neither of us is mad."

It was at that moment that Admiral Chandler and Colonel Frobisher came in. Behind them came Diana.

Hugh Chandler said in a weak, dazed voice:

"This chap says I'm not mad. . . ."

Hercule Poirot said:

"I am happy to tell you that you are entirely and completely sane."

Hugh laughed. It was a laugh such as a lunatic might popularly be supposed to give.

"That's damned funny! It's sane, is it, to cut the throats of sheep and other animals? I was sane, was I, when I killed that parrot? And the cat tonight?"

"I tell you you did not kill the sheep—or the parrot—or the cat."

"Then who did?"

"Someone who has had at heart the sole object of proving you insane. On each occasion you were given a heavy soporific and a blood-stained knife or razor was planted by you. It was someone else whose bloody hands were washed in your basin."

"But why?"

"In order that you should do what you were just about to do when I stopped you."

Hugh stared. Poirot turned to Colonel Frobisher.

"Colonel Frobisher, you lived for many years in India. Did you never come across cases where persons were deliberately driven mad by the administration of drugs?"

Colonel Frobisher's face lit up. He said:

"Never came across a case myself, but I've heard of them often enough. Datura poisoning. It ends up driving a person insane."

"Exactly. Well, the active principle of the datura is very closely allied to, if it is not actually, the alkaloid atropine—which is also obtained from belladonna or deadly nightshade. Belladonna preparations are fairly common and atropine sulphate itself is prescribed freely for eye treatments. By duplicating a prescription and getting it made up in different places, a large quantity of the poison could be obtained without arousing suspicion. The alkaloid could be extracted from it and then introduced into, say, a soothing shaving cream. Applied externally it would cause a rash. This would soon lead to abrasions in shaving and thus the drug would be continually entering the system. It would produce certain symptoms—dryness of the mouth and throat, difficulty in swallowing, hallucinations, double vision—all the symptoms, in fact, which Mr. Chandler has experienced."

He turned to the young man.

"And to remove the last doubt from your mind, I will tell you that that is not a supposition but a fact. Your shaving cream was heavily impregnated with atropine sulphate. I took a sample and had it tested."

White, shaking, Hugh said:

"Who did it? Why?

Hercule Poirot said:

"That is what I have been studying ever since I arrived here. I have been looking for a motive for murder. Diana Maberly gained financially by your death, but I did not consider her seriously—"

Hugh Chandler flashed out:

"I should hope not!"

"I envisaged another possible motive. The eternal triangle: two men and a woman. Colonel Frobisher had been in love with your mother, Admiral Chandler married her."

Admiral Chandler cried out:

"George? George! I won't believe it."

Hugh said in an incredulous voice:

"Do you mean that hatred could go on—to a son?"

Hercule Poirot said:

"Under certain circumstances, yes."

Frobisher cried out:

"It's a damned lie! Don't believe him, Charles."

Chandler shrank away from him. He muttered to himself:

"The datura . . . India—yes, I see. . . . And we'd never suspect poison—not with madness in the family already. . . ."

*"Mais oui!"* Hercule Poirot's voice rose high and shrill. "Madness in the family. A madman—bent on revenge—cunning—as madmen are, concealing his madness for years." He whirled round on Frobisher. "Mon Dieu, you must have known, you must have suspected, that Hugh was your son? Why did you never tell him so?"

Frobisher stammered, gulped.

"I didn't know. I couldn't be sure. . . . You see, Caroline came to me once—she was frightened of something—in great trouble. I don't know, I never have known, what it was all about. She—I—we lost our heads. Afterwards I went away at once—it was the only thing to be done, we both knew we'd got to play the game. I—well, I wondered, but I couldn't be sure. Caroline never said anything that led me to think Hugh was my son. And then when this—this streak of madness appeared, it settled things definitely, I thought."

Poirot said:

"Yes, it settled things! You could not see the way the boy has of thrusting out his face and bringing down his brows—a trick he inherited from you. But Charles Chandler saw it. Saw it years ago—and learnt the truth from his wife. I think she was afraid of him—he'd begun to show her the mad streak—that was what drove her into your arms— you whom she had always loved. Charles Chandler planned his revenge. His wife died in a boating accident. He and she were out in the boat alone and he knows how that accident came about. Then he settled down to feed his concentrated hatred against the boy who bore his name but who was not his son. Your Indian stories put the idea of datura poisoning into his head. Hugh should be slowly driven mad. Driven to the stage where he would take his own life in despair.

The blood lust was Admiral Chandler's, not Hugh's. It was Charles Chandler who was driven to cut the throats of sheep in lonely fields. But it was Hugh who was to pay the penalty!

"Do you know when I suspected? When Admiral Chandler was so averse to his son seeing a doctor. For Hugh to object was natural enough. But the father! There might be treatment which would save his son—there were a hundred reasons why he should seek to have a doctor's opinion. But, no, a doctor must not be allowed to see Hugh Chandler—in case a doctor should discover that Hugh was sane!"

Hugh said very quietly:

"Sane. . . . I am sane?"

He took a step towards Diana. Frobisher said in a gruff voice:

"You're sane enough. There's no taint in our family."

Diana said:

*"Hugh. . . ."*

Admiral Chandler picked up Hugh's gun. He said:

"All a lot of nonsense! Think I'll go and see if I can get a rabbit—"

Frobisher started forward, but the hand of Hercule Poirot restrained him. Poirot said:

"You said yourself—just now—that it was the best way. . . ."

Hugh and Diana had gone from the room.

The two men, the Englishman and the Belgian, watched the last of the Chandlers cross the Park and go up into the woods.

Presently, they heard a shot. . . .

# VIII

# The Horses of Diomedes

## I

THE telephone rang.

"Hullo, Poirot, is that you?"

Hercule Poirot recognized the voice as that of young Dr. Stoddart. He liked Michael Stoddart, liked the shy friendliness of his grin, was amused by his naïve interest in crime, and respected him as a hard-working and shrewd man in his chosen profession.

"I don't like bothering you—" the voice went on and hesitated.

"But something is bothering you?" suggested Hercule Poirot acutely.

"Exactly." Michael Stoddart's voice sounded relieved. "Hit it in one!"

*"Eh bien,* what can I do for you, my friend?"

Stoddart sounded diffident. He stammered a little when he answered.

"I suppose it would be awful c-c-cheek if I asked you to come round. Perhaps you're busy. . . . B-b-but I'm in a bit of a j-j-jam."

"Certainly I will come. To your house?"

"No—as a matter of fact I'm at the Mews that runs along behind. Conningby Mews. The number is 17. Could you really come? I'd be no end grateful."

"I arrive immediately," replied Hercule Poirot.

## 2

Hercule Poirot walked along the dark Mews looking up at the numbers. It was past one o'clock in the morning and for the most part the Mews appeared to have gone to bed, though there were still lights in one or two windows.

As he reached 17, its door opened and Dr. Stoddart stood looking out.

"Good man!" he said. "Come up, will you?"

A small ladderlike stairway led to the upper floor. Here, on the right, was a fairly big room, furnished with divans, rugs, triangular silver cushions and large numbers of bottles and glasses.

Everything was more or less in confusion, cigarette ends were everywhere and there were many broken glasses.

"Ha!" said Hercule Poirot. *"Mon cher Watson,* I deduce that there has been here a party!"

"There's been a party all right," said Stoddart grimly. "Some party, I should say!"

"You did not, then, attend it yourself?"

"No, I'm here strictly in my professional capacity."

"What happened?"

Stoddart said:

"This place belongs to a woman called Patience Grace—Mrs. Patience Grace."

"It sounds," said Poirot, "a charming Old World name."

"There's nothing charming or Old World about Mrs. Grace. She's good-looking in a tough sort of way. She's got through a couple of husbands, and now she's got a boy friend whom she suspects of trying to run out on her. They started this party on drink and they finished it on dope—cocaine, to be exact. Cocaine is stuff that starts off making you feel just grand and with everything in the garden lovely. It peps you up and you feel you can do twice as much as you usually do. Take too much of it and you get violent mental excitement, delusions and delirium. Mrs. Grace had a violent quarrel with her boy friend, an unpleasant person by the name of Hawker. Result, he walked out on her then and there, and she leaned out of the window and took a pot shot at him with a brand new revolver that someone had been fool enough to give her."

Hercule Poirot's eyebrows rose.

"Did she hit him?"

"Not she! Bullet went several yards wide, I should say. What she *did* hit was a miserable loafer who was creeping along the Mews looking in the dustbins. Got him through the fleshy part of the arm. He raised hell, of course, and the crowd hustled him in here quick, got the wind up with all the blood that was spilling out of him and came round and got me."

"Yes?"

"I patched him up all right. It wasn't serious. Then one or two of the men got busy on him and in the end he consented to accept a couple of five-pound notes and say no more about it. Suited him all right, poor devil. Marvellous stroke of luck."

"And you?"

"I had a bit more work to do. Mrs. Grace herself was in raving hysterics by that time. I gave her a shot of something and packed her off to bed. There was another girl who'd more or less passed out— quite young she was, and I attended to her, too. By that time everyone was slinking off as fast as they could leave."

He paused.

"And then," said Poirot, "you had time to think over the situation."

"Exactly," said Stoddart. "If it was an ordinary drunken binge, well, that would be the end of it. But dope's different."

"You are quite sure of your facts?"

"Oh, absolutely. No mistaking it. It's cocaine all right. I found some in a lacquer box—they snuff it up, you know. Question is, where does it come from? I remembered that you'd been talking the other day about a big new wave of drug-taking and the increase of drug addicts."

Hercule Poirot nodded. He said:

"The police will be interested in this party tonight."

Michael Stoddart said unhappily:

"That's just it. . . ."

Poirot looked at him with suddenly awakened interest. He said:

"But you—you are not very anxious that the police should be interested?"

Michael Stoddart mumbled:

"Innocent people get mixed up in things . . . hard lines on them."

"Is it Mrs. Patience Grace for whom you are solicitous?"

"Good Lord, no. She's as hard-boiled as they make them!"

Hercule Poirot said gently:

"It is, then, the other one—the girl?"

Dr. Stoddart said:

"Of course, she's hard-boiled, too, in a way. I mean, she'd *describe* herself as hard-boiled. But she's really just very young—a bit wild and all that—but it's just kid foolishness. She gets mixed up in a racket like this because she thinks it's smart or modern or something like that."

A faint smile came to Poirot's lips. He said softly:

"This girl, you have met her before tonight?"

Michael Stoddart nodded. He looked very young and embarrassed.

"Ran across her in Mertonshire. At the Hunt Ball. Her father's a retired general—blood and thunder, shoot 'em down—pukka sahib— all that sort of thing. There are four daughters and they are all a bit wild—driven to it with a father like that, I should say. And it's a bad part of the county where they live—armaments works near by and a lot of money—none of the old-fashioned country feeling—a rich crowd and most of them pretty vicious. The girls have got in with a bad set."

Hercule Poirot looked at him thoughtfully for some minutes. Then he said:

"I perceive now why you desired my presence. You want me to take the affair in hand?"

"Would you? I feel I ought to do something about it—but I confess I'd like to keep Sheila Grant out of the limelight if I could."

"That can be managed, I fancy. I should like to see the young lady."

"Come along."

He led the way out of the room. A voice called fretfully from a door opposite.

"Doctor—for God's sake, doctor, I'm going crazy."

Stoddart went into the room. Poirot followed. It was a bedroom in a complete state of chaos—powder spilled on the floor—pots and jars everywhere, clothes flung about. On the bed was a woman with unnaturally blond hair and a vacant, vicious face. She called out:

"I've got insects crawling all over me. . . . I have. I swear I have. I'm going mad. . . . For God's sake, give me a shot of something."

Dr. Stoddart stood by the bed, his tone was soothing—professional.

Hercule Poirot went quietly out of the room. There was another door opposite him. He opened that.

It was a tiny room—a mere slip of a room—plainly furnished. On the bed a slim, girlish figure lay motionless.

Hercule Poirot tiptoed to the side of the bed and looked down upon the girl.

Dark hair, a long pale face—and—yes, young—very young. . . .

A gleam of white showed between the girl's lids. Her eyes opened, startled frightened eyes. She stared, sat up, tossing her head in an effort to throw back the thick mane of blue black hair. She looked like a frightened filly—She shrank away a little—as a wild animal shrinks when it is suspicious of a stranger who offers it food.

She said—and her voice was young and thin and abrupt:

"Who the hell are you?"

"Do not be afraid, mademoiselle."

"Where's Dr. Stoddart?"

That young man came into the room at that minute. The girl said, with a note of relief in her voice:

"Oh, there you are! Who's this?"

"This is a friend of mine, Sheila. How are you feeling now?"

The girl said weakly:

"Awful. Lousy. . . . Why did I take that foul stuff?"

Stoddart said drily:

"I shouldn't do it again, if I were you."

"I—I shan't."

Hercule Poirot said:

"Who gave it to you?"

Her eyes widened, her upper lip twitched a little. She said:

"It was here—at the party. We all tried it. It—it was wonderful at first."

Hercule Poirot said gently:

"But who brought it here?"

She shook her head.

"I don't know. . . . It might have been Tony—Tony Hawker. But I don't really know anything about it."

Poirot said gently:

"Is it the first time you have taken cocaine, mademoiselle?"

She nodded.

"You'd better make it the last," said Stoddart brusquely.

"Yes—I suppose so—but it *was* rather marvellous."

"Now look here, Sheila Grant," said Stoddart, "I'm a doctor and I know what I'm talking about. Once start this drug-taking racket and you'll land yourself in unbelievable misery. I've seen some and I know. Drugs ruin people, body and soul. Drink's a gentle little picnic compared to drugs. Cut it right out from this minute. Believe me, it isn't funny! What do you think your father would say to tonight's business?"

"Father?" Sheila Grant's voice rose. "Father?" She began to laugh. "I can just see Father's face! He mustn't know about it. He'd have seven fits!"

"And quite right, too," said Stoddart.

"Doctor—doctor—" the long wail of Mrs. Grace's voice came from the other room.

Stoddart muttered something uncomplimentary under his breath and went out of the room.

Sheila Grant stared at Poirot again. She was puzzled. She said:

"Who are you really? You weren't at the party."

"No, I was not at the party. I am a friend of Dr. Stoddart's."

"You're a doctor, too? You don't look like a doctor."

"My name," said Poirot, contriving as usual to make the simple statement sound like the curtain of the first act of a play, "my name is Hercule Poirot. . . ."

The statement did not fail of its effect. Occasionally Poirot was distressed to find that a callous younger generation had never heard of him.

But it was evident that Sheila Grant had heard of him. She was flabbergasted—dumfounded. She stared and stared. . . .

# 3

It has been said, with or without justification for the statement, that everyone has an aunt in Torquay.

It has also been said that everyone has at least a second cousin in Mertonshire. Mertonshire is a reasonable distance from London. It has hunting, shooting, and fishing, it has several very picturesque but slightly self-conscious villages, it has a good system of railways and a new arterial road facilitates motoring to and from the metropolis. Servants object to it less than they do to other, more rural, portions of the British Isles. As a result, it is practically impossible to live in Mertonshire unless you have an income that runs into four figures, and what with income tax and one thing and another, five figures is better.

Hercule Poirot, being a foreigner, had no second cousins in the county, but he had acquired by now a large circle of friends and he had no difficulty in getting himself invited for a visit in that part of the world. He had, moreover, selected as hostess a dear lady whose chief delight was exercising her tongue on the subject of her neighbours—the only drawback being that Poirot had to submit to hearing a great deal about people in whom he had no interest whatever, before coming to the subject of the people he was interested in.

"The Grants? Oh, yes, there are four of them. Four girls. I don't wonder the poor old General can't control them. What can a man do with four girls?" Lady Carmichael's hands flew up eloquently. Poirot said, "What indeed?" and the lady continued.

"Used to be a great disciplinarian in his regiment, so he told me. But those girls defeat him. Not like when I was young. Old Colonel Sandys was such a martinet, I remember, that his poor daughters—"

(Long excursion into the trials of the Sandys girls and other friends of Lady Carmichael's youth.)

"Mind you," said Lady Carmichael, reverting to her first theme, "I don't say there's anything really wrong about those girls. Just high spirits—and getting in with an undesirable set. It's not what it used to be down here. The oddest people come here. There's no what you might call 'county' left. It's all money, money, money nowadays. And you do hear the oddest stories! Who did you say? Anthony Hawker? Oh, yes, I know him. What I call a very unpleasant young man. But apparently rolling in money. He comes down here to hunt—and he gives parties—very lavish parties—and rather peculiar parties, too, if one is to believe all one is told—not that I ever do, because I do think people are so ill-natured. They always believe the worst. You know, it's become quite a fashion to say a person drinks or takes drugs. Somebody said to me the other day that young girls were natural inebriates, and really I don't think that was a nice thing to say at all. And if anyone's at all peculiar or vague in their manner, everyone says 'drugs' and that's unfair, too. They say it about Mrs. Larkin and though I don't care for the woman, I do really think it's nothing more than absentmindedness. She's a great friend of your Anthony Hawker, and that's why, if you ask me, she's so down on the Grant girls—says they're maneaters! I daresay they do run after men a bit, but why not? It's natural, after all. And they're good-looking pieces, every one of them."

Poirot interjected a question.

"Mrs. Larkin? My dear man, it's no good asking me *who* she is. Who's anybody nowadays? They say she rides well and she's obviously well off. Husband was something in the city. He's dead, not divorced. She's not been here very long, came here just after the Grants did. I've always thought she—"

Old Lady Carmichael stopped. Her mouth opened, her eyes bulged. Leaning forward she struck Poirot a sharp blow across the knuckles with a paper cutter she was holding. Disregarding his wince of pain she exclaimed excitedly:

"Why, of course! So *that's* why you're down here! You nasty deceitful creature, I insist on your telling me all about it."

"But what is it I am to tell you all about?"

Lady Carmichael aimed another playful blow which Poirot avoided deftly.

"Don't be an oyster, Hercule Poirot! I can see your mustache quivering. Of course, it's *crime* brings you down here—and you're just pumping me shamelessly! Now, let me see, can it be murder? Who's died lately? Only old Louisa Gilmore and she was eighty-five and had dropsy, too. Can't be her. Poor Leo Staverton broke his neck in the hunting field and he's all done up in plaster—that can't be it. Perhaps it isn't murder. What a pity! I can't remember any special jewel robberies lately. . . . Perhaps it's just a criminal you're tracking down. . . . Is it Beryl Larkin? *Did* she poison her husband? Perhaps it's remorse that makes her so vague."

"Madame, madame," cried Hercule Poirot, "you go too fast."

"Nonsense. You're up to something, Hercule Poirot."

"Are you acquainted with the classics, madame?"

"What have the classics got to do with it?"

"They have this to do with it. I emulate my great predecessor Hercules. One of the Labors of Hercules was the taming of the wild horses of Diomedes."

"Don't tell me you came down here to train horses—at your age—and always wearing patent leather shoes! You don't look to me as though you'd ever been on a horse in your life!"

"The horses, madame, are symbolic. They were wild horses who ate human flesh."

"How very unpleasant of them. I always do think these ancient Greeks and Romans are very unpleasant. I can't think why clergymen are so fond of quoting from the classics—for one thing one never understands what they mean and it always seems to me that the whole subject matter of the classics is very unsuitable for clergymen. So much incest, and all those statues with nothing on—not that I mind that myself, but you know what clergymen are—quite upset if girls come to church with no stockings on—let me see, where was I?"

"I am not quite sure."

"I suppose, you wretch, you just won't tell me if Mrs. Larkin murdered her husband? Or perhaps Anthony Hawker is the Brighton trunk murderer?"

She looked at him hopefully, but Hercule Poirot's face remained impassive.

"It might be forgery," speculated Lady Carmichael. "I did see Mrs. Larkin in the bank the other morning and she'd just cashed a fifty-pound cheque to self—it seemed to me at the time a lot of money to want in cash. Oh, no, that's the wrong way round—if she was a forger she would be paying it in, wouldn't she? Hercule Poirot, if you sit there looking like an owl and saying nothing, I shall throw something at you."

"You must have a little patience," said Hercule Poirot.

# 4

Ashley Lodge, the residence of General Grant, was not a large house. It was situated on the side of a hill, had good stables, and a straggling, rather neglected garden.

Inside, it was what a house agent would have described as "fully furnished." Cross-legged Buddhas leered down from convenient niches, brass Benares trays and tables encumbered the floor space. Processional elephants garnished the mantelpieces and more tortured brasswork adorned the walls.

In the midst of this Anglo-Indian home from home, General Grant was ensconced in a large shabby armchair with his leg, swathed in bandages, reposing on another chair.

"Gout," he explained. "Ever had the gout, Mr.—er Poirot? Makes a feller damned bad-tempered! All my father's fault. Drank port all his life—so did my grandfather. It's played the deuce with me. Have a drink? Ring that bell, will you, for that feller of mine?"

A turbaned servant appeared. General Grant addressed him as Abdul and ordered him to bring the whisky and soda. When it came he poured out such a generous portion that Poirot was moved to protest.

"Can't join you, I'm afraid, M. Poirot." The General eyed the tantalus sadly. "My doctor wallah says it's poison to me to touch the stuff. Don't suppose he knows for a minute. Ignorant chaps, doctors. Spoil sports. Enjoy knocking a man off his food and drink and putting him on some pap like steamed fish. Steamed fish—pah!"

In his indignation the General incautiously moved his bad foot and uttered a yelp of agony at the twinge that ensued.

He apologised for his language.

"Like a bear with a sore head, that's what I am. My girls give me a wide berth when I've got an attack of gout. Don't know that I blame them. You've met one of 'em, I hear."

"I have had that pleasure, yes. You have several daughters, have you not?"

"Four," said the General, gloomily. "Not a boy amongst 'em. Four blinking girls. Bit of a thought, these days."

"They are all four very charming, I hear?"

"Not too bad—not too bad. Mind you, I never know what they're up to. You can't control girls nowadays. Lax times—too much laxity everywhere. What can a man do? Can't lock 'em up, can I?"

"They are popular in the neighbourhood, I gather."

"Some of the old cats don't like 'em," said General Grant. "A good deal of mutton dressed as lamb round here. A man's got to be careful. One of those blue-eyed widows nearly caught me—used to come round here purring like a kitten. 'Poor General Grant—you must have had such an interesting life.' " The General winked and placed one finger against his nose. "A little bit too obvious, M. Poirot. Oh, well, take it all round, I suppose it's not a bad part of the world. A bit go-ahead and noisy for my taste. I liked the country when it was the country—not all this motoring and jazz and that blasted eternal radio. I won't have one here and the girls know it. A man's got a right to a little peace in his own home."

Gently, Poirot led the conversation round to Anthony Hawker.

"Hawker? Hawker? Don't know him. Yes, I do, though. Nasty-looking fellow with his eyes too close together. Never trust a man who can't look you in the face."

"He is a friend, is he not, of your daughter Sheila's?"

"Sheila? Wasn't aware of it. Girls never tell me anything." The bushy eyebrows came down over the nose—the piercing blue eyes looked out of the red face straight into Hercule Poirot's. "Look here, M. Poirot, what's all this about? Mind telling me what you've come to see me about?"

Poirot said slowly:

"That would be difficult—perhaps I hardly know myself. I would say only this: Your daughter Sheila—perhaps all your daughters—have made some undesirable friends."

"Got into a bad set, have they? I was a bit afraid of that. One hears a word dropped here and there." He looked pathetically at Poirot. "But what am I to do, M. Poirot? What am I to do?"

Poirot shook his head perplexedly.

General Grant went on.

"What's wrong with the bunch they're running with?"

Poirot replied by another question.

"Have you noticed, General Grant, that any of your daughters have been moody, excited—then depressed—nervy—uncertain in their tempers?"

"Damme, sir, you're talking like a patent medicine. No, I haven't noticed anything of the kind."

"That is fortunate," said Poirot gravely.

"What the devil is the meaning of all this, sir?"

"Drugs!"

"WHAT!"

The word came in a roar.

Poirot said:

"An attempt is being made to induce your daughter Sheila to become a drug addict. The cocaine habit is very quickly formed. A week or two will suffice. Once the habit is formed, an addict will pay anything, do anything, to get a further supply of the drug. You can realise what a rich haul the person who peddles that drug can make."

He listened in silence to the spluttering, wrathful blasphemies that poured from the old man's lips. Then, as the fires died down, with a final choice description of exactly what he, the General, would do to the blinkety-blinkety son of a blank when he got hold of him, Hercule Poirot said:

"We have first, as your so admirable Mrs. Beeton says, to catch the hare. Once we have caught our drug peddler, I will turn him over to you with the greatest pleasure, General."

He got up, tripped over a heavily carved small table, regained his balance with a clutch at the General, murmured:

"A thousand pardons, and may I beg of you, General—you understand, *beg* of you—to say nothing whatever about all this to your daughters."

"What? I'll have the truth out of them, that's what I'll have!"

"That is exactly what you will not have. All you will get is a lie."

"But damme, sir—"

"I assure you, General Grant, you *must* hold your tongue. That is vital—you understand? Vital!"

"Oh, well, have it your own way," growled the old soldier.

He was mastered but not convinced.

Hercule Poirot picked his way carefully through the Benares brass and went out.

# 5

Mrs. Larkin's room was full of people.

Mrs. Larkin herself was mixing cocktails at a side table. She was a tall woman with pale auburn hair rolled into the back of her neck. Her eyes were greenish grey with big black pupils. She moved easily, with a kind of sinister grace. She looked as though she were in her early thirties. Only a close scrutiny revealed the lines at the corners of the eyes and hinted that she was ten years older than her looks.

Hercule Poirot had been brought here by a brisk middle-aged woman, a friend of Lady Carmichael's. He found himself given a cocktail and further directed to take one to a girl sitting in the window. The girl was small and fair—her face was pink and white and suspiciously angelic. Her eyes, Hercule Poirot noticed at once, were alert and suspicious.

He said:

"To your continued good health, mademoiselle."

She nodded and drank. Then she said abruptly:

"You know my sister."

"Your sister? Ah, you are then one of the Miss Grants?"

"I'm Pam Grant."

"And where is your sister today?"

"She's out hunting. Ought to be back soon."

"I met your sister in London."

"I know."

"She told you?"

Pam Grant nodded. She said abruptly:

"Was Sheila in a jam?"

"So she did not tell you everything?"

The girl shook her head. She asked:

"Was Tony Hawker there?"

Before Poirot could answer, the door opened and Hawker and Sheila Grant came in. They were in hunting kit and Sheila had a streak of mud on her cheek.

"Hullo, people, we've come in for a drink. Tony's flask is dry."

Poirot murmured:

"Talk of the angels—"

Pam Grant snapped:

"Devils, you mean."

Poirot said sharply:

"Is it like that?"

Beryl Larkin had come forward. She said:

"Here you are, Tony. Tell me about the run? Did you draw Gelert's Copse?"

She drew him away with her skilfully to a sofa near the fireplace. Poirot saw him turn his head and glance at Sheila before he went.

Sheila had seen Poirot. She hesitated a minute, then came over to the two in the window. She said abruptly:

"So it *was* you who came to the house yesterday?"

"Did your father tell you?"

She shook her head.

"Abdul described you. I—guessed."

Pam exclaimed: "You went to see Father?"

Poirot said:

"Ah—yes. We have—some mutual friends."

Pam said sharply:

"I don't believe it."

"What do you not believe? That your father and I could have a mutual friend?"

The girl flushed.

"Don't be stupid. I meant—that wasn't really your reason—"

She turned on her sister.

"Why don't you say something, Sheila?"

Sheila started. She said:

"It wasn't—it wasn't anything to do with Tony Hawker?"

"Why should it be?" asked Poirot.

Sheila flushed and went back across the room to the others.

Pam said with sudden vehemence but in a lowered voice:

"I don't like Tony Hawker. There—there's something sinister about him—and about her—Mrs. Larkin, I mean. Look at them now."

Poirot followed her glance.

Hawker's head was close to that of his hostess. He appeared to be soothing her. Her voice rose for a minute.

"—but I can't wait. I want it now!"

Poirot said with a little smile:

"*Les femmes*—whatever it is—they always want it now, do they not?"

But Pam Grant did not respond. Her face was cast down. She was nervously pleating and repleating her tweed skirt.

Poirot murmured conversationally:

"You are quite a different type from your sister, mademoiselle."

She flung her head up, impatient of banalities. She said:

"M. Poirot, what's the stuff Tony's been giving Sheila? What is it that's been making her—different?"

He looked straight at her. He asked:

"Have you ever taken cocaine, Miss Grant?"

She shook her head.

"Oh, no! So that's it! Cocaine? But isn't that very dangerous?"

Sheila Grant had come over to them, a fresh drink in her hand. She said:

"What's dangerous?"

Poirot said:

"We are talking of the effects of drug-taking. Of the slow death of the mind and spirit—the destroying of all that is true and good in a human being."

Sheila Grant caught her breath. The drink in her hand swayed and spilled a little on the floor. Poirot went on:

"Dr. Stoddart has, I think, made clear to you just what that death in life entails. It is so easily done—so hard to undo. The person who deliberately profits from the degradation and misery of other people is a vampire preying on flesh and blood."

He turned away. Behind him he heard Pam Grant's voice say: "Sheila!" and he caught a whisper—a faint whisper—from Sheila Grant. It was so low he hardly heard it.

"The flask. . . ."

Hercule Poirot said good-bye to Mrs. Larkin and went out into the hall. On the hall table was a hunting flask lying with a crop and a hat. Poirot picked it up. There were initials on it. A. H.

Poirot murmured to himself:

"Tony's flask is empty?"

He shook it gently. There was no sound of liquor. He unscrewed the top.

Tony Hawker's flask was not empty. It was full—of white powder. . . .

# 6

Hercule Poirot stood on the terrace of Lady Carmichael's house and pleaded with a girl.

He said:

"You are very young, mademoiselle. It is my belief that you have not known, not really known, what it is you and your sisters have been doing. You have been feeding, like the mares of Diomedes, on human flesh."

Sheila shuddered and gave a sob. She said:

"It sounds horrible, put like that. And yet it's true! I never realised it until that evening in London when Dr. Stoddart talked to me. He was so grave—so sincere. I saw then what an awful thing it was I had been doing. . . . Before that I thought it was— Oh! rather like drink after hours—something people would pay to get, but not something that really mattered very much!"

Poirot said:

"And now?"

Sheila Grant said:

"I'll do anything you say. I—I'll talk to the others," she added. . . . "I don't suppose Dr. Stoddart will ever speak to me again. . . ."

"On the contrary," said Poirot. "Both Dr. Stoddart and I are prepared to help you in every way in our power to start afresh. You can trust us. But one thing must be done. There is one person who must be destroyed—destroyed utterly, and only you and your sisters can destroy him. It is your evidence and your evidence alone that will convict him."

"You mean—my father?"

"Not your father, mademoiselle. Did I not tell you that Hercule Poirot knows everything? Your photograph was easily recognized in official quarters. You are Sheila Kelly—a persistent young shoplifter who was sent to a reformatory some years ago. When you came out of that reformatory, you were approached by the man who calls himself General Grant and offered this post—the post of a 'daughter.' There would be plenty of money, plenty of fun, a good time. All you had to do was to introduce the 'snuff' to your friends, always pretending that someone else had given it to you. Your 'sisters' were in the same case as yourself."

He paused and said:

"Come now, mademoiselle—this man must be exposed and sentenced. After that—"

"Yes, afterwards?"

Poirot coughed. He said with a smile:
"You shall be dedicated to the service of the gods. . . ."

# 7

Michael Stoddart stared at Poirot in amazement. He said:
"General Grant? General Grant?"

"Precisely, *mon cher*. The whole *mise en scène*, you know, was what you would call 'very bogus.' The Buddhas, the Benares brass, the Indian servant! And the gout, too! It is out of date, the gout. It is old, old gentlemen who have the gout—not the fathers of young ladies of nineteen.

"Moreover, I made quite certain. As I go out, I stumble, I clutch at the gouty foot. So perturbed is the gentleman by what I have been saying that he did not even notice. Oh, yes, he is very, very bogus, that General! *Tout de même*, it is a smart idea. The retired Anglo-Indian General, the well-known comic figure with a liver and a choleric temper, he settles down—not among other retired Anglo-Indian Army officers—oh, no, he goes to a milieu far too expensive for the usual retired Army man. There are rich people there, people from London, an excellent field to market the goods. And who would suspect four lively attractive young girls? If anything comes out, they will be considered as victims—that for a certainty!"

"What was your idea exactly when you went to see the old devil? Did you want to put the wind up him?"

"Yes. I wanted to see what would happen. I had not long to wait. The girls had their orders. Anthony Hawker, actually one of their victims, was to be the scapegoat. Sheila was to tell me about the flask in the hall. She nearly could not bring herself to do so—but the other girl rapped out an angry 'Sheila' at her and she just faltered it out."

Michael Stoddart got up and paced up and down. He said:
"You know, I'm not going to lose sight of that girl. I've got a pretty sound theory about these adolescent criminal tendencies. If you look back into the home life, you nearly always find—"

Poirot interrupted him.

He said:
"*Mon cher*, I have the deepest respect for your science. I have no doubt that your theories will work admirably where Miss Sheila Kelly is concerned."

"The others, too."

"The others, perhaps. It may be. The only one I am sure about is the little Sheila. You will tame her, not a doubt of it! In truth, she eats out of your hand already. . . ."

Flushing, Michael Stoddart said:

"What nonsense you talk, Poirot."

# IX

# The Girdle of Hyppolita

## I

ONE thing leads to another, as Hercule Poirot is fond of saying without much originality.

He adds that this was never more clearly evidenced than in the case of the stolen Rubens.

He was never much interested in the Rubens. For one thing, Rubens is not a painter he admires, and then the circumstances of the theft were quite ordinary. He took it up to oblige Alexander Simpson who was by way of being a friend of his and for a certain private reason of his own not unconnected with the classics!

After the theft, Alexander Simpson sent for Poirot and poured out all his woes. The Rubens was a recent discovery, a hitherto unknown masterpiece, but there was no doubt of its authenticity. It had been placed on display at Simpson's Galleries and it had been stolen in broad daylight. It was at the time when the unemployed were pursuing their tactics of lying down on street crossings and penetrating into the Ritz. A small body of them had entered Simpson's Galleries and lain down with the slogan displayed of "Art is a Luxury. Feed the Hungry." The police had been sent for, everyone had crowded round in eager curiosity and it was not till the demonstrators had been forcibly removed by the arm of the law that it was noticed that the new Rubens had been neatly cut out of its frame and removed also!

"It was quite a small picture, you see," explained Mr. Simpson. "A man could put it under his arm and walk out while everyone was looking at those miserable idiots of unemployed."

The men in question, it was discovered, had been paid for their innocent part in the robbery. They were to demonstrate at Simpson's Galleries. But they had known nothing of the reason until afterwards.

Hercule Poirot thought that it was an amusing trick but did not see what he could do about it. The police, he pointed out, could be trusted to deal with a straightforward robbery.

Alexander Simpson said:

"Listen to me, Poirot. I know who stole the picture and where it is going."

According to the owner of Simpson's Galleries, it had been stolen by a gang of international crooks on behalf of a certain millionaire who was not above acquiring works of art at a surprisingly low price—and no questions asked! The Rubens, said Simpson, would be smuggled over to France where it would pass into the millionaire's possession. The English and French police were on the alert, nevertheless Simpson was of the opinion that they would fail. "And once it has passed into this dirty dog's possession, it's going to be more difficult. Rich men have to be treated with respect. That's where you come in. The situation's going to be delicate. You're the man for that."

Finally, without enthusiasm, Hercule Poirot was induced to accept the task. He agreed to depart for France immediately. He was not very interested in his quest, but because of it, he was introduced to the Case of the Missing Schoolgirl, which interested him very much indeed.

He first heard of it from Chief Inspector Japp who dropped in to see him just as Poirot was expressing approval of his valet's packing.

"Ha," said Japp. "Going to France, aren't you?"

Poirot said:

*"Mon cher,* you are incredibly well informed at Scotland Yard."

Japp chuckled. He said:

"We have our spies! Simpson's got you on to this Rubens business. Doesn't trust us, it seems! Well, that's neither here nor there, but what I want you to do is something quite different. As you're going to Paris anyway, I thought you might as well kill two birds with one stone. Detective Inspector Hearn's over there cooperating with the Frenchies—you know Hearn? Good chap—but perhaps not very imaginative. I'd like your opinion on the business."

"What is this matter of which you speak?"

"Child's disappeared. It'll be in the papers this evening. Looks as though she's been kidnapped. Daughter of a canon down at Cranchester. King, her name is, Winnie King."

He proceeded with the story.

Winnie had been on her way to Paris, to join that select and high-class establishment for English and American girls—Miss Pope's. Winnie had come up from Cranchester by the early train—had been seen across London by a member of Elder Sisters Ltd. who undertook such work as seeing girls from one station to another, had been delivered at Victoria to Miss Burshaw, Miss Pope's second in command, and had then, in company with eighteen other girls, left Victoria by the boat train. Nineteen girls had crossed the channel, had passed through the customs at Calais, had got into the Paris train, had lunched in the restaurant car. But when, on the outskirts of Paris, Miss Burshaw had counted heads, it was discovered that only *eighteen* girls could be found!

"Aha," Poirot nodded. "Did the train stop anywhere?"

"It stopped at Amiens, but at that time the girls were in the restaurant car and they all say positively that Winnie was with them then. They lost her, so to speak, on the return journey to their compartments. That is to say, she did not enter her own compartment with the other five girls who were in it. They did not suspect anything was wrong, merely thought she was in one of the two other reserved carriages."

Poirot nodded.

"So she was last seen—when exactly?"

"About ten minutes after the train left Amiens." Japp coughed modestly. "She was last seen—er—entering the toilette."

Poirot murmured:

"Very natural." He went on, "There is nothing else?"

"Yes, one thing." Japp's face was grim. "Her hat was found by the side of the line—at a spot approximately fourteen miles from Amiens."

"But no body?"

"No body."

Poirot asked:

"What do you yourself think?"

"Difficult to know *what* to think! As there's no sign of her body—she can't have fallen off the train."

"Did the train stop at all after leaving Amiens?"

"No. It slowed up once—for a signal—but it didn't stop, and I doubt if it slowed up enough for anyone to have jumped off without injury. You're thinking that the kid got a panic and tried to run away? It was her first term and she might have been homesick, that's true enough, but all the same she was fifteen and a half—a sensible age, and she'd been in quite good spirits all the journey, chattering away and all that."

Poirot asked:

"Was the train searched?"

"Oh, yes, they went right through it before it arrived at the Nord station. The girl wasn't on the train, that's quite certain."

Japp added in an exasperated manner:

"She just disappeared—into thin air! It doesn't make sense, M. Poirot. It's crazy!"

"What kind of a girl was she?"

"Ordinary normal type as far as I can make out."

"I mean—what did she look like?"

"I've got a snap of her here. She's not exactly a budding beauty."

He proffered the snapshot to Poirot, who studied it in silence.

It represented a lanky girl with her hair in two limp plaits. It was not a posed photograph, the subject had clearly been caught unawares. She was in the act of eating an apple, her lips were parted, showing slightly protruding teeth confined by a dentist's plate. She wore spectacles.

Japp said:

"Plain-looking kid—but then they are plain at that age! Was at my dentist's yesterday. Saw a picture in the Sketch of Marcia Gaunt, this season's beauty. *I* remember her at fifteen when I was down at the Castle over their burglary business. Spotty, awkward, teeth sticking out, hair all lank and anyhow. They grow into beauties overnight—I don't know how they do it! It's like a miracle."

Poirot smiled.

"Women," he said, "are a miraculous sex! What about the child's family? Have they anything helpful to say?"

Japp shook his head.

"Nothing that's any help. Mother's an invalid. Poor old Canon King is absolutely bowled over. He swears that the girl was frightfully keen to go to Paris—had been looking forward to it. Wanted to study painting and music—that sort of thing. Miss Pope's girls go in for Art with a capital A. As you probably know, Miss Pope's is a very well-known establishment. Lots of society girls go there. She's strict—quite a dragon—and very expensive—and extremely particular whom she takes."

Poirot sighed.

"I know the type. And Miss Burshaw who took the girls over from England?"

"Not exactly frantic with brains. Terrified that Miss Pope will say it's her fault."

Poirot said thoughtfully:

"There is no young man in the case?"

Japp gesticulated towards the snapshot.

"Does she look like it?"

"No, she does not. But notwithstanding her appearance, she may have a romantic heart. Fifteen is not so young."

"Well," said Japp, "if a romantic heart spirited her off that train, I'll take to reading lady novelists."

He looked hopefully at Poirot.

"Nothing strikes you—eh?"

Poirot shook his head slowly. He said:

"They did not, by any chance, find her shoes also by the side of the line?"

"Shoes? No. Why shoes?"

Poirot murmured:

"Just an idea. . . ."

## 2

Hercule Poirot was just going down to his taxi when the telephone rang. He took off the receiver.

"Yes?"

Japp's voice spoke.

"Glad I've just caught you. It's all off, old man. Found a message at the Yard when I got back. The girl's turned up. At the side of the main road fifteen miles from Amiens. She's dazed and they can't get any coherent story from her. Doctor says she's been doped—however, she's all right. Nothing wrong with her."

Poirot said slowly:

"So you have, then, no need of my services?"

"Afraid not! In fact—sorrrry you have been trrrroubled. . . ."

Japp laughed at his own witticism and rang off.

Hercule Poirot did not laugh. He put back the receiver slowly. His face was worried.

## 3

Detective Inspector Hearn looked at Poirot curiously.

He said:

"I'd no idea you'd be so interested, sir."

Poirot said:

"You had word from Chief Inspector Japp that I might consult with you over this matter?"

Hearn nodded.

"He said you were coming over on some other business, and that you'd give us a hand with this puzzle. But I didn't expect you, now it's all cleared up. I thought you'd be busy on your own job."

Hercule Poirot said:

"My own business can wait. It is this affair here that interests me. You called it a puzzle, and you say it is now ended. But the puzzle is still there, it seems."

"Well, sir, we've got the child back. And she's not hurt. That's the main thing."

"But it does not solve the problem of how you got her back, does it? What does she herself say? A doctor saw her, did he not? What did he say?"

"Said she'd been doped. She was still hazy with it. Apparently, she can't remember anything much after starting off from Cranchester. All later events seem to have been wiped out. Doctor thinks she might just possibly have had slight concussion. There's a bruise on the back of the head. Says that would account for a complete blackout of memory."

Poirot said:

"Which is very convenient for—someone!"

Inspector Hearn said in a doubtful voice:

"You don't think she is shamming, sir?"

"Do you?"

"No, I'm sure she isn't. She's a nice kid—a bit young for her age."

"No, she is not shamming." Poirot shook his head. "But I would like to know how she got off that train. I want to know who is responsible—and why?"

"As to why, I should say it was an attempt at kidnapping, sir. They meant to hold her to ransom."

"But they didn't!"

"Lost their nerve with the hue and cry—and planted her by the road quick."

Poirot inquired sceptically:

"And what ransom were they likely to get from a Canon of Cranchester Cathedral? English Church dignitaries are not millionaires."

Detective Inspector Hearn said cheerfully:

"Made a botch of the whole thing, sir, in my opinion."

"Ah, that's your opinion."

Hearn said, his face flushing slightly:

"What's yours, sir?"

"I want to know how she was spirited off that train."

The policeman's face clouded over.

"That's a real mystery, that is. One minute she was there, sitting in the dining car, chatting to the other girls. Five minutes later she's vanished—hey presto—like a conjuring trick."

"Precisely, like a conjuring trick! Who else was there in the coach of the train where Miss Pope's reserved compartments were?"

Inspector Hearn nodded.

"That's a good point, sir. That's important. It's particularly important because it was the last coach on the train and as soon as all the people were back from the restaurant car, the doors between the coaches were locked—actually so as to prevent people crowding along to the restaurant car and demanding tea before they'd had time to clear up lunch and get ready. Winnie King came back to the coach with the others—the school had three reserved compartments there."

"And in the other compartment of the coach?"

Hearn pulled out his notebook.

"Miss Jordan and Miss Butters—two middle-aged spinsters going to Switzerland. Nothing wrong with them, highly respectable, well-known in Hampshire where they come from. Two French commercial travellers, one from Lyons, one from Paris. Both respectable middle-aged men. A young man, James Elliot, and his wife—flashy piece of goods she was. He's got a bad reputation, suspected by the police of being mixed up in some questionable transactions—but has never touched kidnapping. Anyway, his compartment was searched and there was nothing in his hand luggage to show that he was mixed up in this. Don't see how he *could* have been. Only other person was an American lady, Mrs. Van Suyder, travelling to Paris. Nothing known about her. Looks O.K. That's the lot."

Hercule Poirot said:

"And it is quite definite that the train did not stop after it left Amiens?"

"Absolutely. It slowed down once, but not enough to let anyone jump off—not without damaging themselves pretty severely and risking being killed."

Hercule Poirot murmured:

"That is what makes the problem so peculiarly interesting. The schoolgirl vanishes into thin air just outside Amiens. She reappears from thin air also just outside Amiens. Where has she been in the meantime?"

Inspector Hearn shook his head.

"It sounds mad, put like that. Oh! By the way, they told me you were asking something about shoes—the girl's shoes. She had her shoes on all right when she was found, but there was a pair of shoes on the line, a signalman found them. Took 'em home with him, as they seemed in good condition. Stout black laced walking shoes."

"Ah," said Poirot. He looked gratified.

Inspector Hearn said curiously:

"I don't get the meaning of the shoes, sir? Do they mean anything?"

"They confirm a theory," said Hercule Poirot. "A theory of how the conjuring trick was done."

# 4

Miss Pope's establishment was, like many other establishments of the same kind, situated in Neuilly. Hercule Poirot, staring up at its respectable façade, was suddenly submerged by a flow of girls emerging from its portals.

He counted twenty-five of them, all dressed alike in dark blue coats and skirts with uncomfortable looking British hats of dark blue velour on their heads, round which was tied the distinctive purple and gold of Miss Pope's choice. They were of ages varying from fourteen to eighteen, thick and thin, fair and dark, awkward and graceful. At the end, walking with one of the younger girls, was a gray-haired, fussy-looking woman whom Poirot judged to be Miss Burshaw.

Poirot stood looking after them a minute, then he rang the bell and asked for Miss Pope.

Miss Lavinia Pope was a very different person from her second in command, Miss Burshaw. Miss Pope had personality. Miss Pope was awe-inspiring. Even should Miss Pope unbend graciously to parents, she would still retain that obvious superiority to the rest of the world which is such a powerful asset to a schoolmistress.

Her grey hair was dressed with distinction, her costume was severe but chic. She was competent and omniscient.

The room in which she received Poirot was the room of a woman of culture. It had graceful furniture, flowers, some framed signed photographs of those of Miss Pope's pupils who were of note in the world—many of them in their presentation gowns and feathers. On the walls hung reproductions of the world's artistic masterpieces and some good water-colour sketches. The whole place was clean and polished to the last degree. No speck of dust, one felt, would have the temerity to deposit itself in such a shrine.

Miss Pope received Poirot with the competence of one whose judgment seldom fails.

"M. Hercule Poirot? I know your name, of course. I suppose you have come about this very unfortunate affair of Winnie King. A most distressing incident."

Miss Pope did not look distressed. She took disaster as it should be taken, dealing with it competently and thereby reducing it almost to insignificance.

"Such a thing," said Miss Pope, "has never occurred before."

"And never will again!" her manner seemed to say.

Hercule Poirot said:

"It was the girl's first term here, was it not?"

"It was."

"You had had a preliminary interview with Winnie—and with her parents?"

"Not recently. Two years ago, I was staying near Cranchester—with the Bishop, as a matter of fact—"

Miss Pope's manner said:

("Mark this, please. I am the kind of person who stays with Bishops!")

"While I was there I made the acquaintance of Canon and Mrs. King. Mrs. King, alas, is an invalid. I met Winnie then. A very well brought-up girl, with a decided taste for art. I told Mrs. King that I should be happy to receive her here in a year or two—when her general studies were completed. We specialize here, M. Poirot, in art and music. The girls are taken to the opera, to the Comédie Française, they attend lectures at the Louvre. The very best masters come here to instruct them in music, singing, and painting. The broader culture, that is our aim."

Miss Pope remembered suddenly that Poirot was not a parent and added abruptly:

"What can I do for you, M. Poirot?"

"I would be glad to know what is the present position regarding Winnie?"

"Canon King has come over to Amiens and is taking Winnie back with him. The wisest thing to do after the shock the child has sustained."

She went on:

"We do not take delicate girls here. We have no special facilities for looking after invalids. I told the canon that in my opinion he would do well to take the child home with him."

Hercule Poirot asked bluntly:

"What, in your opinion, actually occurred, Miss Pope?"

"I have not the slightest idea, M. Poirot. The whole thing, as reported to me, sounds quite incredible. I really cannot see that the member of my staff who was in charge of the girls was in any way to blame— except that she might, perhaps, have discovered the girl's absence sooner."

Poirot said:

"You have received a visit, perhaps, from the police?"

A faint shiver passed over Miss Pope's aristocratic form. She said glacially:

"A Monsieur Lefarge of the Préfecture called to see me, to see if I could throw any light upon the situation. Naturally I was unable to do so. He then demanded to inspect Winnie's trunk which had, of course, arrived here with those of the other girls. I told him that that had already been called for by another member of the police. Their departments, I fancy, must overlap. I got a telephone call, shortly afterwards, insisting that I had not turned over all Winnie's possessions to them. I was extremely short with them over that. One must not submit to being bullied by officialdom."

Poirot drew a long breath. He said:

"You have a spirited nature. I admire you for it, mademoiselle. I presume that Winnie's trunk had been unpacked on arrival?"

Miss Pope looked a little put out of countenance.

"Routine," she said. "We live strictly by routine. The girls are unpacked for on arrival and their things put away in the way I expect them to be kept. Winnie's things were unpacked with those of the other girls. Naturally, they were afterwards repacked, so that her trunk was handed over exactly as it had arrived."

Poirot said:

*"Exactly?"*

He strolled to the wall.

"Surely this is a picture of the famous Cranchester Bridge with the Cathedral showing in the distance."

"You are quite right, M. Poirot. Winnie had evidently painted that to bring to me as a surprise. It was in her trunk with a wrapper round it and *For Miss Pope from Winnie* written on it. Very charming of the child."

"Ah!" said Poirot. "And what do you think of it—as a painting?"

He himself had seen many pictures of Cranchester Bridge. It was a subject that could always be found represented at the Academy each year—sometimes as an oil painting—sometimes in the watercolour room. He had seen it painted well, painted in a mediocre fashion, painted boringly. But he had never seen it quite as crudely represented as in the present example.

Miss Pope was smiling indulgently.

She said:

"One must not discourage one's girls, M. Poirot. Winnie will be stimulated to do better work, of course."

Poirot said thoughtfully:

"It would have been more natural, would it not, for her to do a watercolour?"

"Yes. I did not know she was attempting to paint in oils."

"Ah," said Hercule Poirot. "You will permit me, mademoiselle?"

He unhooked the picture and took it to the window. He examined it, then, looking up, he said:

"I am going to ask you, mademoiselle, to give me this picture."

"Well, really, M. Poirot—"

"You cannot pretend that you are very attached to it. The painting is abominable."

"Oh, it has no artistic merit, I agree. But it is a pupil's work and—"

"I assure you, mademoiselle, that it is a most unsuitable picture to have hanging upon your wall."

"I don't know why you should say that, M. Poirot."

"I will prove it to you in a moment."

He took a bottle, a sponge and some rags from his pocket. He said:

"First I am going to tell you a little story, mademoiselle. It has a resemblance to the story of the Ugly Duckling that turned into a Swan."

He was working busily as he talked. The odour of turpentine filled the room.

"You do not perhaps go much to theatrical revues?"

"No, indeed, they seem to me so trivial. . . ."

"Trivial, yes, but sometimes instructive. I have seen a clever revue artist change her personality in the most miraculous way. In one sketch she is a cabaret star, exquisite and glamorous. Ten minutes later, she is an undersized, anemic child with adenoids, dressed in a gym tunic—ten minutes later still, she is a ragged gypsy telling fortunes by a caravan."

"Very possible, no doubt, but I do not see—"

"But I am showing you how the conjuring trick was worked on the train. Winnie, the schoolgirl, with her fair plaits, her spectacles, her disfiguring dental plate—goes into the *toilette*. She emerges a quarter of an hour later—to use the words of Detective Inspector Hearn—as 'a flashy piece of goods.' Sheer silk stockings, high-heeled shoes—a mink coat to cover a school uniform, a daring little piece of velvet called a hat perched on her curls—and a face—oh, yes, a face. Rouge, powder, lipstick, mascara! What is the real face of that quick-change *artiste* really like? Probably only the good God knows! But, you, mademoiselle, you yourself, you have often seen how the awkward schoolgirl changes almost miraculously into the attractive and well-groomed debutante."

Miss Pope gasped.

"Do you mean that Winnie King disguised herself as—"

"Not Winnie King—no. Winnie was kidnapped on the way across London. Our quick-change *artiste* took her place. Miss Burshaw had never seen Winnie King—How was she to know that the schoolgirl with the lank plaits and the brace on her teeth was not Winnie King at all? So far, so good, but the impostor could not afford actually to arrive here, since you were acquainted with the real Winnie. So hey presto, Winnie disappears in the *toilette* and emerges as wife to a man called Jim Elliot whose passport includes a wife! The fair plaits, the spectacles, the lisle thread stockings, the dental plate—all that can go into a small space. But the thick unglamorous shoes and the hat—that very unyielding British hat—have to be disposed of elsewhere—they go out of the window. Later, the real Winnie is brought across the channel—no one is looking for a sick, half-doped child being brought from England to France—and is quietly deposited from a car by the side of the main road. If she has been doped all along with scopolamine, she will remember very little of what has occurred."

Miss Pope was staring at Poirot. She demanded:

"But *why?* What would be the *reason* of such a senseless masquerade?"

Poirot replied gravely:

"Winnie's luggage! These people wanted to smuggle something from England into France—something that every customs man was on the lookout for—in fact, stolen goods. But what place is safer than a schoolgirl's trunk? You are well known, Miss Pope, your establishment is justly famous. At the Gare du Nord the trunks of Mesdemoiselles the little *Pensionnaires* are passed *en bloc.* It is the well-known English school of Miss Pope! And then, after the kidnapping, what more natural than to send and collect the child's luggage—ostensibly from the Préfecture?"

Hercule Poirot smiled.

"But, fortunately, there was the school routine of unpacking trunks on arrival—and a present for you from Winnie—but not the same present that Winnie packed at Cranchester."

He came towards her.

"You have given this picture to me. Observe now, you must admit that it is not suitable for your select school!"

He held out the canvas.

As though by magic Cranchester Bridge had disappeared. Instead was a classical scene in rich dim colourings.

Poirot said softly:

"*The Girdle of Hyppolita.* Hyppolita gives her girdle to Hercules— painted by Rubens. A great work of art—*mais tout de même* not quite suitable for your drawing room."

Miss Pope blushed slightly.

Hyppolita's hand was on her girdle—she was wearing nothing else. . . . Hercules had a lion skin thrown lightly over one shoulder. The flesh of Rubens is rich voluptuous flesh. . . .

Miss Pope said, regaining her poise:

"A fine work of art. . . . All the same—as you say—after all, one must consider the susceptibilities of parents. Some of them are inclined to be narrow . . . if you know what I mean. . . ."

# 5

It was just as Poirot was leaving the house that the onslaught took place. He was surrounded, hemmed in, overwhelmed by a crowd of girls, thick, thin, dark and fair.

*"Mon Dieu!"* he murmured. "Here, indeed, is the attack by the Amazons!"

A tall fair girl was crying out:

"A rumour has gone round—"

They surged closer. Hercule Poirot was surrounded. He disappeared in a wave of young vigorous femininity.

Twenty-five voices arose, pitched in various keys but all uttering the same momentous phrase:

"M. Poirot, will you write your name in my autograph book . . . ?"

# X

# The Flock of Geryon

## I

"**I** REALLY do apologise for intruding like this, M. Poirot."

Miss Carnaby clasped her hands fervently round her handbag and leaned forward, peering anxiously into Poirot's face. As usual, she sounded breathless.

Hercule Poirot's eyebrows rose.

She said anxiously:

"You do remember me, don't you?"

Hercule Poirot's eyes twinkled. He said:

"I remember you as one of the most successful criminals that I have ever encountered!"

"Oh, dear me, M. Poirot, must you really say such things? You were so kind to me. Emily and I often talk about you, and if we see anything about you in the paper we cut it out at once and paste it in a book. As for Augustus, we have taught him a new trick. We say, 'Die for Sherlock Holmes, die for Mr. Fortune, die for Sir Henry Merrivale, and then die for M. Hercule Poirot' and he goes down and lies like a log—lies absolutely still without moving until we say the word!"

"I am gratified," said Poirot. "And how is *ce cher Auguste?*"

Miss Carnaby clasped her hands and became eloquent in praise of her Pekinese.

"Oh, M. Poirot, he's cleverer than ever. He knows *everything*. Do you know, the other day I was just admiring a baby in a pram and suddenly I felt a tug and there was Augustus trying his hardest to bite through his lead. Wasn't that clever?"

Poirot's eyes twinkled. He said:

"It looks to me as though Augustus shared these criminal tendencies we were speaking of just now!"

Miss Carnaby did not laugh. Instead, her nice plump face grew worried and sad. She said in a kind of gasp:

"Oh, M. Poirot, I'm so *worried.*"

Poirot said kindly:

"What is it?"

"Do you know, M. Poirot, I'm afraid—I really am afraid—that I must be a *hardened criminal*—if I may use such a term. Ideas come to me!"

"What kind of ideas?"

"The most extraordinary ideas! For instance, yesterday, a really most *practical* scheme for robbing a post office came into my head. I wasn't thinking about it—it just came! And another very ingenious way for evading custom duties. . . . I feel convinced—quite convinced—that it would work."

"It probably would," said Poirot drily. "That is the danger of your ideas."

"It has worried me, M. Poirot, very much. Having been brought up with strict principles, as I have been, it is *most* disturbing that such lawless—such really wicked—ideas should come to me. The trouble is partly, I think, that I have a good deal of leisure time now. I have left Lady Hoggin and I am engaged by an old lady to read to her and write her letters every day. The letters are soon done and the moment I begin reading she goes to sleep, so I am left just sitting there—with an idle mind—and we all know the use the devil has for idleness."

"Tcha, tcha," said Poirot.

"Recently I have read a book—a very modern book, translated from the German. It throws a most interesting light on criminal tendencies. One must, so I understand, sublimate one's impulses! That, really, is why I came to you."

"Yes?" said Poirot.

"You see, M. Poirot, I think that it is really not so much wickedness as a craving for excitement! My life has unfortunately been very humdrum. The—er—campaign of the Pekinese dogs, I sometimes feel, was the only time when I really lived. Very reprehensible, of course, but, as my book says, one must not turn one's back on the truth. I came to you, M. Poirot, because I hoped it might be possible to—to sublimate that craving for excitement by employing it, if I may put it that way, on the side of the angels."

"Aha," said Poirot. "It is then as a colleague that you present yourself?"

Miss Carnaby blushed.

"It is very presumptuous of me, I know. But you were so *kind*—"

She stopped. Her eyes, faded blue eyes, had something in them of the pleading of a dog who hopes against hope that you will take him for a walk.

"It is an idea," said Hercule Poirot slowly.

"I am, of course, not at all clever," explained Miss Carnaby. "But my powers of—of dissimulation are good. They have to be—otherwise one would be discharged from the post of companion immediately. And I have always found that to appear even stupider than one is occasionally has good results."

Hercule Poirot laughed. He said:

"You enchant me, mademoiselle."

"Oh, dear, M. Poirot, what a very kind man you are. Then you do encourage me to *hope?* As it happens, I have just received a small legacy—a very small one—but it enables my sister and myself to keep and feed ourselves in a frugal manner so that I am not absolutely dependent on what I earn."

"I must consider," said Poirot, "where your talents may best be employed. You have no idea yourself, I suppose?"

"You know, you must really be a thought reader, M. Poirot. I have been anxious lately about a friend of mine. I was going to consult you. Of course you may say it is all an old maid's fancy—just imagination. One is prone, perhaps, to exaggerate, and to see design where there may be only coincidence."

"I do not think that you would exaggerate, Miss Carnaby. Tell me what is on your mind."

"Well, I have a friend, a very dear friend, though I have not seen very much of her of late years. Her name is Emmeline Clegg. She married a man in the north of England and he died a few years ago, leaving her very comfortably off. She was unhappy and lonely after his death and I am afraid she is in some ways a rather foolish and perhaps credulous woman. Religion, M. Poirot, can be a great help and sustenance—but by that I mean orthodox religion."

"You refer to the Greek church?" asked Poirot.

Miss Carnaby looked shocked.

"Oh, no, indeed. Church of England. And though I do not approve of Roman Catholics, they are at least recognized. And the Wesleyans and Congregationalists—they are all well-known, respectable bodies. What I am talking about are these odd sects. They just spring up. They have a kind of emotional appeal but sometimes I have very grave doubts as to whether there is any true religious feeling behind them at all."

"You think your friend is being victimized by a sect of this kind?"

"I do. Oh, I certainly do! The Flock of the Shepherd, they call themselves. Their headquarters is in Devonshire—a very lovely estate by the sea. The adherents go there for what they term a retreat. That is a period of a fortnight—with religious services and rituals. And there are three big festivals in the year: the Coming of the Pasture, the Full Pasture, and the Reaping of the Pasture."

"Which last is stupid," said Poirot. "Because one does not reap pasture."

"The whole thing is stupid," said Miss Carnaby with warmth. "The whole sect centers on the head of the movement, the Great Shepherd, he is called. A Dr. Andersen. A very handsome-looking man, I believe, with a presence."

"Which is attractive to the women, yes?"

"I am afraid so," Miss Carnaby sighed. "My father was a very handsome man. Sometimes, it was most awkward in the parish. The rivalry in embroidering vestments—and the division of church work—"

She shook her head reminiscently.

"Are the members of the Great Flock mostly women?"

"At least three quarters of them, I gather. What men there are, are mostly cranks! It is upon the women that the success of the movement depends and—and on the funds they supply."

"Ah," said Poirot. "Now we come to it. Frankly, you think the whole thing is a ramp?"

"Frankly, M. Poirot, I do. And another thing worries me. I happen to know that my poor friend is so bound up in this religion that she has recently made a will leaving all her property to the movement."

Poirot said sharply:

"Was that—suggested to her?"

"In all fairness, no. It was entirely her own idea. The Great Shepherd had shown her a new way of life—so all that she had was to go on her death to the great Cause. What really worries me is—"

"Yes—go on—"

"Several very wealthy women have been among the devotees. In the last year three of them, no less, have died."

"Leaving all their money to this sect?"

"Yes."

"Their relations have made no protest? I should have thought it likely that there might have been litigation."

"You see, M. Poirot, it is usually lonely women who belong to this gathering. People who have no very near relations or friends."

Poirot nodded thoughtfully. Miss Carnaby hurried on.

"Of course, I've no right to suggest anything at all. From what I have been able to find out, there was nothing wrong about any of these deaths. One, I believe, was pneumonia following influenza, and another was attributed to gastric ulcer. There were absolutely no suspicious circumstances, if you know what I mean, and the deaths did not take place at Green Hills Sanctuary but at their own homes. I've no doubt it is quite all right, but all the same I—well—I shouldn't like anything to happen to Emmie."

She clasped her hands, her eyes appealed to Poirot.

Poirot himself was silent for some minutes. When he spoke there was a change in his voice. It was grave and deep.

He said:

"Will you give me, or will you find out for me, the names and addresses of these members of the sect who have recently died?"

"Yes, indeed, M. Poirot."

Poirot said slowly:

"Mademoiselle, I think you are a woman of great courage and determination. You have good histrionic powers. Would you be willing to undertake a piece of work that may be attended with considerable danger?"

"I should like nothing better," said the adventurous Miss Carnaby.

Poirot said warningly:

"If there is a risk at all, it will be a grave one. You comprehend— either this is a mare's nest or else it is serious. To find out which it is, it will be necessary for you yourself to become a member of the Great Flock. I would suggest that you exaggerate the amount of the legacy that you recently inherited. You are now a well-to-do woman with no very definite aim in life. You argue with your friend Emmeline about this religion she has adopted—assure her that it is all nonsense. She is eager to convert you. You allow yourself to be persuaded to go down to Green Hills Sanctuary. And there you fall a victim to the persuasive powers and magnetic influence of Dr. Andersen. I think I can safely leave that part to you?"

Miss Carnaby smiled modestly. She murmured:

"I think I can manage that all right!"

## 2

"Well, my friend, what have you got for me?"

Chief Inspector Japp looked thoughtfully at the little man who asked the question. He said ruefully:

"Not at all what I'd like to have, Poirot. I hate these long-haired religious cranks like poison. Filling up women with a lot of mumbojumbo. But this fellow's being careful. There's nothing one can get hold of. All sounds a bit batty but harmless."

"Have you learned anything about this Dr. Andersen?"

"I've looked up his past history. He was a promising chemist and got chucked out of some German university. Seems his mother was Jewish. He was always keen on the study of Oriental myths and religions, spent all his spare time on that and has written various articles on the subject—some of the articles sound pretty crazy to me."

"So it is possible that he is a genuine fanatic?"

"I'm bound to say it seems quite likely!"

"What about those names and addresses I gave you?"

"Nothing doing there. Miss Everitt died of ulcerative colitis. Doctor quite positive there was no hanky-panky. Mrs. Lloyd died of broncho-pneumonia. Lady Western died of tuberculosis. Had suffered from it many years ago—before she even met this bunch. Miss Lee died of typhoid—attributed to some salad she ate somewhere in the north of England. Three of them got ill and died in their own homes, and Mrs. Lloyd died in a hotel in the south of France. As far as those deaths go, there's nothing to connect them with the Great Flock or with Andersen's place down in Devonshire. Must be pure coincidence. All absolutely O.K. and according to Cocker."

Hercule Poirot sighed. He said:

"And yet, *mon cher,* I have a feeling that this is the tenth Labor of Hercules, and that this Dr. Andersen is the Monster Geryon whom it is my mission to destroy."

Japp looked at him anxiously.

"Look here, Poirot, you haven't been reading any queer literature yourself lately, have you?"

Poirot said with dignity:

"My remarks are, as always, apt, sound, and to the point."

"You might start a new religion yourself," said Japp, "with the creed: 'There is no one so clever as Hercule Poirot, Amen, D.C. Repeat ad lib'!"

# 3

"It is the peace here that I find so wonderful," said Miss Carnaby, breathing heavily and ecstatically.

"I told you so, Amy," said Emmeline Clegg.

The two friends were sitting on the slope of a hillside overlooking a deep and lovely blue sea. The grass was vivid green, the earth and the cliffs a deep glowing red. The little estate now known as Green Hills Sanctuary was a promontory comprising about six acres. Only a narrow neck of land joined it to the mainland so that it was almost an island.

Mrs. Clegg murmured sentimentally:

"The red land—the land of glow and promise—where threefold destiny is to be accomplished."

Miss Carnaby sighed deeply and said:

"I thought the Master put it all so beautifully at the service last night."

"Wait," said her friend, "for the festival tonight. The Full Growth of the Pasture!"

"I'm looking forward to it," said Miss Carnaby.

"You will find it a wonderful spiritual experience," her friend promised her.

Miss Carnaby had arrived at Green Hills Sanctuary a week previously. Her attitude on arrival had been: "Now what's all this nonsense? Really, Emmie, a sensible woman like you—etc., etc."

At a preliminary interview with Dr. Andersen, she had conscientiously made her position quite clear.

"I don't want to feel that I am here under false pretences, Dr. Andersen. My father was a clergyman of the Church of England and I have never wavered in my faith. I don't hold with heathen doctrines."

The big golden-haired man had smiled at her—a very sweet and understanding smile. He had looked indulgently at the plump, rather belligerent figure sitting so squarely in her chair.

"Dear Miss Carnaby," he said. "You are Mrs. Clegg's friend, and as such welcome. And, believe me, our doctrines are not heathen. Here all religions are welcomed, and all honoured equally."

"Then they shouldn't be," said the staunch daughter of the late Reverend Thomas Carnaby.

Leaning back in his chair, the Master murmured in his rich voice, "In my Father's House are many mansions. . . . Remember that, Miss Carnaby."

As they left the presence, Miss Carnaby murmured to her friend, "He really is a very handsome man."

"Yes," said Emmeline Clegg. "And so wonderfully spiritual."

Miss Carnaby agreed. It was true—she had felt it—an aura of unworldliness—of spirituality. . . .

She took a grip upon herself. She was not here to fall a prey to the fascination, spiritual or otherwise, of the Great Shepherd. She conjured up a vision of Hercule Poirot. He seemed very far away, and curiously mundane. . . .

"Amy," said Miss Carnaby to herself, "take a grip upon yourself. Remember what you are here for. . . ."

But as the days went on, she found herself surrendering only too easily to the spell of Green Hills. The peace, the simplicity, the delicious though simple food, the beauty of the services with their chants of Love and Worship, the simple moving words of the Master, appealing to all that was best and highest in humanity—here all the strife and ugliness of the world was shut out. Here was only Peace and Love. . . .

And tonight was the great summer Festival, the Festival of the Full Pasture. And at it, she, Amy Carnaby, was to become initiated—to become one of the Flock.

The Festival took place in the white glittering concrete building, called by the Initiates the Sacred Fold. Here the devotees assembled just before the setting of the sun. They wore sheepskin cloaks and had sandals on their feet. Their arms were bare. In the centre of the Fold on a raised platform stood Dr. Andersen. The big man, golden-haired and blue-eyed, with his fair beard and his handsome profile, had never seemed more compelling. He was dressed in a green robe and carried a shepherd's crook of gold.

He raised this aloft and a deathly silence fell on the assembly.

"Where are my sheep?"

The answer came from the crowd:

*"We are here, O Shepherd."*

"Lift up your hearts with joy and thanksgiving. This is the Feast of Joy."

*"The Feast of Joy and we are joyful."*

"There shall be no more sorrow for you, no more pain. All is joy!"

*"All is joy. . . ."*

"How many heads has the Shepherd?"

*"Three heads, a head of gold, a head of silver, a head of sounding brass."*

"How many bodies have the Sheep?"

*"Three bodies, a body of flesh, a body of corruption, and a body of light."*

"How shall you be sealed in the Flock?"

*"By the Sacrament of Blood."*

"Are you prepared for that Sacrament?"

*"We are."*

"Bind your eyes and hold forth your right arm."

The crowd obediently bound their eyes with the green scarves provided for the purpose. Miss Carnaby, like the rest, held her arm out in front of her.

The Great Shepherd moved along the lines of his Flock. There were little cries, moans of either pain or ecstasy.

Miss Carnaby, to herself, said fiercely:

"Most blasphemous, the whole thing! This kind of religious hysteria is to be deplored. I shall remain absolutely calm and observe the reactions of other people. I will not be carried away—I will not. . . ."

The Great Shepherd had come to her. She felt her arm taken, held, there was a sharp stinging pain like the prick of a needle. The Shepherd's voice murmured:

*"The Sacrament of Blood that brings joy. . . ."*

He passed on.

Presently there came a command.

"Unveil and enjoy the pleasures of the spirit!"

The sun was just sinking. Miss Carnaby looked round her. At one with the others, she moved slowly out of the Fold. She felt suddenly uplifted, happy. She sank down on a soft grassy bank. Why had she ever thought she was a lonely, unwanted middle-aged woman? Life was wonderful—she herself was wonderful! She had the power of thought—of dreaming. There was nothing that she could not accomplish!

A great rush of exhilaration surged through her. She observed her fellow devotees round her—they seemed suddenly to have grown to an immense stature.

*"Like trees walking . . ."* said Miss Carnaby to herself reverently.

She lifted her hand. It was a purposeful gesture—with it she could command the earth. Caesar, Napoleon, Hitler—poor miserable little fellows! They knew nothing of what she, Amy Carnaby, could do! Tomorrow she would arrange for World Peace, for International Brotherhood. There should be no more wars—no more poverty—no more disease. She, Amy Carnaby, would design a New World.

But there need be no hurry. Time was infinite. . . . Minute succeeded minute, hour succeeded hour! Miss Carnaby's limbs felt heavy, but her mind was delightfully free. It could roam at will over the whole universe. She slept—but even as she slept she dreamt. . . . Great spaces . . . vast buildings . . . a new and wonderful world. . . .

Gradually the world shrank, Miss Carnaby yawned. She moved her stiff limbs. What had happened since yesterday? Last night she had dreamt. . . .

There was a moon. By it, Miss Carnaby could just distinguish the figures on her watch. To her stupefaction the hands pointed to a quarter to ten. The sun, as she knew, had set at eight-ten. Only an hour and thirty-five minutes ago? Impossible. And yet—

"Very remarkable," said Miss Carnaby to herself.

# 4

Hercule Poirot said:

"You must obey my instructions very carefully. You understand?"

"Oh, yes, M. Poirot. You may rely on me."

"You have spoken of your intention to benefit the cult?"

"Yes, M. Poirot. I spoke to the Master—excuse me, to Dr. Andersen myself. I told him very emotionally what a wonderful revelation the whole thing had been—how I had come to scoff and remained to believe. I—really it seemed quite natural to say all these things. Dr. Andersen, you know, has a lot of magnetic charm."

"So I perceive," said Hercule Poirot drily.

"His manner was most convincing. One really feels he doesn't care about money at all. 'Give what you can,' he said smiling in that wonderful way of his, 'if you can give nothing, it does not matter. You are one of the Flock just the same.' 'Oh, Dr. Andersen,' I said, 'I am not so badly off as that. I have just inherited a considerable amount of money from a distant relative and though I cannot actually touch any of the money until the legal formalities are all complied with, there is one thing I want to do at once.' And then I explained that I was making a will and that I wanted to leave all I had to the Brotherhood. I explained that I had no near relatives."

"And he graciously accepted the bequest?"

"He was very detached about it. Said it would be many long years before I passed over, that he could tell I was cut out for a long life of joy and spiritual fulfilment. He really speaks most movingly."

"So it would seem."

Poirot's tone was dry. He went on:

"You mentioned your health?"

"Yes, M. Poirot. I told him that I had had lung trouble, and that it had recurred more than once, but that a final treatment in a sanitarium some years ago had, I hoped, quite cured me."

"Excellent!"

"Though why it is necessary for me to say that I am consumptive when my lungs are as sound as a bell I really cannot see."

"Be assured it is necessary. You mentioned your friend?"

"Yes. I told him (strictly in confidence) that dear Emmeline, besides the fortune she had inherited from her husband, would inherit an even larger sum shortly from an aunt who was deeply attached to her."

"*Eh bien,* that ought to keep Mrs. Clegg safe for the time being!"

"Oh, M. Poirot, do you really think there *is* anything wrong?"

"That is what I am going to endeavour to find out. Have you met a Mr. Cole down at the Sanctuary?"

"There was a Mr. Cole there last time I went down. A most peculiar man. He wears grass green shorts and eats nothing but cabbage. He is a very ardent believer."

"*Eh bien,* all progresses well—I make you my compliments on the work you have done—all is now set for the Autumn Festival."

## 5

"Miss Carnaby—just a moment."

Mr. Cole clutched at Miss Carnaby, his eyes bright and feverish.

"I have had a vision—a most remarkable vision. I really must tell you about it."

Miss Carnaby sighed. She was rather afraid of Mr. Cole and his visions. There were moments when she was decidedly of the opinion that Mr. Cole was mad.

And she found these visions of his sometimes very embarrassing. They recalled to her certain outspoken passages in that very modern German book on the subconscious mind which she had read before coming down to Devon.

Mr. Cole, his eyes glistening, his lips twitching, began to talk excitedly.

"I had been meditating—reflecting on the Fullness of Life, on the Supreme Joy of Oneness—and then, you know, my eyes were opened and I saw—"

Miss Carnaby braced herself and hoped that what Mr. Cole had seen would not be what he had seen last time—which had been, apparently, a Ritual Marriage in ancient Sumeria between a god and goddess.

"I saw—" Mr. Cole leant towards her, breathing hard, his eyes looking (yes, really they did) quite mad—"the Prophet Elijah descending from Heaven in his fiery chariot."

Miss Carnaby breathed a sigh of relief. Elijah was much better, she didn't mind Elijah.

"Below," went on Mr. Cole, "were the altars of Baal—hundreds and hundreds of them. A voice cried to me: 'Look, write and testify that which you shall see—'"

He stopped and Miss Carnaby murmured politely, "Yes?"

"On the altars were the sacrifices, bound there, helpless, waiting for the knife. Virgins—hundreds of virgins—young beautiful naked virgins—"

Mr. Cole smacked his lips, Miss Carnaby blushed.

"Then came the ravens, the ravens of Odin, flying from the North. They met the ravens of Elijah—together they circled in the sky—they swooped, they plucked out the eyes of the victims—there was wailing and gnashing of teeth—and the Voice cried: 'Behold a Sacrifice—for on this day shall Jehovah and Odin sign blood brotherhood!' Then the Priests fell upon their victims, they raised their knives—they mutilated their victims—"

Desperately Miss Carnaby broke away from her tormentor who was now slavering at the mouth in a kind of sadistic fervour:

"Excuse me one moment."

She hastily accosted Lipscomb, the man who occupied the Lodge which gave admission to Green Hills and who providentially happened to be passing.

"I wonder," she said, "if you have found a brooch of mine. I must have dropped it somewhere about the grounds."

Lipscomb, who was a man immune from the general sweetness and light of Green Hills, merely growled that he hadn't seen any brooch. It wasn't his work to go about looking for things. He tried to shake off Miss Carnaby but she accompanied him, babbling about her brooch, till she had put a safe distance between herself and the fervour of Mr. Cole.

At that moment, the Master himself came out of the Great Fold and, emboldened by his benign smile, Miss Carnaby ventured to speak her mind to him.

Did he think that Mr. Cole was quite—was quite—

The Master laid a hand on her shoulder.

"You must cast out Fear," he said. "Perfect Love casteth out Fear. . . ."

"But I think Mr. Cole is mad. Those visions he has—"

"As yet," said the Master, "he sees Imperfectly . . . through the Glass of his own Carnal Nature. But the day will come when he shall see Spiritually—Face to Face."

Miss Carnaby was abashed. Of course, put like that— She rallied to make a smaller protest.

"And really," she said, "need Lipscomb be so abominably rude?"

Again the Master gave his Heavenly Smile.

"Lipscomb," he said, "is a faithful watchdog. He is a crude—a primitive soul—but faithful—utterly faithful."

He strode on. Miss Carnaby saw him meet Mr. Cole, pause, put a hand on Mr. Cole's shoulder. She hoped that the Master's influence might alter the scope of future visions.

In any case, it was only a week now to the Autumn Festival.

# 6

On the afternoon preceding the Festival, Miss Carnaby met Hercule Poirot in a small teashop in the sleepy little town of Newton Woodbury. Miss Carnaby was flushed and even more breathless than usual. She sat sipping tea and crumbling a rock bun between her fingers.

Poirot asked several questions to which she replied monosyllabically. Then he said:

"How many will there be at the Festival?"

"I think a hundred and twenty. Emmeline is there, of course, and Mr. Cole—really he has been very odd lately. He has visions. He described some of them to me—really most peculiar—I hope, I do hope, he is not insane. Then there will be quite a lot of new members—nearly twenty."

"Good. You know what you have to do?"

There was a moment's pause before Miss Carnaby said in a rather odd voice:

"I know what you told me, M. Poirot. . . ."

*"Très bien!"*

Then Amy Carnaby said clearly and distinctly:

"But I am not going to do it."

Hercule Poirot stared at her. Miss Carnaby rose to her feet. Her voice came fast and hysterical.

"You sent me here to spy on Dr. Andersen. You suspected him of all sorts of things. But he is a wonderful man—a great Teacher. I believe in him heart and soul! And I am not going to do your spying work any more, M. Poirot! I am one of the Sheep of the Shepherd. The Master has a new passage for the World and from now on, I belong to him body and soul. And I'll pay for my own tea, please."

With which slight anticlimax Miss Carnaby planked down one and threepence and rushed out of the teashop.

*"Nom d'un nom d'un nom,"* said Hercule Poirot.

The waitress had to ask him twice before he realized that she was presenting the bill. He met the interested stare of a surly-looking man at the next table, flushed, paid the check and got up and went out. He was thinking furiously.

# 7

Once again the Sheep were assembled in the Great Fold. The Ritual Questions and Answers had been chanted.

"Are you prepared for the Sacrament?"

*"We are."*

"Bind your eyes and hold out your right arm."

The Great Shepherd, magnificent in his green robe, moved along the waiting lines. Mr. Cole, next to Miss Carnaby, gave a gulp of painful ecstasy as the needle pierced his flesh.

The Great Shepherd stood by Miss Carnaby. His hands touched her arm—

"No, you don't. None of that. . . ."

Words incredible—unprecedented. A scuffle, a roar of anger. Green veils were torn from eyes—to see an unbelievable sight—the Great Shepherd struggling in the grasp of the sheep-skinned Mr. Cole aided by another devotee.

In rapid professional tones, the erstwhile Mr. Cole was saying:

"—and I have here a warrant for your arrest. I must warn you that anything you say may be used in evidence at your trial."

There were other figures now at the door of the Sheepfold—blue uniformed figures.

Someone cried:

"It's the police. They're taking the Master away. They're taking the Master. . . ."

Everyone was shocked—horrified. . . . To them the Great Shepherd was a martyr, suffering, as all great teachers suffer, from the ignorance and persecution of the outside world. . . .

Meanwhile Detective Inspector Cole was carefully packing up the hypodermic syringe that had fallen from the Great Shepherd's hand.

# 8

"My brave colleague!"

Poirot shook Miss Carnaby warmly by the hand and introduced her to Chief Inspector Japp.

"First-class work, Miss Carnaby," said Chief Inspector Japp. "We couldn't have done it without you and that's a fact."

"Oh, dear!" Miss Carnaby was fluttered. "It's so kind of you to say so. And I'm afraid, you know, that I've really enjoyed it all. The excitement, you know, and playing my part. I got quite carried away sometimes. I really felt I was one of those foolish women."

"That's where your success lay," said Japp. "You were the genuine article. Nothing less would have taken that gentleman in! He's a pretty astute scoundrel."

Miss Carnaby turned to Poirot.

"That was a terrible moment in the teashop. I didn't know what to do. I just had to act on the spur of the moment."

"You were magnificent," said Poirot warmly. "For a moment I thought that either you or I had taken leave of our senses. I thought for one little minute that you meant it."

"It was such a shock," said Miss Carnaby. "Just when we had been talking confidentially. I saw in the glass that Lipscomb, who keeps the Lodge of the Sanctuary, was sitting at the table behind me. I don't know now if it was an accident or if he had actually followed me. As I say, I had to do the best I could on the spur of the minute and trust that you would understand."

Poirot smiled.

"I did understand. There was only one person sitting near enough to overhear anything we said and as soon as I left the teashop I arranged to have him followed when he came out. When he went straight back to the Sanctuary I understood that I could rely on you and that you would not let me down—but I was afraid because it increased the danger for you."

"Was—was there really danger? What was there in the syringe?"

Japp said:

"Will you explain, or shall I?"

Poirot said gravely:

"Mademoiselle, this Dr. Andersen had perfected a scheme of exploitation and murder—scientific murder. Most of his life has been spent in bacteriological research. Under a different name he has a chemical laboratory in Sheffield. There he makes cultures of various bacilli. It was his practice, at the Festivals, to inject into his followers a small but sufficient dose of Cannabis Indica—which is also known by the names of Hashish or Bhang. This gives delusions of grandeur and pleasurable enjoyment. It bound his devotees to him. These were the Spiritual Joys that he promised them."

"Most remarkable," said Miss Carnaby. "Really a most remarkable sensation."

Hercule Poirot nodded.

"That was his general stock in trade—a dominating personality, the power of creating mass hysteria and the reactions produced by this drug. But he had a second aim in view.

"Lonely women, in their gratitude and fervour, made wills leaving their money to the Cult. One by one, these women died. They died in their own homes and apparently of natural causes. Without being too technical I will try to explain. It is possible to make intensified cultures of certain bacteria. The bacillus Coli Communis, for instance, the cause of ulcerative colitis. Typhoid bacilli can be introduced into the system. So can the Pneumococcus. There is also what is termed Old Tuberculin which is harmless to a healthy person but which stimulates any old tubercular lesion into activity. You perceive the cleverness of the man? These deaths would occur in different parts of the country, with different doctors attending them and without any risk of arousing suspicion. He had also, I gather, cultivated a substance which had the power of delaying but intensifying the action of the chosen bacillus."

"He's a devil, if there ever was one!" said Chief Inspector Japp.

Poirot went on:

"By my orders, you told him that you were a tuberculous subject. There was Old Tuberculin in the syringe when Cole arrested him. Since you were a healthy person it would not have harmed you, which is why I made you lay stress on your tubercular trouble. I was terrified that even now he *might* choose some other germ, but I respected your courage and I had to let you take the risk."

"Oh, that's all right," said Miss Carnaby brightly. "I don't mind taking risks. I'm only frightened of bulls in fields and things like that. But have you enough evidence to convict this dreadful person?"

Japp grinned.

"Plenty of evidence," he said. "We've got his laboratory and his cultures and the whole layout!"

Poirot said:

"It is possible, I think, that he has committed a long line of murders. I may say that it was not because his mother was a Jewess that he was dismissed from that German university. That merely made a convenient tale to account for his arrival here and to gain sympathy for him. Actually, I fancy, he is of pure Aryan blood." Miss Carnaby sighed.

*"Qu'est ce qu'il y a?"* asked Poirot.

"I was thinking," said Miss Carnaby, "of a marvellous dream I had at the First Festival—hashish, I suppose. I arranged the whole world so beautifully! No wars, no poverty, no ill health, no ugliness . . . no crime. . . ."

"It must have been a fine dream," said Japp enviously.

Miss Carnaby jumped up. She said:

"I must get home. Emily has been so anxious. And dear Augustus has been missing me terribly, I hear."

Hercule Poirot said with a smile:

"He was afraid, perhaps, that, like him, you were going to 'die for Hercule Poirot'!"

# XI

# The Apples of
the Hesperides

## I

HERCULE Poirot looked thoughtfully into the face of the man behind the big mahogany desk. He noted the generous brow, the mean mouth, the rapacious line of the jaw and the piercing visionary eyes. He understood from looking at the man why Emery Power had become the great financial force that he was.

And his eyes falling to the long delicate hands, exquisitely shaped, that lay on the desk, he understood, too, why Emery Power had attained renown as a great collector. He was known on both sides of the Atlantic as a connoisseur of works of art. His passion for the artistic went hand in hand with an equal passion for the historic. It was not enough for him that a thing should be beautiful—he demanded also that it should have a tradition behind it.

Emery Power was speaking. His voice was quiet—a small distinct voice that was more effective than any mere volume of sound could have been.

"You do not, I know, take many cases nowadays. But I think you will take this one."

"It is, then, an affair of great moment?"

Emery Power said:

"It is of moment to me."

Poirot remained in an inquiring attitude, his head slightly on one side. He looked like a meditative robin.

The other went on.

"It concerns the recovery of a work of art. To be exact, a gold chased goblet, dating from the Renaissance. It is said to be the goblet used by Pope Alexander VI—Roderigo Borgia. He sometimes presented it to a favoured guest to drink from. That guest, M. Poirot, usually died."

"A pretty history," Poirot murmured.

"Its career has always been associated with violence. It has been stolen more than once. Murder has been done to gain possession of it. A trail of bloodshed has followed it through the ages."

"On account of its intrinsic value or for other reasons?"

"Its intrinsic value is certainly considerable. The workmanship is exquisite (it is said to have been made by Benvenuto Cellini). The design represents a tree round which a jewelled serpent is coiled and the apples on the tree are formed of very beautiful emeralds."

Poirot murmured with an apparent quickening of interest:

"Apples?"

"The emeralds are particularly fine, so are the rubies in the serpent, but of course the real value of the cup is its historical associations. It was put up for sale by the Marchese di San Veratrino in 1929. Collectors bid against each other and I secured it finally for a sum equalling (at the then rate of exchange) thirty thousand pounds."

Poirot raised his eyebrows. He murmured:

"Indeed a princely sum! The Marchese di San Veratrino was fortunate."

Emery Power said:

"When I really want a thing, I am willing to pay for it, M. Poirot."

Hercule Poirot said softly:

"You have no doubt heard the Spanish proverb. *'Take what you want—and pay for it, says God.'* "

For a moment the financier frowned—a swift light of anger showed in his eyes. He said coldly:

"You are by way of being a philosopher, M. Poirot."

"I have arrived at the age of reflection, monsieur."

"Doubtless. But it is not reflection that will restore my goblet to me."

"You think not?"

"I fancy action will be necessary."

Hercule Poirot nodded placidly.

"A lot of people make the same mistake. But I demand your pardon, Mr. Power, we have digressed from the matter in hand. You were saying that you had bought the cup from the Marchese di San Veratrino?"

"Exactly. What I have now to tell you is that it was stolen before it actually came into my possession."

"How did that happen?"

"The Marchese's Palace was broken into on the night of the sale and eight or ten pieces of considerable value were stolen, including the goblet."

"What was done in the matter?"

Power shrugged his shoulders.

"The police, of course, took the matter in hand. The robbery was recognized to be the work of a well-known international gang of thieves. Two of their number, a Frenchman called Dublay and an Italian called Riccovetti, were caught and tried—some of the stolen goods were found in their possession."

"But not the Borgia Goblet?"

"But not the Borgia Goblet. There were, as far as the police could ascertain, three men actually engaged in the robbery—the two I have just mentioned and a third, an Irishman named Patrick Casey. This last was an expert cat burglar. It was he who is said to have actually stolen the things. Dublay was the brains of the group and planned their coups; Riccovetti drove the car and waited below for the goods to be lowered down to him."

"And the stolen goods? Were they split up into three parts?"

"Possibly. On the other hand, the articles that were recovered were those of least value. It seems possible that the more noteworthy and spectacular pieces had been hastily smuggled out of the country."

"What about the third man, Casey? Was he never brought to justice?"

"Not in the sense you mean. He was not a very young man. His muscles were stiffer than formerly. Two weeks later he fell from the fifth floor of a building and was killed instantly."

"Where was this?"

"In Paris. He was attempting to rob the house of the millionaire banker, Duvauglier."

"And the goblet has never been seen since?"

"Exactly."

"It has never been offered for sale?"

"I am quite sure it has not. I may say that not only the police, but also private inquiry agents, have been on the lookout for it."

"What about the money you had paid over?"

"The Marchese, a very punctilious person, offered to refund it to me as the cup had been stolen from his house."

"But you did not accept?"

"No."

"Why was that?"

"Shall we say because I preferred to keep the matter in my own hands?"

"You mean that if you had accepted the Marchese's offer, the goblet, if recovered, would be his property, whereas now it is legally yours?"

"Exactly."

Poirot asked:

"What was there behind that attitude of yours?"

Emery Power said with a smile:

"You appreciate that point, I see. Well, M. Poirot, it is quite simple.

I thought I knew who was actually in possession of the goblet."

"Very interesting. And who was it?"

"Sir Reuben Rosenthal. He was not only a fellow collector but he was at the time a personal enemy. We had been rivals in several business deals—and on the whole I had come out the better. Our animosity culminated in this rivalry over the Borgia Goblet. Each of us was determined to possess it. It was more or less a point of honour. Our appointed representatives bid against each other at the sale."

"And your representative's final bid secured the treasure?"

"Not precisely. I took the precaution of having a second agent—ostensibly the representative of a Paris dealer. Neither of us, you understand, would have been willing to yield to the other, but to allow a third party to acquire the cup, with the possibility of approaching that third party quietly afterwards—that was a very different matter."

"In fact, *une petite déception.*"

"Exactly."

"Which was successful—and immediately afterwards Sir Reuben discovered how he had been tricked?"

Power smiled.

It was a revealing smile.

Poirot said:

"I see the position now. You believed that Sir Reuben, determined not to be beaten, deliberately commissioned the theft?"

Emery Power raised a hand.

"Oh, no, no! It would not be so crude as that. It amounted to this—shortly afterwards Sir Reuben would have purchased a Renaissance goblet, provenance unspecified."

"The description of which would have been circulated by the police?"

"The goblet would not have been placed openly on view."

"You think it would have been sufficient for Sir Reuben to *know* that he possessed it?"

"Yes. Moreover, if I had accepted the Marchese's offer—it would have been possible for Sir Reuben to conclude a private arrangement with him later, thus allowing the goblet to pass legally into his possession."

He paused a minute and then said:

"But by retaining the legal ownership, there were still possibilities left open to me of recovering my property."

"You mean," said Poirot bluntly, "that you could arrange for it to be stolen from Sir Reuben."

"Not stolen, M. Poirot. I should have been merely recovering my own property."

"But I gather that you were not successful?"

"For a very good reason. Rosenthal has never had the goblet in his possession."

"How do you know?"

"Recently there has been a merger of oil interests. Rosenthal's interests and mine now coincide. We are allies and not enemies. I spoke to him frankly on the subject and he at once assured me that the cup had never been in his possession."

"And you believe him?"

"Yes."

Poirot said thoughtfully:

"Then for nearly ten years you have been, as they say in this country, barking up the mistaken tree?"

The financier said bitterly:

"Yes, that is exactly what I have been doing!"

"And now—it is all to start again from the beginning?"

The other nodded.

"And that is where I come in? I am the dog that you set upon the cold scent—a very cold scent."

Emery Power said drily:

"If the affair were easy it would not have been necessary for me to send for you. Of course, if you think it impossible—"

He had found the right word. Hercule Poirot drew himself up. He said coldly:

"I do not recognize the word impossible, monsieur! I ask myself only—is this affair sufficiently interesting for me to undertake?"

Emery Power smiled again. He said:

"It has this interest—you may name your own fee."

The small man looked at the big man. He said softly:

"Do you then desire this work of art so much? Surely not!"

Emery Power said:

"Put it that I, like yourself, do not accept defeat."

Hercule Poirot bowed his head. He said:

"Yes—put that way—I understand. . . ."

## 2

Inspector Wagstaffe was interested.

"The Veratrino cup? Yes, I remember all about it. I was in charge of the business this end. I speak a bit of Italiano, you know, and I went over and had a powwow with the macaronis. It's never turned up from that day to this. Funny thing, that."

"What is your explanation? A private sale?"

Wagstaffe shook his head.

"I doubt it. Of course, it's remotely possible. . . . No, my explanation is a good deal simpler. The stuff was cached—and the only man who knew where it was is dead."

"You mean Casey?"

"Yes. He may have cached it somewhere in Italy, or he may have succeeded in smuggling it out of the country. But *he* hid it and wherever he hid it, there it still is."

Hercule Poirot sighed.

"It is a romantic theory. Pearls stuffed into plaster casts—what is the story—the Bust of Napoleon, is it not? But in this case it is not jewels—it is a large solid gold cup. Not so easy to hide that, one would think."

Wagstaffe said vaguely:

"Oh, I don't know. It could be done, I suppose. Under the floor boards—something of that kind."

"Had Casey a house of his own?"

"Yes—in Liverpool." He grinned. "It wasn't under the floor boards there. We made sure of that."

"What about his family?"

"Wife was a decent sort of woman—tubercular. Worried to death by her husband's way of life. She was religious—a devout Catholic—but couldn't make up her mind to leave him. She died a couple of years ago. Daughter took after her—she became a nun. The son was different—a chip off the old block. Last I heard of him he was doing time in America."

Hercule Poirot wrote in his little notebook. America. He said:

"It is possible that Casey's son may have known the hiding-place?"

"Don't believe he did. It would have come into the fences' hands by now."

"The cup might have been melted down."

"It might. Quite possible, I should say. But I don't know—its supreme value is to collectors—and there's a lot of funny business goes on with collectors—you'd be surprised! Sometimes," said Wagstaffe virtuously, "I think collectors haven't any morals at all."

"Ah! Would you be surprised if Sir Reuben Rosenthal, for instance, were engaged in what you describe as 'funny business'?"

Wagstaffe grinned.

"I wouldn't put it past him. He's not supposed to be very scrupulous where works of art are concerned."

"What about the other members of the gang?"

"Riccovetti and Dublay both got stiff sentences. I should imagine they'll be coming out about now."

"Dublay is a Frenchman, is he not?"

"Yes, he was the brains of the gang."

"Were there other members of it?"

"There was a girl—Red Kate she used to be called. Took a job as lady's maid and found out all about a crib—where stuff was kept and so on. She went to Australia, I believe, after the gang broke up."

"Anyone else?"

"Chap called Yougouian was suspected of being in with them. He's a dealer. Headquarters in Stamboul but he has a shop in Paris. Nothing proved against him—but he's a slippery customer."

Poirot sighed. He looked at his little notebook. In it was written: America, Australia, Italy, France, Turkey. . . .

He murmured:

"I'll put a girdle round the earth—"

"Pardon?" said Inspector Wagstaffe.

"I was observing," said Hercule Poirot, "that a world tour seems indicated."

# 3

It was the habit of Hercule Poirot to discuss his cases with his capable valet, George. That is to say, Hercule Poirot would let drop certain observations to which George would reply with the worldly wisdom which he had acquired in the course of his career as a gentleman's gentleman.

"If you were faced, Georges," said Poirot, "with the necessity of conducting investigations in five different parts of the globe, how would you set about it?"

"Well, sir, air travel is very quick, though some say as it upsets the stomach. I couldn't say myself."

"One asks oneself," said Hercule Poirot, "what would Hercules have done?"

"You mean the bicycle chap, sir?"

"Or," pursued Hercule Poirot, "one simply asks, what did he do? And the answer, Georges, is that he travelled energetically. But he was forced in the end to obtain information—as some say—from Prometheus—others from Nereus."

"Indeed, sir?" said George. "I never heard of either of those gentlemen. Are they travel agencies, sir?"

Hercule Poirot, enjoying the sound of his own voice, went on:

"My client, Emery Power, understands only one thing—action! But it is useless to dispense energy by unnecessary action. There is a golden rule in life, Georges, never do anything yourself that others can do for you.

"Especially," added Hercule Poirot, rising and going to the bookshelf, "when expense is no object!"

He took from the shelf a file labelled with the letter D and opened it at the words "Detective Agencies—Reliable."

"The modern Prometheus," he murmured. "Be so obliging, Georges, as to copy out for me certain names and addresses. Messrs. Hankerton, New York. Messrs. Laden & Bosher, Sydney. Signor Giovanni Mezzi, Rome. M. Nahum, Stamboul. Messrs. Roget et Franconard, Paris."

He paused while George finished this. Then he said:

"And now be so kind as to look up the trains for Liverpool."

"Yes, sir, you are going to Liverpool, sir?"

"I am afraid so. It is possible, Georges, that I may have to go even farther. But not just yet."

# 4

It was three months later that Hercule Poirot stood on a rocky point and surveyed the Atlantic Ocean. Gulls rose and swooped down again with long, melancholy cries. The air was soft and damp.

Hercule Poirot had the feeling, not uncommon in those who come to Inishgowlan for the first time, that he had reached the end of the world. He had never in his life imagined anything so remote, so desolate, so abandoned. It had beauty, a melancholy, haunted beauty, the beauty of a remote and incredible past. Here, in the west of Ireland, the Romans had never marched, tramp, tramp, tramp; had never fortified a camp; had never built a well-ordered, sensible, useful road. It was a land where common sense and an orderly way of life were unknown.

Hercule Poirot looked down at the tips of his patent leather shoes and sighed. He felt forlorn and very much alone. The standards by which he lived were here not appreciated.

His eyes swept slowly up and down the desolate coastline, then once more out to sea. Somewhere out there, so tradition had it, were the Isles of the Blest, the Land of Youth. . . .

He murmured to himself:

*The Apple Tree, the Singing and the Gold* . . .

And suddenly, Hercule Poirot was himself again—the spell was broken, he was once more in harmony with his patent leather shoes and natty dark grey gent's suiting.

Not very far away he had heard the toll of a bell. He understood that bell. It was a sound he had been familiar with from early youth.

He set off briskly along the cliff. In about ten minutes he came in sight of the building on the cliff. A high wall surrounded it and a great wooden door studded with nails was set in the wall. Hercule Poirot came to this door and knocked. There was a vast iron knocker. Then he cautiously pulled at a rusty chain and a shrill little bell tinkled briskly inside the door.

A small panel in the door was pushed aside and showed a face. It was a suspicious face, framed in starched white. There was a distinct moustache on the upper lip, but the voice was the voice of a woman; it was the voice of what Hercule Poirot called a *femme formidable*.

It demanded his business.

"Is this the Convent of St. Mary and All Angels?"

The formidable woman said with asperity:

"And what else would it be?"

Hercule Poirot did not attempt to answer that. He said to the dragon:

"I would like to see the Mother Superior."

The dragon was unwilling, but in the end she yielded. Bars were drawn back, the door opened and Hercule Poirot was conducted to a small bare room where visitors to the convent were received.

Presently a nun glided in, her rosary swinging at her waist.

Hercule Poirot was a Catholic by birth. He understood the atmosphere in which he found himself.

"I apologise for troubling you, *ma mère*," he said, "but you have here, I think, a *religieuse* who was, in the world, Kate Casey."

The Mother Superior bowed her head. She said:

"That is so. Sister Mary Ursula in religion."

Hercule Poirot said:

"There is a certain wrong that needs righting. I believe that Sister Mary Ursula could help me. She has information that might be invaluable."

The Mother Superior shook her head. Her face was placid, her voice calm and remote. She said:

"Sister Mary Ursula cannot help you."

"But I assure you—"

He broke off. The Mother Superior said:

"Sister Mary Ursula died two months ago."

## 5

In the saloon bar of Jimmy Donovan's Hotel, Hercule Poirot sat uncomfortably against the wall. The hotel did not come up to his ideas of what a hotel should be. His bed was broken—so were two of the window panes in his room—thereby admitting that night air which Hercule Poirot distrusted so much. The hot water brought him had been tepid and the meal he had eaten was producing curious and painful sensations in his inside.

There were five men in the bar and they were all talking politics. For the most part Hercule Poirot could not understand what they said. In any case, he did not much care.

Presently he found one of the men sitting beside him. This was a man of a slightly different class from the others. He had the stamp of the seedy townsman upon him.

He said with immense dignity:

"I tell you, sir. I tell you—Pegeen's Pride hasn't got a chance, not a chance . . . bound to finish right down the course—right down the course. You take my tip . . . everybody ought to take my tip. Know who I am, shir, do you know, I shay? Atlas, thatsh who I am—Atlas of the Dublin Sun. . . . Been tipping winnersh all the season. . . . Didn't I give Larry's Girl? Twenty-five to one—twenty-five to one. Follow Atlas and you can't go wrong."

Hercule Poirot regarded him with a strange reverence. He said, and his voice trembled:

"*Mon Dieu,* it is an omen!"

## 6

It was some hours later. The moon showed from time to time, peeping out coquettishly from behind the clouds. Poirot and his new friend had walked some miles. The former was limping. The idea crossed his mind that there were, after all, other shoes—more suitable to country walking than patent leather. Actually George had respectfully conveyed as much. "A nice pair of brogues," was what George had said.

Hercule Poirot had not cared for the idea. He liked his feet to look neat and well shod. But now, tramping along this stony path, he realized that there were other shoes. . . .

His companion said suddenly:

"Is it the way the priest would be after me for this? I'll not have a mortal sin upon my conscience."

Hercule Poirot said:

"You are only restoring to Caesar the things which are Caesar's."

They had come to the wall of the convent. Atlas prepared to do his part.

A groan burst from him and he exclaimed in low poignant tones that he was destroyed entirely!

Hercule Poirot spoke with authority.

"Be quiet. It is not the weight of the world that you have to support—only the weight of Hercule Poirot."

## 7

Atlas was turning over two new crisp five-pound notes.

He said hopefully:

"Maybe I'll not remember in the morning the way I earned this. I'm after worrying that Father O'Reilly will be after me."

"Forget everything, my friend. Tomorrow the world is yours."

Atlas murmured:

"And what'll I put it on? There's Working Lad, he's a grand horse, a lovely horse he is! And there's Sheila Boyne. 7 to 1 I'd get on her."

He paused.

"Was it my fancy now or did I hear you mention the name of a heathen god? Hercules, you said, and glory be to God, there's a Hercules running in the three-thirty tomorrow."

"My friend," said Hercule Poirot, "put your money on that horse. I tell you this, Hercules cannot fail."

And it is certainly true that on the following day Mr. Rosslyn's Hercules very unexpectedly won the Boynan Stakes, starting price 60 to 1.

## 8

Deftly Hercule Poirot unwrapped the neatly done up parcel. First the brown paper, then the wadding, lastly the tissue paper.

On the desk in front of Emery Power he placed a gleaming golden cup. Chased on it was a tree bearing apples of green emeralds.

The financier drew a deep breath. He said:

"I congratulate you, M. Poirot."

Hercule Poirot bowed.

Emery Power stretched out a hand. He touched the rim of the goblet, drawing his finger round it. He said in a deep voice:

"Mine!"

Hercule Poirot agreed.

"Yours!"

The other gave a sigh. He leaned back in his chair. He said in a businesslike voice:

"Where did you find it?"

Hercule Poirot said:

"I found it on an altar."

Emery Power stared.

Poirot went on:

"Casey's daughter was a nun. She was about to take her final vows at the time of her father's death. She was an ignorant but a devout girl. The cup was hidden in her father's house in Liverpool. She took it to the convent wanting, I think, to atone for her father's sins. She gave it to be used to the glory of God. I do not think that the nuns themselves ever realized its value. They took it, probably, for a family heirloom. In their eyes it was a chalice and they used it as such."

Emery Power said:

"An extraordinary story!" He added, "What made you think of going there?"

Poirot shrugged his shoulders.

"Perhaps—a process of elimination. And then there was the extraordinary fact that no one had ever tried to dispose of the cup. That looked, you see, as though it were in a place where ordinary material values did not apply. I remembered that Patrick Casey's daughter was a nun."

Power said heartily:

"Well, as I said before, I congratulate you. Let me know your fee and I'll write you a cheque."

Hercule Poirot said:

"There is no fee."

The other stared at him.

"What do you mean?"

"Did you ever read fairy stories when you were a child? The King in them would say: 'Ask of me what you will'?"

"So you are asking something?"

"Yes, but not money. Merely a simple request."

"Well, what is it? D'you want a tip for the markets?"

"That would be only money in another form. My request is much simpler than that."

"What is it?"

Hercule Poirot laid his hand on the cup.

"Send this back to the convent."

There was a pause. Then Emery Power said:

"Are you quite mad?"

Hercule Poirot shook his head.

"No, I am not mad. See, I will show you something."

He picked up the goblet. With his fingernail, he pressed hard into the open jaws of the snake that was coiled round the tree. Inside the cup a tiny portion of the gold chased interior slid aside leaving an aperture into the hollow handle.

Poirot said:

"You see? This was the drinking cup of the Borgia Pope. Through this little hole the poison passed into the drink. You have said yourself that the history of this cup is evil. Violence and blood and evil passions have accompanied its possession. Evil will perhaps come to you in your turn."

"Superstition!"

"Possibly. But why were you so anxious to possess this thing? Not for its beauty. Not for its value. You have a hundred—a thousand perhaps—beautiful and rare things. You wanted it to sustain your pride. You were determined not to be beaten. *Eh bien,* you are not beaten. You win! The goblet is in your possession. But now, why not make a great—a supreme gesture? Send it back to where it has dwelt in peace for nearly ten years. Let the evil of it be purified there. It belonged to the Church once—let it return to the Church. Let it stand once more on the altar, purified and absolved as we hope that the souls of men shall be also purified and absolved from their sins."

He leaned forward.

"Let me describe for you the place where I found it—the Garden of Peace, looking out over the Western Sea towards a forgotten Paradise of Youth and Eternal Beauty."

He spoke on, describing in simple words the remote charm of Inishgowlan.

Emery Power sat back, one hand over his eyes. He said at last:

"I was born on the west coast of Ireland. I left there as a boy to go to America."

Poirot said gently:

"I heard that."

The financier sat up. His eyes were shrewd again. He said, and there was a faint smile on his lips:

"You are a strange man, M. Poirot. You shall have your way. Take the goblet to the convent as a gift in my name. A pretty costly gift. Thirty thousand pounds—and what shall I get in exchange?"

Poirot said gravely:

"The nuns will have Masses said for your soul."

The rich man's smile widened—a rapacious, hungry smile. He said:

"So, after all, it may be an investment! Perhaps, the best one I ever made. . . ."

# 9

In the little parlour of the convent, Hercule Poirot told his story and restored the chalice to the Mother Superior.

She murmured:

"Tell him we thank him and we will pray for him."

Hercule Poirot said gently:

"He needs your prayers."

"Is he then an unhappy man?"

Poirot said:

"So unhappy that he has forgotten what happiness means. So unhappy that he does not know he is unhappy."

The nun said softly:

"Ah, a rich man. . . ."

Hercule Poirot said nothing—for he knew there was nothing to say. . . .

# XII

# The Capture of Cerberus

## I

HERCULE Poirot, swaying to and fro in the tube train, thrown now against one body, now against another, thought to himself that there were too many people in the world! Certainly there were too many people in the underground world of London at this particular moment (6:30 P.M.) of the evening. Heat, noise, crowd, contiguity—the unwelcome pressure of hands, arms, bodies, shoulders! Hemmed in and pressed around by strangers—and on the whole (he thought distastefully) a plain and uninteresting lot of strangers! Humanity seen thus en masse was not attractive. How seldom did one see a face sparkling with intelligence, how seldom a *femme bien mise!* What was this passion that attacked women for knitting under the most unpropitious conditions? A woman did not look her best knitting; the absorption, the glassy eyes, the restless, busy fingers! One needed the agility of a wild cat, and the willpower of a Napoleon to manage to knit in a crowded tube, but women managed it! If they succeeded in obtaining a seat, out came a miserable little strip of shrimp pink and click-click went the pins!

No repose, thought Poirot, no feminine grace! His elderly soul revolted from the stress and hurry of the modern world. All these young women who surrounded him—so alike, so devoid of charm, so lacking in rich, alluring femininity! He demanded a more flamboyant appeal. Ah! to see a *femme du monde, chic,* sympathetic, *spirituelle*—a woman with ample curves, a woman ridiculously and extravagantly dressed! Once there had been such women. But now—now—

The train stopped at a station; people surged out, forcing Poirot back onto the points of knitting pins; surged in, squeezing him into even more sardinelike proximity with his fellow passengers. The train started off again with a jerk, Poirot was thrown against a stout woman with knobbly parcels, said *"Pardon!"* bounced off again into a long,

angular man whose attaché case caught him in the small of the back.
He said *"Pardon!"* again. He felt his moustaches becoming limp and
uncurled. *Quel enfer!* Fortunately the next station was his!

It was also the station of what seemed to be about a hundred and
fifty other people, since it happened to be Piccadilly Circus. Like a
great tidal wave they flowed out onto the platform. Presently Poirot
was again jammed tightly on an escalator being carried upwards towards the surface of the earth.

Up, thought Poirot, from the Infernal Regions. . . . How exquisitely
painful was a suitcase rammed into one's knees from behind on an
ascending escalator!

At that moment, a voice cried his name. Startled, he raised his eyes.
On the opposite escalator, the one descending, his unbelieving eyes
saw a vision from the past. A woman of full and flamboyant form;
her luxuriant henna red hair crowned with a small plastron of straw
to which was attached a positive platoon of brilliantly feathered little
birds. Exotic-looking furs dripped from her shoulders.

Her crimson mouth opened wide, her rich foreign voice echoed
resoundingly. She had good lungs.

"It *is!*" she screamed. "But it is! *Mon cher Hercule Poirot!* We must
meet again! I insist!"

But Fate itself is not more inexorable than the behaviour of two
escalators moving in an inverse direction. Steadily, remorselessly, Hercule Poirot was borne upward, and the Countess Vera Rossakoff was
borne downwards.

Twisting himself sideways, leaning over the balustrade, Poirot cried
despairingly:

*"Chère madame*—where then can I find you?"

Her reply came to him faintly from the depths. It was unexpected,
yet seemed at the moment strangely apposite.

*"In Hell. . . ."*

Hercule Poirot blinked. He blinked again. Suddenly he rocked on
his feet. Unawares he had reached the top—and had neglected to
step off properly. The crowd spread out round him. A little to one
side a dense crowd was pressing onto the downward escalator. Should
he join them? Had that been the Countess's meaning? No doubt that
travelling in the bowels of the earth at the rush hour *was* hell. If
that had been the Countess's meaning, he could not agree with her
more. . . .

Resolutely Poirot crossed over, sandwiched himself into the descending crowd and was borne back into the depths. At the foot of the
escalator no sign of the Countess. Poirot was left with a choice of
blue, amber, and other lights to follow.

Was the Countess patronizing the Bakerloo or the Piccadilly line?

Poirot visited each platform in turn. He was swept about among surging crowds boarding or leaving trains, but nowhere did he espy that flamboyant Russian figure, the Countess Vera Rossakoff.

Weary, battered, and infinitely chagrined, Hercule Poirot once more ascended to ground level and stepped out into the hubbub of Piccadilly Circus. He reached home in a mood of pleasurable excitement.

It is the misfortune of small, precise men to hanker after large and flamboyant women. Poirot had never been able to rid himself of the fatal fascination the Countess held for him. Though it was something like twenty years since he had seen her last the magic still held. Granted that her make-up now resembled a scene painter's sunset, with the woman under the make-up well hidden from sight, to Hercule Poirot she still represented the sumptuous and the alluring. The little bourgeois was still thrilled by the aristocrat. The memory of the adroit way she stole jewelry roused the old admiration. He remembered the magnificent aplomb with which she had admitted the fact when taxed with it. A woman in a thousand—in a million! And he had met her again—and lost her!

"In hell," she had said. Surely his ears had not deceived him? She had said that?

But what had she meant by it? Had she meant London's Underground Railways? Or were her words to be taken in a religious sense? Surely, even if her own way of life made hell the most plausible destination for her after this life, surely—surely her Russian courtesy would not suggest that Hercule Poirot was necessarily bound for the same place?

No, she must have meant something quite different. She must have meant—Hercule Poirot was brought up short against bewilderment. What an intriguing, what an unpredictable woman! A lesser woman might have shrieked "The Ritz" or "Claridge's." But Vera Rossakoff had cried poignantly and impossibly, "Hell!"

Poirot sighed. But he was not defeated. In his perplexity he took the simplest and most straightforward course on the following morning. He asked his secretary, Miss Lemon.

Miss Lemon was unbelievably ugly and incredibly efficient. To her, Poirot was nobody in particular—he was merely her employer. She gave him excellent service. Her private thoughts and dreams were concentrated on a new filing system which she was slowly perfecting in the recesses of her mind.

"Miss Lemon, may I ask you a question?"

"Of course, M. Poirot." Miss Lemon took her fingers off the typewriter keys and waited attentively.

"If a friend asked you to meet her—or him—in Hell, what would you do?"

Miss Lemon, as usual, did not pause. She knew, as the saying goes, all the answers.

"It would be advisable, I think, to ring up for a table," she said.

Hercule Poirot stared at her in a stupefied fashion.

He said, staccato, "You—would—ring—up—for—a—table?"

Miss Lemon nodded and drew the telephone towards her.

"Tonight?" she asked, and taking assent for granted since he did not speak, she dialled briskly.

"Temple Bar 14578? Is that Hell? Will you please reserve a table for two. M. Hercule Poirot. Eleven o'clock."

She replaced the receiver and her fingers hovered over the keys of her typewriter. A slight—a very slight look of impatience was discernible upon her face. She had done her part, the look seemed to say, surely her employer could now leave her to get on with what she was doing?

But Hercule Poirot required explanations.

"What is it then, this Hell?" he demanded.

Miss Lemon looked slightly surprised.

"Oh, didn't you know, M. Poirot? It's a nightclub—quite new and very much the rage at present—run by some Russian woman, I believe. I can fix up for you to become a member before this evening quite easily."

Whereupon, having wasted (as she made obvious) quite time enough, Miss Lemon broke into a perfect fusillade of efficient typing.

At eleven that evening Hercule Poirot passed through a doorway over which a neon sign discreetly showed one letter at a time. A gentleman in red tails received him and took from him his coat.

A gesture directed him to a flight of wide shallow stairs leading downwards. On each step a phrase was written. The first one ran:

*"I meant well. . . ."*

The second:

*"Wipe the slate clean and start afresh. . . ."*

The third:

*"I can give it up any time I like. . . ."*

"The good intentions that pave the way to hell," Hercule Poirot murmured appreciatively. *"C'est bien imaginé, ça!"*

He descended the stairs. At the foot was a tank of water with scarlet lilies. Spanning it was a bridge, shaped like a boat. Poirot crossed by it.

On his left in a kind of marble grotto sat the largest and ugliest and blackest dog Poirot had ever seen! It sat up very straight and gaunt and immovable. It was perhaps, he thought (and hoped), not real. But at that moment the dog turned its ferocious and ugly head and from the depths of its black body a low, rumbling growl was emitted. It was a terrifying sound.

And then Poirot noticed a decorative basket of small round dog biscuits. They were labeled *"A sop for Cerberus!"*

It was on them that the dog's eyes were fixed. Once again the low rumbling growl was heard. Hastily Poirot picked up a biscuit and tossed it towards the great hound.

A cavernous red mouth yawned; then came a snap as the powerful jaws closed again. Cerberus had accepted his sop! Poirot moved on through an open doorway.

The room was not a big one. It was dotted with little tables, a space of dancing floor in the middle. It was lighted with small red lamps, there were frescoes on the walls, and at the far end was a vast grill at which officiated chefs dressed as devils with tails and horns.

All this Poirot took in before, with all the impulsiveness of her Russian nature, Countess Vera Rossakoff, resplendent in scarlet evening dress, bore down upon him with outstretched hands.

"Ah, you have come! My dear—my *very* dear friend! What a joy to see you again! After such years—so many—how many? No, we will not say how many! To me it seems but as yesterday. You have not changed—not in the least have you changed!"

"Nor you, *chère amie,*" Poirot exclaimed, bowing over her hand.

Nevertheless, he was fully conscious now that twenty years is twenty years. Countess Rossakoff might not uncharitably have been described as a ruin. But she was at least a spectacular ruin. The exuberance, the full-blooded enjoyment of life was still there, and she knew, none better, how to flatter a man.

She drew Poirot with her to a table at which two other people were sitting.

"My friend, my celebrated friend, M. Hercule Poirot," she announced. "He who is the terror of evildoers! I was once afraid of him myself, but now I lead a life of the extreme, the most virtuous dullness. Is it not so?"

The tall, thin, elderly man to whom she spoke said, "Never say dull, Countess."

"The Professor Liskeard," the Countess announced. "He who knows everything about the past and who gave me the valuable hints for the decorations here."

The archaeologist shuddered slightly.

"If I'd known what you meant to do!" he murmured. "The result is so appalling."

Poirot observed the frescoes more closely. On the wall facing him, Orpheus and his jazz band played, while Eurydice looked hopefully towards the grill. On the opposite wall Osiris and Isis seemed to be throwing an Egyptian underworld boating party. On the third wall some bright young people were enjoying mixed bathing in a state of nature.

"The Country of the Young," explained the Countess and added in the same breath, completing her introduction, "And this is my little Alice."

Poirot bowed to the second occupant of the table, a severe-looking girl in a check coat and skirt. She wore horn-rimmed glasses.

"She is very, very clever," said Countess Rossakoff. "She has a degree and she is a psychologist and she knows all the reasons why lunatics are lunatics! It is not, as you might think, because they are mad! No, there are all sorts of other reasons. I find that very peculiar."

The girl called Alice smiled kindly but a little disdainfully. She asked the professor in a firm voice if he would like to dance. He appeared flattered but dubious.

"My dear young lady, I fear I only waltz."

"This *is* a waltz," said Alice patiently.

They got up and danced. They did not dance well.

The Countess Rossakoff sighed. Following out a train of thought of her own, she murmured, "And yet she is not *really* bad-looking. . . ."

"She does not make the most of herself," said Poirot judicially.

"Frankly," cried the Countess, "I cannot understand the young people of nowadays. They do not try anymore to please—always, in my youth, I tried—the colours that suited me—a little padding in the frocks—the corset laced tight round the waist—the hair, perhaps, a more interesting shade—"

She pushed back the heavy Titian tresses from her forehead—it was undeniable that she, at least, was still trying and trying hard!

"To be content with what nature has given you, that—that is *stupid!* It is also arrogant! The little Alice, she writes pages of long words about sex, but how often, I ask you, does a man suggest to her that they should go to Brighton for the weekend? It is all long words and work, and the welfare of the workers, and the future of the world. It is very worthy, but I ask you, is it gay? And look, I ask you, how drab these young people have made the world! It is all regulations and prohibitions! Not so when I was young."

"That reminds me, how is your son, madame?" At the last moment he substituted "son," for "little boy," remembering that twenty years had passed.

The Countess's face lit up with enthusiastic motherhood.

"The beloved angel! So big now, such shoulders, so handsome! He is in America. He builds there—bridges, banks, hotels, department stores, railways, anything the Americans want!"

Poirot looked slightly puzzled.

"He is then an engineer? Or an architect?"

"What does it matter?" demanded the Countess. "He is adorable! He is wrapped up in iron girders, and machinery, and things called stresses. The kind of things that I have never understood in the least. But we adore each other—always we adore each other! And so for his sake I adore the little Alice. But, yes, they are engaged. They meet on a plane or a boat or a train, and they fall in love, all in the midst of talking about the welfare of the workers. And when she comes to London she comes to see me and I take her to my heart." The Countess clasped her arms across her vast bosom, "And I say—'You and Niki love each other—so I too love you—but if you love him why do you leave him in America?' And she talks about her 'job' and the book she is writing, and her career, and frankly I do not understand, but I have always said one must be tolerant." She added all in one breath, "And what do you think, *cher ami,* of all this that I have imagined here?"

"It is very well imagined," said Poirot, looking round him approvingly. "It is *chic!*"

The place was full and it had about it that unmistakable air of success which cannot be counterfeited. There were languid couples in full evening dress, Bohemians in corduroy trousers, stout gentlemen in business suits. The band, dressed as devils, dispensed hot music. No doubt about it, *"Hell"* had caught on.

"We have all kinds here," said the Countess. "That is as it should be, is it not? The gates of hell are open to all?"

"Except, possibly, to the poor?" Poirot suggested.

The Countess laughed.

"Are we not told that it is difficult for a rich man to enter the kingdom of heaven? Naturally, then, he should have priority in hell."

The professor and Alice were returning to the table. The Countess got up.

"I must speak to Aristide."

She exchanged some words with the head waiter, a lean Mephistopheles, then went round from table to table, speaking to the guests.

The professor, wiping his forehead and sipping a glass of wine, remarked:

"She is a personality, is she not? People feel it."

He excused himself as he went over to speak to someone at another table. Poirot, left alone with the severe Alice, felt slightly embarrassed as he met the cold blue of her eyes. He recognized that she was actually quite good-looking, but he found her distinctly alarming.

"I do not yet know your last name," he murmured.

"Cunningham. Dr. Alice Cunningham. You have known Vera in past days, I understand?"

"Twenty years ago it must be."

"I find her a very interesting study," said Dr. Alice Cunningham. "Naturally I am interested in her as the mother of the man I am going to marry, but I am interested in her from the professional standpoint as well."

"Indeed?"

"Yes. I am writing a book on criminal psychology. I find the night life of this place very illuminating. We have several criminal types who come here regularly. I have discussed their early life with some of them. Of course, you know all about Vera's criminal tendencies— I mean that she steals?"

"Why, yes—I know that," said Poirot, slightly taken aback.

"I call it the Magpie complex myself. She takes, you know, always glittering things. Never money. Always jewels. I find that as a child she was petted and indulged but very much shielded. Life was unendurably dull for her—dull and safe. Her nature demanded drama—it craved for *punishment*. That is at the root of her indulgence in theft. She wants the importance, the notoriety of being *punished!*"

Poirot objected, "Her life can surely not have been safe and dull as a member of the *ancien régime* in Russia during the Revolution?"

A look of faint amusement showed in Miss Cunningham's pale blue eyes.

"Ah," she said. "A member of the *ancien régime?* She has told you that?"

"She is undeniably an aristocrat," said Poirot staunchly, fighting back certain uneasy memories of the wildly varying accounts of her early life told him by the Countess herself.

"One believes what one wishes to believe," remarked Miss Cunningham, casting a professional eye on him.

Poirot felt alarmed. In a moment, he felt, he would be told what was *his* complex. He decided to carry the war into the enemy's camp. He enjoyed the Countess Rossakoff's society partly because of her aristocratic *provenance,* and he was not going to have his enjoyment spoiled by a spectacled little girl with boiled gooseberry eyes and a degree in psychology!

"Do you know what I find astonishes me?" he asked.

Alice Cunningham did not admit in so many words that she did *not* know. She contented herself with looking bored but indulgent.

Poirot went on:

"It amazes me that you—who are young, and who could look pretty if you took the trouble—well, it amazes me that you do *not* take the trouble! You wear the heavy coat and skirt with the big pockets as though you were going to play the game of golf. But it is not here, the golf links, it is the underground cellar with the temperature of 71 Fahrenheit, and your nose it is hot and shines, but you do not powder it, and the lipstick you put it on your mouth without interest, without emphasizing the curve of the lips! You are a woman, but you do not draw attention to the fact of being a woman. And I say to you '*Why Not*'? It is a pity!"

For a moment he had the satisfaction of seeing Alice Cunningham look human. He even saw a spark of anger in her eyes. Then she regained her attitude of smiling contempt.

"My dear M. Poirot," she said, "I'm afraid you're out of touch with the modern ideology. It is *fundamentals* that matter—not the trappings."

She looked up as a dark and very beautiful young man came towards them.

"This is a most interesting type," she murmured with zest. "Paul Varesco! Lives on women and has strange depraved cravings! I want him to tell me more about a nursery governess who looked after him when he was three years old."

A moment or two later she was dancing with the young man. He danced divinely. As they drifted near Poirot's table, Poirot heard her say, "And after the summer at Bognor she gave you a toy crane? A *crane*—yes, that's very suggestive."

For a moment Poirot allowed himself to toy with the speculation that Miss Cunningham's interest in criminal types might lead one day to her mutilated body being found in a lonely wood. He did not like Alice Cunningham, but he was honest enough to realize that the reason for his dislike was the fact that she was so palpably unimpressed by Hercule Poirot! His vanity suffered!

Then he saw something that momentarily put Alice Cunningham out of his head. At a table on the opposite side of the floor sat a fair-haired young man. He wore evening dress, his hair shone, his moustache was such as the Guards affect, his whole demeanor was that of one who lived a life of ease and pleasure. Opposite him sat the right kind of expensive girl. He was gazing at her in a fatuous and foolish manner. Anyone seeing them might have murmured, "The idle rich!" Nevertheless Poirot knew very well that the young man was neither rich nor idle. He was, in fact, Detective Inspector Charles Stevens, and it seemed probable to Poirot that Detective Inspector Stevens was here on business. . . .

## 2

On the following morning Poirot paid a visit to Scotland Yard to his old friend, Chief Inspector Japp.

Japp's reception of his tentative inquiries was unexpected.

"You old fox!" said Japp affectionately. "How you get on to these things beats me!"

"But I assure you I know nothing—nothing at all! It is just idle curiosity."

Japp said that Poirot could tell that to the Marines!

"You want to know all about this place *Hell?* Well, on the surface it's just another of these things. It's caught on! They must be making a lot of money, though of course the expenses are pretty high. There's a Russian woman ostensibly running it, calls herself the Countess Something or other—"

"I am acquainted with Countess Rossakoff," said Poirot coldly. "We are old friends."

"But she's just a dummy," Japp went on. "She didn't put up the money. It might be the head waiter chap, Aristide Paaopolous—he's got an interest in it—but we don't believe it's really his show either. In fact, we don't know *whose* show it is!"

"And Inspector Stevens goes there to find out?"

"Oh, you saw Stevens, did you? Lucky young dog landing a job like that at the taxpayers' expense! A fat lot he's found out so far!"

"What do you suspect there is to find out?"

"Dope! Drug racket on a large scale. And the dope's being paid for not in money, but in precious stones."

"Aha?"

"This is how it goes. Lady Blank—or the Countess of Whatnot—finds it hard to get hold of cash—and in any case doesn't want to draw large sums out of the bank. But she's got jewels—family heirlooms sometimes! They're taken along to a place for 'cleaning' or 'resetting'—there the stones are taken out of their settings and replaced with paste. The unset stones are sold over here or on the Continent. It's all plain sailing—there's been no robbery, no hue and cry after them. Say sooner or later it's discovered that a certain tiara or necklace is a fake? Lady Blank is all innocence and dismay—can't imagine *how* or *when* the substitution can have taken place—necklace has never been out of her possession! Sends the poor perspiring police off on wild goose chases after dismissed maids, or doubtful butlers, or suspicious window cleaners.

"But we're not quite so dumb as these social birds *think!* We had several cases come up one after another—and we found a common

factor—all the women showed signs of dope—nerves, irritability—
twitching, pupils of eyes dilated, etcetera. Question was: Where were
they getting the dope from and who was running the racket?"

"And the answer, you think, is this place *Hell?*"

"We believe it's the headquarters of the whole racket. We've discovered where the work on the jewelry is done—a place called Golconda
Limited—respectable enough on the surface, high-class imitation jewelry. There's a nasty bit of work called Paul Varesco—ah, I see you
know him?"

"I have seen him—in *Hell.*"

"That's where I'd like to see him—in the real place! He's as bad
as they make 'em—but women—even decent women—eat out of his
hand! He's got some kind of connection with Golconda, and I'm pretty
sure he's the man behind *Hell.* It's ideal for his purpose—everyone
goes there, society women, professional crooks—it's the perfect meeting place."

"You think the exchange—jewels for dope—takes place there?"

"Yes. We know the Golconda side of it—we want the other—the
dope side. We want to know who's supplying the stuff and where
it's coming from."

"And so far you have no idea?"

"I *think* it's the Russian woman—but we've no evidence. A few
weeks ago we thought we were getting somewhere. Varesco went
to the Golconda place, picked up some stones there and went straight
from there to *Hell.* Stevens was watching him, but he didn't actually
see him pass the stuff. When Varesco left, we picked him up—the
stones weren't on him. We raided the club, rounded up everybody!
Result, no stones, no dope!"

"A fiasco, in fact?"

Japp winced:

"You're telling me! Might have got in a bit of a jam, but luckily in
the roundup we got Peverel (you know, the Battersea murderer). Pure
luck, he was supposed to have got away to Scotland. One of our smart
sergeants spotted him from his photos. So all's well that ends well—
kudos for us—terrific boost for the club—it's been more packed than
ever before!"

Poirot said:

"But it does not advance the dope inquiry. There is, perhaps, a
place of concealment on the premises?"

"Must be. But we couldn't find it. Went over the place with a toothcomb. And between you and me, there's been an unofficial search as
well—" He winked. "Strictly on the Q.T. Spot of breaking and entering.
Not a success, our 'unofficial' man nearly got torn to pieces by that
ruddy great dog! It sleeps on the premises."

"Aha, Cerberus?"

"Yes. Silly name for a dog—to call it after a packet of salt."

"Cerberus," murmured Poirot thoughtfully.

"Suppose you try your hand at it, Poirot," suggested Japp. "It's a pretty problem and worth doing. I hate the drug racket, destroys people body and soul. That really *is* hell, if you like!"

Poirot murmured meditatively:

"It would round off things—yes. . . . Do you know what the twelfth labour of Hercules was?"

"No idea."

*"The Capture of Cerberus.* It is appropriate, is it not?"

"Don't know what you're talking about, old man, but remember, 'Dog eats man' is news." And Japp leaned back roaring with laughter.

# 3

"I wish to speak to you with the utmost seriousness," said Poirot.

The hour was early, the Club as yet nearly empty. The Countess and Poirot sat at a small table near the doorway.

"But I do not feel serious," she protested. *"La petite Alice,* she is always serious and, *entre nous,* I find it very boring. My poor Niki, what fun will he have? None."

"I entertain for you much affection," continued Poirot steadily. "And I do not want to see you in what is called the jam."

"But it is absurd what you say there! I am on the top of the world, the money it rolls in!"

"You own this place?"

The Countess's eye became slightly evasive.

"Certainly," she replied.

"But you have a partner?"

"Who told you that?" asked the Countess sharply.

"Is your partner Paul Varesco?"

"Oh! Paul Varesco! What an idea!"

"He has a bad—a criminal record. Do you realize that you have criminals frequenting this place?"

The Countess burst out laughing.

"There speaks the *bon bourgeois!* Naturally I realize! Do you not see that that is half the attraction of this place? These young people from Mayfair—they get tired of seeing their own kind round them in the West End. They come here, they see the criminals: the thief, the blackmailer, the confidence trickster—perhaps, even, the murderer—the man who will be in the Sunday papers next week! It is exciting, that—they think they are seeing life! So does the prosperous man who all the week sells the knickers, the stockings, the corsets! What a change from his respectable life and his respectable friends! And then, a further thrill—there at a table, stroking his moustache, is the Inspector from Scotland Yard—an Inspector in tails!"

"So you knew that?" said Poirot softly.

Her eyes met his and she smiled.

*"Mon cher ami,* I am not so simple as you seem to suppose!"

"Do you also deal in drugs here?"

"Ah, ça non!" The Countess spoke sharply. "That would be an abomination!"

Poirot looked at her for a moment or two, then he sighed.

"I believe you," he said. "But in that case it is all the more necessary that you tell me who really owns this place."

"I own it," she snapped.

"On paper, yes. But there is someone behind you."

"Do you know, *mon ami,* I find you altogether too curious. Is he not much too curious, Dou dou?"

Her voice dropped to a coo as she spoke the last words and she threw the duck bone from her plate to the big black hound who caught it with a ferocious snap of the jaws.

"What is it that you call that animal?" asked Poirot, diverted.

*"C'est mon petit Dou dou!"*

"But it is ridiculous, a name like that!"

"But he is adorable! He is a police dog! He can do anything—anything— Wait!"

She rose, looked round her, and suddenly snatched up a plate with a large succulent steak which had just been deposited before a diner at a nearby table. She crossed to the marble niche and put the plate down in front of the dog, at the same time uttering a few words in Russian.

Cerberus gazed in front of him. The steak might not have existed.

"You see? And it is not just a matter of *minutes!* No, he will remain like that for *hours* if need be!"

Then she murmured a word and like lightning Cerberus bent his long neck and the steak disappeared as though by magic.

Vera Rossakoff flung her arms around the dog's neck and embraced him passionately, rising on tiptoe to do so.

"See how gentle he can be!" she cried. "For me, for Alice, for his friends—they can do what they like! But one has but to give him the word and presto! I can assure you he would tear a—police inspector, for instance—into little pieces! Yes, into little pieces!"

She burst out laughing.

"I would have but to say the word—"

Poirot interrupted hastily. He mistrusted the Countess' sense of humor. Inspector Stevens might be in real danger.

"Professor Liskeard wants to speak to you."

The professor was standing reproachfully at her elbow.

"You took my steak," he complained. "Why did you take my steak? It was a good steak!"

## 4

"Thursday night, old man," said Japp. "That's when the balloon goes up. It's Andrews' pigeon, of course—Narcotic Squad—but he'll be delighted to have you horn in. No, thanks, I won't have any of your fancy *sirops*. I have to take care of my stomach. Is that whiskey I see over there? That's more the ticket!"

Setting his glass down, he went on:

"We've solved the problem, I think. There's another way out of that Club—and we've found it!"

"Where?"

"Behind the grill. Part of it swings round."

"But surely you would see—"

"No, old boy. When the raid started, the lights went out—switched off at the main—and it took us a minute or two to get them turned on again. Nobody got out the front way because it was being watched, but it's clear now that somebody could have nipped out by the secret way with the doings. We've been examining the house behind the Club—and that's how we tumbled to the trick."

"And you propose to do—what?"

Japp winked.

"Let it go according to plan—the police appear, the lights go out— and somebody's waiting on the other side of that secret door to see who comes through. This time we've got 'em!"

"Why Thursday?"

Again Japp winked.

"We've got the Golconda pretty well taped now. There will be stuff going out of there on Thursday. Lady Carrington's emeralds."

"You permit," said Poirot, "that I, too, make one or two little arrangements?"

Sitting at his usual small table near the entrance on Thursday night, Poirot studied his surroundings. As usual *Hell* was going with a swing!

The Countess was even more flamboyantly made up than usual, if that was possible. She was being very Russian tonight, clapping her hands and screaming with laughter. Paul Varesco had arrived. Sometimes he wore faultless evening dress, sometimes, as tonight, he chose to present himself in a kind of apache get-up, tightly buttoned coat, scarf round the neck. He looked vicious and attractive. Detaching himself from a stout middle-aged woman plastered with diamonds, he leaned over Alice Cunningham, who was sitting at a table writing busily in a little notebook, and asked her to dance. The stout woman scowled at Alice and looked at Varesco with adoring eyes.

There was no adoration in Miss Cunningham's eyes. They gleamed with pure scientific interest, and Poirot caught fragments of their conversation as they danced past him. She had progressed beyond the nursery governess and was now seeking information about the matron at Paul's preparatory school.

When the music stopped, she sat down by Poirot, looking happy and excited.

"Most interesting," she said. "Varesco will be one of the most important cases in my book. The symbolism is unmistakable. Trouble about the vests for instance—for vest read *hair shirt* with all its associations—and the whole thing becomes quite plain. He's a definitely criminal type but a cure *can* be effected—"

"That she can reform a rake," said Poirot, "has always been one of woman's dearest illusions!"

Alice Cunningham looked at him coldly.

"There is nothing *personal* about this, M. Poirot."

"There never is," said Poirot. "It is always pure disinterested altruism—but the object of it is usually an attractive member of the opposite sex. Are you interested, for instance, in where *I* went to school, or what was the attitude of the matron to *me?*"

"You are not a criminal type," said Miss Cunningham.

"Do you know a criminal type when you see one?"

"Certainly I do."

Professor Liskeard joined them. He sat down by Poirot.

"Are you talking about criminals? You should study the criminal code of Hammurabi, M. Poirot. 1800 B.C. Most interesting. *The man who is caught stealing during a fire shall be thrown into the fire.*"

He stared pleasurably ahead of him towards the electric grill.

"And there are older, Sumerian laws. *If a wife hateth her husband and saith unto him 'Thou art not my husband' they shall throw her into the river.* Cheaper and easier than the divorce court. But if a husband says that to his wife he only has to pay her a certain measure of silver. Nobody throws *him* in the river."

"The same old story," said Alice Cunningham. "One law for the man and one for the woman."

"Women, of course, have a greater appreciation of monetary value," said the professor thoughtfully. "You know," he added, "I like this place. I come here most evenings. I don't have to pay. The Countess arranged that—very nice of her—in consideration of my having advised her about the decorations, she says. Not that they're anything to do with me really—I'd no idea what she was asking me questions for— and naturally she and the artist have got everything *quite* wrong. I hope nobody will ever know I had the remotest connection with the dreadful things. I should never live it down. But she's a wonderful woman—rather like a Babylonian, I always think. The Babylonians were good women of business, you know—"

The professor's words were drowned in a sudden chorus. The word "Police" was heard—women rose to their feet, there was a babel of sound. The lights went out and so did the electric grill.

As an undertone to the turmoil, the Professor's voice went on tranquilly reciting various excerpts from the laws of Hammurabi.

When the lights went on again, Hercule Poirot was halfway up the wide, shallow steps. The police officers by the door saluted him, and he passed out into the street and strolled to the corner. Just around the corner, pressed against the wall, was a small and odoriferous man with a red nose. He spoke in an anxious, husky whisper.

"I'm 'ere, guv'nor. Time for me to do my stuff?"

"Yes. Go on."

"There's an awful lot of coppers about!"

"That is all right. They've been told about you."

"I 'ope they won't interfere, that's all?"

"They will not interfere. You're sure you can accomplish what you have set out to do? The animal in question is both large and fierce."

" 'E won't be fierce to me," said the little man confidently. "Not with what I've got 'ere! Any dog'll follow me to hell for it!"

"In that case," murmured Hercule Poirot, "he has to follow you out of *Hell!*"

# 5

In the small hours of the morning the telephone rang. Poirot picked up the receiver.

Japp's voice said:

"You asked me to ring you."

"Yes, indeed. *Eh bien?*"

"No dope—we got the emeralds."

"Where?"

"In Professor Liskeard's pocket."

"Professor Liskeard?"

"Surprises you, too? Frankly I don't know what to think. He looked as astonished as a baby, stared at them, said he hadn't the faintest idea how they got in his pocket, and dammit I believe he was speaking the truth! Varesco could have slipped them into his pocket easily enough in the blackout. I can't see a man like old Liskeard being mixed up in this sort of business. He belongs to all these high falutin' societies. Why he's even connected with the British Museum! The only thing he ever spends money on is books, and musty old secondhand books at that. No, he doesn't fit. I'm beginning to think we're wrong about the whole thing—there never has been any dope in that Club."

"Oh, yes there has, my friend. It was there tonight. Tell me, did no one come out through your secret way?"

"Yes, Prince Henry of Scandenberg and his equerry—he only arrived in England yesterday. Vitamian Evans, the Cabinet Minister. (Devil of a job being a Labour Minister, you have to be so careful! Nobody minds a Tory politician spending money on riotous living because the taxpayers think it's his own money—but when it's a Labour man the public feel it's *their* money he's spending! And so it is, in a manner of speaking.) Lady Beatrice Viner was the last—she's getting married the day after tomorrow to the priggish young Duke of Leominster. I don't believe any of that lot were mixed up in this."

"You believe rightly. Nevertheless, the dope *was* in the Club and someone took it out of the Club."

"Who did?"

"I did, *mon ami*," said Poirot, softly.

He replaced the receiver, cutting off Japp's spluttering noises, as a bell trilled out. He went and opened the front door. The Countess Rossakoff sailed in.

"If it were not that we are, alas, too old, how compromising this would be!" she exclaimed. "You see, I have come as you told me to do in your note. There is, I think, a policeman behind me, but he can stay in the street. And now, my friend, what is it?"

Poirot gallantly relieved her of her fox furs.

"Why did you put those emeralds in Professor Liskeard's pocket?" he demanded. *"Ce n'est pas gentille, ce que vous avez fait la!"*

The Countess' eyes opened wide.

"Naturally, it was in *your* pocket I meant to put the emeralds!"

"Oh, in *my* pocket?"

"Certainly. I cross hurriedly to the table where you usually sit—but the lights they are out and I suppose, by inadvertence, I put them in the professor's pocket."

"And why did you wish to put stolen emeralds in my pocket?"

"It seemed to me—I had to think quickly, you understand—the best thing to do!"

"Really, Vera, you are *impayable!*"

"But, dear friend, *consider!* The police arrive, the lights go out (our little private arrangement for the patrons who must not be embarrassed) *and a hand takes my bag off the table.* I snatch it back, but I feel through the velvet something hard inside. I slip my hand in, I find what I know by touch to be jewels and I comprehend at once who has put them there!"

"Oh, you do?"

"Of course I do! It is that *salaud!* It is that lizard, that monster, that double-faced, double-crossing squirming adder of a pig's son, Paul Varesco."

"The man who is your partner in *Hell?*"

"Yes, yes, it is he who owns the place, who put up the money. Until now I do not betray him—I can keep faith, me! But now that he double-crosses me, that he tries to embroil me with the police—ah! now I will spit his name out—yes, *spit* it out!"

"Calm yourself," said Poirot, "and come with me into the next room."

He opened the door. It was a small room and seemed for a moment to be completely filled with dog. Cerberus had looked out-size even in the spacious premises of *Hell.* In the tiny dining room of Poirot's service flat there seemed nothing else but Cerberus in the room. There was also, however, the small and odoriferous man.

"We've turned up here according to plan, guv'nor," said the little man in a husky voice.

"Dou dou!" screamed the Countess. "My angel Dou dou!"

Cerberus beat the floor with his tail—but he did not move.

"Let me introduce you to Mr. William Higgs," shouted Poirot, above the thunder of Cerberus' tail. "A master in his profession. During the brouhaha tonight," went on Poirot, "Mr. Higgs induced Cerberus to follow him up out of *Hell.*"

"*You* induced him?" The Countess stared incredulously at the small ratlike figure. "But *how? How?*"

Mr. Higgs dropped his eyes bashfully.

" 'Ardly like to say afore a lady. But there's things no dogs won't resist. Follow me anywhere a dog will if I want 'im to. Of course you understand it won't work the same way with bitches. No, that's different, that is."

The Countess Rossakoff turned on Poirot.

"But why? *Why?*"

Poirot said slowly:

"A dog trained for the purpose will carry an article in his mouth until he is commanded to loose it. He will carry it if need be for hours. Will you now tell your dog to drop what he holds?"

Vera Rossakoff stared, turned, and uttered two crisp words.

The great jaws of Cerberus opened. Then, it was really alarming, *Cerberus' tongue dropped out of his mouth.* . . .

Poirot stepped forward. He picked up a small package encased in pink spongebag rubber. He unwrapped it. Inside it was a packet of white powder.

"What is it?" the Countess demanded sharply.

Poirot said softly:

"*Cocaine.* Such a small quantity, it would seem—but enough to be worth thousands of pounds to those willing to pay for it. . . . Enough to bring ruin and misery to several hundred people. . . ."

She caught her breath. She cried out:

"And you think that *I*—but it is not so! I swear to you it is not so! In the past I have amused myself with the jewels, the *bibelots,* the little curiosities—it all helps one to live, you understand. And what I feel is, why not? Why should one person own a thing more than another?"

"Just what I feel about dogs," Mr. Higgs chimed in.

"You have no sense of right or wrong," said Poirot, sadly, to the Countess.

She went on:

"But *drugs—that, no!* For there one causes misery, pain, degeneration! I had no idea—no faintest idea—that my so charming, so innocent, so delightful little *Hell* was being used for *that* purpose!"

"I agrees with you about dope," said Mr. Higgs. "Doping of greyhounds—that's dirty, that is! I wouldn't never have nothing to do with anything like that, and I never *'ave* 'ad!"

"But say you believe me, my friend," implored the Countess.

"But of course I believe you! Have I not taken time and trouble to convict the real organizer of the dope racket? Have I not performed the twelfth Labor of Hercules and brought Cerberus up from Hell to prove my case? For I tell you this, I do not like to see my friends framed—yes, *framed*—for it was *you* who were intended to take the rap if things went wrong! It was in *your* handbag the emeralds would have been found and if anyone had been clever enough (like me) to suspect a hiding place in the mouth of a savage dog—*eh bien,* he is *your* dog, is he not? Even if he *has* accepted *la petite Alice* to the point of obeying her orders also! Yes, you may well open your eyes! From the first I did not like that young lady with her scientific jargon and her coat and skirt with the big pockets. Yes, *pockets.* Unnatural that any woman should be so disdainful of her appearance! And what does she say to me—that it is fundamentals that count! Aha! what is fundamental is *pockets*. Pockets, in which she can carry drugs and take away jewels—a little exchange easily made while she is dancing with her accomplice whom she pretends to regard as a psychological case. Ah, but what a cover! No one suspects the earnest, the scientific psychologist with a medical degree and spectacles. She can smuggle in drugs, and induce her rich patients to form the habit, and put up the money for a night club and arrange that it shall be run by someone with—shall we say, a little weakness in her past! But she despises Hercule Poirot, she thinks she can deceive him with her talk of nursery governesses and vests! *Eh bien,* I am ready for her. The lights go off. Quickly I rise from my table and go to stand by Cerberus. In the darkness I hear her come. She opens his mouth and forces in the package, and I—delicately, unfelt by her, I snip with a tiny pair of scissors a little piece from her sleeve."

Dramatically he produced a sliver of material.

"You observe—the identical checked tweed—and I will give it to Japp to fit it back where it belongs—and make the arrest—and say how clever once more has been Scotland Yard."

The Countess Rossakoff stared at him in stupefaction. Suddenly she let out a wail like a foghorn.

"But my Niki—my Niki. This will be terrible for him—" She paused. "Or do you think not?"

"There are a lot of other girls in America," said Hercule Poirot.

"And but for you his mother would be in prison—in *prison*—with her hair cut off—sitting in a cell—and smelling of disinfectant! Ah, but you are wonderful—*wonderful.*"

Surging forward she clasped Poirot in her arms and embraced him with Slavonic fervour. Mr. Higgs looked on appreciatively. The dog Cerberus beat his tail upon the floor.

Into the midst of this scene of rejoicing came the trill of a bell.

"Japp!" exclaimed Poirot, disengaging himself from the Countess' arms.

"It would be better, perhaps, if I went into the other room," said the Countess.

She slipped through the connecting door. Poirot started towards the door to the hall.

"Guv'nor," wheezed Mr. Higgs anxiously, "better look at yourself in the glass, 'adn't you?"

Poirot did so and recoiled. Lipstick and mascara ornamented his face in a fantastic medley.

"If that's Mr. Japp from Scotland Yard, 'e'd think the worst—sure to," said Mr. Higgs.

He added, as the bell pealed again, and Poirot strove feverishly to remove crimson grease from the points of his moustache: "What do yer want *me* to do—'ook it too? What about this 'ere 'Ell 'ound?"

"If I remember rightly," said Hercule Poirot, "Cerberus returned to Hell."

"Just as you like," said Mr. Higgs. "As a matter of fact I've taken a kind of fancy to 'im. . . . Still, 'e's not the kind I'd like to pinch—not permanent—too noticeable, if you know what I mean. And think what he'd cost me in shin of beef or 'orseflesh! Eats as much as a young lion, I expect."

"From the Nemean Lion to the Capture of Cerberus," murmured Poirot. "It is complete."

## 6

A week later Miss Lemon brought a bill to her employer.

"Excuse me, M. Poirot. Is it in order for me to pay this? *Leonora, Florist. Red Roses.* Eleven pounds, eight shillings and sixpence. Sent to Countess Vera Rossakoff, *Hell,* 13 End St., W.C.1."

As the hue of red roses, so were the cheeks of Hercule Poirot. He blushed, blushed to the eyeballs.

"Perfectly in order, Miss Lemon. A little—er tribute—to—to an occasion. The Countess' son has just become engaged in America—to the daughter of his employer, a steel magnate. Red roses are—I seem to remember—her favorite flower."

"Quite," said Miss Lemon. "They're very expensive this time of year."

Hercule Poirot drew himself up.

"There are moments," he said, "when one does not economize."

Humming a little tune, he went out of the door. His step was light, almost sprightly. Miss Lemon started after him. Her filing system was forgotten. All her feminine instincts were aroused.

"Good gracious," she murmured. "I wonder. . . . Really—at *his* age! . . . Surely not. . . ."

# THREE
# BLIND
# MICE

# The Third-Floor Flat

"**B**OTHER!" said Pat.

With a deepening frown she rummaged wildly in the silken trifle she called an evening bag. Two young men and another girl watched her anxiously. They were all standing outside the closed door of Patricia Garnett's flat.

"It's no good," said Pat. "It's not there. And now what shall we do?"

"What is life without a latchkey?" murmured Jimmy Faulkener.

He was a short, broad-shouldered young man, with good-tempered blue eyes.

Pat turned on him angrily. "Don't make jokes, Jimmy. This is serious."

"Look again, Pat," said Donovan Bailey. "It must be there somewhere."

He had a lazy, pleasant voice that matched his lean, dark figure.

"If you ever brought it out," said the other girl, Mildred Hope.

"Of course I brought it out," said Pat. "I believe I gave it to one of you two." She turned on the man accusingly. "I told Donovan to take it for me."

But she was not to find a scapegoat so easily. Donovan put in a firm disclaimer, and Jimmy backed him up.

"I saw you put it in your bag myself," said Jimmy.

"Well, then, one of you dropped it out when you picked up my bag. I've dropped it once or twice."

"Once or twice!" said Donovan. "You've dropped it a dozen times at least, besides leaving it behind on every possible occasion."

"I can't see why everything on earth doesn't drop out of it the whole time," said Jimmy.

"The point is—how are we going to get in?" said Mildred.

She was a sensible girl, who kept to the point, but she was not nearly so attractive as the impulsive and troublesome Pat.

All four of them regarded the closed door blankly.

625

"Couldn't the porter help?" suggested Jimmy. "Hasn't he got a master key or something of that kind?"

Pat shook her head. There were only two keys. One was inside the flat hung up in the kitchen and the other was—or should be—in the maligned bag.

"If only the flat were on the ground floor," wailed Pat. "We could have broken open a window or something. Donovan, you wouldn't like to be a cat burglar, would you?"

Donovan declined firmly but politely to be a cat burglar.

"A flat on the fourth floor is a bit of an undertaking," said Jimmy.

"How about a fire escape?" suggested Donovan.

"There isn't one."

"There should be," said Jimmy. "A building five stories high ought to have a fire escape."

"I dare say," said Pat. "But what should be doesn't help us. How am I ever to get into my flat?"

"Isn't there a sort of thingummybob?" said Donovan. "A thing the tradesmen send up chops and Brussels sprouts in?"

"The service lift," said Pat. "Oh yes, but it's only a sort of wirebasket thing. Oh, wait—I know. What about the coal lift?"

"Now that," said Donovan, "is an idea."

Mildred made a discouraging suggestion. "It'll be bolted," she said. "In Pat's kitchen, I mean, on the inside."

But the idea was instantly negatived.

"Don't you believe it," said Donovan.

"Not in *Pat's* kitchen," said Jimmy. "Pat never locks and bolts things."

"I don't think it's bolted," said Pat. "I took the dustbin off this morning, and I'm sure I never bolted it afterwards, and I don't think I've been near it since."

"Well," said Donovan, "that fact's going to be very useful to us tonight, but, all the same, young Pat, let me point out to you that these slack habits are leaving you at the mercy of burglars—nonfeline— every night."

Pat disregarded these admonitions.

"Come on," she cried, and began racing down the four flights of stairs. The others followed her. Pat led them through a dark recess, apparently full to overflowing of perambulators, and through another door into the well of the flats, and guided them to the right lift. There was, at the moment, a dustbin on it. Donovan lifted it off and stepped gingerly onto the platform in its place. He wrinkled up his nose.

"A little noisome," he remarked. "But what of that? Do I go alone on this venture or is anyone coming with me?"

"I'll come, too," said Jimmy.

He stepped on by Donovan's side.

"I suppose the lift will bear me," he added doubtfully.

"You can't weigh much more than a ton of coal," said Pat, who had never been particularly strong on her weights-and-measures table.

"And, anyway, we shall soon find out," said Donovan cheerfully, as he hauled on the rope.

With a grinding noise they disappeared from sight.

"This thing makes an awful noise," remarked Jimmy as they passed up through blackness. "What will the people in the other flats think?"

"Ghosts or burglars, I expect," said Donovan. "Hauling this rope is quite heavy work. The porter of Friars Mansions does more work than I ever suspected. I say, Jimmy old son, are you counting the floors?"

"Oh, Lord! No. I forgot about it."

"Well, I have, which is just as well. That's the third we're passing now. The next is ours."

"And now, I suppose," grumbled Jimmy, "we shall find that Pat did bolt the door after all."

But these fears were unfounded. The wooden door swung back at a touch, and Donovan and Jimmy stepped out into the inky blackness of Pat's kitchen.

"We ought to have a torch for this wild nightwork," explained Donovan. "If I know Pat, everything's on the floor, and we shall smash endless crockery before I can get to the light switch. Don't move about, Jimmy, till I get the light on."

He felt his way cautiously over the floor, uttering one fervent "Damn!" as a corner of the kitchen table took him unawares in the ribs. He reached the switch, and in another moment another "Damn!" floated out of the darkness.

"What's the matter?" asked Jimmy.

"Light won't come on. Dud bulb, I suppose. Wait a minute. I'll turn the sitting-room light on."

The sitting room was the door immediately across the passage. Jimmy heard Donovan go out of the door, and presently fresh muffled curses reached him. He himself edged his way cautiously across the kitchen.

"What's the matter?"

"I don't know. Rooms get bewitched at night, I believe. Everything seems to be in a different place. Chairs and tables where you least expected them. Oh, hell! Here's another!"

But at this moment Jimmy fortunately connected with the electric-light switch and pressed it down. In another minute two young men were looking at each other in silent horror.

This room was not Pat's sitting room. They were in the wrong flat.

To begin with, the room was about ten times more crowded than Pat's, which explained Donovan's pathetic bewilderment at repeatedly cannoning into chairs and tables. There was a large round table in the centre of the room covered with a baize cloth, and there was an aspidistra in the window. It was, in fact, the kind of room whose owner, the young men felt sure, would be difficult to explain to. With silent horror they gazed down at the table, on which lay a little pile of letters.

"Mrs. Ernestine Grant," breathed Donovan, picking them up and reading the name. "Oh, help! Do you think she's heard us?"

"It's a miracle she hasn't heard you," said Jimmy. "What with your language and the way you've been crashing into the furniture. Come on, for the Lord's sake, let's get out of here quickly."

They hastily switched off the light and retraced their steps on tiptoe to the lift. Jimmy breathed a sigh of relief as they regained the fastness of its depths without further incident.

"I do like a woman to be a good, sound sleeper," he said approvingly. "Mrs. Ernestine Grant has her points."

"I see it now," said Donovan; "why we made the mistake in the floor, I mean. Out in that well we started up from the basement."

He heaved on the rope, and the lift shot up. "We're right this time."

"I devoutly trust we are," said Jimmy as he stepped out into another inky void. "My nerves won't stand many more shocks of this kind."

But no further nerve strain was imposed. The first click of the light showed them Pat's kitchen, and in another minute they were opening the front door and admitting the two girls who were waiting outside.

"You have been a long time," grumbled Pat. "Mildred and I have been waiting here ages."

"We've had an adventure," said Donovan. "We might have been hauled off to the police station as dangerous malefactors."

Pat had passed on into the sitting room, where she switched on the light and dropped her wrap on the sofa. She listened with lively interest to Donovan's account of his adventures.

"I'm glad she didn't catch you," she commented. "I'm sure she's an old curmudgeon. I got a note from her this morning—wanted to see me sometime—something she had to complain about—my piano, I suppose. People who don't like pianos over their heads shouldn't come and live in flats. I say, Donovan, you've hurt your hand. It's all over blood. Go and wash it under the tap."

Donovan looked down at his hand in surprise. He went out of the room obediently and presently his voice called to Jimmy.

"Hullo," said the other, "what's up? You haven't hurt yourself badly, have you?"

"I haven't hurt myself at all."

There was something so queer in Donovan's voice that Jimmy stared at him in surprise. Donovan held out his washed hand and Jimmy saw that there was no mark or cut of any kind on it.

"That's odd," he said, frowning. "There was quite a lot of blood. Where did it come from?" And then suddenly he realized what his quicker-witted friend had already seen. "By Jove," he said. "It must have come from that flat." He stopped, thinking over the possibilities his words implied. "You're sure it was—er—blood?" he said. "Not paint?"

Donovan shook his head. "It was blood, all right," he said, and shivered.

They looked at each other. The same thought was clearly in each of their minds. It was Jimmy who voiced it first.

"I say," he said awkwardly. "Do you think we ought to—well—go down again—and have—a—a look around? See it's all right, you know?"

"What about the girls?"

"We won't say anything to them. Pat's going to put on an apron and make us an omelette. We'll be back by the time they wonder where we are."

"Oh, well, come on," said Donovan. "I suppose we've got to go through with it. I dare say there isn't anything really wrong."

But his tone lacked conviction. They got into the lift and descended to the floor below. They found their way across the kitchen without much difficulty and once more switched on the sitting-room light.

"It must have been in here," said Donovan, "that—that I got the stuff on me. I never touched anything in the kitchen."

He looked round him. Jimmy did the same, and they both frowned. Everything looked neat and commonplace and miles removed from any suggestion of violence or gore.

Suddenly Jimmy started violently and caught his companion's arm.

"Look!"

Donovan followed the pointing finger, and in his turn uttered an exclamation. From beneath the heavy red curtains there protruded a foot—a woman's foot in a gaping patent-leather shoe.

Jimmy went to the curtains and drew them sharply apart. In the recess of the window a woman's huddled body lay on the floor, a sticky dark pool beside it. She was dead, there was no doubt of that. Jimmy was attempting to raise her up when Donovan stopped him.

"You'd better not do that. She oughtn't to be touched till the police come."

"The police. Oh, of course. I say, Donovan, what a ghastly business. Who do you think she is? Mrs. Ernestine Grant?"

"Looks like it. At any rate, if there's anyone else in the flat, they're keeping jolly quiet."

"What do we do next?" asked Jimmy. "Run out and get a policeman or ring up from Pat's flat?"

"I should think ringing up would be best. Come on, we might as well go out the front door. We can't spend the whole night going up and down in that evil-smelling lift."

Jimmy agreed. Just as they were passing through the door, he hesitated. "Look here; do you think one of us ought to stay—just to keep an eye on things—till the police come?"

"Yes, I think you're right. If you'll stay, I'll run up and telephone."

He ran quickly up the stairs and rang the bell of the flat above. Pat came to open it—a very pretty Pat with a flushed face and a cooking apron on. Her eyes widened in surprise.

"You? But how— Donovan, what is it? Is anything the matter?"

He took both her hands in his. "It's all right, Pat—only we've made rather an unpleasant discovery in the flat below. A woman—dead."

"Oh!" She gave a little gasp. "How horrible. Has she had a fit or something?"

"No. It looks—well—it looks rather as though she had been murdered."

"Oh, Donovan!"

"I know. It's pretty beastly."

Her hands were still in his. She had left them there—was even clinging to him. Darling Pat—how he loved her. Did she care at all for him? Sometimes he thought she did. Sometimes he was afraid that Jimmy Faulkener— Remembrances of Jimmy waiting patiently below made him start guiltily.

"Pat, dear, we must telephone to the police."

"Monsieur is right," said a voice behind him. "And in the meantime, while we are waiting their arrival, perhaps I can be of some slight assistance."

They had been standing in the doorway of the flat, and now they peered out onto the landing. A figure was standing on the stairs a little way above them. It moved down and into their range of vision.

They stood staring at a little man with a very fierce moustache and an egg-shaped head. He wore a resplendent dressing gown and embroidered slippers. He bowed gallantly to Patricia.

"Mademoiselle!" he said. "I am, as perhaps you know, the tenant of the flat above. I like to be up high—the air—the view over London. I take the flat in the name of Mr. O'Connor. But I am not an Irishman. I have another name. That is why I venture to put myself at your service. Permit me." With a flourish he pulled out a card and handed it to Pat. She read it.

"Monsieur Hercule Poirot. Oh!" She caught her breath. *The* Monsieur Poirot! The great detective? And you will really help?"

"That is my intention, mademoiselle. I nearly offered my help earlier in the evening."

Pat looked puzzled.

"I heard you discussing how to gain admission to your flat. Me, I am very clever at picking locks. I could, without doubt, have opened your door for you, but I hesitated to suggest it. You would have had the grave suspicions of me."

Pat laughed.

"Now, monsieur," said Poirot to Donovan. "Go in, I pray of you, and telephone to the police. I will descend to the flat below."

Pat came down the stairs with him. They found Jimmy on guard, and Pat explained Poirot's presence. Jimmy, in his turn, explained to Poirot his and Donovan's adventures. The detective listened attentively.

"The lift door was unbolted, you say? You emerged into the kitchen, but the light it would not turn on."

He directed his footsteps to the kitchen as he spoke. His fingers pressed the switch.

*"Tiens! Voilà ce qui est curieux!"* he said as the light flashed on. "It functions perfectly now. I wonder—" He held up a finger to ensure silence and listened. A faint sound broke the stillness—the sound of an unmistakable snore. "Ah!" said Poirot. *"La chambre de domestique."*

He tiptoed across the kitchen into a little pantry, out of which led a door. He opened the door and switched on the light. The room was the kind of dog kennel designed by the builders of flats to accommodate a human being. The floor space was almost entirely occupied by the bed. In the bed was a rosy-cheeked girl lying on her back with her mouth wide open, snoring placidly.

Poirot switched off the light and beat a retreat.

"She will not wake," he said. "We will let her sleep till the police come."

He went back to the sitting room. Donovan had joined them.

"The police will be here almost immediately, they say," he said breathlessly. "We are to touch nothing."

Poirot nodded. "We will not touch," he said. "We will look, that is all."

He moved into the room. Mildred had come down with Donovan, and all four young people stood in the doorway and watched him with breathless interest.

"What I can't understand, sir, is this," said Donovan. "I never went near the window. How did the blood come on my hand?"

"My young friend, the answer to that stares you in the face. Of what colour is the tablecloth? Red, is it not? And doubtless you did put your hand on the table."

"Yes, I did. Is that—" He stopped.

Poirot nodded. He was bending over the table. He indicated with his hand a dark patch on the red.

"It was here that the crime was committed," he said solemnly. "The body was moved afterwards."

Then he stood upright and looked slowly round the room. He did not move, he handled nothing, but nevertheless the four watching felt as though every object in that rather frowsty place gave up its secret to his observant eye.

Hercule Poirot nodded his head as though satisfied. A little sigh escaped him. "I see," he said.

"You see what?" asked Donovan curiously.

"I see," said Poirot, "what you doubtless felt—that the room is over-full of furniture."

Donovan smiled ruefully. "I did go barging about a bit," he confessed. "Of course, everything was in a different place to Pat's room, and I couldn't make it out."

"Not everything," said Poirot.

Donovan looked at him inquiringly.

"I mean," said Poirot apologetically, "that certain things are always fixed. In a block of flats the door, the window, the fireplace—they are in the same place in the rooms which are below each other."

"Isn't that rather splitting hairs?" asked Mildred. She was looking at Poirot with faint disapproval.

"One should always speak with absolute accuracy. That is a little—how do you say?—fad of mine."

There was the noise of footsteps on the stairs, and three men came in. They were a police inspector, a constable, and the divisional surgeon. The inspector recognized Poirot and greeted him in an almost reverential manner. Then he turned to the others.

"I shall want statements from everyone," he began, "but in the first place—"

Poirot interrupted. "A little suggestion. We will go back to the flat upstairs and mademoiselle here shall do what she was planning to do—make us an omelette. Me, I have a passion for the omelettes. Then, *Monsieur l'Inspecteur*, when you have finished here, you will mount to us and ask questions at your leisure."

It was arranged accordingly, and Poirot went up with them.

"Monsieur Poirot," said Pat, "I think you're a perfect dear. And you shall have a lovely omelette. I really make omelettes frightfully well."

"That is good. Once, mademoiselle, I loved a beautiful young English girl who resembled you greatly—but alas!—she could not cook. So perhaps everything was for the best."

There was a faint sadness in his voice, and Jimmy Faulkener looked at him curiously.

Once in the flat, however, he exerted himself to please and amuse. The grim tragedy below was almost forgotten.

The omelette had been consumed and duly praised by the time that Inspector Rice's footsteps were heard. He came in accompanied by the doctor, having left the constable below.

"Well, Monsieur Poirot," he said. "It all seems clear and aboveboard—not much in your line, though we may find it hard to catch the man. I'd just like to hear how the discovery came to be made."

Donovan and Jimmy between them recounted the happenings of the evening. The inspector turned reproachfully to Pat.

"You shouldn't leave your lift door unbolted, miss. You really shouldn't."

"I shan't again," said Pat with a shiver. "Somebody might come in and murder me like that poor woman below."

"Ah, but they didn't come in that way, though," said the inspector.

"You will recount to us what you have discovered, yes?" said Poirot.

"I don't know as I ought to—but seeing it's you, Monsieur Poirot—"

"*Précisément*," said Poirot. "And these young people—they will be discreet."

"The newspapers will get hold of it, anyway, soon enough," said the inspector. "There's no real secret about the matter. Well, the dead woman's Mrs. Grant, all right. I had the porter up to identify her. Woman of about thirty-five. She was sitting at the table, and she was shot with an automatic pistol of small caliber, probably by someone sitting opposite her at table. She fell forward, and that's how the blood-stain came on the table."

"But wouldn't someone have heard the shot?" asked Mildred.

"The pistol was fitted with a silencer. No, you wouldn't hear anything. By the way, did you hear the screech the maid let out when we told her her mistress was dead? No. Well, that just shows how unlikely it was that anyone would hear the other."

"Has the maid no story to tell?" asked Poirot.

"It was her evening out. She's got her own key. She came in about ten o'clock. Everything was quiet. She thought her mistress had gone to bed."

"She did not look in the sitting room, then?"

"Yes, she took the letters in there which had come by the evening post, but she saw nothing unusual—any more than Mr. Faulkener and Mr. Bailey did. You see, the murderer had concealed the body rather neatly behind the curtains."

"But it was a curious thing to do, don't you think?"

Poirot's voice was very gentle, yet it held something that made the inspector look up quickly.

"Didn't want the crime discovered till he'd had time to make his getaway."

"Perhaps, perhaps—but continue with what you were saying."

"The maid went out at five o'clock. The doctor here puts the time of death as—roughly—about four to five hours ago. That's right, isn't it?"

The doctor, who was a man of few words, contented himself with jerking his head affirmatively.

"It's a quarter to twelve now. The actual time can, I think, be narrowed down to a fairly definite hour."

He took out a crumpled sheet of paper.

"We found this in the pocket of the dead woman's dress. You needn't be afraid of handling it. There are no fingerprints on it."

Poirot smoothed out the sheet. Across it some words were printed in small, prim capitals.

I WILL COME TO SEE YOU THIS EVENING AT HALF-PAST SEVEN.—
J.F.

"A compromising document to leave behind," commented Poirot as he handed it back.

"Well, he didn't know she'd got it in her pocket," said the inspector. "He probably thought she'd destroyed it. We've evidence that he was a careful man, though. The pistol she was shot with we found under the body—and there again no fingerprints. They'd been wiped off very carefully with a silk handkerchief."

"How do you know," said Poirot, "that it was a silk handkerchief?"

"Because we found it," said the inspector triumphantly. "At the last, as he was drawing the curtains, he must have let it fall unnoticed."

He handed across a big white silk handkerchief—a good-quality handkerchief. It did not need the inspector's finger to draw Poirot's attention to the mark on it in the centre. It was neatly marked and quite legible. Poirot read the name out.

"John Fraser."

"That's it," said the inspector. "John Fraser—J.F. in the note. We know the name of the man we have to look for, and I dare say when we find out a little about the dead woman, and her relations come forward, we shall soon get a line on him."

"I wonder," said Poirot. "No, *mon cher*, somehow I do not think he will be easy to find, your John Fraser. He is a strange man—careful, since he marks his handkerchiefs and wipes the pistol with which he has committed the crime—yet careless, since he loses his handkerchief and does not search for a letter that might incriminate him."

"Flurried, that's what he was," said the inspector.

"It is possible," said Poirot. "Yes, it is possible. And he was not seen entering the building?"

"There are all sorts of people going in and out at the time. These are big blocks. I suppose none of you—" he addressed the four collectively—"saw anyone coming out of the flat?"

Pat shook her head. "We went out earlier—about seven o'clock."

"I see." The inspector rose. Poirot accompanied him to the door. "As a little favor, may I examine the flat below?"

"Why, certainly, Monsieur Poirot. I know what they think of you at headquarters. I'll leave you a key. I've got two. It will be empty. The maid cleared out to some relatives, too scared to stay there alone."

"I thank you," said Monsieur Poirot. He went back into the flat, thoughtful.

"You're not satisfied, Monsieur Poirot?" said Jimmy.

"No," said Poirot. "I am not satisfied."

Donovan looked at him curiously. "What is it that—well, worries you?"

Poirot did not answer. He remained silent for a minute or two, frowning, as though in thought, then he made a sudden impatient movement of his shoulders.

"I will say good night to you, mademoiselle. You must be tired. You have had much cooking to do—eh?"

Pat laughed. "Only the omelette. I didn't do dinner. Donovan and Jimmy came and called for us, and we went out to a little place in Soho."

"And then without doubt, you went to a theatre?"

"Yes. *The Brown Eyes of Caroline.*"

"Ah!" said Poirot. "It should have been blue eyes—the blue eyes of mademoiselle."

He made a sentimental gesture, and then once more wished Pat good night, also Mildred, who was staying the night by special request, as Pat admitted frankly that she would get the horrors if left alone on this particular night.

The two young men accompanied Poirot. When the door was shut and they were preparing to say good-bye to him on the landing, Poirot forestalled them.

"My young friends, you heard me say that I was not satisfied? *Eh bien*, it is true—I am not. I go now to make some little investigations of my own. You would like to accompany me—yes?"

An eager assent greeted this proposal. Poirot led the way to the flat below and inserted the key the inspector had given him in the lock. On entering, he did not, as the others had expected, enter the sitting room. Instead he went straight to the kitchen. In a little recess which served as a scullery, a big iron bin was standing. Poirot uncovered this and, doubling himself up, began to rootle in it with the energy of a ferocious terrier.

Both Jimmy and Donovan stared at him in amazement.

Suddenly with a cry of triumph he emerged. In his hand he held aloft a small stoppered bottle.

"*Voilà!*" he said. "I find what I seek." He sniffed at it delicately. "Alas! I am *enrhumé*—I have the cold in the head."

Donovan took the bottle from him and sniffed in his turn, but could smell nothing. He took out the stopper and held the bottle to his nose before Poirot's warning cry could stop him.

Immediately he fell like a log. Poirot, by springing forward, partly broke his fall.

"Imbecile!" he cried. "The idea. To remove the stopper in that foolhardy manner! Did he not observe how delicately I handled it? Monsieur—Faulkener—is it not? Will you be so good as to get me a little brandy? I observed a decanter in the sitting room."

Jimmy hurried off, but by the time he returned, Donovan was sitting up and declaring himself quite all right again. He had to listen to a short lecture from Poirot on the necessity of caution in sniffing at possibly poisonous substances.

"I think I'll be off home," said Donovan, rising shakily to his feet. "That is, if I can't be any more use here. I feel a bit wonky still."

"Assuredly," said Poirot. "That is the best thing you can do. Monsieur Faulkener, attend me here a little minute. I will return on the instant."

He accompanied Donovan to the door and beyond. They remained outside on the landing talking for some minutes. When Poirot at last re-entered the flat, he found Jimmy standing in the sitting room gazing round him with puzzled eyes.

"Well, Monsieur Poirot," he said, "what next?"

"There is nothing next. The case is finished."

"What?"

"I know everything—now."

Jimmy stared at him. "That little bottle you found?"

"Exactly. That little bottle."

Jimmy shook his head. "I can't make head or tail of it. For some reason or other I can see you are dissatisfied with the evidence against this John Fraser, whoever he may be."

"Whoever he may be," repeated Poirot softly. "If he is anyone at all—well, I shall be surprised."

"I don't understand."

"He is a name—that is all—a name carefully marked on a handkerchief!"

"And the letter?"

"Did you notice that it was printed? Now, why? I will tell you. Handwriting might be recognized, and a typewritten letter is more easily traced than you would imagine—but if a real John Fraser wrote that letter, those two points would not have appealed to him! No, it was written on purpose and put in the dead woman's pocket for us to find. There is no such person as John Fraser."

Jimmy looked at him inquiringly.

"And so," went on Poirot, "I went back to the point that first struck me. You heard me say that certain things in a room were always in the same place under given circumstances. I gave three instances. I might have mentioned a fourth—the electric-light switch, my friend."

Jimmy still stared uncomprehendingly. Poirot went on.

"Your friend Donovan did not go near the window—it was by resting his hand on this table that he got it covered in blood! But I asked myself at once—why did he rest it there? What was he doing groping about this room in darkness? For remember, my friend, the electric-light switch is always in the same place—by the door. Why, when he came to this room, did he not at once feel for the light and turn it on? That was the natural, the normal thing to do. According to him, he tried to turn on the light in the kitchen, but failed. Yet when I tried the switch, it was in perfect working order. Did he, then, not wish the light to go on just then? If it had gone on, you would both have seen at once that you were in the wrong flat. There would have been no reason to come into this room."

"What are you driving at, Monsieur Poirot? I don't understand. What do you mean?"

"I mean—this."

Poirot held up a Yale door key.

"The key of this flat?"

"No, *mon ami,* the key of the flat above. Mademoiselle Patricia's key, which Monsieur Donovan Bailey abstracted from her bag sometime during the evening."

"But why—why?"

"*Parbleu!* So that he could do what he wanted to do—gain admission to this flat in a perfectly unsuspicious manner. He made sure that the lift door was unbolted earlier in the evening."

"Where did you get the key?"

Poirot's smile broadened. "I found it just now—where I looked for it—in Monsieur Donovan's pocket. See you, that little bottle I pretended to find was a ruse. Monsieur Donovan is taken in. He does what I knew he would do—unstoppers it and sniffs. And in that little bottle is ethyl chloride, a very powerful instant anaesthetic. It gives me just the moment or two of unconsciousness I need. I take from his pocket the two things that I knew would be there. This key was one of them—the other—"

He stopped and then went on.

"I questioned at the time the reason the inspector gave for the body being concealed behind the curtain. To gain time? No, there was more than that. And so I thought of just one thing—the post, my friend. The evening post that comes at half-past nine or thereabouts. Say the murderer does not find something he expects to find, but that something may be delivered by post later. Clearly, then, he must come back. But the crime must not be discovered by the maid when she comes in, or the police would take possession of the flat, so he hides the body behind the curtain. And the maid suspects nothing and lays the letters on the table as usual."

"The letters?"

"Yes, the letters." Poirot drew something from his pocket. "This is the second article I took from Monsieur Donovan when he was unconscious." He showed the superscription—a typewritten envelope addressed to Mrs. Ernestine Grant. "But I will ask you one thing first, Monsieur Faulkener, before we look at the contents of this letter. Are you or are you not in love with Mademoiselle Patricia?"

"I care for Pat damnably—but I've never thought I had a chance."

"You thought that she cared for Monsieur Donovan? It may be that she had begun to care for him—but it was only a beginning, my friend. It is for you to make her forget—to stand by her in her trouble."

"Trouble?" said Jimmy sharply.

"Yes, trouble. We will do all we can to keep her name out of it, but it will be impossible to do so entirely. She was, you see, the motive."

He ripped open the envelope that he held. An enclosure fell out. The covering letter was brief, and was from a firm of solicitors.

DEAR MADAM,
    The document you enclose is quite in order, and the fact of the marriage having taken place in a foreign country does not invalidate it in any way.

                                        Yours truly, etc.

Poirot spread out the enclosure. It was a certificate of marriage between Donovan Bailey and Ernestine Grant, dated eight years ago.

"Oh, my God!" said Jimmy. "Pat said she'd had a letter from the woman asking to see her, but she never dreamed it was anything important."

Poirot nodded. "Monsieur Donovan knew—he went to see his wife this evening before going to the flat above—a strange irony, by the way, that led the unfortunate woman to come to this building where her rival lived—he murdered her in cold blood, and then went on to his evening's amusement. His wife must have told him that she had sent the marriage certificate to her solicitors and was expecting to hear from them. Doubtless he himself had tried to make her believe that there was a flaw in the marriage."

"He seemed in quite good spirits, too, all the evening. Monsieur Poirot, you haven't let him escape?" Jimmy shuddered.

"There is no escape for him," said Poirot gravely. "You need not fear."

"It's Pat I'm thinking about mostly," said Jimmy. "You don't think— she really cared."

"*Mon ami*, that is your part," said Poirot gently. "To make her turn to you and forget. I do not think you will find it very difficult!"

# The Adventure of
# Johnnie Waverly

"YOU can understand the feelings of a mother," said Mrs. Waverly for perhaps the sixth time.

She looked appealingly at Poirot. My little friend, always sympathetic to motherhood in distress, gesticulated reassuringly.

"But yes, but yes, I comprehend perfectly. Have faith in Papa Poirot."

"The police—" began Mr. Waverly.

His wife waved the interruption aside. "I won't have anything more to do with the police. We trusted to them and look what happened! But I'd heard so much of Monsieur Poirot and the wonderful things he'd done, that I felt he might possibly be able to help us. A mother's feelings—"

Poirot hastily stemmed the reiteration with an eloquent gesture. Mrs. Waverly's emotion was obviously genuine, but it assorted strangely with her shrewd, rather hard type of countenance. When I heard later that she was the daughter of a prominent steel manufacturer of Birmingham who had worked his way up in the world from an office boy to his present eminence, I realized that she had inherited many of the paternal qualities.

Mr. Waverly was a big, florid, jovial-looking man. He stood with his legs straddled wide apart and looked the type of the country squire.

"I suppose you know all about this business, Monsieur Poirot?"

The question was almost superfluous. For some days past the paper had been full of the sensational kidnapping of little Johnnie Waverly, the three-year-old son and heir of Marcus Waverly, Esq., of Waverly Court, Surrey, one of the oldest families in England.

"The main facts I know, of course, but recount to me the whole story, monsieur, I beg of you. And in detail if you please."

"Well, I suppose the beginning of the whole thing was about ten days ago when I got an anonymous letter—beastly things, anyway—that I couldn't make head or tail of. The writer had the impudence to demand that I should pay him twenty-five thousand pounds—

twenty-five thousand pounds, Monsieur Poirot! Failing my agreement, he threatened to kidnap Johnnie. Of course I threw the thing into the wastepaper basket without more ado. Thought it was some silly joke. Five days later I got another letter. "Unless you pay, your son will be kidnapped on the twenty-ninth.' That was on the twenty-seventh. Ada was worried, but I couldn't bring myself to treat the matter seriously. Damn it all, we're in England. Nobody goes about kidnapping children and holding them up to ransom."

"It is not a common practice, certainly," said Poirot. "Proceed, monsieur."

"Well, Ada gave me no peace, so—feeling a bit of a fool—I laid the matter before Scotland Yard. They didn't seem to take the thing very seriously—inclined to my view that it was some silly joke. On the twenty-eighth I got a third letter. 'You have not paid. Your son will be taken from you at twelve o'clock noon tomorrow, the twenty-ninth. It will cost you fifty thousand pounds to recover him.' Up I drove to Scotland Yard again. This time they were more impressed. They inclined to the view that the letters were written by a lunatic, and that in all probability an attempt of some kind would be made at the hour stated. They assured me that they would take all due precautions. Inspector McNeil and a sufficient force would come down to Waverly on the morrow and take charge.

"I went home much relieved in my mind. Yet we already had the feeling of being in a state of siege. I gave orders that no stranger was to be admitted, and that no one was to leave the house. The evening passed off without any untoward incident, but on the following morning my wife was seriously unwell. Alarmed by her condition, I sent for Dr. Dakers. Her symptoms appeared to puzzle him. While hesitating to suggest that she had been poisoned, I could see that that was what was in his mind. There was no danger, he assured me, but it would be a day or two before she would be able to get about again. Returning to my own room, I was startled and amazed to find a note pinned to my pillow. It was in the same handwriting as the others and contained just three words: 'At twelve o'clock.'

"I admit, Monsieur Poirot, that then I saw red! Someone in the house was in this—one of the servants. I had them all up, blackguarded them right and left. They never spilt on each other; it was Miss Collins, my wife's companion, who informed me that she had seen Johnnie's nurse slip down the drive early that morning. I taxed her with it, and she broke down. She had left the child with the nursery maid and stolen out to meet a friend of hers—a man! Pretty goings-on! She denied having pinned the note to my pillow—she may have been speaking the truth, I don't know. I felt I couldn't take the risk of the child's own nurse being in the plot. One of the servants was implicated—of that I was sure. Finally I lost my temper and sacked the whole bunch, nurse and all. I gave them an hour to pack their boxes and get out of the house."

Mr. Waverly's red face was quite two shades redder as he remembered his just wrath.

"Was not that a little injudicious, monsieur?" suggested Poirot. "For all you know, you might have been playing into the enemy's hands."

Mr. Waverly stared at him. "I don't see that. Send the whole lot packing, that was my idea. I wired to London for a fresh lot to be sent down that evening. In the meantime, there'd be only people I could trust in the house: my wife's secretary, Miss Collins, and Tredwell, the butler, who has been with me since I was a boy."

"And this Miss Collins, how long has she been with you?"

"Just a year," said Mrs. Waverly. "She has been invaluable to me as a secretary-companion, and is also a very efficient housekeeper."

"The nurse?"

"She has been with me six months. She came to me with excellent references. All the same, I never really liked her, although Johnnie was quite devoted to her."

"Still, I gather she had already left when the catastrophe occurred. Perhaps, Monsieur Waverly, you will be so kind as to continue."

Mr. Waverly resumed his narrative.

"Inspector McNeil arrived about ten-thirty. The servants had all left by then. He declared himself quite satisfied with the internal arrangements. He had various men posted in the park outside, guarding all the approaches to the house, and he assured me that if the whole thing were not a hoax, we should undoubtedly catch my mysterious correspondent."

"I had Johnnie with me, and he and I and the inspector went together into a room we call the council chamber. The inspector locked the door. There is a big grandfather clock there, and as the hands drew near to twelve, I don't mind confessing that I was as nervous as a cat. There was a whirring sound, and the clock began to strike. I clutched Johnnie. I had a feeling a man might drop from the skies. The last stroke sounded, and as it did so, there was a great commotion outside—shouting and running. The inspector flung up the window, and a constable came running up.

" 'We've got him, sir,' he panted. 'He was sneaking up through the bushes. He's got a whole dope outfit on him.'

"We hurried out on the terrace where two constables were holding a ruffianly looking fellow in shabby clothes, who was twisting and turning in a vain endeavour to escape. One of the policemen held out an unrolled parcel which they had wrested from their captive. It contained a pad of cotton wool and a bottle of chloroform. It made my blood boil to see it. There was a note, too, addressed to me. I tore it open. It bore the following words: 'You should have paid up. To ransom your son will now cost you fifty thousand. In spite of all your precautions he has been abducted at twelve o'clock on the twenty-ninth as I said.'

"I gave a great laugh, the laugh of relief, but as I did so I heard the hum of a motor and a shout. I turned my head. Racing down the drive towards the south lodge at a furious speed was a low, long grey car. It was the man who drove it who had shouted, but that was not what gave me a shock of horror. It was the sight of Johnnie's flaxen curls. The child was in the car beside him.

"The inspector ripped out an oath. 'The child was here not a minute ago,' he cried. His eyes swept over us. We were all there: myself, Tredwell, Miss Collins. 'When did you see him last, Mr. Waverly?'

"I cast my mind back, trying to remember. When the constable had called us, I had run out with the inspector, forgetting all about Johnnie.

"And then there came a sound that startled us, the chiming of a church clock from the village. With an exclamation the inspector pulled out his watch. It was exactly twelve o'clock. With one common accord we ran to the council chamber; the clock there marked the hour as ten minutes past. Someone must have deliberately tampered with it, for I have never known it gain or lose before. It is a perfect time-keeper."

Mr. Waverly paused. Poirot smiled to himself and straightened a little mat which the anxious father had pushed askew.

"A pleasing little problem, obscure and charming," murmured Poirot. "I will investigate it for you with pleasure. Truly it was planned *à merveille.*"

Mrs. Waverly looked at him reproachfully. "But my boy," she wailed.

Poirot hastily composed his face and looked the picture of earnest sympathy again. "He is safe, madame; he is unharmed. Rest assured, these miscreants will take the greatest care of him. Is he not to them the turkey—no, the goose—that lays the golden eggs?"

"Monsieur Poirot, I'm sure there's only one thing to be done—pay up. I was all against it at first—but now! A mother's feelings—"

"But we have interrupted monsieur in his history," cried Poirot hastily.

"I expect you know the rest pretty well from the papers," said Mr. Waverly. "Of course, Inspector McNeil got onto the telephone immediately. A description of the car and the man was circulated all round, and it looked at first as though everything was going to turn out all right. A car, answering to the description, with a man and a small boy, had passed through various villages, apparently making for London. At one place they had stopped, and it was noticed that the child was crying and obviously afraid of his companion. When Inspector McNeil announced that the car had been stopped and the man and boy detained, I was almost ill with relief. You know the sequel. The boy was not Johnnie, and the man was an ardent motorist, fond of children, who had picked up a small child playing in the streets of Edenswell, a village about fifteen miles from us, and was kindly giving him a ride. Thanks to the cocksure blundering of the police, all traces have disappeared. Had they not persistently followed the wrong car, they might by now have found the boy."

"Calm yourself, monsieur. The police are a brave and intelligent force of men. Their mistake was a very natural one. And altogether it was a clever scheme. As to the man they caught in the grounds, I understand that his defense has consisted all along of a persistent denial. He declares that the note and parcel were given to him to deliver at Waverly Court. The man who gave them to him handed him a ten-shilling note and promised him another if it were delivered at exactly ten minutes to twelve. He was to approach the house through the grounds and knock at the side door."

"I don't believe a word of it," declared Mrs. Waverly hotly. "It's all a parcel of lies."

"*En vérité,* it is a thin story," said Poirot reflectively. "But so far they have not shaken it. I understand, also, that he made a certain accusation?"

His glance interrogated Mr. Waverly. The latter got rather red again.

"The fellow had the impertinence to pretend that he recognized in Tredwell the man who gave him the parcel. 'Only the bloke has shaved off his moustache.' Tredwell, who was born on the estate!"

Poirot smiled a little at the country gentleman's indignation. "Yet you yourself suspect an inmate of the house to have been accessory to the abduction."

"Yes, but not Tredwell."

"And you, madame?" asked Poirot, suddenly turning to her.

"It could not have been Tredwell who gave this tramp the letter and parcel—if anybody ever did, which I don't believe. It was given him at ten o'clock, he says. At ten o'clock Tredwell was with my husband in the smoking room."

"Were you able to see the face of the man in the car, monsieur? Did it resemble that of Tredwell in any way?"

"It was too far away for me to see his face."

"Has Tredwell a brother, do you know?"

"He had several, but they are all dead. The last one was killed in the war."

"I am not yet clear as to the grounds of Waverly Court. The car was heading for the south lodge. Is there another entrance?"

"Yes, what we call the east lodge. It can be seen from the other side of the house."

"It seems to me strange that nobody saw the car entering the grounds."

"There is a right of way through, and access to a small chapel. A good many cars pass through. The man must have stopped the car in a convenient place and run up to the house just as the alarm was given and attention attracted elsewhere."

"Unless he was already inside the house," mused Poirot. "Is there any place where he could have hidden?"

"Well, we certainly didn't make a thorough search of the house beforehand. There seemed no need. I suppose he might have hidden himself somewhere, but who would have let him in?"

"We shall come to that later. One thing at a time—let us be methodical. There is no special hiding place in the house? Waverly Court is an old place, and there are sometimes 'priest's holes,' as they call them."

"By gad, there *is* a priest's hole. It opens from one of the panels in the hall."

"Near the council chamber?"

"Just outside the door."

"*Voilà!*"

"But nobody knows of its existence except my wife and myself."

"Tredwell?"

"Well—he might have heard of it."

"Miss Collins?"

"I have never mentioned it to her."

Poirot reflected for a minute.

"Well, monsieur, the next thing is for me to come down to Waverly Court. If I arrive this afternoon, will it suit you?"

"Oh, as soon as possible, please, Monsieur Poirot!" cried Mrs. Waverly. "Read this once more."

She thrust into his hands the last missive from the enemy which had reached the Waverlys that morning and which had sent her posthaste to Poirot. It gave clever and explicit directions for the paying over of the money, and ended with a threat that the boy's life would pay for any treachery. It was clear that a love of money warred with the essential mother love of Mrs. Waverly, and that the latter was at last gaining the day.

Poirot detained Mrs. Waverly for a minute behind her husband.

"Madame, the truth, if you please. Do you share your husband's faith in the butler Tredwell?"

"I have nothing against him, Monsieur Poirot. I cannot see how he can have been concerned in this, but—well, I have never liked him—never!"

"One other thing, madame. Can you give me the address of the child's nurse?"

"One forty-nine Netherall Road, Hammersmith. You don't imagine—"

"Never do I imagine. Only—I employ the little grey cells. And sometimes, just sometimes, I have a little idea."

Poirot came back to me as the door closed.

"So madame has never liked the butler. It is interesting, that, eh, Hastings?"

I refused to be drawn. Poirot has deceived me so often that I now go warily. There is always a catch somewhere.

After completing an elaborate outdoor toilet, we set off for Netherall Road. We were fortunate enough to find Miss Jessie Withers at home. She was a pleasant-faced woman of thirty-five, capable and superior. I could not believe that she could be mixed up in the affair. She was bitterly resentful of the way she had been dismissed, but admitted that she had been in the wrong. She was engaged to be married to a painter and decorator who happened to be in the neighbourhood, and she had run out to meet him. The thing seemed natural enough. I could not quite understand Poirot. All his questions seemed to me quite irrelevant. They were concerned mainly with the daily routine of her life at Waverly Court. I was frankly bored and glad when Poirot took his departure.

"Kidnapping is an easy job, *mon ami*," he observed, as he hailed a taxi in the Hammersmith Road and ordered it to drive to Waterloo. "That child could have been abducted with the greatest ease any day for the last three years."

"I don't see that that advances us much," I remarked coldly.

"*Au contraire*, it advances us enormously, but enormously! If you must wear a tie pin, Hastings, at least let it be in the exact centre of your tie. At present it is at least a sixteenth of an inch too much to the right."

Waverly Court was a fine old place and had recently been restored with taste and care. Mr. Waverly showed us the council chamber, the terrace, and all the various spots connected with the case. Finally, at Poirot's request, he pressed a spring in the wall, a panel slid aside, and a short passage led us into the priest's hole.

"You see," said Waverly. "There is nothing here."

The tiny room was bare enough; there was not even the mark of a footstep on the floor. I joined Poirot where he was bending attentively over a mark in the corner.

"What do you make of this, my friend?"

There were four imprints close together.

"A dog," I cried.

"A very small dog, Hastings."

"A Pom."

"Smaller than a Pom."

"A griffon?" I suggested doubtfully.

"Smaller even than a griffon. A species unknown to the Kennel Club."

I looked at him. His face was alight with excitement and satisfaction.

"I was right," he murmured. "I knew I was right. Come, Hastings."

As we stepped out into the hall and the panel closed behind us, a young lady came out of a door farther down the passage. Mr. Waverly presented her to us.

"Miss Collins."

Miss Collins was about thirty years of age, brisk and alert in manner. She had fair, rather dull hair, and wore a pince-nez.

At Poirot's request, we passed into a small morning room, and he questioned her closely as to the servants and particularly as to Tredwell. She admitted that she did not like the butler.

"He gives himself airs," she explained.

They then went into the question of the food eaten by Mrs. Waverly on the night of the 28th. Miss Collins declared that she had partaken of the same dishes upstairs in her sitting room and had felt no ill effects. As she was departing, I nudged Poirot.

"The dog," I whispered.

"Ah, yes, the dog!" He smiled broadly. "Is there a dog kept here by any chance, mademoiselle?"

"There are two retrievers in the kennels outside."

"No, I mean a small dog, a toy dog."

"No—nothing of the kind."

Poirot permitted her to depart. Then, pressing the bell, he remarked to me, "She lies, that Mademoiselle Collins. Possibly I should, also, in her place. Now for the butler."

Tredwell was a dignified individual. He told his story with perfect aplomb, and it was essentially the same as that of Mr. Waverly. He admitted that he knew the secret of the priest's hole.

When he finally withdrew, pontifical to the last, I met Poirot's quizzical eyes.

"What do you make of it all, Hastings?"

"What do you?" I parried.

"How cautious you become. Never, never will the grey cells function unless you stimulate them. Ah, but I will not tease you! Let us make our deductions together. What points strike us specially as being difficult?"

"There is one thing that strikes me," I said. "Why did the man who kidnapped the child go out by the south lodge instead of by the east lodge where no one would see him?"

"That is a very good point, Hastings, an excellent one. I will match it with another. Why warn the Waverlys beforehand? Why not simply kidnap the child and hold him to ransom?"

"Because they hoped to get the money without being forced to action."

"Surely it was very unlikely that the money would be paid on a mere threat?"

"Also they wanted to focus attention on twelve o'clock, so that when the tramp man was seized, the other could emerge from his hiding place and get away with the child unnoticed."

"That does not alter the fact that they were making a thing difficult that was perfectly easy. If they do not specify a time or date, nothing would be easier than to wait their chance, and carry off the child in a motor one day when he is out with his nurse."

"Ye-es," I admitted doubtfully.

"In fact, there is a deliberate playing of the farce! Now let us approach the question from another side. Everything goes to show that there was an accomplice inside the house. Point number one, the mysterious poisoning of Mrs. Waverly. Point number two, the letter pinned to the pillow. Point number three, the putting on of the clock ten minutes—all inside jobs. And an additional fact that you may not have noticed. There was no dust in the priest's hole. It had been swept out with a broom.

"Now then, we have four people in the house. We can exclude the nurse, since she could not have swept out the priest's hole, though she could have attended to the other three points. Four people, Mr. and Mrs. Waverly, Tredwell the butler, and Miss Collins. We will take Miss Collins first. We have nothing much against her, except that we know very little about her, that she is obviously an intelligent young woman, and that she has only been here a year."

"She lied about the dog, you said," I reminded him.

"Ah, yes, the dog." Poirot gave a peculiar smile. "Now let us pass to Tredwell. There are several suspicious facts against him. For one thing, the tramp declares that it was Tredwell who gave him the parcel in the village."

"But Tredwell can prove an alibi on that point."

"Even then, he could have poisoned Mrs. Waverly, pinned the note to the pillow, put on the clock, and swept out the priest's hole. On the other hand, he has been born and bred in the service of the Waverlys. It seems unlikely in the last degree that he should connive at the abduction of the son of the house. It is not in the picture!"

"Well, then?"

"We must proceed logically—however absurd it may seem. We will briefly consider Mrs. Waverly. But she is rich, the money is hers. It is her money which has restored this impoverished estate. There would be no reason for her to kidnap her son and pay over her money to herself. Her husband, now, is in a different position. He has a rich wife. It is not the same thing as being rich himself—in fact I have a little idea that the lady is not very fond of parting with her money, except on a very good pretext. But Mr. Waverly, you can see at once, he is *bon viveur.*"

"Impossible," I spluttered.

"Not at all. Who sends away the servants? Mr. Waverly. He can write the notes, drug his wife, put on the hands of the clock, and establish an excellent alibi for his faithful retainer Tredwell. Tredwell has never liked Mrs. Waverly. He is devoted to his master and is willing to obey his orders implicitly. There were three of them in it. Waverly, Tredwell, and some friend of Waverly. That is the mistake the police made; they made no further inquiries about the man who drove the grey car with the wrong child in it. He was the third man. He picks up a child in a village nearby, a boy with flaxen curls. He drives in through the east lodge and passes out through the south lodge just at the right moment, waving his hand and shouting. They cannot see his face or the number of the car, so obviously they cannot see the child's face, either. Then he lays a false trail to London. In the meantime, Tredwell has done his part in arranging for the parcel and note to be delivered by a rough-looking gentleman. His master can provide an alibi in the unlikely case of the man recognizing him, in spite of the false moustache he wore. As for Mr. Waverly, as soon as the hullaballoo occurs outside, and the inspector rushes out, he quickly hides the child in the priest's hole, and follows him out. Later in the day, when the inspector is gone and Miss Collins is out of the way, it will be easy enough to drive him off to some safe place in his own car."

"But what about the dog?" I asked. "And Miss Collins lying?"

"That was my little joke. I asked her if there were any toy dogs in the house, and she said no—but doubtless there are some—in the nursery! You see, Mr. Waverly placed some toys in the priest's hole to keep Johnnie amused and quiet."

"Monsieur Poirot—" Mr. Waverly entered the room—"have you discovered anything? Have you any clue to where the boy has been taken?"

Poirot handed him a piece of paper. "Here is the address."

"But this is a blank sheet."

"Because I am waiting for you to write it down for me."

"What the—" Mr. Waverly's face turned purple.

"I know everything, monsieur. I give you twenty-four hours to return the boy. Your ingenuity will be equal to the task of explaining his reappearance. Otherwise, Mrs. Waverly will be informed of the exact sequence of events."

Mr. Waverly sank down in a chair and buried his face in his hands. "He is with my old nurse, ten miles away. He is happy and well cared for."

"I have no doubt of that. If I did not believe you to be a good father at heart, I should not be willing to give you another chance."

"The scandal—"

"Exactly. Your name is an old and honoured one. Do not jeopardize it again. Good evening, Mr. Waverly. Ah, by the way, one word of advice. Always sweep in the corners!"

# Four-and-Twenty
# Blackbirds

HERCULE Poirot was dining with his friend, Henry Bonnington, at the Gallant Endeavour in the King's Road, Chelsea.

Mr. Bonnington was fond of the Gallant Endeavour. He liked the leisurely atmosphere, he liked the food which was "plain" and "English" and "not a lot of made-up messes." He liked to tell people who dined with him there just exactly where Augustus John had been wont to sit and to draw their attention to the famous artists' names in the visitors' book. Mr. Bonnington was himself the least artistic of men—but he took a certain pride in the artistic activities of others.

Molly, the sympathetic waitress, greeted Mr. Bonnington as an old friend. She prided herself on remembering her customers' likes and dislikes in the way of food.

"Good evening, sir," she said, as the two men took their seats at a corner table. "You're in luck today—turkey stuffed with chestnuts—that's your favourite, isn't it? And ever such a nice Stilton we've got! Will you have soup first or fish?"

Mr. Bonnington deliberated the point. He said to Poirot warningly as the latter studied the menu:

"None of your French kickshaws now. Good well-cooked English food."

"My friend," Hercule Poirot waved his hand, "I ask no better! I put myself in your hands unreservedly."

"Ah—hruup—er—hm," replied Mr. Bonnington and gave careful attention to the matter.

These weighty matters, and the question of wine, settled, Mr. Bonnington leaned back with a sigh and unfolded his napkin as Molly sped away.

"Good girl, that!" he said approvingly. "Was quite a beauty once—artists used to paint her. She knows about food, too—and that's a great deal more important. Women are very unsound on food as a rule. There's many a woman if she goes out with a fellow she fancies—

won't even notice what she eats. She'll just order the first thing she sees."

Hercule Poirot shook his head.

"*C'est terrible.*"

"Men aren't like that, thank God!" said Mr. Bonnington complacently.

"Never?" There was a twinkle in Hercule Poirot's eye.

"Well, perhaps when they're very young," conceded Mr. Bonnington. "Young puppies! Young fellows nowadays are all the same—no guts—no stamina. I've no use for the young—and they," he added with strict impartiality, "have no use for me. Perhaps they're right! But to hear some of these young fellows talk you'd think no man had a right to be alive after sixty! From the way they go on, you'd wonder more of them didn't help their elderly relations out of the world."

"It is possible," said Hercule Poirot, "that they do."

"Nice mind you've got, Poirot, I must say. All this police work saps your ideals."

Hercule Poirot smiled.

"*Tout de même,*" he said. "It would be interesting to make a table of accidental deaths over the age of sixty. I assure you it would raise some curious speculations in your mind."

"The trouble with you is that you've started going to look for crime—instead of waiting for crime to come to you."

"I apologise," said Poirot. "I talk what you call 'the shop.' Tell me, my friend, of your own affairs. How does the world go with you?"

"Mess!" said Mr. Bonnington. "That's what's the matter with the world nowadays. Too much mess. And too much fine language. The fine language helps to conceal the mess. Like a highly flavoured sauce concealing the fact that the fish underneath it is none of the best! Give me an honest fillet of sole and no messy sauce over it."

It was given him at that moment by Molly and he grunted approval.

"You know just what I like, my girl," he said.

"Well, you come here pretty regular, don't you, sir? I ought to know what you like."

Hercule Poirot said:

"Do people then always like the same things? Do not they like a change sometimes?"

"Not gentlemen, sir. Ladies like variety—gentlemen always like the same thing."

"What did I tell you?" grunted Bonnington. "Women are fundamentally unsound where food is concerned!"

He looked round the restaurant.

"The world's a funny place. See that odd-looking old fellow with a beard in the corner? Molly'll tell you he's always here Tuesday and

Thursday nights. He has come here for close on ten years now—he's a kind of landmark in the place. Yet nobody here knows his name or where he lives or what his business is. It's odd when you come to think of it."

When the waitress brought the portions of turkey, he said:

"I see you've still got Old Father Time over there?"

"That's right, sir. Tuesdays and Thursdays, his days are. Not but what he came in here on a *Monday* last week! It quite upset me! I felt I'd got my dates wrong and that it must be Tuesday without my knowing it! But he came in the next night as well—so the Monday was just a kind of extra, so to speak."

"An interesting deviation from habit," murmured Poirot. "I wonder what the reason was?"

"Well, sir, if you ask me, I think he'd had some kind of upset or worry."

"Why did you think that? His manner?"

"No, sir—not his manner exactly. He was very quiet as he always is. Never says much except good evening when he comes and goes. No, it was his order."

"His order?"

"I dare say you gentlemen will laugh at me," Molly flushed up, "but when a gentleman has been here for ten years, you get to know his likes and dislikes. He never could bear suet pudding or blackberries and I've never known him take thick soup—but on that Monday night he ordered thick tomato soup, beefsteak and kidney pudding and blackberry tart! Seemed as though he just didn't notice *what* he ordered!"

"Do you know," said Hercule Poirot, "I find that extraordinarily interesting."

Molly looked gratified and departed.

"Well, Poirot," said Henry Bonnington with a chuckle. "Let's have a few deductions from you. All in your best manner."

"I would prefer to hear yours first."

"Want me to be Watson, eh? Well, old fellow went to a doctor and the doctor changed his diet."

"To thick tomato soup, steak and kidney pudding and blackberry tart? I cannot imagine any doctor doing that."

"Don't you believe it, old boy. Doctors will put you onto anything."

"That is the only solution that occurs to you?"

Henry Bonnington said:

"Well, seriously, I suppose there's only one explanation possible. Our unknown friend was in the grip of some powerful mental emotion. He was so perturbed by it that he literally did not notice what he was ordering or eating."

He paused a minute and then said:

"You'll be telling me next that you know just *what* was on his mind. You'll say perhaps that he was making up his mind to commit a murder."

He laughed at his own suggestion.

Hercule Poirot did not laugh.

He has admitted that at that moment he was seriously worried. He claims that he ought then to have had some inkling of what was likely to occur.

His friends assure him that such an idea is quite fantastic.

It was some three weeks later that Hercule Poirot and Bonnington met again—this time their meeting was in the Tube.

They nodded to each other, swaying about, hanging on to adjacent straps. Then at Piccadilly Circus there was a general exodus and they found seats right at the forward end of the car—a peaceful spot since nobody passed in or out that way.

"That's better," said Mr. Bonnington. "Selfish lot, the human race, they won't pass up the car however much you ask 'em to!"

Hercule Poirot shrugged his shoulders.

"What will you?" he said. "Life is too uncertain."

"That's it. Here today, gone tomorrow," said Mr. Bonnington with a kind of gloomy relish. "And talking of that, d'you remember that old boy we noticed at the Gallant Endeavour? I shouldn't wonder if *he'd* hopped it to a better world. He's not been there for a whole week. Molly's quite upset about it."

Hercule Poirot sat up. His green eyes flashed.

"Indeed?" he said. "Indeed?"

Bonnington said:

"D'you remember I suggested he'd been to a doctor and been put on a diet? Diet's nonsense of course—but I shouldn't wonder if he had consulted a doctor about his health and what the doctor said gave him a bit of a jolt. That would account for him ordering things off the menu without noticing what he was doing. Quite likely the jolt he got hurried him out of the world sooner than he would have gone otherwise. Doctors ought to be careful what they tell a chap."

"They usually are," said Hercule Poirot.

"This is my station," said Mr. Bonnington. "Bye, bye. Don't suppose we shall ever know now who the old boy was—not even his name. Funny world!"

He hurried out of the carriage.

Hercule Poirot, sitting frowning, looked as though he did not think it was such a funny world.

He went home and gave certain instructions to his faithful valet, George.

Hercule Poirot ran his finger down a list of names. It was a record of deaths within a certain area.

Poirot's finger stopped.

"Henry Gascoigne. Sixty-nine. I might try him first."

Later in the day, Hercule Poirot was sitting in Dr. MacAndrew's surgery just off the King's Road. MacAndrew was a tall, red-haired Scotsman with an intelligent face.

"Gascoigne?" he said. "Yes, that's right. Eccentric old bird. Lived alone in one of those derelict old houses that are being cleared away in order to build a block of modern flats. I hadn't attended him before, but I'd seen him about and I knew who he was. It was the dairy people got the wind up first. The milk bottles began to pile up outside. In the end the people next door sent word to the police and they broke the door in and found him. He'd pitched down the stairs and broken his neck. Had on an old dressing gown with a ragged cord—might easily have tripped himself up with it."

"I see," said Hercule Poirot. "It was quite simple—an accident."

"That's right."

"Had he any relations?"

"There's a nephew. Used to come along and see his uncle about once a month. Lorrimer, his name is, George Lorrimer. He's a medico himself. Lives at Wimbledon."

"Was he upset at the old man's death?"

"I don't know that I'd say he was upset. I mean, he had an affection for the old man, but he didn't really know him very well."

"How long had Mr. Gascoigne been dead when you saw him?"

"Ah!" said Dr. MacAndrew. "This is where we get official. Not less than forty-eight hours and not more than seventy-two hours. He was found on the morning of the sixth. Actually, we got closer than that. He'd got a letter in the pocket of his dressing gown—written on the third—posted in Wimbledon that afternoon—would have been delivered somewhere around nine-twenty P.M. That puts the time of death at after nine-twenty on the evening of the third. That agrees with the contents of the stomach and the processes of digestion. He had had a meal about two hours before death. I examined him on the morning of the sixth and his condition was quite consistent with death having occurred about sixty hours previously—round about ten P.M. on the third."

"It all seems very consistent. Tell me, when was he last seen alive?"

"He was seen in the King's Road about seven o'clock that same evening. Thursday the third, and he dined at the Gallant Endeavour restaurant at seven-thirty. It seems he always dined there on Thursdays. He was by way of being an artist, you know. An extremely bad one."

"He had no other relations? Only this nephew?"

"There was a twin brother. The whole story is rather curious. They hadn't seen each other for years. It seems the other brother, Anthony Gascoigne, married a very rich woman and gave up art—and the brothers quarrelled over it. Hadn't seen each other since, I believe. But oddly enough, they died on the same day. The elder twin passed away at three o'clock on the afternoon of the third. Once before I've known a case of twins dying on the same day—in different parts of the world! Probably just a coincidence—but there it is."

"Is the other brother's wife alive?"

"No, she died some years ago."

"Where did Anthony Gascoigne live?"

"He had a house on Kingston Hill. He was, I believe, from what Dr. Lorrimer tells me, very much of a recluse."

Hercule Poirot nodded thoughtfully.

The Scotsman looked at him keenly.

"What exactly have you got in your mind, M. Poirot?" he asked bluntly. "I've answered your questions—as was my duty seeing the credentials you brought. But I'm in the dark as to what it's all about."

Poirot said slowly:

"A simple case of accidental death, that's what you said. What I have in mind is equally simple—a simple push."

Dr. MacAndrew looked startled.

"In other words, murder! Have you any grounds for that belief?"

"No," said Poirot. "It is a mere supposition."

"There must be something—" persisted the other.

Poirot did not speak. MacAndrew said:

"If it's the nephew, Lorrimer, you suspect, I don't mind telling you here and now that you are barking up the wrong tree. Lorrimer was playing bridge in Wimbledon from eight-thirty till midnight. That came out at the inquest."

Poirot murmured:

"And presumably it was verified. The police are careful."

The doctor said:

"Perhaps you know something against him?"

"I didn't know that there was such a person until you mentioned him."

"Then you suspect somebody else?"

"No, no. It is not that at all. It's a case of the routine habits of the human animal. That is very important. And the dead M. Gascoigne does not fit in. It is all wrong, you see."

"I really don't understand."

Hercule Poirot murmured:

"The trouble is, there is too much sauce over the bad fish."

"My dear sir?"

Hercule Poirot smiled.

"You will be having me locked up as a lunatic soon, *Monsieur le Docteur*. But I am not really a mental case—just a man who has a liking for order and method and who is worried when he comes across a fact that does not fit in. I must ask you to forgive me for having given you so much trouble."

He rose and the doctor rose also.

"You know," said MacAndrew, "honestly I can't see anything the least bit suspicious about the death of Henry Gascoigne. I say he fell— you say somebody pushed him. It's all—well—in the air."

Hercule Poirot sighed.

"Yes," he said. "It is workmanlike. Somebody has made the good job of it!"

"You still think—?"

The little man spread out his hands.

"I'm an obstinate man—a man with a little idea—and nothing to support it! By the way, did Henry Gascoigne have false teeth?"

"No, his own teeth were in excellent preservation. Very creditable indeed at his age."

"He looked after them well—they were white and well brushed?"

"Yes, I noticed them particularly. Teeth tend to grow a little yellow as one grows older, but they were in good condition."

"Not discolored in any way?"

"No. I don't think he was a smoker if that is what you mean?"

"I did not mean that precisely—it was just a long shot—which probably will not come off! Good-bye, Dr. MacAndrew, and thank you for your kindness."

He shook the doctor's hand and departed.

"And now," he said, "for the long shot."

At the Gallant Endeavour, he sat down at the same table which he had shared with Bonnington. The girl who served him was not Molly. Molly, the girl told him, was away on a holiday.

It was only just seven and Hercule Poirot found no difficulty in entering into conversation with the girl on the subject of old Mr. Gascoigne.

"Yes," she said. "He'd been here for years and years. But none of us girls ever knew his name. We saw about the inquest in the paper, and there was a picture of him. 'There,' I said to Molly. 'If that isn't our "Old Father Time" ' as we used to call him."

"He dined here on the evening of his death, did he not?"

"That's right. Thursday, the third. He was always here on a Thursday. Tuesdays and Thursdays—punctual as a clock."

"You don't remember, I suppose, what he had for dinner?"

"Now let me see, it was mulligatawny soup, that's right, and beef-steak pudding or was it the mutton?—no, pudding, that's right, and blackberry and apple pie and cheese. And then to think of him going home and falling down those stairs that very same evening. A frayed dressing-gown cord they said it was as caused it. Of course, his clothes were always something awful—old-fashioned and put on anyhow, and all tattered, and yet he *had* a kind of air, all the same, as though he was *somebody!* Oh, we get all sorts of interesting customers here."

She moved off.

Hercule Poirot ate his filleted sole. His eyes showed a green light.

"It is odd," he said to himself, "how the cleverest people slip up over details. Bonnington will be interested."

But the time had not yet come for leisurely discussion with Bonnington.

Armed with introductions from a certain influential quarter, Hercule Poirot found no difficulty at all in dealing with the coroner for the district.

"A curious figure, the deceased man Gascoigne," he observed. "A lonely, eccentric old fellow. But his decease seems to arouse an unusual amount of attention?"

He looked with some curiosity at his visitor as he spoke.

Hercule Poirot chose his words carefully.

"There are circumstances connected with it, monsieur, which make investigation desirable."

"Well, how can I help you?"

"It is, I believe, within your province to order documents produced in your court to be destroyed, or to be impounded—as you think fit. A certain letter was found in the pocket of Henry Gascoigne's dressing gown, was it not?"

"That is so."

"A letter from his nephew, Dr. George Lorrimer?"

"Quite correct. The letter was produced at the inquest as helping to fix the time of death."

"Which was corroborated by the medical evidence?"

"Exactly."

"Is that letter still available?"

Hercule Poirot waited rather anxiously for the reply.

When he heard that the letter was still available for examination, he drew a sigh of relief.

When it was finally produced he studied it with some care. It was written in a slightly cramped handwriting with a stylographic pen.

It ran as follows:

*Dear Uncle Henry,*

*I am sorry to tell you that I have had no success as regards Uncle Anthony. He showed no enthusiasm for a visit from you and would give me no reply to your request that he would let bygones be bygones. He is, of course, extremely ill, and his mind is inclined to wander. I should fancy that the end is very near. He seemed hardly to remember who you were.*

*I am sorry to have failed you, but I can assure you that I did my best.*

> *Your affectionate nephew,*
>
> *George Lorrimer.*

The letter itself was dated 3rd November. Poirot glanced at the envelope's postmark—4.30 P.M. 3 Nov.

He murmured:

"It is beautifully in order, is it not?"

Kingston Hill was his next objective. After a little trouble, with the exercise of good-humored pertinacity, he obtained an interview with Amelia Hill, cook-housekeeper to the late Anthony Gascoigne.

Mrs. Hill was inclined to be stiff and suspicious at first, but the charming geniality of this strange-looking foreigner would have had its effect on a stone. Mrs. Amelia Hill began to unbend.

She found herself, as had so many other women before her, pouring out her troubles to a really sympathetic listener.

For fourteen years she had had charge of Mr. Gascoigne's household—*not* an easy job! No, indeed! Many a woman would have quailed under the burdens *she* had had to bear! Eccentric the poor gentleman was and no denying it. Remarkably close with his money—a kind of mania with him it was—and he as rich a gentleman as might be! But Mrs. Hill had served him faithfully, and put up with his ways, and naturally she'd expected at any rate a remembrance. But no—nothing at all! Just an old will that left all his money to his wife and if she predeceased him then everything to his brother, Henry. A will made years ago. It didn't seem fair!

Gradually Hercule Poirot detached her from her main theme of unsatisfied cupidity. It was indeed a heartless injustice! Mrs. Hill could not be blamed for feeling hurt and surprised. It was well known that Mr. Gascoigne was tight-fisted about money. It had even been said that the dead man had refused his only brother assistance. Mrs. Hill probably knew all about that.

"Was it that that Dr. Lorrimer came to see him about?" asked Mrs.

Hill. "I knew it was something about his brother, but I thought it was just that his brother wanted to be reconciled. They'd quarrelled years ago."

"I understand," said Poirot, "that Mr. Gascoigne refused absolutely?"

"That's right enough," said Mrs. Hill with a nod. " 'Henry?' he says, rather weak like. 'What's this about Henry? Haven't seen him for years and don't want to. Quarrelsome fellow, Henry.' Just that."

The conversation then reverted to Mrs. Hill's own special grievances, and the unfeeling attitude of the late Mr. Gascoigne's solicitor.

With some difficulty Hercule Poirot took his leave without breaking off the conversation too abruptly.

And so, just after the dinner hour, he came to Elmcrest, Dorset Road, Wimbledon, the residence of Dr. George Lorrimer.

The doctor was in. Hercule Poirot was shown into the surgery and there presently Dr. George Lorrimer came to him, obviously just risen from the dinner table.

"I'm not a patient, Doctor," said Hercule Poirot. "And my coming here is, perhaps, somewhat of an impertinence—but I'm an old man and I believe in plain and direct dealing. I do not care for lawyers and their long-winded roundabout methods."

He had certainly aroused Lorrimer's interest. The doctor was a clean-shaven man of middle height. His hair was brown but his eyelashes were almost white which gave his eyes a pale, boiled appearance. His manner was brisk and not without humour,

"Lawyers?" he said, raising his eyebrows. "Hate the fellows! You rouse my curiosity, my dear sir. Pray sit down."

Poirot did so and then produced one of his professional cards which he handed to the doctor.

George Lorrimer's white eyelashes blinked.

Poirot leaned forward confidentially. "A good many of my clients are women," he said.

"Naturally," said Dr. George Lorrimer, with a slight twinkle.

"As you say, naturally," agreed Poirot. "Women distrust the official police. They prefer private investigations. They do not want to have their troubles made public. An elderly woman came to consult me a few days ago. She was unhappy about a husband she'd quarrelled with many years before. This husband of hers was your uncle, the late Mr. Gascoigne." George Lorrimer's face went purple.

"My uncle? Nonsense! His wife died many years ago."

"Not your uncle, Mr. *Anthony* Gascoigne. Your uncle, Mr. *Henry* Gascoigne."

"Uncle Henry? But *he* wasn't married?"

"Oh yes, he was," said Hercule Poirot, lying unblushingly. "Not a doubt of it. The lady even brought along her marriage certificate."

"It's a lie!" cried George Lorrimer. His face was now as purple as a plum. "I don't believe it. You're an impudent liar."

"It is too bad, is it not?" said Poirot. "You have committed murder for nothing."

"Murder?" Lorrimer's voice quavered. His pale eyes bulged with terror.

"By the way," said Poirot, "I see you have been eating blackberry tart again. An unwise habit. Blackberries are said to be full of vitamins, but they may be deadly in other ways. On this occasion I rather fancy they have helped to put a rope round a man's neck—your neck, Dr. Lorrimer."

"You see, *mon ami,* where you went wrong was over your fundamental assumption." Hercule Poirot, beaming placidly across the table at his friend, waved an expository hand. "A man under severe mental stress doesn't choose that time to do something that he's never done before. His reflexes just follow the track of least resistance. A man who is upset about something *might* conceivably come down to dinner dressed in his pyjamas—but they will be his *own* pyjamas—not somebody else's.

"A man who dislikes thick soup, suet pudding and blackberries suddenly orders all three one evening. *You* say, because he is thinking of something else. But I say that a man who has got something on his mind will order automatically the dish he has ordered most often before.

"*Eh bien,* then, what other explanation could there be? I simply could not think of a reasonable explanation. And I was worried! The incident was all wrong. It did not fit! I have an orderly mind and I like things to fit. Mr. Gascoigne's dinner order worried me.

"Then you told me that the man had disappeared. He had missed a Tuesday and a Thursday the first time for years. I liked that even less. A queer hypothesis sprang up in my mind. If I were right about it *the man was dead.* I made inquiries. The man *was* dead. And he was very neatly and tidily dead. In other words the bad fish was covered up with the sauce!

"He had been seen in the King's Road at seven o'clock. He had had dinner here at seven-thirty—two hours before he died. It all fitted in—the evidence of the stomach contents, the evidence of the letter. Much too much sauce! You couldn't see the fish at all!

"Devoted nephew wrote the letter, devoted nephew had beautiful alibi for time of death. Death very simple—a fall down the stairs. Simple accident? Simple murder? Everyone says the former.

"Devoted nephew only surviving relative. Devoted nephew will inherit—but is there anything *to* inherit? Uncle notoriously poor.

"But there is a brother. And brother in his time had married a rich wife. And brother lives in a big rich house on Kingston Hill, so it would seem that rich wife must have left him all her money. You see the sequence—rich wife leaves money to Anthony, Anthony leaves money to Henry, Henry's money goes to George—a complete chain."

"All very pretty in theory," said Bonnington. "But what did you do?"

"Once you *know*—you can usually get hold of what you want. Henry had died two hours after a *meal*—that is all the inquest really bothered about. But supposing that meal was not dinner, but *lunch.* Put yourself in George's place. George wants money—badly. Anthony Gascoigne is dying—but his death is no good to George. His money goes to Henry, and Henry Gascoigne may live for years. So Henry must die too— and the sooner the better—but his death must take place *after* Anthony's, and at the same time George must have an alibi. Henry's habit of dining regularly at a restaurant on two evenings of the week suggests an alibi to George. Being a cautious fellow, he tries his plan out first. *He impersonates his uncle on Monday evening at the restaurant in question.* It goes without a hitch. Everyone there accepts him as his uncle. He is satisfied. He has only to wait till Uncle Anthony shows definite signs of pegging out. The time comes. He writes a letter to his uncle on the afternoon of the second November but dates it the third. He comes up to town on the afternoon of the third, calls on his uncle, and carries his scheme into action. A sharp shove and down the stairs goes Uncle Henry. George hunts about for the letter he has written, and shoves it in the pocket of his uncle's dressing gown. At seven-thirty he is at the Gallant Endeavour, beard, bushy eyebrows all complete. Undoubtedly Mr. Henry Gascoigne is alive at seven-thirty. Then a rapid metamorphosis in a lavatory and back full speed in his car to Wimbledon and an evening of bridge. The perfect alibi."

Mr. Bonnington looked at him.

"But the postmark on the letter?"

"Oh, that was very simple. The postmark was smudgy. Why? It had been altered with lamp black from second November to third November. You would not notice it unless you were looking for it. And finally there were the blackbirds."

"Blackbirds?"

"Four-and-twenty blackbirds baked in a pie! Or blackberries if you prefer to be literal! George, you comprehend, was after all not quite a good enough actor. Do you remember the fellow who blacked himself all over to play Othello? That is the kind of actor you have got to be in crime. George *looked* like his uncle and *walked* like his uncle and *spoke* like his uncle and had his uncle's beard and eyebrows, but he forgot to *eat* like his uncle. He ordered the dishes that he himself liked. Blackberries discolor the teeth—the corpse's teeth were not discolored, and yet Henry Gascoigne ate blackberries at the Gallant Endeavour that night. But there were no blackberries in the stomach. I asked this morning. And George had been fool enough to keep the beard and the rest of the makeup. Oh! plenty of evidence once you look for it. I called on George and rattled him. That finished it! He had been eating blackberries again, by the way. A greedy fellow— cared a lot about his food. *Eh bien,* greed will hang him all right unless I am very much mistaken."

A waitress brought them two portions of blackberry and apple tart.

"Take it away," said Mr. Bonnington. "One can't be too careful. Bring me a small helping of sago pudding."

# THE
# UNDER DOG

# The Under Dog

LILY Margrave smoothed her gloves out on her knee with a nervous gesture, and darted a glance at the occupant of the big chair opposite her.

She had heard of M. Hercule Poirot, the well-known investigator, but this was the first time she had seen him in the flesh.

The comic, almost ridiculous, aspect that he presented disturbed her conception of him. Could this funny little man, with the egg-shaped head and the enormous moustache, really do the wonderful things that were claimed for him? His occupation at the moment struck her as particularly childish. He was piling small blocks of colored wood one upon the other, and seemed far more interested in the result than in the story she was telling.

At her sudden silence, however, he looked sharply across at her.

"Mademoiselle, continue, I pray of you. It is not that I do not attend; I attend very carefully, I assure you."

He began once more to pile the little blocks of wood one upon the other, while the girl's voice took up the tale again. It was a gruesome tale, a tale of violence and tragedy, but the voice was so calm and unemotional, the recital was so concise that something of the savor of humanity seemed to have been left out of it.

She stopped at last.

"I hope," she said anxiously, "that I have made everything clear."

Poirot nodded his head several times in emphatic assent. Then he swept his hand across the wooden blocks, scattering them over the table, and, leaning back in his chair, his fingertips pressed together and his eyes on the ceiling, he began to recapitulate.

"Sir Reuben Astwell was murdered ten days ago. On Wednesday, the day before yesterday, his nephew, Charles Leverson, was arrested by the police. The facts against him as far as you know are—you will correct me if I am wrong, mademoiselle.

"Sir Reuben was sitting up late writing in his own special sanctum, the Tower Room. Mr. Leverson came in late, letting himself in with a latchkey. He was overheard quarreling with his uncle by the butler, whose room was directly below the Tower Room. The quarrel ended with a sudden thud as of a chair being thrown over and a half-smothered cry.

"The butler was alarmed, and thought of getting up to see what was the matter, but as a few seconds later he heard Mr. Leverson leave the room gaily whistling a tune, he thought nothing more of it. On the following morning, however, a housemaid discovered Sir Reuben dead by his desk. He had been struck down by some heavy instrument. The butler, I gather, did not at once tell the story to the police. That was natural, I think, eh, mademoiselle?"

The sudden question made Lily Margrave start.

"I beg your pardon?" she said.

"One looks for humanity in these matters, does one not?" said the little man. "As you recited the story to me—so admirably, so concisely— you made of the actors in the drama machines—puppets. But me, I look always for human nature. I say to myself, this butler, this—what did you say his name was?"

"His name is Parsons."

"This Parsons, then, he will have the characteristics of his class, he will object very strongly to the police, he will tell them as little as possible. Above all, he will say nothing that might seem to incriminate a member of the household. A housebreaker, a burglar, he will cling to that idea with all the strength of extreme obstinacy. Yes, the loyalties of the servant class are an interesting study."

He leaned back, beaming.

"In the meantime," he went on, "everyone in the household has told his or her tale, Mr. Leverson among the rest, and his tale was that he had come in late and gone up to bed without seeing his uncle."

"That is what he said."

"And no one saw reason to doubt that tale," mused Poirot, "except, of course, Parsons. Then there comes down an inspector from Scotland Yard, Inspector Miller you said, did you not? I know him, I have come across him once or twice in the past. He is what they call the sharp man, the ferret, the weasel.

"Yes, I know him! And the sharp Inspector Miller, he sees what the local inspector has not seen, that Parsons is ill at ease and uncomfortable, and knows something that he has not told. *Eh bien,* he makes short work of Parsons. By now it has been clearly proved that no one broke into the house that night, that the murderer must be looked for inside the house and not outside. And Parsons is unhappy and frightened, and feels very relieved to have his secret knowledge drawn out of him.

"He has done his best to avoid scandal, but there are limits; and so Inspector Miller listens to Parsons' story, and asks a question or two, and then makes some private investigations of his own. The case he builds up is very strong—very strong.

"Blood-stained fingers rested on the corner of the chest in the Tower Room, and the fingerprints were those of Charles Leverson. The house-maid told him she emptied a basin of blood-stained water in Mr. Lever-son's room the morning after the crime. He explained to her that he had cut his finger, and he *had* a little cut there, oh yes, but such a very little cut! The cuff of his evening shirt had been washed, but they found blood stains in the sleeve of his coat. He was hard pressed for money, and he inherited money at Sir Reuben's death. Oh, yes, a very strong case, mademoiselle." He paused.

"And yet you come to me today."

Lily Margrave shrugged her slender shoulders.

"As I told you, M. Poirot, Lady Astwell sent me."

"You would not have come of your own accord, eh?"

The little man glanced at her shrewdly. The girl did not answer.

"You do not reply to my question."

Lily Margrave began smoothing her gloves again.

"It is rather difficult for me, M. Poirot. I have my loyalty to Lady Astwell to consider. Strictly speaking, I am only her paid companion, but she has treated me more as though I were a daughter or a niece. She has been extraordinarily kind, and whatever her faults, I should not like to appear to criticize her actions, or—well, to prejudice you against taking up the case."

"Impossible to prejudice Hercule Poirot, *ce la ne ce fait pas,*" declared the little man cheerily. "I perceive that you think Lady Astwell has in her bonnet the buzzing bee. Come now, is it not so?"

"If I must say—"

"Speak, mademoiselle."

"I think the whole thing is simply silly."

"It strikes you like that, eh?"

"I don't want to say anything against Lady Astwell—"

"I comprehend," murmured Poirot gently. "I comprehend perfectly." His eyes invited her to go on.

"She really is an awfully good sort, and frightfully kind, but she isn't—how can I put it? She isn't an educated woman. You know she was an actress when Sir Reuben married her, and she has all sorts of prejudices and superstitions. If she says a thing, it must be so, and she simply won't listen to reason. The Inspector was not very tactful with her, and it put her back up. She says it is nonsense to suspect Mr. Leverson and just the sort of stupid, pigheaded mistake the police would make, and that, of course, dear Charles did not do it."

"But she has no reasons, eh?"

"None whatever."

"Ha! Is that so? Really, now."

"I told her," said Lily, "that it would be no good coming to you with a mere statement like that and nothing to go on."

"You told her that," said Poirot, "did you really? That is interesting."

His eyes swept over Lily Margrave in a quick comprehensive survey, taking in the details of her neat black tailor made, the touch of white at her throat, an expensive crepe de Chine blouse showing dainty tucks, and the smart little black felt hat. He saw the elegance of her, the pretty face with its slightly pointed chin, and the dark blue long-lashed eyes. Insensibly his attitude changed; he was interested now, not so much in the case as in the girl sitting opposite him.

"Lady Astwell is, I should imagine, mademoiselle, just a trifle inclined to be unbalanced and hysterical?"

Lily Margrave nodded eagerly.

"That describes her exactly. She is, as I told you, very kind, but it is impossible to argue with her or to make her see things logically."

"Possibly she suspects someone on her own account," suggested Poirot, "someone quite absurd."

"That is exactly what she does do," cried Lily. "She has taken a great dislike to Sir Reuben's secretary, poor man. She says she *knows* he did it, and yet it has been proved quite conclusively that poor Mr. Owen Trefusis cannot possibly have done it."

"And she has no reason?"

"Of course not; it is all intuition with her."

Lily Margrave's voice was very scornful.

"I perceive, mademoiselle," said Poirot, smiling, "that you do not believe in intuition?"

"I think it is nonsense," replied Lily.

Poirot leaned back in his chair.

"*Les femmes,*" he murmured, "they like to think that it is a special weapon that the good God has given them, and for every once that it shows them the truth, at least nine times it leads them astray."

"I know," said Lily, "but I have told you what Lady Astwell is like. You simply cannot argue with her."

"So you, mademoiselle, being wise and discreet, came along to me as you were bidden, and have managed to put me *au courant* of the situation."

Something in the tone of his voice made the girl look up sharply.

"Of course, I know," said Lily apologetically, "how very valuable your time is."

"You are too flattering, mademoiselle," said Poirot, "but indeed—yes, it is true, at this present time I have many cases of moment on hand."

"I was afraid that might be so," said Lily, rising. "I will tell Lady Astwell—"

But Poirot did not rise also. Instead he lay back in his chair and looked steadily up at the girl.

"You are in haste to be gone, mademoiselle? Sit down one more little moment, I pray of you."

He saw the color flood into her face and ebb out again. She sat down once more slowly and unwillingly.

"Mademoiselle is quick and decisive," said Poirot. "She must make allowances for an old man like myself, who comes to his decisions slowly. You mistook me, mademoiselle. I did not say that I would not go down to Lady Astwell."

"You will come, then?"

The girl's tone was flat. She did not look at Poirot, but down at the ground, and so was unaware of the keen scrutiny with which he regarded her.

"Tell Lady Astwell, mademoiselle, that I am entirely at her service. I will be at—Mon Repos, is it not?—this afternoon."

He rose. The girl followed suit.

"I—I will tell her. It is very good of you to come, M. Poirot. I am afraid, though, you will find you have been brought on a wild goose chase."

"Very likely, but—who knows?"

He saw her out with punctilious courtesy to the door. Then he returned to the sitting-room, frowning, deep in thought. Once or twice he nodded his head, then he opened the door and called to his valet.

"My good George, prepare me, I pray of you, a little valise. I go down to the country this afternoon."

"Very good, sir," said George.

He was an extremely English-looking person. Tall, cadaverous, and unemotional.

"A young girl is a very interesting phenomenon, George," said Poirot, as he dropped once more into his armchair and lighted a tiny cigarette. "Especially, you understand, when she has brains. To ask someone to do a thing and at the same time to put them against doing it, that is a delicate operation. It requires finesse. She was very adroit— oh, very adroit—but Hercule Poirot, my good George, is of a cleverness quite exceptional."

"I have heard you say so, sir."

"It is not the secretary she has in mind," mused Poirot. "Lady Astwell's accusation of him she treats with contempt. Just the same she is anxious that no one should disturb the sleeping dogs. I, my good George, I go to disturb them, I go to make the dog fight! There is a drama there, at Mon Repos. A human drama, and it excites me. She was adroit, the little one, but not adroit enough. I wonder—I wonder what I shall find there?"

Into the dramatic pause which succeeded these words George's voice broke apologetically.

"Shall I pack dress clothes, sir?"

Poirot looked at him sadly.

"Always the concentration, the attention to your own job. You are very good for me, George."

When the 4:55 drew up at Abbots Cross station, there descended from it M. Hercule Poirot, very neatly and foppishly attired, his moustache waxed to a stiff point. He gave up his ticket, passed through the barrier, and was accosted by a tall chauffeur.

"Mr. Poirot?"

The little man beamed upon him.

"That is my name."

"This way, sir, if you please."

He held open the door of the big Rolls Royce limousine.

The house was a bare three minutes from the station. The chauffeur descended once more and opened the door of the car, and Poirot stepped out. The butler was already holding the front door open.

Poirot gave the outside of the house a swift appraising glance before passing through the open door. It was a big, solidly built red brick mansion, with no pretentions to beauty, but with an air of solid comfort.

Poirot stepped into the hall. The butler relieved him deftly of his hat and overcoat, then murmured with that deferential undertone only to be achieved by the best servants:

"Her Ladyship is expecting you, sir."

Poirot followed the butler up the soft carpeted stairs. This, without doubt, was Parsons, a very well-trained servant, with a manner suitably devoid of emotion. At the top of the staircase he turned to the right along a corridor. He passed through a door into a little anteroom, from which two more doors led. He threw open the left-hand one of these, and announced:

"M. Poirot, m'lady."

The room was not a very large one, and it was crowded with furniture and knickknacks. A woman, dressed in black, got up from a sofa and came quickly toward Poirot.

"M. Poirot," she said with outstretched hand. Her eye ran rapidly over the dandified figure. She paused a minute, ignoring the little man's bow over her hand, and his murmured "My Lady," and then, releasing his hand after a sudden vigorous pressure, she exclaimed:

"I believe in small men! They are the clever ones."

"Inspector Miller," murmured Poirot, "is, I think, a tall man?"

"He is a bumptious idiot," said Lady Astwell. "Sit down here by me, will you, M. Poirot?"

She indicated the sofa and went on:

"Lily did her best to put me off sending for you, but I have not come to my time of life without knowing my own mind."

"A rare accomplishment," said Poirot, as he followed her to the settee.

Lady Astwell settled herself comfortably among the cushions and turned so as to face him.

"Lily is a dear girl," said Lady Astwell, "but she thinks she knows everything, and as often as not in my experience those sort of people are wrong. I am not clever, M. Poirot, I never have been, but I am right where many a more stupid person is wrong. I believe in *guidance*. Now do you want me to tell you who is the murderer, or do you not? A woman knows, M. Poirot."

"Does Miss Margrave know?"

"What did she tell you?" asked Lady Astwell sharply.

"She gave me the facts of the case."

"The facts? Oh, of course they are dead against Charles, but I tell you, M. Poirot, he didn't do it. I *know* he didn't!"

She bent upon him an earnestness that was almost disconcerting.

"You are very positive, Lady Astwell?"

"Trefusis killed my husband, M. Poirot. I am sure of it."

"Why?"

"Why should he kill him, do you mean, or why am I sure? I tell you I *know* it! I am funny about those things. I made up my mind at once, and I stick to it."

"Did Mr. Trefusis benefit in any way by Sir Reuben's death?"

"Never left him a penny," returned Lady Astwell promptly. "Now that shows you dear Reuben couldn't have liked or trusted him."

"Had he been with Sir Reuben long, then?"

"Close on nine years."

"That is a long time," said Poirot softly, "a very long time to remain in the employment of one man. Yes, Mr. Trefusis, he must have known his employer well."

Lady Astwell stared at him.

"What are you driving at? I don't see what that has to do with it."

"I was following out a little idea of my own," said Poirot. "A little idea, not interesting, perhaps, but original, on the effects of service."

Lady Astwell still stared.

"You *are* very clever, aren't you?" she said in rather a doubtful tone. "Everybody says so."

Hercule Poirot laughed.

"Perhaps you shall pay me that compliment, too, madame, one of these days. But let us return to the motive. Tell me now of your household, of the people who were here in the house on the day of the tragedy."

"There was Charles, of course."

"He was your husband's nephew, I understand, not yours."

"Yes, Charles was the only son of Reuben's sister. She married a comparatively rich man, but one of those crashes came—they do in the city—and he died, and his wife, too, and Charles came to live with us. He was twenty-three at the time, and going to be a barrister. But when the trouble came, Reuben took him into his office."

"He was industrious, M. Charles?"

"I like a man who is quick on the uptake," said Lady Astwell with a nod of approval. "No, that's just the trouble, Charles was *not* industrious. He was always having rows with his uncle over some muddle or other that he had made. Not that poor Reuben was an easy man to get on with. Many's the time I've told him that he had forgotten what it was to be young himself. He was very different in those days, M. Poirot."

Lady Astwell heaved a sigh of reminiscence.

"Changes must come, milady," said Poirot. "It is the law."

"Still," said Lady Astwell, "he was never really rude to me. At least if he was, he was always sorry afterward—poor dear Reuben."

"He was difficult, eh?" said Poirot.

"I could always manage him," said Lady Astwell with the air of a successful lion tamer. "But it was rather awkward sometimes when he would lose his temper with the servants. There are ways of doing it, and Reuben's was not the right way."

"How exactly did Sir Reuben leave his money, Lady Astwell?"

"Half to me and half to Charles," replied Lady Astwell promptly. "The lawyers don't put it simply like that, but that's what it amounts to."

Poirot nodded his head.

"I see—I see," he murmured. "Now, Lady Astwell, I will demand of you that you will describe to me the household. There was yourself, and Sir Reuben's nephew, Mr. Charles Leverson, and the secretary, Mr. Owen Trefusis, and there was Miss Lily Margrave. Perhaps you will tell me something of that young lady."

"You want to know about Lily?"

"Yes, she has been with you long?"

"About a year. I have had a lot of secretary-companions, you know, but somehow or other they all got on my nerves. Lily was different. She was tactful and full of common sense, and besides she looks so nice. I do like to have a pretty face about me, M. Poirot. I am a funny kind of person; I take likes and dislikes straight away. As soon as I saw that girl, I said to myself, 'She'll do.' "

"Did she come to you through friends, Lady Astwell?"

"I think she answered an advertisement. Yes—that was it."

"You know something of her people, of where she comes from?"

"Her father and mother are out in India, I believe. I don't really know much about them, but you can see at a glance that Lily is a lady, can't you, M. Poirot?"

"Oh perfectly, perfectly."

"Of course," went on Lady Astwell, "I am not a lady myself. I know it, and the servants know it, but there is nothing mean-spirited about me. I can appreciate the real thing when I see it, and no one could be nicer than Lily has been to me. I look upon that girl almost as a daughter, M. Poirot, indeed I do."

Poirot's right hand strayed out and straightened one or two of the objects lying on a table near him.

"Did Sir Reuben share this feeling?" he asked.

His eyes were on the knickknacks, but doubtless he noted the pause before Lady Astwell's answer came.

"With a man it's different. Of course they—they got on very well."

"Thank you, madame," said Poirot. He was smiling to himself.

"And these were the only people in the house that night?" he asked. "Excepting, of course, the servants."

"Oh, there was Victor."

"Victor?"

"Yes, my husband's brother, you know, and his partner."

"He lived with you?"

"No, he had just arrived on a visit. He has been out in West Africa for the past few years."

"West Africa," murmured Poirot.

He had learned that Lady Astwell could be trusted to develop a subject herself if sufficient time was given her.

"They say it's a wonderful country, but I think it's the kind of place that has a very bad effect upon a man. They drink too much, and they get uncontrolled. None of the Astwells has a good temper, and Victor's, since he came back from Africa, has been simply too shocking. He has frightened *me* once or twice."

"Did he frighten Miss Margrave, I wonder?" murmured Poirot gently.

"Lily? Oh, I don't think he has seen much of Lily."

Poirot made a note or two in a diminutive notebook; then he put the pencil back in its loop and returned the notebook to his pocket.

"I thank you, Lady Astwell. I will now, if I may, interview Parsons."

"Will you have him up here?"

Lady Astwell's hand moved toward the bell. Poirot arrested the gesture quickly.

"No, no, a thousand times no. I will descend to him."

"If you think it is better—"

Lady Astwell was clearly disappointed at not being able to participate in the forthcoming scene. Poirot adopted an air of secrecy.

"It is essential," he said mysteriously, and left Lady Astwell duly impressed.

He found Parsons in the butler's pantry, polishing silver. Poirot opened the proceedings with one of his funny little bows.

"I must explain myself," he said. "I am a detective agent."

"Yes, sir," said Parsons, "we gathered as much."

His tone was respectful but aloof.

"Lady Astwell sent for me," continued Poirot. "She is not satisfied; no, she is not satisfied at all."

"I have heard her Ladyship say so on several occasions," said Parsons.

"In fact," said Poirot, "I recount to you the things you already know? Eh? Let us then not waste time on these bagatelles. Take me, if you will be so good, to your bedroom and tell me exactly what it was you heard there on the night of the murder."

The butler's room was on the ground floor, adjoining the servant's hall. It had barred windows, and the strong room was in one corner of it. Parsons indicated the narrow bed.

"I had retired, sir, at 11 o'clock. Miss Margrave had gone to bed, and Lady Astwell was with Sir Reuben in the Tower Room."

"Lady Astwell was with Sir Reuben? Ah, proceed."

"The Tower Room, sir, is directly over this. If people are talking in it one can hear the murmur of voices, but naturally not anything that is said. I must have fallen asleep about half past eleven. It was just 12 o'clock when I was awakened by the sound of the front door being slammed to and knew Mr. Leverson had returned. Presently I heard footsteps overhead, and a minute or two later Mr. Leverson's voice talking to Sir Reuben.

"It was my fancy at the time, sir, that Mr. Leverson was—I should not exactly like to say drunk, but inclined to be a little indiscreet and noisy. He was shouting at his uncle at the top of his voice. I caught a word or two here or there, but not enough to understand what it was all about, and then there was a sharp cry and a heavy thud."

There was a pause, and Parsons repeated the last words.

"A heavy thud," he said impressively.

"If I mistake not, it is a *dull* thud in most works of romance," murmured Poirot.

"Maybe, sir," said Parsons severely. "It was a *heavy* thud I heard."

"A thousand pardons," said Poirot.

"Do not mention it, sir. After the thud, in the silence, I heard Mr. Leverson's voice as plain as plain can be, raised high. 'My God,' he said, 'My God,' just like that, sir."

Parsons, from his first reluctance to tell the tale, had now progressed to a thorough enjoyment of it. He fancied himself mightily as a narrator. Poirot played up to him.

*"Mon Dieu,"* he murmured. "What emotion you must have experienced!"

"Yes, indeed, sir," said Parsons, "as you say, sir. Not that I thought very much of it at the time. But it *did* occur to me to wonder if anything was amiss, and whether I had better go up and see. I went to turn the electric light on, and was unfortunate enough to knock over a chair.

"I opened the door, and went through the servants' hall, and opened the other door which gives on a passage. The back stairs lead up from there, and as I stood at the bottom of them, hesitating, I heard Mr. Leverson's voice from up above, speaking hearty and cheery-like. 'No harm done, luckily,' he says. 'Good night,' and I heard him move off along the passage to his own room, whistling.

"Of course I went back to bed at once. Just something knocked over, that's all I thought it was. I ask you, sir, was I to think Sir Reuben was murdered, with Mr. Leverson saying good night and all?"

"You are sure it was Mr. Leverson's voice you heard?"

Parsons looked at the little Belgian pityingly, and Poirot saw clearly enough that, right or wrong, Parsons' mind was made up on this point.

"Is there anything further you would like to ask me, sir?"

"There is one thing," said Poirot, "do you like Mr. Leverson?"

"I—I beg your pardon, sir?"

"It is a simple question. Do you like Mr. Leverson?"

Parsons, from being startled at first, now seemed embarrassed.

"The general opinion in the servants' hall, sir," he said, and paused.

"By all means," said Poirot, "put it that way if it pleases you."

"The opinion is, sir, that Mr. Leverson is an open-handed young gentleman, but not, if I may say so, particularly intelligent, sir."

"Ah!" said Poirot. "Do you know, Parsons, that without having seen him, that is also precisely my opinion of Mr. Leverson."

"Indeed, sir."

"What is your opinion—I beg your pardon—the opinion of the servants' hall of the secretary?"

"He is a very quiet, patient gentleman, sir. Anxious to give no trouble."

*"Vraiment,"* said Poirot.

The butler coughed.

"Her Ladyship, sir," he murmured, "is apt to be a little hasty in her judgments."

"Then, in the opinion of the servants' hall, Mr. Leverson committed the crime?"

"We none of us wish to think it was Mr. Leverson," said Parsons. "We—well, plainly we didn't think he had it in him, sir."

"But he has a somewhat violent temper, has he not?" asked Poirot.

Parsons came nearer to him.

"If you are asking me who had the most violent temper in the house—"

Poirot held up a hand.

"Ah! But that is not the question I should ask," he said softly. "My question would be, who has the best temper?"

Parsons stared at him open-mouthed.

Poirot wasted no further time on him. With an amiable little bow— he was always amiable—he left the room and wandered out into the big square hall of Mon Repos. There he stood a minute or two in thought, then, at a slight sound that came to him, cocked his head on one side in the manner of a perky robin, and finally, with noiseless steps, crossed to one of the doors that led out of the hall.

He stood in the doorway, looking into the room; a small room furnished as a library. At a big desk at the farther end of it sat a thin, pale young man busily writing. He had a receding chin, and wore pince-nez.

Poirot watched him for some minutes, and then he broke the silence by giving a completely artificial and theatrical cough.

"Ahem!" coughed M. Hercule Poirot.

The young man at the desk stopped writing and turned his head. He did not appear unduly startled, but an expression of perplexity gathered on his face as he eyed Poirot.

The latter came forward with a little bow.

"I have the honor of speaking to M. Trefusis, yes? Ah! my name is Poirot, Hercule Poirot. You may perhaps have heard of me."

"Oh—er—yes, certainly," said the young man.

Poirot eyed him attentively.

Owen Trefusis was about thirty-three years of age, and the detective saw at once why nobody was inclined to treat Lady Astwell's accusation seriously. Mr. Owen Trefusis was a prim, proper young man, disarmingly meek, the type of man who can be, and is, systematically bullied. One could feel quite sure that he would never display resentment.

"Lady Astwell sent for you, of course," said the secretary. "She mentioned that she was going to do so. Is there any way in which I can help you?"

His manner was polite without being effusive. Poirot accepted a chair, and murmured gently:

"Has Lady Astwell said anything to you of her beliefs and suspicions?"

Owen Trefusis smiled a little.

"As far as that goes," he said, "I believe she suspects me. It is absurd, but there it is. She has hardly spoken a civil word to me since, and she shrinks against the wall as I pass by."

His manner was perfectly natural, and there was more amusement than resentment in his voice. Poirot nodded with an air of engaging frankness.

"Between ourselves," he explained, "she said the same thing to me. I did not argue with her—me, I have made it a rule never to argue with very positive ladies. You comprehend, it is a waste of time."

"Oh, quite."

"I say, yes, milady—oh, perfectly, milady—*précisément*, milady. They mean nothing, those words, but they soothe all the same. I make my investigations, for though it seems almost impossible that anyone except M. Leverson could have committed the crime, yet—well, the impossible has happened before now."

"I understand your position perfectly," said the secretary. "Please regard me as entirely at your service."

*"Bon,"* said Poirot. "We understand one another. Now recount to me the events of that evening. Better start with dinner."

"Leverson was not at dinner, as you doubtless know," said the secretary. "He had a serious disagreement with his uncle, and went off to dine at the Golf Club. Sir Reuben was in a very bad temper in consequence."

"Not too amiable, *ce monsieur,* eh?" hinted Poirot delicately.

Trefusis laughed.

"Oh! He was a Tartar! I haven't worked with him for nine years without knowing most of his little ways. He was an extraordinarily difficult man, M. Poirot. He would get into childish fits of rage and abuse anybody who came near him. I was used to it by that time. I got into the habit of paying absolutely no attention to anything he said. He was not bad-hearted really, but he could be most foolish and exasperating in his manner. The great thing was never to answer him back."

"Were other people as wise as you were in that respect?"

Trefusis shrugged his shoulders.

"Lady Astwell enjoyed a good row," he said. "She was not in the least afraid of Sir Reuben, and she always stood up to him and gave him as good as she got. They always made up afterward, and Sir Reuben was really devoted to her."

"Did they quarrel that last night?"

The secretary looked at him sideways, hesitated a minute, then he said:

"I believe so; what made you ask?"

"An idea, that is all."

"I don't know, of course," explained the secretary, "but things looked as though they were working up that way."

Poirot did not pursue the topic.

"Who else was at dinner?"

"Miss Margrave, Mr. Victor Astwell, and myself."

"And afterward?"

"We went into the drawing-room. Sir Reuben did not accompany us. About ten minutes later he came in and hauled me over the coals for some trifling matter about a letter. I went up with him to the Tower Room and set the thing straight; then Mr. Victor Astwell came in and said he had something he wished to talk to his brother about, so I went downstairs and joined the two ladies.

"About a quarter of an hour later I heard Sir Reuben's bell ringing violently, and Parsons came to say I was to go up to Sir Reuben at once. As I entered the room, Mr. Victor Astwell was coming out. He nearly knocked me over. Something had evidently happened to upset him. He has a very violent temper. I really believe he didn't see me."

"Did Sir Reuben make any comment on the matter?"

"He said: 'Victor is a lunatic; he will do for somebody someday when he is in one of these rages.' "

"Ah!" said Poirot. "Have you any idea what the trouble was about?"

"I couldn't say at all."

Poirot turned his head very slowly and looked at the secretary. Those last words had been uttered too hastily. He formed the conviction that Trefusis could have said more had he wished to do so. But once again Poirot did not press the question.

"And then? Proceed, I pray of you."

"I worked with Sir Reuben for about an hour and a half. At 11 o'clock Lady Astwell came in, and Sir Reuben told me I could go to bed."

"And you went?"

"Yes."

"Have you any idea how long she stayed with him?"

"None at all. Her room is on the first floor, and mine is on the second, so I would not hear her go to bed."

"I see."

Poirot nodded his head once or twice and sprang to his feet.

"And now, monsieur, take me to the Tower Room."

He followed the secretary up the broad stairs to the first landing. Here Trefusis led him along the corridor, and through a baize door at the end of it, which gave on the servants' staircase and on a short passage that ended in a door. They passed through this door and found themselves on the scene of the crime.

It was a lofty room twice as high as any of the others, and was roughly about thirty feet square. Swords and assegais adorned the walls, and many native curios were arranged about on tables. At the far end, in the embrasure of the window, was a large writing table. Poirot crossed straight to it.

"It was here Sir Reuben was found?"

Trefusis nodded.

"He was struck from behind, I understand?"

Again the secretary nodded.

"The crime was committed with one of these native clubs," he explained. "A tremendously heavy thing. Death must have been practically instantaneous."

"That strengthens the conviction that the crime was not premeditated. A sharp quarrel, and a weapon snatched up almost unconsciously."

"Yes, it does not look well for poor Leverson."

"And the body was found fallen forward on the desk?"

"No, it had slipped sideways to the ground."

"Ah," said Poirot, "that is curious."

"Why curious?" asked the secretary.

"Because of this."

Poirot pointed to a round irregular stain on the polished surface of the writing table.

"That is a blood stain, *mon ami.*"

"It may have splattered there," suggested Trefusis, "or it may have been made later, when they moved the body."

"Very possibly, very possibly," said the little man. "There is only the one door to this room?"

"There is a staircase here."

Trefusis pulled aside a velvet curtain in the corner of the room nearest the door, where a small spiral staircase led upward.

"This place was originally built by an astronomer. The stairs lead up to the tower where the telescope was fixed. Sir Reuben had the place fitted up as a bedroom, and sometimes slept there if he was working very late."

Poirot went nimbly up the steps. The circular room upstairs was plainly furnished, with a camp bed, a chair and dressing table. Poirot satisfied himself that there was no other exit, and then came down again to where Trefusis stood waiting for him.

"Did you hear Mr. Leverson come in?" he asked.

Trefusis shook his head.

"I was fast asleep by that time."

Poirot nodded. He looked slowly round the room.

"*Eh bien!*" he said at last. "I do not think there is anything further here, unless—perhaps you would be so kind as to draw the curtains."

Obediently Trefusis pulled the heavy black curtains across the window at the far end of the room. Poirot switched on the light—which was masked by a big alabaster bowl hanging from the ceiling.

"There was a desk light?" he asked.

For reply the secretary clicked on a powerful green-shaded hand lamp, which stood on the writing table. Poirot switched the other light off, then on, then off again.

"*C'est bien!* I have finished here."

"Dinner is at half-past seven," murmured the secretary.

"I thank you, M. Trefusis, for your many amiabilities."

"Not at all."

Poirot went thoughtfully along the corridor to the room appointed for him. The immovable George was there laying out his master's things.

"My good George," he said presently, "I shall, I hope, meet at dinner a certain gentleman who begins to intrigue me greatly. A man who has come home from the tropics, George. With a tropical temper— so it is said. A man whom Parsons tries to tell me about, and whom Lily Margrave does not mention. The late Sir Reuben had a temper of his own, George. Supposing such a man to come into contact with a man whose temper was worse than his own—how do you say it? The fur would jump about, eh?"

" 'Would fly' is the correct expression, sir, and it is not always the case, sir, not by a long way."

"No?"

"No, sir. There was my Aunt Jemima, sir, a most shrewish tongue she had, bullied a poor sister of hers who lived with her, something shocking she did. Nearly worried the life out of her. But if anyone came along who stood up to her, well, it was a very different thing. It was meekness she couldn't bear."

"Ha!" said Poirot, "it is suggestive—that."

George coughed apologetically.

"Is there anything I can do in any way," he inquired delicately, "to—er—assist you, sir?"

"Certainly," said Poirot promptly. "You can find out for me what color evening dress Miss Lily Margrave wore that night, and which housemaid attends her."

George received these commands with his usual stolidity.

"Very good, sir, I will have the information for you in the morning."

Poirot rose from his seat and stood gazing into the fire.

"You are very useful to me, George," he murmured. "Do you know, I shall not forget your Aunt Jemima?"

Poirot did not, after all, see Victor Astwell that night. A telephone message came from him that he was detained in London.

"He attends to the affairs of your late husband's business, eh?" asked Poirot of Lady Astwell.

"Victor is a partner," she explained. "He went out to Africa to look into some mining concessions for the firm. It *was* mining, wasn't it, Lily?"

"Yes, Lady Astwell."

"Gold mines, I think, or was it copper or tin? You ought to know, Lily, you were always asking Reuben questions about it all. Oh, do be careful, dear, you will have that vase over!"

"It is dreadfully hot in here with the fire," said the girl. "Shall I— shall I open the window a little?"

"If you like, dear," said Lady Astwell placidly.

Poirot watched while the girl went across to the window and opened it. She stood there a minute or two breathing in the cool night air. When she returned and sat down in her seat, Poirot said to her politely:

"So Mademoiselle is interested in mines?"

"Oh, not really," said the girl indifferently. "I listened to Sir Reuben, but I don't know anything about the subject."

"You pretended very well, then," said Lady Astwell. "Poor Reuben actually thought you had some ulterior motive in asking all those questions."

The little detective's eyes had not moved from the fire, into which he was steadily staring, but nevertheless, he did not miss the quick flush of vexation on Lily Margrave's face. Tactfully he changed the conversation. When the hour for good nights came, Poirot said to his hostess:

"May I have just two little words with you, madame?"

Lily Margrave vanished discreetly. Lady Astwell looked inquiringly at the detective.

"You were the last person to see Sir Reuben alive that night?"

She nodded. Tears sprang into her eyes, and she hastily held a black-edged handkerchief to them.

"Ah, do not distress yourself, I beg of you do not distress yourself."

"It's all very well, M. Poirot, but I can't help it."

"I am a triple imbecile thus to vex you."

"No, no, go on. What were you going to say?"

"It was about 11 o'clock, I fancy, when you went into the Tower Room, and Sir Reuben dismissed Mr. Trefusis. Is that right?"

"It must have been about then."

"How long were you with him?"

"It was just a quarter to twelve when I got up to my room; I remember glancing at the clock."

"Lady Astwell, will you tell me what your conversation with your husband was about?"

Lady Astwell sank down on the sofa and broke down completely. Her sobs were vigorous.

"We—qua—qua—quarreled," she moaned.

"What about?" Poirot's voice was coaxing, almost tender.

"L—l—lots of things. It b—b—began with L—Lily. Reuben took a dislike to her—for no reason, and said he had caught her interfering with his papers. He wanted to send her away, and I said she was a dear girl, and I would not have it. And then he s—s—started shouting me down, and I wouldn't have that, so I just told him what I thought of him.

"Not that I really meant it, M. Poirot, and he said he had taken me out of the gutter to marry me, and I said—ah, but what does it all matter now? I shall never forgive myself. You know how it is, M. Poirot, I always did say a good row clears the air, and how was I to know someone was going to murder him that very night? Poor old Reuben."

Poirot had listened sympathetically to all this outburst.

"I have caused you suffering," he said. "I apologize. Let us now be very businesslike—very practical, very exact. You still cling to your idea that Mr. Trefusis murdered your husband?"

Lady Astwell drew herself up.

"A woman's instinct, M. Poirot," she said solemnly, "never lies."

"Exactly, exactly," said Poirot. "But when did he do it?"

"When? After I left him, of course."

"You left Sir Reuben at a quarter to twelve. At five minutes to twelve Mr. Leverson came in. In that ten minutes you say the secretary came down from his bedroom and murdered him?"

"It is perfectly possible."

"So many things are possible," said Poirot. "It could be done in ten minutes. Oh, yes! But was it?"

"Of course he *says* he was in bed and fast asleep," said Lady Astwell, "but who is to know if he was or not?"

"Nobody saw him about," Poirot reminded her.

"Everybody was in bed and fast asleep," said Lady Astwell triumphantly. "Of course nobody saw him."

"I wonder," said Poirot to himself.

A short pause.

"*Eh bien,* Lady Astwell, I will wish you good night."

George deposited a tray of early-morning coffee by his master's bedside.

"Miss Margrave, sir, wore a dress of light green chiffon on the night in question."

"Thank you, George, you are most reliable."

"The third housemaid looks after Miss Margrave, sir. Her name is Gladys."

"Thank you, George. You are invaluable."

"Not at all, sir."

"It is a fine morning," said Poirot, looking out of the window, "and no one is likely to be astir very early. I think, my good George, that we shall have the Tower Room to ourselves if we proceed there to make a little experiment."

"You need me, sir?"

"The experiment," said Poirot, "will not be painful."

The curtains were still drawn in the Tower Room when they arrived there. George was about to pull them, when Poirot restrained him.

"We will leave the room as it is. Just turn on the desk lamp."

The valet obeyed.

"Now, my good George, sit down in that chair. Dispose yourself as though you were writing. *Très bien.* Me, I seize a club, I steal up behind you, so, and I hit you on the back of the head."

"Yes, sir," said George.

"Ah!" said Poirot, "but when I hit you, do not continue to write. You comprehend I cannot be exact. I cannot hit you with the same force with which the assassin hit Sir Reuben. When it comes to that point, we must do the make-believe. I hit you on the head, and you collapse, so. The arms well relaxed, the body limp. Permit me to arrange you. But no, do not flex your muscles."

He heaved a sigh of exasperation.

"You press admirably the trousers, George," he said, "but the imagination you possess it not. Get up and let me take your place."

Poirot in his turn sat down at the writing table.

"I write," he declared, "I write busily. You steal up behind me, you hit me on the head with the club. Crash! The pen slips from my fingers, I drop forward, but not very far forward, for the chair is low, and the desk is high, and, moreover, my arms support me. Have the goodness, George, to go back to the door, stand there, and tell me what you see."

"Ahem!"

"Yes, George?" encouragingly.

"I see you, sir, sitting at the desk."

"*Sitting* at the desk?"

"It is a little difficult to see plainly, sir," explained George, "being such a long way away, sir, and the lamp being so heavily shaded. If I might turn on this light, sir?"

His hand reached out to the switch.

"Not at all," said Poirot sharply. "We shall do very well as we are. Here am I bending over the desk, there are you standing by the door. Advance now, George, advance, and put your hand on my shoulder."

George obeyed.

"Lean on me a little, George, to steady yourself on your feet, as it were. Ah! *Voilà.*"

Hercule Poirot's limp body slid artistically sideways.

"I collapse—so!" he observed. "Yes, it is very well imagined. There is now something most important that must be done."

"Indeed, sir?" said the valet.

"Yes, it is necessary that I should breakfast well."

The little man laughed heartily at his own joke.

"The stomach, George; it must not be ignored."

George maintained a disapproving silence. Poirot went downstairs chuckling happily to himself. He was pleased at the way things were shaping. After breakfast he made the acquaintance of Gladys, the third housemaid. He was very interested in what she could tell him of the crime. She was sympathetic toward Charles, although she had no doubt of his guilt.

"Poor young gentleman, sir, it seems hard, it does, him not being quite himself at the time."

"He and Miss Margrave should have got on well together," suggested Poirot, "as the only two young people in the house."

Gladys shook her head.

"Very stand-offish Miss Lily was with him. She wouldn't have no carryings-on, and she made it plain."

"He was fond of her, was he?"

"Oh, only in passing, so to speak; no harm in it, sir. Mr. Victor Astwell, now he *is* properly gone on Miss Lily."

She giggled.

"*Ah vraiment!*"

Gladys giggled again.

"Sweet on her straight away he was. Miss Lily *is* just like a lily, isn't she, sir? So tall and such a lovely shade of gold hair."

"She should wear a green evening frock," mused Poirot. "There is a certain shade of green—"

"She has one, sir," said Gladys. "Of course, she can't wear it now, being in mourning, but she had it on the very night Sir Reuben died."

"It should be a light green, not a dark green," said Poirot.

"It is a light green, sir. If you wait a minute I'll show it to you. Miss Lily has just gone out with the dogs."

Poirot nodded. He knew that as well as Gladys did. In fact, it was only after seeing Lily safely off the premises that he had gone in search of the housemaid. Gladys hurried away, and returned a few minutes later with a green evening dress on a hanger.

"*Exquis!*" murmured Poirot, holding up hands of admiration. "Permit me to take it to the light a minute."

He took the dress from Gladys, turned his back on her and hurried to the window. He bent over it, then held it out at arm's length.

"It is perfect," he declared. "Perfectly ravishing. A thousand thanks for showing it to me."

"Not at all, sir," said Gladys. "We all know that Frenchmen are interested in ladies' dresses."

"You are too kind," murmured Poirot.

He watched her hurry away again with the dress. Then he looked down at his two hands and smiled. In the right hand was a tiny pair of nail scissors, in the left was a neatly clipped fragment of green chiffon.

"And now," he murmured, "to be heroic."

He returned to his own apartment and summoned George.

"On the dressing table, my good George, you will perceive a gold scarf pin."

"Yes, sir."

"On the washstand is a solution of carbolic. Immerse, I pray you, the point of the pin in the carbolic."

George did as he was bid. He had long ago ceased to wonder at the vagaries of his master.

"I have done that, sir."

"*Très bien!* Now approach. I tender to you my first finger; insert the point of the pin in it."

"Excuse me, sir, you want me to prick you, sir?"

"But, yes, you have guessed correctly. You must draw blood, you understand, but not too much."

George took hold of his master's finger. Poirot shut his eyes and leaned back. The valet stabbed at the finger with the scarf pin, and Poirot uttered a shrill yell.

*"Je vous remercie,* George," he said. "What you have done is ample."

Taking a small piece of green chiffon from his pocket, he dabbed his finger with it gingerly.

"The operation has succeeded to a miracle," he remarked, gazing at the result. "You have no curiosity, George? Now, that is admirable!"

The valet had just taken a discreet look out of the window.

"Excuse me, sir," he murmured, "a gentleman has driven up in a large car."

"Ah! Ah!" said Poirot. He rose briskly to his feet. "The elusive Mr. Victor Astwell. I go down to make his acquaintance."

Poirot was destined to hear Mr. Victor Astwell sometime before he saw him. A loud voice rang out from the hall.

"Mind what you are doing, you damned idiot! That case has got glass in it. Curse you, Parsons, get out of the way! Put it down, you fool!"

Poirot skipped nimbly down the stairs. Victor Astwell was a big man. Poirot bowed to him politely.

"Who the devil are you?" roared the big man.

Poirot bowed again.

"My name is Hercule Poirot."

"Lord!" said Victor Astwell. "So Nancy sent for you, after all, did she?"

He put a hand on Poirot's shoulder and steered him into the library.

"So you are the fellow they make such a fuss about," he remarked, looking him up and down. "Sorry for my language just now. That chauffeur of mine is a damned ass, and Parsons always does get on my nerves, blithering old idiot.

"I don't suffer fools gladly, you know," he said, half apologetically, "but by all accounts you are not a fool, eh, M. Poirot?"

He laughed breezily.

"Those who have thought so have been sadly mistaken," said Poirot placidly.

"Is that so? Well, so Nancy has carted you down here—got a bee in her bonnet about the secretary. There is nothing in that; Trefusis is as mild as milk—drinks milk, too, I believe. The fellow is a teetotaler. Rather waste of your time, isn't it?"

"If one has an opportunity to observe human nature, time is never wasted," said Poirot quietly.

"Human nature, eh?"

Victor Astwell stared at him, then he flung himself down in a chair.

"Anything I can do for you?"

"Yes, you can tell me what your quarrel with your brother was about that evening."

Victor Astwell shook his head.

"Nothing to do with the case," he said decisively.

"One can never be sure," said Poirot.

"It had nothing to do with Charles Leverson."

"Lady Astwell thinks that Charles had nothing to do with the murder."

"Oh, Nancy!"

"Parsons assumes that it was M. Charles Leverson who came in that night, but he didn't see him. Remember nobody saw him."

"You are wrong there," said Astwell. "I saw him."

"You saw him?"

"It's very simple. Reuben had been pitching into young Charles—not without good reason, I must say. Later on he tried to bully me. I told him a few home truths and, just to annoy him, I made up my mind to back the boy. I meant to see him that night, so as to tell him how the land lay. When I went up to my room I didn't go to bed. Instead, I left the door ajar and sat on a chair smoking. My room is on the second floor, M. Poirot, and Charles's room is next to it."

"Pardon my interrupting you—Mr. Trefusis, he, too, sleeps on that floor?"

Astwell nodded.

"Yes, his room is just beyond mine."

"Nearer the stairs?"

"No, the other way."

A curious light came into Poirot's face, but the other didn't notice it and went on:

"As I say, I waited up for Charles. I heard the front door slam, as I thought, about five minutes to twelve, but there was no sign of Charles for about ten minutes. When he did come up the stairs, I saw that it was no good tackling him that night."

He lifted his eyebrows significantly.

"I see," murmured Poirot.

"Poor devil couldn't walk straight," said Astwell. "He was looking pretty ghastly, too. I put it down to his condition at the time. Of course, now I realize that he had come straight from committing the crime."

Poirot interposed a quick question.

"You heard nothing from the Tower Room?"

"No, but you must remember that I was right at the other end of the building. The walls are thick, and I don't believe you would even hear a pistol shot fired from there."

Poirot nodded.

"I asked if he would like some help getting to bed," continued Astwell. "But he said he was all right and went into his room and banged the door. I undressed and went to bed."

Poirot was staring thoughtfully at the carpet.

"You realize, M. Astwell," he said at last, "that your evidence is very important?"

"I suppose so, at least—what do you mean?"

"Your evidence that ten minutes elapsed between the slamming of the front door and Leverson's appearance upstairs. He himself says, so I understand, that he came into the house and went straight up to bed. But there is more than that. Lady Astwell's accusation of the secretary is fantastic, I admit, yet up to now it has not been proved impossible. But your evidence creates an alibi."

"How is that?"

"Lady Astwell says that she left her husband at a quarter to twelve, while the secretary had gone to bed at eleven o'clock. The only time he could have committed the crime was between a quarter to twelve and Charles Leverson's return. Now, if, as you say, you sat with your door open, he could not have come down from his room without your seeing him."

"That is so," agreed the other.

"There is no other staircase?"

"No, to get down to the Tower Room he would have had to pass my door, and he didn't, I am quite sure of that. And, anyway, M. Poirot, as I said just now, the man is as meek as a parson, I assure you."

"But yes, but yes," said Poirot soothingly, "I understand all that." He paused. "And you will not tell me the subject of your quarrel with Sir Reuben?"

The other's face turned a dark red.

"You'll get nothing out of me."

Poirot looked at the ceiling.

"I can always be discreet," he murmured, "where a lady is concerned."

Victor Astwell sprang to his feet.

"Damn you, how did you—what do you mean?"

"I was thinking," said Poirot, "of Miss Lily Margrave."

Victor Astwell stood undecided for a minute or two, then his color subsided, and he sat down again.

"You are too clever for me, M. Poirot. Yes, it was Lily we quarreled about. Reuben had his knife into her; he had ferreted out something or other about the girl—false references, something of that kind. I don't believe a word of it myself.

"And then he went further than he had any right to go, talked about her stealing down at night and getting out of the house to meet some fellow or other. My God! I gave it to him; I told him that better men than he had been killed for saying less. That shut him up. Reuben was inclined to be a bit afraid of me when I got going."

"I hardly wonder at it," murmured Poirot politely.

"I think a lot of Lily Margrave," said Victor in another tone. "A nice girl through and through."

Poirot did not answer. He was staring in front of him, seemingly lost in abstraction. He came out of his brown study with a jerk.

"I must, I think, promenade myself a little. There is a hotel here, yes?"

"Two," said Victor Astwell, "the Golf Hotel up by the links and the Mitre down by the station."

"I thank you," said Poirot. "Yes, certainly I must promenade myself a little."

The Golf Hotel, as befits its name, stands on the golf links almost adjoining the club house. It was to this hostelry that Poirot repaired first in the course of that "promenade" which he had advertised himself as being about to take. The little man had his own way of doing things. Three minutes after he had entered the Golf Hotel he was in private consultation with Miss Langdon, the manageress.

"I regret to incommode you in any way, mademoiselle," said Poirot, "but you see I am a detective."

Simplicity always appealed to him. In this case the method proved efficacious at once.

"A detective!" exclaimed Miss Langdon, looking at him doubtfully.

"Not from Scotland Yard," Poirot assured her. "In fact—you may have noticed it? I am not an Englishman. No, I make the private inquiries into the death of Sir Reuben Astwell."

"You don't say, now!" Miss Langdon goggled at him expectantly.

"Precisely," said Poirot, beaming. "Only to someone of discretion like yourself, would I reveal the fact. I think, mademoiselle, you may be able to aid me. Can you tell me of any gentleman staying here on the night of the murder who was absent from the hotel that evening and returned to it about twelve or half-past?"

Miss Langdon's eyes opened wider than ever.

"You don't think—?" she breathed.

"That you had the murderer here? No, but I have reason to believe that a guest staying here promenaded himself in the direction of Mon Repos that night, and if so he may have seen something which, though conveying no meaning to him, might be very useful to me."

The manageress nodded her head sapiently, with an air of one thoroughly well up in the annals of detective law.

"I understand perfectly. Now, let me see; who did we have staying here?"

She frowned, evidently running over the names in her mind, and helping her memory by occasionally checking them off on her fingertips.

"Captain Swann, Mr. Elkins, Major Blunt, old Mr. Benson. No, really, sir, I don't believe anyone went out that evening."

"You would have noticed if they had done so, eh?"

"Oh, yes, sir, it is not very usual, you see. I mean gentlemen go out to dinner and all that, but they don't go out after dinner, because— well, there is nowhere to go to, is there?"

The attractions of Abbots Cross were golf and nothing but golf.

"That is so," agreed Poirot. "Then, as far as you remember, mademoiselle, nobody from here was out that night?"

"Captain England and his wife were out to dinner."

Poirot shook his head.

"That is not the kind of thing I mean. I will try the other hotel; the Mitre, is it not?"

"Oh, the Mitre," said Miss Langdon. "Of course, anyone might have gone out walking from there."

The disparagement of her tone, though vague, was evident, and Poirot beat a tactful retreat.

Ten minutes later he was repeating the scene, this time with Miss Cole, the brusque manageress of the Mitre, a less pretentious hotel with lower prices, situated close to the station.

"There was one gentleman out late that night, came in about halfpast twelve, as far as I can remember. Quite a habit of his it was, to go out for a walk at that time of the evening. He had done it once or twice before. Let me see now, what was his name? Just for the moment I can't remember it."

She pulled a large ledger toward her and began turning over the pages.

"Nineteenth, twentieth, twenty-first, twenty-second. Ah, here we are. Naylor, Captain Humphrey Naylor."

"He had stayed here before? You know him well?"

"Once before," said Miss Cole, "about a fortnight earlier. He went out then in the evening, I remember."

"He came to play golf, eh?"

"I suppose so," said Miss Cole; "that's what most of the gentlemen come for."

"Very true," said Poirot. "Well, mademoiselle, I thank you infinitely, and I wish you good day."

He went back to Mon Repos with a very thoughtful face. Once or twice he drew something from his pocket and looked at it.

"It must be done," he murmured to himself, "and soon, as soon as I can make the opportunity."

His first proceeding on reentering the house was to ask Parsons where Miss Margrave might be found. He was told that she was in the small study dealing with Lady Astwell's correspondence, and the information seemed to afford Poirot satisfaction.

He found the little study without difficulty. Lily Margrave was seated at a desk by the window, writing. But for her the room was empty. Poirot carefully shut the door behind him and came toward the girl.

"I may have a little minute of your time, mademoiselle, you will be so kind?"

"Certainly."

Lily Margrave put the papers aside and turned toward him.

"What can I do for you?"

"On the evening of the tragedy, mademoiselle, I understand that when Lady Astwell went to her husband you went straight up to bed. Is that so?"

Lily Margrave nodded.

"You did not come down again, by any chance?"

The girl shook her head.

"I think you said, mademoiselle, that you had not at any time that evening been in the Tower Room?"

"I don't remember saying so, but as a matter of fact that is quite true. I was not in the Tower Room that evening."

Poirot raised his eyebrows.

"Curious," he murmured.

"What do you mean?"

"Very curious," murmured Hercule Poirot again. "How do you account, then, for this?"

He drew from his pocket a little scrap of stained green chiffon and held it up for the girl's inspection.

Her expression did not change, but he felt rather than heard the sharp intake of breath.

"I don't understand, M. Poirot."

"You wore, I understand, a green chiffon dress that evening, mademoiselle. This"—he tapped the scrap in his fingers—"was torn from it."

"And you found it in the Tower Room?" asked the girl sharply. "Whereabouts?"

Hercule Poirot looked at the ceiling.

"For the moment shall we just say—in the Tower Room?"

For the first time, a look of fear sprang into the girl's eyes. She began to speak, then checked herself. Poirot watched her small white hands clenching themselves on the edge of the desk.

"I wonder if I did go into the Tower Room that evening?" she mused. "Before dinner, I mean. I don't think so. I am almost sure I didn't. If that scrap has been in the Tower Room all this time, it seems to me a very extraordinary thing the police did not find it right away."

"The police," said the little man, "do not think of things that Hercule Poirot thinks of."

"I may have run in there for a minute just before dinner," mused Lily Margrave, "or it may have been the night before. I wore the same dress then. Yes, I am almost sure it was the night before."

"I think not," said Poirot evenly.

"Why?"

He only shook his head slowly from side to side.

"What do you mean?" whispered the girl.

She was leaning forward, staring at him, all the color ebbing out of her face.

"You do not notice, mademoiselle, that this fragment is stained? There is no doubt about it, that stain is human blood."

"You mean—?"

"I mean, mademoiselle, that you were in the Tower Room *after* the crime was committed, not before. I think you will do well to tell me the whole truth, lest worse should befall you."

He stood up now, a stern little figure of a man, his forefinger pointed accusingly at the girl.

"How did you find out?" gasped Lily.

"No matter, mademoiselle. I tell you Hercule Poirot *knows.* I know all about Captain Humphrey Naylor, and that you went down to meet him that night."

Lily suddenly put her head down on her arms and burst into tears. Immediately Poirot relinquished his accusing attitude.

"There, there, my little one," he said, patting the girl on the shoulder. "Do not distress yourself. Impossible to deceive Hercule Poirot; once realize that and all your troubles will be at an end. And now you will tell me the whole story, will you not? You will tell old Papa Poirot?"

"It is not what you think, it isn't, indeed. Humphrey—my brother—never touched a hair of his head."

"Your brother, eh?" said Poirot. "So that is how the land lies. Well, if you wish to save him from suspicion, you must tell me the whole story now, without reservations."

Lily sat up again, pushing back the hair from her forehead. After a minute or two, she began to speak in a low, clear voice.

"I will tell you the truth, M. Poirot. I can see now that it would be absurd to do anything else. My real name is Lily Naylor, and Humphrey is my only brother. Some years ago, when he was out in Africa, he discovered a gold mine, or rather, I should say, discovered the presence of gold. I can't tell you this part of it properly, because I don't understand the technical details, but what it amounted to was this:

"The thing seemed likely to be a very big undertaking, and Humphrey came home with letters to Sir Reuben Astwell in the hopes of getting him interested in the matter. I don't understand the rights of it even now, but I gather that Sir Reuben sent out an expert to report, and that he subsequently told my brother that the expert's report was unfavorable and that he, Humphrey, had made a great mistake. My brother went back to Africa on an expedition into the interior and was lost sight of. It was assumed that he and the expedition had perished.

"It was soon after that that a company was formed to exploit the Mpala Gold Fields. When my brother got back to England he at once jumped to the conclusion that these gold fields were identical with those he had discovered. Sir Reuben Astwell had apparently nothing to do with this company, and they had seemingly discovered the place on their own. But my brother was not satisfied; he was convinced that Sir Reuben had deliberately swindled him.

"He became more and more violent and unhappy about the matter. We two are alone in the world, M. Poirot, and as it was necessary then for me to go out and earn my own living, I conceived the idea of taking a post in this household and trying to find out if any connection existed between Sir Reuben and the Mpala Gold Fields. For obvious reasons I concealed my real name, and I'll admit frankly that I used a forged reference.

"There were many applicants for the post, most of them with better qualifications than mine, so—well, M. Poirot, I wrote a beautiful letter from the Duchess of Perthshire, who I knew had just gone to America. I thought a Duchess would have a great effect upon Lady Astwell, and I was quite right. She engaged me on the spot.

"Since then I have been that hateful thing, a spy, and until lately with no success. Sir Reuben is not a man to give away his business secrets, but when Victor Astwell came back from Africa he was less guarded in his talk, and I began to believe that, after all, Humphrey had not been mistaken. My brother came down here about a fortnight before the murder, and I crept out of the house to meet him secretly at night. I told him the things Victor Astwell had said, and he became very excited and assured me I was definitely on the right track.

"But after that things began to go wrong; someone must have seen me stealing out of the house and have reported the matter to Sir Reuben. He became suspicious and hunted up my references, and soon discovered the fact that they were forged. The crisis came on the day of the murder. I think he thought I was after his wife's jewels. Whatever his suspicions were, he had no intention to allow me to remain any longer at Mon Repos, though he agreed not to prosecute me on account of the references. Lady Astwell took my part throughout and stood up valiantly to Sir Reuben."

She paused. Poirot's face was very grave.

"And now, mademoiselle," he said, "we come to the night of the murder."

Lily swallowed hard and nodded her head.

"To begin with, M. Poirot, I must tell you that my brother had come down again, and that I had arranged to creep out and meet him once more. I went up to my room, as I have said, but I did not go to bed. Instead, I waited till I thought everyone was asleep, and then stole downstairs again and out by the side door. I met Humphrey and acquainted him in a few hurried words with what had occurred. I told him that I believed the papers he wanted were in Sir Reuben's safe in the Tower Room, and we agreed as a last desperate adventure to try and get hold of them that night.

"I was to go in first and see that the way was clear. I heard the church clock strike twelve as I went in by the side door. I was halfway up the stairs leading to the Tower Room, when I heard a thud of something falling, and a voice cried out, 'My God!' A minute or two afterward the door of the Tower Room opened, and Charles Leverson came out. I could see his face quite clearly in the moonlight, but I was crouching some way below him on the stairs where it was dark, and he did not see me at all.

"He stood there a moment swaying on his feet and looking ghastly. He seemed to be listening; then with an effort he seemed to pull himself together and, opening the door into the Tower Room, called out something about there being no harm done. His voice was quite jaunty and debonair, but his face gave the lie to it. He waited a minute more, and then slowly went on upstairs and out of sight.

"When he had gone I waited a minute or two and then crept to the Tower Room door. I had a feeling that something tragic had happened. The main light was out, but the desk lamp was on, and by its light I saw Sir Reuben lying on the floor by the desk. I don't know how I managed it, but I nerved myself at last to go over and kneel down by him. I saw at once that he was dead, struck down from behind, and also that he couldn't have been dead long; I touched his hand and it was still quite warm. It was just horrible, M. Poirot. Horrible!"

She shuddered again at the remembrance.

"And then?" said Poirot, looking at her keenly.

Lily Margrave nodded.

"Yes, M. Poirot, I know what you are thinking. Why didn't I give the alarm and raise the house? I should have done so, I know, but it came over me in a flash, as I knelt there, that my quarrel with Sir Reuben, my stealing out to meet Humphrey, the fact that I was being sent away on the morrow, made a fatal sequence. They would say that I had let Humphrey in, and that Humphrey had killed Sir Reuben out of revenge. If I said that I had seen Charles Leverson leaving the room, no one would believe me.

"It was terrible, M. Poirot! I knelt there, and thought and thought, and the more I thought the more my nerve failed me. Presently I noticed Sir Reuben's keys which had dropped from his pocket as he fell. Among them was the key of the safe, the combination word I already knew, since Lady Astwell had mentioned it once in my hearing. I went over to that safe, M. Poirot, unlocked it and rummaged through the papers I found there.

"In the end I found what I was looking for. Humphrey had been perfectly right. Sir Reuben was behind the Mpala Gold Fields, and he had deliberately swindled Humphrey. That made it all the worse. It gave a perfectly definite motive for Humphrey having committed the crime. I put the papers back in the safe, left the key in the door of it, and went straight upstairs to my room. In the morning I pretended to be surprised and horror-stricken, like everyone else, when the house-maid discovered the body."

She stopped and looked piteously across at Poirot.

"You do believe me, M. Poirot. Oh, do say you believe me!"

"I believe you, mademoiselle," said Poirot; "you have explained many things that puzzled me. Your absolute certainty, for one thing, that Charles Leverson had committed the crime, and at the same time your persistent efforts to keep me from coming down here."

Lily nodded.

"I was afraid of you," she admitted frankly. "Lady Astwell could not know, as I did, that Charles was guilty, and I couldn't say anything. I hoped against hope that you would refuse to take the case."

"But for that obvious anxiety on your part, I might have done so," said Poirot dryly.

Lily looked at him swiftly, her lips trembled a little.

"And now, M. Poirot, what—what are you going to do?"

"As far as you are concerned, mademoiselle, nothing. I believe your story, and I accept it. The next step is to go to London and see Inspector Miller."

"And then?" asked Lily.

"And then," said Poirot, "we shall see."

Outside the door of the study he looked once more at the little square of stained green chiffon which he held in his hand.

"Amazing," he murmured to himself complacently, "the ingenuity of Hercule Poirot."

Detective Inspector Miller was not particularly fond of M. Hercule Poirot. He did not belong to that small band of inspectors at the Yard who welcomed the little Belgian's cooperation. He was wont to say that Hercule Poirot was much overrated. In this case he felt pretty sure of himself, and greeted Poirot with high good humor in consequence.

"Acting for Lady Astwell, are you? Well, you have taken up a mare's nest in that case."

"There is, then, no possible doubt about the matter?"

Miller winked. "Never was a clearer case, short of catching a murderer absolutely red-handed."

"M. Leverson has made a statement, I understand?"

"He had better have kept his mouth shut," said the detective. "He repeats over and over again that he went straight up to his room and never went near his uncle. That's a fool story on the face of it."

"It is certainly against the weight of evidence," murmured Poirot. "How does he strike you, this young M. Leverson?"

"Darned young fool."

"A weak character, eh?"

The inspector nodded.

"One would hardly think a young man of that type would have the—how do you say it—the bowels to commit such a crime."

"On the face of it, no," agreed the inspector. "But, bless you, I have come across the same thing many times. Get a weak, dissipated young man into a corner, fill him up with a drop too much to drink, and for a limited amount of time you can turn him into a fire eater. A weak man in a corner is more dangerous than a strong man."

"That is true, yes; that is true what you say."

Miller unbent a little further.

"Of course, it is all right for you, M. Poirot," he said. "You get your fees just the same, and naturally you have to make a pretense of examining the evidence to satisfy Her Ladyship. I can understand all that."

"You understand such interesting things," murmured Poirot, and took his leave.

His next call was upon the solicitor representing Charles Leverson. Mr. Mayhew was a thin, dry, cautious gentleman. He received Poirot with reserve. Poirot, however, had his own ways of inducing confidence. In ten minutes' time the two were talking together amicably.

"You will understand," said Poirot, "I am acting in this case solely on behalf of Mr. Leverson. That is Lady Astwell's wish. She is convinced that he is not guilty."

"Yes, yes, quite so," said Mr. Mayhew without enthusiasm.

Poirot's eyes twinkled. "You do not perhaps attach much importance to the opinions of Lady Astwell?" he suggested.

"She might be just as sure of his guilt tomorrow," said the lawyer dryly.

"Her intuitions are not evidence certainly," agreed Poirot, "and on the face of it the case looks very black against this poor young man."

"It is a pity he said what he did to the police," said the lawyer; "it will be no good his sticking to that story."

"Has he stuck to it with you?" inquired Poirot.

Mayhew nodded. "It never varies an iota. He repeats it like a parrot."

"And that is what destroys your faith in him," mused the other. "Ah, don't deny it," he added quickly, holding up an arresting hand. "I see it only too plainly. In your heart you believe him guilty. But listen now to me, to me, Hercule Poirot. I present to you a case.

"This young man comes home, he has drunk the cocktail, the cock-tail, and again the cocktail, also without doubt the English whisky and soda many times. He is full of, what you call it? the courage Dutch, and in that mood he lets himself into the house with his latchkey, and he goes with unsteady steps up to the Tower Room. He looks in at the door and sees in the dim light his uncle, apparently bending over the desk.

"M. Leverson is full, as we have said, of the courage Dutch. He lets himself go, he tells his uncle just what he thinks of him. He defies him, he insults him, and the more his uncle does not answer back, the more he is encouraged to go on, to repeat himself, to say the same thing over and over again, and each time more loudly. But at last the continued silence of his uncle awakens an apprehension. He goes nearer to him, he lays his hand on his uncle's shoulder, and his uncle's figure crumples under his touch and sinks in a heap to the ground.

"He is sobered then, this M. Leverson. The chair falls with a crash, and he bends over Sir Reuben. He realizes what has happened, he looks at his hand covered with something warm and red. He is in a panic then, he would give anything on earth to recall the cry which has just sprung from his lips, echoing through the house. Mechanically he picks up the chair, then he hastens out through the door and listens. He fancies he hears a sound, and immediately, automatically, he pretends to be speaking to his uncle through the open door.

"The sound is not repeated. He is convinced he has been mistaken in thinking he heard one. Now all is silence, he creeps up to his room, and at once it occurs to him how much better it will be if he pretends never to have been near his uncle that night. So he tells his story. Parsons at that time, remember, has said nothing of what he heard. When he does do so, it is too late for M. Leverson to change. He is stupid, and he is obstinate, he sticks to his story. Tell me, monsieur, is that not possible?"

"Yes," said the lawyer, "I suppose in the way you put it that it is possible."

Poirot rose to his feet.

"You have the privilege of seeing M. Leverson," he said. "Put to him the story I have told you, and ask him if it is not true."

Outside the lawyer's office, Poirot hailed a taxi.

"348 Harley Street," he murmured to the driver.

Poirot's departure for London had taken Lady Astwell by surprise, for the little man had not made any mention of what he proposed doing. On his return, after an absence of twenty-four hours, he was informed by Parsons that Lady Astwell would like to see him as soon as possible. Poirot found the lady in her own boudoir. She was lying down on the divan, her head propped up by cushions, and she looked startlingly ill and haggard; far more so than she had done on the day Poirot arrived.

"So you have come back, M. Poirot?"

"I have returned, milady."

"You went to London?"

Poirot nodded.

"You didn't tell me you were going," said Lady Astwell sharply.

"A thousand apologies, milady, I am in error, I should have done so. La prochaine fois—"

"You will do exactly the same," interrupted Lady Astwell with a shrewd touch of humor. "Do things first and tell people afterward, that is your motto right enough."

"Perhaps it has also been milady's motto?" His eyes twinkled.

"Now and then, perhaps," admitted the other. "What did you go up to London for, M. Poirot? You can tell me now, I suppose?"

"I had an interview with the good Inspector Miller, and also with the excellent Mr. Mayhew."

Lady Astwell's eyes searched his face.

"And you think, now—?" she said slowly.

Poirot's eyes were fixed on her steadily.

"That there is a possibility of Charles Leverson's innocence," he said gravely.

"Ah!" Lady Astwell half sprang up, sending two cushions rolling to the ground. "I was right, then, I was right!"

"I said a possibility, madame, that is all."

Something in his tone seemed to strike her. She raised herself on one elbow and regarded him piercingly.

"Can I do anything?" she asked.

"Yes," he nodded his head, "you can tell me, Lady Astwell, why you suspect Owen Trefusis."

"I have told you I *know*—that's all."

"Unfortunately that is not enough," said Poirot dryly. "Cast your mind back to the fatal evening, milady. Remember each detail, each tiny happening. What did you notice or observe about the secretary? I, Hercule Poirot, tell you there must have been something."

Lady Astwell shook her head.

"I hardly noticed him at all that evening," she said, "and I certainly was not thinking of him."

"Your mind was taken up by something else?"

"Yes."

"With your husband's animus against Miss Lily Margrave?"

"That's right," said Lady Astwell, nodding her head; "you seem to know all about it, M. Poirot."

"Me, I know everything," declared the little man with an absurdly grandiose air.

"I am fond of Lily, M. Poirot; you have seen that for yourself. Reuben began kicking up a rumpus about some reference or other of hers. Mind you, I don't say she hadn't cheated about it. She had. But, bless you, I have done many worse things than that in the old days. You have got to be up to all sorts of tricks to get around theatrical managers. There is nothing I wouldn't have written, or said, or done, in my time.

"Lily wanted this job, and she put in a lot of slick work that was not quite—well, quite the thing, you know. Men are so stupid about that sort of thing; Lily really might have been a bank clerk absconding with millions for the fuss he made about it. I was terribly worried all the evening, because, although I could usually get round Reuben in the end, he was terribly pig-headed at times, poor darling. So of course I hadn't time to go noticing secretaries, not that one does notice Mr. Trefusis much, anyway. He is just there and that's all there is to it."

"I have noticed that fact about M. Trefusis," said Poirot. "His is not a personality that stands forth, that shines, that hits you *cr-r-rack*."

"No," said Lady Astwell, "he is not like Victor."

"M. Victor Astwell is, I should say, explosive."

"That is a splendid word for him," said Lady Astwell. "He explodes all over the house, like one of those thingimy-jig firework things."

"A somewhat quick temper, I should imagine?" suggested Poirot.

"Oh, he's a perfect devil when roused," said Lady Astwell, "but bless you, *I'm* not afraid of him. All bark and no bite to Victor."

Poirot looked at the ceiling.

"And you can tell me nothing about the secretary that evening?" he murmured gently.

"I tell you, M. Poirot, I *know*. It's intuition. A woman's intuition—"

"Will not hang a man," said Poirot, "and what is more to the point, it will not save a man from being hanged. Lady Astwell, if you sincerely believe that M. Leverson is innocent, and that your suspicions of the secretary are well-founded, will you consent to a little experiment?"

"What kind of an experiment?" demanded Lady Astwell suspiciously.

"Will you permit yourself to be put into a condition of hypnosis?"

"Whatever for?"

Poirot leaned forward.

"If I were to tell you, madame, that your intuition is based on certain facts recorded subconsciously, you would probably be skeptical. I will only say, then, that this experiment I propose may be of great importance to that unfortunate young man, Charles Leverson. You will not refuse?"

"Who is going to put me into a trance?" demanded Lady Astwell suspiciously. "You?"

"A friend of mine, Lady Astwell, arrives, if I mistake not, at this very minute. I hear the wheels of the car outside."

"Who is he?"

"A Doctor Cazalet of Harley Street."

"Is he—all right?" asked Lady Astwell apprehensively.

"He is not a quack, madame, if that is what you mean. You can trust yourself in his hands quite safely."

"Well," said Lady Astwell with a sigh, "I think it is all bunkum, but you can try if you like. Nobody is going to say that I stood in your way."

"A thousand thanks, milady."

Poirot hurried from the room. In a few minutes he returned ushering in a cheerful, round-faced little man, with spectacles, who was very upsetting to Lady Astwell's conception of what a hypnotist should look like. Poirot introduced them.

"Well," said Lady Astwell good-humoredly, "how do we start this tomfoolery?"

"Quite simple, Lady Astwell, quite simple," said the little doctor. "Just lean back, so—that's right, that's right. No need to be uneasy."

"I am not in the least uneasy," said Lady Astwell. "I should like to see anyone hypnotizing me against my will."

Doctor Cazalet smiled broadly.

"Yes, but if you consent, it won't be against your will, will it?" he said cheerfully. "That's right. Turn off that other light, will you, M. Poirot? Just let yourself go to sleep, Lady Astwell."

He shifted his position a little.

"It's getting late. You are sleepy—very sleepy. Your eyelids are heavy, they are closing—closing—closing. Soon you will be asleep. . . ."

His voice droned on, low, soothing, and monotonous. Presently he leaned forward and gently lifted Lady Astwell's right eyelid. Then he turned to Poirot, nodding in a satisfied manner.

"That's all right," he said in a low voice. "Shall I go ahead?"

"If you please."

The doctor spoke out sharply and authoritatively, "You are asleep, Lady Astwell, but you hear me, and you can answer my questions."

Without stirring or raising an eyelid, the motionless figure on the sofa replied in a low, monotonous voice:

"I hear you. I can answer your questions."

"Lady Astwell, I want you to go back to the evening on which your husband was murdered. You remember that evening?"

"Yes."

"You are at the dinner table. Describe to me what you saw and felt."

The prone figure stirred a little restlessly.

"I am in great distress. I am worried about Lily."

"We know that; tell us what you saw."

"Victor is eating all the salted almonds; he is greedy. Tomorrow I shall tell Parsons not to put the dish on that side of the table."

"Go on, Lady Astwell."

"Reuben is in a bad humor tonight. I don't think it is altogether about Lily. It is something to do with business. Victor looks at him in a queer way."

"Tell us about Mr. Trefusis, Lady Astwell."

"His left shirt cuff is frayed. He puts a lot of grease on his hair. I wish men didn't, it ruins the covers in the drawing room."

Cazalet looked at Poirot; the other made a motion with his head.

"It is after dinner, Lady Astwell, you are having coffee. Describe the scene to me."

"The coffee is good tonight. It varies. Cook is very unreliable over her coffee. Lily keeps looking out of the window, I don't know why. Now, Reuben comes into the room; he is in one of his worst moods tonight, and bursts out with a perfect flood of abuse to poor Mr. Trefusis. Mr. Trefusis has his hand round the paper knife, the big one with the sharp blade like a knife. How hard he is grasping it; his knuckles are quite white. Look, he has dug it so hard in the table that the point snaps. He holds it just as you would hold a dagger you were going to stick into someone. There, they have gone out together now. Lily has got her green evening dress on; she looks so pretty in green, just like a lily. I must have the covers cleaned next week."

"Just a minute, Lady Astwell."

The doctor leaned across to Poirot.

"We have got it, I think," he murmured. "That action with the paper knife, that's what convinced her that the secretary did the thing."

"Let us go on to the Tower Room now."

The doctor nodded, and began once more to question Lady Astwell in his high, decisive voice.

"It is later in the evening; you are in the Tower Room with your husband. You and he have had a terrible scene together, have you not?"

Again the figure stirred uneasily.

"Yes—terrible—terrible. We said dreadful things—both of us."

"Never mind that now. You can see the room clearly, the curtains were drawn, the lights were on."

"Not the middle light, only the desk light."

"You are leaving your husband now, you are saying good night to him."

"No, I was too angry."

"It is the last time you will see him; very soon he will be murdered. Do you know who murdered him, Lady Astwell?"

"Yes. Mr. Trefusis."

"Why do you say that?"

"Because of the bulge—the bulge in the curtain."

"There was a bulge in the curtain?"

"Yes."

"You saw it?"

"Yes. I almost touched it."

"Was there a man concealed there—Mr. Trefusis?"

"Yes."

"How do you know?"

For the first time the monotonous answering voice hesitated and lost confidence.

"I—I—because of the paper knife."

Poirot and the doctor again interchanged swift glances.

"I don't understand you, Lady Astwell. There was a bulge in the curtain, you say? Someone concealed there? You didn't see that person?"

"No."

"You thought it was Mr. Trefusis because of the way he held the paper knife earlier?"

"Yes."

"But Mr. Trefusis had gone upstairs, had he not?"

"Yes—yes, that's right, he had gone upstairs."

"So he couldn't have been behind the curtain in the window?"

"No—no, of course not, he wasn't there."

"He had said good night to your husband some time before, hadn't he?"

"Yes."

"And you didn't see him again?"

"No."

She was stirring now, throwing herself about, moaning faintly.

"She is coming out," said the doctor. "Well, I think we have got all we can, eh?"

Poirot nodded. The doctor leaned over Lady Astwell.

"You are waking," he murmured softly. "You are waking now. In another minute you will open your eyes."

The two men waited, and presently Lady Astwell sat upright and stared at them both.

"Have I been having a nap?"

"That's it, Lady Astwell, just a little sleep," said the doctor.

She looked at him.

"Some of your hocus-pocus, eh?"

"You don't feel any the worse, I hope?" he asked.

Lady Astwell yawned.

"I feel rather tired and done up."

The doctor rose.

"I will ask them to send you up some coffee," he said, "and we will leave you for the present."

"Did I—say anything?" Lady Astwell called after them as they reached the door.

Poirot smiled back at her.

"Nothing of great importance, madame. You informed us that the drawing-room covers needed cleaning."

"So they do," said Lady Astwell. "You needn't have put me into a trance to get me to tell you that." She laughed good-humoredly. "Anything more?"

"Do you remember M. Trefusis picking up a paper knife in the drawing room that night?" asked Poirot.

"I don't know, I'm sure," said Lady Astwell. "He may have done so."

"Does a bulge in the curtain convey anything to you?"

Lady Astwell frowned.

"I seem to remember," she said slowly. "No—it's gone, and yet—"

"Do not distress yourself, Lady Astwell," said Poirot quickly. "It is of no importance—of no importance whatever."

The doctor went with Poirot to the latter's room.

"Well," said Cazalet, "I think this explains things pretty clearly. No doubt when Sir Reuben was dressing down the secretary, the latter grabbed tight hold on a paper knife, and had to exercise a good deal of self-control to prevent himself answering back. Lady Astwell's conscious mind was wholly taken up with the problem of Lily Margrave, but her subconscious mind noticed and misconstrued the action.

"It implanted in her the firm conviction that Trefusis murdered Sir Reuben. Now we come to the bulge in the curtain. That is interesting. I take it from what you have told me of the Tower Room that the desk was right in the window. There are curtains across that window, of course?"

"Yes, *mon ami,* black velvet curtains."

"And there is room in the embrasure of the window for anyone to remain concealed behind them?"

"There would be just room, I think."

"Then there seems at least a possibility," said the doctor slowly, "that someone was concealed in the room, but if so it could not be the secretary, since they both saw him leave the room. It could not be Victor Astwell, for Trefusis met him going out, and it could not be Lily Margrave. Whoever it was must have been concealed there *before* Sir Reuben entered the room that evening. You have told me pretty well how the land lies. Now what about Captain Naylor? Could it have been he who was concealed there?"

"It is always possible," admitted Poirot. "He certainly dined at the hotel, but how soon he went out afterward is difficult to fix exactly. He returned about half-past twelve."

"Then it might have been he," said the doctor, "and if so, he committed the crime. He had the motive, and there was a weapon near at hand. You don't seem satisfied with the idea, though?"

"Me, I have other ideas," confessed Poirot. "Tell me now, *M. le Docteur,* supposing for one minute that Lady Astwell herself had committed this crime, would she necessarily betray the fact in the hypnotic state?"

The doctor whistled.

"So that's what you are getting at? Lady Astwell is the criminal, eh? Of course—it is possible; I never thought of it till this minute. She was the last to be with him, and no one saw him alive afterward. As to your question, I should be inclined to say—No. Lady Astwell would go into the hypnotic state with a strong mental reservation to say nothing of her own part in the crime. She would answer my questions truthfully, but she would be dumb on that one point. Yet I should hardly have expected her to be so insistent on Mr. Trefusis's guilt."

"I comprehend," said Poirot. "But I have not said that I believe Lady Astwell to be the criminal. It is a suggestion, that is all."

"It is an interesting case," said the doctor after a minute or two. "Granting Charles Leverson is innocent, there are so many possibilities, Humphrey Naylor, Lady Astwell, and even Lily Margrave."

"There is another you have not mentioned," said Poirot quietly, "Victor Astwell. According to his own story, he sat in his room with the door open waiting for Charles Leverson's return, but we have only his own word for it, you comprehend?"

"He is the bad-tempered fellow, isn't he?" asked the doctor. "The one you told me about?"

"That is so," agreed Poirot.

The doctor rose to his feet.

"Well, I must be getting back to town. You will let me know how things shape, won't you?"

After the doctor had left, Poirot pulled the bell for George.

"A cup of *tisane*, George. My nerves are much disturbed."

"Certainly, sir," said George. "I will prepare it immediately."

Ten minutes later he brought a steaming cup to his master. Poirot inhaled the noxious fumes with pleasure. As he sipped it, he soliloquized aloud.

"The chase is different all over the world. To catch the fox you ride hard with the dogs. You shout, you run, it is a matter of speed. I have not shot the stag myself, but I understand that to do so you crawl for many long, long hours upon your stomach. My friend Hastings has recounted the affair to me. Our method here, my good George, must be neither of these. Let us reflect upon the household cat. For many long, weary hours, he watches the mouse hole, he makes no movement, he betrays no energy, but—he does not go away."

He sighed and put the empty cup down on its saucer.

"I told you to pack for a few days. Tomorrow, my good George, you will go to London and bring down what is necessary for a fortnight."

"Very good, sir," said George. As usual he displayed no emotion.

The apparently permanent presence of Hercule Poirot at Mon Repos was disquieting to many people. Victor Astwell remonstrated with his sister-in-law about it.

"It's all very well, Nancy. You don't know what fellows of that kind are like. He has found jolly comfortable quarters here, and he is evidently going to settle down comfortably for about a month, charging you two guineas a day all the while."

Lady Astwell's reply was to the effect that she could manage her own affairs without interference.

Lily Margrave tried earnestly to conceal her perturbation. At the time, she had felt sure that Poirot believed her story. Now she was not so certain.

Poirot did not play an entirely quiescent game. On the fifth day of his sojourn he brought down a small thumbograph album to dinner. As a method of getting the thumbprints of the household, it seemed a rather clumsy device, yet not perhaps so clumsy as it seemed, since no one could afford to refuse their thumbprints. Only after the little man had retired to bed did Victor Astwell state his views.

"You see what it means, Nancy. He is out after one of us."

"Don't be absurd, Victor."

"Well, what other meaning could that blinking little book of his have?"

"M. Poirot knows what he is doing," said Lady Astwell complacently, and looked with some meaning at Owen Trefusis.

On another occasion Poirot introduced the game of tracing footprints on a sheet of paper. The following morning, going with his soft catlike tread into the library, the detective startled Owen Trefusis, who leaped from his chair as though he had been shot.

"You must really excuse me, M. Poirot," he said primly, "but you have us on the jump."

"Indeed, how is that?" demanded the little man innocently.

"I will admit," said the secretary, "that I thought the case against Charles Leverson utterly overwhelming. You apparently do not find it so."

Poirot was standing looking out of the window. He turned suddenly to the other.

"I shall tell you something, M. Trefusis—in confidence."

"Yes?"

Poirot seemed in no hurry to begin. He waited a minute, hesitating. When he did speak, his opening words were coincident with the opening and shutting of the front door. For a man saying something in confidence, he spoke rather loudly, his voice drowning the sound of a footstep in the hall outside.

"I shall tell you this in confidence, Mr. Trefusis. There is new evidence. It goes to prove that when Charles Leverson entered the Tower Room that night, Sir Reuben was already dead."

The secretary stared at him.

"But what evidence? Why have we not heard of it?"

"You *will* hear," said the little man mysteriously. "In the meantime, you and I alone know the secret."

He skipped nimbly out of the room, and almost collided with Victor Astwell in the hall outside.

"You have just come in, eh, monsieur?"

Astwell nodded.

"Beastly day outside," he said, breathing hard, "cold and blowy."

"Ah," said Poirot, "I shall not promenade myself today—me, I am like a cat, I sit by the fire and keep myself warm."

"Ça marche, George," he said that evening to the faithful valet, rubbing his hands as he spoke, "they are on the tenterhooks—the jump! It is hard, George, to play the game of the cat, the waiting game, but it answers, yes, it answers wonderfully. Tomorrow we make a further effect."

On the following day, Trefusis was obliged to go up to town. He went up by the same train as Victor Astwell. No sooner had they left the house than Poirot was galvanized into a fever of activity.

"Come, George, let us hurry to work. If the housemaid should approach these rooms, you must delay her. Speak to her sweet nothings, George, and keep her in the corridor."

He went first to the secretary's room, and began a thorough search. Not a drawer or a shelf was left uninspected. Then he replaced everything hurriedly, and declared his quest finished. George, on guard in the doorway, gave way to a deferential cough.

"If you will excuse me, sir?"

"Yes, my good George?"

"The shoes, sir. The two pairs of brown shoes were on the second shelf, and the patent leather ones were on the shelf underneath. In replacing them you have reversed the order."

"Marvelous!" cried Poirot, holding up his hands. "But let us not distress ourselves over that. It is of no importance, I assure you, George. Never will M. Trefusis notice such a trifling matter."

"As you think, sir," said George.

"It is your business to notice such things," said Poirot encouragingly as he clapped the other on the shoulder. "It reflects credit upon you."

The valet did not reply, and when, later in the day, the proceeding was repeated in the room of Victor Astwell, he made no comment on the fact that Mr. Astwell's underclothing was not returned to its drawers strictly according to plan. Yet, in the second case at least, events proved the valet to be right and Poirot wrong. Victor Astwell came storming into the drawing room that evening.

"Now, look here, you blasted little Belgian jackanapes, what do you mean by searching my room? What the devil do you think you are going to find there? I won't have it, do you hear? That's what comes of having a ferreting little spy in the house."

Poirot's hands spread themselves out eloquently as his words tumbled one over the other. He offered a hundred apologies, a thousand, a million. He had been maladroit, officious, he was confused. He had taken an unwarranted liberty. In the end the infuriated gentleman was forced to subside, still growling.

And again that evening, sipping his *tisane*, Poirot murmured to George:

"It marches, my good George, yes—it marches."

"Friday," observed Hercule Poirot thoughtfully, "is my lucky day."

"Indeed, sir."

"You are not superstitious, perhaps, my good George?"

"I prefer not to sit down thirteen at table, sir, and I am adverse to passing under ladders. I have no superstitions about a Friday, sir."

"That is well," said Poirot, "for, see you, today we make our Waterloo."

"Really, sir."

"You have such enthusiasm, my good George, you do not even ask what I propose to do."

"And what is that, sir?"

"Today, George, I make a final thorough search of the Tower Room."

True enough, after breakfast, Poirot, with the permission of Lady Astwell, went to the scene of the crime. There, at various times of the morning, members of the household saw him crawling about on all fours, examining minutely the black velvet curtains and standing on high chairs to examine the picture frames on the wall. Lady Astwell for the first time displayed uneasiness.

"I have to admit it," she said. "He is getting on my nerves at last. He has something up his sleeve, and I don't know what it is. And the way he is crawling about on the floor up there like a dog makes me downright shivery. What is he looking for, I'd like to know? Lily, my dear, I wish you would go up and see what he is up to now. No, on the whole, I'd rather you stayed with me."

"Shall I go, Lady Astwell?" asked the secretary, rising from the desk.

"If you would, Mr. Trefusis."

Owen Trefusis left the room and mounted the stairs to the Tower Room. At first glance, he thought the room was empty, there was certainly no sign of Hercule Poirot there. He was just turning to go down again when a sound caught his ears; he then saw the little man halfway down the spiral staircase that led to the bedroom above.

He was on his hands and knees; in his left hand was a little pocket lens, and through this he was examining minutely something on the woodwork beside the stair carpet.

As the secretary watched him, he uttered a sudden grunt, and slipped the lens into his pocket. He then rose to his feet, holding something between his finger and thumb. At that moment he became aware of the secretary's presence.

"Ah, hah! M. Trefusis, I didn't hear you enter."

He was in that moment a different man. Triumph and exultation beamed all over his face. Trefusis stared at him in surprise.

"What is the matter, M. Poirot? You look very pleased."

The little man puffed out his chest.

"Yes, indeed. See you I have at last found that which I have been looking for from the beginning. I have here between my finger and thumb the one thing necessary to convict the criminal."

"Then," the secretary raised his eyebrows, "it was not Charles Leverson?"

"It was not Charles Leverson," said Poirot. "Until this moment, though I know the criminal, I am not sure of his name, but at last all is clear."

He stepped down the stairs and tapped the secretary on the shoulder.

"I am obliged to go to London immediately. Speak to Lady Astwell for me. Will you request of her that everyone should be assembled in the Tower Room this evening at nine o'clock? I shall be there then, and I shall reveal the truth. Ah, me, but I am well content."

And breaking into a fantastic little dance, he skipped from the Tower Room. Trefusis was left staring after him.

A few minutes later Poirot appeared in the library, demanding if anyone could supply him with a little cardboard box.

"Unfortunately, I have not such a thing with me," he explained, "and there is something of great value that it is necessary for me to put inside."

From one of the drawers in the desk Trefusis produced a small box, and Poirot professed himself highly delighted with it.

He hurried upstairs with his treasure trove; meeting George on the landing, he handed the box to him.

"There is something of great importance inside," he explained. "Place it, my good George, in the second drawer of my dressing table, beside the jewel case that contains my pearl studs."

"Very good, sir," said George.

"Do not break it," said Poirot. "Be very careful. Inside that box is something that will hang a criminal."

"You don't say, sir," said George.

Poirot hurried down the stairs again and, seizing his hat, departed from the house at a brisk run.

His return was more unostentatious. The faithful George, according to orders, admitted him by the side door.

"They are all in the Tower Room?" inquired Poirot.

"Yes, sir."

There was a murmured interchange of a few words, and then Poirot mounted with the triumphant step of the victor to that room where the murder had taken place less than a month ago. His eyes swept around the room. They were all there, Lady Astwell, Victor Astwell, Lily Margrave, the secretary, and Parsons, the butler. The latter was hovering by the door uncertainly.

"George, sir, said I should be needed here," said Parsons as Poirot made his appearance. "I don't know if that is right, sir?"

"Quite right," said Poirot. "Remain, I pray of you."

He advanced to the middle of the room.

"This has been a case of great interest," he said in a slow, reflective voice. "It is interesting because anyone might have murdered Sir Reuben Astwell. Who inherits his money? Charles Leverson and Lady Astwell. Who was with him last that night? Lady Astwell. Who quarreled with him violently? Again Lady Astwell."

"What are you talking about?" cried Lady Astwell. "I don't understand, I—"

"But someone else quarreled with Sir Reuben," continued Poirot in a pensive voice. "Someone else left him that night white with rage. Supposing Lady Astwell left her husband alive at a quarter to twelve that night, there would be ten minutes before Mr. Charles Leverson returned, ten minutes in which it would be possible for someone from the second floor to steal down and do the deed, and then return to his room again."

Victor Astwell sprang up with a cry.

"What the hell—?" He stopped, choking with rage.

"In a rage, Mr. Astwell, you once killed a man in West Africa."

"I don't believe it," cried Lily Margrave.

She came forward, her hands clenched, two bright spots of color in her cheeks.

"I don't believe it," repeated the girl. She came close to Victor Astwell's side.

"It's true, Lily," said Astwell, "but there are things this man doesn't know. The fellow I killed was a witch doctor who had just massacred fifteen children. I consider that I was justified."

Lily came up to Poirot.

"M. Poirot," she said earnestly, "you are wrong. Because a man has a sharp temper, because he breaks out and says all kinds of things, that is not any reason why he should do a murder. I know—I *know*, I tell you—that Mr. Astwell is incapable of such a thing."

Poirot looked at her, a very curious smile on his face. Then he took her hand in his and patted it gently.

"You see, mademoiselle," he said gently, "you also have your intuitions. So you believe in Mr. Astwell, do you?"

Lily spoke quietly.

"Mr. Astwell is a good man," she said, "and he is honest. He had nothing to do with the inside work of the Mpala Gold Fields. He is good through and through, and—I have promised to marry him."

Victor Astwell came to her side and took her other hand.

"Before God, M. Poirot," he said, "I didn't kill my brother."

"I know you did not," said Poirot.

His eyes swept around the room.

"Listen, my friends. In an hypnotic trance, Lady Astwell mentioned having seen a bulge in the curtain that night."

Everyone's eyes swept to the window.

"You mean there was a burglar concealed there?" exclaimed Victor Astwell. "What a splendid solution!"

"Ah!" said Poirot gently. "But it was not *that* curtain."

He wheeled around and pointed to the curtain that masked the little staircase.

"Sir Reuben used the bedroom the night prior to the crime. He breakfasted in bed, and he had Mr. Trefusis up there to give him instructions. I don't know what it was that Mr. Trefusis left in that bedroom, but there was something. When he said good night to Sir Reuben and Lady Astwell, he remembered this thing and ran up the stairs to fetch it. I don't think either the husband or wife noticed him, for they had already begun a violent discussion. They were in the middle of this quarrel when Mr. Trefusis came down the stairs again.

"The things they were saying to each other were of so intimate and personal a nature that Mr. Trefusis was placed in a very awkward position. It was clear to him that they imagined he had left the room some time ago. Fearing to arouse Sir Reuben's anger against himself, he decided to remain where he was and slip out later. He stayed there behind the curtain, and as Lady Astwell left the room she subconsciously noticed the outline of his form there.

"When Lady Astwell had left the room, Trefusis tried to steal out unobserved, but Sir Reuben happened to turn his head, and became aware of the secretary's presence. Already in a bad temper, Sir Reuben hurled abuse at his secretary, and accused him of deliberately eavesdropping and spying.

"Messieurs and mesdames, I am a student of psychology. All through this case I have looked, not for the bad-tempered man or woman, for bad temper is its own safety valve. He who can bark does not bite. No, I have looked for the good-tempered man, for the man who is patient and self-controlled, for the man who for nine years has played the part of the underdog. There is no strain so great as that which has endured for years, there is no resentment like that which accumulates slowly.

"For nine years Sir Reuben has bullied and browbeaten his secretary, and for nine years that man has endured in silence. But there comes a day when at last the strain reaches its breaking point. *Something snaps!* It was so that night. Sir Reuben sat down at his desk again, but the secretary, instead of turning humbly and meekly to the door, picks up the heavy wooden club, and strikes down the man who had bullied him once too often."

He turned to Trefusis, who was staring at him as though turned to stone.

"It was so simple, your alibi. Mr. Astwell thought you were in your room, but *no one saw you go there.* You were just stealing out after striking down Sir Reuben, when you heard a sound, and you hastened back to cover, behind the curtain. You were behind there when Charles Leverson entered the room, you were there when Lily Margrave came. It was not till long after that that you crept up through a silent house to your bedroom. Do you deny it?"

Trefusis began to stammer.

"I—I never—"

"Ah! Let us finish this. For two weeks now I have played the comedy, I have showed you the net closing slowly around you. The fingerprints, footprints, the search of your room with the things artistically replaced. I have struck terror into you with all of this; you have lain awake at night fearing and wondering; did you leave a fingerprint in the room or a footprint somewhere?

"Again and again you have gone over the events of that night wondering what you have done or left undone, and so I brought you to the state where you made a slip. I saw the fear leap into your eyes today when I picked up something from the stairs where you had stood hidden that night. Then I made a great parade, the little box, the entrusting of it to George, and I go out."

Poirot turned toward the door.

"George?"

"I am here, sir."

The valet came forward.

"Will you tell these ladies and gentlemen what my instructions were?"

"I was to remain concealed in the wardrobe in your room, sir, having placed the cardboard box where you told me to. At half-past three this afternoon, sir, Mr. Trefusis entered the room; he went to the drawer and took out the box in question."

"And in that box," continued Poirot, "was a common pin. Me, I speak always the truth. I did pick up something on the stairs this morning. That is your English saying, is it not? 'See a pin and pick it up, all the day you'll have good luck.' Me, I have had good luck, I have found the murderer."

He turned to the secretary.

"You see?" he said gently. *"You betrayed yourself."*

Suddenly Trefusis broke down. He sank into a chair sobbing, his face buried in his hands.

"I was mad," he groaned. "I was mad. But, oh, my God, he badgered and bullied me beyond bearing. For years I had hated and loathed him."

"I knew!" cried Lady Astwell.

She sprang forward, her face irradiated with savage triumph.

"I *knew* that man had done it."

She stood there, savage and triumphant.

"And you were right," said Poirot. "One may call things by different names, but the fact remains. Your 'intuition,' Lady Astwell, proved correct. I felicitate you."

# The Plymouth Express

ALEC Simpson, R.N., stepped from the platform at Newton Abbot into a first-class compartment of the Plymouth Express. A porter followed him with a heavy suitcase. He was about to swing it up to the rack, but the young sailor stopped him.

"No—leave it on the seat. I'll put it up later. Here you are."

"Thank you, sir." The porter, generously tipped, withdrew.

Doors banged; a stentorian voice shouted, "Plymouth only. Change for Torquay. Plymouth next stop." Then a whistle blew, and the train drew slowly out of the station.

Lieutenant Simpson had the carriage to himself. The December air was chilly, and he pulled up the window. Then he sniffed vaguely and frowned. What a smell there was! Reminded him of that time in the hospital, and the operation on his leg. Yes, chloroform; that was it!

He let the window down again, changing his seat to one with its back to the engine. He pulled a pipe out of his pocket and lit it. For a little time he sat inactive, looking out into the night and smoking.

At last he roused himself, and opening the suitcase, took out some papers and magazines, then closed the suitcase again and endeavored to shove it under the opposite seat—without success. Some hidden obstacle resisted it. He shoved harder with rising impatience, but it still stuck out halfway into the carriage.

"Why the devil won't it go in?" he muttered, and hauling it out completely, he stooped down and peered under the seat. . . .

A moment later a cry rang out into the night, and the great train came to an unwilling halt in obedience to the imperative jerking of the communication cord.

*"Mon ami,"* said Poirot, "you have, I know, been deeply interested in this mystery of the Plymouth Express. Read this."

I picked up the note he flicked across the table to me. It was brief and to the point.

Dear Sir,

I shall be obliged if you will call upon me at your earliest convenience.

Yours faithfully,

Ebenezer Halliday

The connection was not clear to my mind, and I looked inquiringly at Poirot.

For answer he took up the newspaper and read aloud: "'A sensational discovery was made last night. A young naval officer returning to Plymouth found under the seat of his compartment the body of a woman, stabbed through the heart. The officer at once pulled the communication cord, and the train was brought to a standstill. The woman, who was about thirty years of age, and richly dressed, has not yet been identified.'

"And later we have this: 'The woman found dead in the Plymouth Express has been identified as the Honourable Mrs. Rupert Carrington.' You see now, my friend? Or if you do not, I will add this—Mrs. Rupert Carrington was, before her marriage, Flossie Halliday, daughter of old man Halliday, the steel king of America."

"And he has sent for you? Splendid!"

"I did him a little service in the past—an affair of bearer bonds. And once, when I was in Paris for a royal visit, I had Mademoiselle Flossie pointed out to me. *La jolie petite pensionnaire!* She had the *joli dot* too! It caused trouble. She nearly made a bad affair."

"How was that?"

"A certain Count de la Rochefour. *Un bien mauvais sujet!* A bad hat, as you would say. An adventurer pure and simple, who knew how to appeal to a romantic young girl. Luckily her father got wind of it in time. He took her back to America in haste. I heard of her marriage some years later, but I know nothing of her husband."

"H'm," I said. "The Honourable Rupert Carrington is no beauty, by all accounts. He'd pretty well run through his own money on the turf, and I should imagine old man Halliday's dollars came along in the nick of time. I should say that for a good-looking, well-mannered, utterly unscrupulous young scoundrel, it would be hard to find his match!"

"Ah, the poor little lady! *Elle n'est pas bien tombée!*"

"I fancy he made it pretty obvious at once that it was her money, and not she, that had attracted him. I believe they drifted apart almost at once. I have heard rumors lately that there was to be a definite legal separation."

"Old man Halliday is no fool. He would tie up her money pretty tight."

"I dare say. Anyway, I know as a fact that the Honourable Rupert is said to be extremely hard up."

"Aha! I wonder—"

"You wonder what?"

"My good friend, do not jump down my throat like that. You are interested, I see. Supposing you accompany me to see Mr. Halliday. There is a taxi stand at the corner."

A few minutes sufficed to whirl us to the superb house in Park Lane rented by the American magnate. We were shown into the library, and almost immediately we were joined by a large, stout man with piercing eyes and an aggressive chin.

"Monsieur Poirot?" said Mr. Halliday. "I guess I don't need to tell you what I want you for. You've read the papers, and I'm never one to let the grass grow under my feet. I happened to hear you were in London, and I remembered the good work you did over those bonds. Never forget a name. I've got the pick of Scotland Yard, but I'll have my own man as well. Money no object. All the dollars were made for my little girl—and now she's gone, I'll spend my last cent to catch the damned scoundrel that did it! See? So it's up to you to deliver the goods."

Poirot bowed.

"I accept, monsieur, all the more willingly that I saw your daughter in Paris several times. And now I will ask you to tell me the circumstances of her journey to Plymouth and any other details that seem to you to bear upon the case."

"Well, to begin with," responded Halliday, "she wasn't going to Plymouth. She was going to join a house party at Avonmead Court, the Duchess of Swansea's place. She left London by the twelve-fourteen from Paddington, arriving at Bristol (where she had to change) at two-fifty. The principal Plymouth expresses, of course, run via Westbury, and do not go near Bristol at all. The twelve-fourteen does a nonstop run to Bristol, afterwards stopping at Weston, Taunton, Exeter, and Newton Abbot. My daughter traveled alone in her carriage, which was reserved as far as Bristol, her maid being in a third-class carriage in the next coach."

Poirot nodded, and Mr. Halliday went on, "The party at Avonmead Court was to be a very gay one, with several balls, and in consequence my daughter had with her nearly all her jewels—amounting in value, perhaps, to about a hundred thousand dollars."

"*Un moment,*" interrupted Poirot. "Who had charge of the jewels? Your daughter, or the maid?"

"My daughter always took charge of them herself, carrying them in a small blue morocco case."

"Continue, monsieur."

"At Bristol the maid, Jane Mason, collected her mistress's dressing bag and wraps, which were with her, and came to the door of Flossie's compartment. To her intense surprise, my daughter told her that she was not getting out at Bristol, but was going on further. She directed Mason to get out the luggage and put it in the cloakroom. She could have tea in the refreshment room, but she was to wait at the station for her mistress, who would return to Bristol by an up-train in the course of the afternoon. The maid, although very much astonished, did as she was told. She put the luggage in the cloakroom and had some tea. But up-train after up-train came in, and her mistress did not appear. After the arrival of the last train, she left the luggage where it was, and went to a hotel near the station for the night. This morning she read of the tragedy, and returned to town by the first available train."

"Is there nothing to account for your daughter's sudden change of plan?"

"Well, there is this: According to Jane Mason, at Bristol, Flossie was no longer alone in her carriage. There was a man in it who stood looking out of the further window so that she could not see his face."

"The train was a corridor one, of course?"

"Yes."

"Which side was the corridor?"

"On the platform side. My daughter was standing in the corridor as she talked to Mason."

"And there is no doubt in your mind—excuse me!" He got up and carefully straightened the inkstand which was a little askew. *"Je vous demande pardon,"* he continued, re-seating himself. "It affects my nerves to see anything crooked. Strange, is it not? I was saying, monsieur, that there is no doubt in your mind as to this probably unexpected meeting being the cause of your daughter's sudden change of plan?"

"It seems the only reasonable supposition."

"You have no idea as to who the gentleman in question might be?"

The millionaire hesitated for a moment, and then replied, "No—I do not know at all."

"Now—as to the discovery of the body?"

"It was discovered by a young naval officer who at once gave the alarm. There was a doctor on the train. He examined the body. She had been first chloroformed, and then stabbed. He gave it as his opinion that she had been dead about four hours, so it must have been done not long after leaving Bristol—probably between there and Weston, possibly between Weston and Taunton."

"And the jewel case?"

"The jewel case, Monsieur Poirot, was missing."

"One thing more, monsieur. Your daughter's fortune—to whom does it pass at her death?"

"Flossie made a will soon after her marriage, leaving everything to her husband." He hesitated for a minute, and then went on, "I may as well tell you, Monsieur Poirot, that I regard my son-in-law as an unprincipled scoundrel, and that, by my advice, my daughter was on the eve of freeing herself from him by legal means—no difficult matter. I settled her money upon her in such a way that he could not touch it during her lifetime, but although they have lived entirely apart for some years, she had frequently acceded to his demands for money, rather than face an open scandal. However, I was determined to put an end to this. At last Flossie agreed, and my lawyers were instructed to take proceedings."

"And where is Monsieur Carrington?"

"In town. I believe he was away in the country yesterday, but he returned last night."

Poirot considered a little while. Then he said, "I think that is all, monsieur."

"You would like to see the maid, Jane Mason?"

"If you please."

Halliday rang the bell and gave a short order to the footman.

A few minutes later Jane Mason entered the room, a respectable, hard-featured woman, as emotionless in the face of tragedy as only a good servant can be.

"You will permit me to put a few questions? Your mistress, she was quite as usual before starting yesterday morning? Not excited or flurried?"

"Oh no, sir!"

"But at Bristol she was quite different?"

"Yes, sir, regular upset—so nervous she didn't seem to know what she was saying."

"What did she say exactly?"

"Well, sir, as near as I can remember, she said, 'Mason, I've got to alter my plans. Something has happened—I mean, I'm not getting out here after all. I must go on. Get out the luggage and put it in the cloakroom; then have some tea, and wait for me in the station.'

" 'Wait for you here, ma'am?' I asked.

" 'Yes, yes. Don't leave the station. I shall return by a later train. I don't know when. It mayn't be until quite late.'

" 'Very well, ma'am,' I says. It wasn't my place to ask questions, but I thought it was very strange."

"It was unlike your mistress, eh?"

"Very unlike her, sir."

"What did you think?"

"Well, sir, I thought it was to do with the gentleman in the carriage. She didn't speak to him, but she turned round once or twice as though to ask him if she was doing right."

"But you didn't see the gentleman's face?"

"No, sir; he stood with his back to me all the time."

"Can you describe him at all?"

"He had on a light fawn overcoat and a traveling cap. He was tall and slender, like, and the back of his head was dark."

"You didn't know him?"

"Oh no, I don't think so, sir."

"It was not your master, Mr. Carrington, by any chance?"

Mason looked rather startled.

"Oh, I don't think so, sir!"

"But you are not *sure?*"

"It was about the master's build, sir—but I never thought of it being him. We so seldom saw him. . . . I couldn't say it *wasn't* him!"

Poirot picked up a pin from the carpet and frowned at it severely; then he continued, "Would it be possible for the man to have entered the train at Bristol before you reached the carriage?"

Mason considered.

"Yes, sir, I think it would. My compartment was very crowded, and it was some minutes before I could get out—and then there was a very large crowd on the platform, and that delayed me too. But he'd only have had a minute or two to speak to the mistress, that way. I took it for granted that he'd come along the corridor."

"That is more probable, certainly."

He paused, still frowning.

"You know how the mistress was dressed, sir?"

"The papers give a few details, but I would like you to confirm them."

"She was wearing a white fox fur toque, sir, with a white spotted veil, and a blue frieze coat and skirt—the shade of blue they call electric."

"Hm, rather striking."

"Yes," remarked Mr. Halliday. "Inspector Japp is in hopes that that may help us to fix the spot where the crime took place. Anyone who saw her would remember her."

"*Précisément!* Thank you, mademoiselle."

The maid left the room.

"Well!" Poirot got up briskly. "That is all I can do here—except, monsieur, that I would ask you to tell me everything—but *everything!*"

"I have done so."

"Are you sure?"

"Absolutely."

"Then there is nothing more to be said. I must decline the case."

"Why?"

"Because you have not been frank with me."

"I assure you—"

"No, you are keeping something back."

There was a moment's pause, and then Halliday drew a paper from his pocket and handed it to my friend.

"I guess that's what you're after, Monsieur Poirot—though how you know about it fairly gets my goat!"

Poirot smiled, and unfolded the paper. It was a letter written in thin sloping handwriting. Poirot read it aloud.

Chère Madame,

It is with infinite pleasure that I look forward to the felicity of meeting you again. After your so amiable reply to my letter, I can hardly restrain my impatience. I have never forgotten those days in Paris. It is most cruel that you should be leaving London tomorrow. However, before very long, and perhaps sooner than you think, I shall have the joy of beholding once more the lady whose image has ever reigned supreme in my heart.

Believe, chère madame, all the assurances of my most devoted and unaltered sentiments—

Armand de la Rochefour.

Poirot handed the letter back to Halliday with a bow.

"I fancy, monsieur, that you did not know that your daughter intended renewing her acquaintance with the Count de la Rochefour?"

"It came as a thunderbolt to me! I found this letter in my daughter's handbag. As you probably know, Monsieur Poirot, this so-called count is an adventurer of the worst type."

Poirot nodded.

"But I want to know how you knew of the existence of this letter?"

My friend smiled. "Monsieur, I did not. But to track footmarks and recognize cigarette ash is not sufficient for a detective. He must also be a good psychologist! I knew that you disliked and mistrusted your son-in-law. He benefits by your daughter's death; the maid's description of the mysterious man bears a sufficient resemblance to him. Yet you are not keen on his track! Why? Surely because your suspicions lie in another direction. Therefore you were keeping something back."

"You're right, Monsieur Poirot. I was sure of Rupert's guilt until I found this letter. It unsettled me horribly."

"Yes. The Count says, 'Before very long, and perhaps sooner than you think.' Obviously he would not want to wait until you should get wind of his reappearance. Was it he who traveled down from London by the twelve-fourteen, and came along the corridor to your daughter's compartment? The Count de la Rochefour is also, if I remember rightly, tall and dark!"

The millionaire nodded.

"Well, monsieur, I will wish you good day. Scotland Yard has, I presume, a list of the jewels?"

"Yes. I believe Inspector Japp is here now if you would like to see him."

Japp was an old friend of ours, and greeted Poirot with a sort of affectionate contempt.

"And how are you, monsieur? No bad feeling between us, though we *have* got our different ways of looking at things. How are the 'little grey cells,' eh? Going strong?"

Poirot beamed upon him. "They function, my good Japp; assuredly they do!"

"Then that's all right. Think it was the Honourable Rupert, or a crook? We're keeping an eye on all the regular places, of course. We shall know if the shiners are disposed of, and of course whoever did it isn't going to keep them to admire their sparkle. Not likely! I'm trying to find out where Rupert Carrington was yesterday. Seems a bit of a mystery about it. I've got a man watching him."

"A great precaution, but perhaps a day late," suggested Poirot gently.

"You always will have your joke, Monsieur Poirot. Well, I'm off to Paddington. Bristol, Weston, Taunton, that's my beat. So long."

"You will come round and see me this evening, and tell me the result?"

"Sure thing, if I'm back."

"That good inspector believes in matter in motion," murmured Poirot as our friend departed. "He travels; he measures footprints; he collects mud and cigarette ash! He is extremely busy! He is zealous beyond words! And if I mentioned psychology to him, do you know what he would do, my friend? He would smile! He would say to himself: 'Poor old Poirot! He ages! He grows senile!' Japp is the 'younger generation knocking on the door.' And *ma foi!* They are so busy knocking that they do not notice that the door is open!"

"And what are you going to do?"

"As we have *carte blanche*, I shall expend threepence in ringing up the Ritz—where you may have noticed our Count is staying. After that, as my feet are a little damp, and I have sneezed twice, I shall return to my rooms and make myself a *tisane* over the spirit lamp!"

I did not see Poirot again until the following morning. I found him placidly finishing his breakfast.

"Well?" I inquired eagerly. "What has happened?"

"Nothing."

"But Japp?"

"I have not seen him."

"The Count?"

"He left the Ritz the day before yesterday."

"The day of the murder?"

"Yes."

"Then that settles it! Rupert Carrington is cleared."

"Because the Count de la Rochefour has left the Ritz? You go too fast, my friend."

"Anyway, he must be followed, arrested! But what could be his motive?"

"One hundred thousand dollars' worth of jewelry is a very good motive for anyone. No, the question to my mind is: why kill her? Why not simply steal the jewels? She would not prosecute."

"Why not?"

"Because she is a woman, *mon ami*. She once loved this man. Therefore she would suffer her loss in silence. And the Count, who is an extremely good psychologist where women are concerned—hence his successes—would know that perfectly well! On the other hand, if Rupert Carrington killed her, why take the jewels, which would incriminate him fatally?"

"As a blind."

"Perhaps you are right, my friend. Ah, here is Japp! I recognize his knock."

The inspector was beaming good-humoredly.

"Morning, Poirot. Only just got back. I've done some good work! And you?"

"Me, I have arranged my ideas," replied Poirot placidly.

Japp laughed heartily.

"Old chap's getting on in years," he observed beneath his breath to me. "That won't do for us young folk," he said aloud.

*"Quel dommage?"* Poirot inquired.

"Well, do you want to hear what I've done?"

"You permit me to make a guess? You have found the knife with which the crime was committed, by the side of the line between Weston and Taunton, and you have interviewed the paper boy who spoke to Mrs. Carrington at Weston!"

Japp's jaw fell. "How on earth did you know? Don't tell me it was those almighty 'little grey cells' of yours!"

"I am glad you admit for once that they are *all mighty!* Tell me, did she give the paper boy a shilling for himself?"

"No, it was half a crown!" Japp had recovered his temper, and grinned. "Pretty extravagant, these rich Americans!"

"And in consequence the boy did not forget her?"

"Not he. Half-crowns don't come his way every day. She hailed him and bought two magazines. One had a picture of a girl in blue on the cover. 'That'll match me,' she said. Oh, he remembered her perfectly. Well, that was enough for me. By the doctor's evidence, the crime *must* have been committed before Taunton. I guessed they'd throw the knife away at once, and I walked down the line looking for it; and sure enough, there it was. I made inquiries at Taunton about our man, but of course it's a big station, and it wasn't likely they'd notice him. He probably got back to London by a later train."

Poirot nodded. "Very likely."

"But I found another bit of news when I got back. They're passing the jewels, all right! That large emerald was pawned last night—by one of the regular lot. Who do you think it was?"

"I don't know—except that he was a short man."

Japp stared. "Well, you're right there. He's short enough. It was Red Narky."

"Who is Red Narky?" I asked.

"A particularly sharp jewel thief, sir. And not one to stick at murder. Usually works with a woman—Gracie Kidd; but she doesn't seem to be in it this time—unless she's got off to Holland with the rest of the swag."

"You've arrested Narky?"

"Sure thing. But mind you, it's the other man we want—the man who went down with Mrs. Carrington in the train. He was the one who planned the job, right enough. But Narky won't squeal on a pal."

I noticed that Poirot's eyes had become very green.

"I think," he said gently, "that I can find Narky's pal for you, all right."

"One of your little ideas, eh?" Japp eyed Poirot sharply. "Wonderful how you manage to deliver the goods sometimes, at your age and all. Devil's own luck, of course."

"Perhaps, perhaps," murmured my friend. "Hastings, my hat. And the brush. So! My galoshes, if it still rains! We must not undo the good work of that *tisane. Au revoir,* Japp!"

"Good luck to you, Poirot."

Poirot hailed the first taxi we met, and directed the driver to Park Lane.

When we drew up before Halliday's house, he skipped out nimbly, paid the driver and rang the bell. To the footman who opened the door he made a request in a low voice, and we were immediately taken upstairs. We went up to the top of the house, and were shown into a small neat bedroom.

Poirot's eyes roved round the room and fastened themselves on a small black trunk. He knelt in front of it, scrutinized the labels on it, and took a small twist of wire from his pocket.

"Ask Mr. Halliday if he will be so kind as to mount to me here," he said over his shoulder to the footman.

The man departed, and Poirot gently coaxed the lock of the trunk with a practiced hand. In a few minutes the lock gave, and he raised the lid of the trunk. Swiftly he began rummaging among the clothes it contained, flinging them out on the floor.

There was a heavy step on the stairs, and Halliday entered the room.

"What in hell are you doing here?" he demanded, staring.

"I was looking, monsieur, for *this.*" Poirot withdrew from the trunk a coat and skirt of bright blue frieze, and a small toque of white fox fur.

"What are you doing with my trunk?" I turned to see that the maid, Jane Mason, had entered the room.

"If you will just shut the door, Hastings. Thank you. Yes, and stand with your back against it. Now, Mr. Halliday, let me introduce you to Gracie Kidd, otherwise Jane Mason, who will shortly rejoin her accomplice, Red Narky, under the kind escort of Inspector Japp."

Poirot waved a deprecating hand. "It was of the most simple!" He helped himself to more caviar.

"It was the maid's insistence on the clothes that her mistress was wearing that first struck me. Why was she so anxious that our attention should be directed to them? I reflected that we had only the maid's word for the mysterious man in the carriage at Bristol. As far as the doctor's evidence went, Mrs. Carrington might easily have been murdered *before* reaching Bristol. But if so, then the maid must be an accomplice. And if she were an accomplice, she would not wish this point to rest on her evidence alone. The clothes Mrs. Carrington was wearing were of a striking nature. A maid usually has a good deal of choice as to what her mistress shall wear. Now if, after Bristol, anyone saw a lady in a bright blue coat and skirt, and a fur toque, he will be quite ready to swear he had seen Mrs. Carrington.

"I began to reconstruct. The maid would provide herself with duplicate clothes. She and her accomplice chloroform and stab Mrs. Carrington between London and Bristol, probably taking advantage of a tunnel. Her body is rolled under the seat; and the maid takes her place. At Weston she must make herself noticed. How? In all probability, a newspaper boy will be selected. She will insure his remembering her by giving him a large tip. She also drew his attention to the color of her dress by a remark about one of the magazines. After leaving

Weston, she throws the knife out of the window to mark the place where the crime presumably occurred, and changes her clothes, or buttons a long mackintosh over them. At Taunton she leaves the train and returns to Bristol as soon as possible, where her accomplice has duly left the luggage in the cloakroom. He hands over the ticket and himself returns to London. She waits on the platform, carrying out her role, goes to a hotel for the night and returns to town in the morning, exactly as she said.

"When Japp returned from this expedition, he confirmed all my deductions. He also told me that a well-known crook was passing the jewels. I knew that whoever it was would be the exact opposite of the man Jane Mason described. When I heard that it was Red Narky, who always worked with Gracie Kidd—well, I knew just where to find her."

"And the Count?"

"The more I thought of it, the more I was convinced that he had nothing to do with it. That gentleman is much too careful of his own skin to risk murder. It would be out of keeping with his character."

"Well, Monsieur Poirot," said Halliday, "I owe you a big debt and the check I write after lunch won't go near to settling it."

Poirot smiled modestly and murmured to me, "The good Japp, he shall get the official credit, all right, but though he has got his Gracie Kidd, I think that I, as the Americans say, have got his goat!"

# The Affair at the Victory Ball

PURE chance led my friend Hercule Poirot, formerly chief of the Belgian force, to be connected with the Sytles Case. His success brought him notoriety, and he decided to devote himself to the solving of problems in crime. Having been wounded on the Somme and invalided out of the Army, I finally took up my quarters with him in London. Since I have a first-hand knowledge of most of his cases, it has been suggested to me that I select some of the most interesting and place them on record. In doing so, I feel that I cannot do better than begin with that strange tangle which aroused such widespread public interest at the time. I refer to the affair at the Victory Ball.

Although perhaps it is not so fully demonstrative of Poirot's peculiar methods as some of the more obscure cases, its sensational features, the well-known people involved, and the tremendous publicity given it by the press, make it stand out as a *cause célèbre*, and I have long felt that it is only fitting that Poirot's connection with the solution should be given to the world.

It was a fine morning in spring, and we were sitting in Poirot's rooms. My little friend, neat and dapper as ever, his egg-shaped head tilted slightly on one side, was delicately applying a new pomade to his mustache. A certain harmless vanity was a characteristic of Poirot's and fell into line with his general love of order and method. The daily *Newsmonger,* which I had been reading, had slipped to the floor, and I was deep in a brown study when Poirot's voice recalled me.

"Of what are you thinking so deeply, *mon ami?*"

"To tell you the truth," I replied, "I was puzzling over this unaccountable affair at the Victory Ball. The papers are full of it."

I tapped the sheet with my finger as I spoke.

"Yes?"

"The more one reads of it, the more shrouded in mystery the whole thing becomes!" I warmed to my subject. "Who killed Lord Cronshaw? Was Coco Courtenay's death on the same night a mere coincidence?

Was it an accident? Or did she deliberately take an overdose of co-caine?" I stopped, and then added dramatically, "These are the ques-tions I ask myself."

Poirot, somewhat to my annoyance, did not play up. He was peering into the glass, and merely murmured, "Decidedly, this new pomade, it is a marvel for the mustache!" Catching my eye, however, he added hastily, "Quite so—and how do you reply to your questions?"

But before I could answer, the door opened, and our landlady an-nounced Inspector Japp.

The Scotland Yard man was an old friend of ours and we greeted him warmly.

"Ah! my good Japp," cried Poirot, "and what brings you to see us?"

"Well, Monsieur Poirot," said Japp, seating himself and nodding to me, "I'm on a case that strikes me as being very much in your line, and I came along to know whether you'd care to have a finger in the pie?"

Poirot had a good opinion of Japp's abilities, though deploring his lamentable lack of method; but I, for my part, considered that the detective's highest talent lay in the gentle art of seeking favors under the guise of conferring them!

"It's this Victory Ball," said Japp persuasively. "Come, now, you'd like to have a hand in that."

Poirot smiled at me.

"My friend Hastings would, at all events. He was just holding forth on the subject, *n'est-ce pas, mon ami?*"

"Well sir," said Japp condescendingly, "you shall be in it too. I can tell you, it's something of a feather in your cap to have inside knowledge of a case like this. Well, here's to business. You know the main facts of the case, I suppose, Monsieur Poirot?"

"From the papers only—and the imagination of the journalist is sometimes misleading. Recount the whole story to me."

Japp crossed his legs comfortably and began.

"As all the world and his wife knows, on Tuesday last a grand Victory Ball was held. Every twopenny-halfpenny hop calls itself that nowa-days, but this was the real thing, held at the Colossus Hall, and all London at it—including young Lord Cronshaw and his party."

"His *dossier?*" interrupted Poirot. "I should say his bioscope—no, how do you call it—biograph'?"

"Viscount Cronshaw was the fifth viscount, twenty-five years of age, rich, unmarried, and very fond of the theatrical world. There were rumors of his being engaged to Miss Courtenay of the Albany Theater, who was known to her friends as 'Coco' and who was, by all accounts, a very fascinating young lady."

"Good. *Continuez!*"

"Lord Cronshaw's party consisted of six people, he himself, his uncle, the Honorable Eustace Beltane, a pretty American widow, Mrs. Mallaby, a young actor, Chris Davidson, his wife, and last but not least, Miss Coco Courtenay. It was a fancy-dress ball, as you know, and the Cronshaw party represented the old Italian Comedy—whatever that may be."

"The *Commedia dell' Arte*," murmured Poirot. "I know."

"Anyway, the costumes were copied from a set of china figures forming part of Eustace Beltane's collection. Lord Cronshaw was *Harlequin*; Beltane was *Punchinello*; Mrs. Mallaby matched him as *Pulcinella*; the Davidsons were *Pierrot* and *Pierrette*; and Miss Courtenay, of course, was *Columbine*. Now, quite early in the evening it was apparent that there was something wrong. Lord Cronshaw was moody and strange in his manner. When the party met together for supper in a small private room engaged by the host, everyone noticed that he and Miss Courtenay were no longer on speaking terms. She had obviously been crying, and seemed on the verge of hysterics. The meal was an uncomfortable one, and as they all left the supper room, she turned to Chris Davidson and requested him audibly to take her home, as she was 'sick of the ball.' The young actor hesitated, glancing at Lord Cronshaw, and finally drew them both back to the supper room.

"But all his efforts to secure a reconciliation were unavailing, and he accordingly got a taxi and escorted the now weeping Miss Courtenay back to her flat. Although obviously very much upset, she did not confide in him, merely reiterating again and again that she would 'make old Cronch sorry for this!' That is the only hint we have that her death might not have been accidental, and it's precious little to go upon. By the time Davidson had quieted her down somewhat, it was too late to return to the Colossus Hall, and Davidson accordingly went straight home to his flat in Chelsea, where his wife arrived shortly afterward, bearing the news of the terrible tragedy that had occurred after his departure.

"Lord Cronshaw, it seems, became more and more moody as the ball went on. He kept away from his party, and they hardly saw him during the rest of the evening. It was about one-thirty A.M., just before the grand cotillion when everyone was to unmask, that Captain Digby, a brother officer who knew his disguise, noticed him standing in a box gazing down on the scene.

" 'Hullo, Cronch!' he called. 'Come down and be sociable! What are you moping about up there for like a boiled owl? Come along; there's a good old rag coming on now.'

" 'Right!' responded Cronshaw. 'Wait for me, or I'll never find you in the crowd.'

"He turned and left the box as he spoke. Captain Digby, who had Mrs. Davidson with him, waited. The minutes passed, but Lord Cronshaw did not appear. Finally Digby grew impatient.

"'Does the fellow think we're going to wait all night for him?' he exclaimed.

"At that moment Mrs. Mallaby joined them, and they explained the situation.

"'Say, now,' cried the pretty widow vivaciously, 'he's like a bear with a sore head tonight. Let's go right away and rout him out.'

"The search commenced, but met with no success until it occurred to Mrs. Mallaby that he might possibly be found in the room where they had supped an hour earlier. They made their way there. What a sight met their eyes! There was *Harlequin,* sure enough, but stretched on the ground with a table knife in his heart!"

Japp stopped, and Poirot nodded, and said with the relish of the specialist:

"*Une belle affaire!* And there was no clue as to the perpetrator of the deed? But how should there be!"

"Well," continued the Inspector, "you know the rest. The tragedy was a double one. Next day there were headlines in all the papers, and a brief statement to the effect that Miss Courtenay, the popular actress, had been discovered dead in her bed, and that her death was due to an overdose of cocaine. Now, was it accident or suicide? Her maid who was called upon to give evidence, admitted that Miss Courtenay was a confirmed taker of the drug, and a verdict of accidental death was returned. Nevertheless we can't leave the possibility of suicide out of account. Her death is particularly unfortunate, since it leaves us no clue now to the cause of the quarrel the preceding night. By the way, a small enamel box was found on the dead man. It had *Coco* written across it in diamonds, and was half full of cocaine. It was identified by Miss Courtenay's maid as belonging to her mistress, who nearly always carried it about with her, since it contained her supply of the drug to which she was fast becoming a slave."

"Was Lord Cronshaw himself addicted to the drug?"

"Very far from it. He held unusually strong views on the subject of dope."

Poirot nodded thoughtfully.

"But since the box was in his possession, he knew that Miss Courtenay took it. Suggestive, that, is it not, my good Japp?"

"Ah!" said Japp rather vaguely.

I smiled.

"Well," said Japp, "that's the case. What do you think of it?"

"You found no clue of any kind that has not been reported?"

"Yes, there was this." Japp took a small object from his pocket and handed it over to Poirot. It was a small pompon of emerald green silk, with some ragged threads hanging from it, as though it had been wrenched violently away.

"We found it in the dead man's hand, which was tightly clenched over it," explained the Inspector.

Poirot handed it back without any comment and asked:

"Had Lord Cronshaw any enemies?"

"None that anyone knows of. He seemed a popular young fellow."

"Who benefits by his death?"

"His uncle, the Honorable Eustace Beltane, comes into the title and estates. There are one or two suspicious facts against him. Several people declare that they heard a violent altercation going on in the little supper room, and that Eustace Beltane was one of the disputants. You see, the table knife being snatched up off the table would fit in with the murder being done in the heat of a quarrel."

"What does Mr. Beltane say about the matter?"

"Declares one of the waiters was the worse for liquor, and that he was giving him a dressing down. Also that it was nearer to one than half-past. You see, Captain Digby's evidence fixes the time pretty accurately. Only about ten minutes elapsed between his speaking to Cronshaw and the finding of the body."

"And in any case I suppose Mr. Beltane, as *Punchinello,* was wearing a hump and a ruffle?"

"I don't know the exact details of the costumes," said Japp, looking curiously at Poirot. "And anyway, I don't quite see what that has got to do with it?"

"No?" There was a hint of mockery in Poirot's smile. He continued quietly, his eyes shining with the green light I had learned to recognize so well, "There was a curtain in this little supper room, was there not?"

"Yes, but—"

"With a space behind it sufficient to conceal a man?"

"Yes—in fact, there's a small recess, but how you knew about it— you haven't been to the place, have you Monsieur Poirot?"

"No, my good Japp, I supplied the curtain from my brain. Without it, the drama is not reasonable. And always one must be reasonable. But tell me, did they not send for a doctor?"

"At once, of course. But there was nothing to be done. Death must have been instantaneous."

Poirot nodded rather impatiently.

"Yes, yes, I understand. This doctor, now, he gave evidence at the inquest?"

"Yes."

"Did he say nothing of any unusual symptom—was there nothing about the appearance of the body which struck him as being abnormal?"

Japp stared hard at the little man.

"Yes, Monsieur Poirot. I don't know what you're getting at, but he did mention that there was a tension and stiffness about the limbs which he was quite at a loss to account for."

"Aha!" said Poirot. "Aha! *Mon Dieu!* Japp, that gives one to think, does it not?"

I saw that it had certainly not given Japp to think.

"If you're thinking of poison, monsieur, who on earth would poison a man first and then stick a knife into him?"

"In truth that would be ridiculous," agreed Poirot placidly.

"Now is there anything you want to see, monsieur? If you'd like to examine the room where the body was found—"

Poirot waved his hand.

"Not in the least. You have told me the only thing that interests me—Lord Cronshaw's views on the subject of drug taking."

"Then there's nothing you want to see?"

"Just one thing."

"What is that?"

"The set of china figures from which the costumes were copied."

Japp stared.

"Well, you're a funny one!"

"You can manage that for me?"

"Come round to Berkely Square now if you like. Mr. Beltane—or His Lordship, as I should say now—won't object."

We set off at once in a taxi. The new Lord Cronshaw was not at home, but at Japp's request we were shown into the "China Room," where the gems of the collection were kept. Japp looked round him rather helplessly.

"I don't see how you'll ever find the ones you want, monsieur."

But Poirot had already drawn a chair in front of the mantlepiece and was hopping up upon it like a nimble robin. Above the mirror, on a small shelf to themselves, stood six china figures. Poirot examined them minutely, making a few comments to us as he did so.

"*Les voilà!* The old Italian Comedy. Three pairs! *Harlequin* and *Columbine, Pierrot* and *Pierrette*—very dainty in white and green,—and *Punchinello* and *Pulcinella* in mauve and yellow. Very elaborate, the costume of *Punchinello*—ruffles and frills, a hump, a high hat. Yes, as I thought, very elaborate."

He replaced the figures carefully, and jumped down.

Japp looked unsatisfied, but as Poirot had clearly no intention of explaining anything, the detective put the best face he could upon the matter. As we were preparing to leave, the master of the house came in, and Japp performed the necessary introductions.

The sixth Viscount Cronshaw was a man of about fifty, suave in manner, with a handsome, dissolute face. Evidently an elderly roué, with the languid manner of a poseur. I took an instant dislike to him. He greeted us graciously enough, declaring he had heard great accounts of Poirot's skill and placing himself at our disposal in every way.

"The police are doing all they can, I know," he said. "But I much fear the mystery of my nephew's death will never be cleared up. The whole thing seems utterly mysterious."

Poirot was watching him keenly. "Your nephew had no enemies that you know of?"

"None whatever. I am sure of that." He paused, and then went on, "If there are any questions you would like to ask—"

"Only one." Poirot's voice was serious. "The costumes—they were reproduced *exactly*, from your figurines?"

"To the smallest detail."

"Thank you, milord. That is all I wanted to be sure of. I wish you good day."

"And what next?" inquired Japp as we hurried down the street. "I've got to report at the Yard, you know."

"*Bien!* I will not detain you. I have one other little matter to attend to, and then—"

"Yes?"

"The case will be complete."

"What? You don't mean it! You know who killed Lord Cronshaw?"

"*Parfaitement.*"

"Who was it? Eustace Beltane?"

"Ah! *mon ami*, you know my little weakness! Always I have a desire to keep the threads in my own hands up to the last minute. But have no fear. I will reveal all when the time comes. I want no credit—the affair shall be yours, on the condition that you permit me to play out the *dénouement* my own way."

"That's fair enough," said Japp. "That is, if the *dénouement* ever comes! But I say, you *are* an oyster, aren't you?" Poirot smiled. "Well, so long. I'm off to the Yard."

He strode off down the street, and Poirot hailed a passing taxi.

"Where are we going now?" I asked in lively curiosity.

"To Chelsea to see the Davidsons."

He gave the address to the driver.

"What do you think of the new Lord Cronshaw?" I asked.

"What says my good friend Hastings?"

"I distrust him instinctively."

"You think he is the 'wicked uncle' of the storybooks, eh?"

"Don't you?"

"Me, I think he was most amiable toward us," said Poirot noncommittally.

"Because he had his reasons!"

Poirot looked at me, shook his head sadly, and murmured something that sounded like, "No method."

The Davidsons lived on the third floor of a block of "mansion" flats. Mr. Davidson was out, we were told, but Mrs. Davidson was at home. We were ushered into a long, low room with garish Oriental hangings. The air felt close and oppressive, and there was an overpowering fragrance of joss sticks. Mrs. Davidson came to us almost immediately, a small, fair creature whose fragility would have seemed pathetic and appealing had it not been for the rather shrewd and calculating gleam in her light blue eyes.

Poirot explained our connection with the case, and she shook her head sadly.

"Poor Cronch—and poor Coco too! We were both so fond of her, and her death has been a terrible grief to us. What is it you want to ask me? Must I really go over all that dreadful evening again?"

"Oh, madame, believe me I would not harass your feelings unnecessarily. Indeed, Inspector Japp has told me all that is needful. I only wish to see the costume you wore at the ball that night."

The lady looked somewhat surprised, and Poirot continued smoothly:

"You comprehend, madame, that I work on the system of my country. There we always 'reconstruct' the crime. It is possible that I may have an actual *représentation,* and if so, you understand, the costumes would be important."

Mrs. Davidson still looked a bit doubtful.

"I've heard of reconstructing a crime, of course," she said. "But I didn't know you were so particular about details. But I'll fetch the dress now."

She left the room and returned almost immediately with a dainty wisp of white satin and green. Poirot took it from her and examined it, handing it back with a bow.

"*Merci, madame!* I see you have had the misfortune to lose one of your green pompons, the one on the shoulder here."

"Yes, it got torn off at the ball. I picked it up and gave it to poor Lord Cronshaw to keep for me."

"That was after supper?"

"Yes."

"Not long before the tragedy, perhaps?"

A faint look of alarm came into Mrs. Davidson's pale eyes, and she replied quickly:

"Oh, no—long before that. Quite soon after supper, in fact."

"I see. Well, that is all. I will not derange you further. *Bonjour, madame.*"

"Well," I said, as we emerged from the building. "That explains the mystery of the green pompon."

"I wonder."

"Why, what do you mean?"

"You saw me examine the dress, Hastings?"

"Yes?"

"*Eh bien,* the pompon that was missing had not been wrenched off, as the lady said. On the contrary, it had been *cut* off, my friend, cut off with scissors. The threads were all quite even."

"Dear me!" I exclaimed. "This becomes more and more involved."

"On the contrary," replied Poirot placidly, "it becomes more and more simple."

"Poirot," I cried, "one day I shall murder you! Your habit of finding everything perfectly simple is aggravating to the last degree!"

"But when I explain, *mon ami,* is it not always perfectly simple?"

"Yes; that is the annoying part of it! I feel then that I could have done it myself."

"And so you could, Hastings, so you could. If you would but take the trouble of arranging your ideas! Without method—"

"Yes, yes," I said hastily, for I knew Poirot's eloquence when started on his favorite theme only too well. "Tell me, what do we do next? Are you really going to reconstruct the crime?"

"Hardly that. Shall we say that the drama is over, but that I propose to add a—Harlequinade?"

P . . . . . . ? . . . . . . ? . . . . . . ? . . . . . . ? . . . . . . ?

*(At this point the reader will perhaps be pleased to pause, make his own solution of the crime—and then see how close he comes to the author's.)*

The following Tuesday was fixed upon by Poirot as the day for his mysterious performance. The preparations greatly intrigued me. A white screen was erected at one side of the room, flanked by heavy curtains at either side. A man with some lighting apparatus arrived next, and finally a group of members of the theatrical profession, who disappeared into Poirot's bedroom, which had been rigged up as a temporary dressing room.

Shortly before eight, Japp arrived, in no very cheerful mood. I gathered that the official detective hardly approved of Poirot's plan.

"Bit melodramatic, like all his ideas. But there, it can do no harm, and as he says, it might save us a good bit of trouble. He's been very smart over the case. I was on the same scent myself, of course,"—I felt instinctively that Japp was straining the truth here,—"but there, I promised to let him play the thing out his own way. Ah! here is the crowd."

His Lordship arrived first, escorting Mrs. Mallaby, whom I had not as yet seen. She was a pretty, dark-haired woman, and appeared perceptibly nervous. The Davidsons followed. Chris Davidson also I saw for the first time. He was handsome enough in a rather obvious style, tall and dark, with the easy grace of the actor.

Poirot had arranged seats for the party facing the screen. This was illuminated by a bright light. Poirot switched out the other lights so that the room was in darkness except for the screen. Poirot's voice rose out of the gloom.

"Messieurs, mesdames, a word of explanation. Six figures in turn will pass across the screen. They are familiar to you. *Pierrot* and his *Pierrette; Punchinello* the buffoon, and elegant *Pulcinella;* beautiful *Columbine,* lightly dancing, *Harlequin,* the sprite, invisible to man!"

With these words of introduction, the show began. In turn each figure that Poirot had mentioned bounded before the screen, stayed there a moment poised, and then vanished. The lights went up, and a sigh of relief went round. Everyone had been nervous, fearing they knew not what. It seemed to me that the proceedings had gone singularly flat. If the criminal was among us, and Poirot expected him to break down at the mere sight of a familiar figure, the device had failed signally—as it was almost bound to do. Poirot, however, appeared not a whit discomposed. He stepped forward, beaming.

"Now, messieurs and mesdames, will you be so good as to tell me, one at a time what it is that we have just seen? Will you begin, milord?"

The gentleman looked rather puzzled. "I'm afraid I don't quite understand."

"Just tell me what we have been seeing."

"I—er—well, I should say we have seen six figures passing in front of a screen and dressed to represent the personages in the old Italian Comedy, or—er—ourselves the other night."

"Never mind the other night, milor'," broke in Poirot. "The first part of your speech was what I wanted. Madame, you agree with Milord Cronshaw?"

He had turned as he spoke to Mrs. Mallaby.

"I—er—yes, of course."

"You agree that you have seen six figures representing the Italian Comedy?"

"Why, certainly."

"Monsieur Davidson? You too?"

"Yes."

"Madame?"

"Yes."

"Hastings? Japp? Yes? You are all in accord?"

He looked around upon us; his face grew rather pale, and his eyes were green as any cat's.

"And yet—*you are all wrong!* Your eyes have lied to you—as they lied to you on the night of the Victory Ball. To 'see things with your own eyes' as they say, is not always to see the truth. One must see with the eyes of the mind; one must employ the little cells of gray! Know, then, that tonight and on the night of the Victory Ball, you saw, not *six* figures but *five!* See!"

The lights went out again. A figure bounded in front of the screen—*Pierrot!*

"Who is that?" demanded Poirot. "Is it *Pierrot?*"

"Yes," we all cried.

"Look again!"

With a swift movement the man divested himself of his loose *Pierrot* garb. There in the limelight stood glittering *Harlequin!* At the same moment there was a cry and an overturned chair.

"Curse you," snarled Davidson's voice. "Curse you! How did you guess?"

Then came the clink of handcuffs and Japp's calm official voice. "I arrest you, Christopher Davidson—charge of murdering Viscount Cronshaw—anything you say may be used in evidence against you."

It was a quarter of an hour later. A *recherché* little supper had appeared; and Poirot, beaming all over his face, was dispensing hospitality and answering our eager questions.

"It was all very simple. The circumstances in which the green pompon was found suggested at once that it had been torn from the costume of the murderer. I dismissed *Pierrette* from my mind (since it takes considerable strength to drive a table knife home) and fixed upon *Pierrot* as the criminal. But *Pierrot* left the ball nearly two hours before the murder was committed. So he must either have returned to the ball later to kill Lord Cronshaw, or—*eh bien,* he must have killed him before he left! Was that impossible? Who had seen Lord Cronshaw after supper that evening? Only Mrs. Davidson, whose statement, I suspected, was a deliberate fabrication uttered with the object of accounting for the missing pompon, which, of course, she cut from her own dress to replace the one missing on her husband's costume. But then, *Harlequin,* who was seen in the box at one-thirty, must have been an impersonation. For a moment, earlier, I had considered the possibility of Mr. Beltane being the guilty party. But with his elaborate costume, it was clearly impossible that he could have doubled the rôles of *Punchinello* and *Harlequin.* On the other hand, to Davidson, a young man of about the same height as the murdered man and an actor by profession, the thing was simplicity itself.

"But one thing worried me. Surely a doctor could not fail to perceive the difference between a man who had been dead two hours and one who had been dead ten minutes! *Eh bien!* the doctor *did* perceive it! But he was not taken to the body and asked 'How long has this man been dead?' On the contrary, he was informed that the man had been seen alive ten minutes ago, and so he merely commented at the inquest on the abnormal stiffening of the limbs for which he was quite unable to account!

"All was now marching famously for my theory. Davidson had killed Lord Cronshaw immediately after supper, when, as you remember, he was seen to draw him back into the supper room. Then he departed with Miss Courtenay, left her at the door of her flat (instead of going in and trying to pacify her as he affirmed) and returned posthaste to the Colossus—but as *Harlequin,* not *Pierrot*—a simple transformation effected by removing his outer costume."

The uncle of the dead man leaned forward, his eyes perplexed.

"But if so, he must have come to the ball prepared to kill his victim. What earthly motive could he have had? The motive, that's what I can't get."

"Ah! There we come to the second tragedy—that of Miss Courtenay. There was one simple point which everyone overlooked. Miss Courtenay died of cocaine poisoning—but her supply of the drug was in the enamel box which was found on Lord Cronshaw's body. Where, then, did she obtain the dose which killed her? Only one person could have supplied her with it—Davidson. And that explains everything. It accounts for her friendship with the Davidsons and her demand that Davidson should escort her home. Lord Cronshaw, who was almost fanatically opposed to drug taking, discovered that she was addicted to cocaine, and suspected that Davidson supplied her with it. Davidson doubtless denied this, but Lord Cronshaw determined to get the truth from Miss Courtenay at the ball. He could forgive the wretched girl, but he would certainly have no mercy on the man who made a living by trafficking in drugs. Exposure and ruin confronted Davidson. He went to the ball determined that Cronshaw's silence must be obtained at any cost."

"Was Coco's death an accident, then?"

"I suspect that it was an accident cleverly engineered by Davidson. She was furiously angry with Cronshaw, first for his reproaches, and secondly for taking her cocaine from her. Davidson supplied her with more, and probably suggested her augmenting the dose as a defiance to 'old Cronch'!"

"One other thing," I said. "The recess and the curtain? How did you know about them?"

"Why, *mon ami,* that was the most simple of all. Waiters had been in and out of that little room, so, obviously, the body could not have been lying where it was found on the floor. There must be some place in the room where it could be hidden. I deduced a curtain and a recess behind it. Davidson dragged the body there, and later, after drawing attention to himself in the box, he dragged it out again before finally leaving the Hall. It was one of his best moves. He is a clever fellow!"

But in Poirot's green eyes I read unmistakably the unspoken remark: "But not quite so clever as Hercule Poirot!"

# The Market Basing Mystery

"A FTER all, there's nothing like the country, is there?" said In
spector Japp, breathing in heavily through his nose and out
through his mouth in the most approved fashion.

Poirot and I applauded the sentiment heartily. It had been the Scotland Yard inspector's idea that we should all go for the weekend to
the little country town of Market Basing. When off duty, Japp was
an ardent botanist, and discoursed upon minute flowers possessed of
unbelievably lengthy Latin names (somewhat strangely pronounced)
with an enthusiasm even greater than that he gave to his cases.

"Nobody knows us, and we know nobody," explained Japp. "That's
the idea."

This was not to prove quite the case, however, for the local constable
happened to have been transferred from a village fifteen miles away
where a case of arsenical poisoning had brought him into contact with
the Scotland Yard man. However, his delighted recognition of the
great man only enhanced Japp's sense of well being, and as we sat
down to breakfast on Sunday morning in the parlour of the village
inn, with the sun shining and tendrils of honeysuckle thrusting themselves in at the window, we were all in the best of spirits. The bacon
and eggs were excellent, the coffee not so good, but passable and boil-
ing-hot.

"This is the life," said Japp. "When I retire, I shall have a little
place in the country. Far from crime, like this!"

"*Le crime, il est partout,*" remarked Poirot, helping himself to a
neat square of bread, and frowning at a sparrow which had balanced
itself impertinently on the windowsill.

I quoted lightly:

> *That rabbit has a pleasant face,*
> *His private life is a disgrace.*
> *I really could not tell to you*
> *The awful things that rabbits do.*

741

"Lord," said Japp, stretching himself backward, "I believe I could manage another egg, and perhaps a rasher or two of bacon. What do you say, Captain?"

"I'm with you," I returned heartily. "What about you, Poirot?"

Poirot shook his head.

"One must not so replenish the stomach that the brain refuses to function," he remarked.

"I'll risk replenishing the stomach a bit more," laughed Japp. "I take a large size in stomachs; and by the way, you're getting stout yourself, Monsieur Poirot. Here, miss, eggs and bacon twice."

At that moment, however, an imposing form blocked the doorway. It was Constable Pollard.

"I hope you'll excuse me troubling the inspector, gentlemen, but I'd be glad of his advice."

"I'm on my holiday," said Japp hastily. "No work for me. What is the case?"

"Gentleman up at Leigh House—shot himself—through the head."

"Well, they will do it," said Japp prosaically. "Debt, or a woman, I suppose. Sorry I can't help you, Pollard."

"The point is," said the constable, "that he can't have shot himself. Leastways, that's what Dr. Giles says."

Japp put down his cup.

"*Can't* have shot himself? What do you mean?"

"That's what Dr. Giles says," repeated Pollard. "He says it's plumb impossible. He's puzzled to death, the door being locked on the inside and the window bolted; but he sticks to it that the man couldn't have committed suicide."

That settled it. The further supply of bacon and eggs were waved aside, and a few minutes later we were all walking as fast as we could in the direction of Leigh House, Japp eagerly questioning the constable.

The name of the deceased was Walter Protheroe; he was a man of middle age and something of a recluse. He had come to Market Basing eight years ago and rented Leigh House, a rambling, dilapidated old mansion fast falling into ruin. He lived in a corner of it, his wants attended to by a housekeeper whom he had brought with him. Miss Clegg was her name, and she was a very superior woman and highly thought of in the village. Just lately Mr. Protheroe had had visitors staying with him, a Mr. and Mrs. Parker from London. This morning, unable to get a reply when she went to call her master, and finding the door locked, Miss Clegg became alarmed, and telephoned for the police and the doctor. Constable Pollard and Dr. Giles had arrived at the same moment. Their united efforts had succeeded in breaking down the oak door of his bedroom.

Mr. Protheroe was lying on the floor, shot through the head, and the pistol was clasped in his right hand. It looked a clear case of suicide.

After examining the body, however, Dr. Giles became clearly perplexed, and finally he drew the constable aside and communicated his perplexities to him, whereupon Pollard had at once thought of Japp. Leaving the doctor in charge, he had hurried down to the inn.

By the time the constable's recital was over, we had arrived at Leigh House, a big, desolate house surrounded by an unkempt, weed-ridden garden. The front door was open, and we passed it once into the hall and from there into a small morning room whence proceeded the sound of voices. Four people were in the room: a somewhat flashily dressed man with a shifty, unpleasant face to whom I took an immediate dislike; a woman of much the same type, though handsome in a coarse fashion; another woman dressed in neat black who stood apart from the rest, and whom I took to be the housekeeper; and a tall man dressed in sporting tweeds, with a clever, capable face, and who was clearly in command of the situation.

"Dr. Giles," said the constable, "this is Detective-Inspector Japp of Scotland Yard, and his two friends."

The doctor greeted us and made us known to Mr. and Mrs. Parker. Then we accompanied him upstairs. Pollard, in obedience to a sign from Japp, remained below, as it were on guard over the household. The doctor led us upstairs and along a passage. A door was open at the end; splinters hung from the hinges, and the door itself had crashed to the floor inside the room.

We went in. The body was still lying on the floor. Mr. Protheroe had been a man of middle age, bearded, with hair grey at the temples. Japp went and knelt by the body.

"Why couldn't you leave it as you found it?" he grumbled.

The doctor shrugged his shoulders.

"We thought it a clear case of suicide."

"Hm!" said Japp. "Bullet entered the head behind the left ear."

"Exactly," said the doctor. "Clearly impossible for him to have fired it himself. He'd have had to twist his hand right round his head. It couldn't have been done."

"Yet you found the pistol clasped in his hand? Where is it, by the way?"

The doctor nodded to the table.

"But it wasn't clasped in his hand," he said. "It was inside the hand, but the fingers weren't closed over it."

"Put there afterwards," said Japp; "that's clear enough." He was examining the weapon. "One cartridge fired. We'll test it for fingerprints, but I doubt if we'll find any but yours, Dr. Giles. How long has he been dead?"

"Sometime last night. I can't give the time to an hour or so, as those wonderful doctors in detective stories do. Roughly, he's been dead about twelve hours."

So far, Poirot had not made a move of any kind. He had remained by my side, watching Japp at work and listening to his questions. Only, from time to time, he had sniffed the air very delicately, and as if puzzled. I too had sniffed, but could detect nothing to arouse interest. The air seemed perfectly fresh and devoid of odor. And yet, from time to time, Poirot continued to sniff it dubiously, as though his keener nose detected something I had missed.

Now, as Japp moved away from the body, Poirot knelt down by it. He took no interest in the wound. I thought at first that he was examining the fingers of the hand that had held the pistol, but in a minute I saw that it was a handkerchief carried in the coatsleeve that interested him. Mr. Protheroe was dressed in a dark grey lounge suit. Finally Poirot got up from his knees, but his eyes still strayed back to the handkerchief as though puzzled.

Japp called to him to come and help to lift the door. Seizing my opportunity, I too knelt down, and taking the handkerchief from the sleeve, scrutinized it minutely. It was a perfectly plain handkerchief of white cambric; there was no mark or stain on it of any kind. I replaced it, shaking my head, and confessing myself baffled.

The others had raised the door. I realized that they were hunting for the key. They looked in vain.

"That settles it," said Japp. "The window's shut and bolted. The murderer left by the door, locking it and taking the key with him. He thought it would be accepted that Protheroe had locked himself in and shot himself, and that the absence of the key would not be noticed. You agree, Monsieur Poirot?"

"I agree, yes; but it would have been simpler and better to slip the key back inside the room under the door. Then it would look as though it had fallen from the lock."

"Ah, well, you can't expect everybody to have the bright ideas that you have. You'd have been a holy terror if you'd taken to crime. Any remarks to make, Monsieur Poirot?"

Poirot, it seemed to me, was somewhat at a loss. He looked round the room and remarked mildly and almost apologetically, "He smoked a lot, this monsieur."

True enough, the grate was filled with cigarette stubs, as was an ashtray that stood on a small table near the big armchair.

"He must have got through about twenty cigarettes last night," remarked Japp. Stooping down, he examined the contents of the grate carefully, then transferred his attention to the ashtray. "They're all the same kind," he announced, "and smoked by the same man. There's nothing there, Monsieur Poirot."

"I did not suggest that there was," murmured my friend.

"Ha," cried Japp, "what's this?" He pounced on something bright and glittering that lay on the floor near the dead man. "A broken cuff link. I wonder who this belongs to? Dr. Giles, I'd be obliged if you'd go down and send up the housekeeper."

"What about the Parkers? He's very anxious to leave the house—says he's got urgent business in London."

"I dare say. It'll have to get on without him. By the way things are going, it's likely that there'll be some urgent business down here for him to attend to! Send up the housekeeper, and don't let either of the Parkers give you and Pollard the slip. Did any of the household come in here this morning?"

The doctor reflected.

"No, they stood outside in the corridor while Pollard and I came in."

"Sure of that?"

"Absolutely certain."

The doctor departed on his mission.

"Good man, that," said Japp approvingly. "Some of these sporting doctors are first-class fellows. Well, I wonder who shot this chap. It looks like one of the three in the house. I hardly suspect the housekeeper. She's had eight years to shoot him in if she wanted to. I wonder who these Parkers are? They're not a prepossessing-looking couple."

Miss Clegg appeared at this juncture. She was a thin, gaunt woman with neat grey hair parted in the middle, very staid and calm in manner. Nevertheless there was an air of efficiency about her which commanded respect. In answer to Japp's questions, she explained that she had been with the dead man for fourteen years. He had been a generous and considerate master. She had never seen Mr. and Mrs. Parker until three days ago, when they arrived unexpectedly to stay. She was of the opinion that they had asked themselves—the master had certainly not seemed pleased to see them. The cuff link which Japp showed her had not belonged to Mr. Protheroe—she was sure of that. Questioned about the pistol, she said that she believed her master had a weapon of that kind. He kept it locked up. She had seen it once some years ago, but could not say whether this was the same one. She had heard no shot last night, but that was not surprising, as it was a big, rambling house, and her rooms and those prepared for the Parkers were at the other end of the building. She did not know what time Mr. Protheroe had gone to bed—he was still up when she retired at half-past nine. It was not his habit to go at once to bed when he went to his room. Usually he would sit up half the night, reading and smoking. He was a great smoker.

Then Poirot interposed a question:

"Did your master sleep with his window open or shut, as a rule?"

Miss Clegg considered.

"It was usually open, at any rate at the top."

"Yet now it is closed. Can you explain that?"

"No, unless he felt a draught and shut it."

Japp asked her a few more questions and then dismissed her. Next he interviewed the Parkers separately. Mrs. Parker was inclined to be hysterical and tearful; Mr. Parker was full of bluster and abuse. He denied that the cuff link was his, but as his wife had previously recognized it, this hardly improved matters for him; and as he had also denied ever having been in Protheroe's room, Japp considered that he had sufficient evidence to apply for a warrant.

Leaving Pollard in charge, Japp bustled back to the village and got into telephonic communication with headquarters. Poirot and I strolled back to the inn.

"You're unusually quiet," I said. "Doesn't the case interest you?"

"*Au contraire*, it interests me enormously. But it puzzles me also."

"The motive is obscure," I said thoughtfully, "but I'm certain that Parker's a bad lot. The case against him seems pretty clear but for the lack of motive, and that may come out later."

"Nothing struck you as being especially significant, although overlooked by Japp?"

I looked at him curiously.

"What have you got up your sleeve, Poirot?"

"What did the dead man have up his sleeve?"

"Oh, that handkerchief!"

"Exactly, the handkerchief."

"A sailor carries his handkerchief in his sleeve," I said thoughtfully.

"An excellent point, Hastings, though not the one I had in mind."

"Anything else?"

"Yes, over and over again I go back to the smell of cigarette smoke."

"I didn't smell any," I cried wonderingly.

"No more did I, *cher ami*."

I looked earnestly at him. It is so difficult to know when Poirot is pulling one's leg, but he seemed thoroughly in earnest and was frowning to himself.

The inquest took place two days later. In the meantime other evidence had come to light. A tramp had admitted that he had climbed over the wall into the Leigh House garden, where he often slept in a shed that was left unlocked. He declared that at twelve o'clock he had heard two men quarrelling loudly in a room on the first floor. One was demanding a sum of money; the other was angrily refusing. Concealed behind a bush, he had seen the two men as they passed and repassed the lighted window. One he knew well as being Mr. Protheroe, the owner of the house; the other he identified positively as Mr. Parker.

It was clear now that the Parkers had come to Leigh House to blackmail Protheroe, and when later it was discovered that the dead man's real name was Wendover, and that he had been a lieutenant in the Navy and had been concerned in the blowing up of the first-class cruiser *Merrythought,* in 1910, the case seemed to be rapidly clearing. It was supposed that Parker, cognizant of the part Wendover had played, had tracked him down and demanded hush money which the other refused to pay. In the course of the quarrel, Wendover drew his revolver, and Parker snatched it from him and shot him, subsequently endeavouring to give it the appearance of suicide.

Parker was committed for trial, reserving his defense. We had attended the police-court proceedings. As we left, Poirot nodded his head.

"It must be so," he murmured to himself. "Yes, it must be so. I will delay no longer."

He went into the post office and wrote off a note which he despatched by special messenger. I did not see to whom it was addressed. Then we returned to the inn where we had stayed on that memorable weekend.

Poirot was restless, going to and from the window.

"I await a visitor," he explained. "It cannot be—surely it cannot be that I am mistaken? No, here she is."

To my utter astonishment, in another minute Miss Clegg walked into the room. She was less calm than usual, and was breathing hard as though she had been running. I saw the fear in her eyes as she looked at Poirot.

"Sit down, mademoiselle," he said kindly. "I guessed rightly, did I not?"

For answer she burst into tears.

"Why did you do it?" asked Poirot gently. "Why?"

"I loved him so," she answered. "I was nursemaid to him when he was a little boy. Oh, be merciful to me!"

"I will do all I can. But you understand that I cannot permit an innocent man to hang—even though he is an unpleasing scoundrel."

She sat up and said in a low voice, "Perhaps in the end I could not have, either. Do whatever must be done."

Then, rising, she hurried from the room.

"Did she shoot him?" I asked, utterly bewildered.

Poirot smiled and shook his head.

"He shot himself. Do you remember that he carried his handkerchief in his *right* sleeve? That showed me that he was left-handed. Fearing exposure, after his stormy interview with Mr. Parker, he shot himself. In the morning Miss Clegg came to call him as usual and found him lying dead. As she has just told us, she had known him from a little boy upward, and was filled with fury against the Parkers, who had driven him to this shameful death. She regarded them as murderers, and then suddenly she saw a chance of making them suffer for the deed they had inspired. She alone knew that he was left-handed. She changed the pistol to his right hand, closed and bolted the window, dropped the bit of cuff link she had picked up in one of the downstairs rooms, and went out, locking the door and removing the key."

"Poirot," I said, in a burst of enthusiasm, "you are magnificent. All that from the one little clue of the handkerchief!"

"And the cigarette smoke. If the window had been closed, and all those cigarettes smoked, the room ought to have been full of stale tobacco. Instead, it was perfectly fresh, so I deduced at once that the window must have been open all night, and only closed in the morning, and that gave me a very interesting line of speculation. I could conceive of no circumstances under which a murderer could want to shut the window. It would be to his advantage to leave it open, and pretend that the murderer had escaped that way, if the theory of suicide did not go down. Of course, the tramp's evidence, when I heard it, confirmed my suspicions. He could never have overheard that conversation unless the window had been open."

"Splendid!" I said heartily. "Now, what about some tea?"

"Spoken like a true Englishman," said Poirot with a sigh. "I suppose it is not likely that I could obtain here a glass of *sirop?*"

# The Lemesurier Inheritance

IN company with Poirot, I have investigated many strange cases, but none, I think, to compare with that extraordinary series of events which held our interest over a period of many years, and which culminated in the ultimate problem that Poirot came to solve. Our attention was first drawn to the family history of the Lemesuriers one evening during the war. Poirot and I had but recently come together again, renewing the old days of our acquaintanceship in Belgium. He had been handling some little matter for the War Office—disposing of it to their entire satisfaction; and we had been dining at the Carlton with a Brass Hat who paid Poirot heavy compliments in the intervals of the meal. The Brass Hat had to rush away to keep an appointment with someone, and we finished our coffee in a leisurely fashion before following his example.

As we were leaving the room, I was hailed by a voice which struck a familiar note, and turned to see Captain Vincent Lemesurier, a young fellow whom I had known in France. He was with an older man whose likeness to him proclaimed him to be of the same family. Such proved to be the case, and he was introduced to us as Mr. Hugo Lemesurier, uncle of my young friend.

I did not really know Captain Lemesurier at all intimately, but he was a pleasant young fellow, somewhat dreamy in manner, and I remembered hearing that he belonged to an old and exclusive family with a property in Northumberland which dated from before the Reformation. Poirot and I were not in a hurry, and at the younger man's invitation, we sat down at the table with our two newfound friends, and chatted pleasantly enough on various matters. The elder Lemesurier was a man of about forty, with a touch of the scholar in his stooping shoulders; he was engaged at the moment upon some chemical research work for the Government, it appeared.

Our conversation was interrupted by a tall, dark young man who strode up to the table, evidently laboring under some agitation of mind.

"Thank goodness I've found you both!" he exclaimed.

"What's the matter, Roger?"

"Your guv'nor, Vincent. Bad fall. Young horse." The rest trailed off, as he drew the other aside.

In a few minutes our two friends had hurriedly taken leave of us. Vincent Lemesurier's father had had a serious accident while trying a young horse, and was not expected to live until morning. Vincent had gone deadly white, and appeared almost stunned by the news. In a way, I was surprised—for from the few words he had let fall on the subject while in France, I had gathered that he and his father were not on particularly friendly terms, and so his display of filial feeling now rather astonished me.

The dark young man, who had been introduced to us as a cousin, Mr. Roger Lemesurier, remained behind, and we three strolled out together.

"Rather a curious business, this," observed the young man. "It would interest M. Poirot, perhaps. I've heard of you, you know, M. Poirot—from Higginson." (Higginson was our Brass Hat friend.) "He says you're a whale on psychology."

"I study the psychology, yes," admitted my friend cautiously.

"Did you see my cousin's face? He was absolutely bowled over, wasn't he? Do you know why? A good old-fashioned family curse! Would you care to hear about it?"

"It would be most kind of you to recount it to me."

Roger Lemesurier looked at his watch.

"Lots of time. I'm meeting them at King's Cross. Well, M. Poirot, the Lemesuriers are an old family. Way back in medieval times, a Lemesurier became suspicious of his wife. He found the lady in a compromising situation. She swore that she was innocent, but old Baron Hugo didn't listen. She had one child, a son—and he swore that the boy was no child of his and should never inherit. I forget what he did—some pleasing medieval fancy like walling up the mother and son alive; anyway, he killed them both, and she died protesting her innocence and solemnly cursing the Lemesuriers forever. No firstborn son of a Lemesurier should ever inherit—so the curse ran. Well, time passed, and the lady's innocence was established beyond doubt. I believe that Hugo wore a hair shirt and ended up his days on his knees in a monk's cell. But the curious thing is that from that day to this, no firstborn son ever has succeeded to the estate. It's gone to brothers, to nephews, to second sons—never to the eldest born. Vincent's father was the second of five sons, the eldest of whom died in infancy. Of course, all through the war, Vincent has been convinced that whoever else was doomed, he certainly was. But strangely enough, his two younger brothers have been killed, and he himself has remained unscathed."

"An interesting family history," said Poirot thoughtfully. "But now his father is dying, and he, as the eldest son, succeeds?"

"Exactly. The curse has gone rusty—unable to stand the strain of modern life."

Poirot shook his head, as though deprecating the other's jesting tone. Roger Lemesurier looked at his watch again, and declared that he must be off.

The sequel to the story came on the morrow, when we learned of the tragic death of Captain Vincent Lemesurier. He had been traveling north by the Scotch mail train, and during the night must have opened the door of the compartment and jumped out on the line. The shock of his father's accident coming on top of shell-shock was deemed to have caused temporary mental aberration. The curious superstition prevalent in the Lemesurier family was mentioned, in connection with the new heir, his father's brother, Ronald Lemesurier, whose only son had died on the Somme.

I suppose our accidental meeting with young Vincent on the last evening of his life quickened our interest in anything that pertained to the Lemesurier family, for we noted with some interest two years later the death of Ronald Lemesurier, who had been a confirmed invalid at the time of his succession to the family estates. His brother John succeeded him, a hale, hearty man with a boy at Eton.

Certainly an evil destiny overshadowed the Lemesuriers. On his very next holiday the boy managed to shoot himself fatally. His father's death, which occurred quite suddenly after being stung by a wasp, gave the estate over to the youngest brother of the five—Hugo, whom we remembered meeting on the fatal night at the Carlton.

Beyond commenting on the extraordinary series of misfortunes which befell the Lemesuriers, we had taken no personal interest in the matter, but the time was now close at hand when we were to take a more active part.

One morning "Mrs. Lemesurier" was announced. She was a tall, active woman, possibly about thirty years of age, who conveyed by her demeanor a great deal of determination and strong common sense. She spoke with a faint transatlantic accent.

"M. Poirot? I am pleased to meet you. My husband, Hugo Lemesurier, met you once many years ago, but you will hardly remember the fact."

"I recollect it perfectly, madame. It was at the Carlton."

"That's quite wonderful of you. M. Poirot, I'm very worried."

"What about, madame?"

"My elder boy—I've two boys, you know. Ronald's eight, and Gerald's six."

"Proceed, madame: why should you be worried about little Ronald?"

"M. Poirot, within the last six months he has had three narrow escapes from death: once from drowning—when we were all down at Cornwall this summer; once when he fell from the nursery window; and once from ptomaine poisoning."

Perhaps Poirot's face expressed rather too eloquently what he thought, for Mrs. Lemesurier hurried on with hardly a moment's pause:

"Of course I know you think I'm just a silly fool of a woman, making mountains out of molehills."

"No, indeed, madame. Any mother might be excused for being upset at such occurrences, but I hardly see where I can be of any assistance to you. I am not *le bon Dieu* to control the waves; for the nursery window I should suggest some iron bars; and for the food—what can equal a mother's care?"

"But why should these things happen to Ronald and not to Gerald?"

"The chance, madame—*le hasard!*"

"You think so?"

"What do you think, madame—you and your husband?"

A shadow crossed Mrs. Lemesurier's face.

"It's no good going to Hugo—he won't listen. As perhaps you may have heard, there's supposed to be a curse on the family—no eldest son can succeed. Hugo believes in it. He's wrapped up in the family history, and he's superstitious to the last degree. When I go to him with my fears, he just says it's the curse, and we can't escape it. But I'm from the States, M. Poirot, and over there we don't believe much in curses. We like them as belonging to a real high-toned old family— it gives a sort of *cachet,* don't you know. I was just a musical-comedy actress in a small part when Hugo met me—and I thought his family curse was just too lovely for words. That kind of thing's all right for telling round the fire on a winter's evening, but when it comes to one's own children—I just adore my children, M. Poirot. I'd do anything for them."

"So you decline to believe in the family legend, madame?"

"Can a legend saw through an ivy stem?"

"What is that you are saying, madame?" cried Poirot, an expression of great astonishment on his face.

"I said, can a legend—or a ghost, if you like to call it that—saw through an ivy stem? I'm not saying anything about Cornwall. Any boy might go out too far and get into difficulties—though Ronald could swim when he was four years old. But the ivy's different. Both the boys were very naughty. They'd discovered they could climb up and down by the ivy. They were always doing it. One day—Gerald was away at the time—Ronald did it once too often, and the ivy gave way and he fell. Fortunately he didn't damage himself seriously. But I went out and examined the ivy: it was cut through, M. Poirot—deliberately cut through."

"It is very serious what you are telling me there, madame. You say your younger boy was away from home at the moment?"

"Yes."

"And at the time of the ptomaine poisoning, was he still away?"

"No, they were both there."

"Curious," murmured Poirot. "Now, madame, who are the inmates of your establishment?"

"Miss Saunders, the children's governess, and John Gardiner, my husband's secretary—"

Mrs. Lemesurier paused, as though slightly embarrassed.

"And who else, madame?"

"Major Roger Lemesurier, whom you also met on that night, I believe, stays with us a good deal."

"Ah, yes—he is a cousin, is he not?"

"A distant cousin. He does not belong to our branch of the family. Still, I suppose now he is my husband's nearest relative. He is a dear fellow, and we are all very fond of him. The boys are devoted to him."

"It was not he who taught them to climb up the ivy?"

"It might have been. He incites them to mischief, often enough."

"Madame, I apologize for what I said to you earlier. The danger is real, and I believe that I can be of assistance. I propose that you should invite us both to stay with you. Your husband will not object?"

"Oh, no. But he will believe it to be all of no use. It makes me furious the way he just sits around and expects the boy to die."

"Calm yourself, madame. Let us make our arrangements methodically."

Our arrangements were duly made, and the following day saw us flying northward. Poirot was sunk in a reverie. He came out of it, to remark abruptly:

"It was from a train such as this that Vincent Lemesurier fell?"

He put a slight accent on the "fell."

"You don't suspect foul play there, surely?" I asked.

"Has it struck you, Hastings, that some of the Lemesurier deaths were—shall we say capable of being arranged? Take that of Vincent, for instance: Then the Eton boy—an accident with a gun is always ambiguous. Supposing this child had fallen from the nursery window and been dashed to death—what more natural and unsuspicious? But why only the one child, Hastings? Who profits by the death of the elder child? His younger brother, a child of seven! Absurd!"

"They may mean to do away with the other later," I suggested, though with the vaguest ideas as to who "they" were.

Poirot shook his head as though dissatisfied.

"Ptomaine poisoning," he mused. "Atropine will produce much the same symptoms. Yes, there is need for our presence."

Mrs. Lemesurier welcomed us enthusiastically. Then she took us to her husband's study and left us with him. He had changed a good deal since I saw him last. His shoulders stooped more than ever, and his face had a curious pale gray tinge. He listened while Poirot explained our presence in the house.

"How exactly like Sadie's practical common sense!" he said at last. "Remain by all means, M. Poirot, and I thank you for coming; but— what is written, is written. The way of the transgressor is hard. We Lemesuriers *know*—none of us can escape the doom."

Poirot mentioned the sawn-through ivy, but Hugo seemed very little impressed.

"Doubtless some careless gardener—yes, yes, there may be an instrument, but the purpose behind is plain; and I will tell you this, M. Poirot, it cannot be long delayed."

Poirot looked at him attentively.

"Why do you say that?"

"Because I myself am doomed. I went to a doctor last year. I am suffering from an incurable disease—the end cannot be much longer delayed; but before I die, Ronald will be taken. Gerald will inherit."

"And if anything were to happen to your second son also?"

"Nothing will happen to him; he is not threatened."

"But if it did?" persisted Poirot.

"My cousin Roger is the next heir."

We were interrupted. A tall man with a good figure and crisply curling auburn hair entered with a sheaf of papers.

"Never mind about those now, Gardiner," said Hugo Lemesurier; then he added, "My secretary, Mr. Gardiner."

The secretary bowed, uttered a few pleasant words and then went out. In spite of his good looks, there was something repellent about the man. I said so to Poirot shortly afterward when we were walking round the beautiful old grounds together, and rather to my surprise, he agreed.

"Yes, yes, Hastings, you are right. I do not like him. He is too good-looking. He would be one for the soft job always. Ah, here are the children."

Mrs. Lemesurier was advancing toward us, her two children beside her. They were fine-looking boys, the younger dark like his mother, the elder with auburn curls. They shook hands prettily enough, and were soon absolutely devoted to Poirot. We were next introduced to Miss Saunders, a nondescript female, who completed the party.

For some days we had a pleasant easy existence—ever vigilant, but without result. The boys led a happy normal life, and nothing seemed to be amiss. On the fourth day after our arrival Major Roger Lemesurier came down to stay. He was little changed, still carefree and debonair as of old, with the same habit of treating all things lightly. He was evidently a great favorite with the boys, who greeted his arrival with shrieks of delight and immediately dragged him off to play wild Indians in the garden. I noticed that Poirot followed them unobtrusively.

On the following day we were all invited to tea, boys included, with Lady Claygate, whose place adjoined that of the Lemesuriers. Mrs. Lemesurier suggested that we also should come, but seemed rather relieved when Poirot refused and declared he would much prefer to remain at home.

Once everyone had started, Poirot got to work. He reminded me of an intelligent terrier. I believe that there was no corner of the house that he left unsearched; yet it was all done so quietly and methodically that no attention was directed to his movements. Clearly, at the end, he remained unsatisfied. We had tea on the terrace with Miss Saunders, who had not been included in the party.

"The boys will enjoy it," she murmured in her faded way, "though I hope they will behave nicely, and not damage the flower-beds, or go near the bees—"

Poirot paused in the very act of drinking. He looked like a man who has seen a ghost.

"Bees?" he demanded in a voice of thunder.

"Yes, M. Poirot, bees. Three hives. Lady Claygate is very proud of her bees—"

"Bees?" cried Poirot again. Then he sprang from the table and walked up and down the terrace with his hands to his head. I could not imagine why the little man should be so agitated at the mere mention of bees.

At that moment we heard the car returning. Poirot was on the doorstep as the party alighted.

"Ronald's been stung," cried Gerald excitedly.

"It's nothing," said Mrs. Lemesurier. "It hasn't even swollen. We put ammonia on it."

"Let me see, my little man," said Poirot. "Where was it?"

"Here, on the side of my neck," said Ronald importantly. "But it doesn't hurt. Father said, 'Keep still—there's a bee on you.' And I kept still, and he took it off, but it stung me first, though it didn't really hurt, only like a pin, and I didn't cry, because I'm so big and going to school next year."

Poirot examined the child's neck, then drew away again. He took me by the arm and murmured:

"Tonight, *mon ami*, tonight we have a little affair on! Say nothing— to anyone."

He refused to be more communicative, and I went through the evening devoured by curiosity. He retired early and I followed his example. As we went upstairs, he caught me by the arm and delivered his instructions:

"Do not undress. Wait a sufficient time, extinguish your light and join me here."

I obeyed, and found him waiting for me when the time came. He enjoined silence on me with a gesture, and we crept quietly along to the nursery wing. Ronald occupied a small room of his own. We entered it and took up our position in the darkest corner. The child's breathing sounded heavy and undisturbed.

"Surely he is sleeping very heavily?" I whispered.

Poirot nodded.

"Drugged," he murmured.

"Why?"

"So that he should not cry out at—"

"At what?" I asked, as Poirot paused.

"At the prick of the hypodermic needle, *mon ami!* Hush, let us speak no more—not that I expect anything to happen for some time."

But in this Poirot was wrong. Hardly ten minutes had elapsed before the door opened softly, and some one entered the room. I heard a sound of quick hurried breathing. Footsteps moved to the bed, and then there was a sudden click. The light of a little electric lantern fell on the sleeping child—the holder of it was still invisible in the shadow. The figure laid down the lantern. With the right hand it brought forth a syringe; with the left it touched the boy's neck—

Poirot and I sprang at the same minute. The lantern rolled to the floor, and we struggled with the intruder in the dark. His strength was extraordinary. At last we overcame him.

"The light, Hastings. I must see his face—though I fear I know only too well whose face it will be."

So did I, I thought, as I groped for the lantern. For a moment I had suspected the secretary, egged on by my secret dislike of the man, but I felt assured by now that the man who stood to gain by the death of his two childish cousins was the monster we were tracking.

My foot struck against the lantern. I picked it up and switched on the light. It shone full on the face of—Hugo Lemesurier, the boy's father!

The lantern almost dropped from my hand.

"Impossible," I murmured hoarsely. "Impossible!"

Lemesurier was unconscious. Poirot and I between us carried him to his room and laid him on the bed. Poirot bent and gently extricated something from his right hand. He showed it to me. It was a hypodermic syringe. I shuddered.

"What is in it? Poison?"

"Formic acid, I fancy."

"Formic acid?"

"Yes. Probably obtained by distilling ants. He was a chemist, you remember. Death would have been attributed to the bee sting."

"My God," I muttered. "His own son! And you expected this?"

Poirot nodded gravely.

"Yes. He is insane, of course. I imagine that the family history has become a mania with him. His intense longing to succeed to the estate led him to commit the long series of crimes. Possibly the idea occurred to him first when traveling north that night with Vincent. He couldn't bear the prediction to be falsified. Ronald's son was already dead, and Ronald himself was a dying man—they are a weakly lot. He arranged the accident to the gun, and—which I did not suspect until now— contrived the death of his brother John by this same method of injecting formic acid into the jugular vein. His ambition was realized then, and he became the master of the family acres. But his triumph was short-lived—he found that he was suffering from an incurable disease. And he had the madman's fixed idea—the eldest son of a Lemesurier could not inherit. I suspect that the bathing accident was due to him—he encouraged the child to go out too far. That failing, he sawed through the ivy, and afterwards poisoned the child's food."

"Diabolical!" I murmured with a shiver. "And so cleverly planned!"

"Yes, *mon ami*, there is nothing more amazing than the extraordinary sanity of the insane! Unless it is the extraordinary eccentricity of the sane! I imagine that it is only lately that he has completely gone over the borderline, there was method in his madness to begin with."

"And to think that I suspected Roger—that splendid fellow."

"It was the natural assumption, *mon ami*. We knew that he also traveled north with Vincent that night. We knew, too, that he was the next heir after Hugo and Hugo's children. But our assumption was not borne out by the facts. The ivy was sawn through when only little Ronald was at home—but it would be to Roger's interest that both children should perish. In the same way, it was only Ronald's food that was poisoned. And today when they came home and I found that there was only his father's word for it that Ronald had been stung, I remembered the other death from a wasp sting—and I knew!"

Hugo Lemesurier died a few months later in the private asylum to which he was removed. His widow was remarried a year later to Mr. John Gardiner, the auburn-haired secretary. Ronald inherited the broad acres of his father, and continues to flourish.

"Well, well," I remarked to Poirot. "Another illusion gone. You have disposed very successfully of the curse of the Lemesuriers."

"I wonder," said Poirot very thoughtfully. "I wonder very much indeed."

"What do you mean?"

"*Mon ami,* I will answer you with one significant word—*red!*"

"Blood?" I queried, dropping my voice to an awe-stricken whisper.

"Always you have the imagination melodramatic, Hastings! I refer to something much more prosaic—the color of little Ronald Lemesurier's hair."

# The Cornish Mystery

"**M**RS. Pengelley," announced our landlady, and withdrew discreetly.

Many unlikely people came to consult Poirot, but to my mind, the woman who stood nervously just inside the door, fingering her feather neckpiece, was the most unlikely of all. She was so extraordinarily commonplace—a thin, faded woman of about fifty, dressed in a braided coat and skirt, some gold jewelry at her neck, and with her grey hair surmounted by a singularly unbecoming hat. In a country town, you pass a hundred Mrs. Pengelleys in the street every day.

Poirot came forward and greeted her pleasantly, perceiving her obvious embarrassment.

"Madame! Take a chair, I beg of you. My colleague, Captain Hastings."

The lady sat down, murmuring uncertainly, "You are Monsieur Poirot, the detective?"

"At your service, madame."

But our guest was still tongue-tied. She sighed, twisted her fingers, and grew steadily redder and redder.

"There is something I can do for you, eh, madame?"

"Well, I thought—that is—you see—"

"Proceed, madame, I beg of you—proceed."

Mrs. Pengelley, thus encouraged, took a grip on herself.

"It's this way, Monsieur Poirot—I don't want to have anything to do with the police. No, I wouldn't go to the police for anything! But all the same, I'm sorely troubled about something. And yet I don't know if I ought—" She stopped abruptly.

"Me, I have nothing to do with the police. My investigations are strictly private."

Mrs. Pengelley caught at the word.

"Private—that's what I want. I don't want any talk or fuss, or things in the papers. Wicked it is, the way they write things, until the family could never hold up their heads again. And it isn't as though I was

759

even sure—it's just a dreadful idea that's come to me, and put it out of my head I can't." She paused for breath. "And all the time I may be wickedly wronging poor Edward. It's a terrible thought for any wife to have. But you do read of such dreadful things nowadays."

"Permit me—it is of your husband you speak?"

"Yes."

"And you suspect him of—what?"

"I don't like even to say it, Monsieur Poirot. But you *do* read of such things happening—and the poor souls suspecting nothing."

I was beginning to despair of the lady's ever coming to the point, but Poirot's patience was equal to the demand made upon it.

"Speak without fear, madame. Think what joy will be yours if we are able to prove your suspicions unfounded."

"That's true—anything's better than this wearing uncertainty. Oh, Monsieur Poirot, I'm dreadfully afraid I'm being *poisoned.*"

"What makes you think so?"

Mrs. Pengelley, her reticence leaving her, plunged into a full recital more suited to the ears of her medical attendant.

"Pain and sickness after food, eh?" said Poirot thoughtfully. "You have a doctor attending you, madame? What does he say?"

"He says it's acute gastritis, Monsieur Poirot. But I can see that he's puzzled and uneasy, and he's always altering the medicine, but nothing does any good."

"You have spoken of your—fears, to him?"

"No, indeed, Monsieur Poirot. It might get about in the town. And perhaps it *is* gastritis. All the same, it's very odd that whenever Edward is away for the weekend, I'm quite all right again. Even Freda noticed that—my niece, Monsieur Poirot. And then there's that bottle of weed killer, never used, the gardener says, and yet it's half empty."

She looked appealingly at Poirot. He smiled reassuringly at her, and reached for a pencil and notebook.

"Let us be businesslike, madame. Now, then, you and your husband reside—where?"

"Polgarwith, a small market town in Cornwall."

"You have lived there long?"

"Fourteen years."

"And your household consists of you and your husband. Any children?"

"No."

"But a niece, I think you said?"

"Yes, Freda Stanton, the child of my husband's only sister. She has lived with us for the last eight years—that is, until a week ago."

"Oho, and what happened a week ago?"

"Things hadn't been very pleasant for some time; I don't know what had come over Freda. She was so rude and impertinent, and her temper something shocking, and in the end she flared up one day, and out she walked and took rooms of her own in the town. I've not seen her since. Better leave her to come to her senses, so Mr. Radnor says."

"Who is Mr. Radnor?"

Some of Mrs. Pengelley's initial embarrassment returned.

"Oh, he's—he's just a friend. Very pleasant young fellow."

"Anything between him and your niece?"

"Nothing whatever," said Mrs. Pengelley emphatically.

Poirot shifted his ground.

"You and your husband are, I presume, in comfortable circumstances?"

"Yes, we're very nicely off."

"The money, is it yours or your husband's?"

"Oh, it's all Edward's. I've nothing of my own."

"You see, madame, to be businesslike, we must be brutal. We must seek for a motive. Your husband, he would not poison you just *pour passer le temps!* Do you know of any reason why he should wish you out of the way?"

"There's the yellow-haired hussy who works for him," said Mrs. Pengelley, with a flash of temper. "My husband's a dentist, Monsieur Poirot, and nothing would do but he must have a smart girl, as he said, with bobbed hair and a white overall, to make his appointments and mix his fillings for him. It's come to my ears that there have been fine goings-on, though of course he swears it's all right."

"This bottle of weed killer, madame, who ordered it?"

"My husband—about a year ago."

"Your niece, now, has she any money of her own?"

"About fifty pounds a year, I should say. She'd be glad enough to come back and keep house for Edward if I left him."

"You have contemplated leaving him, then?"

"I don't intend to let him have it all his own way. Women aren't the downtrodden slaves they were in old days, Monsieur Poirot."

"I congratulate you on your independent spirit, madame; but let us be practical. You return to Polgarwith today?"

"Yes, I came up by an excursion. Six this morning the train started, and the train goes back at five this afternoon."

"*Bien!* I have nothing of great moment on hand. I can devote myself to your little affair. Tomorrow I shall be in Polgarwith. Shall we say that Hastings, here, is a distant relative of yours, the son of your second cousin? Me, I am his eccentric foreign friend. In the meantime, eat only what is prepared by your own hands, or under your eye. You have a maid whom you trust?"

"Jessie is a very good girl, I am sure."

"Till tomorrow then, madame, and be of good courage."

Poirot bowed the lady out, and returned thoughtfully to his chair. His absorption was not so great, however, that he failed to see two minute strands of feather scarf wrenched off by the lady's agitated fingers. He collected them carefully and consigned them to the waste-paper basket.

"What do you make of the case, Hastings?"

"A nasty business, I should say."

"Yes, if what the lady suspects be true. But is it? Woe betide any husband who orders a bottle of weed killer nowadays. If his wife suffers from gastritis, and is inclined to be of a hysterical temperament, the fat is in the fire."

"You think that is all there is to it?"

"Ah—*voilà*—I do not know, Hastings. But the case interests me— it interests me enormously. For, see you, it has positively no new features. Hence the hysterical theory, and yet Mrs. Pengelley did not strike me as being a hysterical woman. Yes, if I mistake not, we have here a very poignant human drama. Tell me, Hastings, what do you consider Mrs. Pengelley's feelings towards her husband to be?"

"Loyalty struggling with fear," I suggested.

"Yet, ordinarily, a woman will accuse anyone in the world—but not her husband. She will stick to her belief in him through thick and thin."

"The 'other woman' complicates the matter."

"Yes, affection may turn to hate, under the stimulus of jealousy. But hate would take her to the police—not to me. She would want an outcry—a scandal. No, no, let us exercise our little grey cells. Why did she come to me? To have her suspicions proved wrong? Or—to have them *proved right?* Ah, we have here something I do not under-stand—an unknown factor. Is she a superb actress, our Mrs. Pengelley? No, she was genuine, I would swear that she was genuine, and therefore I am interested. Look up the trains to Polgarwith, I pray you."

The best train of the day was the one-fifty from Paddington which reached Polgarwith just after seven o'clock. The journey was uneventful, and I had to rouse myself from a pleasant nap to alight upon the platform of the bleak little station. We took our bags to the Duchy Hotel, and after a light meal, Poirot suggested our stepping round to pay an after-dinner call on my so-called cousin.

The Pengelleys' house stood a little way back from the road with an old-fashioned cottage garden in front. The smell of stocks and mi-gnonette came sweetly wafted on the evening breeze. It seemed impossible to associate thoughts of violence with this old-world charm. Poirot rang and knocked. As the summons was not answered, he rang again. This time, after a little pause, the door was opened by a dishevelled-looking servant. Her eyes were red, and she was sniffing violently.

"We wish to see Mrs. Pengelley," explained Poirot. "May we enter?"

The maid stared. Then, with unusual directness, she answered, "Haven't you heard, then? She's dead. Died this evening—about half an hour ago."

We stood staring at her, stunned.

"What did she die of?" I asked at last.

"There's some as could tell." She gave a quick glance over her shoulder. "If it wasn't that somebody ought to be in the house with the missus, I'd pack my box and go tonight. But I'll not leave her dead with no one to watch by her. It's not my place to say anything, and I'm not going to say anything—but everybody knows. It's all over the town. And if Mr. Radnor don't write to the 'Ome Secretary, someone else will. The doctor may say what he likes. Didn't I see the master with my own eyes a-lifting down of the weed killer from the shelf this very evening? And didn't he jump when he turned round and saw me watching of him? And the missus' gruel there on the table, all ready to take to her? Not another bit of food passes my lips while I am in this house! Not if I dies for it."

"Where does the doctor live who attended your mistress?"

"Dr. Adams. Round the corner there in High Street. The second house."

Poirot turned away abruptly. He was very pale.

"For a girl who was not going to say anything, that girl said a lot," I remarked drily.

Poirot struck his clenched hand into his palm.

"An imbecile, a criminal imbecile, that is what I have been, Hastings. I have boasted of my little grey cells, and now I have lost a human life—a life that came to me to be saved. Never did I dream that anything would happen so soon. May the good God forgive me, but I never believed anything would happen at all. Her story seemed to me artificial. Here we are at the doctor's. Let us see what he can tell us."

Dr. Adams was the typical, genial, red-faced country doctor of fiction. He received us politely enough, but at a hint of our errand, his red face became purple.

"Damned nonsense! Damned nonsense, every word of it! Wasn't I in attendance on the case? Gastritis—gastritis pure and simple. This town's a hotbed of gossip—a lot of scandal-mongering old women get together and invent God knows what. They read these scurrilous rags of newspapers, and nothing will suit them but that someone in their town shall get poisoned too. They see a bottle of weed killer on a shelf—and hey presto!—away goes their imagination with the bit between its teeth. I know Edward Pengelley—he wouldn't poison his grandmother's dog. And why should he poison his wife? Tell me that?"

"There is one thing, Monsieur le Docteur, that perhaps you do not know."

And, very briefly, Poirot outlined the main facts of Mrs. Pengelley's visit to him. No one could have been more astonished than Dr. Adams. His eyes almost started out of his head.

"God bless my soul!" he ejaculated. "The poor woman must have been mad. Why didn't she speak to me? That was the proper thing to do."

"And have her fears ridiculed?"

"Not at all, not at all. I hope I've got an open mind."

Poirot looked at him and smiled. The physician was evidently more perturbed than he cared to admit. As we left the house, Poirot broke into a laugh.

"He is as obstinate as a pig, that one. He has said it is gastritis; therefore it is gastritis! All the same, he has the mind uneasy."

"What's our next step?"

"A return to the inn, and a night of horror upon one of your English provincial beds, *mon ami*. It is a thing to make pity, the cheap English bed!"

"And tomorrow?"

"*Rien à faire*. We must return to town and await developments."

"That's very tame," I said, disappointed. "Suppose there are none?"

"There will be! I can promise you that. Our old doctor may give as many certificates as he pleases. He cannot stop several hundred tongues from wagging. And they will wag to some purpose, I can tell you that!"

Our train for town left at eleven the following morning. Before we started for the station, Poirot expressed a wish to see Miss Freda Stanton, the niece mentioned to us by the dead woman. We found the house where she was lodging easily enough. With her was a tall, dark young man whom she introduced in some confusion as Mr. Jacob Radnor.

Miss Freda Stanton was an extremely pretty girl of the old Cornish type—dark hair and eyes and rosy cheeks. There was a flash in those same dark eyes which told of a temper that it would not be wise to provoke.

"Poor Auntie," she said, when Poirot had introduced himself and explained his business. "It's terribly sad. I've been wishing all the morning that I'd been kinder and more patient."

"You stood a great deal, Freda," interrupted Radnor.

"Yes, Jacob, but I've got a sharp temper, I know. After all, it was only silliness on Auntie's part. I ought to have just laughed and not minded. Of course, it's all nonsense her thinking that Uncle was poisoning her. She *was* worse after any food he gave her—but I'm sure it was only from thinking about it. She made up her mind she would be, and then she was."

"What was the actual cause of your disagreement, mademoiselle?"

Miss Stanton hesitated, looking at Radnor. That young gentleman was quick to take the hint.

"I must be getting along, Freda. See you this evening. Good-bye, gentlemen; you're on your way to the station, I suppose?"

Poirot replied that we were, and Radnor departed.

"You are affianced, is it not so?" demanded Poirot, with a sly smile. Freda Stanton blushed and admitted that such was the case.

"And that was really the whole trouble with Auntie," she added.

"She did not approve of the match for you?"

"Oh, it wasn't that so much. But you see, she—" The girl came to a stop.

"Yes?" encouraged Poirot gently.

"It seems rather a horrid thing to say about her—now she's dead. But you'll never understand unless I tell you. Auntie was absolutely infatuated with Jacob."

"Indeed?"

"Yes, wasn't it absurd? She was over fifty, and he's not quite thirty! But there it was. She was silly about him! I had to tell her at last that it was me he was after—and she carried on dreadfully. She wouldn't believe a word of it, and was so rude and insulting that it's no wonder I lost my temper. I talked it over with Jacob, and we agreed that the best thing to do was for me to clear out for a bit till she came to her senses. Poor Auntie—I suppose she was in a queer state altogether."

"It would certainly seem so. Thank you, mademoiselle, for making things so clear to me."

A little to my surprise, Radnor was waiting for us in the street below.

"I can guess pretty well what Freda has been telling you," he remarked. "It was a most unfortunate thing to happen, and very awkward for me, as you can imagine. I need hardly say that it was none of my doing. I was pleased at first, because I imagined the old woman was helping on things with Freda. The whole thing was absurd—but extremely unpleasant."

"When are you and Miss Stanton going to be married?"

"Soon, I hope. Now, Monsieur Poirot, I'm going to be candid with you. I know a bit more than Freda does. She believes her uncle to be innocent. I'm not so sure. But I can tell you one thing: I'm going to keep my mouth shut about what I do know. Let sleeping dogs lie. I don't want my wife's uncle tried and hanged for murder."

"Why do you tell me all this?"

"Because I've heard of you, and I know you're a clever man. It's quite possible that you might ferret out a case against him. But I put it to you—what good is that? The poor woman is past help, and she'd have been the last person to want a scandal—why, she'd turn in her grave at the mere thought of it."

"You are probably right there. You want me to—hush it up, then?"

"That's my idea. I'll admit frankly that I'm selfish about it. I've got my way to make—and I'm building up a good little business as a tailor and outfitter."

"Most of us are selfish, Mr. Radnor. Not all of us admit it so freely. I will do what you ask—but I tell you frankly you will not succeed in hushing it up."

"Why not?"

Poirot held up a finger. It was market day, and we were passing the market—a busy hum came from within.

"The voice of the people—that is why, Mr. Radnor. Ah, we must run, or we shall miss our train."

"Very interesting, is it not, Hastings?" said Poirot, as the train steamed out of the station.

He had taken out a small comb from his pocket, also a microscopic mirror, and was carefully arranging his mustache, the symmetry of which had become slightly impaired during our brisk run.

"You seem to find it so," I replied. "To me, it is all rather sordid and unpleasant. There's hardly any mystery about it."

"I agree with you; there is no mystery whatever."

"I suppose we can accept the girl's rather extraordinary story of her aunt's infatuation? That seemed the only fishy part to me. She was such a nice, respectable woman."

"There is nothing extraordinary about that—it is completely ordinary. If you read the papers carefully, you will find that often a nice respectable woman of that age leaves a husband she has lived with for twenty years, and sometimes a whole family of children as well, in order to link her life with that of a young man considerably her junior. You admire *les femmes*, Hastings; you prostrate yourself before all of them who are good-looking and have the good taste to smile upon you; but psychologically you know nothing whatever about them. In the autumn of a woman's life, there comes always one mad moment when she longs for romance, for adventure—before it is too late. It comes nonetheless surely to a woman because she is the wife of a respectable dentist in a country town!"

"And you think—"

"That a clever man might take advantage of such a moment."

"I shouldn't call Pengelley so clever," I mused. "He's got the whole town by the ears. And yet I suppose you're right. The only two men who know anything, Radnor and the doctor, both want to hush it up. He's managed that somehow. I wish we'd seen the fellow."

"You can indulge your wish. Return by the next train and invent an aching molar."

I looked at him keenly.

"I wish I knew what you considered so interesting about the case."

"My interest is very aptly summed up by a remark of yours, Hastings. After interviewing the maid, you observed that for someone who was not going to say a word, she had said a good deal."

"Oh!" I said doubtfully; then I harped back to my original criticism, "I wonder why you made no attempt to see Pengelley?"

"*Mon ami,* I give him just three months. Then I shall see him for as long as I please—in the dock."

For once I thought Poirot's prognostications were going to be proved wrong. The time went by, and nothing transpired as to our Cornish case. Other matters occupied us, and I had nearly forgotten the Pengelley tragedy when it was suddenly recalled to me by a short paragraph in the paper which stated that an order to exhume the body of Mrs. Pengelley had been obtained from the Home Secretary.

A few days later, and "The Cornish Mystery" was the topic of every paper. It seemed that gossip had never entirely died down, and when the engagement of the widower to Miss Marks, his secretary, was announced, the tongues burst out again louder than ever. Finally a petition was sent to the Home Secretary; the body was exhumed; large quantities of arsenic were discovered; and Mr. Pengelley was arrested and charged with the murder of his wife.

Poirot and I attended the preliminary proceedings. The evidence was much as might have been expected. Dr. Adams admitted that the symptoms of arsenical poisoning might easily be mistaken for those of gastritis. The Home Office expert gave his evidence; the maid Jessie poured out a flood of voluble information, most of which was rejected, but which certainly strengthened the case against the prisoner. Freda Stanton gave evidence as to her aunt's being worse whenever she ate food prepared by her husband. Jacob Radnor told how he had dropped in unexpectedly on the day of Mrs. Pengelley's death, and found Pengelley replacing the bottle of weed killer on the pantry shelf, Mrs. Pengelley's gruel being on the table close by. Then Miss

Marks, the fair-haired secretary, was called, and wept and went into hysterics and admitted that there had been "passages" between her and her employer, and that he had promised to marry her in the event of anything happening to his wife. Pengelley reserved his defense and was sent for trial.

Jacob Radnor walked back with us to our lodgings.

"You see, Monsieur Radnor," said Poirot, "I was right. The voice of the people spoke—and with no uncertain voice. There was to be no hushing up of this case."

"You were quite right," sighed Radnor. "Do you see any chance of his getting off?"

"Well, he has reserved his defense. He may have something—up the sleeve, as you English say. Come in with us, will you not?"

Radnor accepted the invitation. I ordered two whiskies and sodas and a cup of chocolate. The last order caused consternation, and I much doubted whether it would ever put in an appearance.

"Of course," continued Poirot, "I have a good deal of experience in matters of this kind. And I see only one loophole of escape for our friend."

"What is it?"

"That you should sign this paper."

With the suddenness of a conjurer, he produced a sheet of paper covered with writing.

"What is it?"

"A confession that *you* murdered Mrs. Pengelley."

There was a moment's pause; then Radnor laughed.

"You must be mad!"

"No, no, my friend, I am not mad. You came here; you started a little business; you were short of money. Mr. Pengelley was a man very well-to-do. You met his niece; she was inclined to smile upon you. But the small allowance that Pengelley might have given her upon her marriage was not enough for you. You must get rid of both the uncle and the aunt; then the money would come to her, since she was the only relative. How cleverly you set about it! You made love to that plain middle-aged woman until she was your slave. You implanted in her doubts of her husband. She discovered first that he was deceiving her—then, under your guidance, that he was trying to poison her. You were often at the house; you had opportunities to introduce the arsenic into her food. But you were careful never to do so when her husband was away. Being a woman, she did not keep her suspicions to herself. She talked to her niece; doubtless she talked to other women friends. Your only difficulty was keeping up separate relations with the two women, and even that was not so difficult as it looked. You explained to the aunt that, to allay the suspicions of her husband, you had to pretend to pay court to the niece. And the younger lady needed little convincing—she would never seriously consider her aunt as a rival.

"But then Mrs. Pengelley made up her mind, without saying anything to you, to consult *me*. If she could be really assured, beyond any possible doubt, that her husband was trying to poison her, she would feel justified in leaving him, and linking her life with yours—which is what she imagined you wanted her to do. But that did not suit your book at all. You did not want a detective prying around. A favourable minute occurs. You are in the house when Mr. Pengelley is getting some gruel for his wife, and you introduce the fatal dose. The rest is easy. Apparently anxious to hush matters up, you secretly foment them. But you reckoned without Hercule Poirot, my intelligent young friend."

Radnor was deadly pale, but he still endeavoured to carry off matters with a high hand.

"Very interesting and ingenious, but why tell me all this?"

"Because, monsieur, I represent—not the law, but Mrs. Pengelley. For her sake, I give you a chance of escape. Sign this paper, and you shall have twenty-four hours' start—twenty-four hours before I place it in the hands of the police."

Radnor hesitated.

"You can't prove anything."

"Can't I? I am Hercule Poirot. Look out of the window, monsieur. There are two men in the street. They have orders not to lose sight of you."

Radnor strode across to the window and pulled aside the blind, then shrank back with an oath.

"You see, monsieur? Sign—it is your best chance."

"What guarantee have I—"

"That I shall keep faith? The word of Hercule Poirot. You will sign? Good. Hastings, be so kind as to pull that left-hand blind halfway up. That is the signal that Mr. Radnor may leave unmolested."

White, muttering oaths, Radnor hurried from the room. Poirot nodded gently.

"A coward! I always knew it."

"It seems to me, Poirot, that you've acted in a criminal manner," I cried angrily. "You always preach against sentiment. And here you are letting a dangerous criminal escape out of sheer sentimentality."

"That was not sentiment—that was business," replied Poirot. "Do you not see, my friend, that we have no shadow of proof against him? Shall I get up and say to twelve stolid Cornishmen that I, Hercule Poirot, *know*? They would laugh at me. The only chance was to frighten him and get a confession that way. Those two loafers that I noticed outside came in very useful. Pull down the blind again, will you, Hastings? Not that there was any reason for raising it. It was part of the *mise en scène.*

"Well, well, we must keep our word. Twenty-four hours, did I say? So much longer for poor Mr. Pengelley—and it is not more than he deserves; for mark you, he deceived his wife. I am very strong on the family life, as you know. Ah, well, twenty-four hours—and then? I have great faith in Scotland Yard. They will get him, *mon ami;* they will get him."

# The King of Clubs

"**T**RUTH," I observed, laying aside the daily *Newsmonger*, "is stranger than fiction!"

The remark was not, perhaps, an original one. It appeared to incense my friend. Tilting his egg-shaped head on one side, the little man carefully flicked an imaginary fleck of dust from his carefully creased trousers, and observed:

"How profound! What a thinker is my friend Hastings!"

Without displaying any annoyance at this quite uncalled-for gibe, I tapped the sheet I had laid aside.

"You've read this morning's paper?"

"I have. And after reading it, I folded it anew symmetrically. I did not cast it on the floor as you have done, with your so lamentable absence of order and method."

(That is the worst of Poirot. Order and Method are his gods. He goes so far as to attribute all his success to them.)

"Then you saw the account of the murder of Henry Reedburn the impresario? It was that which prompted my remark. Not only is truth stranger than fiction—it is more dramatic. Think of that solid middle-class English family, the Oglanders. Father and mother, son and daughter, typical of thousands of families all over this country. The men of the family go to the city every day; the women look after the house. Their lives are perfectly peaceful, and utterly monotonous. Last night they were sitting in their neat suburban drawing room at Daisymead, Streatham, playing bridge. Suddenly, without any warning, the French window bursts open, and a woman staggers into the room. Her gray satin frock is marked with a crimson stain. She utters one word, "Murder!" before she sinks to the ground insensible. It is possible that they recognize her from her pictures as Valerie Saintclair, the famous dancer who has lately taken London by storm!"

"Is this your eloquence, or that of the daily *Newsmonger?*" inquired Poirot.

"The daily *Newsmonger* was in a hurry to go to press, and contented itself with bare facts. But the dramatic possibilities of the story struck me at once."

Poirot nodded thoughtfully. "Wherever there is human nature, there is drama. *But*—it is not always just where you think it is. Remember that. Still, I too am interested in the case, since it is likely that I shall be connected with it."

"Indeed?"

"Yes. A gentleman rang me up this morning, and made an appointment with me on behalf of Prince Paul of Maurania."

"But what has that to do with it?"

"You do not read your pretty little English scandal papers. The ones with the funny stories, and 'a little mouse has heard—' or 'a little bird would like to know—' See here."

I followed his short stubby finger along the paragraph:

"—whether the foreign Prince and the famous dancer are *really* affinities! And if the lady likes her new diamond ring!"

"And now to resume your so dramatic narrative," said Poirot. "Mademoiselle Saintclair had just fainted on the drawing-room carpet at Daisymead, you remember."

I shrugged. "As a result of Mademoiselle's first murmured words when she came round, the two male Oglanders stepped out, one to fetch a doctor to attend to the lady, who was evidently suffering terribly from shock, and the other to the police station—whence after telling his story, he accompanied the police to Mon Désir, Mr. Reedburn's magnificent villa, which is situated at no great distance from Daisymead. There they found the great man, who by the way suffers from a somewhat unsavory reputation, lying in the library with the back of his head cracked open like an eggshell."

"I have cramped your style," said Poirot kindly. "Forgive me, I pray. . . . Ah, here is *M. le Prince!*"

Our distinguished visitor was announced under the title of Count Feodor. He was a strange-looking youth, tall, eager, with a weak chin, the famous Mauranberg mouth, and the dark fiery eyes of a fanatic.

"M. Poirot?"

My friend bowed.

"Monsieur, I am in terrible trouble, greater than I can well express—"

Poirot waved his hand. "I comprehend your anxiety. Mademoiselle Saintclair is a very dear friend, is it not so?"

The Prince replied simply, "I hope to make her my wife."

Poirot sat up in his chair, and his eyes opened.

The Prince continued, "I should not be the first of my family to make a morganatic marriage. My brother Alexander has also defied the Emperor. We are living now in more enlightened days, free from the old caste prejudice. Besides, Mademoiselle Saintclair, in actual fact, is quite my equal in rank. You have heard hints as to her history?"

"There are many romantic stories of her origin—not an uncommon thing with famous dancers. I have heard that she is the daughter of an Irish charwoman, also the story which makes her mother a Russian grand duchess."

"The first story, is, of course, nonsense," said the young man. "But the second is true. Valerie, though bound to secrecy, has let me guess as much. Besides, she proves it unconsciously in a thousand ways. I believe in heredity, M. Poirot."

"I too believe in heredity," said Poirot thoughtfully, "I have seen some strange things in connection with it—*moi qui vous parle.* . . . But to business, *M. le Prince.* What do you want of me? What do you fear? I may speak freely, may I not? Is there anything to connect Mademoiselle Saintclair with the crime? She knew Reedburn of course?"

"Yes. He professed to be in love with her."

"And she?"

"She would have nothing to say to him."

Poirot looked at him keenly. "Had she any reason to fear him?"

The young man hesitated. "There was an incident. You know Zara, the clairvoyant?"

"No."

"She is wonderful. You should consult her sometime. Valerie and I went to see her last week. She read the cards for us. She spoke to Valerie of trouble—of gathering clouds; then she turned up the last card—the covering card, they call it. It was the king of clubs. She said to Valerie, 'Beware. There is a man who holds you in his power. You fear him—you are in great danger through him. You know whom I mean?' Valerie was white to the lips. She nodded and said, 'Yes, yes, I know.' Shortly afterward we left. Zara's last words to Valerie were, 'Beware of the king of clubs. Danger threatens you!' I questioned Valerie. She would tell me nothing—assured me that all was well. But now, after last night, I am more sure than ever that in the king of clubs Valerie saw Reedburn, and that he was the man she feared."

The Prince paused abruptly. "Now you understand my agitation when I opened the paper this morning. Supposing Valerie, in a fit of madness—oh, it is impossible!"

Poirot rose from his seat, and patted the young man kindly on the shoulder. "Do not distress yourself, I beg of you. Leave it in my hands."

"You will go to Streatham? I gather she is still there, at Daisymead— prostrated by the shock."

"I will go at once."

"I have arranged matters—through the embassy. You will be allowed access everywhere."

"Then we will depart—Hastings, you will accompany me? *Au revoir, M. le Prince.*"

Mon Désir was an exceptionally fine villa, thoroughly modern and comfortable. A short carriage-drive led up to it from the road, and beautiful gardens extended behind the house for some acres.

On mentioning Prince Paul's name, the butler who answered the door at once took us to the scene of the tragedy. The library was a magnificent room, running from back to front of the whole building, with a window at either end, one giving on the front carriage drive, and the other on the garden. It was in the recess of the latter that the body had lain. It had been removed not long before, the police having concluded their examination.

"That is annoying," I murmured to Poirot. "Who knows what clues they may have destroyed?"

My little friend smiled. "Eh—eh! How often must I tell you that clues come from *within?* In the little gray cells of the brain lies the solution of every mystery."

He turned to the butler. "I suppose, except for the removal of the body, the room has not been touched?"

"No sir. It's just as it was when the police came up last night."

"These curtains, now. I see they pull right across the window recess. They are the same in the other window. Were they drawn last night?"

"Yes sir. I draw them every night."

"Then Reedburn must have drawn them back himself?"

"I suppose so, sir."

"Did you know your master expected a visitor last night?"

"He did not say so, sir. But he gave orders he was not to be disturbed after dinner. You see, sir, there is a door leading out of the library onto the terrace at the side of the house. He could have admitted anyone that way."

"Was he in the habit of doing that?"

The butler coughed discreetly. "I believe so, sir."

Poirot strode to the door in question. It was unlocked. He stepped through it onto the terrace which joined the drive on the right; on the left it led up to a red brick wall.

"The fruit garden, sir. There is a door leading into it farther along, but it was always locked at six o'clock."

Poirot nodded, and reentered the library, the butler following.

"Did you hear nothing of last night's events?"

"Well, sir, we heard voices in the library, a little before nine. But that wasn't unusual, especially being a lady's voice. But of course, once we were all in the servants' hall, right the other side, we didn't hear anything at all. And then, about eleven o'clock, the police came."

"How many voices did you hear?"

"I couldn't say, sir. I only noticed the lady's."

"Ah!"

"I beg pardon, sir, but Dr. Ryan is still in the house, if you would care to see him."

We jumped at the suggestion, and in a few minutes the doctor, a cheery, middle-aged man, joined us, and gave Poirot all the information he required. Reedburn had been lying near the window, his head by the marble window-seat. There were two wounds, one between the eyes, and the other, the fatal one, on the back of the head.

"He was lying on his back?"

"Yes. There is the mark." He pointed to a small dark stain on the floor.

"Could not the blow on the back of the head have been caused by his striking the floor?"

"Impossible. Whatever the weapon was, it penetrated some distance into the skull."

Poirot looked thoughtfully in front of him. In the embrasure of each window was a carved marble seat, the arms being fashioned in the form of a lion's head. A light came into Poirot's eyes. "Supposing he had fallen backward on this projecting lion's head, and slipped from there to the ground. Would not that cause a wound such as you describe?"

"Yes, it would. But the angle at which he was lying makes that theory impossible. And besides, there could not fail to be traces of blood on the marble of the seat."

"Unless they were washed away?"

The Doctor shrugged his shoulders. "That is hardly likely. It would be to no one's advantage to give an accident the appearance of murder."

"Quite so," acquiesced Poirot. "Could either of the blows have been struck by a woman, do you think?"

"Oh, quite out of the question, I should say. You are thinking of Mademoiselle Saintclair, I suppose?"

"I think of no one in particular until I am sure," said Poirot, gently.

He turned his attention to the open French window, and the Doctor continued:

"It is through here that Mademoiselle Saintclair fled. You can just catch a glimpse of Daisymead between the trees. Of course, there are many houses nearer to the front of the house on the road, but as it happens, Daisymead, though some distance away, is the only house visible this side."

"Thank you for your amiability, Doctor," said Poirot. "Come, Hastings, we will follow the footsteps of mademoiselle."

Poirot led the way down through the garden, out through an iron gate, across a short stretch of green and in through the garden gate of Daisymead, which was an unpretentious little house in about half an acre of ground. There was a small flight of steps leading up to a French window. Poirot nodded in their direction.

"That is the way Mademoiselle Saintclair went. For us, who have not her urgency to plead, it will be better to go round to the front door."

A maid admitted us and took us into the drawing room, then went in search of Mrs. Oglander. The room had evidently not been touched since the night before. The ashes were still in the gate, and the bridge table was still in the center of the room, with a dummy exposed, and the hands thrown down. The place was somewhat overloaded with gimcrack ornaments, and a good many family portraits of surpassing ugliness adorned the walls.

Poirot gazed at them more leniently than I did, and straightened one or two that were hanging a shade askew. *"La famille,* it is a strong tie, is it not? Sentiment, it takes the place of beauty."

I agreed, my eyes being fixed on a family group comprising a gentleman with whiskers, a lady with a high "front" of hair, a stolid, thickset boy, and two little girls tied up with a good many unnecessary bows of ribbon. I took this to be the Oglander family in earlier days, and studied it with interest.

The door opened, and a young woman came in. Her dark hair was neatly arranged, and she wore a drab-colored sportscoat and a tweed skirt.

She looked at us inquiringly. Poirot stepped forward. "Miss Oglander? I regret to derange you—especially after all you have been through. The whole affair must have been most disturbing."

"It has been rather upsetting," admitted the young lady cautiously. I began to think that the elements of drama were wasted on Miss Oglander, that her lack of imagination rose superior to any tragedy. I was confirmed in this belief as she continued, "I must apologize for the state this room is in. Servants get so foolishly excited."

"It was here that you were sitting last night, *n'est-ce pas?"*

"Yes, we were playing bridge after supper, when—"

"Excuse me—how long had you been playing?"

"Well—" Miss Oglander considered. "I really can't say. I suppose it must have been about ten o'clock. We had had several rubbers, I know."

"And you yourself were sitting—where?"

"Facing the window. I was playing with my mother and had gone one no trump. Suddenly, without any warning, the window burst open, and Miss Saintclair staggered into the room."

"You recognized her?"

"I had a vague idea her face was familiar."

"She is still here, is she not?"

"Yes, but she refuses to see anyone. She is still quite prostrated."

"I think she will see me. Will you tell her that I am here at the express request of Prince Paul of Maurania?"

I fancied that the mention of a royal prince rather shook Miss Oglander's imperturbable calm. But she left the room on her errand without any further remark, and returned almost immediately to say that Mademoiselle Saintclair would see us in her room.

We followed her upstairs, and into a fair-sized light bedroom. On a couch by the window a woman was lying who turned her head as we entered. The contrast between the two women struck me at once, the more so as in actual features and coloring they were not unalike— but oh, the difference! Not a look, not a gesture of Valerie Saintclair's but expressed drama. She seemed to exhale an atmosphere of romance. A scarlet flannel dressing gown covered her feet—a homely garment in all conscience; but the charm of her personality invested it with an exotic flavor, and it seemed an Eastern robe of glowing color.

Her large dark eyes fastened themselves on Poirot.

"You come from Paul?" Her voice matched her appearance—it was full and languid.

"Yes, mademoiselle. I am here to serve him—and you."

"What do you want to know?"

"Everything that happened last night. *But everything!*"

She smiled rather wearily.

"Do you think I should lie? I am not stupid. I see well enough that there can be no concealment. He held a secret of mine, that man who is dead. He threatened me with it. For Paul's sake, I endeavored to make terms with him. I could not risk losing Paul. . . . Now that he is dead, I am safe. But for all that, I did not kill him."

Poirot shook his head with a smile. "It is not necessary to tell me that, mademoiselle. Now recount to me what happened last night."

"I offered him money. He appeared to be willing to treat with me. He appointed last night at nine o'clock. I was to go to Mon Désir. I knew the place; I had been there before. I was to go round to the side door into the library, so that the servants should not see me."

"Excuse me, mademoiselle, but were you not afraid to trust yourself alone there at night?"

Was it my fancy, or was there a momentary pause before she answered?

"Perhaps I was. But you see, there was no one I could ask to go with me. And I was desperate. Reedburn admitted me to the library. Oh, that man! I am glad he is dead! He played with me, as a cat does with a mouse. He taunted me. I begged and implored him on my knees. I offered him every jewel I have. All in vain! Then he named his own terms. Perhaps you can guess what they were. I refused. I told him what I thought of him. I raved at him. He remained calmly smiling. And then, as I fell to silence at last, there was a sound—from behind the curtain in the window. . . . He heard it too. He strode to the curtains and flung them wide apart. There was a man there, hiding—a dreadful-looking man, a sort of tramp. He struck at Mr. Reedburn—then he struck again, and he went down. The tramp clutched at me with his bloodstained hand. I tore myself free, slipped through the window, and ran for my life. Then I perceived the lights in this house, and made for them. The blinds were up, and I saw some people playing bridge. I almost fell into the room. I just managed to gasp out 'Murder!' and then everything went black—"

"Thank you, mademoiselle. It must have been a great shock to your nervous system. As to this tramp, could you describe him? Do you remember what he was wearing?"

"No—it was all so quick. But I should know the man anywhere. His face is burnt in on my brain."

"Just one more question, mademoiselle. The curtains of the *other* window, the one giving on the drive, were they drawn?"

For the first time a puzzled expression crept over the dancer's face. She seemed to be trying to remember.

*"Eh bien, mademoiselle?"*

"I think—I am almost sure—yes, quite sure! They were *not* drawn."

"That is curious, since the other ones were. No matter. It is, I dare say, of no great importance. You are remaining here long, mademoiselle?"

"The doctor thinks I shall be fit to return to town tomorrow." She looked round the room. Miss Oglander had gone out. "These people, they are very kind—but they are not of my world. I shock them! And to me—well, I am not fond of the *bourgeoisie!*"

A faint note of bitterness underlay her words.

Poirot nodded. "I understand. I hope I have not fatigued you unduly with my questions?"

"Not at all, monsieur. I am only too anxious Paul should know all as soon as possible."

"Then I will wish you good day, mademoiselle."

As Poirot was leaving the room, he paused, and pounced on a pair of patent-leather slippers. "Yours, mademoiselle?"

"Yes, monsieur. They have just been cleaned and brought up."

"Ah!" said Poirot, as we descended the stairs. "It seems that the domestics are not too excited to clean shoes, though they forget a grate. Well, *mon ami*, at first there appeared to be one or two points of interest, but I fear, I very much fear, that we must regard the case as finished. It all seems straightforward enough."

"And the murderer?"

"Hercule Poirot does not hunt down tramps," replied my friend grandiloquently.

Miss Oglander met us in the hall. "If you will wait in the drawing room a minute, Mamma would like to speak to you."

The room was still untouched, and Poirot idly gathered up the cards, shuffling them with his tiny, fastidiously groomed hands.

"Do you know what I think, my friend?"

"No?" I said eagerly.

"I think that Miss Oglander made a mistake in going one no trump. She should have gone three spades."

"Poirot! You are the limit."

"*Mon Dieu*, I cannot always be talking blood and thunder!"

Suddenly he stiffened, "Hastings—*Hastings*. See! The king of clubs is missing from the pack!"

"Zara!" I cried.

"Eh?" He did not seem to understand my allusion. Mechanically he stacked the cards and put them away in their cases. His face was very grave.

"Hastings," he said at last, "I, Hercule Poirot, have come near to making a big mistake—a very big mistake."

I gazed at him, impressed, but utterly uncomprehending.

"We must begin again, Hastings. Yes, we must begin again. But this time we shall not err."

He was interrupted by the entrance of a handsome middle-aged lady. She carried some household books in her hand. Poirot bowed to her.

"Do I understand, sir, that you are a friend of—er—Miss Saint-clair's?"

"I come from a friend of hers, madame."

"Oh, I see. I thought perhaps—"

Poirot suddenly waved brusquely at the window.

"Your blinds were not pulled down last night?"

"No—I suppose that is why Miss Saintclair saw the light so plainly."

"There was moonlight last night. I wonder that you did not see Mademoiselle Saintclair from your seat here facing the windows?"

"I suppose we were engrossed with our game. Nothing like this has ever happened before to us."

"I can quite believe that, madame. And I will put your mind at rest. Mademoiselle Saintclair is leaving tomorrow."

"Oh!" The good lady's face cleared.

"And I will wish you good morning, madame."

A servant was cleaning the steps as we went out of the front door. Poirot addressed her.

"Was it you who cleaned the shoes of the young lady upstairs?"

The maid shook her head. "No sir. I don't think they've been cleaned."

"Who cleaned them, then?" I inquired of Poirot, as we walked down the road.

"Nobody. They did not need cleaning."

"I grant that walking on the road or path on a fine night would not soil them. But surely after going through the long grass of the garden, they would have been soiled and stained."

"Yes," said Poirot with a curious smile. "In that case, I agree, they would have been stained."

"But—"

"Have patience a little half hour, my friend. We are going back to Mon Désir."

The butler looked surprised at our reappearance, but offered no objection to our returning to the library.

"Hi, that's the wrong window, Poirot," I cried as he made for the one overlooking the carriage drive.

"I think not, my friend. See here." He pointed to the marble lion's head. On it was a faint discolored smear. He shifted his finger and pointed to a similar stain on the polished floor.

"Some one struck Reedburn a blow with his clenched fist between the eyes. He fell backward on this projecting bit of marble, then slipped to the floor. Afterward, he was dragged across the floor to the other window, and laid there instead, but not quite at the same angle, as the Doctor's evidence told us."

"But why? It seems utterly unnecessary."

"On the contrary, it was essential. Also, it is the key to the murderer's identity—though, by the way, he had no intention of killing Reedburn, and so it is hardly permissible to call him a murderer. He must be a very strong man!"

"Because of having dragged the body across the floor?"

"Not altogether. It has been an interesting case. I nearly made an imbecile of myself, though."

"Do you mean to say it is over, that you know everything?"

"Yes."

A remembrance smote me. "No," I cried. "There is one thing you do *not* know!"

"And that?"

"You do not know where the missing king of clubs is!"

"Eh? Oh, that is droll! That is very droll, my friend."

"Why?"

*"Because it is in my pocket!"* He drew it forth with a flourish.

"Oh!" I said, rather crestfallen. "Where did you find it? Here?"

"There was nothing sensational about it. It had simply not been taken out with the other cards. It was in the box."

"Hm! All the same, it gave you an idea, didn't it?"

"Yes, my friend. I present my respects to His Majesty."

"And to Madame Zara!"

"Ah yes—to the lady also."

"Well, what are we going to do now?"

"We are going to return to town. But I must have a few words with a certain lady at Daisymead first."

The same little maid opened the door to us.

"They're all at lunch now, sir—unless it's Miss Saintclair you want to see, and she's resting."

"It will do if I can see Mrs. Oglander for a few minutes. Will you tell her?"

We were led into the drawing room to wait. I had a glimpse of the family in the dining room as we passed, now reinforced by the presence of two heavy, solid-looking men, one with a mustache, the other with a beard also.

In a few minutes Mrs. Oglander came into the room, looking inquiringly at Poirot, who bowed.

"Madame, we, in our country, have a great tenderness, a great respect for the mother. The *mère de famille*, she is everything!"

Mrs. Oglander looked rather astonished at this opening.

"It is for that reason that I have come—to allay a mother's anxiety. The murderer of Mr. Reedburn will not be discovered. Have no fear. I, Hercule Poirot, tell you so. I am right, am I not? Or is it a wife that I must reassure?"

There was a moment's pause. Mrs. Oglander seemed searching Poirot with her eyes. At last she said quietly, "I don't know how you know—but yes, you are right."

Poirot nodded gravely. "That is all, madame. But do not be uneasy. Your English policemen have not the eyes of Hercule Poirot." He tapped the family portrait on the wall with his fingernail.

"You had another daughter once. She is dead, madame?"

Again there was a pause, as she searched him with her eyes. Then she answered, "Yes, she is dead."

"Ah!" said Poirot briskly. "Well, we must return to town. You permit that I return the king of clubs to the pack? It was your only slip. You understand, to have played bridge for an hour or so, with only fifty-one cards—well, no one who knows anything of the game would credit it for a minute! *Bonjour!*"

"And now, my friend," said Poirot as we stepped toward the station, "you see it all!"

"I see nothing! Who killed Reedburn?"

"John Oglander, Junior. I was not quite sure if it was the father or the son, but I fixed on the son as being the stronger and younger of the two. It had to be one of them, because of the window."

"Why?"

"There were four exits from the library—two doors, two windows; but evidently only one would do. Three exits gave on the front, directly or indirectly. The tragedy had to occur in the back window in order to make it appear that Valerie Saintclair came to Daisymead by chance. Really, of course, she fainted, and John Oglander carried her across over his shoulders. That is why I said he must be a strong man."

"Did they go there together, then?"

"Yes. You remember Valerie's hesitation when I asked her if she was not afraid to go alone? John Oglander went with her—which didn't improve Reedburn's temper, I fancy. They quarreled, and it was probably some insult leveled at Valerie that made Oglander hit him. The rest, you know."

"But why the bridge?"

"Bridge presupposes four players. A simple thing like that carries a lot of conviction. Who would have supposed that there had been only three people in that room all the evening."

I was still puzzled.

"There's one thing I don't understand. What have the Oglanders to do with the dancer Valerie Saintclair?"

"Ah, that I wonder you did not see. And yet you looked long enough at that picture on the wall—longer than I did. Mrs. Oglander's other daughter may be dead to her family, but the world knows her as Valerie Saintclair!"

"*What?*"

"Did you not see the resemblance the moment you saw the two sisters together?"

"No," I confessed. "I only thought how extraordinary dissimilar they were."

"That is because your mind is so open to external romantic impressions, my dear Hastings. The features are almost identical. So is the coloring. The interesting thing is that Valerie is ashamed of her family, and her family is ashamed of her. Nevertheless, in a moment of peril, she turned to her brother for help, and when things went wrong, they all hung together in a remarkable way. Family strength is a marvelous thing. They can all act, that family. That is where Valerie gets her histrionic talent from. I, like Prince Paul, believe in heredity! They deceived *me!* But for a lucky accident, and test question to Mrs. Oglander by which I got her to contradict her daughter's account of how they were sitting, the Oglander family would have put a defeat on Hercule Poirot."

"What shall you tell the Prince?"

"That Valerie could not possibly have committed the crime, and that I doubt if that tramp will ever be found. Also, to convey my compliments to Zara. A curious coincidence, that! I think I shall call this little affair the Adventure of the King of Clubs. What do you think, my friend?"

# The Adventure of
# the Clapham Cook

AT the time that I was sharing rooms with my friend Hercule
Poirot, it was my custom to read aloud to him the headlines
in the morning newspaper, *The Daily Blare*.

*The Daily Blare* was a paper that made the most of any opportunity
for sensationalism. Robberies and murders did not lurk obscurely in
its back pages. Instead they hit you in the eye in large type on the
front page.

> *Absconding Bank Clerk Disappears with Fifty Thousand
> Pounds' Worth of Negotiable Securities,* I read.
> *Husband Puts his Head in Gas Oven. Unhappy Home Life.
> Missing Typist. Pretty Girl of Twenty-One. Where is Edna Field?*

"There you are, Poirot, plenty to choose from. An absconding bank
clerk, a mysterious suicide, a missing typist—which will you have?"

My friend was in a placid mood. He quietly shook his head.

"I am not greatly attracted to any of them, *mon ami*. Today I feel
inclined for the life of ease. It would have to be a very interesting
problem to tempt me from my chair. See you, I have affairs of importance of my own to attend to."

"Such as?"

"My wardrobe, Hastings. If I mistake not, there is on my new grey
suit the spot of grease—only the unique spot, but it is sufficient to
trouble me. Then there is my winter overcoat—I must lay him aside
in the powder of Keatings. And I think—yes, I think—the moment
is ripe for the trimmings of my moustache—and afterwards I must
apply the *pomade*."

"Well," I said, strolling to the window, "I doubt if you'll be able
to carry out this delirious program. That was a ring at the bell. You
have a client."

"Unless the affair is one of national importance, I touch it not,"
declared Poirot with dignity.

A moment later our privacy was invaded by a stout red-faced lady who panted audibly as a result of her rapid ascent of the stairs.

"You're M. Poirot?" she demanded, as she sank into a chair.

"I am Hercule Poirot, yes, madame."

"You're not a bit like what I thought you'd be," said the lady, eyeing him with some disfavour. "Did you pay for the bit in the paper saying what a clever detective you were, or did they put it in themselves?"

"Madame!" said Poirot, drawing himself up.

"I'm sorry, I'm sure, but you know what these papers are nowadays. You begin reading a nice article 'What a bride said to her plain unmarried friend,' and it's all about a simple thing you buy at the chemist's and shampoo your hair with. Nothing but puff. But no offense taken, I hope? I'll tell you what I want you to do for me. I want you to find my cook."

Poirot stared at her; for once his ready tongue failed him. I turned aside to hide the broadening smile I could not control.

"It's all this wicked dole," continued the lady. "Putting ideas into servants' heads, wanting to be typists and what nots. Stop the dole, that's what I say. I'd like to know what *my* servants have to complain of—afternoon and evening off a week, alternate Sundays, washing put out, same food as we have—and never a bit of margarine in the house, nothing but the very best butter."

She paused for want of breath and Poirot seized his opportunity. He spoke in his haughtiest manner rising to his feet as he did so.

"I fear you are making a mistake, Madame. I am not holding an inquiry into the conditions of domestic service. I am a private detective."

"I know that," said our visitor. "Didn't I tell you I wanted you to find my cook for me? Walked out of the house on Wednesday, without so much as a word to me, and never came back."

"I am sorry, Madame, but I do not touch this particular kind of business. I wish you good morning."

Our visitor snorted with indignation.

"That's it, is it, my fine fellow? Too proud, eh? Only deal with government secrets and countesses' jewels? Let me tell you a servant's every bit as important as a tiara to a woman in my position. We can't all be fine ladies going out in our motors with our diamonds and our pearls. A good cook's a good cook—and when you lose her, it's as much to you as her pearls are to some fine lady."

For a moment or two it appeared to be a toss up between Poirot's dignity and his sense of humour. Finally he laughed and sat down again.

"Madame, you are in the right, and I am in the wrong. Your remarks are just and intelligent. This case will be a novelty. Never yet have I hunted a missing domestic. Truly here is the problem of national importance that I was demanding of fate just before your arrival. *En avant!* You say this jewel of a cook went out on Wednesday and did not return. That is the day before yesterday."

"Yes, it was her day out."

"But probably, madame, she has met with some accident. Have you inquired at any of the hospitals?"

"That's exactly what I thought yesterday, but this morning, if you please, she sent for her box. And not so much as a line to me! If I'd been at home, I'd not have let it go—treating me like that! But I'd just stepped out to the butcher."

"Will you describe her to me?"

"She was middle-aged, stout, black hair turning grey—most respectable. She'd been ten years in her last place. Eliza Dunn, her name was."

"And you had had—no disagreement with her on the Wednesday?"

"None whatever. That's what makes it all so queer."

"How many servants do you keep, madame?"

"Two. The house-parlourmaid, Annie, is a very nice girl. A bit forgetful and her head full of young men, but a good servant if you keep her up to her work."

"Did she and the cook get on well together?"

"They had their ups and downs, of course—but on the whole, very well."

"And the girl can throw no light on the mystery?"

"She says not—but you know what servants are—they all hang together."

"Well, well, we must look into this. Where did you say you resided, Madame?"

"At Clapham; 88 Prince Albert Road."

"*Bien, madame,* I will wish you good morning, and you may count upon seeing me at your residence during the course of the day."

Mrs. Todd, for such was our new friend's name, then took her departure. Poirot looked at me somewhat ruefully.

"Well, well, Hastings, this is a novel affair that we have here. The Disappearance of the Clapham Cook! Never, *never*, must our friend Inspector Japp get to hear of this!"

He then proceeded to heat an iron and carefully removed the grease spot from his grey suit by means of a piece of blotting paper. His moustache he regretfully postponed to another day, and we set out for Clapham.

Prince Albert Road proved to be a street of small prim houses, all exactly alike, with neat lace curtains veiling the windows, and well polished brass knockers on the doors.

We rang the bell at No. 88, and the door was opened by a neat maid with a pretty face. Mrs. Todd came out in the hall to greet us.

"Don't go, Annie," she cried. "This gentleman's a detective and he'll want to ask you some questions."

Annie's face displayed a struggle between alarm and a pleasurable excitement.

"I thank you, madame," said Poirot bowing. "I would like to question your maid now—and to see her alone, if I may."

We were shown into a small drawing room, and when Mrs. Todd, with obvious reluctance, had left the room, Poirot commenced his cross-examination.

"*Voyons, Mademoiselle Annie,* all that you shall tell us will be of the greatest importance. You alone can shed any light on the case. Without your assistance I can do nothing."

The alarm vanished from the girl's face and the pleasurable excitement became more strongly marked.

"I'm sure, sir," she said, "I'll tell you anything I can."

"That is good," Poirot beamed approval on her. "Now, first of all what is your own idea? You are a girl of remarkable intelligence. That can be seen at once! What is your own explanation of Eliza's disappearance?"

Thus encouraged, Annie fairly flowed into excited speech.

"White Slavers, sir, I've said so all along! Cook was always warning me against them. *'Don't you sniff no scent, or eat any sweets—no matter how gentlemanly the fellow!'* Those were her words to me. And now they've got her! I'm sure of it. As likely as not, she's been shipped to Turkey or one of them Eastern places where I've heard they like them fat!"

Poirot preserved an admirable gravity.

"But in that case—and it is indeed an idea!—would she have sent for her trunk?"

"Well, I don't know, sir. She'd want her things—even in those foreign places."

"Who came for the trunk—a man?"

"It was Carter Paterson, sir."

"Did you pack it?"

"No, sir, it was already packed and corded."

"Ah! that's interesting. That shows that when she left the house on Wednesday, she had already determined not to return. You see that, do you not?"

"Yes, sir." Annie looked slightly taken aback. "I hadn't thought of that. But it might still have been White Slavers, mightn't it, sir?" she added wistfully.

"Undoubtedly!" said Poirot gravely. He went on: "Did you both occupy the same bedroom?"

"No, sir, we had separate rooms."

"And had Eliza expressed any dissatisfaction with her present post to you at all? Were you both happy here?"

"She'd never mentioned leaving. The place is all right—" The girl hesitated.

"Speak freely," said Poirot kindly. "I shall not tell your mistress."

"Well, of course, sir, she's a caution, Missus is. But the food's good. Plenty of it, and no stinting. Something hot for supper, good outings, and as much frying fat as you like. And anyway, if Eliza did want to make a change, she'd never have gone off this way, I'm sure. She'd have stayed her month. Why, Missus could have a month's wages out of her for doing this!"

"And the work, it is not too hard?"

"Well, she's particular—always poking round in corners and looking for dust. And then there's the lodger, or paying guest as he's always called. But that's only breakfast and dinner, same as master. They're out all day in the city."

"You like your master?"

"He's all right—very quiet and a bit on the stingy side."

"You can't remember, I suppose, the last thing Eliza said before she went out?"

"Yes, I can. 'If there's any stewed peaches over from the dining room,' she says, 'we'll have them for supper, and a bit of bacon and some fried potatoes.' Mad over stewed peaches, she was. I shouldn't wonder if they didn't get her that way."

"Was Wednesday her regular day out?"

"Yes, she had Wednesdays and I had Thursdays."

Poirot asked a few more questions, then declared himself satisfied. Annie departed, and Mrs. Todd hurried in, her face alight with curiosity. She had, I felt certain, bitterly resented her exclusion from the room during our conversation with Annie. Poirot, however, was careful to soothe her feelings tactfully.

"It is difficult," he explained, "for a woman of exceptional intelligence such as yourself, madame, to bear patiently the roundabout methods we poor detectives are forced to use. To have patience with stupidity is difficult for the quick-witted."

Having thus charmed away any little resentment on Mrs. Todd's part, he brought the conversation round to her husband and elicited the information that he worked with a firm in the city and would not be home until after six.

"Doubtless he is very disturbed and worried by this unaccountable business, eh? Is it not so?"

"He's never worried," declared Mrs. Todd. " 'Well, well, get another, my dear.' That's all *he* said! He's so calm that it drives me to distraction sometimes. '*An ungrateful woman,*' he said. '*We are well rid of her.*' "

"What about the other inmates of the house, madame?"

"You mean Mr. Simpson, our paying guest? Well, as long as he gets his breakfast and his evening meal all right, *he* doesn't worry."

"What is his profession, madame?"

"He works in a bank." She mentioned its name, and I started slightly, remembering my perusal of *The Daily Blare.*

"A young man?"

"Twenty-eight, I believe. Nice quiet young fellow."

"I should like to have a few words with him, and also with your husband, if I may. I will return for that purpose this evening. I venture to suggest that you should repose yourself a little, madame, you look fatigued."

"I should just think I am! First the worry about Eliza, and then I was at the Sales practically all yesterday, and you know what *that* is, Mr. Poirot, and what with one thing and another and a lot to do in the house, because of course Annie can't do it all—and very likely she'll give notice anyway, being unsettled in this way—well, what with it all, I'm tired out!"

Poirot murmured sympathetically, and we took our leave.

"It's a curious coincidence," I said, "but that absconding clerk, Davis, was from the same bank as Simpson. Can there be any connection, do you think?"

Poirot smiled.

"At the one end, a defaulting clerk, at the other a vanishing cook. It is hard to see any relation between the two, unless possibly Davis visited Simpson, fell in love with the cook, and persuaded her to accompany him on his flight!"

I laughed. But Poirot remained grave.

"He might have done worse," he said reprovingly. "Remember, Hastings, if you are going into exile, a good cook may be of more comfort than a pretty face!" He paused for a moment and then went on. "It is a curious case, full of contradictory features. I am interested— yes, I am distinctly interested."

That evening we returned to 88 Prince Albert Road and interviewed both Todd and Simpson. The former was a melancholy, lantern-jawed man of forty-odd.

"Oh! yes, yes," he said vaguely. "Eliza. Yes. A good cook, I believe. And economical. I make a strong point of economy."

"Can you imagine any reason for her leaving you so suddenly?"

"Oh! well," said Mr. Todd vaguely. "Servants, you know. My wife worries too much. Worn out from always worrying. The whole problem's quite simple really. 'Get another, my dear,' I say. 'Get another.'

That's all there is to it. No good crying over spilt milk."

Mr. Simpson was equally unhelpful. He was a quiet inconspicuous young man with spectacles.

"I must have seen her, I suppose," he said. "Elderly woman, wasn't she? Of course, it's the other one I see always, Annie. Nice girl. Very obliging."

"Were those two on good terms with each other?"

Mr. Simpson said he couldn't say, he was sure. He supposed so.

"Well, we get nothing of interest there, *mon ami,*" said Poirot as we left the house. Our departure had been delayed by a burst of vociferous repetition from Mrs. Todd, who repeated everything she had said that morning at rather greater length.

"Are you disappointed?" I asked. "Did you expect to hear something?"

Poirot shook his head.

"There was a possibility, of course," he said. "But I hardly thought it likely."

The next development was a letter which Poirot received on the following morning. He read it, turned purple with indignation, and handed it to me.

> *Mrs. Todd regrets that after all she will not avail herself of Mr. Poirot's services. After talking the matter over with her husband she sees that it is foolish to call in a detective about a purely domestic affair. Mrs. Todd encloses a guinea for consultation fee.*

"Aha!" cried Poirot angrily. "And they think to get rid of Hercule Poirot like that! As a favor—a great favor—I consent to investigate their miserable little twopenny halfpenny affair—and they dismiss me *comme ça!* Here, I mistake not, is the hand of Mr. Todd. But I say—No!—thirty-six times no! I will spend my own guineas, thirty-six hundred of them if need be, but I will get to the bottom of this matter!"

"Yes," I said. "But how?"

Poirot calmed down a little.

"*D'abord,*" he said, "we will advertise in the papers. Let me see—yes—something like this:

"'*If Eliza Dunn will communicate with this address, she will hear of something to her advantage.*' Put it in all the papers you can think of, Hastings. Then I will make some little inquiries of my own. Go, go—all must be done as quickly as possible!"

I did not see him again until the evening, when he condescended to tell me what he had been doing.

"I have made inquiries at the firm of Mr. Todd. He was not absent on Wednesday, and he bears a good character—so much for him. Then Simpson, on Thursday he was ill and did not come to the bank, but he was there on Wednesday. He was moderately friendly with Davis. Nothing out of the common. There does not seem to be anything there. No. We must place our reliance on the advertisement."

The advertisement duly appeared in all the principal daily papers. By Poirot's orders it was to be continued every day for a week. His eagerness over this uninteresting matter of a defaulting cook was extraordinary, but I realised that he considered it a point of honour to persevere until he finally succeeded. Several extremely interesting cases were brought to him about this time, but he declined them all. Every morning he would rush at his letters, scrutinize them earnestly, and then lay them down with a sigh.

But our patience was rewarded at last. On the Wednesday following Mrs. Todd's visit, our landlady informed us that a person of the name of Eliza Dunn had called.

*"Enfin!"* cried Poirot. "But make her mount then! At once. Immediately."

Thus admonished, our landlady hurried out and returned a moment or two later, ushering in Miss Dunn. Our quarry was much as described: tall, stout, and eminently respectable.

"I came in answer to the advertisement," she explained. "I thought there must be some muddle or other, and that perhaps you didn't know I'd already got my legacy."

Poirot was studying her attentively. He drew forward a chair with a flourish.

"The truth of the matter is," he explained. "That your late mistress, Mrs. Todd, was much concerned about you. She feared some accident might have befallen you."

Eliza Dunn seemed very much surprised.

"Didn't she get my letter then?"

"She got no word of any kind." He paused, and then said persuasively, "Recount to me the whole story, will you not?"

Eliza Dunn needed no encouragement. She plunged at once into a lengthy narrative.

"I was just coming home on Wednesday night and had nearly got to the house, when a gentleman stopped me. A tall gentleman he was, with a beard and a big hat. 'Miss Eliza Dunn?' he said. 'Yes,' I said. 'I've been inquiring for you at No. 88,' he said. 'They told me I might meet you coming along here. Miss Dunn, I have come from Australia specially to find you. Do you happen to know the maiden name of your maternal grandmother?' 'Jane Emmott,' I said. 'Exactly,' he said. 'Now, Miss Dunn, although you may never have heard of the fact, your grandmother had a great friend, Eliza Leech. This friend went to Australia where she married a very wealthy settler. Her two children died in infancy, and she inherited all her husband's property. She died a few months ago, and by her will you inherit a house in this country and a considerable sum of money.'

"You could have knocked me down with a feather," continued Miss Dunn. "For a minute, I was suspicious, and he must have seen it, for he smiled. 'Quite right to be on your guard, Miss Dunn,' he said. 'Here are my credentials.' He handed me a letter from some lawyers in Melbourne, Hurst and Crotchet, and a card. He was Mr. Crotchet. 'There are one or two conditions,' he said. 'Our client was a little eccentric, you know. The bequest is conditional on your taking possession of the house (it is in Cumberland) before twelve o'clock tomorrow. The other condition is of no importance—it is merely a stipulation that you should not be in domestic service.' My face fell. 'Oh! Mr. Crotchet,' I said. 'I'm a cook. Didn't they tell you at the house?' 'Dear, dear,' he said. 'I had no idea of such a thing. I thought you might possibly be a companion or governess there. This is very unfortunate— very unfortunate indeed.'

"Shall I have to lose all the money?' I said anxious like. He thought for a minute or two. 'There are always ways of getting round the law, Miss Dunn,' he said at last. 'We lawyers know that. The way out here is for you to have left your employment this afternoon.' 'But my month?' I said. 'My dear Miss Dunn,' he said with a smile. 'You can leave an employer any minute by forfeiting a month's wages. Your mistress will understand in view of the circumstances. The difficulty is *time!* It is imperative that you should catch the 11:05 from King's Cross to the North. I can advance you ten pounds or so for the fare, and you can write a note at the station to your employer. I will take it to her myself and explain the whole circumstances.' I agreed, of course, and an hour later I was in the train, so flustered that I didn't know whether I was on my head or my heels. Indeed by the time I got to Carlisle, I was half inclined to think the whole thing was one of those confidence tricks you read about. But I went to the address he had given me—solicitors they were, and it was all right. A nice little house, and an income of three hundred a year. These lawyers knew very little, they'd just got a letter from a gentleman in London instructing them to hand over the house to me and £150 for the first six months. Mr. Crotchet sent up my things to me, but there was no word from Missus. I supposed she was angry and grudged me my bit of luck. She kept back my box too, and sent my clothes in paper parcels. But there, of course if she never had my letter, she might think it a bit cool of me."

Poirot had listened attentively to this long history. Now he nodded his head as though completely satisfied.

"Thank you, mademoiselle. There had been, as you say, a little muddle. Permit me to recompense you for your trouble." He handed her an envelope. "You return to Cumberland immediately? A little word in your ear. *Do not forget how to cook.* It is always useful to have something to fall back upon in case things go wrong."

"Credulous," he murmured, as our visitor departed, "but perhaps not more than most of her class." His face grew grave. "Come, Hastings, there is no time to be lost. Get a taxi while I write a note to Japp."

Poirot was waiting on the doorstep when I returned with the taxi.

"Where are we going?" I asked anxiously.

"First, to despatch this note by special messenger."

This was done and re-entering the taxi Poirot gave the address to the driver.

"Eighty-eight Prince Albert Road, Clapham."

"So we are going there?"

"*Mais oui.* Though frankly I fear we shall be too late. Our bird will have flown, Hastings."

"Who is our bird?"

Poirot smiled.

"The inconspicuous Mr. Simpson."

"What?" I exclaimed.

"Oh! come now, Hastings, do not tell me that all is not clear to you now?"

"The cook was got out of the way, I realise that," I said, slightly piqued. "But why? *Why* should Simpson wish to get her out of the house? Did she know something about him?"

"Nothing whatever."

"Well, then—"

"But he wanted something that she had."

"Money? The Australian legacy?"

"No, my friend—something quite different." He paused a moment and then said gravely, *"A battered tin trunk. . . ."*

I looked sideways at him. His statement seemed so fantastic that I suspected him of pulling my leg, but he was perfectly grave and serious.

"Seriously he could buy a trunk if he wanted one," I cried.

"He did not want a new trunk. He wanted a trunk of pedigree. A trunk of assured respectability."

"Look here, Poirot," I cried, "this really is a bit thick. You're pulling my leg."

He looked at me.

"You lack the brains and the imagination of Mr. Simpson, Hastings. See here: On Wednesday evening, Simpson decoys away the cook. A printed card and a printed sheet of notepaper are simple matters to obtain, and he is willing to pay £150 and a year's house rent to assure the success of his plan. Miss Dunn does not recognise him—the beard and the hat and the slight colonial accent completely deceive her. That is the end of Wednesday—except for the trifling fact that Simpson has helped himself to fifty thousand pounds worth of negotiable securities."

"*Simpson*—but it was *Davis*—"

"If you will kindly permit me to continue, Hastings! Simpson knows that the theft will be discovered on Thursday afternoon. He does not go to the bank on Thursday, but he lies in wait for Davis when he comes out to lunch. Perhaps he admits the theft and tells Davis he will return the securities to him—anyhow he succeeds in getting Davis to come to Clapham with him. It is the maid's day out, and Mrs. Todd was at the Sales, so there is no one in the house. When the theft is discovered and Davis is missing, the implication will be overwhelming. Davis is the thief! Mr. Simpson will be perfectly safe, and can return to work on the morrow like the honest clerk they think him."

"And Davis?"

Poirot made an expressive gesture, and slowly shook his head.

"It seems too cold-blooded to be believed, and yet what other explanation can there be, *mon ami*. The one difficulty for a murderer is the disposal of the body—and Simpson had planned that out beforehand. I was struck at once by the fact that although Eliza Dunn obviously meant to return that night when she went out (witness her remark about the stewed peaches) *yet her trunk was already packed when they came for it*. It was Simpson who sent word to Carter Paterson to call on Friday and it was Simpson who corded up the box on Thursday afternoon. What suspicion could possibly arise? A maid leaves and sends for her box, it is labelled and addressed ready in her name, probably to a railway station within easy reach of London. On Saturday afternoon, Simpson, in his Australian disguise, claims it, he affixes a new label and address and re-despatches it somewhere else, again 'to be left till called for.' When the authorities get suspicious, for excellent reasons, and open it, all that can be elicited will be that a bearded colonial despatched it from some junction near London. There will be nothing to connect it with 88 Prince Albert Road. Ah! here we are."

Poirot's prognostications had been correct. Simpson had left two days previously. But he was not to escape the consequences of his crime. By the aid of wireless, he was discovered on the *Olympia*, en route to America.

A tin trunk, addressed to Mr. Henry Wintergreen, attracted the attention of railway officials at Glasgow. It was opened and found to contain the body of the unfortunate Davis.

Mrs. Todd's cheque for a guinea was never cashed. Instead Poirot had it framed and hung on the wall of our sitting-room.

"It is to me a little reminder, Hastings. Never to despise the trivial—the undignified. A disappearing domestic at one end—a cold-blooded murder at the other. To me, one of the most interesting of my cases."

# DOUBLE SIN

# Double Sin

I HAD called in at my friend Poirot's rooms to find him sadly over-
worked. So much had he become the rage that every rich woman
who had mislaid a bracelet or lost a pet kitten rushed to secure
the services of the great Hercule Poirot. My little friend was a strange
mixture of Flemish thrift and artistic fervor. He accepted many cases
in which he had little interest owing to the first instinct being predomi-
nant.

He also undertook cases in which there was a little or no monetary
reward sheerly because the problem involved interested him. The
result was that, as I say, he was overworking himself. He admitted
as much himself, and I found little difficulty in persuading him to
accompany me for a week's holiday to that well-known South Coast
resort, Ebermouth.

We had spent four very agreeable days when Poirot came to me,
an open letter in his hand.

"*Mon ami*, you remember my friend Joseph Aarons, the theatrical
agent?"

I assented after a moment's thought. Poirot's friends are so many
and so varied, and range from dustmen to dukes.

"*Eh bien*, Hastings, Joseph Aarons finds himself at Charlock Bay.
He is far from well, and there is a little affair that it seems is worrying
him. He begs me to go over and see him. I think, *mon ami*, that I
must accede to his request. He is a faithful friend, the good Joseph
Aarons, and has done much to assist me in the past."

"Certainly, if you think so," I said. "I believe Charlock Bay is a
beautiful spot, and as it happens I've never been there."

"Then we combine business with pleasure," said Poirot. "You will
inquire about the trains, yes?"

"It will probably mean a change or two," I said with a grimace.
"You know what these cross-country lines are. To go from the South
Devon coast to the North Devon coast is sometimes a day's journey."

However, on inquiry, I found that the journey could be accomplished by only one change at Exeter and that the trains were good. I was hastening back to Poirot with the information when I happened to pass the offices of the Speedy cars and saw written up:

Tomorrow. All-day excursion to Charlock Bay. Starting 8:30 through some of the most beautiful scenery in Devon.

I inquired a few particulars and returned to the hotel full of enthusiasm. Unfortunately, I found it hard to make Poirot share my feelings.

"My friend, why this passion for the motor coach? The train, see you, it is sure? The tires, they do not burst; the accidents, they do not happen. One is not incommoded by too much air. The windows can be shut and no drafts admitted."

I hinted delicately that the advantage of fresh air was what attracted me most to the motor-coach scheme.

"And if it rains? Your English climate is so uncertain."

"There's a hood and all that. Besides, if it rains badly, the excursion doesn't take place."

"Ah!" said Poirot. "Then let us hope that it rains."

"Of course, if you feel like that and . . ."

"No, no, *mon ami*. I see that you have set your heart on the trip. Fortunately, I have my great coat with me and two mufflers." He sighed. "But shall we have sufficient time at Charlock Bay?"

"Well, I'm afraid it means staying the night there. You see, the tour goes round by Dartmoor. We have lunch at Monkhampton. We arrive at Charlock Bay about four o'clock, and the coach starts back at five, arriving here at ten o'clock."

"So!" said Poirot. "And there are people who do this for pleasure! We shall, of course, get a reduction of the fare since we do not make the return journey?"

"I hardly think that's likely."

"You must insist."

"Come now, Poirot, don't be mean. You know you're coining money."

"My friend, it is not the meanness. It is the business sense. If I were a millionaire, I would pay only what was just and right."

As I had foreseen, however, Poirot was doomed to fail in this respect. The gentleman who issued tickets at the Speedy office was calm and unimpassioned but adamant. His point was that we ought to return. He even implied that we ought to pay extra for the privilege of leaving the coach at Charlock Bay.

Defeated, Poirot paid over the required sum and left the office.

"The English, they have no sense of money," he grumbled. "Did you observe a young man, Hastings, who paid over the full fare and yet mentioned his intention of leaving the coach at Monkhampton?"

"I don't think I did. As a matter of fact . . ."

"You were observing the pretty young lady who booked No. 5, the next seat to ours. Ah! Yes, my friend, I saw you. And that is why when I was on the point of taking seats No. 13 and 14—which are in the middle and as well sheltered as it is possible to be—you rudely pushed yourself forward and said that 3 and 4 would be better."

"Really, Poirot," I said, blushing.

"Auburn hair—always the auburn hair!"

"At any rate, she was more worth looking at than an odd young man."

"That depends upon the point of view. To me, the young man was interesting."

Something rather significant in Poirot's tone made me look at him quickly. "Why? What do you mean?"

"Oh! Do not excite yourself. Shall I say that he interested me because he was trying to grow a mustache and as yet the result is poor." Poirot stroked his own magnificent mustache tenderly. "It is an art," he murmured, "the growing of the mustache! I have sympathy for all who attempt it."

It is always difficult with Poirot to know when he is serious and when he is merely amusing himself at one's expense. I judged it safest to say no more.

The following morning dawned bright and sunny. A really glorious day! Poirot, however, was taking no chances. He wore a woolly waistcoat, a mackintosh, a heavy overcoat, and two mufflers, in addition to wearing his thickest suit. He also swallowed two tablets of "Antigrippe" before starting and packed a further supply.

We took a couple of small suitcases with us. The pretty girl we had noticed the day before had a small suitcase, and so did the young man whom I gathered to have been the object of Poirot's sympathy. Otherwise, there was no luggage. The four pieces were stowed away by the driver, and we all took our places.

Poirot, rather maliciously, I thought, assigned me the outside place as "I had the mania for the fresh air" and himself occupied the seat next to our fair neighbor. Presently, however, he made amends. The man in seat 6 was a noisy fellow, inclined to be facetious and boisterous, and Poirot asked the girl in a low voice if she would like to change seats with him. She agreed gratefully, and, the change having been effected, she entered into conversation with us and we were soon all three chattering together merrily.

She was evidently quite young, not more than nineteen, and as ingenuous as a child. She soon confided to us the reason of her trip. She was going, it seemed, on business for her aunt who kept a most interesting antique shop in Ebermouth.

This aunt had been left in very reduced circumstances on the death of her father and had used her small capital and a houseful of beautiful things which her father had left to start in business. She had been extremely successful and had made quite a name for herself in the trade. This girl, Mary Durrant, had come to be with her aunt and learn the business and was very excited about it—much preferring it to the other alternative—becoming a nursery governess or companion.

Poirot nodded interest and approval to all this.

"Mademoiselle will be successful, I am sure," he said gallantly. "But I will give her a little word of advice. Do not be too trusting, mademoiselle. Everywhere in the world there are rogues and vagabonds, even it may be on this very coach of ours. One should always be on the guard, suspicious!"

She stared at him open-mouthed, and he nodded sapiently.

"But yes, it is as I say. Who knows? Even I who speak to you may be a malefactor of the worst description."

And he twinkled more than ever at her surprised face.

We stopped for lunch at Monkhampton, and, after a few words with the waiter, Poirot managed to secure us a small table for three close by the window. Outside, in a big courtyard, about twenty *char-a-bancs* were parked—*char-a-bancs* which had come from all over the county. The hotel dining room was full, and the noise was rather considerable.

"One can have altogether too much of the holiday spirit," I said with a grimace.

Mary Durrant agreed. "Ebermouth is quite spoiled in the summers nowadays. My aunt says it used to be quite different. Now one can hardly get along the pavements for the crowd."

"But it is good for business, mademoiselle."

"Not for ours particularly. We sell only rare and valuable things. We do not go in for cheap bric-a-brac. My aunt has clients all over England. If they want a particular period table or chair, or a certain piece of china, they write to her, and, sooner or later, she gets it for them. That is what has happened in this case."

We looked interested and she went on to explain. A certain American gentleman, Mr. J. Baker Wood, was a connoisseur and collector of miniatures. A very valuable set of miniatures had recently come into the market, and Miss Elizabeth Penn—Mary's aunt—had purchased them. She had written to Mr. Wood describing the miniatures and naming a price. He had replied at once, saying that he was prepared to purchase if the miniatures were as represented and asking that someone should be sent with them for him to see where he was staying at Charlock Bay. Miss Durrant had accordingly been dispatched, acting as representative for the firm.

"They're lovely things, of course," she said. "But I can't imagine anyone paying all that money for them. Five hundred pounds! Just think of it! They're by Cosway. Is it Cosway I mean? I get so mixed up in these things."

Poirot smiled. "You are not yet experienced, eh, mademoiselle?"

"I've had no training," said Mary ruefully. "We weren't brought up to know about old things. It's a lot to learn."

She sighed. Then suddenly, I saw her eyes widen in surprise. She was sitting facing the window, and her glance now was directed out of that window, into the courtyard. With a hurried word, she rose from her seat and almost ran out of the room. She returned in a few moments, breathless and apologetic.

"I'm so sorry rushing off like that. But I thought I saw a man taking my suitcase out of the coach. I went flying after him, and it turned out to be his own. It's one almost exactly like mine. I felt like such a fool. It looked as though I were accusing him of stealing it."

She laughed at the idea.

Poirot, however, did not laugh. "What man was it, mademoiselle? Describe him to me."

"He had on a brown suit. A thin weedy young man with a very indeterminate mustache."

"Aha," said Poirot. "Our friend of yesterday, Hastings. You know this young man, mademoiselle. You have seen him before?"

"No, never. Why?"

"Nothing. It is rather curious—that is all."

He relapsed into silence and took no further part in the conversation until something Mary Durrant said caught his attention.

"Eh, mademoiselle, what is that you say?"

"I said that on my return journey I should have to be careful of 'malefactors,' as you call them. I believe Mr. Wood always pays for things in cash. If I have five hundred pounds in notes on me, I shall be worth some malefactor's attention."

She laughed but again Poirot did not respond. Instead, he asked her what hotel she proposed to stay at in Charlock Bay.

"The Anchor Hotel. It is small and not expensive, but quite good."

"So!" said Poirot. "The Anchor Hotel. Precisely where Hastings here has made up his mind to stay. How odd!"

He twinkled at me.

"You are staying long in Charlock Bay?" asked Mary.

"One night only. I have business there. You could not guess, I am sure, what my profession is, mademoiselle?"

I saw Mary consider several possibilities and reject them—probably from a feeling of caution. At last, she hazarded the suggestion that Poirot was a conjurer. He was vastly entertained.

"Ah! But it is an idea that! You think I take the rabbits out of the hat? No, mademoiselle. Me, I am the opposite of a conjurer. The conjurer, he makes things disappear. Me, I make things that have disappeared, reappear." He leaned forward dramatically so as to give the words full effect. "It is a secret, mademoiselle, but I will tell you, I am a detective!"

He leaned back in his chair pleased with the effect he had created. Mary Durrant stared at him spellbound. But any further conversation was barred for the braying of various horns outside announced that the road monsters were ready to proceed.

As Poirot and I went out together I commented on the charm of our luncheon companion. Poirot agreed.

"Yes, she is charming. But, also rather silly?"

"Silly?"

"Do not be outraged. A girl may be beautiful and have auburn hair and yet be silly. It is the height of foolishness to take two strangers into her confidence as she has done."

"Well, she could see we were all right."

"That is imbecile, what you say, my friend. Anyone who knows his job—naturally he will appear 'all right.' That little one she talked of being careful when she would have five hundred pounds in money with her. But she has five hundred pounds with her now."

"In miniatures."

"Exactly. In miniatures. And between one and the other, there is no great difference, *mon ami.*"

"But no one knows about them except us."

"And the waiter and the people at the next table. And, doubtless, several people in Ebermouth! Mademoiselle Durrant, she is charming, but, if I were Miss Elizabeth Penn, I would first of all instruct my new assistant in the common sense." He paused and then said in a different voice, "You know, my friend, it would be the easiest thing in the world to remove a suitcase from one of those *char-a-bancs* while we were all at luncheon."

"Oh! Come, Poirot, somebody will be sure to see."

"And what would they see? Somebody removing his luggage. It would be done in an open and aboveboard manner, and it would be nobody's business to interfere."

"Do you mean—Poirot, are you hinting— But that fellow in the brown suit—it was his own suitcase?"

Poirot frowned. "So it seems. All the same, it is curious, Hastings, that he should have not removed his suitcase before, when the car first arrived. He has not lunched here, you notice."

"If Miss Durrant hadn't been sitting opposite the window, she wouldn't have seen him," I said slowly.

"And since it was his own suitcase, that would not have mattered," said Poirot. "So let us dismiss it from our thoughts, *mon ami.*"

Nevertheless, when we had resumed our places and were speeding along once more, he took the opportunity of giving Mary Durrant a further lecture on the dangers of indiscretion which she received meekly enough but with the air of thinking it all rather a joke.

We arrived at Charlock Bay at four o'clock and were fortunate enough to be able to get rooms at the Anchor Hotel—a charming old-world inn in one of the side streets.

Poirot had just unpacked a few necessaries and was applying a little cosmetic to his mustache preparatory to going out to call upon Joseph Aarons when there came a frenzied knocking at the door. I called "Come in," and, to my utter amazement, Mary Durrant appeared, her face white and large tears standing in her eyes.

"I do beg your pardon—but—but the most awful thing has happened. And you did say you were a detective?" This to Poirot.

"What has happened, mademoiselle?"

"I opened my suitcase. The miniatures were in a crocodile dispatch case—locked, of course. Now, look!"

She held out a small square crocodile-covered case. The lid hung loose. Poirot took it from her. The case had been forced; great strength must have been used. The marks were plain enough. Poirot examined it and nodded.

"The miniatures?" he asked, though we both knew the answer well enough.

"Gone. They've been stolen. Oh! What shall I do?"

"Don't worry," I said. "My friend is Hercule Poirot. You must have heard of him. He'll get them back for you if anyone can."

"Monsieur Poirot. The great Monsieur Poirot."

Poirot was vain enough to be pleased at the obvious reverence in her voice. "Yes, my child," he said. "It is I, myself. And you can leave your little affair in my hands. I will do all that can be done. But I fear—I much fear—that it will be too late. Tell me, was the lock of your suitcase forced also?"

She shook her head.

"Let me see it, please."

We went together to her room, and Poirot examined the suitcase closely. It had obviously been opened with a key.

"Which is simple enough. These suitcase locks are all much of the same pattern. *Eh, bien,* we must ring up the police and we must also get in touch with Mr. Baker Wood as soon as possible. I will attend to that myself."

I went with him and asked what he meant by saying it might be too late. *"Mon cher,* I said today that I was the opposite of the conjurer—that I make the disappearing things reappear—but suppose someone has been beforehand with me. You do not understand? You will in a minute."

He disappeared into the telephone box. He came out five minutes later looking very grave. "It is as I feared. A lady called upon Mr. Wood with the miniatures half an hour ago. She represented herself as coming from Miss Elizabeth Penn. He was delighted with the miniatures and paid for them forthwith."

"Half an hour ago—before we arrived here."

Poirot smiled rather enigmatically. "The Speedy cars are quite speedy, but a fast motor from say, Monkhampton, would get here a good hour ahead of them at least."

"And what do we do now?"

"The good Hastings—always practical. We inform the police, do all we can for Miss Durrant, and—yes, I think decidedly, we have an interview with Mr. J. Baker Wood."

We carried out this program. Poor Mary Durrant was terribly upset, fearing her aunt would blame her.

"Which she probably will," observed Poirot, as we set out for the Seaside Hotel where Mr. Wood was staying. "And with perfect justice. The idea of leaving five hundred pounds' worth of valuables in a suitcase and going to lunch! All the same, *mon ami,* there are one or two curious points about the case. That dispatch box, for instance, why was it forced?"

"To get out the miniatures."

"But was not that a foolishness? Say our thief is tampering with the luggage at lunch time under the pretext of getting out his own. Surely it is much simpler to open the suitcase, transfer the dispatch case unopened to his own suitcase, and get away, than to waste the time forcing the lock?"

"He had to make sure the miniatures were inside."

Poirot did not look convinced, but, as we were just being shown into Mr. Wood's suite, we had no time for more discussion.

I took an immediate dislike to Mr. Baker Wood.

He was a large vulgar man, very much overdressed and wearing a diamond solitaire ring. He was blustering and noisy.

Of course, he'd not suspected anything amiss? Why should he? The woman said she had the miniatures all right. Very fine specimens, too! Had he the numbers of the notes? No, he hadn't. And who was Mr.—er—Poirot, anyway, to come asking him all these questions?

"I will not ask you anything more, monsieur, except for one thing. A description of the woman who called upon you. Was she young and pretty?"

"No, sir, she was not. Most emphatically not. A tall woman, middle-aged, grey hair, blotchy complexion and a budding mustache. A siren? Not on your life."

"Poirot," I cried, as we took our departure. "A mustache. Did you hear?"

"I have the use of my ears, thank you, Hastings."

"But what a very unpleasant man."

"He has not the charming manner, no."

"Well, we ought to get the thief all right," I remarked. "We can identify him."

"You are of such a naive simplicity, Hastings. Do you not know that there is such a thing as an alibi?"

"You think he will have an alibi?"

Poirot replied unexpectedly, "I sincerely hope so."

"The trouble with you is," I said, "that you like a thing to be difficult."

"Quite right, *mon ami*. I do not like—how do you say it—the bird who sits!"

Poirot's prophecy was fully justified. Our traveling companion in the brown suit turned out to be a Mr. Norton Kane. He had gone straight to the Gorge Hotel at Monkhampton and had been there during the afternoon. The only evidence against him was that of Miss Durrant who declared that she had seen him getting out his luggage from the car while we were at lunch.

"Which in itself is not a suspicious act," said Poirot meditatively.

After that remark, he lapsed into silence and refused to discuss the matter any further, saying when I pressed him, that he was thinking of mustaches in general, and that I should be well advised to do the same.

I discovered, however, that he had asked Joseph Aarons—with whom he spent the evening—to give him every detail possible about Mr. Baker Wood. As both men were staying at the same hotel, there was a chance of gleaning some stray crumbs of information. Whatever Poirot learned, he kept to himself, however.

Mary Durrant, after various interviews with the police, had returned to Ebermouth by an early morning train. We lunched with Joseph Aarons, and, after lunch, Poirot announced to me that he had settled the theatrical agent's problem satisfactorily, and that we could return to Ebermouth as soon as we liked. "But not by road, *mon ami;* we go by rail this time."

"Are you afraid of having your pocket picked, or of meeting another damsel in distress?"

"Both those affairs, Hastings, might happen to me on the train. No, I am in haste to be back in Ebermouth, because I want to proceed with our case."

"Our case?"

"But, yes, my friend. Mademoiselle Durrant appealed to me to help her. Because the matter is now in the hands of the police, it does not follow that I am free to wash my hands of it. I came here to oblige an old friend, but it shall never be said of Hercule Poirot that he deserted a stranger in need!" And he drew himself up grandiloquently.

"I think you were interested before that," I said shrewdly. "In the office of cars, when you first caught sight of that young man, though what drew your attention to him I don't know."

"Don't you, Hastings? You should. Well, well, that must remain my little secret."

We had a short conversation with the police inspector in charge of the case before leaving. He had interviewed Mr. Norton Kane, and told Poirot in confidence that the young man's manner had not impressed him favorably. He had blustered, denied, and contradicted himself.

"But just how the trick was done, I don't know," he confessed. "He could have handed the stuff to a confederate who pushed off at once in a fast car. But that's just theory. We've got to find the car and the confederate and pin the thing down."

Poirot nodded thoughtfully.

"Do you think that was how it was done?" I asked him, as we were seated in the train.

"No, my friend, that was not how it was done. It was cleverer than that."

"Won't you tell me?"

"Not yet. You know—it is my weakness—I like to keep my little secrets till the end."

"Is the end going to be soon?"

"Very soon now."

We arrived in Ebermouth a little after six and Poirot drove at once to the shop which bore the name "Elizabeth Penn." The establishment was closed, but Poirot rang the bell, and presently Mary herself opened the door, and expressed surprise and delight at seeing us.

"Please come in and see my aunt," she said.

She led us into a back room. An elderly lady came forward to meet us; she had white hair and looked rather like a miniature herself with her pink-and-white skin and her blue eyes. Round her rather bent shoulders she wore a cape of priceless old lace.

"Is this the great Monsieur Poirot?" she asked in a low charming voice. "Mary has been telling me. I could hardly believe it. And you will really help us in our trouble. You will advise us?"

Poirot looked at her for a moment, then bowed.

"Mademoiselle Penn—the effect is charming. But you should really grow a mustache."

Miss Penn gave a gasp and drew back.

"You were absent from business yesterday, were you not?"

"I was here in the morning. Later I had a bad headache and went directly home."

"Not home, mademoiselle. For your headache you tried the change of air, did you not? The air of Charlock Bay is very bracing, I believe."

He took me by the arm and drew me toward the door. He paused there and spoke over his shoulder.

"You comprehend, I know everything. This little—farce—it must cease."

There was a menace in his tone. Miss Penn, her face ghastly white, nodded mutely. Poirot turned to the girl.

"Mademoiselle," he said gently, "you are young and charming. But participating in these little affairs will lead to that youth and charm being hidden behind prison walls—and I, Hercule Poirot, tell you that that will be a pity."

Then he stepped out into the street and I followed him, bewildered.

"From the first, *mon ami,* I was interested. When that young man booked his place as far as Monkhampton only, I saw the girl's attention suddenly riveted on him. Now why? He was not of the type to make a woman look at him for himself alone. When we started on that coach, I had a feeling that something would happen. Who saw the young man tampering with the luggage? Mademoiselle and mademoiselle only, and remember she chose that seat—a seat facing the window— a most unfeminine choice.

"And then she comes to us with the tale of robbery—the dispatch box forced which makes not the common sense, as I told you at the time."

"And what is the result of it all? Mr. Baker Wood has paid over good money for stolen goods. The miniatures will be returned to Miss Penn. She will sell them and will have made a thousand pounds instead of five hundred. I make the discreet inquiries and learn that her business is in a bad state—touch and go. I say to myself—the aunt and niece are in this together."

"Then you never suspected Norton Kane?"

"*Mon ami!* With that mustache? A criminal is either clean shaven or he has a proper mustache that can be removed at will. But what an opportunity for the clever Miss Penn—a shrinking elderly lady with a pink-and-white complexion as we saw her. But if she holds herself erect, wears large boots, alters her complexion with a few unseemly blotches and—crowning touch—adds a few sparse hairs to her upper lip. What then? A masculine woman, says Mr. Wood, and—'a man in disguise' say we at once."

"She really went to Charlock yesterday?"

"Assuredly. The train, as you may remember telling me, left here at eleven and got to Charlock Bay at two o'clock. Then the return train is even quicker—the one we came by. It leaves Charlock at four:five and gets here at six:fifteen. Naturally, the miniatures were never in the dispatch case at all. That was artistically forced before being packed. Mademoiselle Mary has only to find a couple of mugs who will be sympathetic to her charm and champion beauty in distress. But one of the mugs was no mug—he was Hercule Poirot!"

I hardly liked the inference. I said hurriedly:

"Then, when you said you were helping a stranger, you were willfully deceiving me. That's exactly what you were doing."

"Never do I deceive you, Hastings. I only permit you to deceive yourself. I was referring to Mr. Baker Wood—a stranger to these shores." His face darkened. "Ah! When I think of that imposition, that iniquitous overcharge; the same fare single to Charlock as return, my blood boils to protect the visitor! Not a pleasant man, Mr. Baker Wood, not, as you would say, sympathetic. But a visitor! And we visitors, Hastings, must stand together. Me, I am all for the visitors!"

# Wasps' Nest

OUT of the house came John Harrison and stood a moment on the terrace looking out over the garden. He was a big man with a lean, cadaverous face. His aspect was usually somewhat grim but when, as now, the rugged features softened into a smile, there was something very attractive about him.

John Harrison loved his garden, and it had never looked better than it did on this August evening, summery and languorous. The rambler roses were still beautiful; sweet peas scented the air.

A well-known creaking sound made Harrison turn his head sharply. Who was coming in through the garden gate? In another minute, an expression of utter astonishment came over his face, for the dandified figure coming up the path was the last he expected to see in this part of the world.

"By all that's wonderful," cried Harrison. "Monsieur Poirot!"

It was, indeed, the famous Hercule Poirot whose renown as a detective had spread over the whole world.

"Yes," he said, "it is I. You said to me once, 'If you are ever in this part of the world, come and see me.' I take you at your word. I arrive."

"And I'm delighted," said Harrison heartily. "Sit down and have a drink."

With a hospitable hand, he indicated a table on the veranda bearing assorted bottles.

"I thank you," said Poirot, sinking down into a basket chair. "You have, I suppose, no *sirop?* No, no, I thought not. A little plain soda water then—no whisky." And he added in a feeling voice as the other placed the glass beside him, "Alas: My mustaches are limp. It is this heat!"

"And what brings you into this quiet spot?" asked Harrison as he dropped into another chair. "Pleasure?"

"No, *mon ami*, business."

"Business? In this out-of-the-way place?"

Poirot nodded gravely. "But yes, my friend, all crimes are not committed in crowds, you know?"

The other laughed. "I suppose that was rather an idiotic remark of mine. But what particular crime are you investigating down here, or is that a thing I mustn't ask?"

"You may ask," said the detective. "Indeed, I would prefer that you asked."

Harrison looked at him curiously. He sensed something a little unusual in the other's manner. "You are investigating a crime, you say?" he advanced rather hesitatingly. "A serious crime?"

"A crime of the most serious there is."

"You mean . . ."

"Murder."

So gravely did Hercule Poirot say that word that Harrison was quite taken aback. The detective was looking straight at him and again there was something so unusual in his glance that Harrison hardly knew how to proceed. At last, he said, "But I have heard of no murder."

"No," said Poirot, "you would not have heard of it."

"Who has been murdered?"

"As yet," said Hercule Poirot, "nobody."

"What?"

"That is why I said you would not have heard of it. I am investigating a crime that has not yet taken place."

"But look here, that is nonsense."

"Not at all. If one can investigate a murder before it has happened, surely that is very much better than afterward. One might even—a little idea—prevent it."

Harrison stared at him. "You are not serious, Monsieur Poirot."

"But yes, I am serious."

"You really believe that a murder is going to be committed? Oh, it's absurd!"

Hercule Poirot finished the first part of the sentence without taking any notice of the exclamation.

"Unless we can manage to prevent it. Yes, *mon ami*, that is what I mean."

"We?"

"I said we. I shall need your cooperation."

"Is that why you came down here?"

Again Poirot looked at him, and again an indefinable something made Harrison uneasy.

"I came here, Monsieur Harrison, because I—well—like you."

And then he added in an entirely different voice: "I see, Monsieur Harrison, that you have a wasps' nest there. You should destroy it."

The change of subject made Harrison frown in a puzzled way. He followed Poirot's glance and said in rather a bewildered voice, "As a matter of fact, I'm going to. Or rather, young Langton is. You remember Claude Langton? He was at that same dinner where I met you. He's coming over this evening to take the nest. Rather fancies himself at the job."

"Ah!" said Poirot. "And how is he going to do it?"

"Petrol and the garden syringe. He's bringing his own syringe over; it's a more convenient size than mine."

"There is another way, is there not?" asked Poirot. "With cyanide of potassium?"

Harrison looked a little surprised. "Yes, but that's rather dangerous stuff. Always a bit of risk having it about the place."

Poirot nodded gravely. "Yes, it is deadly poison." He waited a minute and then repeated in a grave voice. "Deadly poison."

"Useful if you want to do away with your mother-in-law, eh?" said Harrison with a laugh.

But Hercule Poirot remained grave. "And you are quite sure, Monsieur Harrison, that it is with petrol that Monsieur Langton is going to destroy your wasps' nest?"

"Quite sure. Why?"

"I wondered. I was at the chemist's in Barchester this afternoon. For one of my purchases I had to sign the poison book. I saw the last entry. It was for cyanide of potassium and it was signed for by Claude Langton."

Harrison stared. "That's odd," he said. "Langton told me the other day that he'd never dream of using the stuff; in fact, he said it oughtn't to be sold for the purpose."

Poirot looked out over the roses. His voice was very quiet as he asked a question. "Do you like Langton?"

The other started. The question somehow seemed to find him quite unprepared. "I—I—well, I mean—of course, I like him. Why shouldn't I?"

"I only wondered," said Poirot placidly, "whether you did."

And as the other did not answer, he went on. "I also wondered if he liked you?"

"What are you getting at, Monsieur Poirot? There's something in your mind I can't fathom."

"I am going to be very frank. You are engaged to be married, Monsieur Harrison. I know Miss Molly Deane. She is a very charming, a very beautiful girl. Before she was engaged to you, she was engaged to Claude Langton. She threw him over for you."

Harrison nodded.

"I do not ask what her reasons were; she may have been justified. But I tell you this, it is not too much to suppose that Langton has not forgotten or forgiven."

"You're wrong, Monsieur Poirot. I swear you're wrong. Langton's been a sportsman; he's taken things like a man. He's been amazingly decent to me—gone out of his way to be friendly."

"And that does not strike you as unusual? You use the word 'amazingly,' but you do not seem to be amazed."

"What do you mean, M. Poirot?"

"I mean," said Poirot, and his voice had a new note in it, "that a man may conceal his hate till the proper time comes."

"Hate?" Harrison shook his head and laughed.

"The English are very stupid," said Poirot. "They think that they can deceive anyone but that no one can deceive them. The sportsman—the good fellow—never will they believe evil of him. And because they are brave, but stupid, sometimes they die when they need not die."

"You are warning me," said Harrison in a low voice. "I see it now—what has puzzled me all along. You are warning me against Claude Langton. You came here today to warn me . . ."

Poirot nodded. Harrison sprang up suddenly. "But you are mad, Monsieur Poirot. This is England. Things don't happen like that here. Disappointed suitors don't go about stabbing people in the back and poisoning them. And you're wrong about Langton. That chap wouldn't hurt a fly."

"The lives of flies are not my concern," said Poirot placidly. "And although you say Monsieur Langton would not take the life of one, yet you forget that he is even now preparing to take the lives of several thousand wasps."

Harrison did not at once reply. The little detective in his turn sprang to his feet. He advanced to his friend and laid a hand on his shoulder. So agitated was he that he almost shook the big man, and, as he did so, he hissed into his ear, "Rouse yourself, my friend, rouse yourself. And look—look where I am pointing. There on the bank, close by that tree root. See you, the wasps returning home, placid at the end of the day? In a little hour, there will be destruction, and they know it not. There is no one to tell them. They have not, it seems, a Hercule Poirot. I tell you, Monsieur Harrison, I am down here on business. Murder is my business. And it is my business before it has happened as well as afterward. At what time does Monsieur Langton come to take this wasps' nest?"

"Langton would never . . ."

"At what time?"

"At nine o'clock. But I tell you, you're all wrong. Langton would never . . ."

"These English!" cried Poirot in a passion. He caught up his hat and stick and moved down the path, pausing to speak over his shoulder. "I do not stay to argue with you. I should only enrage myself. But you understand, I return at nine o'clock?"

Harrison opened his mouth to speak, but Poirot did not give him the chance. "I know what you would say, 'Langton would never,' et cetera. Ah, Langton would never! But all the same I return at nine o'clock. But, yes, it will amuse me—put it like that—it will amuse me to see the taking of a wasps' nest. Another of your English sports!"

He waited for no reply but passed rapidly down the path and out through the door that creaked. Once outside on the road, his pace slackened. His vivacity died down, his face became grave and troubled. Once he drew his watch from his pocket and consulted it. The hands pointed to ten minutes past eight. "Over three quarters of an hour," he murmured. "I wonder if I should have waited."

His footsteps slackened; he almost seemed on the point of returning. Some vague foreboding seemed to assail him. He shook it off resolutely, however, and continued to walk in the direction of the village. But his face was still troubled, and once or twice he shook his head like a man only partly satisfied.

It was still some minutes of nine when he once more approached the garden door. It was a clear, still evening; hardly a breeze stirred the leaves. There was, perhaps, something a little sinister in the stillness, like the lull before a storm.

Poirot's footsteps quickened ever so slightly. He was suddenly alarmed—and uncertain. He feared he knew not what.

And at that moment the garden door opened and Claude Langton stepped quickly out into the road. He started when he saw Poirot.

"Oh—er—good evening."

"Good evening, Monsieur Langton. You are early."

Langton stared at him. "I don't know what you mean."

"You have taken the wasps' nest?"

"As a matter of fact, I didn't."

"Oh!" said Poirot softly. "So you did not take the wasps' nest. What did you do then?"

"Oh, just sat and yarned a bit with old Harrison. I really must hurry along now, Monsieur Poirot. I'd no idea you were remaining in this part of the world."

"I had business here, you see."

"Oh! Well, you'll find Harrison on the terrace. Sorry I can't stop."

He hurried away. Poirot looked after him. A nervous young fellow, good looking with a weak mouth!

"So I shall find Harrison on the terrace," murmured Poirot. "I wonder." He went in through the garden door and up the path. Harrison was sitting in a chair by the table. He sat motionless and did not even turn his head as Poirot came up to him.

"Ah! *Mon ami,*" said Poirot. "You are all right, eh?"

There was a long pause and then Harrison said in a queer, dazed voice, "What did you say?"

"I said—are you all right?"

"All right? Yes, I'm all right. Why not?"

"You feel no ill effects? That is good."

"Ill effects? From what?"

"Washing soda."

Harrison roused himself suddenly. "Washing soda? What do you mean?"

Poirot made an apologetic gesture. "I infinitely regret the necessity, but I put some in your pocket."

"You put some in my pocket? What on earth for?"

Harrison stared at him. Poirot spoke quietly and impersonally like a lecturer coming down to the level of a small child.

"You see, one of the advantages, or disadvantages, of being a detective is that it brings you into contact with the criminal classes. And the criminal classes, they can teach you some very interesting and curious things. There was a pickpocket once—I interested myself in him because for once in a way he has not done what they say he has done—and so I get him off. And because he is grateful he pays me in the only way he can think of—which is to show me the tricks of his trade.

"And so it happens that I can pick a man's pocket if I choose without his ever suspecting the fact. I lay one hand on his shoulder, I excite myself, and he feels nothing. But all the same I have managed to transfer what is in his pocket to my pocket and leave washing soda in its place.

"You see," continued Poirot dreamily, "if a man wants to get at some poison quickly to put in a glass, unobserved, he positively must keep it in his right-hand coat pocket; there is nowhere else. I knew it would be there."

He dropped his hand into his pocket and brought out a few white, lumpy crystals. "Exceedingly dangerous," he murmured, "to carry it like that—loose."

Calmly and without hurrying himself, he took from another pocket a wide-mouthed bottle. He slipped in the crystals, stepped to the table and filled up the bottle with plain water. Then carefully corking it, he shook it until all the crystals were dissolved. Harrison watched him as though fascinated.

Satisfied with his solution, Poirot stepped across to the nest. He uncorked the bottle, turned his head aside, and poured the solution into the wasps' nest, then stood back a pace or two watching.

Some wasps that were returning alighted, quivered a little and then lay still. Other wasps crawled out of the hole only to die. Poirot watched for a minute or two and then nodded his head and came back to the veranda.

"A quick death," he said. "A very quick death."

Harrison found his voice. "How much do you know?"

Poirot looked straight ahead. "As I told you, I saw Claude Langton's name in the book. What I did not tell you was that almost immediately afterward, I happened to meet him. He told me he had been buying cyanide of potassium at your request—to take a wasps' nest. That struck me as a little odd, my friend, because I remember that at that dinner of which you spoke, you held forth on the superior merits of petrol and denounced the buying of cyanide as dangerous and unnecessary."

"Go on."

"I knew something else. I had seen Claude Langton and Molly Deane together when they thought no one saw them. I do not know what lovers' quarrel it was that originally parted them and drove her into your arms, but I realized that misunderstandings were over and that Miss Deane was drifting back to her love."

"Go on."

"I knew something more, my friend. I was in Harley Street the other day, and I saw you come out of a certain doctor's house. I know that doctor and for what disease one consults him, and I read the expression on your face. I have seen it only once or twice in my lifetime, but it is not easily mistaken. It was the face of a man under sentence of death. I am right, am I not?"

"Quite right. He gave me two months."

"You did not see me, my friend, for you had other things to think about. I saw something else on your face—the thing that I told you this afternoon men try to conceal. I saw hate there, my friend. You did not trouble to conceal it, because you thought there were none to observe."

"Go on," said Harrison.

"There is not much more to say. I came down here, saw Langton's name by accident in the poison book as I tell you, met him, and came here to you. I laid traps for you. You denied having asked Langton to get cyanide, or rather you expressed surprise at his having done so. You were taken aback at first at my appearance, but presently, you saw how well it would fit in and you encouraged my suspicions. I knew from Langton himself that he was coming at half past eight. You told me nine o'clock, thinking I should come and find everything over. And so I knew everything."

"Why did you come?" cried Harrison. "If only you hadn't come!"

Poirot drew himself up. "I told you," he said, "murder is my business."

"Murder? Suicide, you mean."

"No." Poirot's voice rang out sharply and clearly. "I mean murder. Your death was to be quick and easy, but the death you planned for Langton was the worst death any man can die. He bought the poison; he comes to see you, and he is alone with you. You die suddenly, and the cyanide is found in your glass, and Claude Langton hangs. That was your plan."

Again Harrison moaned.

"Why did you come? Why did you come?"

"I have told you, but there is another reason. I liked you. Listen, *mon ami*, you are a dying man; you have lost the girl you loved, but there is one thing that you are not: you are not a murderer. Tell me now: are you glad or sorry that I came?"

There was a moment's pause and then Harrison drew himself up. There was a new dignity in his face—the look of a man who has conquered his own baser self. He stretched out his hand across the table.

"Thank goodness you came," he cried. "Oh! Thank goodness you came."

# The Theft of
# the Royal Ruby

"I REGRET exceedingly . . ." said M. Hercule Poirot.

He was interrupted. Not rudely interrupted. The interruption was suave, dexterous, persuasive rather than contradictory.

"Please don't refuse offhand, Monsieur Poirot. There are grave issues of State. Your cooperation will be appreciated in the highest quarters."

"You are too kind," Hercule Poirot waved a hand, "but I really cannot undertake to do as you ask. At this season of the year . . ."

Again Mr. Jesmond interrupted. "Christmas time," he said, persuasively. "An old-fashioned Christmas in the English countryside."

Hercule Poirot shivered. The thought of the English countryside at this season of the year did not attract him.

"A good old-fashioned Christmas!" Mr. Jesmond stressed it.

"Me—I am not an Englishman," said Hercule Poirot. "In my country, Christmas, it is for the children. The New Year, that is what we celebrate."

"Ah," said Mr. Jesmond, "but Christmas in England is a great institution and I assure you at Kings Lacey you would see it at its best. It's a wonderful old house, you know. Why, one wing of it dates from the fourteenth century."

Again Poirot shivered. The thought of a fourteenth-century English manor house filled him with apprehension. He had suffered too often in the historic country houses of England. He looked round appreciatively at his comfortable modern flat with its radiators and the latest patent devices for excluding any kind of draught.

"In the winter," he said firmly, "I do not leave London."

"I don't think you quite appreciate, Monsieur Poirot, what a very serious matter this is." Mr. Jesmond glanced at his companion and then back at Poirot.

Poirot's second visitor had up to now said nothing but a polite and formal "How do you do." He sat now, gazing down at his well-polished shoes, with an air of the utmost dejection on his coffee-colored face.

He was a young man, not more than twenty-three, and he was clearly in a state of complete misery.

"Yes, yes," said Hercule Poirot. "Of course the matter is serious. I do appreciate that. His Highness has my heartfelt sympathy."

"The position is one of the utmost delicacy," said Mr. Jesmond.

Poirot transferred his gaze from the young man to his older companion. If one wanted to sum up Mr. Jesmond in a word, the word would have been discretion. Everything about Mr. Jesmond was discreet. His well-cut but inconspicuous clothes, his agreeable, well-bred voice which rarely soared out of an agreeable monotone, his light-brown hair just thinning a little at the temples, his pale serious face. It seemed to Hercule Poirot that he had known not one Mr. Jesmond but a dozen Mr. Jesmonds in his time, all using sooner or later the same phrase— "a position of the utmost delicacy."

"The police," said Hercule Poirot, "can be very discreet, you know."

Mr. Jesmond shook his head firmly.

"Not the police," he said. "To recover the—er—what we want to recover will almost inevitably involve taking proceedings in the law courts and we know so little. We *suspect,* but we do not *know.*"

"You have my sympathy," said Hercule Poirot again.

If he imagined that his sympathy was going to mean anything to his two visitors, he was wrong. They did not want sympathy, they wanted practical help. Mr. Jesmond began once more to talk about the delights of an English Christmas.

"It's dying out, you know," he said, "the real old-fashioned type of Christmas. People spend it at hotels nowadays. But an English Christmas with all the family gathered round, the children and their stockings, the Christmas tree, the turkey and plum pudding, the crackers. The snowman outside the window . . ."

In the interests of exactitude, Hercule Poirot intervened.

"To make a snowman one has to have the snow," he remarked severely. "And one cannot have snow to order, even for an English Christmas."

"I was talking to a friend of mine in the meteorological office only today," said Mr. Jesmond, "and he tells me that it is highly probably there *will* be snow this Christmas."

It was the wrong thing to have said. Hercule Poirot shuddered more forcefully than ever.

"Snow in the country!" he said. "That would be still more abominable. A large, cold, stone manor house."

"Not at all," said Mr. Jesmond. "Things have changed very much in the last ten years or so. Oil-fired central heating."

"They have oil-fired central heating at Kings Lacey?" asked Poirot. For the first time he seemed to waver.

Mr. Jesmond seized his opportunity. "Yes, indeed," he said, "and a splendid hot water system. Radiators in every bedroom. I assure you, my dear Monsieur Poirot, Kings Lacey is comfort itself in the wintertime. You might even find the house *too* warm."

"That is most unlikely," said Hercule Poirot.

With practiced dexterity Mr. Jesmond shifted his ground a little. "You can appreciate the terrible dilemma we are in," he said, in a confidential manner.

Hercule Poirot nodded. The problem was, indeed, not a happy one. A young potentate-to-be, the only son of the ruler of a rich and important native State had arrived in London a few weeks ago. His country had been passing through a period of restlessness and discontent. Though loyal to the father whose way of life had remained persistently Eastern, popular opinion was somewhat dubious of the younger generation. His follies had been Western ones and, as such, looked upon with disapproval.

Recently, however, his betrothal had been announced. He was to marry a cousin of the same blood, a young woman who, though educated at Cambridge, was careful to display no Western influences in her own country. The wedding day was announced and the young prince had made a journey to England, bringing with him some of the famous jewels of his house to be reset in appropriate modern settings by Cartier. These had included a very famous ruby which had been removed from its cumbersome old-fashioned necklace and had been given a new look by the famous jewelers. So far so good, but after this came the snag. It was not to be supposed that a young man possessed of much wealth and convivial tastes, should not commit a few follies of the pleasanter type. As to that there would have been no censure. Young princes were supposed to amuse themselves in this fashion. For the prince to take the girl friend of the moment for a walk down Bond Street and bestow upon her an emerald bracelet or a diamond clip as a reward for the pleasure she had afforded him would have been regarded as quite natural and suitable, corresponding in fact to the Cadillac cars which his father invariably presented to his favorite dancing girl of the moment.

But the prince had been far more indiscreet than that. Flattered by the lady's interest, he had displayed to her the famous ruby in its new setting, and had finally been so unwise as to accede to her request to be allowed to wear it—just for one evening!

The sequel was short and sad. The lady had retired from their supper table to powder her nose. Time passed. She did not return. She had left the establishment by another door and since then had disappeared into space. The important and distressing thing was that the ruby in its new setting had disappeared with her.

These were the facts that could not possibly be made public without the most dire consequences. The ruby was something more than a ruby, it was a historical possession of great significance, and the circumstances of its disappearance were such that any undue publicity about them might result in the most serious political consequences.

Mr. Jesmond was not the man to put these facts into simple language. He wrapped them up, as it were, in a great deal of verbiage. Who exactly Mr. Jesmond was, Hercule Poirot did not exactly know. He had met other Mr. Jesmonds in the course of his career. Whether he was connected with the Home Office, the Foreign Office or some more discreet branch of public service was not specified. He was acting in the interests of the Commonwealth. The ruby must be recovered.

M. Poirot, so Mr. Jesmond delicately insisted, was the man to recover it.

"Perhaps—yes," Hercule Poirot admitted, "but you can tell me so little. Suggestion—suspicion—all that is not very much to go upon."

"Come now, Monsieur Poirot, surely it is not beyond your powers. Ah, come now."

"I do not always succeed."

But this was mock modesty. It was clear enough from Poirot's tone that for him to undertake a mission was almost synonymous with succeeding in it.

"His Highness is very young," Mr. Jesmond said. "It will be sad if his whole life is to be blighted for a mere youthful indiscretion."

Poirot looked kindly at the downcast young man. "It is the time for follies, when one is young," he said encouragingly, "and for the ordinary young man it does not matter so much. The good papa, he pays up; the family lawyer, he helps to disentangle the inconvenience; the young man, he learns by experience and all ends for the best. In a position such as yours, it is hard indeed. Your approaching marriage . . ."

"That is it. That is it exactly." For the first time words poured from the young man. "You see she is very, very serious. She takes life very seriously. She has acquired at Cambridge many very serious ideas. There is to be education in my country. There are to be schools. There are to be many things. All in the name of progress, you understand, of democracy. It will not be, she says, like it was in my father's time. Naturally she knows that I will have diversions in London, but not the scandal. No! It is the scandal that matters. You see it is very, very famous, this ruby. There is a long trail behind it, a history. Much bloodshed—many deaths!"

"Deaths," said Hercule Poirot thoughtfully. He looked at Mr. Jesmond. "One hopes," he said, "it will not come to that?"

Mr. Jesmond made a peculiar noise rather like a hen who has decided to lay an egg and then thought better of it.

"No, no, indeed," he said, sounding rather prim. "There is no question, I am sure, of anything of *that* kind."

"You cannot be sure," said Hercule Poirot. "Whoever has the ruby now, there may be others who want to gain possession of it, and who will not stick at a trifle, my friend."

"I really don't think," said Mr. Jesmond, sounding more prim than ever, "that we need enter into speculations of that kind. Quite unprofitable."

"Me," said Hercule Poirot, suddenly becoming very foreign, "me, I explore all the avenues, like the politicians."

Mr. Jesmond looked at him doubtfully. Pulling himself together, he said, "Well, I can take it that it's settled, Monsieur Poirot? You will go to Kings Lacey?"

"And how do I explain myself there?" asked Hercule Poirot.

Mr. Jesmond smiled with confidence.

"That, I think, can be arranged very easily," he said. "I can assure you that it will all seem quite natural. You will find the Laceys most charming. Delightful people."

"And you do not deceive me about the oil-fired central heating?"

"No, no, indeed." Mr. Jesmond sounded quite pained. "I assure you you will find every comfort."

*"Tout confort moderne,"* murmured Poirot to himself, reminiscently. *"Eh bien,"* he said, "I accept."

The temperature in the long drawing room at Kings Lacey was a comfortable sixty-eight as Hercule Poirot sat talking to Mrs. Lacey by one of the big mullioned windows. Mrs. Lacey was engaged in needlework. She was not doing *petit point* or embroidering flowers upon silk. Instead, she appeared to be engaged in the prosaic task of hemming dishcloths. As she sewed she talked in a soft, reflective voice that Poirot found very charming.

"I hope you will enjoy our Christmas party here, Monsieur Poirot. It's only the family, you know. My granddaughter and a grandson and a friend of his and Bridget who's my great-niece, and Diana who's a cousin and David Welwyn who is a very old friend. Just a family party. But Edwina Morecombe said that that's what you really wanted to see. An old-fashioned Christmas. Nothing could be more old-fashioned than we are! My husband, you know, absolutely lives in the past. He likes everything to be just as it was when he was a boy of twelve years old, and used to come here for his holidays." She smiled to herself. "All the same old things, the Christmas tree and the stockings hung up and the oyster soup and the turkey—two turkeys, one boiled and one roast—and the plum pudding with the ring and the bachelor's button and all the rest of it in it. We can't have sixpences nowadays because they're not pure silver anymore. But all the old desserts, the Elvas plums and Carlsbad plums and almonds and raisins, and crystallized fruit and ginger. Dear me, I sound like a catalogue from Fortnum and Mason!"

"You arouse my gastronomic juices, madame."

"I expect we'll all have frightful indigestion by tomorrow evening," said Mrs. Lacey. "One isn't used to eating so much nowadays, is one?"

She was interrupted by some loud shouts and whoops of laughter outside the window. She glanced out.

"I don't know what they're doing out there. Playing some game or other, I suppose. I've always been so afraid, you know, that these young people would be bored by our Christmas here. But not at all, it's just the opposite. Now my own son and daughter and their friends, they used to be rather sophisticated about Christmas. Say it was all nonsense and too much fuss and it would be far better to go out to a hotel somewhere and dance. But the younger generation seem to find all this terribly attractive. Besides," added Mrs. Lacey practically, "schoolboys and schoolgirls are always hungry, aren't they? I think they must starve them at these schools. After all, one does know children of that age each eat about as much as three strong men."

Poirot laughed and said, "It is most kind of you and your husband, madame, to include me in this way in your family party."

"Oh, we're both delighted, I'm sure," said Mrs. Lacey. "And if you find Horace a little gruff," she continued, "pay no attention. It's just his manner, you know."

What her husband, Colonel Lacey, had actually said was, "Can't think why you want one of these damned foreigners here cluttering up Christmas? Why can't we have him some other time? Can't stick foreigners! All right, all right, so Edwina Morecombe wished him on us. What's it got to do with *her*, I should like to know? Why doesn't *she* have him for Christmas?"

"Because you know very well," Mrs. Lacey had said, "that Edwina always goes to Claridge's."

Her husband had looked at her piercingly and said, "Not up to something, are you, Em?"

"Up to something?" said Em, opening very blue eyes. "Of course not. Why should I be?"

Old Colonel Lacey laughed, a deep, rumbling laugh. "I wouldn't put it past you, Em," he said. "When you look your most innocent is when you *are* up to something."

Revolving these things in her mind, Mrs. Lacey went on, "Edwina said she thought perhaps you might help us. . . . I'm sure I don't know quite how, but she said that friends of yours had once found you very helpful in—in a case something like ours. I—well, perhaps you don't know what I'm talking about?"

Poirot looked at her encouragingly. Mrs. Lacey was close on seventy, as upright as a ramrod, with snow-white hair, pink cheeks, blue eyes, a ridiculous nose and a determined chin.

"If there is anything I can do I shall only be too happy to do it," said Poirot. "It is, I understand, a rather unfortunate matter of a young girl's infatuation."

Mrs. Lacey nodded. "Yes. It seems extraordinary that I should— well, want to talk to you about it. After all, you *are* a perfect stranger. . . ."

"*And* a foreigner," said Poirot, in an understanding manner.

"Yes," said Mrs. Lacey, "but perhaps that makes it easier, in a way. Anyhow, Edwina seemed to think that you might perhaps know something—how shall I put it—something useful about this young Desmond Lee-Wortley."

Poirot paused a moment to admire the ingenuity of Mr. Jesmond and the ease with which he had made use of Lady Morecombe to further his own purposes.

"He has not, I understand, a very good reputation, this young man?" he began delicately.

"No, indeed, he hasn't! A very bad reputation! But that's no help so far as Sarah is concerned. It's never any good, is it, telling young girls that men have a bad reputation? It—it just spurs them on!"

"You are so very right," said Poirot.

"In my young day," went on Mrs. Lacey. "Oh dear, that's a very long time ago! We used to be warned, you know, against certain young men, and of course it *did* heighten one's interest in them, and if one could possibly manage to dance with them, or to be alone with them in a dark conservatory . . ." she laughed. "That's why I wouldn't let Horace do any of the things he wanted to do."

"Tell me," said Poirot, "exactly what it is that troubles you?"

"Our son was killed in the war," said Mrs. Lacey. "My daughter-in-law died when Sarah was born so that she has always been with us, and we've brought her up. Perhaps we've brought her up unwisely—I don't know. But we thought we ought always to leave her as free as possible."

"That is desirable, I think," said Poirot. "One cannot go against the spirit of the times."

"No," said Mrs. Lacey, "that's just what I felt about it. And, of course, girls nowadays do do these sort of things."

Poirot looked at her inquiringly.

"I think the way one expresses it," said Mrs. Lacey, "is that Sarah has got in with what they call the coffee-bar set. She won't go to dances or come out properly or be a deb or anything of that kind. Instead she has two rather unpleasant rooms in Chelsea down by the river and wears these funny clothes that they like to wear, and black stockings or bright green ones. Very thick stockings. (So prickly, I always think!) And she goes about without washing or combing her hair."

"*Ça, c'est tout à fait naturelle*," said Poirot. "It is the fashion of the moment. They grow out of it."

"Yes, I know," said Mrs. Lacey. "I wouldn't worry about *that* sort of thing. But you see she's taken up with this Desmond Lee-Wortley and he really has a *very* unsavory reputation. He lives more or less on well-to-do girls. They seem to go quite mad about him. He very nearly married the Hope girl, but her people got her made a ward in court or something. And of course that's what Horace wants to do. He says he must do it for her protection. But I don't think it's really a good idea, Monsieur Poirot. I mean, they'll just run away together and go to Scotland or Ireland or the Argentine or somewhere and either get married or else live together without getting married. And although it may be contempt of court and all that—well, it isn't really an answer, is it, in the end? Especially if a baby's coming. One has to give in then, and let them get married. And then, nearly always, it seems to me, after a year or two there's a divorce. And then the girl comes home and usually after a year or two she marries someone so nice he's almost dull and settles down. But it's particularly sad, it seems to me, if there is a child, because it's not the same thing, being brought up by a stepfather, however nice. No, I think it's much better if we did as we did in my young days. I mean the first young man one fell in love with was *always* someone undesirable. I remember I had a horrible passion for a young man called—now what was his name now?—how strange it is, I can't remember his Christian name at all! Tibbitt, that was his surname. Young Tibbitt. Of course, my father more or less forbade him the house, but he used to get asked to the same dances, and we used to dance together. And sometimes we'd escape and sit out together and occasionally friends would arrange picnics to which we both went. Of course, it was all very exciting and forbidden and one enjoyed it enormously. But one didn't go to the—well, to the *lengths* that girls go nowadays. And so, after a while, the Mr. Tibbitts faded out. And do you know, when I saw him four years later I was surprised what I could *ever* have seen in him! He seemed to be such a *dull* young man. Flashy, you know. No interesting conversation."

"One always thinks the days of one's own youth are best," said Poirot, somewhat sententiously.

"I know," said Mrs. Lacey. "It's tiresome, isn't it? I mustn't be tiresome. But all the same I *don't* want Sarah, who's a dear girl really, to marry Desmond Lee-Wortley. She and David Welwyn, who is staying here, were always such friends and so fond of each other, and we did hope, Horace and I, that they would grow up and marry. But of course she just finds him dull now, and she's absolutely infatuated with Desmond."

"I do not quite understand, madame," said Poirot. "You have him here now, staying in the house, this Desmond Lee-Wortley?"

"That's *my* doing," said Mrs. Lacey. "Horace was all for forbidding her to see him and all that. Of course, in Horace's day, the father or guardian would have called round at the young man's lodgings with a horse whip! Horace was all for forbidding the fellow the house, and forbidding the girl to see him. I told him that was quite the wrong attitude to take. 'No,' I said. 'Ask him down here. We'll have him down for Christmas with the family party.' Of course, my husband said I was mad! But I said, 'At any rate, dear, let's *try* it. Let her see him in *our* atmosphere and *our* house and we'll be very nice to him and very polite, and perhaps then he'll seem less interesting to her'!"

"I think, as they say, you *have* something there, madame," said Poirot. "I think your point of view is very wise. Wiser than your husband's."

"Well, I hope it is," said Mrs. Lacey doubtfully. "It doesn't seem to be working much yet. But of course he's only been here a couple of days." A sudden dimple showed in her wrinkled cheek. "I'll confess something to you, Monsieur Poirot. I myself can't help liking him. I don't mean I *really* like him, with my *mind*, but I can feel the charm all right. Oh yes, I can see what Sarah sees in him. But I'm an old enough woman and have enough experience to know that he's absolutely no good. Even if I *do* enjoy his company. Though I do think," added Mrs. Lacey, rather wistfully, "he has *some* good points. He asked if he might bring his sister here, you know. She's had an operation and was in hospital. He said it was so sad for her being in a nursing home over Christmas and he wondered if it would be too much trouble if he could bring her with him. He said he'd take all her meals up to her and all that. Well now, I do think that *was* rather nice of him, don't you, Monsieur Poirot?"

"It shows a consideration," said Poirot, thoughtfully, "which seems almost out of character."

"Oh, I don't know. You can have family affections at the same time as wishing to prey on a rich young girl. Sarah will be *very* rich, you know, not only with what we leave her—and of course that won't be very much because most of the money goes with the place to Colin, my grandson. But her mother was a very rich woman and Sarah will inherit all her money when she's twenty-one. She's only twenty now. No, I do think it was nice of Desmond to mind about his sister. And he didn't pretend she was anything very wonderful or that. She's a shorthand typist, I gather—does secretarial work in London. And he's been as good as his word and does carry up trays to her. Not all the time, of course, but quite often. So I think he has some nice points. But all the same," said Mrs. Lacey with great decision, "I don't want Sarah to marry him."

"From all I have heard and been told," said Poirot, "that would indeed be a disaster."

"Do you think it would be possible for you to help us in any way?" asked Mrs. Lacey.

"I think it is possible, yes," said Hercule Poirot, "but I do not wish to promise too much. For the Mr. Desmond Lee-Wortleys of this world are clever, madame. But do not despair. One can, perhaps, do a little something. I shall at any rate, put forth my best endeavors, if only in gratitude for your kindness in asking me here for this Christmas festivity." He looked round him. "And it cannot be so easy these days to have Christmas festivities."

"No, indeed," Mrs. Lacey sighed. She leaned forward. "Do you know, Monsieur Poirot, what I really dream of—what I would love to have?"

"But tell me, madame."

"I simply long to have a small, modern bungalow. No, perhaps not a bungalow exactly, but a small, modern, easy-to-run house built somewhere in the park here, and live in it with an absolutely up-to-date kitchen and no long passages. Everything easy and simple."

"It is a very practical idea, madame."

"It's not practical for me," said Mrs. Lacey. "My husband *adores* this place. He *loves* living here. He doesn't mind being slightly uncomfortable, he doesn't mind the inconveniences and he would hate, simply *hate*, to live in a small modern house in the park!"

"So you sacrifice yourself to his wishes?"

Mrs. Lacey drew herself up. "I do not consider it a sacrifice, Monsieur Poirot," she said. "I married my husband with the wish to make him happy. He has been a good husband to me and made me very happy all these years, and I wish to give happiness to him."

"So you will continue to live here," said Poirot.

"It's not really too uncomfortable," said Mrs. Lacey.

"No, no," said Poirot, hastily. "On the contrary, it is most comfortable. Your central heating and your bathwater are perfection."

"We spent a lot of money in making the house comfortable to live in," said Mrs. Lacey. "We were able to sell some land. Ripe for development, I think they call it. Fortunately right out of sight of the house on the other side of the park. Really rather an ugly bit of ground with no nice view, but we got a very good price for it. So that we have been able to have as many improvements as possible."

"But the service, madame?"

"Oh, well, that presents less difficulty than you might think. Of course, one cannot expect to be looked after and waited upon as one used to be. Different people come in from the village. Two women in the morning, another two to cook lunch and wash it up, and different ones again in the evening. There are plenty of people who want to come and work for a few hours a day. Of course for Christmas we are very lucky. My dear Mrs. Ross always comes in every Christmas. She is a wonderful cook, really first-class. She retired about ten years ago, but she comes in to help us in any emergency. Then there is dear Peverill."

"Your butler?"

"Yes. He is pensioned off and lives in the little house near the lodge, but he is so devoted, and he insists on coming to wait on us at Christmas. Really, I'm terrified, Monsieur Poirot, because he's so old and so shaky that I feel certain that if he carries anything heavy he will drop it. It's really an agony to watch him. And his heart is not good and I'm afraid of his doing too much. But it would hurt his feelings dreadfully if I did not let him come. He hems and hahs and makes disapproving noises when he sees the state our silver is in and within three days of being here, it is all wonderful again. Yes. He is a dear faithful friend." She smiled at Poirot. "So you see, we are all set for a happy Christmas. A white Christmas, too," she added as she looked out of the window. "See? It is beginning to snow. Ah, the children are coming in. You must meet them, Monsieur Poirot."

Poirot was introduced with due ceremony. First, to Colin and Michael, the schoolboy grandson and his friend, nice polite lads of fifteen, one dark, one fair. Then to their cousin, Bridget, a black-haired girl of about the same age with enormous vitality.

"And this is my granddaughter, Sarah," said Mrs. Lacey.

Poirot looked with some interest at Sarah, an attractive girl with a mop of red hair; her manner seemed to him nervy and a trifle defiant, but she showed real affection for her grandmother.

"And this is Mr. Lee-Wortley."

Mr. Lee-Wortley wore a fisherman's jersey and tight black jeans; his hair was rather long and it seemed doubtful whether he had shaved that morning. In contrast to him was a young man introduced as David Welwyn, who was solid and quiet, with a pleasant smile, and rather obviously addicted to soap and water. There was one other member of the party, a handsome, rather intense-looking girl who was introduced as Diana Middleton.

Tea was brought in. A hearty meal of scones, crumpets, sandwiches and three kinds of cake. The younger members of the party appreciated the tea. Colonel Lacey came in last, remarking in a non-committal voice:

"Hey, tea? Oh yes, tea."

He received his cup of tea from his wife's hand, helped himself to two scones, cast a look of aversion at Desmond Lee-Wortley, and sat down as far away from him as he could. He was a big man with bushy eyebrows and a red, weather-beaten face. He might have been taken for a farmer rather than the lord of the manor.

"Started to snow," he said. "It's going to be a white Christmas all right."

After tea the party dispersed.

"I expect they'll go and play with their tape recorders now," said Mrs. Lacey to Poirot. She looked indulgently after her grandson as he left the room. Her tone was that of one who says, "The children are going to play with their toy soldiers."

"They're frightfully technical, of course," she said, "and very grand about it all."

The boys and Bridget, however, decided to go along to the lake and see if the ice on it was likely to make skating possible.

"I thought we could have skated on it this morning," said Colin. "But old Hodgkins said no. He's always so terribly careful."

"Come for a walk, David," said Diana Middleton, softly. David hesitated for half a moment, his eyes on Sarah's red head. She was standing by Desmond Lee-Wortley, her hand on his arm, looking up into his face.

"All right," said David Welwyn, "yes, let's."

Diana slipped a quick hand through his arm and they turned towards the door into the garden. Sarah said:

"Shall we go, too, Desmond? It's fearfully stuffy in the house."

"Who wants to walk?" said Desmond. "I'll get my car out. We'll go along to the Speckled Boar and have a drink."

Sarah hesitated for a moment before saying:

"Let's go to Market Ledbury to the White Hart. It's much more fun."

Though for all the world she would not have put it into words, Sarah had an instinctive revulsion from going down to the local pub with Desmond. It was, somehow, not in the tradition of Kings Lacey. The women of Kings Lacey had never frequented the bar of the Speckled Boar. She had an obscure feeling that to go there would be to let old Colonel Lacey and his wife down. And why not? Desmond Lee-Wortley would have said? For a moment of exasperation Sarah felt that he ought to know why not! One didn't upset such old darlings as Grandfather and dear old Em unless it was necessary. They'd been very sweet, really, letting her lead her own life, not understanding in the least why she wanted to live in Chelsea in the way she did, but accepting it. That was due to Em of course. Grandfather would have kicked up no end of a row.

Sarah had no illusions about her grandfather's attitude. It was not his doing that Desmond had been asked to stay at Kings Lacey. That was Em, and Em was a darling and always had been.

When Desmond had gone to fetch his car, Sarah popped her head into the drawing-room again.

"We're going over to Market Ledbury," she said. "We thought we'd have a drink there at the White Hart."

There was a slight amount of defiance in her voice, but Mrs. Lacey did not seem to notice it.

"Well, dear," she said, "I'm sure that will be very nice. David and Diana have gone for a walk, I see. I'm so glad. I really think it was a brain wave on my part to ask Diana here. So sad being left a widow so young—only twenty-two—I do hope she marries again *soon*."

Sarah looked at her sharply. "What are you up to, Em?"

"It's my little plan," said Mrs. Lacey gleefully. "I think she's just right for David. Of course I know he was terribly in love with *you*, Sarah dear, but you'd no use for him and I realize that he isn't your type. But I don't want him to go on being unhappy, and I think Diana will really suit him."

"What a matchmaker you are, Em," said Sarah.

"I know," said Mrs. Lacey. "Old women always are. Diana's quite keen on him already, I think. Don't you think she'd be just right for him?"

"I shouldn't say so," said Sarah. "I think Diana's far too—well, too intense, too serious. I should think David would find it terribly boring being married to her."

"Well, we'll see," said Mrs. Lacey. "Anyway, *you* don't want him, do you, dear?"

"No, indeed," said Sarah, very quickly. She added, in a sudden rush, "You *do* like Desmond, don't you, Em?"

"I'm sure he's very nice indeed," said Mrs. Lacey.

"Grandfather doesn't like him," said Sarah.

"Well, you could hardly expect him to, could you?" said Mrs. Lacey reasonably, "but I dare say he'll come round when he gets used to the idea. You mustn't rush him, Sarah dear. Old people are very slow to change their minds and your grandfather *is* rather obstinate."

"I don't care what Grandfather thinks or says," said Sarah. "I shall get married to Desmond whenever I like!"

"I know, dear, I know. But do try and be realistic about it. Your grandfather could cause a lot of trouble, you know. You're not of age yet. In another year you can do as you please. I expect Horace will have come round long before that."

"You're on my side aren't you, darling?" said Sarah. She flung her arms round her grandmother's neck and gave her an affectionate kiss.

"I want you to be happy," said Mrs. Lacey. "Ah! there's your young man bringing his car round. You know, I like these very tight trousers these young men wear nowadays. They look so smart—only, of course, it does accentuate knock knees."

Yes, Sarah thought, Desmond *had* got knock knees, she had never noticed it before. . . .

"Go on, dear, enjoy yourself," said Mrs. Lacey.

She watched her go out to the car, then, remembering her foreign guest, she went along to the library. Looking in, however, she saw that Hercule Poirot was taking a pleasant little nap, and smiling to herself, she went across the hall and out into the kitchen to have a conference with Mrs. Ross.

"Come on, beautiful," said Desmond. "Your family cutting up rough because you're coming out to a pub? Years behind the times here, aren't they?"

"Of course they're not making a fuss," said Sarah sharply as she got into the car.

"What's the idea of having that foreign fellow down? He's a detective, isn't he? What needs detecting here?"

"Oh, he's not here professionally," said Sarah. "Edwina Morecombe, my godmother, asked us to have him. I think he's retired from professional work long ago."

"Sounds like a broken-down old cab horse," said Desmond.

"He wanted to see an old-fashioned English Christmas, I believe," said Sarah vaguely.

Desmond laughed scornfully. "Such a lot of tripe, that sort of thing," he said. "How you can stand it I don't know."

Sarah's red hair was tossed back and her aggressive chin shot up.

"I enjoy it!" she said defiantly.

"You can't, baby. Let's cut the whole thing tomorrow. Go over to Scarborough or somewhere."

"I couldn't possibly do that."

"Why not?"

"Oh, it would hurt their feelings."

"Oh, bilge! You know you don't enjoy this childish sentimental bosh."

"Well, not really perhaps, but . . ." Sarah broke off. She realized with a feeling of guilt that she was looking forward a good deal to the Christmas celebration. She enjoyed the whole thing, but she was ashamed to admit that to Desmond. It was not the thing to enjoy Christmas and family life. Just for a moment she wished that Desmond had not come down there at Christmas time. In fact, she almost wished that Desmond had not come down here at all. It was much more fun seeing Desmond in London than here at home.

In the meantime the boys and Bridget were walking back from the lake, still discussing earnestly the problems of skating. Flecks of snow had been falling, and looking up at the sky it could be prophesied that before long there was going to be a heavy snowfall.

"It's going to snow all night," said Colin. "Bet you by Christmas morning we have a couple of feet of snow."

The prospect was a pleasurable one.

"Let's make a snowman," said Michael.

"Good lord," said Colin, "I haven't made a snowman since—well, since I was about four years old."

"I don't believe it's a bit easy to do," said Bridget. "I mean, you have to know how."

"We might make an effigy of Monsieur Poirot," said Colin. "Give it a big black moustache. There is one in the dressing-up box."

"I don't see, you know," said Michael thoughtfully, "how Monsieur Poirot could ever have been a detective. I don't see how he'd ever be able to disguise himself."

"I know," said Bridget, "and one can't imagine him running about with a microscope and looking for clues or measuring footprints."

"I've got an idea," said Colin. "Let's put on a show for him!"

"What do you mean, a show?" asked Bridget.

"Well, arrange a murder for him."

"What a gorgeous idea," said Bridget. "Do you mean a body in the snow—that sort of thing?"

"Yes. It would make him feel at home, wouldn't it?"

Bridget giggled.

"I don't know that I'd go as far as that."

"If it snows," said Colin, "we'll have the perfect setting. A body and footprints—we'll have to think that out rather carefully and pinch one of Grandfather's daggers and make some blood."

They came to a halt and, oblivious to the rapidly falling snow, entered into an excited discussion.

"There's a paintbox in the old schoolroom. We could mix up some blood—crimson-lake, I should think."

"Crimson-lake's a bit too pink, *I* think," said Bridget. "It ought to be a bit browner."

"Who's going to be the body?" asked Michael.

"I'll be the body," said Bridget quickly.

"Oh, look here," said Colin, "*I* thought of it."

"Oh, no, no," said Bridget, "it must be me. It's got to be a girl. It's more exciting. Beautiful girl lying lifeless in the snow."

"Beautiful girl! Ah-ha," said Michael in derision.

"I've got black hair, too," said Bridget.

"What's that got to do with it?"

"Well, it'll show up so well on the snow and I shall wear my red pajamas."

"If you wear red pajamas, they won't show the bloodstains," said Michael in a practical manner.

"But they'd look so effective against the snow," said Bridget, "and they've got white facings, you know, so the blood could be on that. Oh, won't it be gorgeous? Do you think he will really be taken in?"

"He will if we do it well enough," said Michael. "We'll have just your footprints in the snow and one other person's going to the body and coming away from it—a man's, of course. He won't want to disturb them, so he won't know that you're not really dead. You don't think," Michael stopped, struck by a sudden idea. The others looked at him. "You don't think he'll be *annoyed* about it?"

"Oh, I shouldn't think so," said Bridget, with facile optimism. "I'm sure he'll understand that we've just done it to entertain him. A sort of Christmas treat."

"I don't think we ought to do it on Christmas Day," said Colin reflectively. "I don't think Grandfather would like that very much."

"Boxing Day then," said Bridget.

"Boxing Day would be just right," said Michael.

"And it'll give us more time, too," pursued Bridget. "After all, there are a lot of things to arrange. Let's go and have a look at all the props."

They hurried into the house.

The evening was a busy one. Holly and mistletoe had been brought in in large quantities and a Christmas tree had been set up at one end of the dining room. Everyone helped to decorate it, to put up the branches of holly behind pictures and to hang mistletoe in a convenient position in the hall.

"I had no idea anything so archaic still went on," murmured Desmond to Sarah with a sneer.

"We've always done it," said Sarah, defensively.

"What a reason!"

"Oh, don't be tiresome, Desmond. *I* think it's fun."

"Sarah my sweet, you *can't!*"

"Well, not—not really perhaps but—I do in a way."

"Who's going to brave the snow and go to midnight Mass?" asked Mrs. Lacey at twenty minutes to twelve.

"Not me," said Desmond. "Come on, Sarah."

With a hand on her arm he guided her into the library and went over to the record case.

"There are limits, darling," said Desmond. "Midnight Mass!"

"Yes," said Sarah. "Oh yes."

With a good deal of laughter, donning of coats and stamping of feet, most of the others got off. The two boys, Bridget, David, and Diana set out for the ten minutes' walk to the church through the falling snow. Their laughter died away in the distance.

"Midnight Mass!" said Colonel Lacey, snorting. "Never went to midnight Mass in my young days. *Mass,* indeed! Popish, that is! Oh, I beg your pardon, Monsieur Poirot."

Poirot waved a hand. "It is quite all right. Do not mind me."

"Matins is good enough for anybody, I should say," said the colonel. "Proper Sunday morning service. 'Hark the herald angels sing,' and all the good old Christmas hymns. And then back to Christmas dinner. That's right, isn't it, Em?"

"Yes, dear," said Mrs. Lacey. "That's what *we* do. But the young ones enjoy the midnight service. And it's nice, really, that they *want* to go."

"Sarah and that fellow don't want to go."

"Well, there dear, I think you're wrong," said Mrs. Lacey. "Sarah, you know, *did* want to go, but she didn't like to say so."

"Beats me why she cares what that fellow's opinion is."

"She's very young, really," said Mrs. Lacey placidly. "Are you going to bed, Monsieur Poirot? Good night. I hope you'll sleep well."

"And you, madame? Are you not going to bed yet?"

"Not just yet," said Mrs. Lacey. "I've got the stockings to fill, you see. Oh, I know they're all practically grown up, but they do *like* their stockings. One puts jokes in them! Silly little things. But it all makes for a lot of fun."

"You work very hard to make this a happy house at Christmas time," said Poirot. "I honor you."

He raised her hand to his lips in a courtly fashion.

"Hm," grunted Colonel Lacey, as Poirot departed. "Flowery sort of fellow. Still—he appreciates you."

Mrs. Lacey dimpled up at him. "Have you noticed, Horace, that I'm standing under the mistletoe?" she asked with the demureness of a girl of nineteen.

Hercule Poirot entered his bedroom. It was a large room well provided with radiators. As he went over towards the big fourposter bed he noticed an envelope lying on his pillow. He opened it and drew out a piece of paper. On it was a shakily printed message in capital letters.

DON'T EAT NONE OF THE PLUM PUDDING. ONE AS
WISHES YOU WELL.

Hercule Poirot stared at it. His eyebrows rose. "Cryptic," he murmured, "and most unexpected."

Christmas dinner took place at two o'clock and was a feast indeed.
Enormous logs crackled merrily in the wide fireplace and above their
crackling rose the babel of many tongues talking together. Oyster soup
had been consumed, two enormous turkeys had come and gone, mere
carcasses of their former selves. Now, the supreme moment, the Christmas pudding was brought in, in state! Old Peverell, his hands and
his knees shaking with the weakness of eighty years, permitted no
one but himself to bear it in. Mrs. Lacey sat, her hands pressed together
in nervous apprehension. One Christmas, she felt sure, Peverell would
fall down dead. Having either to take the risk of letting him fall down
dead or of hurting his feelings to such an extent that he would probably
prefer to be dead than alive, she had so far chosen the former alternative. On a silver dish the Christmas pudding reposed in its glory. A
large football of a pudding, a piece of holly stuck in it like a triumphant
flag and glorious flames of blue and red rising round it. There was a
cheer and cries of "Ooh-ah."

One thing Mrs. Lacey had done: prevailed upon Peverell to place
the pudding in front of her so that she could help serve it rather
than hand it in turn round the table. She breathed a sigh of relief as
it was deposited safely in front of her. Rapidly the plates were passed
round, flames still licking the portions.

"Wish, Monsieur Poirot," cried Bridget. "Wish before the flame goes.
Quick, Gran darling, quick."

Mrs. Lacey leant back with a sigh of satisfaction. Operation Pudding
had been a success. In front of everyone was a helping with flames
still licking it. There was a momentary silence all round the table as
everyone wished hard.

There was nobody to notice the rather curious expression on the
face of Monsieur Poirot as he surveyed the portion of pudding on
his plate. *"Don't eat none of the plum pudding."* What on earth did
that sinister warning mean? There could be nothing different about
his portion of plum pudding from that of everyone else! Sighing as
he admitted himself baffled—and Hercule Poirot never liked to admit
himself baffled—he picked up his spoon and fork.

"Hard sauce, Monsieur Poirot?"

Poirot helped himself appreciatively to hard sauce.

"Swiped my best brandy again, eh Em?" said the colonel good-hum-
ouredly from the other end of the table. Mrs. Lacey twinkled at him.

"Mrs. Ross insists on having the best brandy, dear," she said. "She says it makes all the difference."

"Well, well," said Colonel Lacey, "Christmas comes but once a year and Mrs. Ross is a great woman. A great woman and a great cook."

"She is indeed," said Colin. "Smashing plum pudding, this. Mmmm." He filled an appreciative mouth.

Gently, almost gingerly, Hercule Poirot attacked his portion of pudding. He ate a mouthful. It was delicious! He ate another. Something tinkled faintly on his plate. He investigated with a fork. Bridget, on his left, came to his aid.

"You've got something, Monsieur Poirot," she said. "I wonder what it is."

Poirot detached a little silver object from the surrounding raisins that clung to it.

"Oooh," said Bridget, "it's the bachelor's button! Monsieur Poirot's got the bachelor's button!"

Hercule Poirot dipped the small silver button into the fingerbowl of water that stood by his plate, and washed it clear of pudding crumbs.

"It is very pretty," he observed.

"That means you're going to be a bachelor, Monsieur Poirot," explained Colin helpfully.

"That is to be expected," said Poirot gravely. "I have been a bachelor for many long years and it is unlikely that I shall change that status now."

"Oh, never say die," said Michael. "I saw in the paper that someone of ninety-five married a girl of twenty two the other day."

"You encourage me," said Hercule Poirot.

Colonel Lacey uttered a sudden exclamation. His face became purple and his hand went to his mouth.

"Confound it, Emmeline," he roared, "why on earth do you let the cook put glass in the pudding?"

"Glass!" cried Mrs. Lacey, astonished.

Colonel Lacey withdrew the offending substance from his mouth. "Might have broken a tooth," he grumbled. "Or swallowed the damn' thing and had appendicitis."

He dropped the piece of glass into the fingerbowl, rinsed it and held it up.

"God bless my soul," he ejaculated. "It's a red stone out of one of the cracker brooches." He held it aloft.

"You permit?"

Very deftly Monsieur Poirot stretched across his neighbour, took it from Colonel Lacey's fingers and examined it attentively. As the squire had said, it was an enormous red stone the color of a ruby. The light gleamed from its facets as he turned it about. Somewhere around the table a chair was pushed sharply back and then drawn in again.

"Phew!" cried Michael. "How wizard it would be if it was *real.*"

"Perhaps it is real," said Bridget hopefully.

"Oh, don't be an ass, Bridget. Why a ruby of that size would be worth thousands and thousands and thousands of pounds. Wouldn't it, Monsieur Poirot?"

"It would indeed," said Poirot.

"But what *I* can't understand," said Mrs. Lacey, "is how it got into the pudding."

"Oooh," said Colin, diverted by his last mouthful, "I've got the pig. It isn't fair."

Bridget chanted immediately, "Colin's got the pig! Colin's got the pig! Colin is the greedy guzzling *Pig!*"

"I've got the ring," said Diana in a clear, high voice.

"Good for you, Diana. You'll be married first, of us all."

"I've got the thimble," wailed Bridget.

"Bridget's going to be an old maid," chanted the two boys. "Yah, Bridget's going to be an old maid."

"Who's got the money?" demanded David. "There's a real ten-shilling piece, gold, in this pudding. I know. Mrs. Ross told me so."

"I think I'm the lucky one," said Desmond Lee-Wortley.

Colonel Lacey's two next-door neighbours heard him mutter, "Yes, you would be."

"*I've* got a ring, too," said David. He looked across at Diana. "Quite a coincidence, isn't it?"

The laughter went on. Nobody noticed that Monsieur Poirot carelessly, as though thinking of something else, had dropped the red stone into his pocket.

Mince pies and Christmas dessert followed the pudding. The older members of the party then retired for a welcome siesta before the tea-time ceremony of the lighting of the Christmas tree. Hercule Poirot, however, did not take a siesta. Instead, he made his way to the enormous old-fashioned kitchen.

"It is permitted," he asked, looking round and beaming, "that I congratulate the cook on this marvelous meal that I have just eaten?"

There was a moment's pause and then Mrs. Ross came forward in a stately manner to meet him. She was a large woman, nobly built with all the dignity of a stage duchess. Two lean grey-haired women were beyond in the scullery washing up and a tow-haired girl was moving to and fro between the scullery and the kitchen. But these were obviously mere myrmidons. Mrs. Ross was the queen of the kitchen quarters.

"I am glad to hear you enjoyed it, sir," she said graciously.

"Enjoyed it!" cried Hercule Poirot. With an extravagant foreign gesture he raised his hand to his lips, kissed it, and wafted the kiss to the ceiling. "But you are a genius, Mrs. Ross! A genius! *Never* have I tasted such a wonderful meal. The oyster soup . . ." he made an expressive noise with his lips. "—and the stuffing. The chestnut stuffing in the turkey, that was quite unique in my experience."

"Well, it's funny that you should say that, sir," said Mrs. Ross graciously. "It's a very special recipe, that stuffing. It was given me by an Austrian chef that I worked with many years ago. But all the rest," she added, "is just good, plain English cooking."

"And is there anything better?" demanded Hercule Poirot.

"Well, it's nice of you to say so, sir. Of course, you being a foreign gentleman might have preferred the continental style. Not but what I can't manage continental dishes, too."

"I am sure, Mrs. Ross, you could manage anything! But you must know that English cooking—*good* English cooking, not the cooking one gets in the second-class hotels or the restaurants—is much appreciated by gourmets on the continent, and I believe I am correct in saying that a special expedition was made to London in the early eighteen hundreds, and a report sent back to France of the wonders of the English puddings. 'We have nothing like that in France,' they wrote. 'It is worth making a journey to London just to taste the varieties and excellencies of the English puddings. And above all puddings," continued Poirot, well launched now on a kind of rhapsody, "is the Christmas plum pudding, such as we have eaten today. That was a homemade pudding, was it not? Not a bought one?"

"Yes, indeed, sir. Of my own making and my own recipe such as I've made for many, many years. When I came here Mrs. Lacey said that she'd ordered a pudding from a London store to save me the trouble. But no, madame, I said, that may be kind of you but no bought pudding from a store can equal a homemade Christmas one. Mind you," said Mrs. Ross, warming to her subject like the artist she was, "it was made too soon before the day. A good Christmas pudding should be made some weeks before and allowed to wait. The longer they're kept, within reason, the better they are. I mind now that when I was a child and we went to church every Sunday, we'd start listening for the collect that begins 'Stir up O Lord we beseech thee' because that collect was the signal, as it were, that the puddings should be made that week. And so they always were. We had the collect on the Sunday, and that week sure enough my mother would make the Christmas puddings. And so it should have been here this year. As it was, that pudding was only made three days ago, the day before you arrived, sir. However, I kept to the old custom. Everyone in the house had to come out into the kitchen and have a stir and make a wish.

That's an old custom, sir, and I've always held to it."

"Most interesting," said Hercule Poirot. "Most interesting. And so everyone came out into the kitchen?"

"Yes, sir. The young gentlemen, Miss Bridget and the London gentleman who's staying here, and his sister and Mr. David and Miss Diana—Mrs. Middleton, I should say . . . all had a stir, they did."

"How many puddings did you make? Is this the only one?"

"No, sir, I made four. Two large ones and two smaller ones. The other large one I planned to serve on New Year's Day and the smaller ones were for Colonel and Mrs. Lacey when they're alone like and not so many in the family."

"I see, I see," said Poirot.

"As a matter of fact, sir," said Mrs. Lacey, "it was the wrong pudding you had for lunch today."

"The wrong pudding?" Poirot frowned. "How is that?"

"Well, sir, we have a big Christmas mould. A china mould with a pattern of holly and mistletoe on top and we always have the Christmas Day pudding boiled in that. But there was a most unfortunate accident. This morning, when Annie was getting it down from the shelf in the larder, she slipped and dropped it and it broke. Well, sir, naturally I couldn't serve that, could I? There might have been splinters in it. So we had to use the other one—the New Year's Day one, which is in a plain bowl. It makes a nice round but it's not so decorative as the Christmas mould. Really, where we'll get another mould like that I don't know. They don't make things in that size nowadays. All tiddly bits of things. Why, you can't even buy a breakfast dish that'll take a proper eight to ten eggs and bacon. Ah, things aren't what they were."

"No, indeed," said Poirot. "But today that is not so. This Christmas Day has been like the Christmas Days of old, is that not true?"

Mrs. Ross sighed. "Well, I'm glad you say so, sir, but of course I haven't the *help* now that I used to have. Not skilled help, that is. The girls nowadays . . ." she lowered her voice slightly, "—they mean very well and they're very willing but they've not been *trained,* sir, if you understand what I mean."

"Times change, yes," said Hercule Poirot. "I, too, find it sad sometimes."

"This house, sir," said Mrs. Ross, "it's too large, you know, for the mistress and the colonel. The mistress, she knows that. Living in a corner of it as they do, it's not the same thing at all. It only comes alive, as you might say, at Christmas time when all the family come."

"It is the first time, I think, that Mr. Lee-Wortley and his sister have been here?"

"Yes, sir." A note of slight reserve crept into Mrs. Ross's voice. "A very nice gentleman he is but, well—it seems a funny friend for Miss

Sarah to have, according to our ideas. But there—London ways are different! It's sad that his sister's so poorly. Had an operation, she had. She seemed all right the first day she was here, but that very day, after we'd been stirring the puddings, she was took bad again and she's been in bed ever since. Got up too soon after her operation, I expect. Ah, doctors nowadays, they have you out of hospital before you can hardly stand on your feet. Why, my very own nephew's wife . . ." And Mrs. Ross went into a long and spirited tale of hospital treatment as accorded to her relations, comparing it unfavorably with the consideration that had been lavished upon them in older times.

Poirot duly commiserated with her. "It remains," he said, "to thank you for this exquisite and sumptuous meal. You permit a little acknowledgment of my appreciation?" A crisp five-pound note passed from his hand into that of Mrs. Ross who said perfunctorily:

"You really shouldn't do *that,* sir."

"I insist. I insist."

"Well, it's very kind of you indeed, sir." Mrs. Ross accepted the tribute as no more than her due. "And I wish you, sir, a very happy Christmas and a prosperous New Year."

The end of Christmas Day was like the end of most Christmas Days. The tree was lighted, a splendid Christmas cake came in for tea, was greeted with approval but was partaken of only moderately. There was cold supper.

Both Poirot and his host and hostess went to bed early.

"Good night, Monsieur Poirot," said Mrs. Lacey. "I hope you've enjoyed yourself."

"It has been a wonderful day, madame, wonderful."

"You're looking very thoughtful," said Mrs. Lacey.

"It is the English pudding that I consider."

"You found it a little heavy, perhaps?" asked Mrs. Lacey delicately.

"No, no, I do not speak gastronomically. I consider its significance."

"It's traditional, of course," said Mrs. Lacey. "Well, good night, Monsieur Poirot, and don't dream too much of Christmas puddings and mince pies."

"Yes," murmured Poirot to himself as he undressed. "It is a problem certainly, that Christmas plum pudding. There is here something that I do not understand at all." He shook his head in a vexed manner. "Well—we shall see."

After making certain preparations, Poirot went to bed, but not to sleep.

It was some two hours later that his patience was rewarded. The door of his bedroom opened very gently. He smiled to himself. It was as he had thought it would be. His mind went back fleetingly to the cup of coffee so politely handed him by Desmond Lee-Wortley.

A little later, when Desmond's back was turned, he had laid the cup down for a few moments on a table. He had then apparently picked it up again and Desmond had had the satisfaction, if satisfaction it was, of seeing him drink the coffee to the last drop. But a little smile lifted Poirot's moustache as he reflected that it was not he but someone else who was sleeping a good sound sleep tonight. "That pleasant young David," said Poirot to himself, "he is worried, unhappy. It will do him no harm to have a night's really sound sleep. And now, let us see what will happen."

He lay quite still, breathing in an even manner with occasionally a suggestion, but the very faintest suggestion, of a snore.

Someone came up to the bed and bent over him. Then, satisfied, that someone turned away and went to the dressing table. By the light of a tiny torch the visitor was examining Poirot's belongings neatly arranged on top of the dressing table. Fingers explored the wallet, gently pulled open the drawers of the dressing table, then extended the search to the pockets of Poirot's clothes. Finally the visitor approached the bed and with great caution slid his hand under the pillow. Withdrawing his hand, he stood for a moment or two as though uncertain what to do next. He walked round the room looking inside ornaments, went into the adjoining bathroom from whence he presently returned. Then, with a faint exclamation of disgust, he went out of the room.

"Ah," said Poirot, under his breath. "You have a disappointment. Yes, yes, a serious disappointment. Bah! To imagine, even, that Hercule Poirot would hide something where you could find it!" Then, turning over on his other side, he went peacefully to sleep.

He was aroused next morning by an urgent soft tapping on his door.

"*Qui est là?* Come in, come in."

The door opened. Breathless, red-faced, Colin stood upon the threshold. Behind him stood Michael.

"Monsieur Poirot, Monsieur Poirot."

"But yes?" Poirot sat up in bed. "It is the early tea? But no. It is you, Colin. What has occurred?"

Colin was, for a moment, speechless. He seemed to be under the grip of some strong emotion. In actual fact it was the sight of the nightcap that Hercule Poirot wore that affected for the moment his organs of speech. Presently he controlled himself and spoke.

"I think—Monsieur Poirot, could you help us? Something rather awful has happened."

"Something has happened? But what?"

"It's—it's Bridget. She's out there in the snow. I think—she doesn't move or speak and—oh, you'd better come and look for yourself. I'm terribly afraid—she may be *dead*."

"What?" Poirot cast aside his bed covers. "Mademoiselle Bridget—dead!"

"I think—I think somebody's killed her. There's—there's blood and—oh do come!"

"But certainly. But certainly. I come on the instant."

With great practicality Poirot inserted his feet into his outdoor shoes and pulled a fur-lined overcoat over his pajamas.

"I come," he said. "I come on the moment. You have aroused the house?"

"No. No, so far I haven't told anyone but you. I thought it would be better. Grandfather and Gran aren't up yet. They're laying breakfast downstairs, but I didn't say anything to Peverell. She—Bridget—she's round the other side of the house, near the terrace and the library window."

"I see. Lead the way. I will follow."

Turning away to hide his delighted grin, Colin led the way downstairs. They went out through the side door. It was a clear morning with the sun not yet high over the horizon. It was not snowing now, but it had snowed heavily during the night and everywhere around was an unbroken carpet of thick snow. The world looked very pure and white and beautiful.

"There!" said Colin breathlessly. "I—it's—*there!*" He pointed dramatically.

The scene was indeed dramatic enough. A few yards away Bridget lay in the snow. She was wearing scarlet pajamas and a white wool wrap thrown round her shoulders. The white wool wrap was stained with crimson. Her head was turned aside and hidden by the mass of her outspread black hair. One arm was under her body, the other lay flung out, the fingers clenched, and standing up in the center of the crimson stain was the hilt of a large curved Kurdish knife which Colonel Lacey had shown to his guests only the evening before.

"*Mon Dieu!*" ejaculated M. Poirot. "It is like something on the stage!"

There was a faint choking noise from Michael. Colin thrust himself quickly into the breach.

"I know," he said. "It—it doesn't seem *real* somehow, does it? Do you see those footprints—I suppose we mustn't disturb them?"

"Ah yes, the footprints. No, we must be careful not to disturb those footprints."

"That's what I thought," said Colin. "That's why I wouldn't let anyone go near her until we got you. I thought you'd know what to do."

"All the same," said Hercule Poirot briskly, "first, we must see if she is still alive? Is not that so?"

"Well—yes—of course," said Michael, a little doubtfully, "but you see, we thought—I mean, we didn't like . . ."

"Ah, you have the prudence! You have read the detective stories. It is most important that nothing should be touched and that the body should be left as it is. But we cannot be sure as yet if it *is* a body, can we? After all, though prudence is admirable, common humanity comes first. We must think of the doctor, must we not, before we think of the police?"

"Oh yes. Of course," said Colin, still a little taken aback.

"We only thought—I mean—we thought we'd better get you before we did anything," said Michael hastily.

"Then you will both remain here," said Poirot. "I will approach from the other side so as not to disturb these footprints. Such excellent footprints, are they not—so very clear? The footprints of a man and a girl going out together to the place where she lies. And then the man's footsteps come back but the girl's—do not."

"They must be the footprints of the murderer," said Colin, with bated breath.

"Exactly," said Poirot. "The footprints of the murderer. A long narrow foot with rather a peculiar type of shoe. Very interesting. Easy, I think, to recognize. Yes, those footprints will be very important."

At that moment Desmond Lee-Wortley came out of the house with Sarah and joined them.

"What on earth are you all doing here?" he demanded in a somewhat theatrical manner. "I saw you from my bedroom window. What's up? Good lord, what's this? It—it looks like . . ."

"Exactly," said Hercule Poirot. "It looks like murder, does it not?"

Sarah gave a gasp, then shot a quick suspicious glance at the two boys.

"You mean someone's killed the girl—what's-her-name—Bridget?" demanded Desmond. "Who on earth would want to kill her? It's unbelievable!"

"There are many things that are unbelievable," said Poirot. "Especially before breakfast, is it not? That is what one of your classics says. Six impossible things before breakfast." He added, "Please wait here, all of you."

Carefully making a circuit, he approached Bridget and bent for a moment down over the body. Colin and Michael were now both shaking with suppressed laughter. Sarah joined them, murmuring, "What have you two been up to?"

"Good old Bridget," whispered Colin. "Isn't she wonderful? Not a twitch!"

"I've never seen anything look so dead as Bridget does," whispered Michael.

Hercule Poirot straightened up again.

"This is a terrible thing," he said. His voice held an emotion it had not held before.

Overcome by mirth, Michael and Colin both turned away. In a choked voice Michael said:

"What—what must we do?"

"There is only one thing to do," said Poirot. "We must send for the police. Will one of you telephone or would you prefer me to do it?"

"I think," said Colin, "I think—what about it, Michael?"

"Yes," said Michael, "I think the jig's up now." He stepped forward. For the first time he seemed a little unsure of himself. "I'm awfully sorry," he said, "I hope you won't mind too much. It—er—it was a sort of joke for Christmas and all that, you know. We thought we'd—well, lay on a murder for you."

"You thought you would lay on a murder for me? Then this—then this . . ."

"It's just a show we put on," explained Colin, "to—to make you feel at home, you know."

"Aha," said Hercule Poirot. "I understand. You make of me the April fool, is that it? But today is not April the first, it is December the twenty-sixth."

"I suppose we oughtn't to have done it really," said Colin, "but—but—you don't mind very much, do you, Monsieur Poirot? Come on, Bridget," he called, "get up. You must be half-frozen to death already."

The figure in the snow, however, did not stir.

"It is odd," said Hercule Poirot, "she does not seem to hear you." He looked thoughtfully at them. "It is a joke, you say? You are sure this is a joke?"

"Why, yes." Colin spoke uncomfortably. "We—we didn't mean any harm."

"But why then does Mademoiselle Bridget not get up?"

"I can't imagine," said Colin.

"Come on, Bridget," said Sarah impatiently. "Don't go on lying there playing the fool."

"We really are very sorry, Monsieur Poirot," said Colin apprehensively. "We do really apologize."

"You need not apologize," said Poirot, in a peculiar tone.

"What do you mean?" Colin stared at him. He turned again. "Bridget! Bridget! What's the matter? Why doesn't she get up? Why does she go on lying there?"

Poirot beckoned to Desmond. "*You*, Mr. Lee-Wortley. Come here. . . ."

Desmond joined him.

"Feel her pulse," said Poirot.

Desmond Lee-Wortley bent down. He touched the arm—the wrist. "There's no pulse . . ." he stared at Poirot. "Her arm's stiff. Good God, she really *is* dead!"

Poirot nodded. "Yes, she is dead," he said. "Someone has turned the comedy into a tragedy."

"Someone—who?"

"There is a set of footprints going and returning. A set of footprints that bears a strong resemblance to the footprints *you* have just made, Mr. Lee-Wortley, coming from the path to this spot."

Desmond Lee-Wortley wheeled round.

"What on earth . . . Are you accusing me? *ME?* You're crazy! Why on earth should I want to kill the girl?"

"Ah—why? I wonder . . . Let us see. . . ."

He bent down and very gently prised open the stiff fingers of the girl's clenched hand.

Desmond drew a sharp breath. He gazed down unbelievingly. In the palm of the dead girl's hand was what appeared to be a large ruby.

"It's that damn thing out of the pudding!" he cried.

"Is it?" said Poirot. "Are you sure?"

"Of course it is."

With a swift movement Desmond bent down and plucked the red stone out of Bridget's hand.

"You should not do that," said Poirot reproachfully. "Nothing should have been disturbed."

"I haven't disturbed the body, have I? But this thing might—might get lost and it's evidence. The great thing is to get the police here as soon as possible. I'll go at once and telephone."

He wheeled round and ran sharply towards the house. Sarah came swiftly to Poirot's side.

"I don't understand," she whispered. Her face was dead white. "I don't *understand*." She caught at Poirot's arm. "What did you mean about—about the footprints?"

"Look for yourself, mademoiselle."

The footprints that led to the body and back again were the same as the ones just made accompanying Poirot to the girl's body and back.

"You mean—that it was Desmond? Nonsense!"

Suddenly the noise of a car came through the clear air. They wheeled round. They saw the car clearly enough driving at a furious pace down the drive and Sarah recognized what car it was.

"It's Desmond," she said. "It's Desmond's car. He—he must have gone to fetch the police instead of telephoning."

Diana Middleton came running out of the house to join them.

"What's happened?" she cried in a breathless voice. "Desmond just came rushing into the house. He said something about Bridget being killed and then he rattled the telephone but it was dead. He couldn't get any answer. He said the wires must have been cut. He said the only thing was to take a car and go for the police. Why the police . . . ?"

Poirot made a gesture.

"Bridget?" Diana stared at him. "But surely—isn't it a joke of some kind? I heard something—something last night. I thought that they were going to play a joke on you, Monsieur Poirot?"

"Yes," said Poirot, "that was the idea—to play a joke on me. But now come into the house, all of you. We shall catch our deaths of cold here and there is nothing to be done until Mr. Lee-Wortley returns with the police."

"But look here," said Colin, "we can't—we can't leave Bridget here alone."

"You can do her no good by remaining," said Poirot gently. "Come, it is a sad, a very sad tragedy, but there is nothing we can do any more to help Mademoiselle Bridget. So let us come in and get warm and have perhaps a cup of tea or of coffee."

They followed him obediently into the house. Peverell was just about to ring the gong. If he thought it extraordinary for most of the household to be outside and for Poirot to make an appearance in pajamas and an overcoat, he displayed no sign of it. Peverell in his old age was still the perfect butler. He noticed nothing that he was not asked to notice. They went into the dining-room and sat down. When they all had a cup of coffee in front of them and were sipping it, Poirot spoke.

"I have to recount to you," he said, "a little history. I cannot tell you all the details, no. But I can give you the main outline. It concerns a young princeling who came to this country. He brought with him a famous jewel which he was to have reset for the lady he was going to marry, but unfortunately before that he made friends with a very pretty young lady. This pretty young lady did not care very much for the man, but she did care for his jewel—so much so that one day she disappeared with this historic possession which had belonged to his house for generations. So the poor young man, he is in a quandary, you see. Above all he cannot have a scandal. Impossible to go to the police. Therefore he comes to me, to Hercule Poirot. 'Recover for me,' he says, 'my historic ruby.' *Eh bien,* this young lady, she has a friend and the friend, he has put through several very questionable transactions. He has been concerned with blackmail and he has been concerned with the sale of jewelry abroad. Always he has been very clever. He is suspected, yes, but nothing can be proved. It comes to my knowledge that this very clever gentleman, he is spending Christmas here in this house. It is important that the pretty young lady, once she has acquired the jewel, should disappear for a while from circulation, so that no pressure can be put upon her, no questions can be asked her. It is arranged, therefore, that she comes here to Kings Lacey, ostensibly as the sister of the clever gentleman . . ."

Sarah drew a sharp breath.

"Oh, no. Oh, no, not *here!* Not with me here!"

"But so it is," said Poirot. "And by a little manipulation I, too, become a guest here for Christmas. This young lady, she is supposed to have just come out of hospital. She is much better when she arrives here. But then comes the news that I, too, arrive, a detective—a well-known detective. At once she has what you call the wind up. She hides the ruby in the first place she can think of, and then very quickly she has a relapse and takes to her bed again. She does not want that I should see her, for doubtless I have a photograph and I shall recognize her. It is very boring for her, yes, but she has to stay in her room and her brother, he brings her up the trays."

"And the ruby?" demanded Michael.

"I think," said Poirot, "that at the moment it is mentioned I arrive, the young lady was in the kitchen with the rest of you, all laughing and talking and stirring the Christmas puddings. The Christmas puddings are put into bowls and the young lady she hides the ruby, pressing it down into one of the pudding bowls. Not the one that we are going to have on Christmas Day. Oh no, that one she knows is in a special mould. She puts it in the other one, the one that is destined to be eaten on New Year's Day. Before then she will be ready to leave, and when she leaves no doubt that Christmas pudding will go with her. But see how fate takes a hand. On the very morning of Christmas Day there is an accident. The Christmas pudding in its fancy mould is dropped on the stone floor and the mould is shattered to pieces. So what can be done? The good Mrs. Ross, she takes the other pudding and sends it in."

"Good lord," said Colin, "do you mean that on Christmas Day when Grandfather was eating his pudding that that was a *real* ruby he'd got in his mouth?"

"Precisely," said Poirot, "and you can imagine the emotions of Mr. Desmond Lee-Wortley when he saw that. *Eh bien,* what happens next?

The ruby is passed round. I examine it and I manage unobtrusively to slip it in my pocket. In a careless way as though I were not interested. But one person at least observes what I have done. When I lie in bed that person searches my room. He searches me. He does not find the ruby. Why?"

"Because," said Michael breathlessly, "you had given it to Bridget. That's what you mean. And so that's why—but I don't understand quite—I mean . . . Look here, what *did* happen?"

Poirot smiled at him.

"Come now into the library," he said, "and look out of the window and I will show you something that may explain the mystery."

He led the way and they followed him.

"Consider once again," said Poirot, "the scene of the crime."

He pointed out of the window. A simultaneous gasp broke from the lips of all of them. There was no body lying on the snow, no trace of the tragedy seemed to remain except a mass of scuffled snow.

"It wasn't all a dream, was it?" said Colin faintly. "I—has someone taken the body away?"

"Ah," said Poirot. "You see? The Mystery of the Disappearing Body." He nodded his head and his eyes twinkled gently.

"Good lord," cried Michael. "Monsieur Poirot, you are—you haven't—oh, look here, he's been having us on all this time!"

Poirot twinkled more than ever.

"It is true, my children, I also have had my little joke. I knew about your little plot, you see, and so I arranged a counterplot of my own. Ah, *voilà* Mademoiselle Bridget. None the worse, I hope, for your exposure in the snow? Never should I forgive myself if you *attrapped une fluxion de poitrine.*"

Bridget had just come into the room. She was wearing a thick skirt and a woollen sweater. She was laughing.

"I sent a *tisane* to your room," said Poirot severely. "You have drunk it?"

"One sip was enough!" said Bridget. *"I'm* all right. Did I do it well, Monsieur Poirot? Goodness, my arm hurts still after that tourniquet you made me put on it."

"You were splendid, my child," said Poirot. "Splendid. But see, all the others are still in the fog. Last night I went to Mademoiselle Bridget. I told her that I knew about your little *complot* and I asked her if she would act a part for me. She did it very cleverly. She made the footprints with a pair of Mr. Lee-Wortley's shoes."

Sarah said in a harsh voice:

"But what's the point of it all, Monsieur Poirot? What's the point of sending Desmond off to fetch the police? They'll be very angry when they find out it's nothing but a hoax."

Poirot shook his head gently.

"But I do not think for one moment, mademoiselle, that Mr. Lee-Wortley went to fetch the police," he said. "Murder is a thing in which Mr. Lee-Wortley does not want to be mixed up. He lost his nerve badly. All he could see was his chance to get the ruby. He snatched that, he pretended the telephone was out of order and he rushed off in a car on the pretence of fetching the police. I think myself it is the last you will see of him for some time. He has, I understand, his own ways of getting out of England. He has his own plane, has he not, mademoiselle?"

Sarah nodded. "Yes," she said. "We were thinking of . . ." She stopped.

"He wanted you to elope with him that way, did he not? *Eh bien*, that is a very good way of smuggling a jewel out of the country. When you are eloping with a girl, and that fact is publicized, then you will not be suspected of also smuggling a historic jewel out of the country. Oh yes, that would have made a very good *camouflage*."

"I don't believe it," said Sarah. "I don't believe a word of it!"

"Then ask his sister," said Poirot, gently nodding his head over her shoulder. Sarah turned her head sharply.

A platinum blonde stood in the doorway. She wore a fur coat and was scowling. She was clearly in a furious temper.

"Sister my foot!" she said, with a short unpleasant laugh. "That swine's no brother of mine! So he's beaten it, has he, and left me to carry the can? The whole thing was *his* idea! *He* put me up to it! Said it was money for jam. They'd never prosecute because of the scandal. I could always threaten to say that Ali had *given* me his historic jewel. Des and I were to have shared the swag in Paris—and now the swine runs out on me! I'd like to murder him!" She switched abruptly. "The sooner I get out of here . . . Can someone telephone for a taxi?"

"A car is waiting at the front door to take you to the station, mademoiselle," said Poirot.

"Think of everything, don't you?"

"Most things," said Poirot complacently.

But Poirot was not to get off so easily. When he returned to the dining room after assisting the spurious Miss Lee-Wortley into the waiting car, Colin was waiting for him.

There was a frown on his boyish face.

"But look here, Monsieur Poirot. *What about the ruby?* Do you mean to say you've let him get away with it?"

Poirot's face fell. He twirled his moustache. He seemed ill at ease.

"I shall recover it yet," he said weakly. "There are other ways. I shall still . . ."

"Well, I do think!" said Michael. "To let that swine get away with the ruby!"

Bridget was sharper.

"He's having us on again," she cried. "You are, aren't you, Monsieur Poirot?"

"Shall we do a final conjuring trick, mademoiselle? Feel in my left-hand pocket."

Bridget thrust her hand in. She drew it out again with a scream of triumph and held aloft a large ruby blinking in crimson splendor.

"You comprehend," explained Poirot, "the one that was clasped in your hand was a paste replica. I brought it from London in case it was possible to make a substitution. You understand? We do not want the scandal. Monsieur Desmond will try and dispose of that ruby in Paris or in Belgium or wherever it is that he has his contacts, and then it will be discovered that the stone is not real! What could be more excellent? All finishes happily. The scandal is avoided, my princeling receives his ruby back again, he returns to his country and makes a sober and we hope a happy marriage. All ends well."

"Except for me," murmured Sarah under her breath.

She spoke so low that no one heard her but Poirot. He shook his head gently.

"You are in error, Mademoiselle Sarah, in what you say there. You have gained experience. All experience is valuable. Ahead of you I prophesy there lies happiness."

"That's what you say," said Sarah.

"But look here, Monsieur Poirot," Colin was frowning. "How did you know about the show we were going to put on for you?"

"It is my business to know things," said Hercule Poirot. He twirled his moustache.

"Yes, but I don't see how you could have managed it. Did someone split—did someone come and tell you?"

"No, no, not that."

"Then how? Tell us how?"

They all chorused, "Yes, tell us how."

"But no," Poirot protested. "But no. If I tell you how I deduced that, you will think nothing of it. It is like the conjurer who shows how his tricks are done!"

"Tell us, Monsieur Poirot! Go on. Tell us, tell us!"

"You really wish that I should solve for you this last mystery?"

"Yes, go on. Tell us."

"Ah, I do not think I can. You will be so disappointed."

"Now, come on, Monsieur Poirot, tell us. *How did you know?*"

"Well, you see, I was sitting in the library by the window in a chair after tea the other day and I was reposing myself. I had been asleep and when I awoke you were discussing your plans just outside the window close to me, and the window was open at the top."

"Is that all?" cried Colin, disgusted. "How simple!"

"Is it not?" cried Hercule Poirot, smiling. "You see? You *are* disappointed!"

"Oh well," said Michael, "at any rate we know everything now."

"Do we?" murmured Hercule Poirot to himself. "*I* do not. *I*, whose business it is to know things."

He walked out into the hall, shaking his head a little. For perhaps the twentieth time he drew from his pocket a rather dirty piece of paper. "DON'T EAT NONE OF THE PLUM PUDDING. ONE AS WISHES YOU WELL."

Hercule Poirot shook his head reflectively. He who could explain everything could not explain this! Humiliating. Who had written it? *Why* had it been written? Until he found that out he would never know a moment's peace. Suddenly he came out of his reverie to be aware of a peculiar gasping noise. He looked sharply down. On the floor, busy with a dustpan and brush was a tow-headed creature in a flowered overall. She was staring at the paper in his hand with large round eyes.

"Oh sir," said this apparition. "Oh, *sir. Please*, sir."

"And who may you be, *mon enfant?*" inquired Poirot genially.

"Annie Bates, sir, please sir. I come here to help Mrs. Ross. I didn't mean, sir, I didn't mean to—to do anything what I shouldn't do. I did mean it well, sir. For your good, I mean."

Enlightenment came to Poirot. He held out the dirty piece of paper.

"Did you write that, Annie?"

"I didn't mean any harm, sir. Really I didn't."

"Of course you didn't, Annie." He smiled at her. "But tell me about it. Why did you write this?"

"Well, it was them two, sir. Mr. Lee-Wortley and his sister. Not that she *was* his sister, I'm sure. None of us thought so! And she wasn't ill a bit. We could all tell *that*. We thought—we all thought—something queer was going on. I'll tell you straight, sir. I was in her bathroom taking in the clean towels, and I listened at the door. *He* was in her room and they were talking together. I heard what they said plain as plain. 'This detective,' he was saying. 'This fellow Poirot who's coming here. We've got to do something about it. We've got to get him out of the way as soon as possible.' And then he says to her in a nasty, sinister sort of way, lowering his voice, 'Where did you put it?' And she answered him, *'In the pudding.'* Oh, sir, my heart gave such a leap I thought it would stop beating. I thought they meant to poison you in the Christmas pudding. I didn't know *what* to do! Mrs. Ross, she wouldn't listen to the likes of me. Then the idea came to me as

I'd write you a warning. And I did and I put it on your pillow where you'd find it when you went to bed." Annie paused breathlessly.

Poirot surveyed her gravely for some minutes.

"You see too many sensational films, I think, Annie," he said at last, "or perhaps it is the television that affects you? But the important thing is that you have the good heart and a certain amount of ingenuity. When I return to London I will send you a present."

"Oh thank you, sir. Thank you very much, sir."

"What would you like, Annie, as a present?"

"Anything I like, sir? Could I have anything I like?"

"Within reason," said Hercule Poirot prudently, "yes."

"Oh sir, could I have a vanity box? A real posh slap-up vanity box like the one Mr. Lee-Wortley's sister, wot wasn't his sister, had?"

"Yes," said Poirot, "yes, I think that could be managed.

"It is interesting," he mused. "I was in a museum the other day observing some antiquities from Babylon or one of those places, thousands of years old—and among them were cosmetics boxes. The heart of woman does not change."

"Beg your pardon, sir?" said Annie.

"It is nothing," said Poirot, "I reflect. You shall have your vanity box, child."

"Oh, thank you, sir. Oh, thank you very much indeed, sir."

Annie departed ecstatically. Poirot looked after her, nodding his head in satisfaction.

"Ah," he said to himself. "And now—I go. There is nothing more to be done here."

A pair of arms slipped round his shoulders unexpectedly.

"If you *will* stand just under the mistletoe . . ." said Bridget.

Hercule Poirot enjoyed it. He enjoyed it very much. He said to himself that he had had a very good Christmas.

# The Double Clue

"**B**UT above everything—no publicity," said Mr. Marcus Hardman for perhaps the fourteenth time.

The word *publicity* occurred throughout his conversation with the regularity of a leitmotif. Mr. Hardman was a small man, delicately plump, with exquisitely manicured hands and a plaintive tenor voice. In his way, he was somewhat of a celebrity and the fashionable life was his profession. He was rich, but not remarkably so, and he spent his money zealously in the pursuit of social pleasure. His hobby was collecting. He had the collector's soul. Old lace, old fans, antique jewelry—nothing crude or modern for Marcus Hardman.

Poirot and I, obeying an urgent summons, had arrived to find the little man writhing in an agony of indecision. Under the circumstances, to call in the police was abhorrent to him. On the other hand, not to call them in was to acquiesce in the loss of some of the gems of his collection. He hit upon Poirot as a compromise.

"My rubies, Monsieur Poirot, and the emerald necklace—said to have belonged to Catherine de Medici. Oh, the emerald necklace!"

"If you will recount to me the circumstances of their disappearance?" suggested Poirot gently.

"I am endeavoring to do so. Yesterday afternoon I had a little tea party—quite an informal affair, some half a dozen people or so. I have given one or two of them during the season, and though perhaps I should not say so, they have been quite a success. Some good music—Nacora, the pianist, and Katherine Bird, the Australian contralto—in the big studio. Well, early in the afternoon, I was showing my guests my collection of medieval jewels. I keep them in the small wall safe over there. It is arranged like a cabinet inside, with colored velvet background, to display the stones. Afterward we inspected the fans—in that case on the wall. Then we all went to the studio for music. It was not until after everyone had gone that I discovered the safe rifled! I must have failed to shut it properly, and someone had seized the opportunity to denude it of its contents. The rubies, Monsieur Poirot, the emerald necklace—the collection of a lifetime! What would I not give to recover them! But there must be no publicity! You fully understand that, do you not, Monsieur Poirot? My own guests, my personal friends! It would be a horrible scandal!"

"Who was the last person to leave this room when you went to the studio?"

"Mr. Johnston. You may know him? The South African millionaire. He has just rented the Abbotburys' house in Park Lane. He lingered behind a few moments, I remember. But surely, oh, surely it could not be he!"

"Did any of your guests return to this room during the afternoon on any pretext?"

"I was prepared for that question, Monsieur Poirot. Three of them did so. Countess Vera Rossakoff, Mr. Bernard Parker, and Lady Runcorn."

"Let us hear about them."

"The Countess Rossakoff is a very charming Russian lady, a member of the old régime. She has recently come to this country. She had bade me goodbye, and I was therefore somewhat surprised to find her in this room apparently gazing in rapture at my cabinet of fans. You know, Monsieur Poirot, the more I think of it, the more suspicious it seems to me. Don't you agree?"

"Extremely suspicious; but let us hear about the others."

"Well, Parker simply came here to fetch a case of miniatures that I was anxious to show to Lady Runcorn."

"And Lady Runcorn herself?"

"As I daresay you know, Lady Runcorn is a middle-aged woman of considerable force of character who devotes most of her time to various charitable committees. She simply returned to fetch a handbag she had laid down somewhere."

"*Bien, monsieur.* So we have four possible suspects. The Russian countess, the English *grand dame,* the South African millionaire, and Mr. Bernard Parker. Who *is* Mr. Parker, by the way?"

The question appeared to embarrass Mr. Hardman considerably.

"He is—er—he is a young fellow. Well, in fact, a young fellow I know."

"I had already deduced as much," replied Poirot gravely. "What does he do, this Mr. Parker?"

"He is a young man about town—not, perhaps, quite in the swim, if I may so express myself."

"How did he come to be a friend of yours, may I ask?"

"Well—er—on one or two occasions he has—performed certain little commissions for me."

"Continue, monsieur," said Poirot.

Hardman looked piteously at him. Evidently the last thing he wanted to do was to continue. But as Poirot maintained an inexorable silence, he capitulated.

"You see, Monsieur Poirot—it is well known that I am interested in antique jewels. Sometimes there is a family heirloom to be disposed of—which, mind you, would never be sold in the open market or to a dealer. But a private sale to me is a very different matter. Parker arranges the details of such things, he is in touch with both sides, and thus any little embarrassment is avoided. He brings anything of that kind to my notice. For instance, the Countess Rossakoff has brought some family jewels with her from Russia. She is anxious to sell them. Bernard Parker was to have arranged the transaction."

"I see," said Poirot thoughtfully. "And you trust him implicitly?"

"I have had no reason to do otherwise."

"Mr. Hardman, of these four people, which do you yourself suspect?"

"Oh, Monsieur Poirot, what a question! They are my friends, as I told you. I suspect none of them—or all of them, whichever way you like to put it."

"I do not agree. You suspect one of those four. It is not Countess Rossakoff. It is not Mr. Parker. Is it Lady Runcorn or Mr. Johnston?"

"You drive me into a corner, Monsieur Poirot, you do indeed. I am most anxious to have no scandal. Lady Runcorn belongs to one of the oldest families in England; but it is true, it is most unfortunately true, that her aunt, Lady Caroline, suffered from a most melancholy affliction. It was understood, of course, by all her friends, and her maid returned the teaspoons, or whatever it was, as promptly as possible. You see my predicament!"

"So Lady Runcorn had an aunt who was a kleptomaniac? Very interesting. You permit that I examine the safe?"

Mr. Hardman assenting, Poirot pushed back the door of the safe and examined the interior. The empty velvet-lined shelves gaped at us.

"Even now the door does not shut properly," murmured Poirot, as he swung it to and fro. "I wonder why? Ah, what have we here? A glove, caught in the hinge. A man's glove."

He held it out to Mr. Hardman.

"That's not one of my gloves," the latter declared.

"Aha! Something more!" Poirot bent deftly and picked up a small object from the floor of the safe. It was a flat cigarette case made of black moiré.

"My cigarette case!" cried Mr. Hardman.

"Yours? Surely not, monsieur. Those are not your initials."

He pointed to an entwined monogram of two letters executed in platinum.

Hardman took it in his hand.

"You are right," he declared. "It is very like mine, but the initials are different. A 'P' and a 'B.' Good heavens—Parker!"

"It would seem so," said Poirot. "A somewhat careless young man— especially if the glove is his also. That would be a double clue, would it not?"

"Bernard Parker!" murmured Hardman. "What a relief! Well, Monsieur Poirot, I leave it to you to recover the jewels. Place the matter in the hands of the police if you think fit—that is, if you are quite sure that it is he who is guilty."

"See you, my friend," said Poirot to me, as we left the house together, "he has one law for the titled, and another law for the plain, this Mr. Hardman. Me, I have not yet been ennobled, so I am on the side of the plain. I have sympathy for this young man. The whole thing was a little curious, was it not? There was Hardman suspecting Lady Runcorn; there was I, suspecting the Countess and Johnston; and all the time, the obscure Mr. Parker was our man."

"Why did you suspect the other two?"

"*Parbleu!* It is such a simple thing to be a Russian refugee or a South African millionaire. Any woman can call herself a Russian countess; anyone can buy a house in Park Lane and call himself a South African millionaire. Who is going to contradict them? But I observe that we are passing through Bury Street. Our careless young friend lives here. Let us, as you say, strike while the iron is in the fire."

Mr. Bernard Parker was at home. We found him reclining on some cushions, clad in an amazing dressing gown of purple and orange. I have seldom taken a greater dislike to anyone than I did to this particular young man with his white, effeminate face and affected lisping speech.

"Good morning, monsieur," said Poirot briskly. "I come from Mr. Hardman. Yesterday, at the party, somebody has stolen all his jewels. Permit me to ask you, monsieur—is this your glove?"

Mr. Parker's mental processes did not seem very rapid. He stared at the glove, as though gathering his wits together.

"Where did you find it?" he asked at last.

"Is it your glove, monsieur?"

Mr. Parker appeared to make up his mind.

"No, it isn't," he declared.

"And this cigarette case, is that yours?"

"Certainly not. I always carry a silver one."

"Very well, monsieur. I go to put matters in the hands of the police."

"Oh, I say, I wouldn't do that, if I were you," cried Mr. Parker in some concern. "Beastly unsympathetic people, the police. Wait a bit.

I'll go round and see old Hardman. Look here—oh, stop a minute."

But Poirot beat a determined retreat.

"We have given him something to think about, have we not?" he chuckled. "Tomorrow we will observe what has occurred."

But we were destined to have a reminder of the Hardman case that afternoon. Without the least warning the door flew open, and a whirlwind in human form invaded our privacy, bringing with her a swirl of sables (it was as cold as only an English June day can be) and a hat rampant with slaughtered ospreys. Countess Vera Rossakoff was a somewhat disturbing personality.

"You are Monsieur Poirot? What is this that you have done? You accuse that poor boy! It is infamous. It is scandalous. I know him. He is a chicken, a lamb—never would he steal. He has done everything for me. Will I stand by and see him martyred and butchered?"

"Tell me, madame, is this his cigarette case?" Poirot held out the black moiré case.

The Countess paused for a moment while she inspected it.

"Yes, it is his. I know it well. What of it? Did you find it in the room? We were all there; he dropped it then, I suppose. Ah, you policemen, you are worse than the Red Guards—"

"And is this his glove?"

"How should I know? One glove is like another. Do not try to stop me—he must be set free. His character must be cleared. You shall do it. I will sell my jewels and give you much money."

"Madame—"

"It is agreed, then? No, no, do not argue. The poor boy! He came to me, the tears in his eyes. 'I will save you,' I said. 'I will go to this man—this ogre, this monster! Leave it to Vera.' Now it is settled, I go."

With as little ceremony as she had come, she swept from the room, leaving an overpowering perfume of an exotic nature behind her.

"What a woman!" I exclaimed. "And what furs!"

"Ah, yes, *they* were genuine enough! Could a spurious countess have real furs? My little joke, Hastings. . . . No, she is truly Russian, I fancy. Well, well, so Master Bernard went bleating to her."

"The cigarette case is his. I wonder if the glove is also—"

With a smile Poirot drew from his pocket a second glove and placed it by the first. There was no doubt of their being a pair.

"Where did you get the second one, Poirot?"

"It was thrown down with a stick on the table in the hall in Bury Street. Truly, a very careless young man, Monsieur Parker. Well, well, *mon ami*—we must be thorough. Just for the form of the thing, I will make a little visit to Park Lane."

Needless to say, I accompanied my friend. Johnston was out, but we saw his private secretary. It transpired that Johnston had only recently arrived from South Africa. He had never been in England before.

"He is interested in precious stones, is he not?" hazarded Poirot.

"Gold mining is nearer the mark," laughed the secretary.

Poirot came away from the interview thoughtful. Late that evening, to my utter surprise, I found him earnestly studying a Russian grammar.

"Good heavens, Poirot!" I cried. "Are you learning Russian in order to converse with the Countess in her own language?"

"She certainly would not listen to my English, my friend!"

"But surely, Poirot, well-born Russians invariably speak French?"

"You are a mine of information, Hastings! I will cease puzzling over the intricacies of the Russian alphabet."

He threw the book from him with a dramatic gesture. I was not entirely satisfied. There was a twinkle in his eye which I knew of old. It was an invariable sign that Hercule Poirot was pleased with himself.

"Perhaps," I said sapiently, "you doubt her being really a Russian. You are going to test her?"

"Ah, no, no, she is Russian all right."

"Well, then—"

"If you really want to distinguish yourself over this case, Hastings, I recommend *First Steps in Russian* as an invaluable aid."

Then he laughed and would say no more. I picked up the book from the floor and dipped into it curiously, but could make neither head nor tail of Poirot's remarks.

The following morning brought us no news of any kind, but that did not seem to worry my little friend. At breakfast, he announced his intention of calling upon Mr. Hardman early in the day. We found the elderly society butterfly at home, and seemingly a little calmer than on the previous day.

"Well, Monsieur Poirot, any news?" he demanded eagerly.

Poirot handed him a slip of paper.

"That is the person who took the jewels, monsieur. Shall I put matters in the hands of the police? Or would you prefer me to recover the jewels without bringing the police into the matter?"

Mr. Hardman was staring at the paper. At last he found his voice.

"Most astonishing. I should infinitely prefer to have no scandal in the matter. I give you *carte blanche,* Monsieur Poirot. I am sure you will be discreet."

Our next procedure was to hail a taxi, which Poirot ordered to drive to the Carlton. There he inquired for Countess Rossakoff. In a few minutes we were ushered up into the lady's suite. She came to meet us with outstretched hands, arrayed in a marvelous negligee of barbaric design.

"Monsieur Poirot!" she cried. "You have succeeded? You have cleared that poor infant?"

"Madame la Comtesse, your friend Mr. Parker is perfectly safe from arrest."

"Ah, but you are the clever little man! Superb! And so quickly too."

"On the other hand, I have promised Mr. Hardman that the jewels shall be returned to him today."

"So?"

"Therefore, madame, I should be extremely obliged if you would place them in my hands without delay. I am sorry to hurry you, but I am keeping a taxi—in case it should be necessary for me to go on to Scotland Yard; and we Belgians, madame, we practice the thrift."

The Countess had lighted a cigarette. For some seconds she sat perfectly still, blowing smoke rings, and gazing steadily at Poirot. Then she burst into a laugh, and rose. She went across to the bureau, opened a drawer, and took out a black silk handbag. She tossed it lightly to Poirot. Her tone, when she spoke, was perfectly light and unmoved.

"We Russians, on the contrary, practice prodigality," she said. "And to do that, unfortunately, one must have money. You need not look inside. They are all there."

Poirot arose.

"I congratulate you, madame, on your quick intelligence and your promptitude."

"Ah! But since you were keeping your taxi waiting, what else could I do?"

"You are too amiable, madame. You are remaining long in London?"

"I am afraid not—owing to you."

"Accept my apologies."

"We shall meet again elsewhere, perhaps."

"I hope so."

"And I—do not!" exclaimed the Countess with a laugh. "It is a great compliment that I pay you there—there are very few men in the world whom I fear. Goodbye, Monsieur Poirot."

"Goodbye, Madame la Comtesse. Ah—pardon me, I forgot! Allow me to return you your cigarette case."

And with a bow he handed to her the little black moiré case we had found in the safe. She accepted it without any change of expression—just a lifted eyebrow and a murmured, "I see!"

"What a woman!" cried Poirot enthusiastically as we descended the stairs. "*Mon Dieu, quelle femme!* Not a word of argument—of protestation, of bluff! One quick glance, and she had sized up the position correctly. I tell you, Hastings, a woman who can accept defeat like that—with a careless smile—will go far! She is dangerous; she has the nerves of steel; she—" He tripped heavily.

SC    Christie, Agatha

      Hercule Poirot's
      casebook